Center Stage

L.M. NELSON

Center Stage
Copyright © 2017 L.M. Nelson

ISBN-10:0-9985135-2-0
ISBN-13:978-0-9985135-2-2

1 2 3 4 5 6 7 8 9 10

This is a work of fiction. The events and characters described herein are imaginary and are not intended to refer to specific places or living people.

Cover Design Assistance by: Rachael Ritchey
Photos Courtesy of:
James DeMers, ptdh, Hermann,
vloveland, noskill1343 @ pixabay.com CC0
Stage Floor: Warton Center CC-BY-SA 3.0

Chapter One

Theater is a calling, an art, and the Juilliard School in New York City was one of the most respected and renowned places in the world to perfect this art. Known for its rigorous program and extensive admission requirements, Juilliard only accepted eight to ten new candidates into the actor training program each year. Ever since she was a little girl, Lauren Hanson dreamed of singing on a Broadway stage. Gaining admittance into Juilliard led her one step closer to fulfilling that dream.

This year's incoming freshmen had the opportunity to go on an educational tour through various theatres in New York City. While touring the Ambassador Theatre, Lauren and her classmates were invited to act out impromptu or perform a monologue on the stage if they wanted to. But Lauren didn't do either of those things. Instead, she confidently stood before an empty house and belted out the song 'Defying Gravity' from the musical *Wicked*.

Roger Zellers, a professional Broadway actor, was backstage retrieving his cellphone when he heard Lauren's heavenly voice echo through the theatre. He roamed onto the stage wing to investigate. Standing center stage, singing her heart out, was an incredibly attractive young woman wearing a Juilliard tee-shirt and jeans. He watched in rapt attention, mesmerized by the intense emotion she projected through her performance. He had to find out who this woman was.

When the class was about to exit the theatre, Roger intercepted her at the door. "Excuse me, Ma'am?"

Lauren turned around. "Yes?"

"I'm sorry. I know you don't know me, but I just heard you sing, and you have the most beautiful voice I have ever heard."

She offered him a small, shy smile. "Thank you."

"I am correct to assume that you're a student at Juilliard?"

"Yes, I am."

He extended an open palm and graciously shook her hand. "I'm Roger Zellers, and if you'd allow me, I'd like to offer my assistance."

"Assistance with what?"

"I would like to provide you with an opportunity that will help you gain exposure and allow you to meet and work with people in the Broadway community."

She asked for clarification. "What do you mean?"

"I'm an actor currently doing a show here at the Ambassador. I happen to know that the manager of this theatre is looking to hire theatre arts students as interns. You'll be behind the scenes during productions, you'll get to work directly with Broadway performers, and you'll learn a few tricks of the trade. It'll get your foot in the door, and people will get to know you. I'd like to give your name to the manager. You certainly captured my attention, I know you'll capture hers as well. You interested?"

The chance to meet and work with Broadway actors and be backstage during shows was a once in a lifetime opportunity toward fulfilling her dream of performing on Broadway. As excited as Lauren was about this opportunity, she was a bit apprehensive because she knew nothing about this man and didn't know if she could trust him.

Sensing this woman's reluctance, Roger offered her an alternative. "Tell you what, why don't you stop by tomorrow afternoon and talk to her." He pulled a business card out of his wallet and grabbed a pen to write something on the back. "We have rehearsal tomorrow at 3:30. When you get here, go around the back and enter through the stage door. Show the security guard this card and tell him Roger sent you."

He handed her the card and she carefully examined it. Printed on the front in huge block letters were the words *Roger Zellers, Broadway Vocalist/Actor/Dancer.* A phone number and website followed.

"So will you stop by tomorrow?"

She smiled with satisfaction. "I'll be here."

After class the next day, Lauren headed over to West 49th Street. She wasn't sure what to expect and wasn't totally convinced this Roger guy was telling the truth about who he was or his connections with Broadway. But as soon as the cab pulled up to the Ambassador Theatre, any doubts Lauren had about Roger quickly disappeared. The marquee out front promoted the musical *Chicago.* Larger than life still shots from the show, one of which captured Roger posing in a black suit, were displayed on the walls outside. Obviously he had been honest with her about his involvement on Broadway, and she felt less reluctant about blindly walking into the theatre.

Once Lauren gained access inside, she took a seat in the back and watched the performers rehearse. Roger, dressed in black jazz pants and a tee-shirt with

Chicago printed on the front, danced around the stage with a black fedora on his head and a cane in his hand while he sang a song called 'Razzle Dazzle.' He had a powerful baritone voice and quite the stage presence. He was incredibly entertaining to watch.

At the conclusion of rehearsal, Roger gulped down a bottle of water and peered out to the rows of empty seats. When he saw Lauren seated in the back row, a huge grin brightened his features. Removing his fedora, he stepped off the stage and strolled to the back to greet her. "I'm glad you made it," he said. "I told Carmen about your remarkable performance yesterday. She's looking forward to meeting you. Come with me and I'll introduce you."

Lauren stood up and followed him.

The theatre manager, Carmen Hollister, discussed details with Lauren. Job responsibilities included cleaning up props, helping with costumes, and basically running around making sure the performers had everything they needed before and during the show. Carmen was willing to work around Lauren's class schedule and offered her twenty hours a week during nighttime and weekend performances. After chatting with Carmen for about thirty minutes, Lauren gladly accepted the job.

When Roger found out Lauren took the position, he beamed with excitement. "That's fantastic. Congratulations!"

"Thank you so much for your help."

"No problem. When do you start?"

"Monday night."

He flashed her an irresistibly captivating grin. "I guess I'll see you on Monday."

On her first day at the Ambassador, Lauren arrived early, eager to get started. Several cast and crew members were already there, including Roger. He leaned against the makeup counter conversing with another man. The moment Lauren walked in, conversation ceased and Roger's eyes drifted her direction. "Well, look who's here. Hello, Lauren. It's good to see you again." He motioned for her to come closer. "Have you met Jason? He's our lead dancer."

Jason welcomed her with a firm handshake. "Welcome aboard. Always good to have a helping hand around here."

"Thanks. I'm looking forward to it."

Roger stood up straight. "Let me show you around." He said goodbye to Jason then led Lauren back to the dressing rooms. He introduced her to several performers from the show and she met one of the makeup artists. Roger showed her where props and costume racks were stored then guided her back to the main gathering area. Several dancers were now warming up, and crew members busily began to prepare for the show. "Do you have any questions?" he asked her.

She looked around the theatre feeling a bit overwhelmed. "This is a lot to take in."

"It is, but things run pretty smoothly around here. We'll help you figure it out." He checked the time on his watch. "I have to get ready for the show. Have fun tonight."

"I'm sure I will. Break a leg, Roger."

"I'll try not to."

During intermission, Roger reached into the mini-fridge to grab a bottle of water. As he unscrewed the lid, he caught sight of Lauren. With the bottle in his hand, he moseyed her direction. "How's it going?"

Lauren looked up. "Busy, but I love it. Everyone has been so helpful."

"I'm glad to hear that." He leaned against the wall with his hand in his pocket and gulped down a huge drink. "How are you getting home tonight? Is someone coming to pick you up?"

"I was going to take a cab."

His eyes widened. "By yourself?"

"Yes."

He rubbed his hand across his chin. "Traveling alone at night in New York City can be dangerous. Please allow me to escort you home after the show."

"You don't have to do that."

"I insist. I won't be able to sleep tonight if I don't see you home safely. Meet me by my dressing room after the show and I'll take you home."

Grateful that he cared so much about her safety, she agreed. "That's very kind. Thank you."

"It's my pleasure."

Throughout the week, Lauren worked three evening shows and all day Saturday. Prior to Saturday's matinee, Lauren tapped on Roger's dressing room door to see if he needed anything.

"It's open," he called out.

She walked in to find Roger clothed only in a pair of black trousers, holding a white button-up dress shirt in his hand. "I'm sorry. I didn't realize you weren't dressed."

Roger shrugged it off. "It's alright. Come on in." He slipped the shirt over his shoulders, leaving it unbuttoned.

In her hand, Lauren held the black fedora Roger needed for his opening number. "You left your hat by the makeup counter again."

"Did I?" He chuckled at his own forgetfulness. "Silly me."

She stepped closer and placed the fedora on his head.

"Thank you for returning it. I appreciate the way you keep tabs on the items I'm always misplacing. Keeps me in check."

"Someone has to."

"And I'm glad that someone is you." He turned away and began to button his shirt. "You're doing a great job, by the way."

"Thank you." Gaining his approval boosted her confidence. "Do you need anything before the show starts?"

"No, thanks. I'm fine."

"Alright. I'm going to check on the others then. See you later."

During a break between the afternoon and evening show, Roger bounded backstage, rubbing his growling stomach. "My tummy is rumbling. We should do a Schmackary's run."

"I'm in." Jason reached for his wallet and handed Roger twenty dollars.

Several other performers added to the fund.

Lauren overheard the conversation and joined them. "What's at Schmackary's?"

"Only the best cookies on the planet." Roger slipped the wad of money in his pocket. "Do you want to come with me? I could use some help carrying the boxes back over here."

"How far is it?"

"About half a mile. We have plenty of time."

Lauren willingly agreed to go with him.

When they arrived at the bakery, Roger ordered two dozen cookies—Sch'mores, Carmel Apple Crisp,

Chocolate Chip, and his personal favorite, Peanut Butter Cup. Once the boxes were filled with everyone's favorites, he asked Lauren, "Any kind in particular you'd like to try?"

She peered into the glass case, eyeing the huge selection of sweet treats. "I want one of those sprinkle cookies."

"Good choice." He added one to the box just for her.

On the way back to the theatre, Roger struck up a conversation. "Have you seen much of New York City?"

"My sister and I went exploring when we first got here. We saw Central Park and quite a bit of Times Square."

"Experienced any nightlife?"

She shook her head. "Other than working in the theatre, no."

"Some of us are going to 54 Below tonight. Would you like to come with us?"

"What's 54 Below?"

"A dinner club with live performances and drinks. It's open stage night, Broadway Sings the Blues. Do you want to come?"

Uncertain, she lifted a shoulder. "I don't know."

Hoping to entice her, he offered, "I'll pay your cover and buy you dinner."

"That's really not necessary, Roger."

He did his best to convince her. "C'mon, Lauren. Come cabaret with us. You're in New York. You need to get out and experience what this city has to offer."

"Are you sure the others won't mind?"

"Of course not. We'd love to have you."

After a bit of persuasion, she agreed to go.

Around 11:00 P.M., Roger, Lauren, and two other *Chicago* cast members strolled over to West 54th Street. As soon as they arrived, they descended a narrow wooden staircase, enclosed by walls plastered with red-patterned wallpaper. At the bottom of the stairs, they were greeted by a 54 Below doormat. The maître d' met them at the entrance and graciously invited them inside.

This intimate and classy restaurant was full of sophisticated New York City glam. The décor was stylish and inviting—leather backed chairs, archival pictures, and a central stage complete with grand piano. The entire place had a 1920's ambience. Every detail from the wallpaper to the molding to the art was reminiscent of a speakeasy.

The group was led to a four-person banquette table. Lauren took a seat next to Roger.

"Do you want a drink?" he asked, hanging his jacket over the back of a chair. "They have a ginger lemonade that's pretty tasty."

Being adventurous, she decided to give it a try.

Once everyone was situated and the waiter took their orders, Roger updated the group on the latest news. "*Holiday Inn* premiers in a few weeks."

"Yes, I saw that," Jason said. "I'm surprised you aren't involved in that."

"Don't have time right now. With eight shows a week, benefit concerts, and recording sessions, I barely have time to breathe."

"Recording sessions for what?" Lauren asked, curious about Roger's activities outside the theatre.

"A collaborative benefit Christmas album. It occupies a lot of my time, but it's for a good cause. That alone makes it worth the hours I devote to it." He took a sip of his wine then set the glass on the table.

While they ate, several performers took turns singing, each entertaining the crowd with their own rendition of various classic blues songs. When it was Roger's turn to take the stage, he sat at the piano and began pounding away at the keys with effortless eloquence. He boisterously sang 'Walking in Memphis', pouring his heart into every word. The intensity of his performance gradually increased until it reached its powerful crescendo. He ended the final note with his eyes fixated right at Lauren.

The restaurant patrons applauded, and Roger slowly rose from the piano bench and shuffled off the stage.

When he returned to the table, Lauren praised his performance. "I had no idea you could play the piano."

"A little something I do in my spare time. It helps me unwind."

At closing time, Roger offered Lauren an escort home. When they arrived at Lincoln Center, he walked her up to the main building of the Juilliard dormitory. "Did you have fun tonight?"

"I did. Thank you for inviting me."

"Thank you for joining us."

She pulled her keys out of her purse. "I appreciate you going out of your way to walk me home."

"It's my pleasure, and it's not out of my way. My apartment is only a few blocks from here." Hoping to get her to mingle with some of his Broadway connections, Roger suggested, "Some friends and I are meeting at Tavern on the Green for brunch tomorrow morning. You're welcome to join us."

"I appreciate the offer, but my sister and I made plans to hang out tomorrow, and I have some studying to do."

"Alright. I just wanted to throw the invitation out there, help you meet some new people."

"Thank you for being so welcoming."

"It's not a problem. Enjoy the rest of your weekend, Lauren."

"You too. I'll see you on Monday."

He smiled charmingly then stepped away from the entrance, whistling as he made his way home

Chapter Two

At the theatre the following week, the cast and crew of *Chicago* decided to order takeout between shows. Everyone pitched in for fresh salads, flatbread sandwiches, and a variety of homemade soups.

Roger claimed a foldup chair and pulled it over to a nearby table. Jason took a seat beside him. With warm lentil soup and kale salad in front of them, they dug in while they talked.

"My sister called me last night," Jason said, pouring balsamic vinaigrette dressing over his salad. "Apparently, she and Leo split up."

"I'm sorry to hear that." Roger dipped his spoon into his soup and took a bite. "I thought they were engaged?"

"They were. It's complicated. According to my sister, Leo only proposed to her because he was afraid to admit he was gay. When he finally realized he couldn't suppress the truth any longer, he broke off the engagement and openly came out."

Roger set his spoon down and wiped his mouth with a napkin. "Oh man. What an awful way to discover the truth about someone. How's she handling that? Is she doing ok?"

"As good as can be expected, I guess. That's a lot to soak in."

"The next time you talk to her, wish her well for me." Lauren was sitting nearby munching on a sandwich. Encouraging her to be social, Roger said, "Would you like to sit with us? I promise we don't bite." He set up another chair to make room for her.

She rose to her feet and slowly trekked over to the table.

"So," Roger said, popping the top off his cranberry and pomegranate juice. "Anything exciting going on at Juilliard?"

They chatted about Juilliard news and happenings on Broadway before Roger retreated to his dressing room to make a few phone calls and prepare for the 7:00 P.M. show.

After the curtain call that night, Roger, still dressed in stage attire, ran into Lauren at the costume rack. "Hello, Lauren."

She pivoted to the sound of his voice. "Great show tonight, Roger."

"Thanks. Can I talk to you for a minute?"

"Sure." She placed a few costumes on the rack then gave him her full attention. "What's up?"

He chuckled at her innocence. "Not here. Come with me." Seeking a more private location, he led her into his dressing room and closed the door.

Being shut in here with him made her a bit uneasy. "What are we doing in here?"

Since Lauren started working at the Ambassador, Roger made several attempts to get to know more about her. He included her in conversations and encouraged her to hang out before and after shows, but with their busy schedules, they had difficulty finding time to connect outside of work. In an attempt to become better acquainted with her, he offered a suggestion. "Have dinner with me."

This comment took her by surprise. "Roger, I..."

"I know what you're thinking," he cut in, sensing her uncertainty. "But I just want to talk."

Lauren had serious doubts about this. Not only was this man far more experienced than she was, he was also ten years older than her. Although Roger was always kind and quite often went out of his way to help her, the thought of spending an evening alone with him made Lauren's nerves shaky.

He didn't want to pressure her or make her feel uncomfortable, but he was sincere in his invitation. "Just dinner. That's all I'm asking."

Reluctant at first, she gave in to his request.

"Fantastic! Are you available Wednesday night?"

"As far as I know, I am."

"Do you like Mexican food?" he suggested.

"Love it."

"Great! I'll make reservations at Rosa's. Will six o'clock work for you?"

"Six o'clock is fine."

Wanting her sister's opinion about this situation, Lauren paid her a visit. She told Lacy all about Roger, explaining how he was the one who hooked her up with the theatre job at the Ambassador. "So what do you think?"

"He's taking you someplace public, isn't he?" Lacy asked, concerned about her sister's safety.

"Yes."

"Is he cute?"

Picturing Roger's incredibly handsome face, mysterious hazel eyes, and adorable smile made Lauren's cheeks flush. "He's gorgeous, and he's an amazing performer. You should hear his voice. The man has some serious pipes."

Taking everything into consideration, Lacy offered her opinion. "Go for it, but keep your phone on. Excuse yourself to the restroom and call me if anything weird happens."

A few minutes before 6:00 P.M. Wednesday night, Roger promptly arrived at the Rose Building at Lincoln Center. This building had twenty-nine floors. Eleven of them housed the students of Juilliard. To enter the building, Roger had to pass through two security stations, one of which questioned his reason for being at the residence halls. Roger stated his intentions, and the guard allowed him access through the crossover to a private bank of elevators that led up to the Juilliard housing suites. Carrying a dozen red roses in his hand, he took the elevator to the eighteenth floor. At the end of the hall, a large bay window overlooked the city. He took a quick peek to admire the view then confidently headed down the hall to Lauren's room.

When Roger knocked, Lauren's tummy grew queasy and her hands began to shake. To calm her nerves, she took a few deep breaths before she opened the door.

Roger greeted her with a pleasant smile. "Good evening." Lauren was beautifully accessorized in a knee-length floral tea dress. She had on black slingback sandals, a pair of delicate rose quartz flowered earrings, and carried a sparkly clutch evening bag. "You look lovely."

This compliment made her blush.

To express his good intentions, he presented her with the roses. "These are for you."

No one, other than her father, had ever given her flowers before, so she was surprised Roger had taken the time to do that. "Thank you."

"You're welcome."

She took in their sweet aroma then set the bouquet on the table near the door.

"Are you ready?"

"Uh huh."

"Then let's go."

Since Rosa's Mexicano was located only blocks away from Lincoln Center, they walked the short distance to get there. This restaurant was one of Roger's favorite locations in New York City to share a meal with someone. The warm ambiance and outstanding cuisine were always a hit with his guests. Traditional amate gods watched over them and brightly colored *papel picado* hung from the ceiling. The delicious aroma of homemade corn tortillas tantalized the senses. On this particular evening, a mariachi band serenaded the diners.

He ordered a glass of wine, which he savored over dinner, along with the stimulating conversation he and Lauren shared. "As much as I love theatre, I can always watch a Bogart classic. Humphrey Bogart is by far my favorite cinema actor. He was on Broadway in the 1920's and 30's, but was one of those actors who was more successful on the big screen. His wife, however, was a Tony award-winning actress. Talented woman. Gotta love the old femme fatale characters Lauren Bacall portrayed."

Lauren agreed with his analysis. "She and Bogart were incredible together. But do you know who I really admire?"

Interested in everything Lauren had to say, Roger couldn't wait to hear more. "Who?"

"Julie Andrews. Definitely one of my idols. Talk about vocal range. She was fabulous in My Fair Lady."

"She was," Roger added. "You say you admire Julie Andrews. For me, it's Gregory Hines, Fred Astaire, and the unmistakable dancing skills of the ultimate tap legend, Bill Robinson."

"Do you tap dance?" Lauren asked.

"I do. Have since I was four. Performed in some children's tap ensembles as a kid and was in Radio City Music Hall's Tap Extravaganza many years ago."

"You're a man of many talents, aren't you?"

"I'd like to think I am."

The dinner conversation continued with Roger talking about his favorite literature works and music he enjoyed. He also mentioned his involvement in the Broadway Cares HIV/AIDS Foundation fundraising efforts.

Lauren spoke highly of her family, bragged about her NCAA basketball playing brother, and shared her connection with her twin sister. She told him about her experience with the Seattle Musical Playhouse and her high school's production of *Phantom of the Opera*, where she won two Fifth Avenue Theatre Awards for her performance in the leading role of Christine Daaé.

"Phantom huh?" Roger remarked. "I am completely obsessed with that show. Have you seen it at the Majestic?"

"No."

"You need to. You are missing the best musical production of all time. I'll get some tickets if you'd like to accompany me."

Thrilled with his invitation, she willingly accepted.

Roger had a great sense of humor, and as the evening progressed, Lauren felt more comfortable around him. Through their conversation, she learned that they shared many common interests besides love of theatre. Musicals, old Hollywood film noir movies, show tunes, beaches, classic literature, and poetry were among them.

To appease Lauren's curiosity, Roger told her about his experience on Broadway. Over the last eight years, he had made an appearance in many productions, including *Cats*, *Les Misérables*, and *Newsies*. He earned a Tony nomination for his role as Scrooge in *A Broadway Christmas Carol* and won a Tony and Drama Desk Award for his portrayal of Huey Calhoun in *Memphis*. He also performed as a tap dancer in Broadway's revival of *Sophisticated Ladies*. His most recent role, however, was as *Chicago*'s slickster lawyer, Billy Flynn.

"Wow," Lauren exclaimed, impressed with his resume. "That's incredible. I would give anything to be on Broadway."

"You will be," Roger affirmed. "With your talent and the education you're receiving from Juilliard, you are going to be a star, Lauren Hanson. There's no doubt in my mind about that."

Lauren's contagious smile brightened the entire room.

Throughout the evening, Roger and Lauren were able to maintain fascinating conversation. Lauren openly joked around with him, and they shared many laughs together. She had a great deal of enthusiasm and made the cutest facial expressions. Roger immensely enjoyed her company.

Roger was easy to talk to. He was fun to be around and was extremely laidback. With the attractive qualities he possessed, Lauren wondered why this 28-year-old Broadway heartthrob chose to spend the evening with her. There were many women in New York City with much more experience who would have easily fallen into his arms given the chance. Daringly, she probed for more information. "Can I ask you something?"

"Absolutely," he replied. "Anything you'd like."

She cocked her head slightly. "There's something I don't understand."

"What's that?"

"You are an amazing man, Roger. You have incredible talent, a fun-loving disposition, and the sweetest smile I've ever seen. Yet at twenty-eight, I find it hard to believe that a woman hasn't swept you up. What's your story?" she asked, hoping to gain some insights into what made this man tick.

No one had ever asked him that before, and he wasn't sure how to respond. Finding her comment both cute and courageous, he chuckled a little. "That's bold."

She could tell he felt a bit uncomfortable about her inquiry into his personal life. She wished now that she hadn't so carelessly pried her nose into his private affairs. "I'm sorry. I didn't mean to…"

"It's alright. You're boldness intrigues me," he interjected. "I don't share personal information about myself with many people. I'm a pretty private guy, and I prefer to keep my personal life separate from my career. But since you asked, I'm going to be totally honest with you." He took a sip of his wine and gently set the glass on the table. "I've been involved in relationships in my past, and I've been in love. I've also been deceived, lied to, and led to believe that a woman I loved actually cared about me, which ended up being a fabrication to fulfill other motives—money and a chance at the spotlight among them."

Lauren began to understand why Roger was slightly reserved. Obviously he had gotten close to someone who hurt him.

"But as a result of everything I've been through, I've learned what I want and don't want."

"And what's that?"

Opening up a bit more, he explained, "I don't believe in leading people on. I will never put on a false front and won't pretend to have feelings for someone if I don't. I'm not the kind of guy who drags out a relationship if it isn't working. For me, a relationship has to go beyond the surface. It has to grow and be meaningful for both of us. Honesty and trust are very important to me. They are the catalysts that build a relationship and keep it growing strong. Without trust, it's next to impossible for a relationship to grow. And a relationship cannot endure if the person you love doesn't reciprocate those feelings. I will give one-hundred percent of myself to the woman I'm with. I'll support her and always put her first, but I expect her to do the same for me. For a relationship to work, it has to be mutual, and feelings we have for one another must be genuine. Too many times I've had a woman say those three words to me when she didn't really mean them. And I won't say them unless I sincerely feel that way. So, in response to your comment, I haven't been swept up because I haven't found the right woman...yet." With that last word, he looked straight into her beautiful green eyes. "But that doesn't mean I'm not looking."

Chapter Three

The following evening, Lauren worked the 8:00 P.M. performance of *Chicago*. When Roger strolled past her, her whole face lit up. "Stop by my dressing room when you get a chance," he said. "I want to show you something." He flashed a charming smile then headed off to change into stage attire.

Later, when Lauren popped in to give Roger a bottle of water, he pulled two theatre tickets for *Phantom of the Opera* out of his wallet and waved them at her. "I picked up tickets for Sunday's matinee." He placed the tickets in her hand. "Why don't you hang onto these. We'll talk details later."

As usual, Roger escorted Lauren to the Juilliard residence halls that night. He joyfully shimmied down the sidewalk taking in the New York City atmosphere. "I'm looking forward to Sunday. I was thinking we could share lunch together before the show, if you have time."

"I don't have any other plans."

"Good. Do you mind giving me your number so we can finalize everything?"

"Not at all."

Once her number was successfully added to his contact list, he shoved his cellphone back in his pocket. "I'll give you a call tomorrow."

Roger bid her farewell then leisurely strolled a few blocks west to his apartment.

Sunday morning, around eleven o'clock, Roger stepped off the elevator onto the eighteenth floor of the Rose Building. On the opposite end of the hallway, a tall, muscular, African American man exited Lauren's dorm room. Lauren hugged him right there in her doorway.

This took Roger by surprise. Lauren never struck him as the type of woman to invite random men into her room, nor did he expect her to be with a man right before they were scheduled to go out.

The man walked past Roger, politely greeting him. "Good morning."

Roger reciprocated then continued down the hall to Lauren's room. Her door was still open, so he lightly tapped on the doorjamb. "Hello?"

Lauren peeked around the corner. "Hi, Roger."

Tilting his head to the side, he pointed down the hallway. "Who was that?"

"Trey. He and I are working on a project together."

Roger tightened his lips and shoved his hands in his pockets. "What kind of project?"

"We're studying Valperga by Mary Shelley."

"Ah yes. Ethanasia and Beatrice, bound together by their love for one who loved only himself."

"You've read it?"

"Many years ago. It's a timeless classic." Roger took a seat on a nearby chair. "We are still having lunch today, aren't we?"

"Of course. Let me grab a sweater first."

Throughout the afternoon, the conversation between them flowed steadily, and on several occasions, Roger caught himself gazing into Lauren's eyes. When the theatre house lights dimmed during the second act of *Phantom of the Opera*, Roger placed his hand over Lauren's. She exchanged a smile with him. Encouraged, he clasped her hand and held it for the remainder of the show.

After the curtain dropped, Roger escorted Lauren home. When they got to her door, he asked, "Have you ever been ballroom dancing?"

"Yes," she confirmed. "But it's been a while."

"A friend of mine is conducting tango classes on Wednesday nights. Since I don't have performance commitments that night, I've considered signing up for a few sessions. Do you know how to tango?"

Lauren shook her head. "No."

"Would you like to learn? I need a dance partner."

"Sure. That sounds like fun."

"Fabulous! The first class is next Wednesday at 7:00. I'll sign us up." Roger had to report to the Ambassador for the Sunday evening showing of *Chicago*. Before he left, he gave Lauren a hug. "I have a show to do, but I'll give you a call later."

As soon as Lauren was safely inside, Roger headed down Broadway toward the Ambassador Theatre, ready to take on another performance as Billy Flynn.

Over the next few weeks, Lauren and Roger dated casually. They had good and constant communication, both face to face and through either text messaging or phone calls. As they got to know each other on a more personal level, Roger hoped to spend more quality time with her. To accomplish this, he came up with a brilliant idea. "I have a suggestion for this weekend if you're interested."

"What did you have in mind?"

"I'd like to cook dinner for you."

"At your apartment?"

"Yes. I have a collection of Bogart movies we can watch and a bottle of wine chilling in my refrigerator. It will give us a chance to talk more privately without other people hanging about." Since Lauren didn't respond right away, Roger had the impression that she was uncomfortable about this. He wished now that he hadn't made such a bold suggestion. "If you don't want to…"

"I do," she cut in. "I'd love to see where you live."

Hoping to make a huge impression, Roger planned an elaborate meal, complete with his best porcelain dishes, crystal wineglasses, and glowing candles. While the salmon baked in the oven, he went into the bedroom to change. Moments later, a knock resounded through his apartment. Anticipating Lauren's arrival, he rushed to answer the door.

Lauren stood before him with a decorative cookie box in her hand. "I brought some cookies. I hope that's ok."

"That's perfect." He took the box from her and showed her inside. "May I take your jacket?"

"Yes, please."

He slipped her jacket off her shoulders and hung it in a nearby coat closet. "I'm going to check on dinner. Feel free to look around."

Roger stepped into the kitchen and Lauren checked out some of the decorative features of his apartment. This place was the epitome of manly glam. With an Art Deco-inspired look, Roger's interior decorating incorporated luxe materials like velvet, Lucite, chrome, and mirror alongside contemporary accessories and art. His clever use of trays, stacks of books, boxes, bowls, and vases created interesting layered vignettes, giving the room character.

Fun contemporary wall art adorned the sitting area, including an attention-grabbing canvas painting of red wine being poured into a wineglass. Matching cylindrical Miro-Chrome Tiffany table lamps accented each glass-topped end table. Various decorative throw pillows, clearly chosen to match the colors of the large stylish imported Oriental area rug, were tossed on the sofa and adjacent loveseat. In the middle of the room, atop a Lucite and chrome-based coffee table, was a layered design of beveled mirror, a book entitled *Wine Wise*, and a unique red wineglass gel candle.

A white brick fireplace was the main feature in the room. On the mantle, Roger had strategically displayed his Tony and Drama Desk Award along with a ceramic vase full of fragrant yellow roses. In the opposite corner was a shiny black piano with open sheet music displayed on the music rack.

He had a large flat screen TV mounted to the wall in the living room. On the floor beneath it was a low standing entertainment shelf unit that held electronics and a collection of DVDs, most of which were various musicals and classic movies like *Casablanca* and *The Maltese Falcon*. Showing off Roger's playful side, an exquisitely detailed mini Lego grand piano sat on a shelf, accompanied by a little Lego man dressed in a tuxedo. Several novels, poetry selections, and books from Broadway plays, including Victor Hugo's *Les Misérables, The Phantom of the Opera* by Gaston Leroux, and Charles Dickens' immortal classic *A Christmas Carol*, were neatly displayed on the bookshelf, along with a vast collection of Broadway Playbills. Decorative boxes, sculptures, and glass bowls were displayed throughout the shelving unit, and Roger had what appeared to be production scripts placed neatly in a fancy black box. An interesting hexagonal-shaped fine Chinese porcelain vase sat on top of the entertainment unit along with a chrome-framed photo of two young boys.

Lauren took a closer look at the photograph. "Who are the little boys in this picture? They're adorable."

"Those are my nephews," he called to her from the kitchen. "Matthew and Gabriel."

"You're an uncle?"

Roger grinned proudly. "Yes, I am. They're my brother's kids."

"I didn't know you had a brother."

"Yup. His name is Peter. He and Amy have been married for eight years now. They're good boys. Their uncle spoils them."

"Yes, I bet you do."

Over dinner, their conversation ranged from discussing family and friendships to sharing embarrassing moments. "I grew up in upstate New York," Roger said, pouring another glass of wine. "My parents still live there, but I've made New York City my home for the past ten years."

"Have you always lived in this apartment?"

"No. Started off sharing a loft with Jason, but as both of us became more established in our careers, and Jason developed a serious relationship with a dancer he'd been dating, we each got our own place."

"Jason is a friend of yours?"

"Oh yeah. We've known each other for years. Met during the production of Newsies. We've been in a couple of shows together and have had a few interesting adventures along the way."

"What kind of adventures?"

Reluctant at first, he decided to divulge the truth. "After Newsies closed, he and I spent a month together in Canada. We went to see a show in Toronto, took in some sights, and got a little rambunctious in Montreal."

"Rambunctious how?"

He attempted to ease his embarrassment by hiding behind a glass of wine. "We went to a tiki lounge and had way too much to drink. In our drunken state, we did some pretty stupid things, some of which I don't even remember now. Somehow we woke up in a hotel on the opposite side of the St. Lawrence River."

Lauren burst out laughing. "I can't picture you as the kind of guy who would stir up trouble like that."

"You'd be surprised. I didn't always make the brightest decisions in my youth, but I've learned from my mistakes. Two days after the tiki bar incident, he and I hopped a plane back to New York. I started rehearsals for Memphis, and he began the production of A Chorus Line. We kind of went our own ways professionally for a while, but ended up working together again in Chicago. We didn't really plan it that way, it just happened."

Lauren found Roger's theatre stories fascinating. Aside from general backstage banter, he was always telling her about makeup mishaps, costume failures, or other funny stage blunders. Tonight, he told her about an accident he had during a fight scene. Apparently he and his supporting actor got a little too rowdy during Les Mis rehearsal and Roger ended up breaking his hand because of it.

"Ow. That must have been painful," Lauren said, cringing at the thought.

"Oh, it was. Put me out of commission for a few days, and I couldn't perform without my hand wrapped in a splint."

Lauren continued with a story of her own. "Lacy twisted her knee on a family ski trip once and had to sit out during a dance performance. She wasn't very happy about it, but my father wouldn't let her perform until it healed."

"Makes sense." He neatly folded his napkin and set it on the table. "Speaking of Lacy, when are you going to introduce me to your sister?"

"Our schedules never seem to be in sync. She has a dance recital next week, if you'd like to come."

"When is it?"

"Sunday night."

With his Sunday night show commitments, this posed a problem. "Hmm, that's not going to work. Maybe we can meet her for brunch?"

"I can ask her, but I think she's working in the morning."

Roger chuckled at this predicament. "I see what you mean about schedule conflicts. We need to make plans at some point to get together so I can meet her."

After dinner dishes were cleared, Roger quickly changed to get ready for the 8:00 show. He escorted Lauren home and gave her a long, lingering hug. His cheek grazed hers, and for a moment he could feel her breath on his skin. His heart danced with excitement. Although they had been dating for a while, Roger and Lauren had never kissed. Roger longed to feel that physical bond with her, and every time he was around her, the pull was stronger. But he wanted to make their first kiss memorable, not forced or rushed, so he fought the urge and slowly pulled away.

They stared at each other for a second or two before Roger broke the silence. "I need to get going. What time do you get out of class tomorrow?"

"3:00."

"Will you have time to meet me for dinner before the show?"

"I should."

They confirmed plans and decided to meet at Francesco's Pizzeria the following evening.

While Roger changed into costume that night, one of his fellow cast members knocked on his dressing room door.

Roger answered holding a black fedora in his hand. "Hey, Brody. What's up?"

"You hang out with Lauren Hanson, right?"

"Yes, I do. Why do you want to know?"

"I was thinking about asking her out."

This comment hammered at Roger's heart. Brody rarely acknowledged Lauren. Why was he suddenly so interested in her?

"What do you know about her? Is she involved with anyone? Has she mentioned anything to you about a boyfriend?"

"As a matter of fact she has."

"Do you know who he is?" Brody asked, overflowing with confidence. "I'd like to know who my competition is."

The cheerful disposition Roger held all day instantly turned black. "You're looking at him."

Brody laughed out loud, not believing a word he said. "I'm serious, Roger. Who is he?"

Roger didn't find this conversation nearly as funny as Brody seemed to think it was. He folded his arms across his chest and stared Brody down.

When Brody realized Roger was telling the truth, he quickly wiped the smile off his face. "You and Lauren?"

Roger stood stiffly and simply nodded.

"Are you serious? You're dating Lauren Hanson?"

"Why are you so surprised by that?"

"I don't know. I thought…" Obviously he had rubbed Roger the wrong way. He slowly inched away. "I'm sorry. I didn't mean to offend."

The incident with Brody tormented Roger all night. When he saw Lauren the next day, he expressed his concerns. "What's going on with you and Brody?"

Lauren raised an eyebrow, wondering where that absurd comment came from. "There's nothing going on with me and Brody. Why would you think that?"

"He and I had an interesting conversation last night."

"About what?"

"About you. He's interested in you."

Lauren wrinkled her forehead. "How do you know that?"

"Because he told me." Roger scooped a slice of spinach, mushroom, and tomato pizza onto Lauren's plate then served himself a slice. "He asked if you had a boyfriend."

"What did you tell him?"

"I told him you and I were dating." He shot her a cockeyed glance. "That is what this is, isn't it?"

"Yes."

Good. At least they were on the same page. "Since Brody now knows, others will soon find out."

"Is that a problem?"

"It's not necessarily a problem, I just know how people are."

She didn't follow his logic. "What do you mean?"

"People talk, Lauren. And sometimes they say things that aren't very nice. Misleading information travels from one person to another, rumors spread, and before you know it all kinds of false accusations are flying around. I don't want you caught in the middle of that."

"I'm a big girl, Roger. I'm sure I can handle it."

"I know you can handle it. I'm not saying that. I'm just expressing my concerns." He switched to a more pleasant topic. "Are you going to be in a hurry to get home tonight?"

"Not really. Why?"

"Because I'd like to show you something."

Eager to find out what it was, she bounced in her seat. "What is it?"

He chuckled at her impatience. "You'll have to wait and see. Stop by my dressing room after curtain call and I'll show you."

As per Roger's request, Lauren made her way to his dressing room as soon as the show was over. The door was closed, so she tapped lightly on the frame. "Roger, it's me."

"Come in, Lauren. It's unlocked."

She stepped inside to find Roger tucking in his shirt. "Great show tonight."

"Thanks." He slipped his cellphone and wallet into his back pockets then reached over to the vanity and grabbed his keys.

"What is it you wanted to show me?"

"Actually, it's not here. We have to hop in a cab to see it."

She crinkled her nose and dropped her eyebrows.

Her reaction made him laugh. "I promise it will be worth it."

Roger flagged down a taxi and the two of them crawled into the back seat together. "Fifth Avenue and 34th Street, please," he told the cab driver.

As the cab pulled away from the curb, Lauren scooted a bit closer. "Where are we going?"

"You mentioned once that you haven't had a chance to visit the Empire State Building. I'm taking you there tonight."

This plan seemed a bit irrational this time of night. "It's almost one o'clock in the morning."

"I know that, but a friend of mine is the tour director. I called her yesterday and arranged to have a private viewing." Roger grinned slyly, waiting for Lauren to respond.

"Are you serious?"

"Yes I am. She's waiting for us inside the building. Just need to call her when we get there."

When they arrived, Lauren stepped onto the sidewalk and looked up at the glorious steel structure, illuminated in its signature white lights. "Wow. That is magnificent."

"Wait 'til you see the view from the top."

Roger's friend, Shaundra, met them at the back entrance. She greeted Roger with a huge hug. "Roger. It's good to see you."

"It's good to see you too." He slid his arm around Lauren's waist. "This is Lauren, the intern at the Ambassador I told you about."

Lauren had a hard time containing her excitement. "Thank you so much for doing this."

"It's my pleasure. I owed Roger a favor anyway." Shaundra led them to the express elevator, and they took a two minute ride up to the eighty-sixth floor.

When the elevator came to a stop, Roger held Lauren's hand and led her out to the observation deck.

The deck wrapped around the building's spire, providing 360-degree views of the entire city. Lauren rushed to the edge to take a peek. Skyscraper lights illuminated all around her. "Look at this view."

Roger stood by her side, taking in the sights along with her.

The city lights reflected off the Hudson River, and in the distance, a brightly glowing tower lit up the skyline. It was the most awe-inspiring scene she had ever witnessed. "I have never seen anything like this in my life." Beaming with excitement, Lauren dashed over to the other side.

Roger trailed behind her, enjoying the child-like joy in Lauren's eyes. He slipped his arm around her and admired the candy-colored hues of the nighttime cityscape. The Chrysler Building, Radio City Music Hall, and Rockefeller Center were clearly visible. Off to the left, bright lights radiated in vibrant purples, pinks, and yellows. Roger pointed them out to her. "Times Square is right over there."

Lauren turned her head to look.

"You know, people complain all the time about how dirty, noisy, and crowded New York City is. But when you come up here and see it all from this perspective, you have to admit, there's nothing quite like it."

"This is the most remarkable thing I've ever seen."

"It's beautiful, isn't it? I love New York City at night. And the best part is we have our own private show."

"It pays to have friends in high places."

Roger chuckled at her statement. "That it does."

Roger's eyes met hers, and his heart turned over in response. He longed to kiss her, and the prolonged anticipation was almost unbearable. His gaze dropped from her eyes to her lips and back to her eyes again. The mood tonight was perfect—they were alone, standing close to one another, and he could feel her body heat. With the city lights illuminating all around them, the atmosphere couldn't have been more romantic. Taking a risk, Roger leaned closer and softly kissed her.

Feeling Lauren's lips on his was a purely sensual experience. It gave him chills, and for a long moment, he felt as if he was floating. She melted into him, and as cliché as it sounded, butterflies fluttered in his tummy. Sharing this intimacy with her was powerful, bonding. He felt happier and more alive than he had in years, and the chill in the air seemed to intensify the feeling.

Fearing he may have pushed things too far, he slowly pulled away from her. "What are you thinking?"

Lauren began to breathe erratically.

His gaze traveled over her face and searched her eyes. "It's ok. You don't have to be afraid." Offering reassurance, he wrapped his arms around her like a warm blanket. "I want to be with you, Lauren. But I don't want to push you to jump into something you're not ready to jump into. I don't want to do anything to make you feel uncomfortable."

"I don't feel uncomfortable."

The glow of his smile was as bright as the lights that surrounded them. "Good. Let's keep it that way."

He reclaimed her lips, but this time she surrendered to him completely, letting go of her fear and taking in every tingly sensation he offered.

It was close to 3:00 A.M. by the time Roger walked Lauren up to her door. "Thank you for sharing that experience with me tonight," he said. "I've always wanted to do that."

"Do what?"

"Kiss someone on top of the Empire State Building. Guess I can scratch that off my bucket list." He chuckled at his own words. "You said your brother plays basketball. You into sports at all?"

"A little. Depends on what it is."

"The Knicks are playing next week. Would you like to go to the game with me?"

"I would love to."

"Alright. I'll call you later with details." As he leaned in to kiss her goodnight, his heart throbbed. His breathing escalated, and his entire body developed chills. He was swept away with a complete feeling of euphoria. He drew out the kiss for as long as possible before they finally parted ways.

Chapter Four

As Roger suspected, word traveled through the Ambassador that he and Lauren were seeing each other outside of work, but they were only rumors until tonight. Prior to the evening performance of *Chicago*, Roger stood outside his dressing room and departed from Lauren with a kiss. Several people witnessed this, including Jason.

When Lauren was out of sight, Jason followed Roger inside his dressing room. He sat down on the loveseat and put his feet up on the table. "What are you doing, Rog?"

"What do you mean?"

Roger was Jason's best friend, and he trusted the man with his life. But after witnessing this recent development, he seriously questioned Roger's sanity. "She's almost half your age. Don't do this to her."

"What do you think I'm doing to her, Jason?"

"She's naïve in the ways of this business, and you're going to get her caught up in it. You told me yourself to never mix business with pleasure."

"This is different," Roger argued.

"Yeah," Jason rebutted. "What you're doing is way worse."

"Lauren is the one thing in my life right now that is stable, dependable, and not totally surrounded by chaos. For the first time in a long time I found someone I can love. I haven't felt this way in years."

"Love?"

"Yes, Jason, love," Roger confirmed. "I have fallen head over heels for this woman and I really want to make this work."

"She's a baby, Rog."

"She's a woman," he argued. "And she's an amazing woman at that."

"You're not sleeping with her, are you?"

"Not that it's any of your business, but no, I'm not," Roger confirmed. "We are taking this slow. So far our relationship is progressing nicely."

"Have you got a screw loose in that head of yours?" Jason asked, not agreeing with any of this. "She's eighteen for Christ sake!"

"What difference does it make how old she is?" Roger demanded to know. "Why are you so hung up on her age?"

Trying to get Roger to reconsider his actions, Jason said, "You honestly don't see anything wrong with a 28-year-old man getting seriously involved with an 18-year-old girl?"

"Woman," Roger corrected. "She's a woman, Jason." He grabbed his costume off the hanger and began to change. "And I'd really like to know at what point I asked you or anyone else for their opinion about this?"

Sensing Roger's frustration, Jason got up to leave. "I hope you know what you're doing."

"I know exactly what I'm doing."

Jason shook his head and left Roger alone to get ready for the show.

Bundled up in jackets, Roger and Lauren held hands as they strolled across the Gapstow Bridge in Central Park. The air was crisp and they could see their breath. Trying to stay warm, Roger gathered Lauren in his arms and held her snugly. "Feels like winter is creeping in on us."

She slid her hands in her jacket pockets. "It does."

"Winters in New York can get bitterly cold. Makes it tough for those who don't have a warm place to go home to. Every year, particularly this time of year, people go hungry, freeze to death, or get sick out on the streets."

"That's awful," Lauren added.

"It is," Roger declared. "Many things in life we take for granted, like a warm place to sleep at night, jackets, gloves, or even a pair of shoes. There are kids out there, by no fault of their own, who don't get a decent meal every day. I find that heartbreaking. Which is why I make it a point to donate food, blankets, and shoes to the less fortunate. I want to do what I can to help."

"You're such a generous person, Roger," she said to him. "Always thinking of others."

He didn't think his actions were anything magnanimous. Donating to charities and freely giving his time was something he did on a regular basis. "I have the means right now to give to those in need. It's the least I can do."

Over the last six weeks, Roger's feelings for Lauren had deepened and intensified exponentially. He wanted nothing more than to protect her, offer his heart to her, and show her all the wonderful things about love. Although he felt this way, he hadn't told her. And he wasn't sure if he should tell her, fearing that her lack of experience would make her apprehensive about diving in that deep.

Lauren nuzzled in closer, and without a second thought, he moved his mouth to hers. Her lips were warm and inviting, and her kiss sent shivers down his spine. Sharing this moment of intimacy with Lauren confirmed what he already knew. He had completely fallen for her and could no longer ignore his feelings. He had to tell her. He gazed upon her with loving eyes and said, "I am head over heels in love with you."

Lauren exhaled heavily. "I'm so glad you said that."

"Why is that?"

"Because I feel the same way about you."

Roger's heart raced. He held her close, gently caressing the small of her back. He couldn't remember the last time he felt this way. "This feels so good, and it feels right." She looked at up him, and he gently grazed his thumb across her lips. "What's your father going to say about us?"

"I'll handle my father."

He clenched her hand in his and continued their walk. "You said he's pretty overprotective. That doesn't sound very promising for me."

"As long as we are honest and don't try to hide this from him, he'll be fine with us," Lauren assured him.

Roger was still worried. "I don't want him to think I'm some kind of cradle-robbing pervert who stalks young women. That's not my intention."

"If Daddy believes you care about me, there won't be a problem."

"I'm more concerned about what you believe." He took both of Lauren's hands in his and looked her in the eye. "Do you believe I care about you? Do you believe I love you?"

Since the day they met, Roger's actions proved that he was sincere about his professed feelings for her. The way he looked at her revealed it. The little things he did for her displayed it. The way he touched her strengthened it. The way he kissed her confirmed it. Their love had deepened every day, and there was no denying how they felt about each other.

"Yes," she replied.

The corners of his mouth arched upward. "That's all that matters."

Lifting her chin, he kissed her again. Mid-kiss, a snowflake fell on their noses, which made Lauren giggle. Roger held his hand out and turned his eyes toward the sky. "Snuggled in blankets of wool inside, I watch blankets of snowflakes fall fast and wide, veiling each hill like a lacy bride, calling me to grab my sled and ride."

"You can ride your sled later," Lauren said. "It's cold out here."

Roger laughed. "You read my mind." He rubbed his hands over her arms to warm her. "Come on. Let's get some cocoa."

While Roger was at the theatre that night, Lauren called her father. Dr. Randal Hanson wasn't sure how to react to the news that his daughter was seriously involved with an older man.

"How much older are we talking here, Lauren?"

"He's twenty-eight," she clarified.

Dr. Hanson sat silently on the other end of the line.

"Daddy?" Lauren asked, hoping to regain his attention.

He released a worried sigh. "I think he might be trying to take advantage of you. You don't have the experience he does. You're an easy target for him."

She argued against this assumption. "It's not like that, Daddy. He's a wonderful man, and he cares about me."

"He's ten years older than you. What can you two possibly have in common?"

Lauren stood her ground. "Aren't you the one who said love knows no boundaries?"

"Yes, but love can also be blind."

Upset by her father's lack of understanding, Lauren protested, "I was hoping to have your support with this."

"I don't know the man, Lauren. I can't trust someone I've never met, especially when my daughter is concerned. If I ever meet the man and he can prove to me that he's sincere and trustworthy, then maybe I'll change my mind. In the meantime, I'm suspicious of a 28-year-old man pursuing my 18-year-old daughter."

When Lauren met Roger for dinner the following evening, he asked her, "What did your father say when you told him?"

Lauren expressed her father's concerns. "He's apprehensive about it. He thinks you're trying to take advantage of me."

"I was afraid of that." He reached across the table and held her hand, trying to make light of the situation. "Help me out here. How do I convince your father that I'm not a wayward scumbag seeking debauchery on innocent young women pursuing their Broadway dreams in New York City?"

"He needs to know he can trust you."

"Ok." With his other hand, he reached for his glass of wine and took a sip. "How do I do that?"

"Just be honest with him. Let him know your true intentions. Show him you're trustworthy."

"Show him?" Roger moved the wineglass away from his lips. "How am I supposed to show him when he's all the way across the country?"

"By being who you are. Don't put on a show for him. He'll respect the fact that you're sincere and not hiding behind a mask."

Since Roger was always wearing costumes and standing on a stage entertaining thousands of people every night, he found Lauren's analogy funny. "But I always put on a show and wear a mask."

Lauren laughed. "That's not what I mean."

"I knew what you meant." He set his wineglass down and came up with a plan. "Are you going home for Christmas break?"

"I was planning to. Why?"

"Let me come with you," he suggested. "It'll give your father and me the opportunity to talk. I'll show him he can indeed trust me."

"What about your show?"

"I can break away for a few days to fly to Seattle with you. And I'll get a hotel. That way your father doesn't have to be suspicious."

She thought his idea was insane. "You don't think that's a little extreme?"

In desperation, he said, "How else can I show him I'm trustworthy? I'm not playing games here, Lauren, and I'm not trying to lead you on or deceive you in any way. My feelings for you are genuine."

"You don't have to explain that to me."

"I don't want your father's opinion of me to come between us," he feared.

"It's not going to," she reassured him.

"Our relationship is meaningful to me. It's worth fighting for, and I'm going to do whatever it takes to fight for it."

Hearing those words from him brought tears to her eyes. No one had ever said anything like that to her before.

Roger cupped his hands around Lauren's. "Sweetheart, I love you, and when I say that, I mean it. I am willing to do whatever it takes to make this relationship work, and if that means flying to Seattle to convince your father, then that is what I will do."

Chapter Five

As the holidays approached, Roger's schedule became more and more hectic. Aside from eight shows a week of *Chicago*, he committed to a one-night-only live benefit Christmas concert at the Palace Theatre. Also on his schedule was a performance in Times Square with the *Chicago* company and an appearance on the Today Show to promote the Toys for Tots program. Broadway.com asked him to film an eight-week 'Behind the Scenes of *Chicago*' video blog, and he was scheduled to perform in the Macy's Day Parade.

Walking home from a Sunday morning stroll through Central Park, Roger updated Lauren on his upcoming events. "My schedule is about to get nuts. With the holidays coming up, I have a ton of things going on, and Broadway Bakes is next week."

"What's that?"

"Working behind the Schmackary's counter selling cookies. We sing and dance for the customers, and any tips we get go directly to Broadway Cares, as well as half the proceeds from the cookies we sell."

"That sounds like fun."

"I enjoy it, and we usually raise quite a bit of money. My schedule is pretty full for the next couple of months. If you try to reach me and I don't get back to you right away, don't take it personally. I'm just busy."

"I think it's great that you do so much to support Broadway Cares. Your selflessness is one of the things I love about you."

Roger's lips formed a smile. "Thank you, Sweetheart. I love you, too."

When he and Lauren turned the corner, they spotted something unusual. A black curly-haired dog was curled up in a ball, shivering in the corner of the apartment stoop. Roger crept closer, trying not to frighten the animal.

"Do you suppose he has an owner?" Lauren asked, worried about the animal.

"I don't know." He tried to coax the dog to come closer. "Come here, Boy."

The dog whined.

Roger squatted to the dog's level and tried again. "Come on. I'm not going to hurt you."

The dog stood up, hobbling across the snow-covered stoop.

"Poor thing. We can't leave him out here. He'll freeze. Let's bring him inside." Cautiously, Roger lifted the dog out of the snow and carried him into shelter.

Once inside, Roger checked for identifying tags. None. The frightened dog was skin and bones, and his fur was all matted. He looked like he hadn't eaten in weeks. Roger fed the short-legged animal some leftover chicken he had in the refrigerator then laid a warm, comfortable blanket on the floor for him to snuggle in. Offering reassurance, he pet his wiry fur. Before the dog fell asleep, he licked Roger's hand.

"It breaks my heart that someone would do this to an innocent animal," Roger said. "This little guy is scared to death."

"I wonder how he got here."

"Don't know, but we need to find out who he belongs to."

Over the next week or so, Roger called the local animal shelters and checked the entire neighborhood for lost pet posters. No one had reported a missing Scottish Terrier. "Looks like I'm adopting a dog," he said to Lauren.

Lauren beamed with excitement. "What are you going to name him?"

After careful consideration, he decided on, "Oliver."

Later that week, Roger's mother came into New York City. Roger wasn't expecting her, so when he opened the door and saw her standing at his doorstep, he was pleasantly surprised. "Mom! What are you doing here?" He hugged her and showed her inside.

"I wanted to see your show. I haven't seen Chicago yet, and I've heard it's a good one, especially since you're the leading man." Roger took her jacket and hung it in the closet while she made herself comfortable on his couch. A small black dog with erect ears and a pointy tail hopped onto her lap, startling her. "Oh my. When did you get a dog?"

"Ollie, get down." Roger shooed the dog off the couch and encouraged him to lie in his dog bed instead. "Found him outside my apartment building in the freezing cold. No one claimed him, so I took him in."

"Of course you did." She scanned Roger's apartment as if she was expecting someone else to be there. "Where is this woman you seem to be so hung up on? She must be pretty special if she's stolen my Roger's heart."

Roger chuckled at his mother's statement. "She's in class right now. But if you join us for dinner tonight, you'll get to meet her."

"Oh good."

Before prepping for dinner, Roger picked up his cellphone. According to the clock, Lauren's last class just ended. Knowing she would be meeting his mother for the first time, he called her to give her a heads up. "Hi, Honey. You out of class?"

"Uh huh. Just got out," she chimed.

Since Lauren was free to talk, Roger explained what was happening. "Something's come up and there's going to be a slight change in our plans tonight."

"What's going on?"

"My mother is in town," he told her. "I wasn't expecting her, but she came in to see the show. We're still going to dinner, but if you don't mind, I'd like her to join us."

"Your mother?"

The nervous tone in Lauren's voice made Roger laugh. "Lauren, relax. It's just my mom."

"Does she know about us?"

"Yes, she does. In fact, she's looking forward to meeting you."

"She is?"

"Yes. She's going to love you."

"What am I supposed to say to her? How am I supposed to act?"

"Just be yourself," he suggested. "Let her see who you are and why I love you so much."

Lauren didn't respond.

Roger hoped she wasn't upset with him. "Are you ok with this?"

"Yes, I'm just nervous."

He offered reassurance. "It's gonna be fine. I'll pick you up in about an hour."

"Ok," she confirmed. "I love you."

"I love you too, Honey. I'll see you in little bit."

Rather than trying to flag down taxis all night, Roger decided to take the car. Before he went in to get Lauren, he turned to his mother and said, "She's nervous about meeting you."

"Why would she be nervous about that?"

"Because you're my mother." He tapped his hand on the steering wheel. "I know I told you about Lauren, but there's one thing I didn't tell you."

"What's that?"

Roger knew what he was about to say wasn't going to be an issue with his mother, but he didn't want her to be surprised when she actually saw Lauren. "She's quite a bit younger than me."

"Should I be concerned about this? She's of legal age, isn't she?"

"Yes, she's eighteen," he clarified.

"Then what difference does it make? If she makes my Roger happy, that's what matters."

He knew she'd understand.

When Roger met Lauren at the door, he greeted her with a kiss.

Since Roger specifically told her they were having dinner with his mother tonight, Lauren was surprised she wasn't with him. "Where's your mom?"

"Waiting in the car."

Lauren fidgeted with her fingers.

Trying to calm her down before she had a panic attack, Roger wrapped his arms around her. "Honey, relax. Don't be so edgy."

"But I'm about to meet your mother."

"Yes, and she's going to adore you. My mother is extremely supportive, and she trusts my judgment. You have nothing to be nervous about."

Throughout dinner, Roger's mother was quite talkative. And, as Roger explained, she supported him and his career, boasting about how proud she was of everything he had accomplished. As the evening progressed, Lauren learned many things about Roger. Evidently he was involved in playhouse theatre from the time he was four and took the stage in *Oliver* for his first public performance at the tender age of five. His mother told stories about how Roger would entertain family members during the holidays by singing show tunes and dancing around the living room with a cane and top hat. She claimed he was a natural performer, and had been from the day he was born. According to his mother, he was an accomplished tap dancer and knew how to play the piano, which Lauren already knew.

Roger was a little embarrassed that his mother spoke about his childhood like that, but every time he glanced Lauren's direction, she had a smile on her face. Obviously she enjoyed the conversation.

After the show, Roger dropped his mother off at the hotel. When he and Lauren were finally alone, he said, "See, I told you not to worry."

"Your mom is nice."

"Yes, she is," he concurred. "And she really likes you. Nice performance, Honey."

"I didn't put on a performance. You told me to be myself."

"I know, and you played the part perfectly. Every sweet ounce of you came out tonight."

Lauren giggled at his flattery.

"You've met my mother. When do I get to meet yours?"

"I thought you wanted to come to Seattle over Christmas break?" she reminded him.

"Well, that all depends. Are you inviting me?" he asked, wanting her to be the one to say it.

"Yes."

"Good. I'll plan accordingly."

For the Macy's Thanksgiving Day Parade, Roger sang 'Give My Regards to Broadway' atop the M&M's Chocolate Candies float. The theatre-themed float featured each of the M&M's characters taking lead roles in Broadway productions. Green took on the role of Elphaba in *Wicked*, Orange and yellow starred in *Cats*, blue was Phantom from The *Phantom of the Opera*, and red portrayed *Camelot's* King Arthur. As much as Roger loved being in the Macy's Parade, standing on a float singing in the frosty air for several hours made his fingers numb and put serious strain on his voice.

Santa Claus making his appearance at the end of the parade was a surefire indicator that the holiday season had begun. Roger, excited about his favorite holiday, spent an afternoon putting up Christmas decorations. He tossed red and green motif throw pillows on the sofa and loveseat then draped a green pine garland across the fireplace mantle. White and red candles of various heights were strategically layered on top of the mantle, and on the wall above, he hung a large Christmas wreath with sparkly white lights around it to brighten it up. Two fuzzy red stockings dangled from the fireplace—one with Roger's name and another that said Oliver. Across the middle of the coffee table, he draped a decorative red runner tablecloth, upon which sat a sterling silver serving tray.

In the center of the tray, he set another white candle, positioned inside a clear glass brandy snifter with poinsettia flowers and holly leaves encircled all around it.

After class that day, Lauren paid Roger a visit. The apartment looked festive with patterns of green, red, and white everywhere. "Wow, Rog, it looks nice in here."

"Thank you."

Roger awkwardly attempted to hold up a giant Christmas tree. Watching him struggle with this task made Lauren giggle. "What are you doing?"

"Putting up this tree," he replied.

"Do you need help?"

"That would be great."

She dropped her backpack on the floor and came over to assist him.

"Here," he said. "Hold this upright so I can straighten it out."

She held the tree while Roger crawled underneath and screwed on the tree stand. He was in an exceptional mood, busting out lyrics to the Christmas songs that played in the background. "Someone has the holiday spirit," Lauren observed.

"Christmas is my favorite time of year."

Once the tree was straight, Roger reached into a plastic tub filled with unopened boxes of ornaments and other Christmas décor and pulled out several strings of white twinkle lights. Lauren helped him untangle the first string and they hung them around the tree. While they decorated, the song 'Baby, It's Cold Outside' came on.

"I love this song," Roger said, and he started to sing.

Lauren chimed in. They continued to duet together as they hung the rest of lights around the tree. When the song was over, Roger looked at Lauren with a delighted grin on his face. "Wow!"

"What?" Lauren asked, wondering what he was so enthusiastic about.

"I love your voice. I always have. I hope someday I will have the opportunity to do a show with you. That would be the pinnacle of my career." He flirtingly winked at her.

She drew her lip between her teeth shyly.

"Which reminds me. A bunch of us are meeting this Sunday to kick off the holiday season by caroling through Central Park."

"Who's us?" Lauren asked.

"Me and a bunch of my Broadway friends. It's something we do for fun to spread holiday cheer throughout the city. You should join us."

Lauren was surprised Roger suggested that. "You want me join in a Christmas caroling party with a bunch of Broadway stars? Are you sure the others want me to come?"

He stopped what he was doing, wondering why she asked him that. "Of course they want you to come. You are a powerhouse soprano, Lauren. We need your voice."

She agreed to tag along.

When the tree was trimmed, they sat on the sofa to admire their masterpiece. "Gorgeous," Roger said. "We did well together. It looks great."

"That's because we make a great team," Lauren added.

"Yes we do."

New York City at Christmastime was one of the most spectacular sights to see. Lauren had never spent Christmas in New York before, so Roger was excited to share this unforgettable experience with her. The entire city had a festive atmosphere indicated by Manhattan's glittering holiday season lights which came alive at night. Snow blanketed the streets of Manhattan, and snowmen made their appearances throughout the city. Wearing hats and scarves, children created snow angels, and ice skaters glided across the ice rink at Rockefeller Center. New York City became a winter wonderland during the holidays.

Some of the best things about New York City this time of year were the department stores with their annual holiday displays. Each store put together beautifully designed windows to celebrate the season. Lord and Taylor's world-famous animated windows brought wide eyes of wonder to children and adults alike. One of Roger's favorite stops was FAO Schwartz, where together he and Lauren tapped toes on the giant floor piano keyboard. They also visited Macy's, stopping in to check out the elaborate Santaland, a stunner of a scene of Christmas trees, elves, toy trains, and snow-filled wonders.

Roger took Lauren to the New York Botanical Garden in the Bronx to witness one of the city's great Christmas traditions, the Holiday Train Show. Displayed here, a quarter-mile toy train track passed by 140 miniature New York icons like the Brooklyn Bridge, Yankee Stadium, and St. Patrick's Cathedral. After their Bronx excursion, they saw The New York City Ballet perform *The Nutcracker* at Lincoln Center. Christmas shows appeared on Broadway this time of year, so Roger and Lauren spent their off night at the Lunt-Fontanne Theatre watching *A Christmas Story: The*

Musical. And the Christmas season wasn't complete without attending the New York Pops annual holiday celebration at Carnegie Hall.

Since it was the season of giving, Roger purchased several pairs of gloves, coats, hats, and scarves and donated them to a homeless shelter. At Mount Sinai Children's Hospital, he and Jason dressed up in Santa Claus suits and distributed a bag of toys to the children. Roger and Lauren spent an evening at a soup kitchen feeding the homeless warm soup on a cold wintry day. For a local orphanage, Roger purchased a bunch of candy canes, stuffed animals, and warm slippers then brightened the children's day by singing Christmas songs with them, like 'Frosty the Snowman' and 'Rudolph the Red Nosed Reindeer.' Every time Roger passed a Salvation Army bell ringer, he dumped money in their red bucket. T'was definitely the season.

An event Roger was involved in that he dearly loved was the Annual Christmas Tree Lighting Ceremony in Rockefeller Plaza. No holiday highlight was quite like the Rockefeller Center Christmas tree. Giant in stature and sentiment, the tree had been a crowd delighter for many years. Decked out in more than 30,000 lights, the great 80-year-old, 80-foot-tall Norway spruce was topped with a ten-foot, 550-pound Swarovski star composed of 25,000 crystals. It was the pillar of incandescent Christmas spirit. The tree lighting ceremony attracted star-studded names and floods of eager faces every year. It was iconic to New York City.

This year, the Rockefeller Center Christmas tree would be lit for the first time on December 4th. Tens of thousands crowded the sidewalks for this event and hundreds of millions watched it live across the globe. Typically, the Radio City Rockettes performed for this event, and many celebrities sang Christmas songs and performed on stage for the lighting of the Christmas tree. The talent here was impeccable, and the holiday spirit soared.

Roger was truly honored when he was asked to sing at the Christmas tree lighting. Lauren came with him. He performed 'I'm Dreaming of a White Christmas' on a cold, snowy stage in front of an oversized tree. By the time he was finished, he desperately needed a cup of warm tea with honey to soothe his throat.

Anxious to get home, he and Lauren hopped in a cab and headed to the warm comfort of his apartment. With his busy schedule, Roger cherished every minute he spent with Lauren. But time always went by too quickly when they were together.

Trying to unthaw, they snuggled on the couch listening to Christmas music. "It's late," he said. "I need to get you home."

"I don't want to go home." She nuzzled in closer. "I wanna stay here with you."

"Good," he whispered. "'Cause I don't want you to leave."

Affectionately, he kissed her on the lips, but Lauren took the kiss deeper—much deeper—increasing the intensity. Roger could tell things were going to swelter soon if he wasn't careful. Fighting back incensed desire, he attempted to come up for air. "Take it easy, Honey."

"But I want to be close to you."

Roger opened his eyes, breathing hard from the fervent mood that had developed. "I want to be close to you too."

Taking matters into her own hands, Lauren reached her hand up his shirt and rubbed her fingers across his bare chest. She worked her way to his shoulders and around his lower back. Taking him by surprise, she grabbed his shirt and pulled it over his head.

Normally Roger was a gentleman in every way, but right now, he had a hard time behaving like one. He peered at her intently, dropping his eyes to her breasts.

Lauren clasped her hands around his neck and pressed her lips against his.

He responded by exploring the contours of her mouth with his tongue. Satisfying an overwhelming need to be close to her, he gathered her into his arms, encompassing her whole body. He roamed his hands up her blouse, feeling her soft, silky skin beneath his fingers. Taking a moment to breathe, he raised his lips to her ear. "What do you say we move this party into the bedroom?"

Lauren bit her lip seductively. "Sounds good."

Roger held out his hands and lifted her off the couch. "Come on."

Once in the room, Roger eased her onto the bed. He took in the delicious sensation of her lips, yearning for more. As his grip tightened, the fire between them grew stronger. He locked his hands against her spine and reached for the latch of her bra. When it was loose, his hand gradually made its way to the curve of her breast. As he slowly undressed her, he explored the soft lines of her back, waist, and thighs. His hands roamed freely, caressing every inch of her beautiful body. Requesting permission to pursue, he reached for the lacy fabric of her panties and tugged at them. "Can we take these off?"

She stared at him with longing in her eyes. "Yes."

He carefully slid them over her hips and down her silky legs, tossing them on the floor behind him. He gave her body a raking stare, photographing her with his eyes. Her shapely curves taunted him. One hand slid down her stomach to the swell of her hips while the other caressed the skin of her thigh. He paused to make a path with his tongue and lips, tasting her salty skin from her belly button all the way to her chin.

Lauren's breath buckled and her body squirmed beneath him. "Roger?"

Panting from the intensity, his lips brushed against hers as he spoke. "Yes?"

"I'm a virgin."

He immediately stopped what he was doing. Drawing her closer, he kissed the top of her head, carefully considering the implications of this situation. "My sweet Lauren." After a minute or two, he lifted her chin and looked her in the eye. "You're not obligated to do this. I love you and want to be with you regardless." With his hand on her cheek, he gently rubbed his thumb across her lips. "Are you sure you want to do this?"

She couldn't deny the spark of excitement she felt. The prolonged anticipation gave her tingles. "Yes."

"You're absolutely positive? Because if you're not one-hundred percent certain this is what you want, I don't want to do this."

"I want to." She lifted her head to kiss him.

He closed his eyes and absorbed her luscious lips, giving in to the searing need that had been building for months.

She helped him undress, and he maneuvered himself on top of her. Propped up on his elbow, he cradled her head in the crook of his arm. "Communicate with me, both with your body and by telling me what you like. Tell me what feels good. Let me know right away if I'm hurting you. I want this experience to be pleasurable for both of us."

He slid his hand across her breast and down to her silken belly while his tongue traced a path over each part of her body.

She touched the bare skin of his back, slowly working her way lower.

While she explored with her hands, he explored with his, searching for pleasure points and taking time to arouse her. When he felt she was ready, he placed his hands on her hips and scooted her down to the corner of the bed. With his feet on the floor, he kissed her knee, slowly working his way up her thigh, to her tummy and breasts, and eventually to her neck. "Relax," he whispered, his breath hot against her ear. "I promise I'll make you feel good." Reassuring her that he would be gentle, he softly kissed her.

His body burned, longing to be close to her. He slipped on a condom then inched his hand up her leg. Her chest heaved and her lips parted, staring at him with longing eyes. His body pressed against hers, and instinctively, she arched toward him. He eased in gently, taking it nice and slow.

Her breath shuddered, and she made a gasping sound.

Roger gazed at her adoringly. "You ok?" he asked, hoping he wasn't hurting her.

"Yes."

Without looking away, he tucked himself neatly into her contours, face to face so they could gaze into each other's eyes and kiss while their bodies intertwined. Lauren melted against him, and together, they found a pleasing tempo. A delicious sensation heated his skin. His whole body throbbed.

To maximize pleasure, they switched positions several times. Being bound to her like this was the most powerful feeling in the world. He felt more connected to her than any person he had ever been with. They not only had an emotional bond, but a physical one as well. As he continued this slow, sensuous rhythm, he felt honored to be the man she chose to give her body to.

Communicating his deep love for her, he sealed the act with a kiss then looked down at her and smiled. "It is my lady, oh, it is my love. Two of the fairest stars in all the heavens do entreat her eyes. The brightness of her cheek would shame those stars, as daylight doth a lamp. See how she leans her cheek upon her hand? Oh, that I were a glove upon that hand, that I might touch that cheek."

Lauren giggled at his soliloquy. "Romeo and Juliet."

"Yes, Ma'am."

"Do you have any idea how many times I've performed in that play?"

"Everyone at some point in their acting career has done Shakespeare. It's a rite of passage into the profession." Roger reclined on the bed, taking Lauren with him. "It's a wonderful composition, though. Shakespeare was a creative genius."

"He was a pervert," Lauren added.

This comment made him chuckle. "Yes, that too. But Romeo and Juliet is a timeless classic."

"It would be much better if it was a musical." Lauren laid her head on Roger's chest, getting more comfortable in his arms.

"Oh man, can you imagine? The classic tragedy of forbidden love set to music. That would be epic. I'd jump right on that."

"Maybe you should write that musical."

He burst out laughing. "I'm not that creative, although I wish I were. I'll leave that kind of creativity to you."

"I would love to be involved in an original composition like that," she said dreamy-eyed.

Roger reflected on her statement. "You know, Juilliard has a special program for that. They'll provide you with the training and skills you need to compose a musical score, and they'll even give you the opportunity to work with professional composers and lyricists. They're quite supportive. In fact, they will allow you to take on the full production of your own work and perform it in front of an audience."

This comment baffled her. She attended classes at Juilliard, yet he seem to know more about the school than she did. "How do you know so much about Juilliard?"

He simply replied, "I was once a student there."

She looked up at him, more curious now. "You were?"

"Yes," he explained. "Left after my second year."

"Why?"

He proceeded to explain, "Well, I kicked around the idea of doing some Broadway auditions. With hundreds of people auditioning, most of whom had more formal training than I did, I knew it wouldn't amount to anything, but I wanted the experience. I attended a casting call for Newsies, and to my surprise, I received a callback. Needless to say, I was in total shock. I decided I had nothing to lose and went for the callback. Unexpectedly, they offered me the part."

Lauren propped herself up on her elbow, excited to hear more of this story.

"Of course I was ecstatic. Being on Broadway had always been a dream of mine and this part just landed in my lap. It was a principal role and would definitely give me stage time. But performing on Broadway required a huge time commitment with rehearsals and shows. As you well know, getting into Juilliard had its own challenges, and I felt honored to have been chosen to receive training there. Yet I knew it would be difficult to maintain the commitment level involved with a major Broadway production while going to school full time. I didn't want to leave Juilliard, but didn't want to give up this once in a lifetime opportunity either, which left me in a bind."

"So what did you do?"

"I accepted the part. The show received a lot of publicity and really took off. It was highly acclaimed by critics. We got rave reviews and even received a few Tony nominations that year, including best musical. It ended up being bigger than any of us possibly imagined."

Lauren beamed with delight, hopeful that one day she would stand on a Broadway stage. "That's amazing."

"That was my debut on Broadway. I've been consistently offered jobs ever since, so I never went back to school."

With her head cocked sideways, she stared down at him. "You never told me you went to Juilliard."

"You never asked." He kissed her lightly on the lips. "You'll get on stage, Lauren. I know you will. Get as much experience as you can. Look into theatre opportunities outside of school. The more stage presence you have, the better."

She nodded in understanding, listening to every piece of advice he offered.

"Take to heart everything Juilliard is teaching you. You'll appreciate it in the end. They're showing you the professional aspects of this industry, and believe me, professionalism is very important," he explained. "A glut of eligible candidates flock to New York City every year looking for their big break. Certain things will help you stand out from the rest, and that one little thing could be what facilitates your first big job."

"Like what?" She rolled onto her tummy and folded her hands across his chest, propping her chin up so she could see his face.

"Your resume is critical," Roger explained as he rested his hand on her bare back. "Jazz it up and keep it current. Stay informed about upcoming plays and musicals by checking Playbill daily. They list auditions in the area and update it regularly. Start off with smaller shows that are off-Broadway to get your name out there. Word of mouth is quite powerful for landing jobs. Getting on Broadway requires jumping through hoops and dodging hurdles, but I can help you navigate through those."

Wanting to learn all she could about this industry and knowing she was talking to an expert, she asked, "Anything else?"

"Being a triple threat really grabs people's attention and can land you jobs others may not have the skills to undertake. Besides ballroom dancing, what other dance experience do you have?"

"I've had some tap, ballet, and jazz training," she replied. "Not a lot, but enough."

"Good. Keep up on those," he advised. "Being a triple threat will turn heads your direction and get you good money when you finally make contract."

"How much does a Broadway performer make?" she wondered.

"It depends on the job," he clarified. "Even with an ensemble role, the minimum is 1,800 a week. Feature and lead roles can make anywhere from two to ten grand a week, depending on your experience, what musical it is, and the type of role you have. A featured actor with proper Broadway credits and a decent agent should be able to get as least 2.5K, and a leading actor who's a Broadway veteran makes even more. Bigger, longer running shows pay more. Musicals that require specific dancing skills offer more pay. If you've been nominated for or have won a Tony Award, you have more promotional clout and can usually negotiate a higher salary fairly successfully. Having extra responsibility in a show equates to additional pay too. Actors selected as understudies or dance captains, roles with higher-than-average risks or fight scenes, or those who have to move set pieces earn additional money per week. And all actors in musicals are entitled to a media fee that covers use of the actor's image on websites, TV commercials, or other publicity material."

"I'm not trying to probe, but how much do you make as a performer?" she asked.

Her innocence amused him. "You're not probing, Sweetheart. You're my girlfriend. You have every right to ask me about money."

"Well, I don't want you to think that's all I care about, because it's not. I'm just curious."

"I'm considered a Broadway veteran. I've also won a Tony Award. Chicago is a big-name, long-running show, and I'm playing a lead role. For this particular show, I'm bringing in about 6K a week."

Lauren's eyes got huge. "Are you serious?"

"It seems like a lot, but keep in mind there are some weeks, between contracts, when I don't have work. And it's not particularly cheap to live in Manhattan."

"Yes, I've noticed."

"This apartment alone is over 5,000 a month." Roger lived in an indulgent two bedroom, two bath apartment on the twelfth floor of a twenty-four story high-rise in Upper West Side Manhattan. This was convenient for him because it was close to the Theatre District and within walking distance of Central Park, shopping, the subway, and any other needed amenities. As an added bonus, it was only blocks away from Juilliard.

"That much?" she remarked, shocked by the high cost of everything in this city.

"New York City is an expensive place to live, and good apartments are hard to come by, so they're pricey." They shifted slightly so they were both lying on their sides. "It's late," he said with a yawn. "I need to get some sleep." He snuggled in behind her and tucked one arm under his pillow. With the other arm, he reached over and turned off the lamp. "Goodnight, Sweetheart. I love you."

"I love you, too," she replied.

It wasn't long before they both drifted off to sleep.

Roger awoke with Lauren in his arms. Seeing her beautiful face and feeling her warm body against his brought a blissful smile to his face. He stretched glamorously and sat up, which in turn woke Lauren up. He looked down at her and gently moved the stray hair off her face. "Good morning, my love. Did you sleep well?"

She stretched and rolled over. "I slept like a baby."

"Sex has a tendency to do that." He gently touched the curve of her waist then slowly worked his way up to the soft skin of her breast. "I learned a few things about you last night."

"Like what?" she asked playfully.

"First of all, you are very comfortable with your body and confident with your sexuality. You're also a woman who's not afraid to take charge. Normally I like to be in control in the bedroom, but I have to admit, when you took over for a while, I rather enjoyed that."

This conversation made her blush.

"There's nothing to be embarrassed about, Honey. It's one of the things I love about you. But now you have me curious."

"About what?"

With his eyebrows bowed forward, he asked, "You claimed you were a virgin, but you didn't act like it. You really got into it with me." He grinned mischievously and positioned his body over hers. "And you know what? You and I are pretty hot in the sack."

"Oh my god. I can't believe you said that."

"It's true." Nibbling on her neck, he whispered, "I could go for round two." He wrapped his arms around her and leaned forward to kiss her.

Starting off the day indulging in sexual fulfillment left Roger winded. He glanced over at the alarm clock, surprised they had stayed in bed so late. "It's almost 10:00."

"Is it?" Lauren turned to look.

"Know what we should do today? Let's snag some Coneys, dink around downtown, and maybe take the ferry to see Lady Liberty. What do you think?"

"Sounds fun," Lauren said.

"I have to be back in time for my show tonight though." Energetically he hopped up and sat on his knees. "Need to take Ollie for a walk first, and a shower is definitely in order." He took her hands and pulled her up with him.

That afternoon, they strolled around Lower Manhattan, popping into several retail stores. Inside a hat store, Roger's playful side began to surface. He put on a blue and white pinstriped train engineer's hat and called out, "All aboard!"

This immediately attracted attention. Lauren put her finger up to her lip trying to get him to lower his voice. "Everyone's staring at us."

"So what? I'm having fun." He slipped on a cowboy hat and tipped it forward. Using his best Texas accent, he said, "Howdy, Ma'am."

Roger was the kind of person who tried to find humor in life. He had a positive attitude and loved to joke around with Lauren. Being around him always made her smile.

"You don't like that one?" He rummaged through the hats to find one he thought she might enjoy. Being silly, he put on an oversized plush green hat with a large pink flower sticking out of it. "What about this one?" In a high pitched Irish dialect, he said, "Oh no, they're after me Lucky Charms."

"That hat is ridiculous," she laughed.

He took it off and picked up a wide rimmed Southern Belle tea hat instead. With a playful grin on his face, he put it on Lauren's head. "Well butter my biscuit. If it ain't Scarlett O'Hara!"

Lauren posed with a pouty face.

"Cute, Honey." He clasped her hand and pivoted toward the door. "Let's get out of here."

She removed the hat and placed it back on the hat rack on the way out.

When they walked past a jewelry store, Lauren glanced in the window at a gold necklace with a heart-shaped ruby and diamond pendant. "Ooh, that's pretty."

Roger came over to see what sparked her interest. "You like that?"

"It's gorgeous." But when she saw the $525 price tag, she lost all enthusiasm. "Is there a ladies' room around here?"

Roger pointed to the department store next door. "I'm sure there's one in there that's suitable for usage."

"I'm gonna run in there real quick. Be right back."

While she was taking care of business, Roger snuck inside the jewelry store and purchased that necklace for her. He had the store clerk hold it for him, making arrangements to pick it up later so he could surprise Lauren with it.

Prior to the next night's show, Roger snuck up behind Lauren and whispered, "Stop by my dressing room later."

She eyed him curiously, wondering what he was up to.

When Lauren made her rounds to check on performers, she knocked on Roger's door.

"It's open," he called out.

She walked inside, and he was already dressed in his black Billy Flynn suit, minus the shoes and hat. "Hi, Sweetie."

"Close the door and come over here. I have something for you."

"What is it?"

He handed her a small box wrapped in blue paper with a small silver bow. "This."

She stood there staring at it.

He openly laughed at her. "You gonna open it?"

She ripped the paper off, anticipating what was inside. But as soon as she removed the lid, the expression on her face was far from enthusiastic. "It's that necklace from yesterday."

"Yes, I know that," he replied.

"Why did you do that?"

Her reaction confused him. She seemed more upset than excited. "I thought you'd be happy, but your tone suggests otherwise. It sounds like you're reprimanding me for buying you something you wanted."

"I'm not reprimanding you, I just know how expensive this is. I wasn't expecting this."

"I will buy you gifts and give you flowers and plan romantic dinner dates with you, Lauren. That's how I am." He removed the necklace from box and clipped it around her neck. "Do you like it?"

"I love it. Thank you."

"You're welcome." He leaned in to kiss her. "Now, on a work related note, my hat is missing."

"Again?" She looked around for it. "Where did it go?"

"I don't know. I was hoping you could help me with that."

"I swear, I'm going to attach it to you with a string."

"You might have to."

She shook her head as his forgetfulness. "I'll find it for you."

"Thanks, Sweetheart."

She left the room in search of a black fedora.

Chapter Six

Since moving to New York, Lauren and her twin sister communicated daily and took the time to see each other as often as possible, but not being together every day was a challenging adjustment for both of them. Even though Lacy was a dance student at Columbia University and the twins were only three miles away from each other, class and work schedules often made it difficult for them to spend time together.

Lauren and Lacy had some kind of special communication—intuitive in nature—that Roger didn't fully understand. Although he had never met Lacy, he witnessed the connection Lauren had with her twin almost daily. Lauren desperately needed some sister time. To assist with this, Roger offered a suggestion. He and Lauren planned to go shopping on Fifth Avenue. They invited Lacy to go with them. Not only would this give Lauren some much needed bonding time with her sister, it would also allow Roger the opportunity to finally meet her.

Lauren and Lacy looked almost identical, which made it easy for Roger to recognize Lacy. There were, however, subtle differences between them. Lauren's hair was longer and she was slightly taller than Lacy. And Lauren had a cute little dimple on her cheek when she smiled that Lacy didn't have.

When Lacy saw Roger, she could see right away why her sister liked him. He was a good looking man with the muscularly toned body of a dancer, and the most captivating smile she'd ever seen. "You must be Roger."

Roger shook her hand. "It is a pleasure to finally meet you, Lacy."

Curious about this man who had managed to capture her sister's heart, Lacy conversed with Roger throughout the morning and watched his interactions with Lauren. He had subtle ways of displaying his affection for Lauren that Lacy found to be quite charming. Generally speaking, he was a positive person. He had a playful nature, tons of energy, and really seemed to enjoy life. He often joked around and had some funny one-liners that would make her laugh. He was articulate and poised in pretty much everything he did. Randomly, he would break out in song or dance down the sidewalk, and he appeared to constantly have a rhythm running through his head. He knew a great deal about the entertainment industry, Broadway in particular, and he was a diehard Yankees and Knicks fan. She witnessed his generous nature when she saw him dump ten dollar bills into the red Salvation Army buckets in front of department stores. He was confident, friendly, and easygoing. And he was chivalrous, holding doors for both of them and offering his hand on slippery sidewalks so they wouldn't fall. He even offered to buy Lacy lunch.

In the heart of Midtown Manhattan, Roger stopped dead in his tracks when they came across a piano showroom. He peered in the window, drooling over a beautifully polished black Steinway concert grand piano. He took Lauren's hand and roamed into the store.

The inside of this building was a breathtaking two-story rotunda that featured a 35-foot domed ceiling. The walls were adorned with fluted white Italian columns and green pilasters of highly polished Greek marble. Original oil paintings of great composers hung on the walls, creating a rich visual landscape that transformed this stunning hall into an opulent art museum. Descending from the ceiling was an elegant, glittering nineteenth century Viennese crystal chandelier. Roger didn't even notice the magnificent architecture of this showroom because he was fixated on the room's dramatic centerpiece—the Steinway.

Roger approached the extraordinary craftsmanship of this one-of-a-kind custom-made piano and gently rubbed his hands across the side, caressing the Steinway with pure love. "Look at this beauty." He circled around it, admiring the beautiful powerhouse of an instrument, while inspecting every fabulous detail. He was like a child in a candy store in the center of this piano universe. Lauren had never seen him so excited.

He let go of her hand and took a seat at the bench. At first, he just sat there staring at the keys as if he was afraid to touch them. Slowly, he placed his fingers on the ivory and began to play a bluesy song with a catchy tune. Then, as Roger often did, he burst into song, singing 'Memphis Lives in Me' which was a song he performed in his Tony award-winning role from the musical *Memphis*. As he sang and plucked away at the keys, he began to draw a crowd. People walked in from the street just to hear him play. The more people gathered, the more of a show Roger put on for them. He was always a showman, even during a routine shopping trip.

When the song was finished, his audience applauded. But Roger didn't hear their applause. He had drifted into his piano dream world. He sat on the piano bench, took in a deep breath, and slowly roamed his fingers across the ivory keys. Then, very carefully, he got off the bench and neatly tucked it back into place. He rubbed the smooth edge one more time before he took Lauren's hand and continued their walk through Manhattan. "That is a beautiful instrument."

"Have you ever owned one?" Lacy asked him.

"A Steinway?" Roger questioned with a laugh. "I would love to own one of those beauties, but they are not cheap."

"How much are they?" she asked.

"You have about a hundred grand lying around?"

Lacy gasped at the god forsaken cost. "Ouch!"

"Yeah, which is why I don't own one, but I can certainly dream."

Lacy adored Roger, and the more she hung around him, the more she realized what a fun, laidback, all around good guy he was. He expressed multiple times through his actions that he loved and cared for Lauren very much. The way he looked at her, interacted with her, and kissed her was warm and affectionate. Lacy encouraged her sister and supported her in every way as far as Roger was concerned.

Roger held Lauren in his arms, panting from the exhilaration of the moment. He lovingly caressed her bare skin while he brought his heartrate back to normal. "This might not be the most opportune time to discuss this, but I feel we need to because it's been weighing heavily on my mind."

"What is it?"

Kissing the top of her head, he tried to figure out how to bring up this sensitive topic. "Sweetheart, I love you dearly, but I really don't want to father a child right now. My career is in full swing, and I know you have goals and dreams of Broadway, and you have school to think about. Neither one of us can afford to have an unplanned pregnancy on our hands."

"But we've been using condoms," she reminded him.

"I know we have," he confirmed. "But those aren't always one-hundred percent effective. I don't want to get you pregnant." Along with his concern, he offered a solution. "Have you considered getting on birth control pills?"

"It won't be that hard for me to arrange that. My dad is a gynecologist. I'll call him."

Roger snorted cynically, disagreeing with this idea. "Do you really think that's wise?"

Lauren shrugged. "What's the problem?"

"I'm trying to earn his trust. I don't think your dad is going to take too kindly to the fact that I'm sleeping with his daughter."

"Well, I don't think we should lie to him. It's better to tell him the truth than try to hide it."

Despite Lauren's lack of concern, Roger was worried. "So I'm supposed to earn his trust by admitting to his face that you and I share a bed?"

"Being honest about it shows you're trustworthy, and that's important to my dad."

"What am I supposed to do, Lauren, walk up to him and say, gee, Dr. Hanson, I am madly in love with your daughter. Oh, and by the way, she and I are having sex. Can you put her on the pill so she doesn't get pregnant? Thank you, Sir. Nice to meet you."

Roger's facetious attitude led Lauren to believe he was far more troubled about this than she was. "Well, don't be that blunt about it. A little subtlety can go a long way."

"I have to be honest with you, Honey, I'm a little in fear for my life here."

"My father isn't out for blood or vengeance."

"No, but he might hang me by the balls and castrate me. He does have access to scalpels, you know."

Lauren laughed at him. "We're both adults, Roger, and we have an adult relationship. My father is not naïve, and he certainly doesn't walk around with blinders on. As long as we're honest with him, everything will be fine." She gently touched his face, trying to ease his worry. "Let me talk to him."

Roger was still apprehensive about this plan. "Are you sure about this?"

"Yes." She reassured him with a kiss. "You always tell me to trust you, now I'm asking you to trust me."

He couldn't argue with that logic. Looking her in the eye, he humbly gave in. "Alright."

Lauren called her father the following afternoon. Although she talked to him about twice a week, Dr. Hanson was happy to hear her voice. "Hi, Baby. How's New York?"

"I love it. My theatre group is putting together a musical for Christmas."

"That's right up your alley. Which musical?

"Holiday Inn."

He wasn't familiar with that one, but then again he wasn't into musicals like Lauren was. "That's great."

"Daddy," she began. "I need a favor from you."

"What's up?"

"I need you to send me a scrip for the pill." Lauren could hear her father tapping his pen on the table, which usually meant he was contemplating what was just said and trying not to get upset about it.

"The pill?"

"Yes," she declared confidently.

After a long, awkward silence, he replied, "So you and Roger have a sexual relationship now, is that it?"

"Yes, Daddy, and we didn't want to hide it from you."

He tried to keep his cool. "Let me get this straight. You go off to New York City, supposedly fall madly in love with some 28-year-old Broadway performer who coaxes you into his bed, and you give in and sleep with him?"

"He didn't coax me," Lauren argued. "It was my decision."

"And I suppose he had nothing to do with that decision either, did he?"

"He wasn't pressuring me, if that's what you're asking," Lauren calmly explained. "Roger and I love each other. We have an intimate relationship, but we want to be safe and responsible about it. Part of that responsibility means not getting pregnant."

As much as he didn't like it, he agreed with her. "Please tell me you've been using condoms."

"Of course we have."

Maybe Roger was more sensible than Randy gave him credit for. At least the man was thinking about Lauren and trying to be responsible about their relationship.

"Daddy, you told me to come to you if I ever needed anything. I'm coming to you now. Will you help us?" Lauren asked.

His daughter had grown up. Not only was she involved in an adult relationship with a man, not a boy, she was talking like an adult too, reasoning with him and making valid arguments. The fact that she came forward with this took a lot of courage on her part. She wasn't trying to pull the wool over his eyes; she was being open and completely honest. Taking a cleansing breath, he told her, "Get me the pharmacy information. I'll send it in."

"Thank you, Daddy."

Adding his last tidbit of fatherly dialogue, Dr. Hanson stated, "I'm not particularly happy about this, but I'm glad you were honest with me about it."

"I know," she acknowledged. "I love you, Daddy."

"I love you too, Baby. Please be careful. And tell your sister to call us once in a while."

As soon as Lauren got off the phone, she texted Roger, who was having lunch with Jason.

Jason couldn't help but notice the grin on Roger's face when he received her message. "Who are you talking to?"

"Lauren." Roger sent her a quick reply then slipped his phone back in his pocket.

Jason didn't want to offend Roger or cause strife between him and his best friend, but he didn't understand what Roger could possibly see in a woman so much younger than him. Women her age tended to be insecure, indecisive, and immature. "I don't get it."

"What would you like me to explain to you?"

"She's eighteen, Rog, fresh out of high school, and you're obsessed with her."

Roger denied this accusation. "I'm not obsessed with her, I'm in love with her. There's a big difference."

"How serious are you about her? Puppy love? Infatuation?"

Roger tried to explain, "Jason, I told you already. This is not infatuation and not a one night fling. We're in a serious, committed relationship, one I have no qualms about exposing."

"If the media finds out how old she is, they're gonna run all over that."

"Why would they care how old she is?" Roger demanded to know.

"Because she's eighteen."

"So? It's not like she's underage. She's an adult. I'm an adult." In his defense, Roger laid it on the line. "Lauren and I have a lot in common, we get along well, and we have a connection with one another. She's not hung up on the fact that I'm a Broadway performer; she loves me for who I am. She's a strong woman who's not afraid to call me out when I'm wrong, and she openly expresses her opinion even if it's different from mine. She's completely supportive, fun to hang out with, and we enjoy our time together. I'm not going to let a petty thing like age keep me from the best relationship I've ever had. The fact that she's eighteen has no relevance to me. I love her. I want to be with her, and not you, the press, or anyone else can prevent that from happening. I have found love in an amazing woman. She's the best thing that's ever happened to me, and I am going to do whatever it takes to make this relationship work." Roger folded his arms across his chest, slightly perturbed at Jason for pestering him about this so much. "I'm floating on cloud nine here and you're rocking my boat. Why can't you just let me enjoy this?"

"I'm not trying to rock your boat," Jason replied. "You know I care about you, and I love to see you happy like this. I'm just afraid that you're floating so high in the clouds that you'll fail to navigate through the icebergs. I don't want to see you sink."

Roger combed his fingers through his hair. "I appreciate your concern."

"Do me a favor. Don't dive off any cliffs or do anything insane, alright?"

"You need not worry. I'm not going to jump into marriage or fatherhood, at least not yet. I want to see how things progress between us. What I'm hoping is that our relationship develops into one of complete trust, genuine understanding, and unconditional mutuality. She's a woman I'm willing to dig in deep with, and she's doing the same with me. This exchange Lauren and I share, it's unlike anything I've ever experienced before. It's deep, Jason."

"Just don't drown," Jason warned, genuinely concerned.

"I won't."

Chapter Seven

The week Lauren and Lacy were scheduled to fly home for Christmas break, Lauren called her brother and explained to him that Roger would be coming to Seattle for a few days, and she was going to need someone to take her to the airport to pick him up.

Nathan questioned his sister about this. "Do Mom and Dad know he's coming?"

"No. I haven't told them yet."

He didn't think this was very wise on her part. "Lauren, Dad's gonna be pissed if Roger shows up unannounced like that. Don't you think you should tell them before he gets here?"

"I was going to tell them."

"When?" Nathan asked. "The sooner you tell them, the better. You know Dad doesn't like having things thrown at him at the last minute."

Lauren considered this advice. "I know."

"You better call him."

"I will."

Jason overheard that Roger's understudy, Adam Millet, was playing Roger's role in *Chicago* all next week. Roger rarely missed a performance, so the fact that he was missing an entire week's worth of shows made

Jason suspicious. "Why is Adam filling in for you next week?"

"Because I'm going out of town."

"Where are you going?"

"Seattle." Roger reached into his refrigerator to pull out a bottle of sparkling water.

"Seattle? What the hell is in Seattle?"

"Lauren's family."

Roger seemed to be dedicating a lot of time and energy into this relationship. Even though he claimed he was taking things slow, Jason was concerned that his friend was trying to dive in too deep too quickly. "You're meeting her family?"

"Yes," Roger explained. "She's already met my mother."

"She's met your mother?"

"Yes, and I've met her sister. I'm going to meet her parents and her brother next week."

Jason shook his head. "Flying off to Seattle to meet her parents sounds pretty damn serious."

Roger plopped on the sofa and put his feet up. "I am serious about her, Jason. I tried to tell you that, but you've done nothing but give me a hard time about this from day one."

"You're jumping in with both feet, aren't you?" Jason warned with a cynical timbre in his voice.

Roger didn't see what the problem was. He unscrewed the lid to his bottle and took a drink. "So?"

"You're not even testing the water first."

"I've already tested the water. When the water's comfortable, you jump in. Lauren and I dated for almost six weeks before I kissed her. How is that not testing the water?" Roger didn't understand why Jason was badgering him about this. Jason knew very little about Lauren, yet he was constantly making judgment calls at her expense. "What is your issue with her?"

"I have no issues with Lauren."

"There must be something, because you are trying to discourage me in every possible way."

"I have nothing against Lauren," Jason repeated.

"Then what is the problem?"

Jason was blatantly honest. "I don't want to see what happened to me happen to you."

Roger knew exactly what Jason was talking about. "No offense, Jason, but Lauren is nothing like Cassandra."

Jason closed his eyes trying to hide the pain and humiliation he once felt from the events that unfolded several years ago. "You told me how much Lauren's dying to succeed on Broadway, and she knows you have connections. She's going to use you to get on stage then ditch you once she gets what she wants."

Roger disputed this claim. "That's not going to happen."

"Lauren is young and inexperienced and very eager to break into this industry. Women like her are erratic, Rog."

"No, Cassandra was erratic," Roger corrected. "Being inexperienced had nothing to do with it. You would have caught her in bed with another man regardless. Simply put, she was two-faced and unfaithful."

Jason didn't disagree. "She totally played me for a fool."

Roger felt his best friend's pain. He remembered how devastated Jason was when he walked in on his ex-girlfriend having sex with a fellow dancer she was working with at the time. What made matters worse was it was a man Jason had known for years. Come to find out later, Cassandra was only with Jason because of his connections, and she used him to gain auditions, meet other performers, network with casting agents, and make a name for herself on Broadway. In the meantime, she was sleeping with this other man behind his back. After all of this went down, Roger had to help Jason pick up the pieces and put his life back together. "I know. I was there, remember?"

"Watch out for yourself, Rog. I don't want to see you get hurt."

Realizing Jason was acting out of pure love and respect for him, Roger said, "I won't."

On December 27th, Roger flew up to Seattle. Nathan agreed to take Lauren to the airport to pick him up, but before he did, Dr. Hanson pulled him aside and gave him a directive. "Keep an eye on Roger. Look for suspicious behavior. Make sure he's treating Lauren with respect."

Nathan thought this was an absurd request. "Are you asking me to spy on him?"

"I'm asking you to be a responsible older brother and look out for your sister. I want assurance that he's not putting on some kind of act for her."

"Lacy seems to think he's a cool guy. She says he cares about Lauren, and she's completely convinced he loves her."

"He's sleeping with her, Nathan. That doesn't mean he's in love with her."

Nathan thought his father was being irrational and pigheaded. "Really? That's your argument? You sleep with Mom. I'm sleeping with Gabby. That means we don't love them?"

"That's different."

Nathan begged to differ. "No it's not."

"Yes it is."

Nathan had to laugh, although he knew doing so would probably upset his father, but this ridiculous rationale was amusing. "How do you figure that?"

"Your mother is my wife, and Gabby..."

"Is my girlfriend," Nathan interrupted. "Just like Lauren is Roger's girlfriend. It's not any different, Dad."

Demanding that his son follow his directive, Dr. Hanson said, "Just keep an eye on him, please."

Nathan didn't see the point. "And do what? Report back to you everything I see?"

"Don't fight me on this."

"I'm not fighting you, I just think you're overreacting. You haven't even met the guy yet and already you're judging him. I think you should at least give him the benefit of the doubt here."

"Did Lauren tell you how old Roger is?"

Nathan didn't care. "Yeah. So? What's the big deal? There are a lot of couples with several years between them. Isn't Dr. Hutchins nine years older than his wife?"

"What's your point?"

"A ten year age difference doesn't mean jack. I'm not meaning any disrespect, Dad, but I think you're being ridiculous about this."

Nathan's tone was becoming increasingly more argumentative. Dr. Hanson didn't like it one bit. "Oh really?"

"Yes," Nathan argued. "You're evaluating their entire relationship on the fact that he's ten years older than her and not basing your opinion on anything else. You haven't met the man or talked to him face to face. Lacy has. She's met Roger. She's talked to him. She's witnessed their interaction. And you and I both know that if Lacy had any doubts, she would have said something, not only to us, but to Lauren as well. Do you really think Lace would keep anything from us if she suspected Lauren was in any kind of danger?"

Nathan had a good point. "Well, no."

"At least get to know the man before you post judgment on him."

Nathan and his girlfriend drove Lauren to the airport. As they headed south on Interstate 405, Nathan glanced at his sister in the rearview mirror. "You know Dad's freaking out, don't you?"

"Is he?"

"Yup," Nathan replied half-heartedly. "I'm supposed to be watching Roger and reporting everything back to him."

Lauren rolled her eyes, hoping her father would restrain himself. "Great."

"I think he's being overly melodramatic, so don't worry. I'm not complying with his request."

When they arrived at the airport, Nathan dropped Lauren off at the entrance. "I'm gonna park the car. We'll be right behind you."

"Thank you, Nathan." Lauren closed the car door and went inside the terminal to wait for Roger. He texted her when he landed, which happened to be right when Nathan and his girlfriend walked in.

"Has he landed yet?" Nathan asked.

"They're taxiing now."

"Oh good. We won't be here as long as I thought."

When passengers started to exit, Lauren anxiously waited for Roger.

Nathan stood a distance back, offering the couple a little privacy while they reunited. Curious about this guy, his girlfriend asked, "What does Roger do?"

"He's a performer on Broadway," Nathan replied.

"Like actual Broadway in New York City?"

"Yeah. He's won a Tony Award, so apparently he's pretty good. It makes sense that they're together. Broadway is her passion, obviously it's his as well. From what Lauren's told me, they share a lot of common interests." Nathan turned his eyes to his sister, hoping she wasn't getting in over her head. "I guess we'll see."

The moment Roger saw Lauren, he rushed to greet her, sweeping her into his arms. "Hello, Beautiful."

Lauren threw her arms around him and they joined together in a kiss.

Overjoyed to see her, Roger said, "I missed you."

"I missed you too."

He gave her one more kiss, then with his carryon bag over his shoulder, he clasped Lauren's hand and headed toward the baggage carousel.

Nathan stepped up to them wearing a grey and purple Washington Basketball tee-shirt. He looked exactly like the pictures Lauren had shown him. "Hello, Nathan." Roger firmly shook his hand.

"Hey, Roger."

Nathan was standing next to a pretty, petite blonde woman. Roger assumed this was his girlfriend. "And this lovely lady must be Gabriella."

"Gabby," she corrected.

After introductions were made, the two couples headed toward the baggage claim. "How was your flight?" Nathan asked, trying to be friendly.

"It wasn't bad. They said to expect turbulence, but it was surprisingly calm."

"That's good," Nathan said. "I was on a bad flight once. The turbulence was so severe the flight attendants couldn't stand upright, and anything that wasn't attached to the plane was rolling around all over the place."

"That doesn't sound pleasant," Roger remarked.

"No," Nathan concurred. "It most certainly was not."

Once Roger had his suitcase, he followed Nathan, Gabby, and Lauren out to the parking garage. In an attempt to become better acquainted with the Hanson family, he started with a topic he knew Nathan would be interested in. "Lauren tells me you play basketball for the University of Washington."

Nathan grinned proudly. "Yes, I do."

"Point guard," Roger added. "That's an important position. Bob Cousy, Isaiah Thomas, and Magic Johnson were among the best."

Impressive. Roger knew his basketball. Nathan liked this guy already. "You a basketball fan?"

"New York Knicks."

"Sweet! You follow college hoops?"

"Yes. Always been a Syracuse fan, no offense intended."

After losing to Syracuse in the playoffs last year, Nathan had to laugh. "None taken."

"Perhaps you can make me a Huskies fan as well. Lauren says you're good."

The corner of Nathan's mouth quirked up. "My sister worships me."

Lauren snorted at him. "Ha! You wish!"

Gabby cut in with her two cents worth. "She is right though. He is good. He just doesn't like to admit it."

This sounded all too familiar. "I know how that goes." Roger chuckled and turned his head toward Lauren. "Must run in the family."

Nathan popped the trunk of his Mustang and put Roger's bags inside. "Have you had lunch?"

"No, I have not."

"Let's snag some food then."

Over lunch, Nathan and Roger discussed basketball and cars, and although Roger didn't want to bore Nathan with theatre talk, they conversed a bit about the entertainment industry. This dialogue led to a discussion about dancing, which got Gabby involved, who in turn carried the conversation over to the world of cheering. Roger listened attentively as Nathan and Gabby spoke. Both seemed very dedicated to their chosen career paths, and each had their own passion they pursued. For Nathan is was basketball; for Gabby it was cheerleading. Based on what he observed today, and what Lauren told him about the family, Roger came to the conclusion that the Hansons were diversely talented.

Roger planned to check into a hotel, but decided he would be courteous and make an appearance with Lauren's parents first. The Hanson house was one of the nicest homes Roger ever had the privilege to view. It was located on a huge plot of lakefront property with a private beach, boat dock, and a beautifully landscaped yard. The view of the lake was breathtaking. Evergreen trees and a beautiful mountain formed a backdrop to the distant cityscape. The calm silence of the lake water took his breath away. He took in a big breath of fresh air and exhaled slowly, taking in the scenery. He listened for a minute to the sounds around him. No taxis, no sirens, no noise of the masses. Just calm, peaceful hums of nature. This was definitely not Manhattan. "Wow. This is beautiful. You grew up here?"

Lauren bobbed her head.

"It is gorgeous out here." Roger peered across the lake at the Seattle skyline, one of the most picturesque he'd ever seen. "Still is the mirror of the lake, floating on skies of blue. Endless shores stretch across the scene, purely placid in view."

Lauren eyed him curiously. "I've never heard that poem before."

"That's because I wrote it," he replied.

"You did?"

"Yup. I've been inspired." He stared out at the lake and inhaled another big breath. This was going to be a relaxing couple of days. Letting out a calm, stress-free sigh, Roger said, "Thank you for inviting me here. I really needed some time to unwind."

"You're welcome."

"Time to meet your parents," he suggested, feeling confident. "Let's do this."

She took his hand and led him into the house.

The inside of the house was just as nice as the outside—open concept, abundant large windows, elaborate furnishings, and top-quality appliances. The Hansons had good taste. As Roger cast an eye over the main room, it became obvious that a doctor lived here. A white lab coat was draped across the back of a chair, and medical books and magazines were spread out across the table, along with a stethoscope and open laptop.

When Dr. Hanson heard the front door, he stepped into the living room. Standing next to his daughter was a dark-haired man dressed in a pair of jeans, black leather loafers, and a black *Phantom of the Opera* tee-shirt. Over his clothes he wore a grey woolen peacoat. He was clean-shaven and clean cut—a respectable looking young man.

Roger graciously offered a handshake. "Dr. Hanson. It's a pleasure, Sir."

Despite the fact that this young man appeared to be polite, Dr. Hanson wasn't sure how he felt about all of this, but to be courteous, he accepted Roger's gracious greeting. "Roger."

The tee-shirt Dr. Hanson was wearing had a picture on the front of a cartoonish looking doctor slipping a latex glove over his abundantly oversized hand. Printed above the picture were the words, *Don't try this at home*. Roger found this amusing. Obviously Dr. Hanson had a sense of humor.

Doing his best to make a tense situation more lighthearted, Roger said, "Love your shirt."

Dr. Hanson glanced down at it. "A buddy of mine gave this to me."

"It's definitely good advice."

When Lacy heard Roger's voice, she trotted down the stairs to greet him. "I thought I heard you down here." She gave him a hug then quickly looked him over. He was handsome and well-dressed, as usual—a good first impression for the family.

Dr. Hanson's wife had been upstairs prepping the guestroom, but when she heard all the excitement, she joined the rest of the family. The minute she saw Roger, she developed a kind and inviting smile. "Hello, Roger. Welcome."

Mrs. Hanson was a beautiful and elegant woman. Roger could definitely see where Lauren got her gorgeous looks from. "Mrs. Hanson. It's a pleasure to meet you, Ma'am."

She didn't shake Roger's hand like her husband did. Instead, she gave him a hug.

This overly enthusiastic greeting took Roger by surprise. Remaining courteous, he said, "You have a lovely home."

"Thank you. Please make yourself comfortable. I set up the guestroom for you."

Although he appreciated her kind gesture, he was taken off guard by her request. "I do appreciate that, but I made hotel reservations."

"Oh, no need," she said. "You are more than welcome to stay here."

"That's really not necessary. I wouldn't want to impose."

"I insist," Mrs. Hanson said. "Please stay."

Wondering what to do, he shot a glance Lauren's direction.

Lauren's nod encouraged him to accept the offer.

Taking Lauren's advice, Roger decided to stay. "Thank you for your hospitality, Ma'am. Much obliged." He removed his coat and got more comfortable.

Dr. Hanson spent the majority of the evening carefully watching Roger's interaction with not only Lauren, but the rest of the family as well. Roger instantly connected with the family. He had engaged in many conversations with everyone, except Dr. Hanson. But Dr. Hanson hadn't made a conscious effort to talk to him. Instead, he held up his guard and watched from a distance.

The awkward silence between them made Roger uncomfortable. He wanted to have a conversation with Dr. Hanson so they could get to know one another, but he sensed the man's hesitation and didn't force himself on him. He hoped, that with time, the tension would lift.

After dinner, Dr. Hanson slipped into the garage. Roger looked at Lauren. Right away she knew what he was thinking. With an encouraging smile, she urged him to go out there.

He nodded in compliance and followed Dr. Hanson into the garage.

When Dr. Hanson heard Roger walk in, he stared at him but didn't say anything.

As Roger closed the door behind him, he noticed a Jaguar parked in the garage. On several occasions, Lauren had mentioned that her father was obsessed with sports cars. She also told him about the Jaguar convertible her father owned and loved. Trying to break the ice, Roger said, "Five liter supercharged 550 horsepower V-8 engine. Zero to sixty in 4.2 seconds. That's a powerful ride."

Apparently this singing, dancing, piano-playing Broadway guru knew a thing or two about cars. "Yes it is."

"How fast can this thing go?"

"Never opened it up all the way, but it's been known to go north of 180."

"Impressive. You ever driven it that fast?" Roger grinned cunningly, knowing Dr. Hanson had to have put the pedal down on this vehicle.

"I've taken it up to 105, but don't tell my wife. She'll kill me if she knows I was driving that fast."

Roger laughed. "Your secret's safe with me."

"Would you like to see the interior?" Dr. Hanson offered.

"Absolutely."

Roger and Dr. Hanson were in the garage together for over twenty minutes, which made Lauren wonder what was going on. "Why is Daddy being so standoffish toward Roger?" she asked her mother. "He's hardly said two words to him."

"He's just concerned, Honey," her mother responded. "You know how your father is."

She nervously peered over at the door. "What do you suppose they're doing out there?"

"Leave them out there and let them talk." Mrs. Hanson sat next to her daughter. "He's a nice man. Friendly, well spoken, and very polite."

"Which is why I don't understand why Daddy is acting this way," Lauren complained.

She shuffled in her seat, facing Lauren. "When your dad and I were dating, my father was like that too. But he eventually came around. Your dad doesn't know Roger. Of course he's a bit suspicious. Give them time to get to know each other."

Before breakfast the next morning, Roger sat at the dining room table with an iPad, checking out critic reviews and keeping up with happenings on Broadway.

Dr. Hanson moseyed into the kitchen with an empty coffee cup in his hand. "Good morning," he said to Roger as he walked past him.

Roger looked up. "Good morning, Doctor."

Dr. Hanson set his cup on the kitchen counter and poured coffee into it. "Was the room comfortable enough for you?"

"It was fine, Sir. Thank you." Roger turned off his tablet and fully engaged in the conversation. "I was serenaded by your bird this morning. I had no idea he sang show tunes."

"Yeah. He's a loudmouth sometimes."

"I think he's great," Roger declared, chuckling under his breath. "My dog howls when I play the piano. We should pair them up. They would make quite an entertaining duo."

Roger had on a peculiar shirt. It was dark brown with the number 24601 written across the front. "What's with the shirt?" Dr. Hanson asked as he stirred sugar into his coffee.

"It's Valjean's prison number from Les Mis."

Not being up on musicals, Dr. Hanson had no idea what that meant. "Anything exciting happening on Broadway?"

"The man who plays Phantom is leaving the production the end of May. I would love to have a shot at that role."

"Go audition for it. Based on your reputation, I'm sure you're a shoein."

"It's not that simple," Roger explained. "There are a lot of hurdles to dodge, especially for a show that big."

"What kind of hurdles?"

"Broadway is big business. Millions of dollars can be either gained or lost with one production, and a lot of it depends on the musical composition, choreography, the director, how much publicity the show gets, and the quality of the actors who perform on stage. Phantom is the biggest moneymaker for Broadway. In a production like that, a certain persona is required. Not everyone can pull off portraying Phantom. He's a complex character. You have to have the voice and be able to ignite the emotion that's within him."

Dr. Hanson grabbed his cup of coffee and joined Roger at the table. "I thought you were good at that sort of thing?"

"I've made my rounds. Played the lead for several major productions, earned a few Tony nominations, and even have a Tony displayed on my fireplace mantle. Phantom's not completely out of my grasp, and it's definitely a role I can get into. I just have to cut through the red tape to get there."

Dr. Hanson considered what Roger was saying, concerned about how all of this would affect his daughter in the future. "Getting on stage is difficult?"

"Not if the talent's there," Roger claimed. "The casting agents and directors will recognize that talent right away and you'll get your shot on stage. It may not be a major role at first, but even an ensemble role is a good start. It's the business aspect of this industry that's challenging. It helps to have connections. The longer you're in the industry, the easier that becomes."

Dr. Hanson rubbed his hand across his chin. "And you've been in this business for how long?"

"Formally, eight years."

"And informally?" Whatever that meant. He really had no clue.

"I've been involved in local and regional theatre, off-Broadway productions, tap ensembles, and Shakespearean Festivals since I was four."

"Sounds like Lauren."

"Lauren has amazing talent," Roger said. "She'll get herself on a Broadway stage. That is not going to be a problem for her. Navigating through the business aspects of Broadway is where she'll need some guidance."

"And I suppose you want to be the one to help her with that?" Dr. Hanson took a sip of his coffee.

"Yes, Sir, I do. I've made theatre my profession, and I've learned to traverse through it quite successfully. I can certainly steer her in the right direction."

Lauren heard the conversation going on and hobbled down the stairs in her baby blue Snoopy pajamas. Her hair was out of place and her eyelids were heavy.

Roger grinned when he saw her. "Good morning, Sleepyhead."

She groggily made her way to Roger's lap, resting her head on his shoulder.

Roger put his arm around her and kissed her lightly on the lips.

She just groaned and closed her eyes.

Dr. Hanson had to admit, seeing them together was adorable. It was pretty apparent that Roger cared about Lauren. As he watched them, he couldn't help but smile. "You want some coffee?"

"I would love some, but I can't get up right now," Roger said, trying not to disturb Lauren's slumber, which quite frankly didn't look very comfortable.

"I'll get you a cup. How do you like it?"

"One cream, two sugars, please." Dr. Hanson was going out of his way to be hospitable. Perhaps the man was learning to trust him. "Thank you, Doctor."

The family spent the day at Seattle Center, which included picking up a box of Seattle Fudge, viewing a model train village, and walking past the Seattle mural. They visited Seattle's famous Pike Place Market, checked out the unique pieces at The Sculpture Garden, browsed through a pottery gallery, and saw a show at the Pacific Science Center's Planetarium. For lunch, they introduced Roger to the Crab Pot, which was a fun place to eat because the restaurant staff took a variety of fresh Pacific Northwest seafood, steamed with mouth-watering spices, and poured it out onto a butcher paper covered table. Each person was given a mallet, a bib, a seafood fork, and a small stainless steel dipping bowl full of melted butter. Even though it was messy, Roger enjoyed this experience with the family. Everyone was having a blast, and the food was good. After lunch, they explored the waterfront, perused through eclectic souvenir shops, hopped on the scenic Great Wheel, and took a walk along the pier enjoying the spectacular view of Elliott Bay. When the sun went down, they headed over to UW to watch Nathan play basketball.

Roger thoroughly enjoyed his time with the Hansons. They were a kind and open family who were very welcoming toward him, and he felt that he and Dr. Hanson had made quite a bit of progress during his short visit. The trip had definitely been worthwhile.

As much as Roger enjoyed being around Lauren's family, he had a show to return to. Before he went through security, he reached into his bag and handed Dr. Hanson an envelope. "Thank you for your kindness."

Dr. Hanson stared at the envelope, wondering what it was.

"It's not much," Roger explained. "Just a way to express my gratitude."

Inside the envelope were two Broadway ticket vouchers for *Chicago*. "Oh wow," Dr. Hanson said, showing them to his wife.

"Those are for front row, center stage, orchestra level seats," Roger explained. "Let me know what show you'd like to attend and I'll have the tickets waiting for you when you get to New York."

Dr. Hanson and his wife grinned at each other. New York would be a great mini vacation. "Thank you. That's very thoughtful."

"You're welcome. When you come out, you'll have a personal tour guide," Roger said. "And maybe we can catch a Knicks or a Yankees game."

"That would be great."

Roger firmly shook his hand. "It was wonderful meeting you, Sir. I look forward to seeing you again soon."

"It's been a pleasure."

"And thank you, Ma'am, for your hospitality," he said to Mrs. Hanson. "You were very warm and welcoming toward me, and I appreciate that."

"You're welcome any time, Roger," she stated, giving him a hug.

Finally, Roger made his way to Lauren, dreading this moment. "Well, Sweetheart, I'm off."

"I know." Lauren put her arms around him. "Please be safe."

"Always." Holding her tightly, he kissed her on the lips. He didn't want to leave her, but he had no choice. "I'll miss you."

"I'll miss you too."

They nuzzled forehead to forehead, gazing into each other's eyes. "We'll be together soon. Enjoy the rest of your time with your family." He gave her one last kiss before he released her. "I love you, Honey. I'll call you tonight."

She waved at him as he exited through security to the boarding gates.

As soon as Roger was out of sight, Dr. Hanson directed his attention to his daughter. "Alright, I admit. He's a nice guy."

Lauren hugged her father tightly, thankful for his approval. "Thank you, Daddy."

Dr. Hanson peeked over at his wife, who stood watching them with a grin on her face. He knew he had done right by her and his daughter, and that's what mattered to him most.

Chapter Eight

Basketball season was in full swing. And for Nathan, that meant his schedule was insanely busy. With his Biology classes, satisfying pre-med requirements, working part time, and all the volunteer work and physician shadowing he was doing, he rarely had time for himself. Any slight break he had in his schedule, he dedicated to studying. On this particular day, he sat on the stairs outside the gym with an open textbook in his lap.

Gabby, dressed in a Washington Cheer jacket, met him outside Alaska Airlines Arena. "Hey, Sweetie."

He looked up from his textbook. "Hey."

A television van full of video equipment was parked nearby, and people wearing security badges ran around the area carrying clipboards. "What's going on?" Gabby asked.

"They're televising the game on ESPN." Nathan closed his book and slipped it into his backpack. "We're going up against Wichita State. If we win this game, it will boost our national ranking."

"Have you played them before?"

"Not this season," Nathan explained. "We met them last year though, in a non-conference invitational. They're a tough team." Nathan stood up and tossed his backpack over his shoulder. He took Gabby's hand and together they walked toward Nathan's apartment. "This is an important game. The results count toward our record and our rank."

"What are you guys ranked right now?"

"At the moment, twelfth nationally. But we have a shot at beating them tonight, if I can get past their point guard. David is good."

Wichita's point guard, David Warren, was a tough competitor. Even though Nathan generally played a fast-paced game, Warren gave him a run for his money. Nathan had a hard time getting shots in over him, and David was so quick on the return that Nathan struggled against him defensively. The Huskies had the home court advantage, but despite this, they were behind throughout most of the game.

With 6:33 left in the second half, Nathan was able to fight his way to an open spot and make a three pointer to get the Huskies within one point and bring the score to 61-60. Warren tried to contest the shot, but his leg buckled when he landed and bent in such an awkward angle that it left him screaming in pain in the middle of the court. All game play stopped as trainers ran onto the court.

Horrified, Nathan covered his mouth with his hand and stared at his opponent's leg. He was badly injured. Skin was broken and the bone was sticking out. Nathan never wished injury on any player, especially a gruesome injury like this. This injury plunged Alaska Airlines Arena into devastated silence.

Several of Wichita's players were overcome with emotion. Two of them fell to the floor crying, and another kneeled on his hands and knees, looking as if he was going to be sick. Clearly Wichita was upset by the injury, embracing each other and crying. Even the coach wiped tears from his eyes.

Nathan had to walk away. He was getting emotional during the nine-minute delay.

They lifted Warren onto a stretcher and carried him off the court as Wichita fans chanted his name. When Wichita returned to the court, they went more than three minutes without scoring and had a hard time getting back into the game. Although David Warren was instrumental in the first half, Washington went on to win with an 85-83 victory.

After the game, Gabby met Nathan by the locker room. "Oh my god, did you see his leg?" she said.

"I was standing right next to him, Gab. That was the worst game injury I've ever seen. And the bad thing is he was trying to block my shot when he broke it. I feel awful."

"It's not your fault," Gabby told him.

"I know, but with an injury like that, he'll be out the rest of the season. And he's a senior, so his college basketball career is over. That's a horrible way to go out."

Gabby tried to get him to focus on something else. "You guys won though."

He sighed, wishing the game hadn't gone down like that. "Yes we did. But when the starting point guard from the opposing team goes out with an injury, I don't want to win like that."

This victory brought the Huskies one step closer to nationals, and even though Nathan sympathized with Wichita State, Gabby knew he was happy about this win. Nathan desperately wanted a national champ-ionship title. She redirected him toward that goal. "You're one game closer now."

A smile slowly crept on his face. "I would love to have an NCAA championship title under my belt before I graduate."

"You guys are well on your way."

"Yes we are." He kissed her lovingly and put his arm around her. "Come on. I'm starving."

Gabby giggled at his incessant appetite. "Why am I not surprised?"

He held Gabby's hand, and together they walked out of the arena.

Over the last six months, Nathan spent a considerable amount of time looking over information about various medical schools he was interested in. University of Washington was his first choice, but he needed other options. He looked into Oregon Health and Science University in Portland and the University of California at San Francisco, where his father studied medicine in a joint program with UC Berkeley.

Nathan not only worked in his father's clinic, he also completed many volunteer hours working in hospital triage, training people in CPR and First Aid, and tutoring fellow students in science and math courses. His father allowed him to observe during routine exams and deliveries and arranged for Nathan to shadow an ER physician. Nathan had taken the required pre-med courses, completed the volunteer hours needed for the application process, and had solid experiences in the medical field. He prepared his personal statement, drafted essays, collected letters of recommendation, and diligently studied for the MCAT, which he was scheduled to take in February. He was ready for the final stages of the application process.

Gabby hadn't really been involved in Nathan's process of preparing for all of this, other than offering support and allowing him time to study when he needed it. But Nathan wanted her to contribute to his decision.

Sunday morning, Nathan awoke when he heard someone rummaging around. He opened his eyes and saw Gabby digging in an athletic bag. Still half asleep, he stretched and looked over at the alarm clock. "Morning, Babe."

"Good morning, Superstar."

He propped himself up on his elbow and reached his hand out to Gabby, pulling her onto the bed with him. "Sit down for a minute. I need to talk to you."

"About what?"

"I'm at the point where I'm ready to apply to medical schools."

"I know. You've been working hard on that, and I'm really proud of you."

He sat up. "There is the possibility that I might not get accepted into UW. I need other options in case it comes down to that."

"You'll get accepted," she said, blowing off his concerns.

"We have to be realistic about this, Gab. Thousands of people apply and only about a hundred or so get in."

"And you'll be one of them." She didn't understand why Nathan was being so negative about this. In her eyes, he was a prime candidate.

"We have to consider every option," he told her. "I've been looking at other med schools besides UW."

"What other med schools?"

"That's what I wanted to talk to you about. I'd like to apply to UCSF and OHSU. I know they're not ideal choices, but they are options I would like to consider." He held her hand and looked her in the eye. "Are you willing, if it comes down to it, to come with me to a school that isn't in Seattle? I know it's asking a lot for you to put everything on hold…"

She didn't let him continue. "Nathan, getting you into medical school is top priority for us."

"What about your career?"

"If I know ahead of time where we're going, I can get certified in that state and find a teaching job there. I told you before, I'm going to support you anyway I can."

"But you've sacrificed so much for me already."

She disagreed. "We make sacrifices for each other, for the benefit of our future together. That's the way it's always been."

Gabby was more than his girlfriend. She was the most supportive and understanding person he knew. She was his rock in times of weakness and his motivation when he felt like giving up. She was his best friend. He didn't want to push her needs and wants aside, but in this case, she was completely willing to stand by his side, regardless of the sacrifices. "I love you, Gab. You are the most selfless person I've ever known."

"Do what you need to do, Nathan. We'll make it work." She pulled a folded towel out of his laundry basket then leaned in to kiss him. "I'm going to hop in the shower."

As she was about to walk out the door, Nathan put his hand on her waist and pulled her on top of him. "Oh no you don't."

Kicking and screaming, she played along. "Let me go!"

He rolled them over. "Never."

She squirmed and laughed and tried to break loose. "Nathan."

"Ssh. My roommate can hear us."

She wiggled her way free and ran into the bathroom. Nathan trailed right behind her.

Dr. Hanson was well aware that Nathan had been extensively researching various medical schools. Knowing how complicated the application process was, he did whatever he could to help his son navigate through the confusion. This included reading through his personal statement. "Your strong commitment to the medical field is definitive in your statement. You displayed solid evidence of personal growth, and your leadership qualities really shine through. However, you might want to emphasize your experience as team captain on the high school basketball team. Don't downplay that. Being captain was an important leadership role, and experience like that is significant."

"Alright." Nathan jotted that down on his paper.

"Have you narrowed down your choices?"

"I think so," Nathan sighed, flustered by the entire process. "Why do medical schools make this so difficult?"

"They're selective, Nate. You know that."

"I know, but with everything they require, I have no time for myself. I've dedicated so much time and energy into this. What if I don't get in?"

"Don't get discouraged. You're a good candidate. You have quality experience, competitive grades, and excellent recommendations. Your medical foundation and philosophy are solid."

Nathan wasn't as convinced. "I guess."

"There is no reason to doubt yourself. You have a lot to offer them," Dr. Hanson encouraged. "Have you been studying those MCAT books I gave you?"

"Yes," Nathan confirmed.

"Good. Keep using them. And keep your grades up."

"Speaking of which…" Nathan pulled out a printout of his semester grades and handed it to his father. He carried mostly A's and B's, but had a C in one of his science classes. Not his best performance. "Neuroscience kicked my butt," he complained. "I barely squeaked by to pull off a C in that class."

Dr. Hanson laughed at his son's lack of enthusiasm. "That wasn't my favorite course either. You know who you need to talk to about Neuroscience? Bruce. He is the master of the human brain. In med school, he killed the rest of us when it came to Neurobiology. He knows his stuff."

"Of course he does, Dad. He's a neurosurgeon." Nathan sat in the chair at the dining room table and gave his father a look of unrest. Even though he was excited about where his future might take him, he was also afraid of what might happen if he couldn't pull this off. Being dyslexic, reading and studying for long periods of time was physically exhausting. He could only focus for an hour at a time before he had to take a break to recharge. "I've heard stories about all the stress you went through and the time commitment involved with medical school. That's a lot of work and a lot of pressure. I'm not sure if I can handle that."

Dr. Hanson gripped his coffee cup. "You have been under more stress and had more pressure put on you as a student athlete than you ever will in medical school. You've performed against highly ranked opponents in high stakes national championship games. And you're taking advanced, upper division Biology courses on top of it all. You've already proven that you have the self-discipline and determination required for medical school. I'm certainly impressed with what you have accomplished."

"Medical school is expensive though. I won't have my basketball scholarship after next year, and I don't know how much time I'm going to have to carry a job."

Dr. Hanson eased his worry. "You get into med school, and I'll pay for it. You don't need to stress over that."

Nathan didn't like relying on his father for finances. He felt more comfortable working to earn money rather than having his father just hand it to him. "I appreciate that, Dad, but I think you've done enough."

"I haven't contributed much toward your education."

"What are you talking about?" Nathan laughed. "You have done nothing but support me. You hooked me up with a job in your clinic and arranged for me to shadow Dr. Ryan. You've helped me navigate through all the pre-med and medical school requirements, bought me an MCAT study guide, and helped me get through the application process."

"I will pay for medical school," Dr. Hanson insisted. "You just get yourself accepted."

"I'm working on that," Nathan replied.

Chapter Nine

There wasn't really a rhyme or reason to determine which Broadway shows would run for long periods and which ones wouldn't. The majority of shows on Broadway lasted anywhere from ten months to a year, and shows closed for various reasons. Some received many pre-sales, had an all-star cast, and were sold out every night, yet they closed in only a few months. Others closed due to actor/actress issues or production reasons. Sometimes low ticket sales or bad reviews caused a show to close. When the cost to produce the show was more than it made in ticket sales, there was no profit for Broadway in keeping it open. But just because a show closed earlier than expected didn't mean it wasn't successful.

Several shows on Broadway were considered long runs. Shows like *Cats* and *Wicked* stayed open for extended periods of time, closed for a year of two, then reopened. Other long-running shows stayed open continually but underwent several cast changes. *Chicago* was one such show.

When Roger landed the role of Billy Flynn, he only agreed to be in the production for twelve months. His contract included the three weeks of rehearsals prior to his premiere, as well as eight performances a week. Rehearsals for *Chicago* began way back in March of the previous year. Since that time, he had taken the stage for over 300 performances. As much as he loved this production, he never promised to be with the show indefinitely. He liked the option of participating in other productions as the new season approached.

Knowing his contract with *Chicago* was soon expiring, Roger spent several months searching for other work options. Through one of his many connections, he found out about a brand new romantic comedy that was coming to Broadway. Intrigued by this production, he read through the storyline and character descriptions. The song lyrics were fun, and several dance routines were incorporated throughout. It had the potential for being a popular production that would bring in heavy revenue for Broadway. Roger wanted to be a part of it.

Rehearsals for this musical were scheduled to start shortly after Roger's stint with *Chicago* ended. The timing was perfect, so he decided to audition.

When they offered him the leading role, he immediately called Lauren. "As an actress, you know how certain roles require emotion, and sometimes romantic portrayals are involved. If I take this part, I'll be required to kiss my female counterpart. Are you going to be okay with that?"

Letting him know she understood, Lauren replied, "It's just a stage kiss. It's no big deal."

"Are you sure? I don't want to take the job if you're going to be uncomfortable about it."

"I'm not," she assured him.

He questioned her sincerity. He wished he could see her face. Her expression would tell him how she really felt. "Just because I kiss someone on stage doesn't mean anything. You know I love you."

"I know," she reiterated. "It's alright, Roger. I trust you."

Lauren was always honest with him, but something in her tone made Roger suspect she wasn't okay with this. Instead of making assumptions, he wanted to speak with her face to face. "We'll talk tonight. Meet me for dinner?"

She agreed to his proposition.

Later that day, Roger heard that his ex, Melinda Richardson, was also in this production. This complicated things. When he met Lauren for dinner that night, they talked about the circumstances involved with this production. "I found out this afternoon that my ex is in this show. I didn't know she was auditioning."

Lauren simply stared at him.

Her silence worried him. "Honey, did you hear what I said?"

"I heard you."

With apologetic eyes, sensing her discomfort with this situation, he stated, "If this is going to cause an issue between us, I won't accept the job. Our relationship is more important. I don't want to do anything to upset you." He reached across the table and held her hand.

"You're the one who seems upset about this. I told you it's okay."

He looked into her eyes and tenderly kissed the back of her fingers. "If you are even the slightest bit uncomfortable about this, I won't take the job."

She insisted. "Take the job, Roger."

"Are you sure?"

"Yes."

He took a deep breath and exhaled slowly. "Alright. I'll confirm with them tomorrow."

Roger's final night with the *Chicago* company was full of emotion. Following the curtain call, he stood on the stage and looked around at the empty seats, giving the Ambassador Theatre a final farewell. Although he was excited about the new opportunities he had in store, he was kind of sad to be leaving. Roger immensely enjoyed this show. He made many friends through this production and met Lauren because of his involvement in *Chicago*.

Feeling nostalgic, he slipped on the black fedora that Billy Flynn wore and started to dance across the stage singing 'Razzle Dazzle.'

Lauren stood behind the curtain and watched. Roger always put his entire heart and soul into every performance. Although Billy Flynn was the only role she ever saw him play, she knew that when Roger put on the suit and hat of the silver-tongued prince of the courtroom, he was transformed into the character.

When Roger spotted Lauren standing stage left, he held his hand out, luring her to join him.

Lauren stepped onto the stage with him.

Turning her body to the theatre seats, he stood behind her and whispered, "Close your eyes."

She did.

"Here you are, standing center stage in the middle of a Broadway theatre after the biggest performance of your life. Can you hear that applause?"

Lauren bit her lip and giggled.

"One by one, the cast reappears for the curtain call. You take your bow and the entire audience rises to its feet. Echoes of applause ricochet off the walls, all for you, Lauren."

Letting out a dreamy sigh, she opened her eyes. "Someday, I hope."

"That will be you. You'll see. And I'm going to be right by your side when it happens." Roger took both of Lauren's hands in his and scanned the room. "I'm gonna miss this place. I have so many memories from this theatre that I will cherish forever. I had the opportunity to work with Jason in this show, had amazing bonding time with incredible cast members, and I met the love of my life." He placed the fedora on her head and pulled her into his arms. "I love you with all my heart, Lauren Hanson." They shared a kiss.

The few cast members still in the building came out of hiding to witness this warm display of affection, cheering and applauding at Roger and Lauren's emotional and positively heart-warming performance. Their applause made Roger laugh. He broke away from Lauren and turned to their audience, taking a graceful bow. As their audience cheered and whistled, Lauren gracefully bowed with him.

Throughout the first and second years of acting training at Juilliard, students were cast in plays and rehearsed them under the guidance of professional staff and guest directors. Plays were selected to challenge students in a variety of demanding ways. The projects were done with basic rehearsal clothes, props, and furniture, and were shared only with an audience from the Juilliard community. This was a great way for Lauren to get stage experience and learn from the best teachers in the business. The downside to this was that the majority of the productions Juilliard put on were classical plays, namely Shakespeare. And since the only people who ever saw Lauren perform were Juilliard students, professors, and staff, no one in the general community had the opportunity to witness how talented she truly was.

Roger loved classics and had no problem with Shakespeare, but he knew Lauren's true talent was not being showcased. In order to get her name out to the masses, he encouraged her to get involved in stage productions outside Juilliard. This way other people, besides the school's exclusive community, could see her perform.

As an extra-curricular activity, Lauren became involved in the West Avenue Musical Theatre Club. A variety of staged musical productions were performed with this club. Lauren enjoyed this experience because she was able to stretch beyond classical theatre and participate in musicals. The club loved having her too. Her unparalleled talent on this local stage was unlike any they had encountered before.

Lauren was getting plenty of stage experience through Juilliard and plenty of exposure in the theatrical community through both her job at the Ambassador and her involvement in the West Avenue Musical Theatre Club. Being involved in local community theatre allowed Lauren to perform in larger venues with bigger audiences. This was a good way for her talent to be spread via word of mouth. Lauren had to get herself on Broadway, but Roger brought her one step closer by helping her navigate through the tricky business aspects; this included promotion.

Roger had been promoting her current show, *South Pacific*, to all of the casting agents, directors, and production team members he knew. He spent several weeks prior to her show handing out fliers, sending personal invitations, and calling friends and colleagues encouraging them to come.

Dr. and Mrs. Hanson flew into New York City to see Lauren perform in *South Pacific*. Lauren's parents were very hospitable toward Roger when he spent a few days in Seattle over Christmas break. While they were on his home turf, he was going to reciprocate that hospitality. Back in February, when they visited New York to redeem their *Chicago* ticket vouchers, they were so busy with the show, seeing a Knicks game, spending time with their daughters, and getting the grand tour of New York City that they didn't have time in their itinerary to stop by Roger's place for dinner. Roger intended to remedy that tonight.

As soon as the Hanson's plane landed in Newark, Roger arranged to have a luxury town car pick them up and bring them to their hotel. That evening, he invited them, along with Lauren and Lacy, over to his apartment for dinner. He wanted Lauren's parents to feel comfortable and welcome in his home, so he spent the entire afternoon preparing for this. He made prime rib with mushroom sauce and garlic potatoes for dinner, tossed a salad together, and purchased a bottle of red wine. Along with this, he prepared an elegant table setting with linen napkins, candles, crystal wineglasses, sterling silver flatware, and bone china dinnerware. It wasn't often that he entertained dinner guests so when he did, he made a grand production out of it. And for Lauren's parents, he wanted to make a big impression.

After preparing dinner, he dressed for the event, going with casual but stylish layers—a pair of grey Armani slacks, grey suede oxfords, and a white and grey striped dress shirt. He slipped a charcoal-colored, multi-textured cashmere knit pullover sweater over his shirt to top off the look.

As requested, Lauren and Lacy brought their parents over to Roger's place promptly at 6:00 P.M.

"Welcome," Roger said as he showed them inside. "Please, make yourselves comfortable. Restroom is

114

around this corner if you need it." He took their jackets and hung them in a nearby closet. "Can I get you something to drink? Water? Sprite? A glass of wine?"

"A glass of wine would be great."

While Roger popped the cork, Dr. Hanson nosed around the apartment. Everything this man owned was high quality and well kept. It was obvious, from first impressions, that Roger made decent money. No one making a mediocre salary would have been able to afford the extravagant furnishings he had in this place. The apartment was classy, comfortable, and abundantly creative. With all the movie, theatre, and music décor displayed throughout, there was no doubt an entertainer resided here. "Nice place," Dr. Hanson remarked.

"Thank you." Roger handed Dr. Hanson a long-stemmed glass full of red wine.

The piano in the room was intriguing. Dr. Hanson moved closer to get a better look at it. "Would you mind playing something?"

This request made Roger grin. He loved to play for people, but rarely had the opportunity to do so. "Not at all," he decreed. "I'd love to." He took a quick sip of his wine then set the glass on a nearby table. He took position on the bench behind the keys and began to play the Gershwin composition 'I Got Rhythm' which, although the sheet music was right in front of him, he had memorized.

Dr. Hanson didn't know a lot about music, but this guy was brilliant. He was completely in awe by Roger's fast-paced, dynamic performance. As Roger played, Dr. Hanson looked over at Lauren, who stood there grinning proudly at her handsome, multi-talented man. Her father mouthed the word 'damn', without actually saying it, which made Lauren giggle. Clearly, her father was impressed.

When Roger finished his personal recital, Dr. Hanson exclaimed, "Extraordinary. You've obviously been playing for a while."

"Started taking lessons when I was five." Roger stood up and pushed the piano bench back into place. "I can play pretty much anything—Beethoven, Ellington, Gershwin."

"Ever play in your shows?"

"We usually have professional orchestration for shows. I did get to play during the production of Memphis though. When the director heard me fiddling around with the piano during rehearsal one day, he adapted a scene to give me the opportunity to play. Best director I ever worked with. He was good at finding people's strengths and working them into the show."

"Isn't that what they're supposed to do?" Dr. Hanson asked.

"Well," Roger said as he picked up his glass. "It depends on the director. Some are better than others. Most I've worked with really know how to run a show, but occasionally we get these new people who don't understand the inner workings of Broadway or the dynamics of live stage performances. There are no retakes or do-overs in theatre. It's live. Quirks need to be worked out before the show opens."

"I'm sure unexpected things happen on stage though," Dr. Hanson assumed.

"Occasionally." Roger took a sip of his wine. "I was doing a show once when my co-star tripped on the steps during her entrance and fell flat on her ass. She stood right back up and did a little 'ta da' as if to say, boy, do I know how to make an entrance. The rest of the show continued without a glitch."

This made Dr. Hanson laugh.

"And during the premiere of Les Mis, a tray fell into the orchestra pit, stopping the music while the conductor handed it back. In character, the actor replied with a 'thank you' and the orchestra continued. Mishaps do happen, but the show goes on," Roger said.

"Anything like that ever happen to you?"

Roger chuckled. "Nothing that drastic. Had a slight makeup mishap once when I was playing Scrooge. Worst thing that ever happened to me was a tap shoe malfunction, which wasn't a huge issue and no one really noticed except me. Incidents do happen. I've learned to always expect the unexpected."

"Keeps you on your toes."

"Definitely."

The following evening was Lauren's show. She was unaware of the number of Broadway connections Roger had invited to this performance. He didn't want to make her nervous by telling her that big name Broadway production managers, directors, casting agents, and fellow actors were watching her, so he let her go on stage and shine, oblivious to the potential possibilities that awaited her.

Roger was enthralled watching Lauren play a leading role. She was talented in many ways—the extensive range of her lovely soprano voice, her incredible acting ability, the cute facial expressions she made, and her rhythmic dance steps. Roger enjoyed this show immensely, and the audience obviously did too because they were laughing and applauding throughout the performance.

Jason came to the show with Roger. When Lauren was singing 'I'm in Love With a Wonderful Guy' and joyfully dancing around the stage with a hat in her hands, Jason leaned toward Roger and whispered, "You know, don't you, that she's thinking about you while she's singing this."

Roger grinned. "I know she is."

"She's good, Rog," Jason admitted. "We need to get her on a Broadway stage."

Glad his friend recognized Lauren's talent, Roger declared, "I'm working on that."

Later that evening, after a post-show dinner with Lauren's parents, Roger stood on his balcony staring out over the lights of Manhattan. The Big Apple, The Metropolis of America—everyone referred to New York City as something different, as this wonderful place meant something different to everyone who visited. With an event, parade, exhibition, or attraction taking place each and every day of the year, New York City seemed to be continually changing. However, one aspect never changed—New York City at night.

The sun had set several hours ago and the lights of the city could be seen vividly. With lights blazing from every skyscraper on every office block, it appeared that New York was constantly alive, working, and living— the perfect reason why it was often nicknamed the City That Never Sleeps. New York City was astonishing at night. The radiating glow from Times Square in the center of Manhattan was a constant reminder of the vibrancy of the city. The many electronic advertising boards were on constantly, twenty-four hours a day, seven days a week, 365 days a year. Times Square's nighttime glow of yellow, pink, green, and blue augmented the liveliness of New York City. There weren't many words or phrases other than breathtaking and awe-inspiring that could do New York at night justice.

Stirring a complete mix of emotions, from confusion to fascination and captivation, the city was seemingly normal—a side of New York that not many tourists got to see. For those who lived here, wherever you looked, people carried out normal, everyday tasks in a city that was considered anything but normal. The busyness and intrigue of New York City, the bright lights, the absolute boldness of it all might not have been calm and tranquil, but it was the place where millions of people choose to go on vacation every year. And to Roger, it was home.

Lauren joined him on the balcony, placing her hands on his shoulders.

"Hey, Sweetheart." Taking advantage of the view, he pulled her into his arms. "Beautiful night tonight."

"It is."

He moved his lips to her ear. "Your performance tonight was spectacular."

"Thank you," she replied. "I can't believe how many people were there. The theatre was packed. I saw Jason sitting next to you."

"I invited him." Admitting what he had done, he said, "He wasn't the only one there tonight that I invited."

Lauren looked up. "Who else did you invite?"

"Quite a few people, actually. I kinda advertised your show."

She lowered her eyebrows, wondering what he meant by that. "Advertised it how?"

"I handed out fliers, made a few phone calls, and personally invited directors, casting agents, and production managers to come see your talent firsthand."

Lauren nervously fidgeted with her hands. "Why did you do that?"

"Because I wanted to help you. This will get your name out there."

"Why didn't you tell me you were inviting all of those people?"

"I thought it better that you didn't know. Your nerves were shaky enough without knowing they were there. I didn't need to combat your nervousness by informing you that Broadway big names were coming to watch you."

She placed her hand on her forehead, a bit befuddled by his actions.

Roger had a feeling Lauren was bothered by what he did. Wondering what she was thinking, he asked, "Are you mad?"

She took a deep breath and sighed. "No. I'm not mad. I just wasn't expecting all of this. I wish you would have told me." She stood by the balcony railing and looked out over the city.

He stood behind her, lovingly wrapping her in his arms. "I didn't mean to upset you. I was only trying to help."

She touched his hand, letting him know it was okay. "I know. It's a little overwhelming though. I'm astounded that all of those people came to see me."

"Your performance tonight was superb. Your talent was truly showcased, and everyone I spoke to afterwards was quite impressed." He gently rubbed her arms to reassure her. "Word's going to get out and more people are going to come see your shows. I can pretty much guarantee that. You're going to make a name for yourself, Lauren Hanson. I always knew you would."

Thankful for his help, but not convinced she was worthy of the audience, she said, "I appreciate you inviting all of those people, but you really didn't have to do that, Roger."

He tried to downplay it. "All I did was hand out some fliers and make a few phone calls. The rest was up to you."

She lifted her chin and looked him in the eye. "Thank you, Sweetie."

"You're welcome."

In the morning, Roger brought coffee and pastries over to the Hanson's hotel room. "Dr. Hanson, do you fish, Sir?"

Dr. Hanson grinned. "Yes, as a matter of fact I do."

"Feel like tossing in some lines tomorrow?"

"In New York City?"

"No," Roger chuckled. "Up at Sylvan Lake. It's a great fishing spot."

"How far is it?"

"About eighty miles from here. It'll take us about an hour and a half to get there. We leave in the morning, fish all day, then drive back. It's great scenery too. Thought you might enjoy it."

"Alright. You have equipment?"

"Yup," Roger declared. "Everything we need. A buddy of mine lives in that area, and he has a boat he's willing to lend me for the day."

"Cool." Dr. Hanson loved fishing. It was one of his favorite things to do. He fished with his dad on Lake Washington as often as he could, and he and Nathan had fished together since Nathan was old enough to hold a rod and reel. "Sounds fun."

Bright and early the next morning, Roger loaded his Aston Martin with fishing poles, necessary tackle, and a cooler which he planned to fill with water bottles, iced tea, and ice cold beer.

Lauren was thrilled that Roger took the initiative to go fishing with her father, especially since Dr. Hanson was an avid fisherman. "Thank you for doing this with Daddy."

"I'm looking forward to it. Haven't been fishing in years."

"Do you have your fishing license?"

"Yup. And your dad got his yesterday, so we are good to go." He grabbed his cellphone and wallet off the dresser. "What are you and Lacy doing with your mom today?"

"Shopping around Manhattan, and we're taking her to lunch."

"Can you do me a favor while you're out and about?"

"Sure, Sweetie. What do you need?"

"I had new tips put on my tap shoes," he said. "Can you stop at Capezio's and pick them up for me?"

"Absolutely. Any idea what time you guys will be back?"

"Not sure," Roger replied, searching through his wallet to give her the claim ticket for his shoes. "Kinda depends on your dad. We'll try to be back in time to meet you ladies for dinner tonight, so think about where you would like to go."

"Sounds good. Have a good conversation with Daddy. Really open up to him and let him get to know you."

"That's the plan." He found the claim ticket and handed it to her. "Love you, Honey. Thank you for doing that for me."

"It's no problem."

Roger gave her a kiss and grabbed his car keys. "Have fun today. I'll see you this evening."

Familiar with Dr. Hanson's coffee addiction, Roger stopped at Starbucks before he drove to the Hanson's hotel. When Dr. Hanson answered the door, Roger presented him with a hot cup of cappuccino. "Good morning, Doctor."

"Good morning, Roger." The aroma of coffee instantly brightened his day. He took the cup of steaming java from Roger and took a sip. "Thank you."

"You're very welcome, Sir."

With coffee in his hand, Dr. Hanson followed Roger out to the car. When he saw the midnight blue Aston Martin, he gawked at it covetously. "Nice car. Is it yours?"

"Yes, Sir."

He circled around and admired the vehicle from all angles. The Aston Martin Vantage was an unprecedented engineering achievement. Combining a V12 engine with the lightest sports car frame, this vehicle was a package of pure aggression. It hit a top speed of 205 miles per hour, creating the fastest series production model ever made. With extreme performance and extreme styling, this car was opulent and dramatic. A spectacular piece of machinery. "I've always wanted one of these," Dr. Hanson said.

Roger dangled the keys in front of him. "Would you like to drive?"

"You can't be serious."

Roger placed the keys in his hand. "See how it feels behind the wheel."

Grinning with excitement, he took position in the driver's seat.

Driving this car was pure heaven. They leisurely cruised the highway, sipped on coffee, and talked, getting to know one another. Come to find out, they had more in common than either one of them imagined—love of fast cars, basketball, fishing, and beach-covered vacation spots were among the main topics of conversation. They had similar taste in clothing and food, both were benevolent benefactors of various charities, and both completely believed in romancing the woman they loved. The more Dr. Hanson spoke with Roger, the more he realized what a down to earth, kind-hearted person he was.

"The Huskies look really good this year," Roger said.

"They do," Dr. Hanson replied. "Nate's stats have gone up quite a bit. He's definitely having one of his best seasons."

"It'll be nice to see a team that doesn't get as much recognition as some of the others blow away the playoffs this year," Roger said confidently. "I'd like to see Nathan and his team hold that trophy."

"So would I. I know that's something he's been hoping for."

"Well, he's certainly turned my attention toward Washington. There are some talented players on that team."

"Yes there are."

"Nathan is one of the highest ranked college point guards out there," Roger declared. "He's an instinctual and intuitive player. Sports Illustrated put him on the top ten list."

Dr. Hanson grinned proudly. "He gets some of that from his mother, but most of it is just his genuine skill and talent with the game. Nathan's always been a basketball player. He lives it and breathes it. His mother was always the same way."

"Your wife plays basketball?"

"She did in college. She was starting point guard for Cal. Both Jane and Nathan are powerhouses on the court. Nathan has raw grit and determination. He's a natural leader with impeccable passing skills and solid accuracy at the net. My wife was always an aggressive player who had amazing ball handling skills. One of the funniest things to witness is when Jane and Nate play one-on-one. Neither one of them like to lose. They get downright mean and fight it out sometimes. Funny as hell."

Roger had to laugh. "I can imagine. Your wife is one of the nicest women I've ever had the privilege to meet."

"Yeah, she's a good woman, an incredible wife, and a wonderful mother. She's always been supportive of me and my career goals, as well as those of the kids."

"Lauren's lucky she has such supportive and loving parents. Not everyone can say that," Roger said. "My mother supports me, as does Gary, but unfortunately I never knew my biological father."

"Really? Why is that?"

Roger proceeded to explain, "My father was Lieutenant Andrew Zellers, United States Air Force. He was a test pilot. One day during a routine test flight, the engine of his plane malfunctioned. He was unable to recover from it and his plane went down. Killed him on impact. My mother was six months pregnant with me at the time, so I never knew my father."

"I'm sorry to hear that."

"It's alright," Roger claimed. "Gary's a good man. My mother met him when I was young, and they married when I was eight years old. He's the only father I've ever known."

"It's good to have someone like that in your life who was willing to take on being a father figure for you."

Roger agreed. "Yes. I'm very grateful."

When they arrived at the lake, they pulled into the driveway. Roger's friend was not home at the time, but had left a key to the cabin under the doormat. They loaded up the aluminum boat, equipped with trolling motor, and headed out to the water.

Sylvan Lake was shaped like a deep bowl and had beautiful clear water with a well-defined weed line along its edge, ideal for fishing. This lake offered a variety of species to catch—crappie, walleye, catfish, trout, and largemouth bass. The cold, deep water provided a good trout habitat, and the shallow weed beds provided great cover for largemouth bass. Overall, it was a successful day; the men returned home with four trout, all weighing nearly ten pounds.

After meeting the women for dinner, Lauren, Lacy, and Roger said goodbye to Randy and Jane Hanson. Before they went their separate ways, Dr. Hanson shook Roger's hand. "I had a great time today. Thank you, Roger."

"Any time, Sir. Thank you for listening to the story about my father."

"I feel honored that you shared it with me," he replied. "Thank you also for looking after Lauren. I feel a lot safer knowing she has you here."

All those months of working to gain Dr. Hanson's trust finally paid off. "It's my pleasure, Sir."

Roger and Lauren bid her parents farewell then got in the car to head back to his apartment. As Roger drove home, Lauren questioned him about something she overheard him say. "What did you tell my dad about your father?"

"That I never knew him."

On several occasions, Roger mentioned a man named Gary. He always called him Dad, thus Lauren assumed Gary was his father. Apparently this was not the case. "I thought Gary was your father?"

"Gary is my mother's husband. Technically he's my step-father." Roger proceeded to tell Lauren about his biological father's plane crash and how his mother met Gary, who had raised him from the time he was eight years old.

Roger had never spoken of his biological father before, so Lauren was surprised to hear about this. "You never told me that."

"No, I didn't," Roger confessed. "From what I've heard, my father was a pretty amazing man. I'll have to show you a picture of him when we get home. I've been told I look just like him."

Roger never ceased to amaze her with the interesting stories he always told. He led a fascinating life and brought excitement into hers in many ways.

Chapter Ten

One thing the Huskies men's basketball team was notorious for was ending strong in the second half of gameplay. They were good under pressure and able to pour it on offensively when stakes were high. They demonstrated this exceptionally well during the playoffs. Since Nathan joined UW, the Dawg Pack had made it into a National Championship playoff contention bracket every year. Last year, they made it into the Final Four. This season they proceeded further in the competition than they ever had in Washington history—the final game against Virginia.

Aside from working on medical school requirements, collecting recommendation letters, writing essays for his applications, and preparing for the MCAT, Nathan had this game to focus on.

The Huskies performed well, but despite their gallant efforts, they finished second in the tournament, losing to Virginia by four points. "Dammit!" Nathan cursed as he headed to the locker room.

Gabby overheard his frustration and ran to catch up with him. "Nathan?"

He stormed off as if he didn't hear her.

She called to him again. "Nathan, wait."

He turned around and snapped at her. "What?"

"Don't take this out on me."

In a harsh, testy tone he said, "We should have won that game. Our defense was awful tonight. It should have been much tighter than it was."

Gabby tried to uplift his spirits. "You guys played hard and really pulled together. You didn't go down without a fight. You should be proud of that. Finishing second in the entire country is a respectable position, Nathan."

"We should have won. We got sloppy and fell apart, and it's my fault."

Wow, he was taking this loss hard, being irrational and oversensitive about it, which made the entire situation worse. "How is that your fault? You're not the only player on the team."

"Because I'm their leader, their point. It's my job to keep the team together."

"It's also their job to guard the person they're assigned to and make shots when they're open. Stop putting this whole thing on your shoulders."

He glared at her. "You don't get it do you? I dropped the ball. I wasn't focused on the game."

She tried to convince him this wasn't his fault. "You were going up against the top ranked team in the nation, Nathan. Cut yourself a little slack. I thought you guys did well."

"Not well enough." He turned his back to her and stormed off to the locker room.

Gabby hated it when Nathan acted like that. He often took losses hard, but he wasn't normally snappy with her about it. She hoped a shower and a pep talk from his coach would put him in a better mood, because right now he was unbearable.

When the team headed back to the hotel, Nathan realized he had unnecessarily taken his frustrations out on Gabby. He went to her hotel room and knocked on her door, hoping to apologize for the way he acted. When she answered, she gave him a harsh look. Feeling guilty, he let out a pitiful sigh. "I'm sorry."

She stared at him with her hands on her hips. "Did you get it out of your system?"

"I acted like a jerk and had no right to take it out on you. I'm sorry, Gab."

She stepped out into the breezeway, closing the door to her room. "Don't be so hard on yourself all the time," she instructed. "And certainly don't carry the weight of the world on your shoulders. I'm here to help you."

"I know," he admitted as he sat on the floor, leaning against the wall. "I should have come and talked to you instead of snapping at you like that. I apologize."

His mood, the tone he was setting, and the expression on his face told Gabby something was bothering him. She sat down next to him, trying to get him to talk. "Nathan, what's wrong?"

Letting out a big sigh, he expressed what was on his mind. "I'm more nervous about these medical school applications and interviews than I was about this game tonight."

"But you won't have interviews until next fall."

"Doesn't mean I'm not preparing for them already." The medical school interview was one of the most crucial elements of the medical school application process. This interview would allow Nathan to go beyond what was written on his application and show them he was more than an MCAT score. "My whole life people have judged me by my stats. There's more to me than that, Gab."

She was surprised he said that. People knew he wasn't just a 'jock' on a basketball court. He was an intelligent, hard-working, altruistic man with strong people skills who had a genuine concern for others. Anyone who truly knew Nathan knew that about him. "I know," she assured him. "And other people know that too, Sweetie."

"Med school is extremely competitive. It is much more demanding than any playoff game I could ever be involved in. They'll critically review my personal statement, letters of recommendation, professional experience, and interview responses to develop a complete picture of who I am and why I want to pursue a life in medicine. I can't afford to screw this up. One false statement or even the smallest mishap on my application could instantly take me out of the pool of candidates. I need to stay focused on this."

"That's all you've been focused on for the last three years," she reminded him.

"But I need to be," he explained. "Medical school is extensive, challenging, and physically strenuous. Admissions committees need to know I can handle the pressure and commit to something like that over a long period of time."

"And you don't think basketball constitutes as that?" she told him. "Don't sneeze at your court experience, Nathan. You've pursued it for several years and have proven your leadership skills on the court. The fact that you've been successful with basketball, along with the B minus grade point average you have, proves you can handle the demands of medical school. I don't think you realize the significance of that."

He chuckled at her statement. "My dad said that exact same thing."

"And he knows what he's talking about. He's been through this process. I would certainly heed his advice."

"I am," Nathan said. "Believe me. I am listening to every damn word he says. But I've got to be honest with you, Babe." He looked her in the eye and bluntly declared, "I'm terrified."

"Of what?" she wondered.

"That I'm not going to get in. That all the hard work and time I've dedicated to this has been a waste of time. That I've busted my butt and made sacrifices for nothing." He took her hand and said, "I want you to be proud of me."

She lovingly touched his arm. "Sweetie, I'm always proud of you. You work hard and have accomplished so much."

"But our future depends on this." With a troubled look on his face, Nathan asked, "What happens if I don't make it? What do we do then?"

"You keep trying, because you, Nathan Hanson, are not a quitter and you don't give up. I know you can do this." She gave him an encouraging smile. "I will always be here for you. You know you can talk to me when you get frustrated or need to vent. You're not in this alone."

Staring at her for a moment, he replied, "I need you. I can't do this without you."

"And I will be here to support you, no matter what."

Her constant dedication and faith in him offered encouragement. Slowly, he leaned in and kissed her.

After completing the three-point contest, in which Nathan defended his title, and Gabby's National Cheerleading competition, which placed Washington sixth and left Gabby and her partner with the coed stunt trophy for the second year in a row, they happily returned to Seattle. However, Nathan didn't rest easy until he received notice that his MCAT scores were in. Before he checked his results, he called Gabby over for moral support. Sputtering his breath, he clicked on the link to view his scores.

He passed with flying colors.

"See," Gabby declared as she touched the tip of his nose. "You can do this, Nathan. I know you can."

Breathing a sigh of relief, he finally showed signs of confidence.

"Now, get your applications finished and start practicing for your interviews. I'll help you."

"You already have," he stated. "More than you know."

Chapter Eleven

Roger was the first one to arrive at the rehearsal studio on West 41st Street. This particular studio brought back memories for him. The first Broadway show he was involved in held rehearsals here. He stood in the middle of the venue and looked around for a minute, taking in the sentimental connection he had to this place. With a rhythm playing in his head, he danced across the floor singing, "Look at me. I'm the king of New York…"

He was interrupted when a woman he hadn't seen in years stepped into the room. "Well, well. If it isn't Roger Zellers."

He stared at her for a minute unsure what to say. Roger had a history with this woman, but the last time they spoke, the words they said to one another weren't very nice. "Melinda."

"You still have the moves, don't you?" She smiled flirtatiously and slowly walked toward him. "It's been a long time, Roger. How have you been?"

He didn't want to be around her, let alone talk to her. Hoping she'd keep her distance, he simply said, "Busy."

"You've made quite a name for yourself, haven't you? A Tony, performing at Rockefeller, and several appearances on the Today Show. You've been involved in some pretty big shows too. The lead in Chicago? That's quite an accomplishment." She took a few steps closer—far too close for Roger's comfort.

"Yes, I guess it is." Uncomfortable with her close proximity, Roger backed away.

He hoped the tenseness he felt would disappear, but as the week progressed, the tension only escalated. Although this show looked good on paper and had a unique concept, daily rehearsals were a disaster. Everything about it felt wrong. The musical score sounded horrible, the director kept changing the scenes, the choreography needed more flare, and every time Roger tried to express his opinion about changes that would make the show better, his ideas were immediately shot down. To make matters worse, working with his ex and being forced to do a kissing scene with her made him uncomfortable. Normally he didn't have a problem making a scene look believable, but performing this scene with his ex was awkward.

The director was far from impressed with Roger's performance. "I'm not feeling the emotion here, Roger."

Roger had the reputation of being cheerful, energetic, and easygoing. He was always professional and cooperative with production crews and generally got along well with his fellow cast members. But he couldn't swallow the lack of creative insight and poor direction involved in this show. The whole production was subpar, not at all the high-caliber, professional quality he was accustomed to. The shoddy rehearsals, eight hour days, five day a week, were putting a strain on his voice, pushing his patience level, and making him edgy.

"Take five," the director announced to the cast.

Roger immediately left the rehearsal studio and stepped outside. Trying to release some tension, he sat on the stairs with his elbows on his knees.

The director stepped outside, and when he saw Roger, he questioned him with a scolding tone. "I can sense some strain between you and Melinda. I don't know what the issue is, Roger, but if working with her is going to cause problems…"

"It's not," Roger combed his fingers through his hair then looked up at the director. "It's not."

"Then what's the problem?"

"What's the problem?" The problem was Roger and the creative team didn't see eye to eye. And if that wasn't bad enough, he had a difficult time working under this director. Roger did not like the man. He was unorganized, inexperienced, and indecisive—by far the worst director he had ever worked with. Roger had an earful of words he wished he could say to this man, but he didn't want to be rude and risk getting fired, so he bit his tongue instead. "I'm just having a hard time getting into this role. I can't find my groove."

"Well, you better find it quick because I don't want any setbacks." The director walked away in a tizzy.

Roger was a professional Tony award-winning theatrical performer with years of experience on Broadway. This show was raw, to say the least, and it seriously lacked creative insight and flare. He was certain this director and the creative team were out to doom the success of this show, and continuing to be in this amateur-like production was going to jeopardize his career. In an attempt to clear his head, he called Lauren.

Since Roger was at rehearsal, Lauren was surprised to receive his call. "Hi, Sweetie. I thought you were at rehearsal?"

"God, it's good to hear your voice."

She could tell something was wrong. "What's the matter?"

Roger exhaled heavily. "Everything! This whole thing is just...wrong."

"What is?" she asked.

"This rehearsal. This show. I can't get into it, and it's frustrating. And to add to everything else, the director's mad at me."

"Why?"

"He says I lack emotion, and I don't know how to fix it." He paused for a moment and collected his thoughts. "Help me."

Lauren tried to bring him out of his funk. "Close your eyes."

He did as she asked.

"Now, imagine you're with me at the most calming place you can think of."

Smiling at her suggestion, he said, "I wish I could be with you right now. That would be so much better than what I'm enduring today."

"You need to focus, Roger."

"That's easier said than done," he complained with a sarcastic titter.

"Pull yourself into your happy place. Once you've cleared your mind, go back to rehearsal refreshed."

This was actually good advice. "That's a fantastic idea. Thanks for your help, Honey."

"You're welcome."

"I have to go, but I'll see you tonight."

"I love you, Roger."

"I love you too." He slipped his cellphone back in his pocket and returned to rehearsal.

Thinking about being alone on a beach with Lauren, surrounded by sand and sun, helped Roger refocus his energy, making the scene they'd been working on more believable. The cast applauded, praising the performance.

"Incredible!" the director commended. "Best scene I've seen all day. We'll wrap it up there."

While the studio began to clear, Melinda moved closer to Roger. "You've still got it," she professed.

He looked up. "Still got what?"

"That fire. That passion," she replied. "You can't tell me that you didn't feel anything with that kiss."

He denied her accusation. "It's called acting, and I'm good at it."

Melinda crept behind him and rubbed her fingers down his back. "What happened between us, Roger?" she whispered in his ear.

Dodging her attempt to seduce him, he stepped away from her. "Do you really have to ask? The lies, the false accusations, rubbing my face in the tabloid dirt. I don't trust you, Melinda." He unzipped his bag and packed his belongings, hurrying to leave.

"Got some kind of hot date tonight, Rog?"

If she only knew.

"Who is she?" Melinda probed. "Anyone I know?"

"Goodnight, Mel." Hastily, he darted out the door, disregarding her remarks.

The next day, Melinda snooped around, questioning people about a young performing arts student Roger was allegedly in a relationship with. She badgered him too, trying to get him to reveal more information. "What's her name, Roger?"

He refused to tell her anything.

The more silent he remained, the more she hounded him. "Are you serious about her?"

Fed up with her stupid game of twenty questions, Roger told her, "Look, I am not here to discuss my personal life with you. What I do in my off time is my business, not yours. We are trying to put on a Broadway show. Will you drop this please and focus on the task at hand?" He ignored any further comments and went back to rehearsal.

After rehearsal, a reporter interviewed Melinda about her upcoming reappearance on the stage following several years in hiatus. Roger Zellers was a big name on Broadway now, so in an attempt to get back into the limelight, Melinda made it a point to emphasize that she was in this production with him. But she did it in such a way that she smeared Roger's name in the process.

Roger was changing out of dance attire at the time this interview occurred, therefore he didn't hear the exchange between Melinda and the reporter. But a friend of his overheard the whole thing and immediately told Roger.

"You have got to be kidding me?"

"Sorry, Rog," his friend said. "Just thought you should know."

"Thanks, Lance."

Before he left that evening, Roger confronted Melinda out in the parking lot. "What did you tell the press?"

"Only what I needed to."

Roger pursed his lips together, trying not blow up at her. "You will say anything to draw attention to yourself, won't you? Dammit, Melinda, don't even start this deceitful crap again."

"Tell me who this woman is, and I'll recall my statement."

"Oh no," he warned. "There is no way am I letting you drag her into this."

Grinning haughtily, she stated, "Oh. So there is a woman." Outraged that Roger wouldn't tell her anything, she gave him a glassy stare. "Who is she, Roger?"

"This is not going to work," he said, sneering at her plaguing nosiness. "I know you blame me for the downfall of your career, but you brought all of this on yourself when you decided to blatantly lie to my face. You're the one who devised that ridiculous story and lied to the press about the extent of our relationship. You can try whatever tricks and gimmicks you want, and you can concoct whatever fabricated tale you'd like, but there is no way in hell you can get to me through her."

"We'll see about that." Melinda pretentiously walked away.

Roger walked into his apartment that evening visibly tense. His posture was rigid and he had a pinched expression on his face. He threw his script on the coffee table and sat on the sofa rubbing his brow as if warding off a headache. "Son-of-a-bitch!"

When Lauren heard foul language come out of Roger's mouth, she grew concerned. She had never heard him swear before. She stood behind him and rubbed his shoulders, trying to get him to relax. "What's the matter?"

He reached up and touched her hand. "I'm sorry. I had a bad day." He took a deep breath to calm himself. "This production is terrible. The choreography is off, the sound doesn't work properly, and every time I make a suggestion, the creative team shoots me down. The damn director changed the script three times today, and to top it all off, my female counterpart is finding any way she can to push my buttons."

Lauren sat on the sofa and reached for his hand. "What happened?"

He proceeded to tell her. "She's getting word out to the local tabloid magazines that being in this production together has rekindled our relationship."

"Is that true?"

Roger scowled in disgust. "No. Not even in the slightest. I assure you there is nothing going on between Melinda and me. She keeps asking about you, but I refuse to tell her anything."

"Why is she asking about me?"

"She wants to use you to get to me," he explained. "She's manipulative. She excels at putting on a sob story and is very capable of getting the public to believe her lies. There is no way I'm giving away any information about you, because she will use any means necessary, including raking you over the coals, to get to me. I refuse to let her drag you into this."

"She's done this before?" Lauren assumed, not quite sure she understood what was going on.

"You have no idea," he said derisively. "She's a pro at blowing up tabloids and stirring up storms. And she's at it again."

"Why would she do that?"

"Personal gain. Revenge," he said.

"Revenge? Against who?"

"Me. In the prime of her career, her popularity dwindled. She lost jobs and a fan base because of it. To this day she blames me for her downfall."

"Why does she blame you?"

He explained, "It's a long story, but basically she fabricated a lie in an attempt to boost her popularity. In the process, she made me look bad."

"What did she say about you?"

Not wanting to hide anything from Lauren, Roger divulged the truth. "She told the press she was carrying my child, which was a blatant lie. She then proceeded to say we were planning a wedding together."

"You and Melinda were engaged?"

"No, that's what I'm trying to tell you. The entire story was a lie. Bottom line is she wasn't getting enough attention, so she made up a juicy tale to gain sympathy points and draw a bigger fan base. When I found out she openly lied about the extent of our relationship, I immediately broke it off. And since the tabloids thought she was pregnant, I was labeled as abandoning her in her time of need. When the truth finally came out, the public saw how manipulative and deceptive she was. From that point on, her career went down the toilet."

"That's terrible! I can't believe she did that."

"Believe me, Lauren, this is nothing new for her."

The emotional rollercoaster Roger had been on lately was wearing him down. He loved being on stage, but this show was causing him unnecessary stress and anxiety. He looked like he was about to pop a vein. "This show is really stressing you out."

"Tell me about it. I thought all of this was behind me, but she refuses to let it go." He closed his eyes and took in her tension-releasing touch. "I seriously need to de-stress."

"I know what we can do. Come with me." She took his hands and pulled him off the couch.

"Where are we going?"

"You'll see."

They ended up at the New York Botanical Gardens wine festival. The festival offered palate-pleasing wine from local wineries. Sommeliers and vintners gave demonstrations and informative discussions about winemaking, and live bands performed amidst the vibrant colors and fragrances of the botanical gardens. This was definitely up Roger's alley. It helped him refresh and unwind.

Days later, Roger met Lauren for dinner. As soon as they claimed their seats, Lauren dunked her ice cube into her water and watched it pop back up. She hadn't said much all night and seemed to drift in and out of the conversation. Roger sensed something was bothering her.

"Is something wrong?" he asked.

"What makes you think something's wrong?"

"Because you're playing with your ice cubes, and you're awfully quiet tonight. What's going through your head?"

She took a deep breath to gather her thoughts. "All these things the magazines are saying. Why would they print stories about you and Melinda getting back together if it wasn't true?"

He quickly interjected. "They're tabloids, Lauren, stories specifically printed to stir up drama. Unfortunately, that is one of the downfalls of this business. I am in the public eye. When the media receives hearsay from unreliable sources, the public perceives it as truth, whether it's true or not. Melinda is trying to stir up trouble. She has some delusion in her head that her fabricated lies will cause tension between us. She seems to think that if she can drift us apart, she'll be able to slip right in. But that is never going to happen." Roger defended his stance. "There is absolutely nothing going on with me and Melinda. I've already told you that."

"Then why do I keep getting hostile messages from people?"

"What messages?"

Lauren pulled out her phone and scrolled through her text messages. When she found what she was looking for, she showed Roger. "These messages."

As Roger skimmed through several texts from an unknown number, his lips drew a hard line, growing angrier with each word he read. "How the hell did she get your number?"

Surprised that Roger recognized the origin of these obscure messages, Lauren questioned his involvement. "You know who's doing this?"

"I have a hunch, if my intuition is correct." He handed Lauren's phone back to her.

"Who?"

"Melinda."

Lauren dropped her jaw. "She's the one sending these?"

"It certainly sounds like something she would do."

"Why would she…"

Roger's cynical voice surfaced. "Because she's a jealous, vindictive, psycho she-bitch."

With a heavy heart, Lauren stared at the table. She didn't know what to make of all this, and wasn't sure she wanted to be a part of it. "I can't do this, Roger."

She stood up to leave, but Roger reached out to stop her. "Honey, please."

Lauren stared at his hand.

"Don't condemn me for Melinda's actions. I can't control what she does, and I'm not responsible for the things she says. Please, sit down. Let's talk about this."

Wavering, she sat back down.

Roger struggled for the right words. "I don't care what the magazines say or what kind of ridiculous allegations Melinda makes. I am not about to let her or anyone else pull us apart. I love you and only you, Lauren. You're the woman of my dreams and the love of my life. I don't want to lose you."

She wanted to believe him, but had a hard time swallowing all of this. Hoping to evade this confrontation, she avoided direct eye contact.

"Sweetheart, look at me."

Reluctantly, she raised her chin.

"Melinda seems to think she can manipulate people through threatening remarks and negative publicity, but we can't let her have that kind of control over us." He lovingly kissed the back of her hand. "I'll take care of this. I promise."

"What are you going to do?"

"Forward those messages to me then block that number. Tomorrow morning, I'll confront Melinda and put an end to this."

Roger arrived at rehearsal early the next day with the specific intent of interrogating Melinda. He immediately sought her out and shoved this incident right in her face. "Can you explain to me please what gives you the right to send threatening messages to my girlfriend?"

With a self-satisfied smirk, she replied, "I'm getting to you, aren't I?"

"You're pissing me off is what you're doing. How did you get her number?"

"You have a bad habit of leaving your cellphone lying around. It was pretty obvious which number was hers. She's on the top of your contact list, and you had over 300 messages to her."

Roger's eyes filled with fury. "You snooped through my cellphone messages?"

"Oh yes," she said smugly. "And they were so sweet, Roger. Sending her kisses and little heart shaped emoji's. She's a lucky girl."

His hand closed into a fist, squashing the anger he felt. "You stole my phone and read my private messages?"

"It wasn't that hard."

He stared at her, disgusted. "You are unbelievable. That is a severe invasion of privacy, and I'm almost a hundred percent certain that sending threatening messages is considered harassment. You need to back off."

Before he returned to his apartment that evening, Roger called Lauren and made plans to meet her for dinner. "We'll meet at 6:30?" he asked, anticipating sharing a pleasant meal with her.

"I should be done by then. I'll call you later to confirm."

"Alright. I'll see you tonight."

After her last class, Lauren made her way to the dorms. She was stopped by someone calling out her name. She whirled around and saw a woman in dark sunglasses looming toward her. Lauren had never seen this woman before, yet somehow this person knew who she was. "May I help you?"

"All he needed was a little push, but he won't budge if you're in the way."

Lauren narrowed her eyes. "Excuse me?"

This woman increased her stride, quickly closing in on Lauren. Lauren's frantic gaze stumbled across the area. The campus was surprisingly empty. Not a soul was anywhere in sight. Struggling to comprehend what was happening, she searched for an escape route. She drew a shallow breath and quickened her pace, trying to sneak to a more populated area.

She didn't get far before this woman lunged toward her with an extended hand and pinned her against the wall, holding her by the throat. Lauren attempted to scream, but her voice seized up. She gripped this woman's hand and desperately tried to pry her fingers away from her neck. Every skin cell tingled, every neuron fired. Her heart rapped against her ribs, ringing in her ears. Fear clenched like a tight fist in her chest.

"You better watch your back, because I will make certain you never step foot on a Broadway stage." With a quick release of her hand, the woman darted out of sight.

Lauren trembled in fear. Her body stiffened and her stomach tightened, forcing her to lean over and vomit in a nearby bush. Her throat clogged, as if she had swallowed cotton balls. She held her hands up to her neck and took in a gulp of air. Once her lungs were full, her shaky legs carried her home. Still uneasy from this ordeal, she sank onto the corner of the bed, curled her legs into her chest, and hugged her knees.

When Lauren didn't show up for dinner, Roger pulled out his phone to see if she had left him a message. She hadn't. It wasn't like her to not show up for a planned dinner date. It also wasn't in her nature not to inform him if she was running late. Concerned about her tardiness, he called to check on her. When she answered, her voice was shaky. "You alright?" Roger asked.

"My stomach is queasy."

"I'm sorry to hear that, but you could have called and told me. I've been waiting here for thirty minutes."

"I'm sorry, Roger. I didn't realize what time it was."

Something wasn't right. Lauren's voice stretched high and tight and she hesitated in her responses, almost as if struggling to speak. "Are you sure you're alright?"

"I'm fine. I just need to rest."

Although he wasn't sure he fully believed her, he took her at her word. "I'll call you in the morning."

She didn't have much to say, and was quick to dismiss the conversation. He figured it was because she wasn't feeling well. He hoped by morning she would be more sociable.

When he called her at 9:00 A.M., she didn't answer her phone. He assumed she was asleep, so he left a voicemail. "Hi, Sweetheart. Just called to see how you're feeling. I'm going to head over to the gym for a bit. Give me a ring when you get this."

He spent about an hour working up a sweat before he headed to the showers. Once he was dressed, he checked his messages. Nothing from Lauren. He tried calling again, but she still didn't answer, which struck him as odd. She always responded to his messages and promptly returned his phone calls. Yet today, she disregarded his attempts to communicate. Concerned about her wellbeing, he headed over to Juilliard to make sure she was okay.

When he arrived, Lauren looked a bit pale. Her arms crossed her midsection, as if she was going to be sick. "How you feeling?"

She drew in a shallow breath and rubbed her red, watery eyes. "Tired. I couldn't sleep last night."

Withdrawn and distant, she sat on the bed with a closed posture, sheltering herself with pillows. Her

148

jawline was taut, and she refused to make eye contact with him. Roger knew something was wrong. "You haven't spoken to me much lately. What's going on?"

Hesitant to tell him, she choked through her words. "I know I told I was okay with all of this, but I'm not. The media, the messages I keep getting, and I'm pretty sure I ran into Melinda yesterday."

"Melinda?" How was this possible? Lauren had never met her before, and Roger made every effort to make sure they never encountered one another. "Are you sure it was her?"

"At first I didn't realize it was her, until she pinned me against the wall and threatened to sabotage my career."

Roger's eyes widened. "What?"

Lauren proceeded to tell him every detail of what happened, from the stalking to the verbal threats she made.

Roger couldn't believe what he heard. He ran his fingers through his hair and released a heavy sigh. "I am so sorry you got dragged into this."

"It's not your fault."

"Yes it is. With Melinda, I should have suspected something like this would happen. The minute I heard she was involved with this show, I should have looked the other way. I knew the kind of person she was and how vindictive she could be. I made the mistake of thinking she might have changed. I shouldn't have done that."

"You couldn't have known, Roger."

"I should have known," he huffed cynically. "Especially after the threatening messages she sent you. We should have taken them more seriously."

"You didn't know it would escalate to this."

"This has gotten way out of hand. We're going to the authorities and filing a complaint."

They went to the local NYC police precinct and filed a harassment complaint against Melinda. The police took down all the information and suggested that Lauren not travel alone for a while. Roger agreed to that plan.

"From now on, I'll walk you to and from class," he insisted.

She protested. "I don't need an escort."

"I'm not debating this with you. Your safety comes first." His statement was absolute, and he wasn't backing down. "And I've decided to terminate my contract."

"I don't want you to quit your job because of me."

"This show is causing too much strife and friction. It's not worth it."

"I don't want to be the reason you…"

He didn't let her finish. "I'm done, Lauren. They'll be other jobs." He drew his mouth to hers and kissed her. "In the morning, I'll talk to my union rep. I'm sure he'll find a loophole to get me out of this."

"What if he can't?"

"We'll figure something out."

Roger had never dropped out of a Broadway production before. But with the unnecessary stress, personal turmoil, constant harassment, and general annoyance this current show caused him, he and his union rep called a meeting with the producer, director, and other production staff, at which time Roger left the show for what he said were personal reasons. They immediately cancelled his contract.

News of this incident spread quickly, which made Melinda's devious plan backfire in her face. Broadway fans found it suspicious that Roger quit shortly after her press announcement of their rekindled love affair. Once again, people questioned her integrity and recognized she was fraudulent in her claim.

Chapter Twelve

Back in January, the Broadway League announced that after more than 1,500 performances, the actor playing the lead in *Phantom of the Opera* was leaving the production. Broadway needed a new Phantom. This was a job Roger had auditioned for years ago, but he lost the part to the actor currently playing the role. Now that he had more experience and was a bigger name on Broadway, he tried again. He really wasn't expecting to get the part, but to his surprise, he received several callbacks. About a week after his final callback, he received a phone call from the production crew offering him the title role.

Anxious to tell Lauren, he barged through her dorm room door singing, "Oh what a beautiful mornin'. Oh what a beautiful day. I've got a beautiful feelin'. Everything's goin' my way."

Lauren giggled at his giddiness. "You're in a good mood."

"Guess who the new masked man in town is going to be?" he boasted proudly.

Lauren gasped in excitement. "Are you serious?"

"Yes I am." He took her in his arms and spun her around. "I got the part."

"Oh Roger, that's wonderful!"

"And since you know the role of Christine so well, I was hoping you could help me rehearse."

"Of course."

"Awesome!" he exclaimed. "Today is a good day. I feel like celebrating."

She wrapped her arms around his neck. "What did you have in mind?"

"Do you like lobster?"

"Love it."

"Great! I know the perfect place."

He took her to City Lobster, the best lobster restaurant in the Big Apple. This place was conveniently located between Times Square and Rockefeller Center, close to the Theatre District, and not far from Juilliard or Roger's apartment. They specialized in delicacies such as Live North Atlantic Lobsters, fresh Alaskan King Crab Legs, and authentic Maryland Lump Crab Cakes. And their a la carte menu offered the finest contemporary New England seafood and Prime Angus Steaks. It was the perfect way to celebrate this long awaited opportunity.

Phantom was the legendary role on Broadway, and *Phantom of the Opera* was the longest running Broadway production in history. For years, it had been the Broadway musical all others were measured against. The timeless story, the unforgettable score, the undeniable greatness of *Phantom of the Opera* made it the most popular show on Broadway. Roger was honored to be a part of it.

Over dinner, he solicited Lauren's opinion on this. "It's a twelve month contract, and once I sign, I'm locked in."

"I know how long you've wanted Phantom, Roger." She reached out and touched his hand. "I think you should take it."

He lifted his glass and took a sip of his wine. "Alright. I'll call them in the morning."

The following afternoon, Roger met with the production manager of *Phantom of the Opera* and accepted the offer for the lead role. Contract negotiations quickly ensued.

Phantom of the Opera was not a new production; the show was already in progress. Roger was merely taking over as the lead. Because of that, rehearsals for this show would be different than they were for new productions. Instead of the typical four to six weeks of rehearsals, learning choreography and mastering musical scores, Roger had two weeks to prepare.

When Roger looked up at the Majestic Theatre's billboard marquee, a picture of the infamous white mask flashed in front of the building. Above that, in bold white letters, was the word *Phantom*. He had been in this theatre many times before, but this time it was a much more emotional experience for him. He wasn't coming to watch the *Phantom of the Opera*. He was the Phantom of the Opera.

After the initial sink in, he went around back to the stage door entrance. Stepping inside this theatre felt surreal. Rows of 1,645 seats lined the elegant theatre with one orchestra and two mezzanine levels. The red velvet curtain and shimmering chandelier added to the majestic look of it all, hence the theatre's name. This theatre was grandiose in appearance, reputation, and production.

Phantom was the most legendary character on Broadway, and Roger was obsessed with him. He had read the book, saw the production numerous times, and listened to the score regularly. He knew the musical inside and out, but he needed to work on interacting with his costars, get timing down on pyrotechnics, and become familiar with the stage setup and props. Sound tests needed to be performed, and he wanted to get a feel for how his voice sounded in this great hall.

He met the cast and was assigned a dressing room. Then, with musical score in hand, he took the stage to do a run through. He knew the part well, but it would take a few more rehearsals to perfect the role.

Besides beginning his run in *Phantom of the Opera*, spring brought many other things—warmer weather, the opening of lingcod season, and the official announcement of the Tony Award nominees.

Roger had recently received word that not only would he be performing the opening number at the Tony Awards, he was also invited to host this event, something he had never done before. He had performed on stage at the Tony's before, but having the opportunity to kick off the show and serve as host at the glorious Radio City Music Hall was truly an honor. He couldn't wait to share this experience with Lauren.

Randy and Jane Hanson never really followed Broadway until their daughter became involved in it. While Jane was reading the Entertainment section of the morning newspaper, she stumbled upon an article about the upcoming Tony Awards. After reading the article, she said, "Roger's hosting the Tony's this year."

Randy didn't seem to care. He turned to the sports section, checking out NBA scores.

"Are you listening?"

"I heard you," Randy replied.

"Then why didn't you answer?"

"I'm concerned about Lauren's involvement in all this." He neatly folded the paper and set it on the table.

"Roger is constantly in the limelight. Since Lauren is closely associated with him, she's going to get caught up in this. I hope she can handle it."

"She'll be fine," Jane replied, thinking Randy was fussing over nothing.

"She's young, Jane, and she doesn't have the experience in the entertainment industry that he does. He's used to the press and the critics and being in the public eye. She's not."

"She'll learn. Doesn't Juilliard teach them that?" she asked.

"I believe they do, but that's not my point," he argued. "You and I both know how badly Lauren wants to get on a Broadway stage. That's all she's talked about since she was little. Roger's successful on Broadway, and because of that, I'm not sure Lauren's getting a realistic view of how the entertainment industry works. It's a competitive business, and I think she's viewing the entire thing through rose-colored glasses, not seeing the harsh reality of it all. She needs to remember that Roger is a professional who has years of experience on stage. He consistently lands lead roles and somehow gets himself into pretty big productions. Lauren sees his success and is going to think it will come just as easy for her. She's expecting to jump into something big right away, but when it doesn't happen, she'll quickly get discouraged. Or suppose she does manage to land a big role, she doesn't have the stage smarts in the professional world. The pressure of being in the public eye or the critical reviews or the demands of performance will be too much for her to handle."

"You don't think Roger has advised her about all of that?"

"I have no idea what he has said to her," Randy said. "I would hope, if he really cares about her, that he would want her to know the downsides as well as the glamor of it all. He did tell me he wanted to help guide her through that."

"You don't believe him?"

"I didn't say that," he refuted. "I just hope that when he does give her advice, she takes every damn word he says to heart."

Before he headed up to the maternity ward, Randy popped into the Emergency Department hoping to catch his best friend, Jim Ryan, during some down time, which was a rare occurrence in the ER.

When Jim spotted Randy, he acknowledged him with a quick nod. Since the ER wasn't overloaded, Jim made some quick scheduling adjustments to make time for his friend.

Over a cup of coffee, Randy told Jim about Roger. He explained how he recently got the lead in *Phantom of the Opera*, was the recipient of the prestigious Tony Award, and was apparently some big name star on Broadway. He also expressed his concerns about his daughter's involvement with it all. "Jane seems to think I'm overreacting. Nathan says I'm getting too hung up on it and told me I should let it go. But I don't know. Should I be worried about my daughter?"

Jim tried to ease his worry. "Lauren is a sensible woman. I wouldn't worry about her too much."

Randy wasn't convinced.

"Didn't you tell me once that you wanted your daughters to pursue their dreams, find happiness, and when either one of them chose a man, you wanted to make sure he treated her with the respect she deserved?"

"Yes, I did say that."

"Heed your own words then." Jim took a sip of his coffee. "Is she happy?"

As much as Randy hated to admit it, he couldn't deny the truth. "Yes. She loves New York. She's learning a lot at Juilliard. She has a part time theatre job that allows her to meet people in the industry while she's making money. She's able to perform on stage, which is all she's ever wanted to do. And…" Randy couldn't believe these words were about to come out of his mouth. "She has met a nice young man who cares about her, supports her, and gives her the respect I demand."

"Then answer your own question. Should you be worried about her?" Jim waited for an honest answer.

Randy exhaled heavily. "Probably not."

"Now, if Roger would have been a punk kid with no job, ragin' hormones, and a pimp mobile with loud exhaust and thumpin' bass, then yes, I would have been concerned."

Randy had to laugh. "Oh, hell no. I would have stomped that fire out quick."

"See? It coulda been a helluva lot worse." Jim raised an eyebrow. "You know, a Broadway star is actually kinda cool, especially for Lauren. He'll certainly show her the ropes, won't he? And I've heard those people, at least the good ones, can make pretty decent money."

"It's funny you say that because he lives in an expensive ass apartment in Upper Westside Manhattan and drives an Aston Martin."

"Are you serious?"

"Yup."

"Damn," Jim complained. "You mean to tell me that I spent all that money on tuition and dedicated all that time in medical school to save people's lives and all this kid does is put on a mask and sing in front of thousands of people every night, and he makes more damn money than I do?"

"Yup, pretty much."

"Ok," Jim chuckled. "Maybe he is a punk kid."

Jim's lack of enthusiasm made Randy laugh.

Chapter Thirteen

With a new actor taking over the lead, the cast of *Phantom of the Opera* met Friday morning to do one final run through to fix any bugs so the production would run smoothly for Roger's debut. At the conclusion of rehearsal, Roger stepped into his dressing room to change back into street clothes. On the table, a ceramic replica of the infamous white mask nestled neatly inside a black velvet box. A note was attached, written on the same parchment paper Phantom uses in the production. *Phantom is a legacy, a legacy which has aged divinely over the years and has been portrayed by some of the most talented people on Broadway. After four years of being Phantom, I pass the mask to you. Best of luck tomorrow, Roger. May the Music of the Night be forever in your heart.*

It was signed by the actor who was carrying out his last performance tonight. Roger picked up the mask and stared at it. After years of waiting, he would finally be at the heart of this timeless tale. Tomorrow, in front of 1,645 dedicated fans, he would wear the mask and transform into the Phantom. He was now a part of the legacy.

Roger's debut as Phantom was a much anticipated event. His parents and many of his friends came out to support him. Lauren, Lacy, and Jason took a seat among them.

This show was sold out, which wasn't surprising considering it was one of the most famous and popular musicals ever made. Every week it grossed over a million dollars. The *Phantom of the Opera*, which opened at the Majestic Theatre in 1988, was the winner of seven Tony Awards, including Best Musical. The show's melodramatic production numbers had struck audiences for years and was currently the longest-running production in Broadway history.

Phantom of the Opera was operatic in scope, utilizing a large cast and orchestra to tell Phantom's obsessive love story. The show was awe-inspiring with its glowing candelabras, creepy Gothic scenery, special effects, and the signature chandelier crashing to the stage.

Before the masked man even appeared on stage, his mysterious voice captivated the audience. When Roger finally made his stage appearance, he immediately entranced the theatre patrons. Phantom's deepest feelings came out. He was romantic, mournful, haunting. But when Roger belted out his rendition of 'Music of the Night', the house sat in silent reverence. He put so much emotion and power into the song, his voice resonated through the theatre. His profound and heart-rending interpretation of Phantom gave Lauren chills.

During intermission, Jason stared at the stage mesmerized. "Wow! That was the most intense per-formance I've ever seen him do."

Roger's mother grinned with pride. "My Roger is such an emotional actor. He puts his heart into every performance."

"Yes he does," Jason agreed. "That man can sing!"

As the performance progressed, Lauren couldn't get over the intensity and emotion Roger displayed on stage. Phantom's agony, rage, and heartbreak brought tears to her eyes.

Two hours and thirty minutes after the show started, the performers took their bows on stage. Roger was the last one to come out. The audience roared and gave him a very loud standing ovation as he took his bow in Phantom's black suit and the white mask. He had brought the house down.

The theatre cleared and Lauren bid the family farewell. But she stuck around, hoping to catch Roger backstage.

In his dressing room, Roger removed the famous white mask and gently set it in its storage box. Still dressed in Phantom's classic black suit, he responded to a knock at his door.

"Hey, Roger," a man in a masquerade costume said. "There's a woman named Lauren out here looking for you."

Roger grinned. "Oh good. I was hoping she'd stay behind."

"You want me to send her back here?" the man suggested.

"Could you, please?"

Anticipating Lauren's arrival, Roger thanked the man then removed the prosthetic latex that covered his face. Finally, his skin could breathe. He placed the black suitcoat on a hanger and hung it on the costume rack of his armoire before Lauren poked her head in the door. She immediately embraced him, almost knocking him over.

"Wow," he exclaimed. "What did I do to merit such a grand welcoming?"

"Oh my god, Rog! You were amazing!" She plopped down on the loveseat.

"Thank you." He closed the door then picked up the eerie latex and moved it over to the vanity.

Lauren curled her lip, repulsed. "That's kind of creepy."

"You don't think it's sexy?"

Lauren eyeballed the box on the table, bouncing forward to get a closer look. "Ooh," she said, staring at the infamous white mask. "Can I touch it?"

He chuckled at her star-struck playfulness. "If you are so inclined."

Lauren took the mask out of the box and admired it. "Do you know what this is?"

"Of course I know what it is," he said, finding her excitement over a mask incredibly cute. "I was wearing it through most of the show."

She held it against her chest. "I can't believe my boyfriend is the Phantom of the Opera."

Roger looked at her as if she'd lost her mind. "You feeling okay?"

"You are so talented, Roger." She placed the mask back in the box then stood up to kiss him. "And charming." She meandered her finger down his chest. "And amazingly sexy."

He gave her an evocative stare. Realizing the door was unlocked, he said, "Hold on a minute."

"What are you doing?"

"Locking the door. Don't want anyone walking in on us." Once the door was secure, he returned to Lauren. "Now, where were we?"

As their kissing session gradually turned more passionate, Roger removed the rest of his costume, letting it drop to the floor. Lauren's clothes came off next, leaving a trail across his dressing room. Roger sat on the loveseat and Lauren straddled his lap. They gazed into each other's eyes and exchanged smiles.

"Are we supposed to be doing this in here?" Lauren whispered, feeling naughty for engaging in this pleasurable act in Roger's dressing room.

"Technically, no. But," he kissed her tenderly on the lips. "If we're quiet, no one will know."

She covered her mouth and giggled, trying hard to be as silent as possible. He laughed right along with her.

In the middle of the act, someone knocked on Roger's door. "Hey, Rog?" a voice on the other end called out.

Gritting his teeth, he stopped briefly and panted. "Yeah?"

"There's a caterer out here if you want to grab a bite before the next performance."

Roger didn't give a rat's ass about food right now. He was partaking in the pleasures of the flesh. Trying to hide what they were doing, he replied, "I'll be out in a minute."

He and Lauren tittered to themselves before they continued, using incredible restraint to remain silent during their entire interlude.

As Roger regained air, he glanced over at the clock. It was a little after 5:30 P.M. His next performance was at 8:00, and with makeup, latex, costumes, and sound wiring, it would take him at least an hour to prep for that. He looked at Lauren and couldn't help but laugh.

She wondered what was so funny. "What?"

Carefully, he maneuvered his body to separate himself from her. He let out a satisfied sigh and leaned back to relax. "That's something I've never done before."

"What is?" she asked, wondering what he was talking about.

"Sex in my dressing room." He flashed her a sexy smile and softly kissed her on the lips.

"Is that bad?"

"Oh no!" he retorted playfully. "Not at all."

Lauren hopped off his lap and searched for her clothes.

As she collected articles of clothing, Roger sized her up from head to toe. Her body was perfect—feminine, curvy, soft, and sexy. Her legs were toned and defined, her butt was firm and round. The hourglass figure she possessed, from her ample breasts all the way to her curvy hips, enticed him. To Roger, Lauren was a natural work of art. "You really are a beautiful woman. I don't tell you that enough."

She tossed him his pants.

Roger planted his feet on the floor and walked over to her, placing his hand gently on her arm. She turned around, arms full of clothes. He took them out of her hands and set them on the loveseat. "I don't take you for granted."

She cocked her head, wondering why he said that.

He pulled her into his arms and locked his eyes on hers. "And I don't ever want you to think you're not important to me. I know I don't always get to see you every day or hold you and show how much I love you, but I do love you."

His words were sentimental and sincere, yet the insecurity in his voice made Lauren question his statement. "Why are you telling me that?"

"Because not a day goes by that I'm not grateful for you. The best day of my life was the day you came into it. I love you with all my heart." He gently grazed the back of his hand across her cheek.

His earnest and loving words brought tears to her eyes. "I love you, too."

Every time Lauren said that to him, his heart pounded. The love he felt for her was deep, unwavering. Being with her made all the coiled up places in his heart unwind. She activated his inner being, filling him with warmth and light and beauty. Being in love with Lauren, and knowing in his heart that she loved him in return, empowered him. It penetrated his deepest depths and incased splendor in his heart. With her, he was able to trust in love again.

Roger longed to be with her, and when they weren't together, he was thinking about being with her. He wanted nothing more than for Lauren to be happy, because that's how much he cared about her. Her needs came before his own. He hid nothing from her because she accepted him and loved him just the way he was. He needed her, and without her, his life was incomplete.

"Where are you going to be tonight?" he asked. "Your place or mine?"

"Probably yours."

Roger reached into his wallet and handed Lauren a twenty dollar bill. Here's some cab money. You going to be alright by yourself?"

"Yes, Sweetie. I'll be fine."

He chuckled at his own worry over her. After all, she was an independent woman perfectly capable of taking a cab home. "Alright."

Lauren grabbed her sweater and gave Roger a hug. "You were phenomenal today. I know you'll be just as amazing with your performance tonight."

"Thanks." He softly kissed her on the lips. "There's some leftover Thai food in the fridge if you're hungry later."

She clutched her purse and headed toward the door. "I'll see you tonight after the show."

As Lauren was about to leave, Roger called out, "Lauren?"

She turned around. "Yes?"

"I love you."

"I love you too." She blew him a kiss and walked out of the room.

It finally dawned on him that he was hungry. He left his dressing room and scoped the theatre searching for this caterer so he could grab some nourishment before prepping for tonight's performance.

Several reviews of the production were posted in the paper the next day. Roger was all too familiar with critic reviews. He had been on the receiving end of them multiple times. Some critics were friendlier than others. But one review in particular caught his attention. *Roger Zellers' emotional portrayal of the Phantom was superbly beautiful and powerful; I have to tip my hat. Judging by sheer invention, emotional punch, and onstage talent, the venerable blockbuster still delivers the goods. The flamboyant gothic design and fantastic staging still have the gleam of finely polished professionalism. The musical score still has a visceral tug, and the chandelier still falls on cue. The Phantom of the Opera remains as fresh and spectacular as ever. It continues to rise to the top of all the musicals ever to appear on Broadway. I hope I listen to the music of the night forever!*

Roger was having the time of his life being Phantom, and his performance was moving people. He quickly became recognized for bringing a different interpretation of Phantom to the show. A deep, emotional Phantom rang out strong, and fans were enthralled by it. Surely, he would go down in the books as one of the best Phantoms of all time.

Chapter Fourteen

Lounging on the sofa watching the NBA playoffs, Nathan answered his cellphone. "Hello?"

"Nathan! How you been, man?"

Nathan wasn't sure who he was talking to, but obviously this person knew him. "Doing well."

"I was able to catch the playoffs against Virginia. Tough break. Close game though. You showed them one hell of a fight."

When he figured out who this person was, a huge smile filled his face. "Chris. It's good to hear your voice. It's been a long time."

"Yes, it has," Christopher declared.

"How's life in Africa?"

"Actually, Jasmine and I are heading back to the states."

"Really?" Nathan replied. "When?"

"Catching a flight Saturday afternoon. Stopping in New York City overnight before we head to Seattle."

Christopher Ryan was finally coming home. Nathan hadn't seen him in years. "That's awesome. Both of my sisters are in New York now. They'll be excited to see you. I'll let them know you're coming."

"Great, but you can't tell my dad, which means you can't tell your dad. I want it to be a surprise."

"Your parents don't know you're coming home?"

"Nope!" Chris declared.

Nathan chuckled. "That will be quite the surprise."

The Ryan and the Hanson families grew up together and knew each other well. Chris's homecoming was something Jim and Jill Ryan had been looking forward to for a long time. This would definitely be a pleasant surprise.

Nathan called Lauren to let her know Chris would be in New York, hoping she and Lacy would plan accordingly. "Will you let Lacy know and make some kind of arrangements to pick them up from the airport?"

"No problem," Lauren said.

"He sent me his flight information. I'll e-mail it to you."

As soon as Lauren got off the phone, she told Roger what was going on. He was a bit confused as to what exactly was happening and why it was significant. "Wait a minute. Who did you say these people were?" he asked, wanting clarification.

Lauren explained, "Chris Ryan is a friend of the family."

"And he's been where?"

"Botswana," Lauren replied.

That was an odd place to make a homestead, considering seventy percent of the country was covered in the Kalahari Desert and suffered from severe drought and poverty. "What on earth was he doing in that god forsaken place?"

"I don't know. Some kind of Peace Corps work or something. I'm not exactly sure."

"Not the best place to raise a child," Roger decided.

"No," Lauren agreed. "Which is probably one of the reasons why he's coming home."

"I would hope so," Roger remarked. "Do they need a place to stay? I have a guestroom they can use."

Roger didn't even know these people, yet he graciously offered them room and board. "That's sweet of you," Lauren replied with a smile.

"It's no big deal. We'll both be home on Sunday. I'm sure we can work something out."

Roger loved entertaining people, and playing host to Christopher Ryan was yet another opportunity for him to do so. When he met Christopher at the airport, he offered a friendly handshake. "Hello, Christopher. I'm Roger Zellers. I've heard a lot about you."

Chris shook his hand. "Pleasure."

Since Chris's hands were full with two carryons and a diaper bag, and his girlfriend had a baby in her arms, Roger kindly offered to carry their baggage out to the cab. "You been to New York before?"

"Nope," Chris replied. "Hoping to take a bite of this Big Apple before we leave."

Thrilled with the opportunity to play tour guide, Roger replied, "I think I can arrange that."

Once they settled in, Lacy offered to look after baby Madeline while Roger and Lauren took Christopher and Jasmine on a ferry tour around New York Harbor. They also went up to the top of the Empire State Building to take in the view from that miraculous height.

"Wow," Chris declared looking down at the city from the tallest point in New York. "This is quite the view."

"Definitely an eye opener," Roger said. "Being way up here makes you realize how small you really are in the world."

"No kidding," Chris agreed. "This is spectacular."

The men chatted throughout the night and became better acquainted. They were both close in age, had some of the same interests, and really hit it off as far as developing a friendship went. The two men exchanged phone numbers and e-mail addresses and promised to keep in touch. Roger even extended his hospitality and offered to take them to a Broadway show next time they visited New York.

In the morning, before Chris and Jasmine left, Roger gave little Madeline a fluffy pink teddy bear and firmly shook Chris's hand. "Have a safe flight. Give us a ring next time you're in New York."

"Will do."

Once they boarded their plane, Roger said to Lauren, "Glad I had the opportunity to meet them. Really nice people."

"Yes they are," Lauren concurred. "Chris's dad has been friends with my father for years."

"Is he a doctor too?"

"Uh huh," Lauren replied with a smile. "The two of them went to Berkeley together."

"That's cool," Roger said. "What kind of doctor is he?"

"ER."

"Oh wow," Roger proclaimed. "Bet he's busy."

"Jim is a really cool guy. I love the Ryans. I can't wait for you to meet the rest of them."

Jim took a brief break from the ER to snag a quick cup of coffee with Randy. "Some dude came into the ER last night wasted and pukin' everywhere, complainin' of severe stomach cramps."

Randy grimaced. "That doesn't sound pleasant."

"Oh it gets better. As I'm doin' an examination on this guy, I come to find out that he drank the fluid from sixteen glow sticks."

Randy found this amusing, yet incredibly asinine. "What the hell? Why would anyone be dumb enough to do that?"

"Stupid assmunch was tryin' to make himself glow in the dark."

"Idiot," he laughed. "Doesn't he know that stuff is toxic?"

"Evidently not," Jim deduced. "Guy was havin' a narf fest and we ended up havin' to pump his stomach because he nearly poisoned himself to death. It didn't help that his blood alcohol level was through the roof."

"Was he aware of what he was drinking?"

"Hell if I know. But I was bogged down with other issues last night and really didn't need that on top of everything else that was goin' on. Some other guy came in at about the same time with a damn fork jabbed into his skull."

Randy considered how that was even possible. "Do I dare ask?"

"Some domestic squabble, and his wife stabbed him with a fork. The cops got involved with that one."

"Man, you see some crazy shit, Jim. Definitely not a dull moment."

"Nope," Jim agreed. "Most definitely not."

While Jim enjoyed a bonding moment with his best friend, Jill was closing out paperwork in the ER. As she stood at the front desk, a voice called out, "Excuse me, Ma'am. I was wondering if you could be of some assistance."

Jill looked up, and a young man with dishpan blonde hair and hazel eyes smiled down at her. "Oh my god! Chris!" She rushed to give him a hug. "What are you doing here?"

"Jasmine and I decided to come home." Jasmine joined his side with the baby in her arms, and Chris reached an arm around her. "Mom, meet Jasmine and your granddaughter, Madeline."

Jill went gaga over the baby, and in the midst of the conversation came to find out that Chris and Jasmine were planning on getting married within the next six months. She also learned that Chris had accepted a job as a social worker for the City of Seattle.

"That's great, Honey," Jill said to her son. "Are you guys home to stay?"

"Yup. I'd like to tell Dad myself." Christopher scanned the ER looking for his father. "Where is he?"

"He went on a coffee break. I'll page him."

Jim was laughing over a story Randy told about his parrot when they both overheard, "Dr. Ryan, please report to the ER. Dr. Ryan to the ER."

"Are you kidding me?" Jim complained. "Not even a fifteen minute break."

Randy chuckled, "Sorry, Man."

Jim grabbed his coffee and headed back down to the ER, flashing Randy a shaka sign as he left. When Jim got there, little was going on. Certainly nothing a resident physician or the nurses couldn't handle. He saw Jill back by the exam rooms and questioned her about this. "Why did you have me paged? Is there a code comin' in or something?"

"No," she replied with a devious smile.

Jim didn't understand. "Then what's goin' on?"

"Go out front and look in the waiting room, please."

"Why?" Jim asked.

"Just do it," she insisted.

To humor her, he went out there. He immediately froze in his tracks when a young blonde man with a baby in his arms stood right in front of him. "I'll be damned." A smile slowly crept onto his face. "Christopher!"

"Hey, Dad."

Jim hugged him tightly. "Oh man, it's good to see you."

"It's good to see you too."

After releasing the death grip he had on his son, Jim scolded, "Dammit, Chris, it has been far too long."

"I know," Chris apologized. "I'm sorry."

"Are you home permanently?"

With a grin, Chris nodded. "Yes, Sir."

This was incredible news. "It's about damn time."

Christopher introduced his father to Jasmine and let him hold Madeline, then he updated him on recent life changes. "My job with the city starts next week, but we need somewhere to crash for a while until we can find our own place and get settled."

"Absolutely," Jim agreed. "Mi casa es tu casa."

Chris was delighted to be home. He had missed his family terribly. "Thanks, Dad."

"Anytime, Son. Welcome home!"

The Ryans were invited to the Hanson's house for a barbecue that Sunday. Nathan and Gabby came too. Everyone hovered over the baby and had wonderful conversations, hearing all about Chris's adventures in Botswana.

"When I first got there, I would lie awake for nights on end wondering if sounds I heard were normal," Chris explained, "like a dog shaking the burglar bars or a bird that sounded like a jackhammer trying to rip open my roof. It was a big adjustment from living in Seattle."

"I bet," Nathan replied.

"And sanitation was definitely a challenge. I attempted to use conventional cleaning methods until I figured out that my pocketknife was the most effective tool for scrubbing the toilet and cleaning the stove."

Randy was completely grossed out by the lack of cleanliness. "Please tell me you washed the pocketknife after you cleaned the toilet."

"Yes, I did," Chris assured him. "Then there was the joy of hand washing clothes. The first couple times it was more like splashing around my bathtub like when I was a child with my rubber ducky, but eventually I developed a system that worked."

Nathan said, "Bet you really missed the conveniences of modern machinery."

"Sometimes," Chris admitted. "It got a little rough when we had to walk to a pit latrine in the middle of the night dodging cows on the way. We were two to three hours away from the closest grocery store and lacked water and electricity. Our kitchen, which was actually a standalone stove with a giant gas tank, was one of only two rooms in our orange, thatched-roof house. To get our water for drinking or taking a bath, we had to walk down to the river. Women cooked over open fires and walked miles to forage for firewood. Men drove cattle to the reservoir while children ran to school along dusty red-dirt roads. It's just the way life was."

Nathan replied, "Sounds pretty remote."

"They had computers, cellphones, a few televisions, and ATMs in larger towns, but electricity was unreliable in rural areas. We had access to cellphone service and e-mail about once every two weeks. A 90-minute bus ride was required to reach the closest city with Internet capabilities. And our bus got seriously delayed once because an elephant was standing in the middle of the road and refused to move," Chris chuckled.

Nathan shook his head. "That is not my kettle of fish. Doesn't sound like a place I would want to spend six years of my life. What exactly were you doing there?"

Chris explained, "My primary role was in a clinic, assisting in systems strengthening and information management. The clinic I was working in was severely understaffed and had an infrastructure that desperately needed improvement. Part of my responsibility was educating people about HIV and AIDS as well as creating community programs, such as after-school and peer-mentoring initiatives. I ran a support group, conducted outreach efforts, and organized events that allowed people to be tested for the deadly disease and hear health care experts speak about it."

"That's good," Nathan said. "I heard there's a huge epidemic over there."

"There is, but it's because they lack education and facts about HIV. Some still think it's transmitted by mosquitoes. Part of it is cultural too. They recognize multiple partners as normal, and even if a mother is HIV positive, she still continues to have children. I came up with a slogan that we used all over the village: Be Faithful and Condomize."

Nathan found that funny. "That's great."

"The other volunteers seemed to like it." Christopher cut a piece off of his steak and savored every morsel. "Man, this is one thing I've really missed. Fresh meat and produce."

"What did you eat?" Nathan wondered, knowing that he would have suffered and died without legitimate food.

"Fresh fruits were pretty much unavailable in Botswana. But spiky, colorful pane worms, the natives ate those like potato chips," he grinned devilishly.

Gabby looked like she was about to be sick. "Ew."

"I didn't care for them much," Chris confessed. "Regularly we ate fatcakes and seswaa, which is fried dough and stewed goat meat. The villagers considered those a delicacy."

Nathan was not impressed. Cringing, he proclaimed, "I'll stick with my steak, thank you." And he cut into his juicy ribeye.

"We ate what was available," Chris explained. "They did make their own bread though, baked it in an earthen oven. It was actually really good. Despite the many people in Botswana who live in extreme poverty, they made quite well with what they had."

"That sounds like quite an experience, Chris," Randy declared.

"It was a great experience. I had some awkward moments where my Setswana wasn't good and carrying on a conversation was challenging, but the people there were really open and friendly. The locals seemed to like us and gave us a huge goodbye when we left. A village couple I was working with even gave me a pair of goat hair sandals."

Nathan asked, "What are you going to do with those?"

"I don't know. Jasmine and I collected quite a few memorabilia during our adventure." He looked at Jasmine and winked. "Glad to be home though."

She went to get the baby, who was now awake from her nap.

After the meal, the two families lounged on the back deck in lawn chairs, enjoying the beautiful spring weather and the calmness of the lake while they sipped on Coronas and lemonade. "I'm gonna run inside and grab another beer," Randy said. "You want one, Jim?"

"Sure," Jim replied. "Thanks, Bro."

"Nate?" Randy asked.

"I'll take one," Nathan replied.

While Randy stepped away, Jim directed his attention to Nathan. "How's the medical school search goin'?"

Nathan shrugged. "It's going alright. Narrowed my choices down to three. Working on secondary applications now, then just waiting to hear about interviews."

"You prepared for that?" Jim asked.

"I think so. My dad's been helping me out."

"Remember to be honest with them," Jim advised. "Don't try to be someone you're not. They want to see who you really are and know that you are a real person who has more goin' on in his life than just medicine. What they don't want is a medical geek who thinks only about medicine 24/7. Show them your versatility."

"That's what Dad said too," Nathan replied.

"Listen to that man," Jim advised. "He's the best doctor I know and was a damn good medical student. He knows what he's talkin' about. Take his advice seriously."

"I am." Nathan expressed his honest concerns. "My dad's better at that kind of stuff than I am. He seems to be a natural with interviews and speeches and being put on the spot like that. It's not as easy for me."

Jim didn't understand what Nathan was talking about. He was a confident young man who was good around crowds and people. He had a natural ability to stay calm in stressful situations and had proved on many occasions that he could easily handle pressure. "I don't agree with that. You are constantly put on the spot, Kiddo. You are a pro at performing under pressure. Many times a game was on the line and you were the one who pulled through to nail those last minute buckets and win it for your team. Don't even tell me that you aren't good at bein' put on the spot. If anyone can handle a high-stakes situation where the pressure is on, it's you."

Nathan tittered. "You sound like my dad."

"Your dad's right," Jim said.

Randy came back with three Coronas in his hand. He handed a beer to Jim and another to his son before he sat back down on his lawn chair and popped the top off his bottle. "What am I so right about?"

Jim and Nathan looked at each other and grinned.

When they went inside the house, Randy's parrot flew down and took Jim's shades off the top of his head. The clever bird squawked, "Surf's up," then flew to the top of his cage with Jim's sunglasses gripped in his talons.

"Dude," Jim complained. "I'm gonna kill that mangy featherhead one of these days."

Randy laughed hysterically.

Jim sneered at him. "You taught him that, didn't you, you son-of-a-bitch?"

Playing innocent, Randy denied this accusation. "Now why would I teach him that?"

"To irritate the crap out of me. I swear that bird hates me." The bird was about to chew on his Oakley aviator sunglasses. Jim jumped out of his seat to chase the bird down. "If he ruins those, you owe me one-hundred fifty bucks."

But Randy didn't care. One-hundred fifty dollars was well worth the price of watching his friend wrestle with an African Grey, who was obviously more cunning than James Ryan was. "I thought it was a rather ingenious trick he pulled on you there, Bud."

Fighting the bird for possession of his sunglasses, Jim said, "What the fuck is a damn feather-brained parrot gonna do with a pair of shades?" After finally winning the battle with the bird, he examined his sunglasses to make sure they weren't scratched.

"Maybe he wants to be stylish like you, 'cause you're the king of fashion," Randy teased, referring to Jim's Hawaiian button up shirt, bright blue tee-shirt, baggy jeans, shark tooth pukka shell necklace, and flip flops.

"Shut up, Asshole." Jim cleaned the smears off the lenses with a Teflon rag then slipped his sunglass back on the top of his head.

Randy laughed as Jim re-spiked his bleach blonde hair with his fingers and tried to reassemble himself.

Chapter Fifteen

Roger had been busy lately with several events on his calendar. Aside from the eight performances a week he had with Phantom, Roger was involved in several fundraising events. One was a charity softball game hosted by Yankee Stadium, where various Broadway stars got together to play a game to raise money for the Broadway Cares/Equity Fights AIDS Foundation.

To raise more funds for Broadway Cares, several cast, crew, and orchestra members from *Phantom of the Opera* joined the Broadway Softball League. Various Broadway shows formed competitive teams and played games against one another in Central Park. The league usually played a ten-game regular season schedule, followed by playoffs to determine the champions in various categories. They played special games for charity and had an All Star series. The league was co-ed, and it was an embedded part of the tradition of Central Park and the New York theatre community. The life of a showman was unstable, but this softball league offered stability, and it was fun. Roger loved it and had participated in it for many years now.

Lauren's Juilliard group was in the midst of performing William Shakespeare's *Love's Labours Lost*. She was also preparing for her appearance at the New York Shakespeare Festival at Delacorte Theatre in

Central Park in a few weeks. Her class and performance schedule at Juilliard, her commitment to the theatre club she was involved in, and her part-time job at the Ambassador, in combination with Roger's schedule, gave the two of them little time to be together. Since the Majestic Theatre was dark on Sunday, and Lauren didn't work on Sundays, they took advantage of this shared day off and spent the entire day together.

They started off with lunch at Grimaldi's Pizzeria, where they enjoyed coal-fired brick oven pizza. This pizza was the best in New York City with its freshly made dough, fresh mozzarella, and fresh San Marzano tomatoes. For an after lunch dessert, they hit up the Brooklyn Ice Cream parlor right across the street.

After indulging in savory frozen delights, Lauren and Roger toured the Museum of Modern Art, located on 53rd Street between Fifth and Sixth Avenues. The Museum of Modern Art, or MoMa, was often identified as the most influential museum of modern art in the world. The museum's collection offered an overview of modern and contemporary art, including works of architecture and design, drawings, paintings, sculpture, photography, prints, illustrated books, film, and electronic media. Van Gogh, Monet, and Pollock were among their favorite exhibits.

Roger and Lauren stood outside in the sculpture garden and eyed a four-and-half foot bronze statue standing in a negligent pose wearing only a derby hat and a bowtie. Lauren laughed when she saw it.

"What's so funny?" Roger wondered.

"You know what this reminds me of?"

"What?"

"You."

"Me?" Trying to see from her point of view, Roger eyed the sculpture again. He didn't see any resemblance. "How does this even remotely look like me?"

"It kinda looks like Billy Flynn." She posed with her hand on the statue's hat. "See? He's wearing the hat."

Roger laughed at her logic. "I like that hat."

"Phantom's hat is better."

"Which one?" he wondered.

"The one with the feathers in it."

"The Masque of the Red Death or the one with ostrich plumes he wears at the cemetery?"

"The black one he wears at the cemetery," she clarified.

"I like that hat too, except when the feathers poke me in the eye." Roger pondered this for a moment. "That Red Death costume is heavy, and it's really hard to move around in. There's a reason we have intermission right before that scene. Getting that thing on is a pain."

"That and they have to put the chandelier back."

"True."

As the evening closed, Roger and Lauren returned to his apartment. He left the lights low, but picked up the remote for the sound system and clicked it on. Soft music began to play. Lauren noticed he had two wineglasses and a bottle of wine set out on the coffee table. She raised an eyebrow at his mysteriousness. "What are you up to?"

"Just setting the scene." He stood behind her and wrapped her in his arms. "Dim lights, romantic music, a comfortable couch, a bottle of wine, you, me...sounds like a scene I could get into." His lips grazed across her ear. "Care to join me?"

She bit her lip in anticipation. "So romantic."

"That's what I was going for." He nibbled on her neck then slowly caressed his hand down her tummy. "Share a glass of wine with me."

They made their way to the couch.

After sipping half his glass, Roger took Lauren's glass out of her hand and set it on the table next to his. He leaned back onto the throw pillows and pulled Lauren with him. Snuggling closer, Roger moved his lips to hers and closed his eyes, soaking in every luscious sensation. "I could lie here like this, with you in my arms, and kiss you all night."

The tender kisses he offered gradually became more and more intense. Lauren lay back, enjoying every moment.

"Ok, I lied," he confessed between breaths. "All this kissing is turning me on. What do you say we move into the bedroom?"

She consented with a smile.

Roger held her in his arms, trying not to stumble over his shoes, while they navigated their way to the bed. Roger eased Lauren onto the mattress then carefully crawled over her, supporting his body weight with his arms and knees.

They maneuvered slightly, centralizing their bodies more before Roger pulled his shirt off and threw it on the floor. He portrayed the role of lover quite well. His soft, gentle hands drove her wild. The way he made her feel every time they were intimate together had Lauren walking on the clouds. He made the act of sex into a well-choreographed dance.

Snuggled under the covers with Lauren in his arms, Roger said, "The opening number for the Tony Awards is going to be cool. The production team is putting together quite a spectacular show. I'm excited for you to see it."

"What are you performing?"

"Razzle Dazzle. We're doing the whole stage show but adding a twist specifically for the Tony's." He drew her hand to his lips and gently kissed her wrist. "You were planning on coming with me, weren't you?"

"To the Tony's?"

"Yes."

Lauren had never attended the Tony Awards before, or anything even remotely close to that magnitude of stardom. She watched it on TV every year and always dreamed that one day she'd attend an event like that, but now that she actually had the opportunity to do so, she didn't know what to say. "Oh my god, Roger. I've never been to an event like that before."

Hoping he could convince her, he declared, "It's a big night for me. They asked me to host the show, and I'm performing the opening number. I'd like to have you by my side for that."

"Do you know how prestigious that is?"

"Yes. It's a formal, red carpet event. I've attended every year for the last eight years."

Her heartbeat escalated and her breathing became shallow. "I have nothing to wear for an event like that."

Easing her anxiety, he said, "We'll get you something to wear."

"They'll be television cameras and the press and…"

"It's a major televised event. There will be cameras." She was about to have an anxiety attack. Trying to get her to calm down, he tenderly kissed her on the lips. "I need you there, Sweetheart. Will you attend with me?"

Taking a deep breath to relax her nerves, she nodded in agreement. "Yes."

"Good. Why don't you go shopping with Lacy tomorrow. She can help you pick out a dress."

The next day, Roger sent Lauren off with her sister to find a formal evening gown for this prestigious event. Not only did this give Lauren an opportunity to go dress shopping, it also gave the twins some much needed bonding time.

They had lunch together, got manicures and pedicures, and used the time to talk. "I can't believe Roger invited you to the Tony's," Lacy exclaimed.

"I'm nervous," Lauren admitted. "Anybody who's anybody on Broadway is going to be there."

"I'm excited for you. The whole world is going to see you and Roger together."

"I know," Lauren replied, anxious about this.

"That man loves you, Lauren, and he's not afraid to let everyone know."

As they dodged hordes of shoppers and tourists, Lauren said, "I want to stay in New York this summer so I can keep working at the Ambassador and continue to perform with the Musical Theatre Club."

"That's cool, but you know Dad's not going to like that if you don't have a legitimate place to live."

Lauren told Lacy what her plans were. "Roger invited me to stay with him."

Lacy's mouth gaped open in surprise. "Are you serious?"

"I'm going to take him up on the offer too."

"Daddy is going to freak out!" she warned.

"I know. That's why I haven't told him yet. Think I'll hold off on that as long as possible."

Several hours later, Lauren arrived at Roger's apartment with two shopping bags in her hand. He greeted her with a kiss. "You're carrying bags. That's a good sign."

She set her bags on the table. "You wanna see what I got?"

"I would love to."

Excited about her purchases, she ran into the bedroom to change.

When Lauren paraded out of the bedroom in a purple strapless sequined gown with a side slit that went midway up her thigh, Roger's eyes widened. The sweetheart bodice was covered with purple and silver sequins and adorned with rhinestones around the neckline. To accessorize the dress, she had on a pair of sparkly silver high-heeled sandals. This gown accentuated her feminine figure and made her look glamorous. Roger stared at her, speechless.

She posed for him. "What do you think? Do you like it?"

Finally able to breathe, he said, "That dress is magnificent." He put his arm around her waist and moved his lips to her ear. "You look stunning. I will be very proud to have you by my side at the Tony's, Lauren."

"Thank you."

"I have the perfect thing for you to wear with that." He gave her a small black box. "While you were out with Lacy, I did a little shopping of my own."

Inside was a pair of round-cut diamond dangle earrings in shimmering white gold, along with a matching bracelet. Lauren's hand covered her mouth, marveled by the elegant and gorgeous gift he presented her with. "Roger, these are beautiful."

He pulled the bracelet out of the box and latched it around her wrist. "A glamorous outfit isn't complete without appropriate accessories." He took the earrings in his hand and handed them to her. "Put these on so we can see the full effect."

She removed the earrings she was wearing and put these in her ears instead.

Lauren was a dazzling beauty, ready to walk the red carpet. "Perfect," Roger declared with a huge smile on his face. He suggested she look in the mirror to see for herself.

Lauren went into the bedroom and peered in the full length mirror. She couldn't believe the elegant and sophisticated image staring back at her. She looked like a movie star.

Roger snuck in behind her and put his hand on her waist. "Look at you," he said, gazing into the mirror. "You're gorgeous, and you are most definitely going to turn heads." Without looking away, his arms encircled her. He brushed a gentle kiss across her forehead then lowered his mouth to meet her kiss. The touch of her lips was a delicious sensation. It satisfied an aching desire, and left him with the burning need for another kiss.

As they were getting dressed to report to Radio City Music Hall for the big event, Roger reminded Lauren, "This is your first public appearance at a major red carpet event."

"I know. That scares me a little."

"There's no need to be nervous." He buttoned up his formal white dress shirt and tied a black tie around his neck. "Being seen at an event of this caliber is good publicity. Make your presence known and shine like the diamond you are."

"Is there some sort of protocol for something like this? Guidelines? Etiquette?"

"Not really," he answered. "You just need to remember that it is a black tie event, and people are watching."

"How does this red carpet stuff work?"

"It's not complicated," he explained, making certain that she fully understood what was happening tonight. "When we get there, we'll step out of the car and onto the red carpet together. Be prepared to see cameras and flashing lights everywhere when we pull up because the press will snap pictures. I'm not shy about revealing our relationship to the public, Lauren, just so you know." He turned his head and winked at her. "I might even kiss you in front of the cameras." He grabbed his black suit coat and slipped it on over his shirt. "Don't be surprised if the press pulls us aside and asks me some questions. It's happened before."

She nodded in understanding. "Ok."

"Once we find our seats, I'm going to have to head backstage to do a quick sound check and get set up to open the show. I've reserved a front row seat for you."

Trying to soak all of this in, Lauren asked, "How long does this usually last?"

"A couple hours. I might need you to help me shake sequins out of my hair when we get home," he chuckled.

"Are you using a confetti cannon?"

"Yup," Roger grinned.

"Oh lovely."

"It's messy, but makes a good show."

When they approached the red carpet area in the designated limousine, Lauren's hands became shaky. "Honey, relax," Roger said. "You have nothing to be nervous about."

She peeked out the window at the abundant crowd. "There are so many people here."

"I know. That's normal for an event like this." Roger tried to calm her nerves by holding her hand. "When we pull up, I'll step out first. Take my hand when I offer it to you and step out beside me. We'll pose for a brief moment to allow the press to snap a few pictures, then we'll walk up to the entrance together. I want to get inside as quickly and orderly as possible."

Lauren understood.

"You ready?" Roger asked with a reassuring smile.

"I guess so."

"You got this, Sweetheart. Just follow my lead."

When their limo pulled up, Roger gracefully stepped out with a charming smile as cameras flashed all around him. He held out his hand and helped Lauren out of the vehicle. Proudly, he put one arm around her and kissed her, which kept the cameras busy for a few minutes. After a brief question and answer session, they walked up to the entrance holding hands. The whole episode took less than thirty minutes. "See?" he whispered to her. "No big deal."

"That's it?" Lauren asked, thinking that was not as spectacular as she thought it was going to be.

"That's it," he replied. "Quick and painless, just the way I like it." They found her seat at the front of the hall. "Ok. I have to get backstage. Mingle and chat," he encouraged. "I'll see you in a bit." He kissed her and left to prepare for the opening number.

Following the initial speech and a flattering introduction, all television cameras turned to Roger and the *Chicago* company, who opened the ceremony with Roger's rendition of 'Razzle Dazzle'. Scantily clad jazz dancers, including Jason, danced across the stage while Roger, dressed in his sequin-collared Billy Flynn suit and black fedora, belted out the song. For the final part of the performance, a drumroll began and a giant Tony Award statue slowly rose up from the stage. With both hands extended towards it, Roger held out the last note of the song until the Tony was completely exposed. With the last measure, he folded his arms across his chest and lowered his head to the final drum beat. The confetti cannon went off, scattering multi-colored confetti and sequin pieces all over the stage. It was a fun and entertaining performance that brought the entire Music Hall to its feet. Roger was always a flamboyant and energetic crowd pleaser. His opening performance tonight at the Tony Awards was just as flashy.

After all nominated shows performed and all awards were presented, Roger and Lauren attended the afterhours party, which lasted well into morning. It was close to 3:00 A.M. by the time they returned home. Roger got more comfortable by loosening his tie and kicking off his shoes. "I saw you talking to some of the people around you tonight."

Lauren sat on the sofa and unfastened her shoes, placing them on the living room floor by the coffee table. "That woman at the party was really nice."

"You know who that is, don't you?" Roger asked as he walked toward the bedroom to lose layers of clothing.

Lauren got up and followed him. "No. Who is she?"

"Miriam Jones. She's an incredible actress and a skilled dancer. I've worked with her before. She played opposite me in Memphis and played the role of Elphaba in Wicked for a while. She's a pretty big name on Broadway. She's going to be in Flashdance with Jason soon."

"Flashdance? When did he start doing that?"

"He signed on with that production a few weeks ago. He's pretty jacked about it," Roger proclaimed. "It's one he's been hoping to get involved in for a while."

"What about Chicago?"

"Tonight was his last performance with Chicago."

"I didn't know that. Congratulate him for me."

"You should congratulate him yourself."

"I would," Lauren said. "But he won't be at the Ambassador anymore. I won't see him."

Roger unbuttoned his shirt and slipped it off his shoulders. "Jason and I have been friends for a long time, Lauren. It would be nice if my best friend and my girlfriend would become better acquainted."

"He doesn't seem that interested in talking to me. Even at the theatre, he doesn't go out of his way to strike up a conversation."

"Then you initiate it," he recommended.

"How do I do that? It's almost like he deliberately avoids me. Is he afraid of me or something?"

Her comment made him laugh. "No, he's not afraid of you. I just don't think he knows what to say. He might feel uncomfortable talking to my girlfriend when I'm not there. Knowing Jason, he probably thinks he's invading my privacy if he talks to you. Maybe we should invite him over for dinner so you two can get to know each other."

"We'll have to wait until I get back," she reminded him.

He abruptly turned his head, wishing she hadn't brought up the fact that she was leaving tomorrow to go on vacation with her family for ten days. "I know. I wish I could come with you."

"Why don't you?"

"You know I can't. I have commitments here." He tossed his shirt in the hamper and hung his coat and dress pants on the hanger on back of the door. "Besides, you need to spend time with your family." When he turned around, Lauren had removed her dress, leaving her in her undergarments. Seeing her standing nearly naked in the middle of his bedroom made him temporarily lose his breath. "You are a beautiful woman, Lauren."

She stepped closer and placed both hands on his chest, stroking his muscles. Roger was fit and toned. He took care of his body, worked out regularly, and looked spectacular without a shirt. Many fans considered him to be the sexiest man on Broadway. "Not lookin' too bad yourself, Mr. Zellers."

Flirting with her, he flashed a crooked smile. "Oh yeah?"

She moved behind him, skimming her hands across the skin of his shoulder. "You were amazing tonight."

"You are amazing every night." He pulled her closer and kissed her. From the corner of his eye, he saw that the curtains were wide open, which made him snicker under his breath.

"What?" Lauren asked.

"I love to entertain people but really don't want an audience right now." He broke away from her long enough to draw the curtains.

"Who's going to see anything up this far?" she teased.

"You'd be surprised. Some people are nosy enough to try to sneak a peek. Let's not give their prying eyes the opportunity." He returned to Lauren's side and continued where they left off.

Roger awoke to Lauren's naked body sprawled out all over him. Somehow, her legs were intertwined with his and her long, dark hair was spread across his chest and arm. Waking up next to her put a smile on his face. He kissed the top of her head and snuggled in closer.

Feeling Roger's touch made Lauren open her eyes and stretch. Positioned the way she was, she could hear his heart beating and feel his chest rise and fall with each breath.

Now that Lauren was awake, Roger said, "I could get used to this."

Lauren groaned sleepily. "Used to what?"

"Waking up with you in my arms." It was 8:06 A.M. Lauren's flight was schedule to leave at 12:30. "We need to get up. I don't want you to miss your flight."

Lacy had already flown home, but Lauren stayed behind to attend the Tony Awards with Roger. She planned to spend the summer in New York working at the Ambassador and performing with the West Avenue Musical Theatre Club building up her stage experience. The problem was the Juilliard dorms were closed during the summer months. Since Roger offered his apartment to Lauren, she had already moved her belongings in. However, she hadn't told her father about this arrangement.

"Does your dad know you're moving in with me?" Roger asked, gently moving stray hairs out of her eyes.

"No."

"Are you planning to tell him?"

"Yes."

"How do you think he's going to react?"

Lauren knew she had to tell her father what her intentions were, but wasn't sure how she was going to approach giving him this news. She would have to tread carefully. "I don't know. Hopefully he'll be grateful that you offered me shelter so I'm not living on the street corner in a cardboard box."

"You know I would never let that to happen," Roger declared. "My apartment is always open to you, and to Lacy if she needs it."

"I know," Lauren replied. "And thank you for that. You're always very kind to her."

"Why wouldn't I be? She's your sister."

"I know, but you go out of your way to be courteous. She was totally surprised when you gave her cab money last week."

"She needed it, and I happened to have the cash on me," he justified. "It's not a big deal."

"She told me yesterday she's going to pay you back when she returns to New York."

"And I told her I didn't want it back. If she tries to give it to me, I won't take it. It was my pleasure to help her." He ran his fingers through her hair and kissed her on the lips. "Please talk to your father."

"I will," she promised.

Right before Lauren headed through security, Roger held her tightly and gave her a long, lingering kiss. "I miss you already. Have fun with your family. Tell everyone I said hello, and take lots of pictures."

She promised she would.

"Call or text me when you get to San Francisco." He cradled her face with his hands and kissed her once more. "I love you, Lauren. Be safe please."

"I love you too."

Reluctantly, he released her. She blew him a kiss before she faded out of sight.

Chapter Sixteen

Touching down in Hawaii, the Hansons were welcomed by women in hula skirts who draped flower leis around their necks.

"Mohalo," Nathan greeted his welcoming committee.

Gabby gave him a funny look. "Mohalo? What does that mean?"

"It means thank you in Hawaiian."

"How do you know that?" she asked.

"I had a conversation with Dr. Ryan before we left. He knows all about Hawaiian history and the surfing community. He gave me a few pointers."

She rolled her eyes. "Oh, great. Are you planning on becoming a surfer now?"

"Not necessarily. Just trying to fit in with the locals." He held his hands out and attempted to hula dance.

Gabby laughed at him.

He took her hand, and together they walked away from the gate, excited about their vacation opportunity in Hawaii.

The family was staying at the Marriott Resort and Spa in Oahu, situated only steps away from world-famous Waikiki Beach. This tropical playground retreat blended the spirit of aloha with a warm, comfortable, and inviting atmosphere. Being here was truly paradise.

Dr. Hanson reserved three separate rooms this year. A suite for him and Jane, another for Nathan and Gabby, and a room for Lauren and Lacy to share.

While Lauren and Lacy got settled into their room, Lacy asked, "Did you tell Daddy about moving in with Roger?"

Lauren shook her head. "When I told him I had a place to stay over the summer, he assumed I was rooming with friends."

"Are you planning to tell him the truth?" Lacy asked, knowing how negatively her father reacted to dishonesty.

"Yes, but I want Daddy to enjoy his vacation before I drop that on him."

The bottom floor of the hotel had a coffee shop. After flying all day and combatting crowded airports and rental car facilities, Randy desperately needed caffeine. "I'm gonna head downstairs and grab a cup of coffee," he said to his wife. "You want anything?"

"No thank you," she replied.

Before he headed downstairs, he made his rounds, stopping first at his daughters' room then Nathan and Gabby's. "We're leaving for dinner in an hour, Nathan. Don't be late," Randy warned his son.

"We won't." Watching his dad trek toward the elevator, Nathan asked, "Where you going?"

"Coffee."

"Wait up. I'll come with you." He ran to catch up with him.

The two of them stepped into the elevator, and Randy pushed the button to the bottom floor. As the elevator descended, Randy said, "I met with Dr. Slate the other day."

Nathan didn't know who that was. "Who's Dr. Slate?"

"One of the doctors on UW's medical school admissions board. He received your application. You listed all the experience you gained from working in my clinic, and he contacted me to check your references."

"Is that good or bad?"

"It's good. Means they're looking at your application," Randy reassured him.

"Emphasizing my experience with you isn't going to hurt my application, is it?" Nathan asked, hoping he hadn't made a mistake to include that.

Randy reassured him. "The experience you had with me was legitimate and definitely worth including. Anyway, back to Dr. Slate. He and I talked for a while. He seemed quite impressed with you."

This perked Nathan up a bit. "He did?"

"Yup. Jim told me Dr. Slate spoke with him too. Maybe you'll get a phone call about an interview soon."

The elevator door opened, and the two of them stepped out to the main lobby. Randy walked over to the front desk, but Nathan stopped in his tracks and stared blankly at his father.

Randy wondered why the sudden change in posture. "What's wrong?"

"I don't want to get into medical school because of my father's connections."

"It doesn't work like that, Nate," Randy swore, shocked by his son's accusation. "You have to get into med school on your own accord. All I did was tell him about the work you do in the clinic. He mentioned that you had included your basketball experience on your application, which turned the conversation to basketball."

"Basketball?" Nathan questioned.

"Yes. He follows college basketball and watched you play in the playoffs. He knew everything about your stats and is looking forward to speaking with you personally."

"That's good, right?"

"Most likely means he wants to interview you."

Nathan grinned from ear to ear, silently celebrating with a fist pump. "Yes!"

Nathan's excitement made Randy laugh. "Just make sure you are sincere and honest with him when he calls you."

"I will be."

Randy curved his arm around his son's shoulder. "Come on. Coffee is calling my name."

After dinner, Nathan and Gabby returned to their room, where Nathan checked his voicemail. He had a message from Dr. Slate, who left a personal cellphone number and asked Nathan to call him back. Nathan immediately returned his call.

Gabby overheard the conversation but couldn't figure out who Nathan was talking to. When he hung up, she asked. "Who was that?"

"Dr. Slate from UW. Guess who has a medical school interview when we get back?"

"Seriously?"

"Yup," Nathan said, grinning.

She rushed to give him a hug. "That's great! Congratulations!"

"Thank you for your support through this, Gab. I never could have done this without you."

"You're welcome, Sweetie. The ride isn't over yet."

"I know," he admitted. "But at least I'm one step closer."

"Yes you are."

Feeling adventurous, Nathan chose to take advantage of the resort's Riding Company Surf School to learn from surfing pros about how to catch a wave.

Gabby questioned this haphazard decision. "You can't be serious?"

"Why wouldn't I be?" he countered. "It's like wakeboarding and skiing all wrapped into one. You should do it with me."

She shook her head. "I don't think so."

"Come on, Gab. It'll be fun. We can ride the waves together and you can be my surfing goddess."

Gabby thought he was crazy. "You have lost your mind."

"We're in Hawaii, Babe. This is the surfing capital of the world."

During this trip, Nathan had purchased a brightly colored Hawaiian shirt. Gabby didn't know why he made this purchase, because she knew he wouldn't wear it once they returned to Seattle. Despite this, he stood in front of the bathroom mirror and admired the way it looked.

"What do you think?" he asked, modeling it for her.

"Oh good god," she teased him. "I'm not letting you hang out with Dr. Ryan anymore."

"Why not?"

"Look what he's done to you. You're corrupted."

"If I'm gonna be in Hawaii, I'm going to soak up the local culture, go surfing, eat pineapple, and wear a Hawaiian shirt." He smiled mischievously. "You should get one of those grass hula skirts with the coconut bikini tops."

"Um…no," she replied firmly.

He laughed at her. "You know I'm teasing." He grabbed his sunglasses and pulled a towel off the towel rack. "Come on, Babe. The beach, the sun, and the waves await us."

Gabby giggled at his silly nature and walked with him down to the beach.

While the Hansons were having an aloha good time in Hawaii, Roger carried on with life in New York City. He and Jason met for lunch and coffee one afternoon when they were both off.

"How's the new show going?" Roger asked.

Happily, Jason replied, "Very well, thank you for asking. The choreography is fantastic, and the entire company is fun to work with. There are some talented people in this show."

"I know. One of them is Jason Preen."

"I wasn't talking about me, although I appreciate your flattery." Jason took a sip from his coffee. "She looked amazing, Rog."

"Who did?"

"Lauren at the Tony's. People have been talking about it."

Roger grinned. "They have?"

"Lots of rumors going around about you two."

Roger wasn't sure he liked what Jason was implying. "What kind of rumors?"

"People speculating, wondering who she is. There's a lot of talk about the kiss you shared on the red carpet."

At least people had noticed. "Why does it not surprise me that they would focus on that?"

"I have to admit, she's a beautiful and elegant young woman."

"Which reminds me," Roger said. "You and Lauren spent months working in the same theatre together and hardly said two words to each other the entire time. It wouldn't hurt for you to get to know the woman I love, Jason. She's not going away."

Jason chuckled at Roger's insistence. "She's your girlfriend. Why do I have to get to know her?"

"Because you're my friend. You're a big part of my life and so is she. It would mean a lot to me if you two would become friends, or at least talk to each other. You have more in common than you realize."

Jason explained, "I don't want to say anything that might give her the wrong impression. I know how much she means to you. I don't want to be the reason she…"

"I have nothing to hide," Roger cut in. "There's nothing you and I have done together or anything you could possibly say that I would be ashamed to have Lauren find out about. Most of the experiences you and I had together, I've already told her about."

"Did you tell her about Montreal?" Jason questioned with a devilish smile.

Roger laughed remembering the stupid, juvenile ignorance he and Jason experienced together in Canada. "Montreal. What the hell were we thinking?"

"What would Lauren say if she knew what happened in Montreal?"

Roger replied, "She knows I have a past, Jason. She knows about me and Mel and the bullshit attached with that. She knows about my father and the fact that I'm a Juilliard dropout. I've touched on Montreal. I never got into explicit details with her, but I have no shame in telling her. It's not something I'm particularly proud of, but we were young. People do stupid things in their youth."

"No kidding," Jason chuckled.

"Why don't you come over to my place next week and have dinner with us," Roger suggested. "It'll give you and Lauren a chance to get to know each other."

"Can I bring a date?"

"Absolutely." That's when he noticed the smile on Jason's face. "You have someone in mind?"

Jason's grin grew a bit wider. "Maybe."

Roger knew what that meant. "Uh oh. Who is she?"

"Her name is Bailey Metcalf. She's one of the dancers I'm working with in Flashdance. Extremely talented."

"Bring her next week. We'll have dinner and get acquainted."

"Alright," Jason agreed. "I'll supply the wine."

"Sounds great."

On their last night in Hawaii, the entire family met at Sunset on the Beach for an outdoor movie screening. Lauren sat next to her father, finally prepared to tell him about the situation with Roger. "Daddy, I need to tell you something."

"What is it, Honey?"

Admitting the truth, she said, "When I told you I had a place to stay in New York over the summer, I didn't exactly tell you everything."

"Oh?"

"I do have living arrangements, but not where you think."

The fact that she wasn't completely honest didn't bother him as much as her questionable housing arrangements in New York City. "So if you're not housing with a group of your friends then where are you going to live, Lauren?"

"I have an apartment."

Not the news he wanted to hear. "In New York City? I'm not comfortable with you living in some cheap, rundown apartment across town or taking the subway alone at night after work. That scares me, Baby."

"I have access to an apartment right in Manhattan. It's a ten minute cab ride from the theatre, and it's safe."

"Manhattan? Do you have any idea how expensive apartments are in Manhattan? You won't be able to afford that."

"I know, but I won't be alone. I'll be sharing it with someone who's already living there."

"A roommate?" Before Lauren even had to tell him, Randy put the pieces together. "You're planning on staying with Roger, aren't you?"

Hoping her father wasn't upset, she asked, "Are you mad?"

Roger made good money. Lauren would certainly be taken care of living with him. His apartment was clean, well-cared for, and safe, and the building itself was homestead to many Broadway big names, which meant Lauren would be among her colleagues. And she wouldn't be coming home alone after late night shows. She'd have Roger with her. Randy felt she'd be safe, but was worried that their relationship was taking a serious shift. He hoped she was emotionally ready for that. "No, Baby, I'm not mad. I'm just concerned. Are you certain you and Roger are ready for that level of commitment? That's boosting your relationship up a pretty big notch."

Thinking Randy was fretting over nothing, Lauren replied, "Daddy, we'll be fine."

"I don't want to see you jump into something that's too deep for you to swim in. Roger is older than you are and has a lot more experience in relationships than you do. He may be ready to make that jump, but are you?"

She tried to reassure him. "I'm not going to leap recklessly without a parachute. Roger is my parachute. I feel safe with him, and I'm happy, Daddy. Roger and I support each other. He's my best friend."

Although Randy understood where Lauren was coming from, the fact that his daughter was stepping into a very serious commitment made him realize she could very well be involved with the man who was going to be her future husband. He wasn't sure how he felt about this. He liked Roger, and he trusted the man, but they had been together less than a year. To him, this seemed like a huge leap forward way too early in their relationship.

Later that night, after settling into their room, Randy questioned Jane about this development. "Did you know Lauren was planning on staying with Roger during the summer?"

"She had mentioned something to me about it, but I didn't know if she was serious or not," Jane said, looking away from the book she was reading. "Why? Did she tell you that's what she was planning on doing?"

"Yes. She told me tonight." He kicked off his shoes and lay back on the bed with his hands clasped behind his head. "I'm not sure that's a good idea."

"What harm can it do?"

"She'll be sharing an apartment with him, Jane. Do you really think she's old enough and mature enough to handle that?"

"It's only temporary, isn't it?"

"That's what she says," Randy argued. "But what happens when she gets comfortable being there and doesn't want to leave? Suddenly our 19-year-old daughter is living with her 29-year-old boyfriend."

"You can't shelter the girls forever, you know," Jane reminded him.

"I don't want to shelter her. I just worry that she's jumping in too deep. I don't want to see her end up with a broken heart over this guy."

"Do you doubt his sincerity?"

"I think he loves her," he replied. "But I wonder how long that feeling is going to last. Does he want a serious commitment, or is he just stopping by for the ride until that feeling wears off?"

"You are doubting his sincerity then."

"He seems like he's serious about her, but is he going to have the patience to stick this out and let their relationship grow or is he going to get tired of waiting and move on to someone who's more ready to take on something permanent? I wish I knew what his intentions were."

"Hypothetically speaking, how would you feel if Roger proposed to Lauren?"

Randy's eyes widened. "Oh god, Jane, don't even suggest that."

"I thought you liked Roger?"

"I do, but I don't want my daughter getting married yet. If that is Roger's intention, I hope he doesn't try to rush into that before Lauren's ready. Their relationship needs to develop more." Deep down, Randy knew it was a matter of time before one of his daughters committed to marriage, but he wasn't ready for his little girl to walk down that aisle quite yet.

Chapter Seventeen

After a busy day with patients, Randy was about to leave the clinic to start his weekend when he received a page from Jim. *Get to the hospital STAT. It's your dad.* Randy's heart plummeted to his stomach. He dropped everything, and without delay hollered at his sister to come with him. Together, they hurried across the street.

Randy stormed the Emergency Room demanding to see Jim. "Where the hell is Dr. Ryan? Get him out here now!"

One of the nurses intercepted him. "Dr. Hanson, please calm down."

But Randy wasn't about to wait. He pushed his way into the exam room area. His mother, crying and shaking, immediately clung to him. "What the hell is going on?" he demanded to know.

Then he saw for himself. In a nearby room, his father was strapped to a gurney with a dozen doctors and nurses surrounding him on all sides. He was hooked up to IV lines and an EKG that was slowly losing rhythm. Jim and the Emergency Room staff frantically worked on him. Randy immediately released his mother and barged into the room where his father was barely hanging on.

Jim met him at the door, holding him back. "Randy, step back."

"Dammit, Ryan! Move the hell out of my way!"

"Step back!" Jim insisted. "Let me and my staff handle this."

"BP dropping," the nurse called out.

"For god's sake, do something!" Randy aggressively tried to shove his way forward.

Jim looked him in the eye. "Please, Randy, let me do my job."

Completely trusting his best friend, Randy stood down.

Jim quickly returned to his patient, treating him with every possible life-saving effort on the list. This was the most emotional experience of his life. He knew the man on the gurney in front of him, and he knew him well. Losing this patient would be devastating on many levels.

Randy watched the fading EKG. His heart pounded in fear. "No!" he cried out. "God dammit, no!"

Jim tried every advanced cardiovascular life support option available. At this point, however, he was limited in his options, and he was running out of time. The EKG V-fibbed. Immediately, he had the staff hook up the defibrillator and shoot his patient with epinephrine.

Randy stood helpless, watching the EKG linger in cardiac dysrhythmia. He wanted to jump in and help. In desperation, he begged, "Jim!"

But Jim didn't hear him. He was too busy trying to save his best friend's father. "Clear!" he yelled at the staff as he threw an electrical pulse to the heart trying to jump start it again. Nothing. He recharged the line and tried again.

Randy began to panic. His breathing became erratic and his pulse rate shot through the roof. His father lay lifeless on the gurney, his heart rate out of rhythm. As the reality of what was happening hit, Randy's eyes filled with tears. "Dad."

"Clear!" Jim hollered again. Another electric pulse shot through the heart. Still nothing. He recharged for a third time. Then his worst fears came true. The EKG went flatline. In a desperate effort to resuscitate, Dr. Ryan ordered forty units of Vasopressin and immediately began CPR.

Randy stared at the asystole EKG lead and knew what it meant. His father's heart no longer had a shockable rhythm—using a defibrillator was pointless. Survival rates in cardiac arrest patients who went asystole was less than two percent. If asystole persisted for fifteen minutes or more, the brain would be deprived of oxygen and death would occur. In anguish, Randy's hands began to shake. His heart sank, crying out to anyone who would listen. "Oh Jesus, please."

Over and over, longer than usually sustained, Jim continued chest compression, praying that a rhythm would reappear and miraculously make the EKG beep that lovely sound. Nothing. Fifteen minutes of nothing. The heart was unresponsive.

Realizing that Jim had exhausted all lifesaving measures and there was nothing more that could be done, Randy broke down in tears. He had lost his father before his very eyes. The only position he could muster was to curl up in a ball on the floor. Losing all strength, he collapsed and buried his face in his hands, giving vent to the agony of his loss.

Jim didn't want to give up. In a desperate effort, he continued CPR.

Randy watched Jim's persistent efforts, knowing there was no chance of reviving the heart. Trying to be strong, he took a deep breath and regained his composure long enough to mutter, "Jim, stop."

Jim ignored him, refusing to call it when the rest of the staff had already ceased life-saving efforts.

Randy knew it was to no avail. He lifted his head and with a shattered voice said, "Stop."

Panting, Jim looked over at Randy, exhausted from this failed attempt. The tears in Randy's eyes and the pain on his face tore at his heart. With shaky hands, he walked over to his best friend and sat on the floor next to him. He felt horribly guilty. What did he overlook? What treatment did he miss? What test did he fail to make? What option did he fail to utilize? His emotions wouldn't stop tormenting him. He removed his latex gloves and put his hand on his forehead, which now throbbed. Trying to justify this devastating loss, he said, "Oh dear god, Randy, I am so sorry." His voice cracked and the tears he tried to suppress flowed steadily. One of the finest men he knew was lying lifeless in his ER under his watch.

Randy swallowed hard from the depths of his throat. Wiping tears away, he looked over at his best friend. "You did all you could."

As soon as the room cleared, the Hanson family moved into a private room, trying to figure out how to deal with this. Through her own pain, Stephanie desperately tried to soothe her mother, who was hysterical. Between the tears, the hugs of condolence, and leaning on each other during this time of mourning, Randy somehow managed to contact Nathan and Jane, who had now joined them at the hospital.

Jane sat next to Randy and placed her hand on his arm, trying to console him.

When things settled down a bit, Nathan realized that the rest of the family needed to be notified. To save his father, aunt, and grandmother from that horrendous turmoil, he graciously offered to make the calls. "I can call Uncle Rob if you want."

Exhausted from the emotional turmoil and stress over the events of the last hour, Randy couldn't think straight. His senses were incapacitated and he felt numb. He didn't even hear what Nathan said.

"At least let me call Lauren and Lacy," Nathan offered.

Randy sat there lifeless, unresponsive.

"Dad?" Nathan cried, trying to get his father's attention.

Randy looked up. "Did you say something?"

"Yes." Nathan reached out and touched his father's hand. "I'll call Uncle Robby."

Emotionally run down, Randy stared at his son and nodded. He wasn't up to coping with this.

Nathan squeezed his father's hand and kissed him on the cheek. "I'll take care of it." He stepped into the hall and made two phone calls. The first was to his uncle, Randy's younger brother. The second was to Lauren.

"Sweetheart, have you seen my cellphone?" Roger called out, hoping he hadn't lost it.

Lauren emerged from the bedroom with Roger's phone in her hand. "What would you do without me?"

"Be lonely and miserable." He took the phone from her and gave her a kiss. "Thanks, Honey."

When Lauren's cellphone rang, she was thrilled to see her brother's number pop up on the screen. She hadn't spoken to him in a while. "Hey, Hotshot!"

"Hey." Nathan's voice was far from cheerful.

"What's the matter with you?" she teased, having no clue what he was about to tell her.

Shattered, Nathan asked, "How soon can you get to Seattle?"

"Why am I going to Seattle?"

"I'm at the hospital with Mom, Dad, Grandma, and Aunt Stephanie."

"Why? What's going on?"

Nathan wasn't sure how to tell her. "It's Grandpa."

Breathing erratically, she began to fear the worst. "Is he ok?"

Nathan had a hard time containing his emotions. He sat on the other end, unable to speak.

"Nathan?"

"He's gone, Lauren."

Lauren put her trembling hand over her mouth. She had a hard time piecing together what her brother had told her. "Oh my god. Grandpa."

"I'll call Lacy," Nathan stated. "Just get here."

Roger had just finished dressing and was ready to head to the Majestic Theatre when he came out of the bathroom and saw Lauren sitting on the sofa staring at her phone, crying. The smile instantly left his face. "Honey?" He rushed over to her. "Honey, what's wrong?"

She looked up at him with pain in her eyes.

The look on her face told him that something horrible had happened. "Sweetheart, what is it?"

"It's my grandfather. My entire family is at the hospital. He…" She sobbed uncontrollably.

Roger knew what that meant. He gathered her in his arms and held her close. "Oh, Honey. I'm sorry." He tenderly kissed the top of her head, his heart breaking right along with hers. "I'm so sorry."

After a few minutes, she wiped her tears. All she could think about at the moment was her father, who had to be devastated. "I need to get to Seattle."

"Of course," he concurred. "I'm coming with you. Let's book a flight as soon as possible."

He was about to head to his laptop and look up flight information, but Lauren stopped him. "You need to do your show. I'll talk to Lacy while you're gone and we'll book a flight."

He was worried about her and didn't think she should be left alone right now. "You sure you don't want me to stay here tonight?"

"No! Go!" she clamored. "Be Phantom. I'll get us packed, and by the time you get home from the show, everything will be ready."

Lauren was adamant in her request. He opted not to argue with her. "Get a red-eye. We'll leave tonight right after the show." He hugged her tightly and kissed her forehead. "I love you, Honey. I'm so sorry."

The next day was rough for the entire family. Shock kicked in, and many tears were shed. Randy seemed to be hit the hardest. The entire day, he hadn't spoken to anyone, didn't display any kind of emotion, and isolated himself from the people he cared about the most.

His lack of interaction with anyone or anything had Roger concerned. Nathan also looked worried. Roger walked over to him and asked, "Is your dad going to be okay?"

Nathan shook his head. "I don't know. I've never seen him like this before."

Roger glanced at Dr. Hanson, feeling the heavy heart he was bearing. He wished he could take his pain away.

Final arrangements for Mark Hanson needed to be taken care of. To save her husband and in-laws from enduring any more pain than necessary, Jane took charge of that torturous endeavor. Besides family members, many others showed up for Mark Hanson's memorial service. Randy's medical partner and friend Greg Hutchins and his wife came, as well as his dear friends Jim and Jill Ryan and Bruce and Mandy Buckman.

For Bruce and Mandy, this tragic event struck very close to home. Not only was Randy their dear friend, but due to a previous marriage with Randy's sister, two of Bruce's daughters were Mark Hanson's grandchildren.

When Bruce's oldest daughter, Emily, saw her father walk into the funeral home, she immediately clung to him. "Daddy."

Bruce put his arm around her and let her cry on his shoulder. "Hey, Baby." Then he reached for his other daughter, Alyssa, who seemed a little more reclusive. "Come here, Princess." Alyssa wrapped her arms around her father and sobbed. "I'm sorry, Honey," he said, letting his girls release their emotions. "I know this is hard."

When Stephanie saw Bruce with the girls, a glazed look of despair spread over her face. She approached him, moving slowly and with heavy steps. Bruce expected a confrontation with his ex-wife, but instead of reprimanding him and causing a scene like she usually did, she stood in front of him, choking down tears. Bruce knew Stephanie was in extreme pain over losing her father, and although the two of them had their differences, he did something he hadn't done in a long time. With his girls watching, Bruce gave her a comforting hug. "I'm so sorry, Steph."

Stephanie whimpered and wiped her eyes. "Thank you for coming."

"Of course," he replied. "Your father was an extraordinary man. He will be sorely missed."

Stephanie cast Bruce a grateful smile and went to join her grieving mother's side.

Bruce turned to his girls. "Why don't you sit with Grandma. She's going to need a lot of support today."

Alyssa and Emily agreed this was a good idea.

He kissed each of his daughter's on the cheek and sent them on their way. He looked across the room and saw Randy sitting in silence at the front of the memorial hall. His head was bowed and his body slumped in despair. Jane sat right next to him, holding his hand. "Mandy," Bruce said, trying to get his wife's attention. "Look at Randy."

Amanda spun that direction and her heart sank to the floor. Randy wasn't interacting with anyone; he was completely numb. She couldn't bear the sight of him without breaking down herself. "Oh god," she cried, sympathizing with her friend's aching heart. "Poor guy. I can't even comprehend what he must be going through right now."

Jim made his way toward them, and Bruce shook his hand. "Hey, Jim."

Jim greeted them both with a hug. "Yo, Buckmans. It's good to see you. Crappy circumstances though."

"For sure." Concerned about Randy's state of mind, Bruce asked, "How's he doing?"

Jim was blatantly honest. "I'm worried about him. He hasn't spoken to anyone in days, not even Jane."

"That's bad," Bruce replied, almost in tears. "Have you talked to Jane?"

"Yeah," Jim said. "She's worried about him too. She says he's in some kind of funk and can't snap out of it. He hasn't been sleepin' and paces the floor all night. He won't eat much and hasn't touched a cup of coffee in days."

Mandy listened in on this conversation. This situation was serious. "He's heartbroken," she said sympathetically.

"I haven't had a chance to talk to him yet," Jim replied. "I want to give him some time to grieve first. He needs to get that out of his system."

Randy sat lifelessly, staring at his father's casket. Bruce's eyes welled with tears, thinking of the horrible grief his friend was enduring. "Oh, Randy. I'm so sorry." Seeing Randy in extreme pain was more than he could bear. He had to turn away.

"You gonna try to talk to him later?" Mandy asked.

"Yeah," Jim released a heavy sigh. "Let's just get him through this service first. This is gonna be rough."

During the memorial service, Randy said nothing, made no eye contact with anyone, and showed no emotion. He wrapped himself in a cocoon of anguish; misery held him down like a steel weight. When it was time for the eulogies, Randy listened but didn't react to anything anyone said. Then, to everyone's surprise, he stood up and took position at the podium. With all eyes on him, he carefully opened a piece of paper and took a deep breath, trying to maintain his composure. After clearing his throat, he began, "God took the strength of a mountain, the majesty of a tree, the warmth of a summer sun, the calm of a quiet sea. The generous soul of nature, the comforting arms of night, the wisdom of the ages, the power of the eagle's flight. The joy of a spring morning, the faith of a mustard seed, the patience of eternity, the depth of a family in need. He combined these qualities, and when there was nothing more to add, His masterpiece was complete. We called him Dad." Randy swallowed the lump in his throat, staggering through his words. "Our father kept a garden of the heart. He was fostering and nurturing and…" His voice cracked through the swell of tears. He tried to continue but couldn't. The pain of this loss was too much to handle. Swallowing the sob in his throat, he looked up. His eyes darkened and a look of tired sadness passed over his features.

Feeling Dr. Hanson's heartache, Roger took charge of this situation. With everyone at the memorial service watching, Roger stepped up to the podium and put his hand on Randy's shoulder.

Randy stared at him, his face bleak with sorrow.

Trying to ease some of Randy's pain, Roger held out his hand, offering to take the eulogy and read for him.

Desperately clinging to the paper, as if it was the only way of holding onto his father, Randy floundered, held mute and almost immobile by sinking despair.

"It's ok," Roger assured him.

Hesitantly, and without saying a word, Randy handed him the paper.

Roger took the eulogy in his hand, stood behind the podium, and with a heavy heart, continued to read where Dr. Hanson left off. "He encouraged us to dream. When the winds and rain came, he protected us enough, but not too much, because he knew we would stand up strong against the storms. He was the marker for our pathways and the light that helped us grow. He was a warm heart and a caring hand. And he gave us unconditional love…love that will last a lifetime. We are our father's garden. Thank you, Dad, for planting the seeds. I love you, and I miss you."

Randy mournfully beheld Roger's compassion, grateful that he stepped up to help the family in their time of need. Shattered by grief, he gave Roger a hug. Together, they sat down with the rest of the family.

When Randy returned home after the service, the band of emotions he had bottled up over the last few days finally escaped, and they escaped with a vengeance. With his hand on his forehead, he leaned against the wall of the living room, shaking. Unable to maintain his strength any longer, he slid down the wall, hugged his knees, and sobbed.

Jane rushed to his side, holding him and trying to ease his sorrow.

Desperately needing her, Randy gripped his wife for dear life, squeezing her as tightly as he could.

She let him cry, something he desperately needed to do.

Randy took the rest of the week off, trying to find a way to muster up the strength to move on with his life. Trapped in crushing despair, everything brought about an emotional meltdown. Something he'd see or hear, even simple things like a ballpoint pen he'd pick up or the parrot singing in his cage triggered tears. He was miserable, overcome by acute physical and emotional pain. Hoping to help Randy cope with this devastating loss, Jane turned to the only person in the world capable of reaching him—his best friend, Jim Ryan.

When Jim came over that afternoon, Jane was overjoyed to see him. "Thank God you're here. He needs you."

"Where is he?"

"Sitting out on the deck. He's been out there all morning."

Jim made his way out to the deck, where Randy sat lifeless in a patio chair staring out at the lake. Treading carefully, so as not to shatter the delicate emotional state his friend was in, he pulled up a chair and sat next to Randy without saying a word. He stared out at the water for a few minutes, wondering what his best friend was thinking.

Randy finally acknowledged him. "I can't do this, Jim," he cried, overwhelmed by the torment of the last week. "I don't know how to let him go."

Randy broke down his defenses and wept. Jim hugged his best friend and let him release his emotions. "If I could take this horrid pain away from you, you know I would." Tears slowly found their way to Jim's eyes. "I love you, man. You know I'm here for you."

After several minutes of release, Randy took a cleansing breath and wiped his tears away. Desperately trying to regain his composure, he swallowed the knot in his throat. Little by little, warmth crept back into his body. "You can't really prepare yourself for something like this. All those classes we took about death and dying and the grieving process…when it hits this close to home, it gives you a whole different perspective on what families go through."

Through his pain and grief-stricken heart, Randy somehow managed to talk about medicine. Jim didn't know how he had gathered up the strength to even conceive that kind of thinking, but he offered a listening ear and let him rant.

"And let me tell you something, this really sucks."

The next day, Randy insisted that he visit his father's grave. Jane wasn't convinced this was a good idea, but Randy wouldn't budge. He told her that if she didn't want to go, he would go on his own. Leaving him alone in his fragile emotional state was not a wise thing to do, so she decided to go with him. She asked Nathan to join them, just in case she needed help with her husband.

When they pulled into the cemetery and up to the gravesite where his father was buried, Randy stopped the car and turned off the ignition. He stared across the grass at the fresh dirt mound in the distance.

Nathan worried that his father was jumping on this too soon. "Dad, are you sure you wanna do this?"

"I need to do this." Randy opened the car door and stepped out.

Nathan tried to get out with him.

"No," Randy insisted. "I want to be alone." He closed the door and slowly walked over to the mound of dirt.

Nathan turned to his mother. "Shouldn't we go with him?"

Jane knew exactly what Randy was going through, as she had lost her mother many years ago. Grief was very personal and different for everybody. Randy was experiencing it in his own way. "Leave him. He'll be fine."

After picking a few leaves off the grave marker, Randy rubbed some dirt off of it then stared at it for a minute before he spoke. "Hi Dad." That alone was difficult to get out, but Randy had some unfinished business with his father he needed to attend to. Tears formed as he sat in the grass and spoke to this dirt mound. "I heard the fish were biting this morning. Water looked nice and clear. Bet the fishing was intense." He paused to collect his thoughts. After a long silence, he continued to speak. "I have so many things I want to say to you, but I don't even know where to begin." He looked down at the grass and picked a strand, fiddling with it for a minute before he dropped it on the ground. Taking a big breath, he poured his heart out. "You told me once that being a man means having the strength to stand up to your biggest fears, even if you don't want to. I don't want to go through this life without the most amazing, supportive, and loving man I've ever known." He couldn't hold back his emotions. Every ounce of pain and heartache he'd felt over the last week flowed through him. "But you taught me to be a man, and part of my responsibility with that means picking myself up and facing these fears. I won't let you down in that regard." Trying to calm himself, he took a few deep breaths and exhaled heavily. "I try to instill all of your life lessons into my kids. Nathan…" Randy smiled as he thought about his son. "He's a good kid. Becoming a responsible, caring man. He's determined to follow the family career choice you began, and he'll make it too. He's smart, disciplined, capable, and an incredible basketball player. He definitely gets that from Jane," Randy chuckled. "I couldn't have asked for a better son. And Lauren, what a talented young woman. She'll make her mark on Broadway one day, I have no doubt about that. She has such a beautiful voice. Oh man, Roger really stepped up this week. He proved to me that he not only cares about Lauren, but about this entire family. I like that kid." Randy beamed with pride. "And my beautiful dancing queen, Lacy. I hope I have given her enough guidance to find her place in this world. Whatever path she chooses, she'll do it with style, that's for sure." Randy compiled his thoughts, trying to make sense of the week's events. His head was a mess. He was still in shock and uncertain as to how or if he would be able to carry on without this man in his life. "I try to be a good father, but no one will ever compare to you and the support, encouragement, and love you always gave to me. I will never forget that."

While Randy continued to talk to the wind, Nathan sat in the car and waited, wondering what Randy was doing up there. "I really don't think he should be doing this."

Jane tried to explain, "Your father needs closure."

Nathan watched intently, worried about his father's emotional state of mind. "Are you sure this is healthy?"

"He needs to say things to Grandpa he didn't get a chance to say. Give him this time."

Randy's heart was heavy, but getting some things off his chest lightened the load a little. He continued to pour his heart out. "Mom's doing ok. She can't bring herself to clean out your things yet. I don't blame her. She isn't ready. But when she is, I'll be the man you taught me to be. I'll stand up, dust myself off, and help her move on." He wiped his eyes and took in some much needed oxygen, sniffling as he spoke. "I didn't get to tell you how grateful and proud I am to be your son. I didn't get to tell you what a pleasure and a joy it was to know you and be such a big part of your life. I didn't get to tell you…" Through blurry, tear-soaked eyes, he cried, "I didn't get to say goodbye." Slowly he stood up and dusted the loose dirt off his pants. Exhaling heavily he vowed, "I'll make you proud. I promise." Taking in one more big breath, he let out a heavy sigh. "Thanks for the talk, Dad. And thanks for listening. You were always good at that." With tears in his eyes, he glanced over at the car and managed to muster up a smile. "I have to go. My wife and son are waiting for me." For about thirty seconds, he fixed his eyes on the Hanson grave marker. "I miss you so much. I'll stop by next week and we'll chat again. I love you, Dad." He blew a kiss to this entity before he left.

When Randy returned to the car, he sat with his hands on the steering wheel staring out the windshield.

"Dad?" Nathan said, trying to get his father to snap out of his zone-out mode.

Randy turned his head. "Who's hungry?"

Randy hadn't eaten anything substantial in days. The fact that his appetite was returning was a good sign. Perhaps having a conversation with his father was the closure he needed to help him move on. Jane smiled at her husband, who had more life in him at this moment that she had witnessed from him in days.

Lying in bed that night, Randy held his wife in his arms. Looking back on the week's events, he declared, "For better or worse. I think this week definitely qualifies as worse." He kissed her forehead, grateful for her loving support. "Thank you for being here for me this week. I really needed you."

"You have nothing to thank me for," Jane replied.

He disagreed. "I do. This week has been hell, and you were so strong." He gently ran his fingers through her hair. "I've had the personality of a wet mop lately, and I'm sorry."

Jane had experienced the death of a parent and completely understood the pain Randy was going through. "For god's sake, Randy, do not apologize. I understand. It would've concerned me if you wouldn't have reacted the way you did."

"I think I'll go back to work on Monday."

"I think that's a good idea. It will keep you busy and get your mind off things."

He kissed her and rolled them over, positioning Jane on her back with him over top of her. "I love you," he said. "I really want to make love to you right now."

She had no objection to his request.

Saturday, Randy went to check on his mother. While he was there, he asked her about symptoms his father had prior to his attack. She told him that while they were out running errands, he suddenly complained of chest pain radiating to his left arm. Within seconds he couldn't breathe, began sweating profusely, became nauseated, then started vomiting uncontrollably. In less than a minute, he collapsed to the ground. Randy considered everything his mother told him. This sounded like classic heart attack symptoms, but Randy had never heard of them coming on that quickly before in a person with no prior history or symptoms of heart disease. Searching for answers, he turned to his colleagues and friends.

Over a cup of coffee, he went to his most trusted and dearest friend first. Since Dr. Ryan was the attending physician in the ER when his father was wheeled in, he hoped Jim had some insights for him. "My father had MI symptoms that spontaneously hit him in less than a minute. Within ten minutes of arriving at the hospital, he went into cardiac arrest. Before that, he had no prior symptoms of heart disease, no previous history of heart problems, and for his age he was a pretty healthy guy. Any idea what would cause symptoms to come on that quickly?" Randy asked, begging for answers.

"I don't know, Randy," Jim admitted, tormented over this crappy set of circumstances. "With no initial symptoms, it's hard to tell. It could have been a lot of things. A spontaneous coronary artery dissection or an undetected blood clot that broke free, which might have caused instantaneous coronary arterial blockage or an embolism. Could have been undiagnosed cardiomyopathy as well. I wish I had answers for you, but I don't. I'm not a cardiologist. You know as much as I do."

"Hmm," Randy pondered as he sipped on his coffee. "I buried my father this week. Yet last night Jane and I had the most intense lovemaking session we'd had in a long time. I feel like some kind of sick bastard."

"Why?"

"Because my family is grieving over the loss of my father while my wife and I are having a carnal pleasure party in the sheets. I'm a heartless ass."

"No you're not," Jim assured him. "You've been under a lot of stress. You needed the release. Lots of couples have sex during times of disaster or trauma. It's like clingin' to each other's lifeline. You went through a traumatic experience. It's natural for you to want to make love to your wife after goin' through somethin' like that."

Randy snorted under his breath, not as certain of Jim's analysis. "I guess."

"And this experience has brought you and Jane closer together. You leaned on each other, and truly demonstrated what a marriage and partnership is all about."

Jim definitely had a strong argument. Randy and his wife had bonded more because of this experience. "That's true."

"That guy your daughter is involved with, I'm impressed with him," Jim said.

"Roger?"

"Yeah. He really stepped up to the plate for you and your family, Bro. The dude's got some class."

"He's a good man, and he's good to Lauren."

"Future son-in-law?" Jim teased.

"Oh good god, Jim. I am not ready to go there yet."

"It's gonna happen sooner or later, Dude."

"I know," Randy admitted. "But let's not rush it."

"What about Nathan and Gabby?"

"Nathan's a little preoccupied right now with prepping for medical school. I don't think he's in any hurry to jump on that boat."

"It was good to see your kids together again," Jim declared. "Lacy still a rebel rouser?"

Randy had to laugh at Jim's statement. "Spunky, sassy, slightly rebellious. She's definitely a woman who knows what she wants and doesn't take crap from anyone."

"Sounds like Jane."

Randy agreed. "She's certainly capable of holding her own. One thing's for sure, I don't have to worry about a man taking advantage of her. She'll crotch shot him and push him up an octave or two. I've seen her do it before."

Jim busted out laughing. "Seriously?"

"Oh hell yeah. Don't mess with that girl. She's got attitude, and she's not afraid to use it." Randy thought about his kids. They were his greatest accomplishment and his most treasured gift. "I hope I've shown them over the years how much I care and how much I love them."

"You have, Dude. You're a good dad," Jim remarked.

"I want to see them fulfill their dreams."

"They will," Jim assured him. "Believe me. They will."

Chapter Eighteen

Fall brought about not only a change in weather and the color of the leaves, but also the beginning of the healing process for the Hanson family. Despite the personal turmoil the family had undergone, they were optimistic that the upcoming months would bring positive changes in their lives. Randy stayed busy with deliveries, gynecological appointments, and working with University of Washington medical students. Nathan and Gabby began their final year of college, engrossed not only in their studies but also in cheering and basketball. Nathan anxiously awaited word from the medical schools he had applied to while Gabby looked forward to student teaching in the spring. Both Lauren and Lacy returned to the world of performing arts school.

As Randy suspected, Lauren chose not to return to the dorms for her second year of Juilliard. By living with Roger, she was being introduced to people in the theatre industry on a daily basis. Roger rarely attended a social function or Broadway event without Lauren.

This particular Saturday was busy for Roger. He had an interview in the morning with Broadway.com then met Lauren for lunch prior to reporting to the Majestic for the first of two performances that day. The afternoon matinee began at two o'clock and ended around 4:30. After the performance, Roger greeted fans and signed Playbills at the stage door.

Every dual performance day seemed to include a different activity between shows. Tonight, one of the cast members cranked 'Bohemian Rhapsody' backstage, which got everyone singing, especially Roger because this was one of his favorite songs. Gradually, cast members began to emerge from dressing rooms into the main gathering area to join in. This experience of loud and not particularly pleasant harmony by the ensemble, cast, and crew was proceeded by a catered dinner. Roger used this time to bond with his fellow cast members. Cast bonding was a standard practice between shows and often involved swarms of actors and dancers clothed in *Phantom of the Opera* costumes gathering near Roger's dressing room bringing various types of cookies for all to share.

After getting a quick prosthetic and makeup touch up, Roger stepped out the back door of the theatre and into the alleyway to get some fresh air before the show. It was nightfall now. The only light came from faint glow of a nearby street lamp, which spread shadows amidst the darkness. Roger took a sip from a water bottle to moisten his throat.

The caterer stood in the partially lit alleyway with her cellphone in her hand. At first Roger didn't see her, but she certainly saw him. The vision of a creepy, monster-looking figure sneaking up on her in the blackened alley made her scream and nearly jump out of her skin. Her instinct to run kicked in.

Roger, realizing he had scared the living hell out of this woman, called after her. "Ma'am! It's ok! Come back!"

Her heart pounded a hundred miles a minute, yet hearing his voice made her stop and turn around.

Keeping her distance, she stared him down. "Mr. Zellers?"

"Yes, it's me." To ease her fear, he stepped out of the shadows and into the light of the streetlamp. "I am so sorry. I did not mean to frighten you."

She put her hand on her heart as the adrenaline careened through her body. Her heart rate slowly began to settle. "You scared the hell out of me."

"I'm sorry. I didn't know anyone else was out here."

She took a closer look at his eerie, prosthetic-covered face and curled her lip. "That is the creepiest, scariest thing I have ever seen."

"In a dark alley at night anyway," he added, trying to lighten the mood.

She playfully smacked him on the arm. "Don't ever do that again."

He couldn't help but laugh. "What were you doing out here by yourself?"

"I needed to make a phone call and wasn't getting good reception in the building, so I stepped out here."

"Are you okay?"

"Yes, I'm fine," she assured him, exhaling to release the tension. "Thank you."

He took another sip of his water then pointed toward the back door of the theatre. "I'm going to head back inside now. You gonna be alright out here by yourself?"

"Oh no!" she shook her head. "I'm right behind you."

Roger escorted the caterer back inside and prepared for the start of the second show.

After another successful performance, Roger made his way home. He walked in the apartment to find

230

Lauren sound asleep on the couch. Several textbooks, a script, and some notebooks were spread out all over the floor. Apparently she'd been studying.

Trying not to wake her, Roger quietly set his keys and cellphone on the table then removed his jacket and draped it over the back of a chair. He grabbed a glass of water from the kitchen and returned to the living room, where he sat on the chair near the sofa.

He stared at Lauren, watching her sleep. It had been a year since Roger first heard her beautiful voice and saw her lovely face at the Ambassador Theatre, the best year of his life. With a content smile on his face, he reflected back on all the wonderful memories he and Lauren had made together over the past twelve months. He was a better man and the world was a better place to live in because of her.

He set his glass on a coaster on the coffee table then knelt down on the floor next to her. He moved a stray hair off her face and kissed her forehead.

She rolled around and let out a cute groan, but didn't fully wake up.

Affectionately, he rubbed his hand across her cheek. "Hello, my sleeping angel."

She opened her weary eyes and looked up at him. "Hey."

"How was your night?"

She stretched and rolled over. "Finally finished that paper I've been working on."

"That's good," he replied.

She sat up, still groggy. "How was the show tonight?"

"Went well," Roger proclaimed. "Audience received it positively."

"They always do."

He took both of her hands in his and helped her off the couch. "Off to bed with you, my sweet." He led her to the bedroom, where she removed all of her clothing, except the tee-shirt and underwear she was wearing. She crawled into bed and Roger tucked her in with a kiss. "I'll come to bed in a little while. I love you, Honey."

She snuggled with her blanket and closed her eyes.

Before Roger exited the room, he shut off the light, leaving her in peaceful slumber. He returned to the living room and read for a while before turning in for the night.

Roger spent a few hours the following afternoon plucking away at the piano. While he played, Oliver sidestepped on his hind legs, howling to the melody. "Hey, Honey. Check this out."

Lauren stepped into the room to look. "Aww. Did you teach him that?"

"No. He just likes music." He rose from the piano and slid the bench back into place before he stepped into the kitchen to get a bone for Ollie. "I've been thinking. How would you feel about spending Thanksgiving in New York this year?"

"I've never been away from home during the holidays before."

He figured she'd say that. "I know. But I'd really like you to meet the rest of my family. With Macy's going on, I can't get away during Thanksgiving. I was thinking maybe you could spend Thanksgiving with me and I'd spend Christmas in Seattle with you. That way we can be together over the holidays instead of thousands of miles apart. What do you think?" He watched her facial expression, waiting for her reaction.

"I'll have to call my parents and tell them."

"Is that a yes?"

Slowly, the corners of her mouth perked up. "Yes."

He responded with a smile of his own. "Fantastic. I'll plan accordingly." While Oliver chomped on a dog bone, Roger grabbed a wineglass from the cupboard and poured red wine into it. "I heard from a friend of mine that they're holding open casting calls for It's a Wonderful Life. It's an off-Broadway seasonal production, but it's a start." He reached into his wallet and handed Lauren a business card with contact information and directions to the casting studio where they were holding auditions. "Auditions are next Saturday."

Lauren didn't take the card from him like he thought she would. Instead, she turned the other way and retreated into the bedroom.

Roger stood there mind-boggled, trying to figure out what he did that caused her to react that way. He replayed the conversation in his head, but nothing struck a chord. Baffled by her behavior, he released a heavy sigh and followed her into the bedroom.

Lauren sat on the edge of the bed with her back facing the door. Fearing he had done something that somehow caused her pain, he sat next to her. "Did I say something that…"

With misty eyes, she interjected, "You don't understand."

"Then help me understand." He reached out and touched her thigh.

She tried to explain, "You know how much I want to be on a Broadway stage."

"Yes, and I can help you get there," he replied.

She shook her head. "No! I want to get on stage because of my talent and my voice, not because I'm Roger Zellers' girlfriend"

Roger wasn't sure how to react to that. A million thoughts ran through his head as he considered the implications of her words. "So what are you telling me? That you don't want my help?"

She looked him in the eye, choking back tears. "I don't want you to exert your influence and use professional connections to pull strings on my behalf."

That was a ridiculous allegation, and he was offended that she assumed that. "Is that what you think I'm doing?"

She looked away.

Shocked and hurt by her accusation, he became defensive. "I am NOT pulling strings for you. I can't get you on a Broadway stage. The only person who can do that is you—you, Lauren Hanson, with your impeccable talent and incredible voice. The fact that you are my girlfriend won't have a damn thing to do with it."

"The only reason people even know my name is because of you," she claimed.

Roger disputed this claim. "No, they know your name because they've seen you perform and heard you sing. All I did was promote your shows. They took it upon themselves to come out and see your talent firsthand. Obviously they liked what they saw and spread the word. I've told you before that word of mouth travels quickly in this industry."

"I don't understand why you go through all this trouble for me. You have your own career to think about. You shouldn't have to worry about mine."

"Honey, look at me." He lifted her chin so they were eye to eye. "I'm helping you because I want to. I have experience and I have connections. I know the right people to talk to. I can lead you through the barriers of this business and give you a clearer path to your own success. But you have to get out from behind the curtain for that to happen. All I'm doing is opening the curtain and allowing you to take center stage."

"But I don't want people to think I'm relying on your name and your connections. I want to do this on my own."

Upset that she felt that way, he offered her some serious advice. "Let me explain something to you, my dear, and you better listen. This business is rough and it's raw. It can either make or break you both as a performer and as a person. It takes years to get a shot at the Broadway stage, and most people try their whole lives and never get a break. There are so many barricades to navigate, hurdles to cross, and hoops to jump through that it will make your head spin. I have been dealing with the business end of this industry for years, and over the years I have learned a few tricks that can knock down those barriers and jump over those hurdles to make the process of getting your shot on stage as quick and painless as possible. I can't get you on stage. Only you can do that. You're the one at the auditions performing in front of the casting directors, not me. But getting a chance to make an audition takes knowing where to look, knowing who to talk to, and knowing how to work the system. You'll get on stage, I truly believe that, but I can help you get there faster because I know how to navigate through the landmines."

"But Roger…"

He didn't let her finish. "Dammit, Lauren, do you want to perform on Broadway?"

"Yes," she said.

"Then listen to me. You can't do this alone. No one can. You need a support system and people who know the ropes around here. I can help you. I want to help you. But you have to want my help, because the last thing I want to do is stand in your way and hold you back."

Roger had never developed crossness in his tone before. That fact that he was being sarcastic and snarky was not in character for him. Lauren was horribly hurt by this.

Roger felt like a jerk for snapping at her like that. "I'm sorry. That was uncalled for." He took a deep breath to calm down. "Honey, let me help you. We can do this faster and easier together, side by side, supporting each other every step of the way. I thought you and I were a team?"

"We are."

"Then let's do this together, as partners. Together we can accomplish much more than we ever will alone." He handed her the card with audition information. "Take the audition. We'll go from there."

She took the card from him and swung into the circle of his arms. His grip tightened, and she could feel his uneven breathing on her cheek. "I'm sorry, Roger."

"Don't worry about it, Sweetheart. Misunderstandings happen."

She relaxed, sinking into the cushion of his embrace.

"And you know what? I can't think of anyone else I'd rather hash things out with than you. I love you, Lauren."

"I love you too." Closing her eyes, she raised herself to meet his kiss.

Chapter Nineteen

For the majority of his career, Randy had worked part time as an adjunct clinical professor for the University of Washington's School of Medicine. He loved working with medical students but wanted freedom in his schedule to still practice medicine in his own clinic. He dedicated two days a week to working with medical students in conjunction with performing surgeries and being on-call for his patients. The deliveries and surgeries he performed on these days were used as teaching tools for his students to observe, practice necessary skills, and gain insights into the field of Obstetrics and Gynecology. Randy took his work with the university seriously, seeing it as an opportunity to shape future doctors and hone their skills.

Randy's work as a clinical professor and medical mentor had become renowned throughout the department. The medical students he worked with praised him as being fair, patient, and knowledgeable in his field. He was always open to offer advice and give insights into his specialty.

Wednesday morning, after running hospital rounds and initiating Grand Rounds with his medical students, Randy received a phone call from Dr. William Iverson, the Dean of the School of Medicine. "Good morning,

Dr. Hanson. Will you have some time later to stop by my office for a few minutes?"

"I can clear my schedule and make time."

"Please do. I have something I would like to discuss with you."

Before he reported to the Dean's office, Randy performed a gynecological surgical procedure and a Caesarian section under the watchful eyes of his students. He then had them complete an analysis of these procedures and assigned them various patient files to research and discuss.

Once his medical students were situated, Randy reported to Dr. Iverson's office. The Dean greeted him with a firm handshake. "Good afternoon, Randy. Thank you for stopping by."

"It's not a problem, Bill."

Dr. Iverson showed Randy into his office. "Please, have a seat."

"Thank you." Randy claimed a chair across from Bill's desk. "What can I do for you?"

Bill took a seat beside him. "First of all, I would like to give my sincere condolences to you and your family for the loss of your father. I'm truly sorry. He was a great man and a wonderful physician."

"Yes, he was."

"I also wanted to thank you for all of your years of service helping us out with the medical students."

"It's my pleasure. I enjoy working with them."

"I know you do, and your enthusiasm shows. The students have learned a lot from you, and your name seems to come up in their conversations quite often," Bill claimed.

"It's good to know I've made a lasting impression on them."

"Along those lines," Bill explained. "We have a resident doctor who has specifically asked for a mentor who is affiliated with a university hospital, but has a private practice. In an attempt to accommodate this particular physician, your name was the first that came up. We know that you, as well as your partner Greg Hutchins, are both former UW residents. And since you have many years of experience working with our medical students, we thought you would be the perfect placement for this resident doctor. Would you be willing to host a resident next term?"

Randy was thrilled that the university instilled this kind of trust in him. "Absolutely."

"Fantastic! I will give her your contact information. Also, we are searching for someone to run the clinical OB/GYN department. We would like to recommend you for this position."

Randy didn't necessarily agree with this decision. "I'm flattered, Bill, but a commitment like that won't give me a lot of time for my own practice. My patients are important to me."

"We know, Randy, and we've considered that," Bill clarified. "The position won't require much more than what you're doing now. You'll still provide clinical experience to the students, but you'll also be involved in helping us place students and determine essential curriculum and necessary textbooks for the OB/GYN aspect of their clinical training. You'll basically be responsible for overseeing the general training and supervision of the medical students as they go through their OB/GYN rotation."

Randy contemplated the time commitment involved with this position. "My kids are grown now, but I do have a wife, Bill," Randy chuckled. "How much time will this require?

"Other than the time you already dedicate, you'll have an occasional evening department meeting to discuss curriculum with the other clinical supervisors. We'll also want to sit down with you to determine textbook choices for our medical students. It's a tenured position with the university, with a pay raise attached."

Randy seriously considered all that Bill Iverson said. "Let me talk to my wife tonight, and I'll give you a call in the morning."

Over a homemade meal and a glass of wine, Randy spoke with Jane about this opportunity. "Bill Iverson called me into his office today."

"What did he want?"

"He offered me a promotion with the university."

"What kind of promotion?"

Randy explained, "They want me to head the clinical OB/GYN department and act as primary supervisor to medical students going through their clerkship training."

"What does that entail?" she asked, then she took a bite of her salad.

"I'll have authoritative say in placement of medical students during their clinical rotations. I'll also be responsible for examining the medical school standards to determine how to best approach what the students should be learning and what resources will best help them learn it."

"So you'll be in charge of their entire clinical experience," Jane summarized.

"Pretty much."

"And how do you feel about that?"

"Well," he said. "It's different from anything I've ever done before. Usually the medical students just follow me around and help with procedures and patient files as I assign them. This is much more direct and explicit."

"Sounds like something you would enjoy."

"Yes, but there is a downside," he explained. "It's going to require me to spend some evenings collaborating with other professors and clinical supervisors, and I'll have to attend medical school department meetings. On the plus side, my schedule won't change much, my practice will still be my priority. Bill says it's a tenured position with the department and includes a pretty substantial pay raise."

"How substantial?"

"About 50K a year, that's over and above what I make through my practice."

"50K?" she asked, impressed with that number.

"It will require a few more hours than what I've been doing, but most of it will be done through my clinic. We're going to work it out so the students get at least one rotation of their practical and clinical experience through me and my patients. That way the medical students get their training, and my patients get their doctor. I teach while I'm overseeing my patients. It's a win-win situation."

"And Bill was ok with this?" she wondered.

"Yes, he and I discussed it over lunch. I wasn't about to commit to anything without getting more specific information about it." He picked up his wineglass and took a sip. "So, what do you think?"

Randy had always said he wanted to get more involved in the medical school. This was his opportunity to do so. "It sounds like a wonderful opportunity," Jane advised him.

"Alright. I'll give Bill a call in the morning."

The anticipation of waiting to hear from medical schools was driving Nathan crazy. His applications had been completed long ago and he had conducted several interviews, both primary and secondary. Now, all he had to do was wait for what seemed like an eternity. His constant pacing and incessant nervous twitchiness was counterproductive, and it was starting to get on Gabby's nerves. "Would you stop that?"

"Stop what?" he asked, as he paced around his living room again.

"You're pacing around like a lion in a cage. Sit down."

Nathan glanced at his watch. "What time does the mail get here?"

"Nathan," Gabby begged, "Please stop worrying."

"Stop worrying? Really, Gab? This is only my life we're talking about."

"And what good is pacing around doing besides making you a nervous wreck?"

He checked his watch again. "I'm going to run over and see if the mail has come yet."

After months of waiting, Nathan came back with a letter in his hand from University of Washington School of Medicine. The much awaited letter that had caused him turmoil for months had finally arrived, but he was too nervous to open it.

Gabby recognized the anxious expression on his face. "What's the matter?"

He handed her the envelope. "Look."

"Oh good, maybe now you'll relax." She gave the envelope back to him. "Open it."

"I can't."

"Why not?"

"I just can't. You do it."

"Are you sure?"

He insisted. "Please, Gab. Open it for me."

Nathan nervously watched as she pulled a folded letter out of the legal sized envelope and read it. From Gabby's reaction, he couldn't tell what the letter said. Growing impatient, he asked, "Well?"

She read the letter out loud. "Dear Mr. Hanson, we congratulate you on your acceptance into the University of Washington's School of Medicine."

He stopped her, making sure he heard her correctly. "What did you say?"

"You got in."

"Seriously?" He snatched the letter from her hand and read for himself.

"That's what it says," she confirmed.

After reading the entirety of the letter, he stood in shock. "I got in."

"That's what I just said," she teased.

Excited about his accomplishment, he grabbed Gabby into his arms and squeezed her. "I did it!" He spun her around, laughing and celebrating. "This is awesome! I can't believe it."

"I knew you would," Gabby told him. "The only person who had doubts was you."

Nathan set her down gently. "I could not have done this without you." In joyous celebration, he kissed her. "Thank you so much, Gab."

"You're welcome, Sweetie. Does this mean you'll stop pacing now?"

Nathan chuckled, "Yes."

"Good, because that was driving me crazy."

Nathan reported to work that afternoon in an impeccable mood. When Randy saw the joyful grin painted on his son's face, he had to comment on it. "Someone is in a good mood. You've got that I just had sex look on your face."

Randy's remark made Nathan laugh. "Nope. The smile on my face is from something better than sex."

"What could possibly be better than sex?" Randy asked with a skeptical smirk.

Nathan pulled an envelope out of his backpack and handed it to his father. "This."

Randy stared at it in anticipation. "Is this what I think it is?" He pulled the letter out and began to read it. "Well, well. Congratulations, Nate! Nicely done." He refolded the letter and stuffed it back inside the envelope. "Did you tell your mom?"

"Not yet. I wanted you to be the first to know."

"Thank you for thinking about me." He tapped his watch. "You're five minutes late. Get to work."

Nathan slipped the envelope back in his backpack and grinned. Even though Dr. Hanson didn't actually say it, Nathan could tell his father was proud of him. "Yes, Sir."

To celebrate Nathan's acceptance into medical school, Jane, Randy, and Gabby collaborated to plan a surprise congratulatory party for him. Jane did most of the preliminary planning but relied on Gabby to make a guest list for this event. Helping Nathan's mother, Gabby secretly invited his coach and entire basketball team, as well as some former players who had graduated. Aside from family members, Randy invited Jim and Jill Ryan, Christopher and his fiancé, and Greg and Raquel Hutchins. The Hanson house was buzzing as friends and family arrived.

"We have to get over to your parents' house," Gabby said, trying to get Nathan to hurry up so he wouldn't miss his own party.

"Why are you in such a hurry to get over there?" Nathan thought they were just going over there for dinner, and he couldn't figure out why Gabby insisted on rushing out the door. "My parents will wait for us, Gab. When Mom says 5:30, that's an estimated time. It's not carved in stone."

"I don't want to be late," she tried to justify.

Nathan laughed. "Usually it's me who's rushing out the door to get food. This is a role reversal."

"Can we just go?" She handed him the car keys.

"Alright, alright. Geez!" Gabby was being pushy tonight, which was not like her at all. "Let's go before you freak out on me."

This celebration had a lighthearted feel. Aside from finger foods and various drinks, Jane prepared a white frosted layer cake with a Caduceus and stethoscope painted on the top. She also made cupcakes topped with little Red Cross candies. She strung a large *Congratulations* banner across the French doors and hung several red, silver, and white helium-filled balloons around the living room and dining area.

For fun, and to add an element of humor to this party, Randy set out several Operation games for people to play at their discretion. He also added other board games, such as Medical Monopoly, The Health Education Game, Medical School Madness, and a card game called Hospital, to the game table. Prior to the party, he prepared a Pictionary game with nothing but medical terminology in it. These were certain to keep their guests entertained.

When Nathan and Gabby arrived, many cars were parked outside. "What the hell?" Nathan questioned. "Did my parents invite the whole neighborhood over for dinner?" The not-so-innocent smirk on Gabby's face told him that more was going on here than just dinner. "Is this why you were in such a hurry to get over here?"

Gabby grinned devilishly, revealing her involvement. "Maybe."

Nathan parked the car and turned off the ignition. "Why are all these people here?"

"I'm not supposed to tell you," she declared.

He stubbornly folded his arms across his chest. "Talk."

"I can't. It's a surprise. Why don't you just go inside and find out for yourself."

When he walked in the house, many voices yelled, "Surprise!"

With the banner and the cake and all these people standing around, Nathan easily figured out what was going on. "Gee, thanks."

Jane gave him a huge hug. "Congratulations, Sweetie. We're so proud of you."

Nathan was mingling with a group of friends when a face he hadn't seen in years walked through the door. With a deer in the headlights look, he stared at the man in awe. "You have got to be kidding." A smile of not only surprise but extreme joy filled his face. He set his cup down on the nearest table and rushed to the door, greeting this man with a hug. "Brett!"

"Hey, Nathan."

Brett Sorenson was the starting point guard for the University of Washington when Nathan was a freshmen. Nathan considered him a mentor and a friend. When Brett graduated, Nathan took over as the starting point guard and led the team in Brett's absence. Although they had kept in touch, they hadn't seen each other since Brett graduated. "What the hell are you doing here?"

Brett explained, "A little bird told me that you were accepted into med school. I heard there was some sort of party going on, and since I was in the neighborhood, I thought I'd stop by and see what all the excitement was about."

Nathan peered over at Gabby, knowing she was the culprit who invited him. "Is this little bird's name Gabriella by any chance?"

Brett grinned. "How'd you guess?"

"Just a hunch." He walked over to the table to get his drink. "How you been?"

"Doing well. Just got a promotion. They made me the assistant manager of the marketing division."

Nathan went into the kitchen to grab a beer out of the refrigerator. He popped the top and handed it to Brett. "It's good to see you."

"It's good to see you too."

As a gag gift, the Huskies basketball team chipped in to get Nathan a tote bag with *Medical Student* printed on the side in big, bold, black letters. They wrapped a *Medical Student: because other sports require only one ball* tee-shirt and stuffed it inside the bag along with a Lego doctor USB drive, a fun coffee cup that looked like a prescription bottle, a book called 'Medical Terminology for Dummies', and a couple of ballpoint syringe pens. For a more serious gift, Randy, Greg, and Jim joined together to get Nathan a medical supply bag. The bag itself was black leather with a Caduceus emblem and the name *Hanson* sewn on the side. They filled it with a new stethoscope, a portable blood pressure monitor, an otoscope kit, an MID pocket reference guide, and other vital medical supplies.

This party was not only a fun surprise, but also a big pick-me-up for Nathan. After all the stress and sacrifice he made to get into medical school, he was glad his family and friends recognized his efforts.

Returning to his apartment that night, Nathan said, "Thank you for doing this for me tonight, Gab."

"It wasn't just me," Gabby told him. "Your parents coordinated most of it."

"I can't believe Brett showed up." He was still stunned that his old friend and mentor was at this celebration.

"Were you surprised?"

Nathan grabbed her by the waist and pulled her close to him. "Very surprised. That made my day." He nibbled on her ear then sent sweet kisses down her neck.

"I'm really proud of you, Nathan."

"Thank you." In loving adoration, he rubbed his thumb across her lips. "Everything you and I have been through, all the goals we set, the dreams we've pursued, I'm glad I got to share all of this with you. Who would have thought that when we first met in eighth grade we would've come this far?"

"Who would have thought that the brat kid who used to tease me all time would turn out to be the man I love?"

"I only teased you because I liked you," Nathan declared. "And I would have asked you out sooner, but your mother wouldn't let you date until you were sixteen."

"I'll never forget that night. That was the first time you and I went out alone together," she recalled, feeling nostalgic.

"I know. I was there."

"That was also the first time you kissed me."

Thinking about that night gave him a warm, fuzzy feeling. "I waited a long time to be alone with you. I wasn't about to let the moment pass without taking advantage of it. Corey had just asked you to the homecoming dance too. Do you remember?"

Gabby laughed. "Uh huh. You were so jealous."

He admitting to her that yes, he was a bit envious. "That's because I wanted you to go with me."

"And I did, didn't I?" she reminded him.

"Yes you did. Corey was pissed too."

"He should have known I'd go with you if you asked me. Everyone knew I liked you."

"You were beautiful that night. You're always beautiful." He softly grazed his hand down her cheek. "I felt proud walking the halls with you, holding your hand. Do you know how many guys would have died to be in my shoes?"

"Other guys weren't you," Gabby proclaimed. "All I ever wanted was you, Nathan."

Overwhelmed by her devotion, he replied, "And all I ever wanted was you. The rest of this is just icing on the cake." Giving her a suggestive stare, he said, "And let me tell you something, it's pretty tasty cake."

Chapter Twenty

"Oh man, today is gonna be nuts," Roger complained, realizing that he had incorporated too many activities into his daily schedule.

"Isn't Thanksgiving usually like that?" Lauren asked, wrapped up in her robe with a cup of cocoa in her hand.

"Yes, but today even more so." He gulped down his cup of coffee and quickly checked the time. It was 7:10 A.M.—much later than he thought it was. "I'm gonna be late." He set his coffee cup in the sink and grabbed his keys. "I have to be there in twenty minutes."

"Central Park West is going to be blocked off," Lauren reminded him.

"You're right. I'll have the cab driver go the other way." He frantically shoved his keys and cellphone into his pocket. "I have to go."

"You should be fine, as long as traffic cooperates."

He snorted derisively. "With the parade blocking every street, it might be faster if I walk."

She loved his subtle wit. "It might."

"I wanna head out as soon as I get back." Roger planned to drive to his parent's house the moment he returned home from the parade.

"I'll be ready," Lauren said.

He grabbed his jacket, scarf, and a pair of leather gloves then kissed Lauren goodbye.

"Be careful," Lauren called out to him. "And stay warm please."

"I'll try. Love you, Honey." And he rushed out the door.

Once again Roger was performing at the Macy's Day Parade. This year he was singing 'Lullaby of Broadway' atop the Broadway Theatre float. Although Roger loved this gig and didn't mind winter weather, he didn't like singing in cold temperatures. The dry, wintry air strained his vocal chords.

More than fifty million people tuned in to the television broadcast of the Macy's parade, and another 3.5 million viewed it live along the parade route. The two-and-a-half mile parade route would only take about two hours to complete, but prior to the parade, Roger had to force his way through crowds to get to his designated area, warm up his voice, and do a sound check with the wireless sound system. At the conclusion of the parade, he would have to push his way through millions of people, all of whom would be trying to get out of closed off areas by swarming subways and hailing taxis.

Instead of fighting the crowds, Lauren chose to watch this event from the comfort of her living room. This would allow her to finish prepping for Thanksgiving dinner. She and Roger had prepared an apple and pumpkin pie the day before, but she still had to bake the cornbread, make deviled eggs, and throw together a multi-green salad with cranberries, diced green apple, and walnuts to take to Roger's parents' house that afternoon, which was 198 miles west of New York City.

Roger's family lived in Owego, New York, which was about a three-hour drive from Manhattan. The parade started at 9:00 in the morning and usually didn't end until noon. By the time Roger navigated through the crowds, it would be close to 1:00 P.M before he got home. They were going to cut it close to get there by 4:00. Despite this tightness in scheduling, Lauren looked forward to meeting the rest of Roger's family.

While Lauren made last minute Thanksgiving preparations, she watched the parade, waiting to see Roger's performance. His float was positioned in the middle of the parade, and when she saw him, he was all bundled up in his jacket, scarf, and gloves. She hoped he was dressed warm enough.

When Santa Claus made his arrival at the parade's finale, the start of the Christmas season was officially marked. And since the parade was over, that meant Roger was on his way home. They planned to stay in Owego overnight, so Lauren packed a bag for them. As soon as Roger walked in the door, they tossed their bag in the car and went on their way.

Once they were out of New York City, they traveled east on Interstate 80 then north onto 81. The drive to Owego was pretty scenic with rolling hills, mountainsides, flowing rivers, and rows upon rows of thick green trees. It reminded Lauren of the state highways of Washington—roads she had traveled many times. The Pocono Mountains were breathtaking, and the rivers, state forests, and wilderness through the Pennsylvania game lands were serene and relaxing. The three-hour car ride gave Roger and Lauren a lot of time to talk and belt out songs they heard on the radio. It was a fun ride.

Lauren was a bit nervous about meeting Roger's family. He didn't understand why, since the only person who would have been critical was his mother, and Lauren already met her. "My nephews might be a little shy around you because you're new to them," Roger explained. "But if you give them each a dollar, you'll be their best friend for the rest of the night."

Lauren found this amusing. "You bribe your nephews with money?"

"I don't bribe them, they just know that when Uncle Roger is around, their piggy banks get a little heavier."

Roger had added a small white paper bag to the already full backseat of the car. "What's in that bag?" Lauren asked.

"I snagged a ceramic Phantom mask for my mom and signed it for her. She likes to get artifacts from my Broadway experiences. Last year I brought her a Chicago promotional poster with a picture of me as Billy Flynn printed on it. She still has it hanging on her wall. In fact, she has an entire room dedicated to my Broadway shows. It's like a Roger Zellers shrine or something."

"Well, you're her son. She's proud of you."

"Something like that."

"You never told me what your brother does for a living."

"Pete?" Roger said. "He's a police officer in Baltimore. Made Lieutenant this year."

"That's a dangerous job," she stated.

"It can be. Peter's good at what he does though. He does a lot of undercover work, which has risks involved, but he usually catches the bad guy."

"What kind of undercover work?" Lauren asked.

"Homeland security infiltration, drug trafficking, suspected gang activity. Things that jeopardize the safety of the public."

"That must be scary for his wife."

"Amy knows the risks he takes. He can't always tell her what he's doing. That would put her and the boys at risk. And Pete doesn't wear his wedding ring on the job because he doesn't want the people he's involved with to know that he has a family. He doesn't carry pictures of them or have his personal cellphone on him when he's running an operation. Just his badge, his gun, his work phone, and a pair of handcuffs. Everything else stays in his locker. He does what he can to keep them safe."

"Sounds like a good man," Lauren remarked.

"We're proud of him." Roger turned on the blinker, glanced in the rearview mirror, checked his blind spot to make sure the lane was clear, then switched lanes to go around a big rig. "They're expecting again."

"That's exciting."

"Yes it is. Another Zellers. Our family's growing bigger all the time."

Located in the foothills of upstate New York, Owego was nestled in a bowl between the Adirondack Mountains and the Susquehanna River. A picturesque bridge arched over the river connecting the town to the road on the adjoining side. Roger drove across the bridge which brought them into town. The first thing that caught Lauren's attention was the beautiful, historic Tioga County courthouse, which sat right in the middle of town. This town was full of large historic homes, buildings, and shops dating back to the nineteen century. As soon as they got across the bridge, Roger turned left on Front Street. He drove down the street a ways before he pulled into the driveway of a yellow two-story colonial-looking house right alongside the Susquehanna River. The historic home had been meticulously maintained. It had a Mansard style roof with elegant decorative accents. The oak double front doors were accented by a beautiful arched casement. A large and inviting front porch with beautiful columns and intricate handrails encircled the entire front of the house.

Roger turned off the ignition and stepped out of the car.

Lauren scanned the surrounding area, focusing primarily on this beautiful home. "This is nice."

"Yup," Roger agreed. "House was built in 1872. Back in the late 1800's, the president of the First National Bank lived here."

Roger's mother and step-father greeted them at the car and helped them unload their belongings. It wasn't long before two small boys raced out of the house and mauled Roger.

"Hey! It's the munchkin brothers!" Roger squatted down to their level, and they both jumped on him, squeezing him with death grips.

Lauren found this downright adorable. Obviously these two young boys were quite fond of their Uncle Roger.

Peter and his wife soon joined them. The boys stared at Lauren, not sure what to make of this foreign woman standing in their grandma's driveway. "Who's she?" the oldest boy asked.

Roger stood by Lauren's side with his arm around her waist. "This is Lauren."

"Is she your girlfriend?" the boy asked with a thoughtful expression on his face.

The seriousness in his nephew's tone made Roger laugh. "Yes, she is."

The older boy eyeballed Lauren while the smaller boy bashfully hid behind his mother's leg.

Roger proceeded to introduce everyone. "Lauren, these are Pete's boys. The oldest one is Gabriel and the little one hiding over there is Matthew."

Lauren waved at them. "Hello."

"Go on," Peter encouraged his boys. "Be polite. Shake her hand and welcome her."

Gabriel followed his father's directive and confidently offered Lauren a handshake.

"Why thank you," she said with a playful curtsy.

Roger pulled out his wallet and knelt down by his nephews, who immediately came to his side. He handed each boy a five dollar bill. "Here you go," he said. "Keep it in a safe place. And if you rub it each night, it will multiply."

The oldest boy, Gabriel, got all starry-eyed. "How does it do that?"

Roger told him, "It's magic money."

The two boys looked at each other, enthralled. They clung tightly to their money and ran into the house.

Roger rose to his feet.

"Roger," Amy said. "Why do you tell them stories like that?"

"Uncle Roger is the money genie," he said with a chuckle. "And as long as I'm here, it will magically multiply."

"It's good to see you," she declared, giving him a hug.

He placed his hand on Amy's tummy. "You look good. How you feeling?"

"Feel great. We told the boys last night. They're super excited."

"That's fantastic." Roger grinned. "I'm happy for you guys. Congratulations." Roger gave his brother a firm hug. "Hey, Pete."

"You're looking good, Roger." Peter looked over at Lauren. "Looks like this woman is taking good care of you."

"That she is," Roger proudly proclaimed. "Pete, this is Lauren."

"I figured as much," he extended an open palm. "Welcome."

Lauren shook his hand. "Thank you."

Once Roger finished introducing everyone, Amy openly gave Lauren a hug. "It's wonderful to finally meet you."

"Thank you, it's wonderful to be here," Lauren replied.

"Come on in," Peter offered, escorting them up to the porch. "Make yourself at home."

Roger's family displayed immense hospitality and gladly welcomed Lauren into their home. Roger's mother and step-father had already met her, but this was the first time Peter and Amy had the chance to talk to her. Peter fell in love with her instantly. She was spunky and cheerful and complemented Roger well. He was happier and more content than Peter had ever seen him. The family adored her.

Roger had never invited anyone home for Thanksgiving before. The fact that he had done this was a pretty big deal. When Peter and Roger had some time alone, Peter questioned his brother about this. "So, Roger..." He put his hand on Roger's shoulder. "You've never brought a woman home to meet the family before."

Roger turned a dining room chair around and sat straddling the back of it. "I know, but it's Lauren."

"I know her name," Peter snickered, taking a seat next to his brother. "This thing you have with her sounds serious. What's going on?"

"I found her." He sipped from his glass of wine. "Took me almost thirty years, but I finally found her."

Peter knew his brother well and could see the gears turning in Roger's head. "Are you thinking what I think you're thinking?"

"What do you think I'm thinking?" Roger asked for clarification.

"You're thinking about a marriage proposal, aren't you?"

Roger set his glass on the table and folded his hands along the back of the chair. "Yes, I am."

Overjoyed by this news, Peter asked, "Have you told Mom about this?"

"No, not yet. I want to get a ring first. I already have one picked out."

Peter looked over at Lauren who was sitting on the sofa carrying on a pleasant conversation with their mother. "I like her, Rog. She's a great girl. Sweet, funny, and she gets along well with Mom." Then Peter said something he wasn't sure Roger wanted to hear. "But she is young. Are you sure she's ready for marriage?"

"I have considered that," Roger admitted. "And I believe she is. We have a wonderful relationship, Pete. She's the woman I've been waiting my whole life for. She's a woman I know I can trust. She's my partner in crime, my rock, my inspiration, and my biggest fan. No one knows me as well as she does—and she knows me inside and out, faults and all. We share everything together, and when I think about my future, I honestly can't picture my life without her in it. She's the woman I want to spend the rest of my life with. The woman I want to raise a family with. The woman I want to share my name with." Roger looked his brother in the eye and said, "Lauren is without a doubt the woman I want to marry."

"She's the one, huh?"

Roger grinned, confident in his decision. "Yup. She's definitely the one."

"That's great!" Peter encouraged, a little too overzealously. "I'm really happy for you."

Peter's enthusiasm made Roger laugh.

"When are you planning to pop the big question?" Peter asked, wondering when and how his little brother was making this marriage proposal.

"I'm thinking Christmas. It's a joyful time of year. We'll celebrate with a joyful occasion."

"You going to Seattle this year?"

"Yup. She's spending Thanksgiving with my family, I'll spend Christmas with hers."

"Fair exchange," Peter remarked.

"We thought so."

After gluttonously devouring pie, Roger took Lauren to the historic Owego marketplace where they went on a peaceful walk down the historic tree-lined streets to view the beautiful nineteenth century architecture and burn off some of the huge meal they had eaten. They viewed some of the other historic homes, visited the Civil War Soldiers and Sailors Monument in front of the courthouse, and Roger stole a kiss on the gazebo erected on the northeast corner of Courthouse Square.

They held hands as they strolled the riverwalk, admiring the view and soaking up the romantic atmosphere. "So, what do you think?" Roger asked.

Owego was an authentic historical village with hometown hospitality. Lauren thought it was charming. "This is an appealing little town. I like it."

"I'm glad you like it, but I was referring to my family," Roger corrected. "Now that you've had a chance to meet all of them, what do you think?"

"Oh," She giggled at her error. "I like them too. They're friendly people, inviting, kind."

"Good," he said, pleased that she felt that way. "That's what I like to hear."

"Your nephews are so cute. Gabriel's an inquisitive one and little Matthew is so sweet."

"They're good boys. Pete and Amy are doing a good job with them."

"Your brother's wife is one of the nicest women I've ever met."

Roger agreed. "I've always liked Amy, and I'm glad you and Mom get along so well."

"Your mom is so funny. I just love her," Lauren replied.

He couldn't have been more pleased. After all, if all went as planned, his family would soon be her family too.

Christmas had come to New York. Carolers spread joy singing Christmas songs under the giant Rockefeller tree, outside the cathedral, and throughout Central Park. Roger and Lauren were among one of the Central Park caroling groups which consisted mostly of Broadway performers. Their song repertoire ranged from spiritual selections like 'God Rest Ye Merry Gentlemen' to more lighthearted traditional carols like 'Sleigh Ride'.

Roger was asked to sing at the Rockefeller Center Christmas Tree Lighting Ceremony again this year. Over the years, he had become a crowd-favorite at this event.

He and Lauren spent Sunday morning putting up the Christmas tree. With an ornament in his hand, Roger reminded her, "I have Rockefeller next week."

"What song are you singing?"

Instead of telling her, he sang the words, "Have yourself a merry little Christmas..."

"That's a good one," Lauren said.

"I'm bummed you didn't get a part in It's a Wonderful Life. That's a great show. I would have loved to see you in that."

"I didn't have enough experience."

"But you'll get more. And the audition experience is good for you. The more you do, the more confident you'll become."

Roger and Lauren finished hanging up decorations then stood back to admire their handiwork. "It's a beautiful tree. Nice job, Sweetheart." They high fived each other then sat on the sofa with Oliver lying between them. "We need to get another stocking."

"Why?" Lauren asked.

He thought it was obvious. "Because you need one."

"But we won't be here for Christmas."

"Doesn't matter." He rose from the couch and began to clean up the empty ornament boxes. "I've been single, living alone for so long that I never had a need for more than one stocking until you and Ollie came around."

Hearing his name made the Scottie's ears perk up. Roger reached over and pet him.

"Except for the two years I was at Juilliard and the six months at the beginning of my career when I shared a flat with Jason, I've always lived alone."

"You're not alone now," she reminded him.

"No I'm not. I have a loving woman and loyal dog. Couldn't ask for anything more. I love sharing an apartment with you, by the way."

"I love being here," she added.

"I guess that means you'll stick around for a while?" he teased.

"Forever and always."

Those words made Roger's heart skip a beat. "Always and forever," he promised in return. He was in the Christmas spirit, and Christmas shopping on Fifth Avenue was calling his name. "I'm hungry. Let's grab something to eat and do a little shopping."

"I'm craving Chinese food," Lauren remarked, getting excited about one of her favorite foods.

"Ooh, that sounds good," he concurred.

They dressed Ollie in a red kilt sweater and tamoshanter hat and took him for a walk through Central Park. After which, they ate cashew chicken and fried rice then headed over to Fifth Avenue to engage in a holiday shopping excursion.

Their first stop was FOA Schwartz Toy Store in the GM Building on Fifth Avenue. Two stories of toys, games, and hobbies made this department store a mansion among toy stores. This store had a magnificent menagerie of cute and cuddly stuffed animals, Legos and Star Wars merchandise, children's books, puppets and board games, and an entire section devoted just to Barbie. Roger grabbed a cart and together, he and Lauren browsed through the store. Roger stopped to play with many of the toys before he tossed them in the cart. He grabbed stuffed animals, toy trucks, books, Playdough, Lego sets, action figures, dolls, and sporting goods. He was having entirely too much fun, and their cart was overflowing.

About an hour and a half into toy shopping, Lauren questioned Roger about the randomness of the items in the cart. "Roger, Honey, why are you getting all these toys?"

"Because, my dear, there are children whose families can't afford to buy gifts for them. It is heartbreaking and unfair for Santa to bypass their house simply because their family has no money to put gifts under their tree. With all these toys, we are going to make some needy kids very happy this year," he explained.

Roger had such a caring heart, and he especially seemed to have a soft spot for children. This was one of the things Lauren always loved about him. "You have a heart of pure gold," she said.

He didn't think it was a big deal. "I have the means to make Christmas magical for some kids. I'm going to do what I can to help."

Before they checked out, Roger stopped at the Schweetz shop located within the store. This section of FOA Schwartz offered signature candy sold by the pound. Inside were dancing jelly beans, a walk-in bubble-gum machine, and nearly one-thousand kinds of candy sure to satisfy any sweet tooth. Roger and Lauren perused through dozens of delicious candies from bears, worms, fruit and anything else gummy, to classic candies such as Jawbreakers and Whoppers. He ended up purchasing a large Jelly Belly filled truck, four smiley face lollipops, bottles of candy bubbles which were just like the soapy kind except you could swallow the flavored bubbles, two enormously oversized chocolate Santas, and a three-pound bag of gummy sea creatures.

Lauren laughed at him. "Have a bit of a sweet tooth?"

"These aren't for me. I'd be wired and sick to my stomach if I ate all of this. These are for Pete's boys."

"Uncle Roger bribing them with candy again?" she teased him.

"I don't bribe them. They're kids, and it's Christmas. I'm just exposing them to the finer things in life."

"I bet your brother loves you for hyping them up on sugar," she mocked.

Roger lifted a shoulder. "He doesn't seem to mind. It's not like they get a ton of candy all the time. They get an overabundance on Halloween and Easter, and they always get a bunch from me at Christmastime. Christmas only comes once a year. Let the kids enjoy it. It won't hurt them."

On the shelf, perched in miniature splendor, was a chocolate baby grand piano. With the top opened, a handful of musical notes and treble clef shaped candies were clearly visible. Roger beamed with excitement. "Now this I want." He picked it up and put in the cart.

Lauren thought Roger's excitement was cute. And the boys were going to love all the sweets their uncle bought for them.

Chapter Twenty-One

Roger and Lauren hopped on an airplane and headed to Seattle for Christmas. They had one layover in Denver, which allowed them a bit of time to grab lunch before they took to the air again.

When they arrived in Seattle, Roger could plainly see that the Hansons liked Christmas as much as he did. Their home was full of holiday spirit, and the entire house smelled like cookies. They were served on a silver platter along with crystal moose glasses full of eggnog and candy cane swizzle sticks. A gorgeous tree was trimmed in gold and red with multi-colored lights. It sparkled brightly and really brought the holiday spirit alive. A big red bow was tied to the top of the parrot's cage, and the bird happily sang 'Jingle Bells.' Even the parrot was in a holiday mood.

Lauren planned to do the bulk of her Christmas shopping in Seattle with her mother and sister. This was easier than trying to transport boxes on an airplane. Roger, on the other hand, had everything he needed as far as gifts were concerned and was able to fit the gifts he had purchased into his carryon bag.

While the girls were out shopping, the men had a chance to do some bonding. For months now, Randy had wondered what Roger's intentions were in regards to Lauren. The fact that they were living together, and

Roger had taken time out his busy performance schedule to spend a major holiday with Lauren, made Randy suspect that Roger planned to bring their relationship to a more serious level. Randy had suspected for a while that this was Roger's intention, but had no confirmation that it was true. That was about to change. Roger's true intentions were about to be revealed.

As Randy and Roger lounged on the sofa flipping back and forth between the football playoffs and basketball, Roger struck up a conversation. "These cookies are incredible." He took a bite of a chocolate chip one, savoring every soft, chewy morsel.

Randy kicked back and put his feet up on the ottoman. "Jane definitely knows how to bake a cookie. I'm convinced I married Betty Crocker."

"How long have you and your wife been married?"

"Twenty-six years now."

"And still going strong, I might add," Roger commended. "What's the secret?"

"What's the secret?"

"To a long and happy marriage. You and your wife have been married for twenty-six years. You must be doing something right."

Randy gladly offered his insights. "Let me give you a piece of advice, Roger. Marriage is a bed of roses, thorns and all. There's no such thing as a perfect marriage, only perfect moments. Any time two individuals live together, especially over many years, there are bound to be annoying, irritating, and frustrating experiences. It will lead to friction. But you have to have friction. You can't get any heat without friction. Whether it's the toothpaste cap, toilet seat, dirty socks on the floor, or the last-minute pull the car over to check the score of the game at the local bar move, one thing that has stuck with me is that the best marriages are served with an extra helping of acceptance for one another's imperfections. That's the beauty of marriage. Our individualities, all of our wonderful differences."

"Makes sense," Roger said. "It's those differences that you fall in love with in the first place. I wouldn't want to be married to someone who was exactly like me."

"Of course not. No one would," Randy agreed. "But along with those differences comes respect. You can't have a successful marriage without respect. Respect is the catalyst for everything else that makes a marriage wonderful—trust, connection, authenticity, and love. The most important of these is love. Love is a four letter word, and it's spelled G-I-V-E. Most people have the misconception that marriage is fifty-fifty. It's not. It's sixty-forty. You give sixty, take forty. But both spouses have to believe that. It's not just about me or just about her, it's about us."

"As it should be," Roger claimed.

"And the great part is that when us gets first priority, I get everything I need, and so does Jane."

Curiously, Roger asked, "How did you propose to your wife?"

"Took her out to dinner at the restaurant where we had our first date. Now mind you, this was right after I found out about my residency match. Jane had lived in San Francisco her whole life up to that point, but my residency was here in Seattle which meant I was leaving. I told her I wanted her to come to Seattle with me, presented her with a ring, and asked her to marry me."

"That's awesome!" Roger declared. "Obviously it worked."

Randy grinned. "Yes it did."

Glancing over at the pile of colorfully wrapped gifts under the Christmas tree, Roger developed a more somber expression. "There's one more gift that needs to go under that tree. It's something I got for Lauren, but I didn't want to put it under there until I spoke with you, Sir."

"If it's a gift for Lauren, what does that have to do with me?"

Roger told him, "It's an engagement ring."

Randy wasn't sure how to react to this news. He knew this was coming, but still wasn't prepared for it.

"Dr. Hanson," Roger readjusted and sat up straighter. "With your permission, Sir, I'd like to ask for Lauren's hand."

Randy rubbed his fingers over his mouth and chin. This old-fashioned, gentlemanly gesture was not a common occurrence this day in age, and quite frankly, Randy was surprised Roger had done it. "You're asking me for permission to marry my daughter?"

"Yes, Sir."

The seriousness on Roger's face made Randy chuckle. "You do realize, don't you, that guys don't do things like this anymore."

"I am aware of that, Sir. But I know how much Lauren respects you and values your opinion," Roger explained. "I know how important Lauren is to you and your wife, and I know how much you love her. But I love her too, and I want to spend the rest of my life with her. I have every intention of proposing to Lauren, but before I do, I wanted you be aware of my intentions and hopefully have your permission."

"You don't need my permission," Randy claimed. "But you do have my approval."

That was the answer he hoped for. "Thank you, Doctor."

Trying to gain more information, Randy asked, "When is this happening?"

"Christmas morning. I'm going to slip the box under the tree and wait for her to open it."

Simple marriage proposal, but effective. "Cool."

"I'd like this to be a surprise. Can I ask a favor from you?"

"Sure."

"Please don't tell anyone," Roger begged. "Right now this is just between you and me. I'd like to keep it that way."

"I won't say a word."

"Thank you, Sir."

Early Christmas morning, before anyone else was awake, Roger carefully slipped a shiny red box with Lauren's name on it under the tree, tucked neatly between two other boxes.

Randy poured coffee into a cup and greeted Roger. "Good morning."

Roger turned his head. Apparently Randy had been awake for a while because he was already dressed and had a pot of coffee brewing. "Good morning, Dr. Hanson. I didn't think anyone else was up yet."

Randy dumped sugar and creamer into his coffee. "How you doing?"

Roger took a seat on one of the barstools at the kitchen island and released a cleansing breath. "You know, I have done hundreds of auditions, and I perform in front of thousands of people every night. Yet none of that ever made me as nervous as I am this morning. I didn't sleep well last night."

Randy flashed him a crooked smile. "Nerve racking, isn't it?"

"Very."

Trying to help Roger relax, Randy pulled another cup out of the cupboard and poured coffee into it. He plopped in two sugar cubes and stirred in a little creamer then handed the cup to Roger. "See if this helps."

"Thank you." He took a sip. "Although I think this might actually make it worse. If I drink too much of this stuff, I'll develop the shakes, which really won't settle my nerves much."

Randy pushed a Dunkin' Donuts box toward him. "Doughnut?"

"Thanks." Roger reached inside and grabbed a white frosted doughnut with red and green sprinkles.

During the gift exchange, Roger's nerves became more and more shaky. He hid it well, however. No one suspected a thing. As the final gift, Lauren was given a shiny red box with her name printed on it. She unwrapped the box to reveal a smaller velvet box and a poem written in Roger's handwriting. While Lauren read the poem, Roger sat across from her with his elbows resting on his knees and hands folded under his chin, nervously rubbing his knuckles across his lips. Carefully, he watched Lauren's reaction. The smile on her face and the tears in her eyes melted his heart. Realizing how incredibly close he was to that famous happy ending, Roger began to develop butterflies in his stomach. His heartrate accelerated and his breathing deepened.

After reading the sentimental testament of love and devotion he had written for her, Lauren looked over at Roger. "Oh, Sweetie. That was beautiful."

Roger immediately got out of his seat, took the velvet box in his hand, and got down on one knee in front of Lauren. Randy already knew what Roger was planning on doing, but to Lauren and the rest of the family this was a complete surprise. As soon as the others realized what was happening, they gasped in surprise. Jane looked like she was about cry. Nathan sat slack-jawed, and Lacy covered her mouth, soaking in every precious moment.

Lauren teared up even more. Their love was so pure and genuine that she knew exactly what Roger was about to do. With a hopeful heart, she scooted up to the edge of the chair and allowed him to put on his show.

"Lauren, the last fifteen months with you have been the most joyful of my life. You have inspired me in many ways and have shown me love that I never imagined possible. You've reignited a doused flame and gave me a newfound belief and hope in true love. Thinking about you keeps me awake. Dreaming about you keeps me asleep, and being with you keeps me alive. I want to fall asleep every night with you by my side, wake up to your beautiful face every morning, and spend every moment of every day with you." He opened the box and presented her with a diamond ring. "Sweetheart, will you marry me?"

Lauren's heart pounded out of control. She reached over and touched his hand, nodding as a tear flowed down her cheek.

Hoping he knew what she meant, he asked, "Yes?"

"Yes!"

Roger sank to his knees. He could barely breathe, yet somehow he managed to spread his arms, completely elated as she joined him on the floor. He allowed the passion and adoration he felt for her to be shown in every way, including through his own tears of joy. At this moment, on this day, he was the happiest man in the world.

Lauren's family cheered and applauded.

Wiping tears away, Lauren lifted her chin. Roger had staged an amazing show. In anticipation, she watched as he took the ring out of the box and held it in between his thumb and forefinger. Holding her left hand in his, he carefully slipped the ring on her finger.

Lauren's mouth opened with a wide smile of excitement as she awed over the ring on her hand. This was the happiest day of her life.

Even though it was simple, this was the most heartwarming and beautiful marriage proposal Randy had ever witnessed. Being an old romantic softy himself, he couldn't hold back tears as he watched this true testament of love. The intimacy they shared for one another was apparent in every way. He saw the love in their eyes as they looked at each other; true, abiding love. Lauren and Roger were meant to be together.

The ring Roger bought for Lauren was elegant and elaborate. Randy figured he probably paid up to five grand for it. It was a dazzling one carat center-cut diamond with round, brilliant-cut diamonds circled all around the white gold band. Roger certainly didn't mess around when it came to buying an engagement ring. Obviously he had done some research and had been thinking about this for a while.

On such a joyous occasion during such a jolly holiday, Nathan's mood was far from cheerful. Randy knew something was bothering him. After brunch, Randy pulled Nathan aside. "Grab some coffee with me."

"I'm not thirsty, Dad," Nathan retorted.

"Then come out on the deck and talk to me while I drink coffee."

Nathan snorted cynically then slipped on his jacket and joined his father on the deck. He took a seat at the patio table right across from Randy, who sipped from his steaming mug.

"Penny for your thoughts?" Randy asked.

Nathan acted like he didn't know what his father was talking about. "What?"

"What's on your mind, Son?"

"Nothing."

Randy didn't buy it. "You've been Sulky Sam for the last hour. What's up?"

Nathan exhaled with a disconcerting sigh. "Gabby."

"That's an awfully big sigh. Everything okay?"

"Yeah," Nathan assured. "Everything's great between us."

"Then what's the problem?"

"That is the problem," Nathan stated.

Randy had no idea what Nathan was talking about. "That doesn't make a whole lot of sense, Son. If things are great between you and Gabby then what are you so gloomy about?"

Nathan tried to explain. "My little sister just got engaged. She and Roger have only been together for a little over a year. Gabby and I have been together a lot longer than that."

"So?"

"I haven't gotten her a ring yet, and I feel horrible about it."

Randy tried to offer his fatherly advice. "Nate, Roger is older than you, and he's stable in his career, makes a good living doing what he does, and he feels confident that he can take care of Lauren. I believe that if he were younger and not as established in his career, he would have waited."

"But Gabby and I have been together for five years. I don't want her to think that I don't want to make that commitment to her, because I do."

Randy reassured him. "Son, you're still in school. Gabby's still in school. You're receiving training for your career so you can make the money necessary to support yourself and potentially a wife. Are you financially stable enough to support both yourself and Gabby right now?"

Nathan considered this. "Well, no."

"Ok then. Keep in mind that Roger and Lauren's situation is different than yours and Gabby's. He is in a position where he has the money to support not only himself quite comfortably, but Lauren as well. The two of them definitely won't be in want."

This wasn't making Nathan feel any better. "Gabby and I should have been first. Not Lauren."

Randy saw the look on his son's face and knew that Nathan was still distressed by this. He tried a different approach. "Have you and Gabby ever talked about marriage?"

"We've talked about it. I've never officially proposed to her, but yes, the topic has come up on several occasions. But that's the problem. We talk about marriage and having a life together, but I never do anything about it. I'm all talk and no action."

Trying to get his son to think rationally, Randy posed a question. "What do you think Gabby would say if you tried to propose to her right now, knowing that neither one of you is financially ready to take that on?"

Nathan grumbled, "She'd probably think I was crazy."

"Because she knows not to rush into something you're not ready for," Randy advised. "Your mom and I were together for four years before I asked her to marry me. And that was after I had secured a residency position and knew I could support us financially. Marriage isn't just about love. It's much more complex than that. If you try to jump into marriage with no means of supporting yourselves, you will crash and burn. Finances have been known to cause many issues and arguments in even the strongest of relationships. Many marriages end over money problems. Be careful that you don't jump into marriage when you're not prepared for it financially."

His father had an excellent point. The last thing he wanted was to argue with Gabby over petty issues like money. Although that still didn't solve his conundrum. "I understand that, Dad, but I want Gabby to be certain that I do plan to make that commitment to her. Even if we don't get married right away, I want my intentions to be known on a more palpable level instead of just talking about it all the time."

Trying to make Nathan feel better about this, Randy offered the only advice he had left. "Nathan, listen, Gabby loves you. And if you two are meant to be together, she'll wait until you both feel financially comfortable enough to take on a big commitment like marriage. Right now, just enjoy the love you share. Have fun together, make love often, and spend quality time building your relationship. Then when both of you are ready, go ahead and make that commitment."

Nathan managed to crack a grin at his father's wisecrack. "Make love often, huh?"

"I would advise so, yes," Randy chuckled with a devilish grin.

"Is that your advice to everyone?"

"Pretty much," Randy replied. "Sex relieves stress. It can be quite a workout too, if you do it right. It's a fun way to kill time, and it gets the dopamine flowing."

His father's nonchalant attitude about sex made him laugh. "Wow! Does Mom know you talk like that?"

Teasing Nathan, he replied, "Most of the time I'm referring to her when I say things like that."

Nathan had heard enough. "Ok, Dad. TMI. I really don't want to know the intimate details of yours and Mom's marriage."

"Sensitive this morning, are we?" Randy taunted him. "Maybe you need a little stress relief. Go home and make love to your girlfriend, Nathan."

"Dad!"

"I'm serious," Randy declared. "You seem tense and uptight. Sex will cure that."

Nathan tried to hide his face, pretending he didn't know this man.

"I'm trying to help you."

"Thank you, Dad, but I think I can handle my own stress relief."

"Your own stress relief?" Randy teased with a taunting grin. "I certainly hope you're not doing it alone. Please tell me Gabby is involved somehow."

"Of course she's involved!" Nathan retorted, annoyed by his father's bantering.

"Oh good. You had me a bit concerned there for a minute."

That night, after everyone else had gone to bed, Lauren and Roger snuggled together on the sofa. The soft light from the fireplace flickered off the walls and Christmas music played softly in the background. Roger held Lauren's hand and fiddled with the diamond ring on her finger. "Do you remember what you asked me on our first date?"

"I asked you a lot of things," she replied.

"Yes, but one thing in particular stood out to me." He affectionately kissed her fingers, one by one. "You asked me why I hadn't been swept up yet. Do you remember?"

Her face flushed, embarrassed that she had asked him that. "Yes. And I think I took you by surprise."

"I thought it was cute, and courageous," he chuckled. "It was definitely something no one had ever asked me before. Do you remember what my response was?"

Thinking back to his reply, she said, "You explained to me your philosophy about relationships."

"And then I told you I hadn't met the right woman yet. Little did I know that the woman sitting across from me at that moment was the woman I'd be spending the rest of my life with." He kissed her ever so gently on the lips. "For a while there, I was beginning to believe that marriage wasn't in the cards for me. Every relationship I'd been in ended in disaster. The dating scene was frustrating, and I'd completely lost faith in love. Misplacing my cellphone that day completely turned my life around."

His comment made her laugh. "You're always losing your phone."

"Yes, but in this case losing it was a good thing. It led me to you. You came into my life when I least expected it, but at a time when I needed you the most." He brushed his lips against her ear, raising goose bumps across her skin. "You had me from hello."

"I did not," she said, not believing him.

"Yes you did," he admitted. "Your voice cap-tivated me from the moment I heard it."

Lauren stared at the ring on her finger, still in shock that Roger had proposed to her. "I was not expecting this from you today."

Roger grinned cunningly. "Surprise!"

"Yes, I was very surprised."

"Good. Then my plan worked."

Lauren drew her lip between her teeth. "I always dreamed that someday I'd marry my best friend. You are the most kindhearted, patient, and understanding man I've ever known. I couldn't help but fall in love with you."

Bringing their mouths within the same breathing space, he said, "I easily fell in love with you."

"This is the best Christmas ever."

Meeting her gaze, he smiled at her. "Yes it is. Merry Christmas, Sweetheart."

"Merry Christmas." Surrounded by the romantic glow of the fire, they joined together in a tender kiss.

Chapter Twenty-Two

Returning home to a snowstorm slowed down air traffic in Newark, which made Roger and Lauren's flight come in several hours late. This storm brought howling winds and more than a foot of snow, making travel treacherous. All of New York City was under a blizzard warning, and they were forecast to get up to twenty more inches of snow within the next two days. Luckily, Roger and Lauren made it home before the storm got worse.

Overnight, the storm dumped fourteen more inches across the city and left thousands without power. Due to thick snow accumulation, more than 141 flights had been canceled for LaGuardia airport and 106 were cancelled at Newark. Amtrak train routes out of New York remained closed as crews cleared snow and fallen trees off the tracks. New York City's subways were running, but with scattered delays. Service on the Long Island Railroad was suspended because of heavy snow. Hourly service was limited on the Metro, and most of the city's bus service was suspended due to treacherous driving conditions. Clearing major thoroughfares and most secondary streets was a challenging chore. While roads near the Upper West Side neighborhood were well-plowed, in the Bronx the roads were packed with ice. Police had to use snowmobiles to reach stranded motorists. Ambulances, fire trucks, police vehicles, and utility trucks got stuck throughout the area despite the fact that more than 2,200 vehicles plowed streets overnight. Trying to get anywhere was nearly impossible. It was imperative that people stayed off the roads.

In the morning, Roger slipped on warm clothes and stepped onto his snow-covered balcony. The city was completely blanketed in white. The scene was pretty, but it was a sloshy, slippery mess. Due to weather conditions and lack of public transportation, Roger's 8:00 P.M. show was canceled that night. In fact, all Broadway shows were canceled because of the storm. As it stood, he had the night off. It was the perfect time to relax by the fire with a warm cup of cocoa. "Honey?" he called to Lauren.

She stepped into the room. "Yes?"

"Grab your appointment calendar and come here for a minute. I want to set a date."

Lauren dug through her backpack to get her planner then sat on the sofa with Roger. "We have to wait until after basketball season if we want Nathan and Gabby to be there."

"Duly noted," he replied.

"And we need enough time to plan our wedding. I don't want to rush."

"I don't want to wait too long either." He thumbed through his calendar at his crazy-busy schedule. He had Phantom performances, a scheduled interview, two TV appearances, a Broadway Live performance, a benefit concert for a children's charity, and several Broadway premieres to attend almost every day from now until the end of May.

Lauren's schedule wasn't much clearer. "What about June?" she suggested as she flipped to a month

280

that was a bit less cluttered. "School will be out by then, your contract with Phantom will be done, basketball season will be over, and Nathan and Gabby's graduation will have passed. We won't have any commitments."

Roger scrolled to June on his calendar—a little over five months away. A reasonable enough amount of time to plan a wedding, but not too far off. "We can pull this off in five months, right?"

"I think so."

As they tried to decide on the best date, Roger pondered the complexity of wedding planning. "I want to be involved in the planning process, Lauren. I know a lot of guys aren't into that kind of thing, but this is our wedding. I want it to reflect who we are. Most weddings are somber and serious. To me, it's a celebration. I'd like to add a little more pizzazz to ours."

"Ooh, I like that. What did you have in mind?"

"Both of us are theatre performers. Why don't we go with some sort of Broadway theme? It will make it more fun and lighthearted."

She liked what she was hearing.

"People like to be entertained. Let's give them a show." Roger waited for her reaction, hoping to get her opinion about this. "What do you think?"

"That sounds fun. I love it."

"Great!" He looked at his calendar again. "We're set for June 3rd then?"

Lauren nodded. "Yup."

"Fabulous!" Roger typed the word wedding in all capital letters and added a heart emoji. "There. It is now officially on my calendar." He set his phone down and leaned over to kiss her.

They awoke the next day to surprisingly clear skies. The city was still covered in snow, but some of the roads had managed to get plowed to a drivable condition. The city was becoming alive again with people walking down the snowy sidewalks while several cabs, cars, and busses started to fill the streets. After being cooped up inside the day before, they had to get out of the apartment.

They took Oliver for a walk, then Lauren decided to spend the day with Lacy. On the way to meet her, Lauren walked Roger a few blocks down the street to a deli, where he planned to join Jason for lunch. Following a brief conversation, Lauren put her arms around Roger's neck and kissed him goodbye before she hopped in a cab to meet her sister.

When Roger came inside and sat in the booth, Jason gave his best friend a funny look.

"Why are you staring at me like that?" Roger asked, removing his jacket and scarf and placing them neatly on the bench beside him.

"Correct me if I'm wrong, but was that an engagement ring I saw on Lauren's finger?"

Roger grinned. "Yes, it was."

Jason had no clue that Roger and Lauren were engaged and was a bit offended that he had been left out of the loop. "When did this happen?"

"Christmas."

"Is there some reason why you didn't tell me about this?"

With a joking banter, Roger explained, "You have been giving me a hard time about my relationship with Lauren from day one. I really didn't think you'd be that interested."

"Not interested?" he huffed. "Rog, you're my best friend. You're getting married. Of course I'm interested." The waitress came by and took their orders. As soon as she left, Jason said, "I can't believe you didn't tell me."

Sensing that Jason was hurt by this, Roger offered an apology. "I'm sorry. You're right. I should have entrusted you with that knowledge. Which brings up a point." Roger took a sip of his water. "Do you have time in your busy schedule to be my Best Man?"

"For you, I'll clear my calendar and make time. Just let me know when."

"June 3rd," Roger answered.

"I am definitely there. Congratulations, man."

"Thank you."

The contract Roger signed for *Phantom of the Opera* was scheduled to end in a few months and once again, he needed to look for work. As much as he loved playing Phantom, Roger was ready for a change. In search for a new production to be involved in, he read synopses from several upcoming shows and revivals. One struck his interest—a revival of *Crazy For You*. It was set to begin production the middle of June and open August first. This was the perfect change of pace, and perfect timing.

This Gershwin musical was a comedy, something more light and airy. This role would also give him a chance to use his tap dancing talent on stage again, which was something he desperately missed. He read up on audition information, where and when readings for this part were occurring, and gained insights into the composition itself. The production looked like something enjoyable, and he loved Gershwin. He decided to give it a shot and audition for the lead role.

Lauren had expressed an interest in this musical and had mentioned to Roger how fun she thought it would be to take part in a singing, dancing comedy extravaganza of this nature. To help her out, Roger went on a quest to find more information regarding general auditions for this show.

He happened to have a personal connection with the casting director. As soon as his audition was over, he took time to catch up with her. "Denise. It's good to see you again. It's been a long time."

"Yes it has."

They exchanged pleasantries then Roger proceeded to tell her about Lauren's talent and experience on the stage. "She's the perfect person for a show like this. She can sing, dance, and she's an emotional actress. A natural talent."

"Who is this person?"

"Her name is Lauren Hanson."

"Another woman you know came in here last week and asked about auditions. Do you know someone named Melinda Richardson?"

His excitement immediately faded. He couldn't escape that woman no matter how hard he tried. "Melinda Richardson is interested in this show?"

"Yes. She claims to know you."

His lips drew a hard line, losing all enthusiasm. "Unfortunately, yes. She and I have a history, but be mindful that if Melinda is involved in this show, I won't be."

"Why is that?"

"She's impossible to work with. She constantly harasses people, argues with cast and crew members, and I had to have her number blocked and file a harassment complaint against her because she sent intimidating text messages to my fiancé and threatened her with violence."

Denise cringed at the immature nature of those actions. "That doesn't sound like someone I want working on this show."

"Probably not, but don't let my opinion influence your decision."

The woman handed Roger a business card with audition information printed on the back. "Have Lauren come in next Friday."

Roger shoved it in his wallet. "Thank you, Denise. You won't be disappointed."

Enthusiastic about his findings, Roger came home that night eager to tell Lauren what he discovered. "I have another audition opportunity for you. I spoke with the casting director of Crazy For You today and she gave me dates and times for open auditions." He pulled the card out of his wallet and gave it to her. "She's interested, and wants you to come in."

Lauren nervously bit her lip.

"You can do this Lauren. Go in confidently and show them what you've got."

After several callbacks and readings, Roger landed the lead role for this production. He would be playing Bobby Childs, heir to a wealthy banking family who yearned to be in show business. Now that he'd been confirmed, they waited to see if Lauren was going to get in.

A week later, Lauren received the call offering her an ensemble role. It wasn't a huge part, but it got her on stage. When she saw Roger that evening, she couldn't wait to tell him.

"See?" he said, ecstatic about her news. "I told you you'd get on stage."

"It's not much of a role," she admitted, kind of disappointed.

"No," he agreed, "But it's a good way to get started. Now shine, Lauren, and let people see what you can do on the big stage."

When Melinda found out Lauren got an ensemble role and she didn't, she filed a formal complaint with the Broadway Commission, stating that the casting director showed favoritism because Roger had a personal connection with Lauren.

Fed up with Melinda's bothersome, constant badgering, Roger remarked, "I am so done with her. Does she really have nothing better to do with her life then pester me?"

"I won't lose this job because of her, will I?" Lauren asked.

"She has no case, Lauren. She can't justify her claim or provide any proof that Denise made a biased decision. The Broadway Commission won't act on it anyway, no matter how much Melinda complains."

They celebrated Lauren's new contract over dinner, followed by her hanging around backstage at *Phantom of the Opera*. As soon as the show was over, they walked out of the theatre together holding hands and laughing. From behind a dark corner, a woman in a black coat appeared.

Roger recognized her right away. "What are you doing here, Melinda?"

Melinda snarled at Lauren. "How dare you barge into my domain and steal this job from me?"

Roger immediately intervened, stepping between them. "Back off."

"No, I will not back off. That woman has taken everything from me."

"She has done nothing to you. This business is fair game to anyone who has the talent."

Fiery rage filled Melinda's eyes. She reached for a metal pipe propped up on a nearby dumpster and gripped it tightly in her hands.

Roger stepped back, sheltering Lauren with his body. "Whoa. Just calm down. Drop the pipe."

She charged at him, swinging violently.

He dodged her attack, barely ducking out of her reach. "What the hell is wrong with you?" he questioned, visibly shaken by her act of aggression. "Have you lost your mind?"

She swung at him again, this time connecting with his upper left arm. The impact knocked him to the ground.

"You ruined my life!" Melinda wailed, then she barreled toward Lauren with a crazed look in her eye.

Adrenaline careened through Roger's body and his reflex to fight back and protect kicked in. Even though his arm hurt like hell, he managed to hop to his feet and grip the pipe in his hands. He and Melinda fought for possession of it. Pushing her backwards, he forced her against the dumpster. "Get a grip, Melinda. You are acting like a freak."

Melinda tried to push back, but Roger's strength overpowered her. Bursting into hysterics, she tightened her grip on the pipe. "How could you do this to me? We were partners, Roger, lovers, and you turned your back on me."

"Clearly you have lost all sense of reality. You've gone way over the line and have crossed the barrier into unmerited territory. If you don't stand down in about five seconds, I will call the police and file assault charges."

Defenseless, she let go of the pipe.

It fell to the ground and Roger kicked it aside. "If you ever come near me or Lauren again, I'll have you arrested."

Melinda huffed and straightened her coattail. With shaking hands, she disappeared down the street.

Lauren held her hand on her chest, staring at Roger in shock. "Are you alright?"

Roger lifted his shirt sleeve to examine his arm. A four-inch welt began to swell and bruise his skin. He gritted his teeth and rubbed it. "Damn."

"What is going on, Roger?"

"There's nothing going on that I haven't already told you. She's crazy, and I'm convinced she's bipolar."

Lauren shook her head, flabbergasted that Roger was associated with such a bitter, self-seeking pest. "What were you doing with a woman like that?"

"She wasn't always like that. She didn't start behaving that way until I received more attention than she did. Then she became a jealous freak."

Roger's arm had a giant red contusion and looked horribly painful. "That looks bad. You need to have it examined by a doctor."

"Yeah, I probably should. We're also making an appointment with an attorney in the morning and having a protection order issued against her. I'm tired of dodging her insanity."

Their dinner date was put on hold that night to allow Roger to collect himself and ice his injured arm.

Chapter Twenty-Three

Later that week, when Lauren came home from class, Roger rushed to meet her at the door. "I came up with the most remarkable idea today."

Lauren set her backpack down, curious about his thoughts. "What is it?"

"Tell me what you think of this." He used hand gestures and motions to describe his vision. "Picture a red carpet with red velvet VIP ropes that lead into the reception area. A Broadway billboard poster with our picture all lit up in white lights." He moved his hands above his head as if outlining a theatre marquee sign. "One night only, come see A Wedding Story, starring Roger Zellers and Lauren Hanson." He put his hands down and looked directly at her. "What do you think?"

"That's a great idea."

"And I was thinking, what if we find a venue that is an actual theater so people get the full Broadway experience."

"Can you rent out theatres like that?"

"I don't know," he admitted. "But I am now on a quest to find out."

Roger's quest to find the perfect wedding venue was one he took quite seriously. After much searching, he was convinced he finally found it. Wednesday afternoon, when Lauren walked in the door, he bounded out of his seat excited to show her what he had found. "I need to show you something. Come with me." He clasped her hand and led her toward the front door.

She dropped her backpack on the floor. "What's the big hurry?"

"You are going to love this."

The venue he discovered was the Hudson Theatre, situated between the Millennium Broadway and the Premier Hotel in the heart of Times Square. Not only was it in a prime location, it was also the second-oldest theatre house on Broadway. Accented by an elegant and classical interior, the Hudson Theatre evoked the splendor of 1903. Red velvet curtains with golden tassels, mint-condition Tiffany glass tiles, gorgeous tables and chairs, elegant balconies and lighting, Broadway quality theatrical lighting and sound—this was the perfect wedding reception venue. They could inspire their guests with Broadway splendor and cut their wedding cake in the gilded queen's box.

"Oh my god, Roger. This place is fantastic."

"I knew you'd love it," he said. "They have the ability to accommodate three-hundred guests with banquet style seating. They'll offer us customized menu options with award-winning cuisine. They'll also cater our rehearsal dinner, offer valet parking for our guests, and..." He grazed his lips on her ear. "If we book this venue for our reception, we'll get a complimentary bridal suite for our wedding night."

Lauren sexily bit her lip at his suggestion.

"I had them hold it for us, but they need a decision and a deposit by tomorrow morning or they're going to give it to someone else." He stood in the middle of the floor, held out his arms, and spun around, looking up at the ceiling. "So, what do you think? Is this not magnificent?"

"I love it." This place was beautiful and perfect for their needs, but an elegant and elaborate venue like this was bound to be expensive. "How much is the deposit?"

"Twenty-five hundred to get the ball rolling. We have to pay another four grand before our wedding."

Lauren raised her eyebrows. "They want over six-thousand dollars for this?"

"Yes, but consider everything that's included. We can personalize the décor, choose our own menu, have access to a Broadway quality sound system, and you can't deny that this is exactly what we've been looking for. We couldn't ask for anything with more splendor." Roger put his hands on her shoulders and turned her so she was looking right at him. "It's our wedding, Honey. I want to make this day special for both of us. If we're gonna do this, let's do it right."

Excited that Roger was doing whatever he could to make their dream wedding a reality, she smiled the biggest, most beautiful smile Roger had ever seen. "Book it."

"Alright!" He took her in his arms and spun her around, laughing joyfully. "This is awesome."

Together, they headed to the office to pay the deposit and secure the venue for their big day.

Over dinner that night, they continued to discuss wedding plans. "I was thinking," Lauren stated. "We met at the Ambassador theatre. Wouldn't it be cool if we could get married there?"

"I might be able to arrange that," Roger said with a sly grin. "Let me talk to Carmen."

"Do they do things like that at Broadway theatres?"

Roger shrugged. "Don't know. Carmen knows us. I'm sure, as long as we're not disrupting any performances, she'll work with us. I'm pretty good at convincing people. Let me work my magic."

In the morning, while Lauren was in class, Roger set up an appointment to speak with Carmen. She greeted him with a hug. "We miss you, Roger. How's Phantom going?"

"I really enjoy it," he stated. "He's one of my favorite roles to play. Have you been able to sneak away to catch a show?"

"Yes. I saw the show last week. You were spectacular, as usual. Don't you have a performance this afternoon?"

"I do, but I need to talk to you." He sat in a chair across from her.

"What can I do for you?"

"I don't know if you were aware, but Lauren Hanson and I were recently engaged."

Carmen cracked a grin. "I heard. Congratulations!"

"Thank you. As you know, Lauren and I met at this theatre. Because of that, she and I were wondering if it would be possible for us to exchange our wedding vows here."

She folded her hands in front of her. "I have a Broadway show to host here, Roger."

"I know," he concurred. "But we'll work around the show schedule." Roger could tell the gears were spinning in Carmen's head. He did his best to lure her in. "It will only be for the ceremony, an hour max, and it will be a private event. General public will be strictly forbidden. We'll even pay you a rental fee for use of the theatre."

She tilted her head from side to side. "Hmm. What day?"

"Saturday, June 3rd. We'll schedule it in the morning, that way we won't disrupt the afternoon performance."

"What about the flowers or confetti or whatever else you're planning on doing to my theatre?"

He tried to bargain with her. "The theater will be returned to its original condition once the ceremony is complete. I promise. I'll even throw in a round of drinks and dinner for you and your husband."

She eyed him inquisitively, contemplating his proposition. "Do I get a wedding invitation?"

"You're the first one on my list." He flashed his sexy smile at her. "Come on, Carmen. Lauren's one of your employees. She's loyal and she's dedicated, and she really wants this. Help me out here."

"Okay. But only if I get an invitation."

Roger breathed a sigh of relief. "Thank you. You have no idea how much this means to us."

She chuckled at his boyish enthusiasm. "Now get out of my theatre. I have a show to prepare for."

He shook her hand and stood up. "We'll talk details later. I'll give you a call."

"Alright. Break a leg today, Roger."

"Thanks."

Wedding plans were beginning to come together nicely. So far they had a venue secured, a working theme, and had selected a date. They were also looking at invitations and flowers and working on securing the guest list. They still had a lot to do. With everything else on her schedule, the complexities of wedding planning was starting to weigh Lauren down.

Roger did his best to calm her. "We can lessen the load if we divvy this out. Let me focus on aspects that involve human resources. I'll use my connections, make some phone calls, and schedule meetings. I have more free time on my schedule during the day than you do, and I'm sure, through the networking I have, that I can probably get things a lot cheaper."

Lauren agreed that was a good idea.

"I won't book anything or make any confirmations until I speak with you. Meanwhile, you can focus on details like flowers and centerpieces. Get Lacy to help you. I'm sure she would love to be involved in this."

"That sounds good," she concurred, feeling a bit less stressed.

Assuring her that everything was going to be alright, he said, "When we work together, we'll accomplish more and no one bears the load. Just share with me anything you find, please,"

When Roger met Jason for lunch the next day, he expressed his concerns in regards to Lauren's stress level about the wedding. "She feels like we're being rushed," Roger explained. "And with her upcoming exams and performances with Juilliard, not to mention her involvement with the Musical Theatre Club, I think she's feeling a little overwhelmed. She seems to think we should be further along in our plans by now."

"You still have three and half months."

"I know," Roger said. "But we're focusing on details. I want to make sure she gets the wedding she wants, and I'm willing to do whatever is necessary to make that happen."

"What do you still have left to do?"

Roger snickered mirthlessly. "Everything. Music, photography, cake, flowers…we haven't found invitations we like yet either."

"Does Lauren have her dress?"

"No."

Jason tried not to laugh at Roger's panic-stricken reaction. To relieve some of Roger's stress, he suggested, "I might be able to help you solve your music problem."

Roger looked at Jason with a curious gaze. "How?"

"My brother."

"Your brother?"

"He has a band, remember? And they play 80's, classic rock, big band, modern music, oldies, the samba, whatever you want. They just need time to rehearse."

Roger sighed in relief. "Oh Jason, I love you."

"Do you want me to give him a call?"

"Yes, please. See if you can set up a time for them to come play for us. I want Lauren to hear how they sound," Roger submitted.

"When?"

"Sunday, if they're available."

Jason nodded. "Alright. I'll set it up."

"Thank you. You are a life saver."

After lunch, Roger stopped by to see an old friend of his by the name of Brandon Schaefer. Brandon was a well-known professional photographer in Manhattan who did most of the photography for Broadway shows and events. Many of the photographs from Playbill programs, actor profiles, promotional posters, and the Broadway.com website were taken by him. Brandon was exceptionally good at his job, and his schedule was usually full.

When Roger waltzed into Brandon's studio that afternoon, Brandon was wrapping up cables and carefully storing camera lenses in their proper place. Roger peeked inside and cleared his throat, trying to get Brandon's attention.

The minute Brandon saw Roger, a huge smile lit up his face. "Hey, Roger. How's it going?" They greeted with a firm handshake.

"Doing quite well, actually. Been busy lately."

"No doubt Phantom is keeping you on your toes. I snapped some still shots at your first performance." He set the wire inside an insulated bag and zipped it up.

"I thought I recognized your work."

Brandon directed Roger to a cushioned leather sofa. "Please, have a seat."

Roger sat down, and Brandon pulled a chair over to him. "What brings you over here?"

"I'm looking for a photographer."

"You've come to the right place." Brandon reached for his appointment book. "You need to schedule a photo shoot?"

"Actually, this isn't business related. It's personal."

"Personal?"

"Yes," Roger replied. "You ever photographed a wedding before?"

"No. Why?"

"Would you consider shooting one?" Roger asked.

"I don't know." He crossed his legs. "Depends whose wedding it is."

"What if I told you it was mine?"

"Yours?" A huge grin decorated Brandon's face. "You're engaged?"

Smiling proudly, Roger said, "Yes, I am."

"Wow!" Brandon exclaimed. "Congrats, man."

"Thank you." Roger took a deep breath, hoping to convince his friend. "Look, Brandon, you do fantastic work. You're the best photographer I know. We could really use your creativity. You would do a beautiful job with our wedding."

Rubbing his chin, Brandon considered Roger's offer. "It's certainly something I've never done before."

Roger added, "You'll still be involved with Broadway, just on a different level."

"Alright." Brandon smiled in agreement. "Sounds fun. I'll give it a shot."

"Awesome!" Roger shook Brandon's hand, sealing the deal. "Let's talk details."

While Brandon and Roger discussed photography issues, Lauren and Lacy were perusing through books of invitations to see what they could find. Nothing sparked Lauren's interest. Lacy browsed the internet and saw something on-line she thought Lauren would like. "Lauren, look at this."

Lauren peeked over Lacy's shoulder to see what she was looking at. What she saw undoubtedly gave her that spark of excitement she was looking for. The wedding invitations Lacy found looked like Broadway Playbill covers. "Yes!" Lauren exclaimed. "Those are perfect."

Lacy pointed to the information on the website. "And look, you can customize them and include a photo on the front if you want."

"These are great. I have to show these to Roger." She copied the website and sent it to Roger.

By late afternoon, Lauren and Roger reunited at the apartment to share their wedding finds of the day.

"Did you see that website I sent you?" Lauren asked him.

"Yes I did," he replied, enthusiastic about her find. "Those are perfect. I have an idea for our cake. The design we want is very specific and unique, but I have the perfect place to go. This woman customizes cakes to your requests and she's not far from here. I've seen her work before. She can make a cake look like a dog or the leaning tower of Pisa or a dragon or whatever you want. She's done a few for Broadway show openings, anniversaries, and such. Her cakes are world renowned."

"Who is it?" Lauren asked, wondering who this cake guru was that Roger spoke so highly about.

"Ever heard of Gina's Cake Shop?"

"The Cake Connoisseur?" The owner of this popular bakery in White Plains, New York was a famous cake designer who had her own TV show. Lauren had watched her show many times.

"Her name's Gina Russo. Let's set up an appointment with her and see if she can hook us up."

Lauren squinted her eyebrows. "You want to get our wedding cake from the Cake Connoisseur?"

"Yes," Roger confirmed.

"That's insane," she declared.

"Why?"

"Because she's Gina Russo."

He had to laugh. "What difference does that make? She's good, Lauren, and I think she can get us what we want. It won't hurt to at least talk to her."

They set up an appointment to meet with a cake consultant. After taste testing many different cake samples, they opted for black and white cake with chocolate fudge filling. The consultant collected information regarding specific things they wanted in their cake design and how many people were on their guest list then told them to expect a phone call by the end of the week.

On the drive back from White Plains, Roger strongly suggested that Lauren start shopping for a wedding dress. "See if your mom can hop a flight over here. Take her and Lacy with you."

"Do you think your mom will want to come?"

"My mom?" Roger questioned.

"Yes, I want her to come too."

Roger smiled at Lauren's thoughtful gesture. "I bet she would love that."

Being in the public eye had the potential for bringing unwanted guests to their private event if word got out. Roger and Lauren tried to stay as discreet as possible in regards to date, time, location, and details of their wedding, but Roger knew from experience that discreetness wasn't always successful. He was concerned about fans, theatregoers, and even unwanted press photographers attempting to invade their private wedding function. To resolve this issue, he came up with an ingenious plan. He and Lauren decided to enclose tickets for admission to the ceremony inside the invitations and made a formal guest list, just like at a real red carpet event. If potential guests didn't have a ticket and were not on the guest list, they would not be allowed admittance. He wasn't doing this to be rude or express distrust, he simply wanted to keep their wedding ceremony and reception private, limited only to invited friends and family members. These tickets were essential in their wedding plans, because without them, fans and paparazzi, who had no business being at this private event, would most likely try to find their way in if they discovered the location.

As it stood now, they had about 250 people on their guest list. But trying to keep out unwanted guests was going to be challenging. Roger offered a suggestion. "Honey, I think we should hire security, just to be safe. That will prevent uninvited people from swarming and invading our wedding."

Lauren agreed. "I think that's a good idea."

"Good. I'll make some calls."

Their custom-made wedding invitations finally arrived. In anticipation, Roger opened the box and pulled one out. The front of the invitation displayed the yellow Playbill logo with a picture of Roger and Lauren underneath. Inside, the invitation read:

The Ambassador Theatre
Proudly Presents
A Wedding Story,
Starring
Roger Zellers & Lauren Hanson
Saturday, June 3rd

ACT I

Following a romantic engagement which began with a misplaced cellphone, a business card, and a black fedora, Roger and Lauren have made it to the altar. Join them for their wedding ceremony at 11:00 A.M. at the Ambassador Theatre, 219 West 49th Street, New York City, New York. Entrance by admittance ticket only.

THE CAST:
The Bride.....................…....Lauren Hanson
The Groom....................….......Roger Zellers
Mother of the Bride....…......Jane Hanson
Father of the Bride...........Dr. Randal Hanson
Mother of the Groom.......Sharon Pennington
Father of the Groom.........Gary Pennington
Maid of Honor…....…...........Lacy Hanson
Best Man....................…….Jason Preen

ACT II

From 3:00 to 7:00 P.M., rejoin the happy couple at the Hudson Theatre, 145 West 44th Street, New York City, New York for their wedding reception. Don't forget to RSVP for this exclusive event by May 20th, and remember to save your ticket for admittance. You won't want to miss it!

"These are cool," Roger said, impressed with the way the invitations turned out.

Lauren carefully examined one. "They turned out nice, didn't they?"

"Yes they did."

Lauren placed the invitation back in the box. "Now we have to address all of them."

Roger curled his lip. "Yuk."

But the monotonous task needed to be done. Inside every invitation, they enclosed RSVP information and one admittance ticket for each person at the residence. These unique tickets looked just like the ones purchased at the ticket box office of Broadway theatres. These tickets, as well as the security Roger was going to hire, were a surefire way to ensure their private event remained private. Roger read over the tickets for completeness. *Admit one: June 3rd, Ambassador Theatre. The red carpet is rolled out! The pleasure of your company is requested for a one day only premiere event of Roger and Lauren's wedding ceremony. Post-nuptial reception following at the Hudson Theatre. Ticket required.*

"We're doing pretty well with wedding plans now," Roger assured her, trying to get her to relax more and worry less.

"Yes, we are." She breathed a little easier and felt much better about their progress over the last several weeks.

"What do we still have left to do?"

Lauren grabbed their checklist and sat down to go over it with Roger.

Running through their to-do list, Roger's eyes shifted to Lauren's hand, admiring the diamond on her finger. That's when he realized they had neglected to include one very crucial element. "What were we thinking?" Roger exclaimed, moving his hand to his forehead. "How could we forget about that?"

"Forget about what?" she asked, wondering what he was panicking about.

"My ring." He felt like an idiot for overlooking such an important component.

"I need one too," she reminded him.

He denied that statement. "No you don't. You already have one. Your engagement ring came with a wedding band. I have it in a box in my sock drawer."

One less thing to worry about. "In that case, we need to go ring shopping for you."

"Definitely."

Wedding ring shopping with Roger was quite the adventure because he was exceptionally picky and had very specific taste. He wanted something that matched with Lauren's yet was still elegant and masculine. Many of the rings he looked at seemed fine under the glass case, but as soon as he put it on, he either didn't like the way it looked on his finger or he didn't like the way it felt—it was either too heavy or uncomfortable when he wore it. Searching for the perfect ring was becoming a long and tiring ordeal.

They were about to give up for the day when they decided to make one final stop. Roger scanned the displays in this store scrutinizing every ring he saw. One ring caught his eye. It was a classy men's diamond wedding ring. The seven sparkling emerald-cut diamonds were set invisibly on the gorgeous 18K white gold band, meeting Roger's style requirements.

Roger slipped it on and inspected it. It was lightweight and comfortable to wear, and it looked fabulous on his hand. "Ok, now this one I like." He held out his hand to show Lauren. "What do you think?"

"It looks good," Lauren said.

He held his hand next to hers to see what their rings looked like together. They complemented each other perfectly. The only problem was the $2,100 price tag, but for a ring Roger was going to wear for the rest of his life, it was well worth the cost. "It's classy, comfortable, and it already fits, so it won't have to be sized."

"Is that the one you want?" Lauren asked, hoping Roger had finally made up his mind.

"This is the one." He removed the ring, paid the store clerk, and walked out of the store with a velvet ring box in his hand.

.

Chapter Twenty-Four

March was a busy time of year for both Nathan and Gabby. Nathan had work commitments, was studying for upcoming finals, and the Huskies were once again involved in March Madness. He also had two papers due at about the same time the tournament was scheduled. Needless to say, he was stressed.

Gabby's schedule wasn't much better. She was busy with cheer season, but had to adapt her schedule to accommodate student teaching. During the season, she didn't travel to away games because she couldn't be out of the classroom that long. Therefore, she only cheered at home games. Since the playoffs occurred on weekends and during spring break, and she wanted to support Nathan and the team during the final games of the season, she made arrangements to travel with her cheer squad. The national championships was an important event, and she was not going to miss it.

The Huskies had a successful season. They made it to the final NCAA game for the second year in a row, but this time they were playing Duke. The Blue Devils were known for being an aggressive team and had one of the highest all-time win records in the NCAA. They were currently ranked as the number one seed, and many predicted they would walk away with the championship. Nathan wasn't about to give in to the publicity of sports predictions. He thought they had a good shot at winning this thing, but to do so they had to get past Duke, and they were going to be a tough team to beat.

Despite the fact that Duke's overall ranking was higher than the Huskies, Nathan was a stronger point guard. His stats were better than Duke's starting point, and he was faster on the court. He averaged eighteen points and nine assists per game and connected on fifty-two percent of his field goals, hitting nearly every three-point shot he attempted. Nationally, Nathan was ranked as the third best point guard in the NCAA. He was exceptionally poised under pressure and made shots when the game was on the line. With his accuracy from three-point range, he could easily overpower Duke's point guard and cut through the defense to hopefully get some outside shots. The problem was Duke's other players. They were bigger than the Huskies and were going to try to double-team him. To overcome Duke's strong defense, Nathan would have to use his passing game, utilize the pick and roll, and focus on looking for the open man.

Nathan sat in his living room and watched a recording of Duke's last game, hoping to see a weakness in their defense. In this particular game, the Blue Devils had their poorest defensive performance of the NCAA tournament. They won because their offense stepped up and scored points. Throughout this tournament, the Huskies' defensive stride was winning games. At the moment, they were unstoppable. But Nathan knew Duke was analyzing the Huskies' weaknesses, just as Washington was studying theirs.

With the remote control in his hand, Nathan sat on the edge of the sofa in deep concentration. He had rewound and reviewed this video multiple times now.

Gabby watched him from the kitchen. He didn't seem as stressed about the final game this year as he was last year. He did, however, seem fixated on one particular stream of plays that he kept reviewing over and over again. Wondering what was on his mind, she put her hands on his shoulders. "How's it going?"

When Nathan felt her touch him, he paused the recording and looked up. "You know, Duke has some gaps in their defense," he told her. "Their point guard keeps it together offensively, but can't hold up in the defense department. I think I can overpower that guy."

"That's good, isn't it?"

"Yes, it is. As long as I can keep him under control, I really think we have a decent shot at this."

She encouraged him, "Wouldn't that be fantastic if you could end your college basketball career with a national championship?"

"Oh, man. That would be the epic. Definitely icing on the cake."

This game against Duke was Nathan's final game as a college athlete. This brought about a swarm of emotions for him. Nathan loved basketball. From a very young age, he had wanted to play college ball for the Washington Huskies. It was a dream he pursued since childhood. He had played competitively since he was young, with his mother coaching him on fundamentals in the peewee league. From there, he played on his middle school team and learned more about the essentials of teamwork. When he started high school, he immediately made the varsity team and played his way through the years to earn a starting position, team captain status, and graduate with a state championship. His experience with the Huskies led him to four straight seasons of making the national playoffs, two of which took him all the way to the final game.

He was going to miss basketball. It had been such a huge part of his life. Through his basketball experience, Nathan met the love of his life, made lifelong friends, earned a full ride scholarship through college, and had the opportunity to see many parts of the country and the world.

Nathan confidently walked onto the court in the final NCAA game. The arena was packed. Cheerleaders from both teams took their position, and the crowd was already making noise, waving pompoms and banging noisemakers. There was a lot of energy flowing through this arena, and things were going to get loud. Television cameras were set up, and sports announcers had begun their commentary. Nathan did his best to tune everything out.

He looked over at Gabby, who was standing with the other cheerleaders. Knowing he was seeking reassurance and encouragement from her, she flashed him a pretty smile and gave him a thumbs up, her way of telling him, 'you got this.' He nodded in complete understanding then joined his team for warmups and shootarounds.

Gabby carefully watched Nathan while he warmed up. He was loose and confident, making his warmup shots and talking with his teammates. His overall attitude was cheerful and positive. However, he kept peering over at Duke's players, giving them a 'come get a piece of me' snarl. The Blue Devils did not intimidate him, and he made sure they knew that.

When it came time to announce the teams, the Huskies stepped onto the court first. Nathan led his team. "Point guard and team captain, number twenty-three, Nathan Hanson!"

The Washington fans' cheers echoed through the arena. Gabby shook her pompoms and led the crowd in welcoming the other four starters onto the court.

While Duke's players were announced, Nathan and his teammates removed their warmup suits. He stretched to loosen up then waited to take his position on the court.

The ref blew his whistle, set the ball for tipoff, and the game began with the Blue Devils receiving the jump ball possession. The first half of the game remained fairly close. The teams were pretty evenly matched, trading off the lead several times and finally ending the half with the Huskies on top by only two points.

The second half seemed to go in the same direction.

Six minutes into the second half, the game took a drastic turn when the ball got loose on a steal attempt. Fighting over possession, Nathan was bashed in the face by an opposing player's elbow. He fell backwards, slid across the floor, and held his hand up to nose, wincing in pain. Immediately, blood gushed from the nasal cavity and dripped all over the court.

Gabby gasped and covered her mouth as if holding in a scream. "Nathan," she called out. Her heart rate accelerated and she began breathing heavily, worried that he had been seriously injured. Feeling his pain, her eyes began to well with tears.

The team doctor, equipped with latex gloves and a medical bag, rushed onto the court. Nathan cursed under his breath and covered his nose with his hand to try to keep blood from spilling onto the hardwood floor. With the doctor and a teammate's help, he slowly rose to his feet and was escorted back to the locker room.

They cleaned the blood off the court and gameplay resumed, without Nathan.

Randy and Jane witnessed this from the stands. Jane began to worry, hoping he hadn't broken his nose. "Is he alright? That was a lot of blood."

"He did take an elbow, Jane," Randy said. "He got bashed pretty hard too."

"Do you think he broke it?"

"Maybe. Can't tell from here."

Jane clenched her jaw, thinking about how much pain Nathan felt. "Ow!"

"Definitely ow. If it is broken, he'll be out the rest of the game."

Jane felt horrible. Nathan had waited his whole life for the opportunity to take home an NCAA championship trophy, and this was his last chance to make that happen. "He'll be crushed if he misses this."

Back in the locker room, the team doctor sat Nathan down and began the workup on his nose, which hurt like hell. The first step was to stop the immense bleeding. The doctor stuffed gauze up the nasal cavity then applied mild pressure. In a sitting position, Nathan tilted his head forward, causing the blood to drain out of the nose instead of down the back of his throat.

"You need to get me back out there," Nathan insisted, knowing the high stakes of this game.

"Not so fast, Hanson. I want to make sure you don't have a head injury." While Nathan applied pressure to his nose, Dr. Whittier checked him for signs and symptoms of a concussion. He had none.

"Am I clear?" Nathan asked, determined to get back into the game.

The doctor got a closer look at his nose. It wasn't disfigured and didn't appear to be broken. "Not as long as you're bleeding. Can't have you on the court like that."

After several minutes of direct pressure, the doctor checked his nose again. The bleeding seemed to have stopped. By this time, Nathan had missed eight minutes of gameplay—vital minutes. He was going to be pissed if they lost the game because of this. "I need to get back out there, Doc. This game is on the line!"

"You need to relax." Dr. Whittier applied a petroleum gauze balloon pack up his nose to allow pressure to continue. He cleaned the blood off his nose and face and had Nathan wash the blood off his hands. While Nathan was doing that, the doctor made him an icepack. He had him hold it on the bridge of his nose to reduce swelling and help restrict the blood vessels. In the meantime, the doctor covered the two blood drops on Nathan's jersey with purple duct tape.

The assistant coach rushed in to see what was going on. "How's he doing? Is it broken?"

The doctor said, "No. Just need to stabilize this so he isn't bleeding all over the court."

The assistant coach looked over at Nathan. "You ready to come back in?"

Nathan's nose hurt like hell, but he didn't care. He'd rather play through the pain than miss this game. "Definitely, if I can get this stupid icepack off my face."

The doctor removed the ice and checked his nose one more time. "You're good."

With balloon pack still stuffed up his nose, Nathan hopped off the exam table and returned to the court. The crowd cheered when they saw him.

With a little over five minutes left in the game, the Huskies called timeout. They were now down by six points. Coach Spoleda put Nathan back in to finish the game.

After reviewing the game plan and a quick pep talk, the Huskies met Duke on the floor. Nathan was loaded with aggressive energy, first off because he missed so much of the game, secondly because Duke's power forward bashed him in the nose. He used his anger productively and channeled it all into the game.

Several plays later, the Huskies closed the gap and were down by only two points. Then Nathan got fouled, which meant he was going to the line. He eyed the net, dribbled twice, and eyed the net again. Focusing only on this shot, he took a deep breath and released the ball—swish. One down. One to go. His teammates congratulated him and he prepared for his second shot. Following his same ritual, he fired shot number two. It too went in. The game was now tied with less than three minutes on the clock.

Duke inbounded the ball and dribbled down the court. Nathan was all over their point guard, making it difficult for him to shoot and forcing him to pass the ball. In turn, another Duke player attempted to make a fade away shot but missed, giving the Huskies the opportunity to snag the ball. In a quick turnaround, they passed the ball to Nathan, who dribbled down to the other end as he carefully read the court. The ball moved around several times. Then Duke made the mistake of leaving Nathan wide open in three-point range. The ball was quickly passed back to him and he nailed a three-point jump shot—boom! They were now up by three. The Huskies fans went wild.

Duke called a twenty second timeout.

The Huskies refocused and reexamined their game plan. With only two minutes left in the game, Washington had to stay focused. They made it this far last year and panicked in the final minutes, causing them to make costly mistakes and lose to Virginia. The coach warned them and gave them a solid game plan. Strong defense was going to be crucial.

The team was tired, but they only had to hold out for two more minutes. Despite trying to fend off the Blue Devil's offense, Duke answered Nathan's three pointer with a layup, reducing Washington's lead to one. Time for Nathan to kick into overdrive. He dribbled down court, making hand motions and hollering something at his teammates on the other end, trying to set up a screen. When they switched formation, Nathan sped in, did a quick half spin as he dribbled, and broke through Duke's point guard. The Huskies' defense held Duke's players back just long enough for Nathan to sneak inside and make a layup. Three point lead regained.

Duke was unable to answer on the other end, and their defense was starting to falter. Either they were beginning to lose focus under the pressure or they were having a bad second half. Nathan didn't care what the reason was. He just knew he needed to get the ball to the net. On their next offensive play, he passed the ball inside to an open player. Duke was unable to answer, bringing the Huskies lead to five points. With only seconds left in game play, Duke would have to make a miracle play to pull this off.

Nathan's heart pounded. The championship trophy was within their grasp, only seconds away.

Duke gained possession of the ball. After some good movement, the ball was handed to their best three-point shooter. He fired a jump shot at three-point range. It bounced off the rim. With fifteen seconds on the clock, Washington's center grabbed the rebound and passed to Nathan at half court. Nathan took it from there. He dribbled around, trying to take time off the clock, before he passed to his shooting guard, who dribbled and switched positions. His teammate had no access to the hoop and quickly passed back to him.

Six seconds.

In one final shooting attempt, Nathan performed a spin move, pushed his way through the defense, and attempted a fade away. It didn't go in, but it didn't matter. The buzzer sounded and the arena exploded with Huskies fans. The team gathered around each other, jumping up and down in elation. This was a dream come true. For the first time in history, the Washington Huskies walked away with the NCAA championship trophy.

Gabby ran over to Nathan and threw her arms around him, screaming in excitement.

He tried to kiss her but realized it hurt to do so. The area around his nose was beginning to swell and it was extremely sore. He needed to put ice on it before it got worse. "We did it, Gab!" Nathan rejoiced. "What a great way to end my college basketball career."

"Oh my god, Nathan, this is incredible. I'm so proud of you."

The Huskies had a remarkable season. And overall, Nathan had a successful four years of college basketball. He was sad it was all ending, but he had other avenues to pursue. He was on his way to medical school.

Back at the hotel, the celebration continued. Through all the reveling, Nathan spent the majority of the night with ice on and off his nose. It wasn't broken, thank God, but it was unbearably sore and extremely tender.

Gabby couldn't help but notice that Nathan was being a lone wolf. Concerned about his state of mind, she came over and sat on his lap. "How's the nose?" she asked.

"Hurts like hell."

Gabby leaned closer to get a better look. It was slightly swollen and starting to bruise. But at least it wasn't gushing blood anymore. "You look a little like Rudolph," she teased him.

"Oh, fantastic."

Offering her sympathy, she leaned in to kiss him.

Being that close to her and moving his lips and tongue in sync with hers made his nose hurt. He pulled away with a grimace on his face. "That actually hurts," he complained. "Can't even kiss you without being in pain."

"I have some Tylenol if you want it," she suggested.

"Doc gave me some."

"Did you take it?" she asked, knowing Nathan had a tendency not to take pain medication when he needed it.

"No," he admitted.

"You're just going to sit here in pain all night?"

He ignored her.

"I thought you wanted to be a doctor?" she questioned him.

"What's that have to do with anything?"

"Did Dr. Whittier tell you to take the Tylenol?"

"Yes."

Gabby figured as much. "So you ignored his advice?"

Nathan wondered where she was going with this. "No."

She laughed. "Yes you did. He said to take it. You didn't do it. You disobeyed your doctor's orders. How would you feel if your patients did that? And what would your dad say?"

"Those are two different, completely unrelated questions," he argued.

"No they're not," Gabby justified. "Your dad would be upset if he knew you were ignoring doctor's orders. And you wouldn't like it if your patients did that. Admit it."

Gabby was right, and he hated that. "So?"

Nathan's stubbornness forced Gabby to use her womanly influence on him. "Take the damn Tylenol, Nathan. Quit trying to be Mr. Macho."

"Fine." He reached into his pocket and pulled out the bottle of Tylenol. He popped two pills in his mouth then chugged down the rest of the water he had. "There. Happy now?"

"Yes." She hopped off his lap and pulled him out of his seat. "Now quit being a party pooper and come celebrate with us."

Nathan grinned at her efforts, which hurt to do. In fact, his whole face hurt. But he stood up anyway and joined her in the festivities.

In the morning, the alarm clock buzzed its shrill noise, undoubtedly waking everyone on the entire hotel floor. Nathan sat up and stretched.

Fellow point guard, Keeton Sullivan, rolled over to turn off the alarm. As he did, his eyes focused in on Nathan's face. "Blimey!" He gawped in surprise. "You resemble a raccoon this morning."

Nathan hopped out of bed and looked in the mirror. He had two black eyes, and his swollen nose was bruised and red. In a cynical tone, he griped, "Lovely."

"You took a hard hit. You're fortunate it isn't broken."

Nathan poked around at his face. It was still sore, and the tissue around his nose was tender. "I was thinking the same thing."

"That was a nice nick on the ball, mate. We gained possession after that," Keeton told him.

"Did we?" Nathan had to chuckle. "Ha, in your face, Duke!"

Keeton laughed. "Left you with one smashing shiner though."

"Hope his elbow is as sore as my nose," Nathan stated, wanting at least a little payback.

"Not bloody likely."

Nathan came back and sat on the bed. "That was quite the game, man. What a rush."

Keeton gathered his eyebrows, giving Nathan a very serious stare down. "We are going to miss you next season, my friend."

Nathan tried not to get emotional. "I'm gonna miss you guys too."

Upon returning to UW, Gabby decided to go home with Nathan. As soon as they walked in the door, they dropped all of their bags on the floor. Nathan clasped Gabby's hands in his, kissed her rather fervently, and forced her up against the wall. They were making out heavily, to the point where Nathan was grabbing Gabby's leg and pressing his pelvis on hers. His roaming hands snuck up her blouse as she pulled Nathan's shirt off.

They were completely oblivious of his roommate, who was sitting on the sofa trying to watch the game. He thought they were going to have sex right there in front of him, which he really didn't want to witness. He cleared his throat to get Nathan's attention.

Apparently Nathan didn't hear him, because instead of stopping, Nathan reached down and unfastened his pants.

"Nathan, Dude!" his roommate exclaimed. "I'm sitting here."

When Nathan realized he and Gabby weren't alone, he froze. "Elliot! I'm sorry, man. I didn't see you."

"That's obvious," Elliot retorted. "If you're gonna have sex, at least do it where I don't have to watch. I don't want that image in my head."

Nathan gave Gabby a kiss and patted her on the butt, shooing her into the bedroom. With a devilish grin, he apologized to Elliot. "Sorry."

Elliot caught sight of Nathan's black eyes and swollen, red nose. "Damn! That guy nailed you."

"Yeah, bled like a bitch."

"I saw." Right at eye level, Nathan stood with his pants unfastened, subjecting Elliot to his obvious erection. Elliot curled his lip. "Dude, take care of that please, before I gag."

Nathan joined Gabby in the bedroom, closed the door, and laughed.

Gabby didn't find humor in this at all. "Oh god, Nathan, that's so embarrassing."

To ease her discomfort, he pulled her into his arms. "We were just kissing. He didn't see anything."

She slid her hand into his pants. "Then how do you explain this?"

"That's just a little swelling problem I have." He nibbled on her neck and playfully moved his hands down to her butt and squeezed. "I was hoping you could help me with that."

"That's not the only thing that's swollen. I think your head is swollen too."

"Haha," he teased. "Aren't you full of jokes?" She had on a skirt, making it easy for him to slide a finger into her panties. He began to explore, trying to get a rise out of her. She made a cute moaning noise, obviously enjoying what he was doing. He slid his finger in further.

"Don't tease me like that," Gabby begged.

"It gets you hot," he said in his seductive bedroom voice. "You always squirm when I touch you like that. I love to make you squirm."

He stripped her panties off and meshed his lips with hers, building the intensity. Gabby moved her hands down to Nathan's pants and helped him step out of them. He then lifted her off the floor. She wrapped her legs around his torso, and he carried her over to the bed.

Normally Nathan and Gabby were pretty discreet, but today neither one of them seemed to care who heard or saw them. Elliot heard loud and clear. He wished he could gouge out his eardrums. The thought of his roommate getting down and dirty like that made him cringe. He knew Nathan and Gabby had been sleeping together, but he really didn't want to hear it. He grabbed the TV remote and turned up the volume to drown out the noise.

To put a climactic end to Nathan's basketball career, he was named to the National Association of Basketball Coaches Honors Court. To be eligible, a student athlete had to be a junior or senior and have a cumulative 3.2 GPA or higher at the conclusion of the season. In his four years at the University of Washington, Nathan demonstrated the true essence of the student athlete. He had reached the pinnacle of competition by competing in the national championships, while also achieving high academic standards.

It wasn't just Nathan who received recognition, the entire Huskies team was honored with a Team Academic Excellence Award. This award recognized outstanding academic achievement by a men's basketball team with a cumulative grade point average of 3.0 or better for all of its competing student athletes. The Huskies managed to produce a collective 3.4 grade point average for the academic year, the highest ever for the team. They didn't just take their basketball seriously, they excelled in the classroom as well.

As Nathan and Gabby walked across campus together to get some dinner, he remembered something he wanted to ask her. "Did you get the results from your certification exam yet?"

"Yes," she replied, celebrating her success. "I passed."

"Good job, Babe. What happens now?"

"I polish up my resume and collect letters of recommendation. Once I get those back, I can send these applications off."

"Good," Nathan replied.

"I start my lead teaching next week."

"I bet you're excited." Nathan knew she was going to do well. He always had the utmost respect for his teachers. He didn't always show it, but he did none the less. Having Gabby go through student teaching gave him an entirely new outlook on how important teachers were and how much they actually did. Knowing this now made him feel guilty for all the crap he put his teachers through. He was excited and anxious for Gabby to get her own classroom and start her career. She was great with kids, had a passion for education, and was going to be a wonderful teacher. "I hope you don't get any students like me."

"Why? You weren't a bad student."

"Come on now," he said trying to shake her memory. "I was a brat. How many times did I make a smartass comment to a teacher or finish my work in ten minutes making the teacher's lesson plans void? Mr. Long hated me."

"Only because you knew more than he did. I don't think he hated you though, I just don't think he knew what you were talking about half the time."

Nathan laughed. "Probably not. He had an AP Calculus student sitting through his ridiculously easy and horribly boring economics class. Every assignment he gave me, I finished in five minutes and got 100 every time. I think it pissed him off."

"It didn't help that you would sit there and stare at him with that inquisitive look on your face after you were done. Probably made him paranoid, wondering what the hell you were up to."

"Probably," Nathan chuckled. "I don't think he liked my basketball analogies either. The guy had no sense of humor. He was the driest person ever, and he wasn't a very good teacher. I could have taught that class better than he did, and I certainly would have made it more interesting. He should have just retired and put all of us out of our misery."

"That's mean," Gabby reprimanded.

"It's true," Nathan defended. "I hated that class."

"It wasn't that bad."

"Maybe not for you. For me it was a waste of time, but I had to have the stupid economics credit to graduate. I wish he could have let me take the final at the beginning of the year. I would have aced it, then I wouldn't have had to sit through that torturous hell. I could have been studying for my AP Physics exam or doing something productive instead."

Gabby tried to defend Mr. Long. "Let me see you step into a classroom and do what teachers do all day."

"There's no way I could do that," Nathan admitted. "You have to have the patience of a saint to deal with kids all day. This is why you're the education major and I'm not. I'd go crazy doing that. I wouldn't last ten minutes in a classroom."

"Then why are you picking on teachers?"

"I'm not picking on teachers, Gab, I'm picking on Mr. Long," he corrected. "I totally respect teachers. I think teaching is one of the most overworked and underpaid professions out there. I've had some amazing teachers, but Mr. Long wasn't one of them."

She admitted he was right. "No, he was pretty terrible."

"See? That's my point." Nathan chuckled. "I think I drove him out of the profession, because I heard that he retired after we graduated."

Chapter Twenty-Five

Nathan was exhausted from a tough and physical basketball season, and his brain was fried from writing papers, preparing lab reports, and studying for exams. He desperately needed a break. Since Gabby and the rest of Lauren's bridesmaids were asked to help pick out bridesmaids' dresses, he and Gabby spent a weekend in New York City.

Lauren wanted each of her bridesmaids to choose a dress they liked, as long as they were all the same color. After spending a day at the dress shop trying on many types of dresses, each woman had a very elegant rose red gown, designed to fit their individual styles. To complete the look, they purchased matching heels and jewelry.

These dresses matched perfectly with the flowers Lauren chose. Since rose red was their wedding color, the bouquets would include red and white roses, pink tulips, and greenery wrapped up in white ribbon. She and Roger didn't want a lot of flowers at their wedding, just enough to add some color and spark. Thus, they opted for flower tips and pedals instead of traditional flower arrangements.

To Roger, the majority of weddings were incredibly dull and lacked entertainment value. He did not want his wedding to be classified among those that were considered uninspiring. He was a performer and was determined to give his guests an entertaining show. Rather than just walking in with his groomsmen and standing on the altar waiting for his bride to arrive, Roger spoke to Jason, his brother, and two other Broadway friends about the possibility of making a more grandiose entrance. Of course his Broadway performing buddies were psyched about this idea and ate it right up. Peter, on the other hand, was not a dancer, but was willing to play along.

Roger needed someone to come up with a creative choreography sequence for this entrance. He turned to Lacy for help. On Roger's off night, while Lauren was working at the Ambassador, Roger secretly met with Lacy to discuss this.

He explained to her what he wanted, but she was a little confused by his request. "You want me to do what?"

"I want you to plan the choreography for this."

Of all the connections he had on Broadway, why did he choose her? "I'm not a professional choreographer. Why did you want me?"

"Two reasons. First, you're Lauren's sister. You're family. Secondly, you are a dance and choreography student, aren't you?"

"Well, yes," she replied.

"Okay. Then here's your chance to develop an original routine. Lacy Hanson's debut as a choreographer," he pointed out.

She tipped her head, reluctant about taking on this task. "These are Broadway performers, Roger. They're used to working with professionals."

She needed some convincing and a pep talk. Roger put his hands on her shoulders and looked her in the eye. "I have faith that you can do this. I wouldn't have asked you if I didn't think so."

Lacy released a deep, weighted sigh.

"If you won't do it for me, then do it for Lauren," he said. "You're her sister and her Maid of Honor. Aren't you supposed to do whatever needs to be done to help her prepare for this wedding?"

She smiled at his tenacity. "You are persistent, aren't you?"

"Come on, Lace. I need you. I know you can do this. All the guys have faith in you."

After much persuasion, she agreed to help him. "How many guys are there?"

"Five, including me."

She pulled out a notepad and wrote down all of this information. "Are all of them experienced dancers?"

"All but one. My brother."

Lacy gave Roger a funny look. "Is he okay with this?"

"Yes. He's not a dancer, but he's a good sport."

"So four professionals and one not."

"Exactly," Roger affirmed.

"I can work with that. Any particular style you're going for?"

"I want something fun that will break the mundane doldrums of a wedding ceremony. Add a little humor, the element of surprise maybe. Modern dance, jazz, or even tap even would be fine."

"How many of you can tap dance?" she asked.

"Two. Jason and me."

She shook her head and turned up her nose. "Probably not tap then."

"I'm totally leaving this in your hands, Lacy," Roger proclaimed confidently. "I know you will come up with something great. But please remember, no one else can know about this, especially Lauren. I want it to be a surprise."

"Alright," she said with a chuckle. "Let me work on this and I'll be in touch."

He kissed her on the cheek. "Thank you. You're awesome!"

Randy told Roger that he would pay the remaining balance on rental fees for the venue and cover the cost of any and all decorations or entertainment required for the reception, this included flowers, table centerpieces, small miscellaneous items, and the red runner rug and velvet barrier ropes for the entrance. Randy also insisted on paying the band to provide entertainment at this ceremony. Roger didn't want to argue with his future father-in-law so he had no choice but to allow Randy to do this.

A month ago, Lauren had gone dress shopping with Roger's mother, Lacy, and Jane. After a day's excursion of searching for the perfect wedding dress, Lauren found one that was elegant, yet sexy. This was another wedding purchase Randy and Jane made. The dress itself was $4,300. The accessories added a bit more to the final cost, but for his daughter's wedding, Randy willingly paid it.

The dress needed a few fitting adjustments, however. When the bridal shop called to let Lauren know that the alterations had been completed, she and Lacy went together to see how it turned out. The moment Lauren paraded out of the dressing room in her dress, Lacy's jaw hit the floor. Her sister was by far the most elegant and beautiful bride she had ever seen. A tear came to her eye. "You look incredible."

Lauren stood in front of the full length mirror and checked the alteration job on the dress. She turned from side to side to view it from all angles. It was a perfect figure-forming fit. "Do you think he'll like it?"

"Oh god, yes! You are going to blow his mind." Lacy fiddled with the train and asked, "Do you want a veil?"

"I think I just want a clip or something."

Lacy pulled several hairpieces off the shelf and held them up to Lauren's hair to see what each one looked like. After careful consideration, they found one that matched perfectly with the details of the dress.

The alterations seamstress carefully bagged up the dress then Lacy and Lauren searched for shoes to complement the look. Overall, they had a successful day.

Even though their wedding was going to be more modern and unique than most, Lauren still wanted to keep some of the old traditions. One of these was not allowing Roger to see the dress until their wedding. Lacy agreed to keep it safe and hidden for her.

When Lauren returned home that afternoon, Roger was surprised she waltzed in empty handed. No dress, no apparel bags, no signs of a shopping excursion at all. He questioned this odd anomaly. "Where's your dress? I thought you were picking it up today."

"I did. Lacy has it."

"I don't get to see it?" Roger asked.

"No," Lauren replied with a cynical laugh. "You have to wait until our wedding."

Disappointed, yet understanding Lauren's logic behind this decision, he whined, "Oh, man."

"Sorry. That's the way it is. Makes it more anticipatory for you if you're surprised."

"You're going to look gorgeous no matter what," Roger commented with a suggestive wink. "I can't wait."

Chapter Twenty-Six

Roger and his groomsmen coordinated a day to look at tuxes for the wedding. Roger had a specific style he was going for—comfort and class. In an attempt to find the perfect tux, he put on comfortable black dress pants and a white dress shirt accessorized with Victorian mother of pearl cufflinks that once belonged to his father. He tried on several suit coats, vests, and ties to get the full effect. After much debate, he went with a Ralph Lauren six button coat with a white spectrum vest and white silk long tie. The other men would be dressed in a similar fashion except their vests and ties were black instead of white. Roger's shoes were black and white two-toned patent leather dress shoes with black laces and brogue detailing, adding that extra touch of class. Knowing he was doing a dance routine, and wanting to make a dramatic entrance, he also snagged a pair of white dress gloves.

While all of his groomsmen were in town, Roger used the opportunity to gather his wedding posse together and rehearse with Lacy. He was able to secure a rehearsal studio for a few hours to give them space and a little discreetness. Since Lauren thought he was spending the entire day tux shopping, keeping this practice session secret was easier than Roger thought it was going to be.

They all met at the studio around 1:30 that afternoon, with the sole purpose of perfecting their dance routine for the big entrance.

Lacy nervously stood in the middle of the studio while Roger, Jason, and the others looked over her choreography plan.

"Wow," Jason said, impressed with Lacy's creativity. "This is good. I've worked with many choreographers, and most of them wouldn't have been able to come up with this."

Hearing a professional dancer say that boosted her confidence.

This routine was set to the song 'Gangnam Style', definitely not your typical wedding song. That alone added a touch of humor. Roger chuckled under his breath as he pictured the five of them performing this dance routine. "This is gonna be funny as hell. And no one is going to suspect a thing."

"You said you wanted to add an unexpected humorous element," Lacy reminded him. "I gave you what you wanted."

"Yes you did," he assured her. "This is great! You hit the nail right on the head. Thank you, Lacy." He handed the plans back to her then excitedly rubbed his hands together. "Alright, gentlemen, let's give this a whirl."

The men lined up according to Lacy's plans. Roger eyed her, waiting for directions. "Okay, Lace, let's see what you got."

They practiced for several hours, laughing and teasing each other every time they messed up, until they were able to go through the entire routine, music included, with no major errors. This bold entrance was certainly going to bring some laughs, not only because the choreography and song choice were hilarious, but because, despite Roger's efforts to help him, Peter couldn't dance. He was certainly trying, but his sense of rhythm was off. Lacy had to simplify his part to something with less steps involved.

A little after 5:00 P.M. they all parted ways, promising to keep it between them so not only Lauren, but the rest of the wedding guests would be surprised by this unexpected twist.

Chapter Twenty-Seven

Graduating from college was a day Nathan and Gabby had anticipated for a long time. This was the day they would finally wear their beautifully ironed black graduation gowns and caps adorned with tassels. Gabby had earned the privilege of wearing golden tassels and cords across the stage. She was graduating with cum laude honors from the College of Education.

Family members flew into Seattle for this event, including Lauren and Roger. Since the Ryans were such a big part of their lives, Nathan invited Jim and Jill to attend as well. Gabby only had her mother, father, and step-mother committed to attending, making seventeen total guests between the two of them.

Since they were graduating from different departments, Nathan and Gabby were unable to sit together during the ceremony. Nathan's assigned spot was in the front and Gabby was sitting more towards the middle. A few minutes before the ceremony began, Nathan squeezed his way through the rows of Education graduates to find Gabby. She thought he had already found his position in line so she didn't understand what he was doing in her department. "Nathan, why are you over here?"

"I wanted to give this to you before we walk the stage." He handed her a small green box.

Inside was a pretty bracelet with seven charms dangling from it—a rolled up diploma, a graduation cap, a stack of books, an apple, a cheering megaphone, a capital G, and a key. Each charm had personal meaning for Gabby, except for the key. The significance of that charm was unclear. "What's the key for?"

He answered, "Because you hold the key to my heart. You always have."

"Aw, thank you, Sweetie." She latched the bracelet around her wrist. "I love this."

"You're welcome, but I gotta go." He leaned over and kissed her then headed back to his place in line with the rest of the Biology graduates.

Despite Nathan's lack of romantic knowhow, he did his best to express his feelings for her. The unexpected things he did, like meticulously choosing specific charms, melted her heart the most. He really was a sweet man.

Walking across that stage to collect their college degrees—a B.A. in Elementary Education for Gabby, a B.S. in Biology for Nathan—was the most prideful moment of their lives. This day marked a significant milestone. They were moving on to a higher level of life experience, where new challenges and changes awaited them.

After making their walk, Nathan and Gabby found each other and squeezed together with a warm hug. "Congratulations, Babe," Nathan said.

"Congratulations to you too." She gave him a kiss then together they searched for their family members.

As the family slowly migrated toward them, Roger shook Nathan's hand, "Congratulations, Nathan."

"Thank you," he replied.

With a smile, Roger joked, "Maybe at this point we should call each other brother."

"You still have two weeks before you get to claim that title."

Gabby spent so much time around the Hanson family over the years that she was like a daughter to them. Randy and Jane had 'adopted' her years ago. To celebrate this event and make the occasion memorable for both Nathan and Gabby, Randy invited Gabby's family to join them for dinner that night. With the large dinner party they had, he reserved a private dining room at Salty's Waterfront Seafood Grill in Seattle.

The dinner conversation ranged from baseball to sports cars to people talking about various aspects of their careers. Stories about stage calamities, interesting cases in the ER, computer malfunctions, and funny things some of Gabriella's students said dominated the dinner banter. In the middle of the conversation, Nathan announced, "Gabby secured a teaching position."

The entire table directed its attention to Gabby.

Her mother, shocked by this news, asked, "Is this true?"

Happily, Gabby nodded. "Yes."

Excitement filled the room, and everyone offered congratulatory well wishes. Nathan just sat there with a proud grin on his face while everyone asked Gabby questions about her new job.

"What grade?" Lacy wondered.

"Kindergarten. It's at Montlake Elementary in the Seattle Public School District," Gabriella explained.

"I know where that is," Randy said. "I drive past it every morning on my way to the clinic. A colleague of mine has a daughter who goes to school there. They have a strong Science curriculum."

Rather than sharing in this excitement, Gabby's mother interrupted the question and answer session by blurting out, "How come you didn't tell me about this?"

The room fell silent.

Embarrassed by her mother's outburst, Gabby's smile instantly turned upside down.

With piercing eyes, Gabby's mom demanded an explanation. "At what point did I stop being informed about your life, Gabriella? I'm your mother. I have a right to know what's going on."

Gabby's lip quivered. She really didn't want to have an argument here, but her mother kept pushing the issue.

"Are you going to answer me?" her mother insisted.

In Gabby's defense, Nathan stepped in. "She just found out this afternoon. I'm the only one who knew."

But her mother didn't care. She glared at Nathan and snarled, "She could have called!"

This huge, unjustified scene upset Gabby, which made Nathan angry. No one spoke to his woman that way. "We were a little preoccupied trying to get ready for graduation."

Gabby's mother ignored him. "Gabby, is there some reason why you didn't call me?"

Gabby rose from the table and darted out the door, wanting to get as far away from her mother as possible.

Everyone stared at the woman, appalled by the disrespectful way she spoke to her daughter.

Nathan couldn't hold back any longer. He pursed his lips together and sneered, trying not to snap. "Was that really necessary? Tonight of all nights?" Infuriated, he tossed his napkin on the table and stood up. "She's worked hard for this. Why can't you be proud of her for once?" Without a second thought, he exited the room and searched for Gabby.

With everyone staring at her, Gabriella's mother thought it best to leave. She gathered her belongings and, without delay, stormed out of the restaurant.

Randy, being host to this dinner party, wasn't sure what to say. Trying to make light of the situation, he held up his glass of wine. "Never a dull moment in this family. Cheers." He quickly downed the glass and attempted to carry on.

Nathan found Gabby sitting under a tree next to the parking lot hugging her legs, sobbing. He sat down next to her, holding her in his arms. "Calm down, Honey." He pulled her closer and kissed the top of her head.

Sniffling, Gabby said, "I hate when she gets like that."

"I know, Baby. I do too." Nathan gently rubbed her back to soothe her.

Several minutes later, Roger came out to find Nathan cradling Gabby under this tree. He approached them cautiously and squatted down to their level. "You guys want to come back inside?"

"Is her mother still in there?" Nathan questioned, not wanting Gabby anywhere near her right now.

Roger shook his head. "No. She left."

Nathan kissed Gabby's forehead. "Hey," he whispered in a soothing voice. "Your mom's gone, Honey. We can go back inside if you want. We don't have to, though, if you don't feel like it."

She wiped her eyes with the back of her hand.

Nathan moved the hair off her pretty face then fixed his eyes on Roger. "Give us a minute."

"Of course." Roger stood up and went back inside to join the family.

After dinner, Gabby's father pulled Nathan aside. "Thank you for standing up for Gabriella tonight."

Nathan looked the man dead in the eye. "I will always stand up for Gabby. My question, Sir, is why didn't you?" Without uttering another word, Nathan put his arm around Gabby and led her out to the car.

Chapter Twenty-Eight

With Lauren straddling his lap, Roger dug his fingers into the flesh of her hips. Their bodies moved in perfect sync. As the heat of the moment intensified, Roger roamed his hands up her back and pulled her against him. Flesh on flesh, Lauren cried out in pleasure. Roger followed with a moan of his own. Savoring this bonding moment, he clung to her for a minute or two, feeling her breath on his skin. Gradually, his heartrate slowed and his breathing returned to normal. He leaned against the headboard, taking Lauren with him. His arms completely encased her.

As he regained air, a sly smile filled his face. For several weeks now, Roger had been hinting about a honeymoon, but refused to tell Lauren where they were going. She bugged him about it every day to no avail. Trying not to break the position they were in, Roger leaned over and opened the bedside table drawer. He reached inside and pulled out an envelope. "Ok. I know you've been waiting a long time for this, so here it is."

She sat upright and took the envelope from him. "What's this?"

His hands rested on her thighs. "Every time I give you something, you ask me what it is. If you would open it, you'd find out."

Bright-eyed, she bit her lip and pulled the contents out of the envelope. In her hand were two roundtrip airline tickets to the Exuma International Airport in the Bahamas and hotel reservations for a honeymoon beachfront suite at Sandals Emerald Bay Resort. Her hand covered her mouth with a gasp. "We're going to the Bahamas?"

"Yes, Ma'am. Two full weeks. No commitments, no hustle and bustle of the city. Just you and me."

She threw her arms around him. "Oh, Roger!"

Her reaction made him laugh. "Are you happy?"

"Yes," she exclaimed. "So happy. Thank you."

"You're welcome," he replied with a wide grin.

Still interlocked in position, she leaned in to kiss him. His heart pounded in erratic rhythm. The kiss lingered in dreamy intimacy, sending currents of desire through his entire body. He took the envelope and its contents from her hand and set them on the nightstand. His arms encased her again and she moaned softly as he lay her down. He lowered his body over hers and reassumed the position. Sinking into her, he began a second round.

Roger regularly extended their intimacy beyond a single session, but Lauren had no complaints. She thoroughly enjoyed the intimacy they shared. Roger was an incredible lover—gentle, passionate, intense, and very capable of making her peak every time. He always made her pleasure his first priority before satisfying his own needs.

Today was Lauren's last day at the Ambassador Theatre. She had given her notice several weeks ago, allowing another Performing Arts student to have the unforgettable experience of working behind the scenes. Carmen completely understood. After all, Lauren was marrying Roger Zellers. She no longer needed this job. She was getting plenty of Broadway exposure through Roger's connections.

Chicago played two shows on Saturday, a matinee and a nighttime show. *Phantom of the Opera* had two shows on Saturday as well, which meant Lauren and Roger both had to work that afternoon. Before heading to the Majestic, Roger arranged to meet Jason for lunch.

Jason picked up a copy of the New York Times to stay updated on Broadway news. There were several articles in the Entertainment section about changes in cast and upcoming premieres for various shows. One article specifically focused on Roger.

In the world of theatrical performers, Roger Zellers is known as one of the most formidable talents in the industry. Heralded for his portrayal of leading roles, Zellers is a musical force unlike any other. His unbridled reputation has led him to a Tony Award win for Best Leading Actor in a Musical, a Drama Desk Award, and the prestigious Theatregoer's Choice Award. Zellers, a New York-born actor, singer, and dancer, is recognized as the favorite leading man to perform on Broadway.

The article went on to list the various productions he'd been involved in, the Macy's and Rockefeller performances he'd done, and his latest recording projects. It emphasized his volunteer work with Broadway Cares, Toys For Tots, and the local children's hospital, and commended him for his food and blanket collecting efforts for the local homeless shelter.

The end of the article read, *At this year's Tony Awards, Roger will portray the Phantom for the last time, performing the unmistakable song, Music of the Night. June 1st he will remove the illustrious white mask to make some personal changes in his life before returning to the Broadway stage in a revival of the Gershwin musical Crazy For You.*

When questioned about the nature of the personal changes he was making, Roger hinted to the fact that he and his long-term girlfriend, Lauren Hanson, who will make her Broadway debut in the upcoming production of Crazy For You with Zellers, were exchanging vows and taking an extended vacation in the Bahamas.

Jason dropped this article on the table in front of Roger's face. "This was all over the newsstands this morning. So much for discreetness."

Roger chuckled. "It's not like it's a secret, Jason. Most people already knew Lauren and I were engaged."

"Relentless fans are going to barge in on your honeymoon," Jason teased.

"I seriously doubt that. None of them are that ambitious. The public knows I'm getting married, and obviously I'm going on a honeymoon with my new wife, but nowhere in that article does it mention when or where either of these events are occurring."

"Still wouldn't surprise me." Jason set his coffee cup on the table. "What are you up to tomorrow?"

"Don't know yet. Why?"

"I know you have a lot going on next week with family coming into town and your last week of Phantom, so," he grinned mischievously as he drew out the o sound. "How would you like to hang out with me, enjoying your last fling as a single man?"

"It's not like I'll never hang out with you again. I'm getting married, I'm not dead."

"I know, but I'm your Best Man. It's my duty to give you some sort of farewell to bachelorhood."

Not sure he liked this plan, Roger replied, "None of that juvenile crap, Jason. I don't want to drink myself to oblivion or even get remotely drunk. No strippers, no showgirls, no bikini clad women popping out of giant cakes."

Roger's sarcasm made Jason laugh. "Actually, I was thinking more along the lines of a Yankees game and stopping at Buffalo Wild Wings for hot wings and a few beers."

Much more to his liking. "Now that I like."

"Think your fiancé will let you sneak away tomorrow?"

"Won't be a problem," Roger said. "Lauren is having her bridal shower tomorrow. Hanging out with you will give me something to do."

"Cool. I'll meet you at your place around noon."

"They're having the shower at my place," Roger corrected. "I'm going to want to be long gone from there before that happens. I'll come to you."

"Sounds good."

With the wedding only days away, Roger and Lauren received a call that their cake was ready. Gina Russo met them at the bakery to do the honors herself. When the White Plains Cake Connoisseur came out of the kitchen area dressed in her white baking apron, she smiled at Roger and offered him a friendly handshake. "Mr. Zellers, pleasure to meet you."

"The pleasure's all mine."

Gina greeted Lauren as well. "Welcome, Ms. Hanson. Thank you for stopping by."

"Thank you," Lauren said.

Gina refocused her attention on Roger. "I understand you're a Broadway performer and have been in some pretty big shows."

"Yes. I have my final performance of Phantom tonight."

"That explains why you chose Broadway as the theme for your wedding cake."

"Yes, Ma'am," Roger confirmed.

"Come on back." She motioned with her hand for them to follow her to a small viewing room at the back of the bakery. "Have a seat and I'll bring it right out."

"Thank you." While Gina was gone, Roger held Lauren's hand. "You excited?"

"Yes."

"Me too. She does great work," Roger said confidently. "Can't wait to see what she did."

When two of Gina's bakery workers carried out the cake, Roger and Lauren were amazed by the detailed precision of each element. The airbrushed black, dark purple, and midnight blue frosting around the edge of the giant four-tiered cake was painted to look exactly like the Manhattan skyline under a nighttime starry sky. Spread throughout the surface of the cake, covering each layer, were exact mini replicas of various Broadway billboard posters. The specifics on these tiny billboards, which included all the shows Roger had been in, were intricately detailed right down to the last cat whisker. On the very top of the cake was a black and white comedy/tragedy theatre mask made from modeling chocolate. Roger was in complete awe over the creative artistry. "Wow, Gina. This looks fantastic!"

Lauren focused on the ornate details of the skyline. "Look, it's the Empire State Building."

The excitement in Lauren's voice brought a smile to Roger's face. "I see."

Lauren pointed out a cute little Phantom mask. "The details are incredible."

"So you like it?" Roger asked, already knowing the answer to that question.

"I love it. It's great!"

"There you have it. The woman is impressed."

"I'm glad you like it," Gina replied.

After collecting final fees for the craftsmanship and labor on this superbly crafted cake, Gina offered to deliver it to their reception venue the morning of their wedding.

Roger agreed.

On the way back from Gina's Bakery, Roger and Lauren stopped at the Newark Airport to pick up Lauren's family. More guests were expected to fly into both LaGuardia and Newark the following day, but for now, at least part of the Hanson family was here.

Roger performed his final show of *Phantom of the Opera* that night. The Hansons had the privilege of seeing this final performance. This was a nostalgic moment for Roger. He waited his entire career to play Phantom and felt blessed to have had the opportunity to play the role of a lifetime. It was an experience he thoroughly enjoyed, and one he was going to miss.

Following the performance, the cast and crew held a party in Roger's honor. He changed out of costume, and with Lauren by his side, partied with the *Phantom of the Opera* family.

Around 2:00 A.M., as the cast party came to a close, Roger passed the mask to the next actor portraying Phantom, as the actor before him had done. He placed a ceramic Phantom mask and a note he had handwritten on the vanity in what was now his former dressing room. The note read, *Maurice, The legacy lives on, and the Music of the Night will continue to take flight.*

343

Congratulations on your new adventure, and best of luck on your journey as the Phantom. Enjoy this experience! Roger.

Right before leaving the Majestic that night, he took Lauren's hand and walked onto the stage of this glorious theatre one final time. "Well," he said with sadness in his voice. "This is it."

"This was your decision, Roger. You could have extended your contract."

"No. It's time to move on. Can't be Phantom forever." He put his arms around her waist and leaned in to kiss her. "Besides, you and I have a new production to work on."

"Yes we do." She rested her head on his shoulder.

"In two days, you'll be my wife."

"I know. I'm so excited."

"So am I," he concurred. "Can't wait to kiss you on the altar."

"Why wait?"

He moved closer, taking in the same air. "No reason."

"Then shut up and kiss me."

With a chuckle, he gladly obeyed.

The next day's agenda was so full that Roger wasn't sure how he was going to fit everything into his schedule. More friends and family members were either flying or driving into New York City, which meant Roger had three airport runs to make that morning. One to LaGuardia and two to Newark. After making three trips to the airport and ensuring everyone checked into their hotels, Roger had to pick up all the tuxes. On the way to the tux shop, he dropped Lauren off at her parents' hotel so she, Lacy, her mom, and Gabby could get manicures and pedicures done.

After grabbing a quick bite to eat, he returned to the apartment to drop the tuxes off, hanging them carefully to ensure they didn't get damaged or wrinkled. He had purchased five black fedoras for the men to wear as part of their dance entrance. He slipped them and the white gloves on the top shelf of the closet and hid them in the corner so Lauren wouldn't find them.

Part of last minute prep for the wedding meant putting final touches on the reception hall. The Hudson Theatre provided tablecloths, napkins, flatware, plates, and glasses, but decorating the reception hall was very specific to their needs. They opted to do it themselves. Roger picked Lauren and the girls up from their beauty salon expedition then met the rest of the family and wedding party at the Hudson Theatre to get the place spruced up for the reception. As busy as he was on this particular day, Roger was actually looking forward to doing this. All the thorough planning he and Lauren had done for their wedding was going to take shape this afternoon.

Over the last month, the staff at the Hudson had met with Lauren and Roger several times to ensure that every detail and desire they had was met so they could have the perfect wedding. The theatre staff didn't disappoint. Upon entrance into the reception hall, the tables had already been set up banquet style, leaving the area closest to the stage open as a dance floor. Ten high-backed black cushioned chairs surrounded each table. Pristine and immaculately clean white linen tablecloths covered each table, and in front of each chair was a neatly folded red linen napkin. Formal table settings of white ceramic bread plates, delicate lace-patterned silver flatware, and crystal wineglasses garnished each spot. Already the place was full of opulence and classiness, and they didn't even have table centerpieces, flowers, or any other décor up yet.

"Looks nice in here," Roger said as he walked inside with a large plastic tub in his arms. He set the tub on the floor and did a quick scan of the room. Everything was set up just as he and Lauren specified.

Jason followed Roger inside, carrying another tub. "Where do you want this?" he asked.

"Just set it down over here."

They unloaded the rest of the decorations and set them on the floor with the others. "Where do we start?"

The first of two scheduled deliveries from the flower shop quickly resolved that question. They began working on the table centerpieces. This was something Roger and Lauren had meticulously planned out. The design they came up with was simple, yet effective. They ordered twenty-two oval-shaped, gold-plated, mirrored vanity trays with floral frames and footed bottoms to use as bases for these centerpieces. Together, he and Lauren worked to layer two dozen red rose tips on top of it. When they had the flowers arranged the way they wanted them, they attached a silk top hat, tilted at an angle and situated in such a way that it appeared the hat was submerged in the roses. Beside the hat, they hot glued a gold and black comedy/tragedy mask. On the other side, attached to a small black dowel, was a laminated Playbill program cover. For grouping and seating purposes, they planned to have each centerpiece represent a different cover, subsequently each table would to be assigned its own musical. After placing this carefully constructed centerpiece on the table to see what it looked like, Roger and Lauren sprinkled red rose pedals and pink tulip tips inside the hat itself. When complete, they stood back to look at it.

"Looks great," Roger boasted. "We did well, my dear."

"Only twenty-one more to go."

He laughed at the complexity of this task. Each centerpiece only took about five to seven minutes to construct, but with twenty-one more to put together, it would take two and a half hours to construct them all. For the effect they offered, it was well worth the extensive use of hot glue and the time required to create them.

To keep the flowers fresh, the theatre cordially offered to store these centerpieces in their restaurant-sized refrigerator until morning, when the theatre staff would set one in the center of every table. While Lauren and Lacy spent two and half hours constructing these centerpieces, Roger and other family members set up the rest of the decorations and entertainment items.

Roger and his groomsmen set up a photo booth. They made it fun by offering several prop boxes and racks full of colorful feathered Mardi Gras masks, various hats, feather boas of different colors, oversized Mickey Mouse gloves, flowered leis, capes, oversized glasses in fun shapes, headbands with antlers and bunny ears attached, and a variety of scarves, ascots, clip on neckties, and big bow ties. Having this available during the reception would allow wedding guests to express themselves and get their photo taken as they stepped into another world for a while.

Along with the photo booth, Roger and Lauren had a party favor box prepared for each table. Inside each box were several plastic masquerade masks in various colors, carnival bead necklaces, fuzzy stick on mustaches, and plastic glasses with large noses attached. These particular items allowed wedding guests to unwind by putting on a mask or wearing a mustache during the reception if they felt like it. Also inside the box were small bottles of bubbles, which they hoped guests would blow at random. There was nothing Roger hated more than sitting through lackluster, humdrum weddings. He and Lauren were making theirs into a fun-filled celebratory party.

The guestbook area they set up was also unique and fun. Roger thought guestbooks were impersonal, so instead of the traditional sign-your-name-to-let-the-bride-and-groom-know-you-were-here book, they set out a wooden box full of parchment paper. Next to this, they had a can full of red feather pens and laid out several types of smiley face and heart-shaped stickers. This was far more personal than just writing a name on a list.

To go along with their Broadway theme, Lauren and Roger wanted to give their wedding guests red carpet treatment. Inside the main theatre doors, they set up a red velvet VIP rope barrier and spread a long red carpet across the floor. The wedding party and several family members spent an hour blowing up white, gold, and black balloons. They attached each balloon bouquet to individual golden rope poles. At the very end of the red carpet road was a large framed Broadway-style billboard poster with a photo of Roger and Lauren. It was surrounded by shiny white lights and the words, *A Wedding Story, June 3rd at the Hudson Theatre in NYC, New York. Starring Lauren Hanson as Blushing Bride and Roger Zellers as Dashing Groom! One night only!*

With family members and the entire wedding party working together, all decorations and reception necessities were set up in a little less than three hours.

The reception hall looked fabulous. "This is my kind of party!" Roger said. "Definitely fun and festive."

After doing a final check on the reception dinner menu, everyone headed over to the Ambassador Theatre for wedding rehearsal. The Justice of the Peace, who had the honor of marrying them, was a cheerful man in his mid-40's. When Roger informed him that he and Lauren had written their own vows and scripted their own ring exchange, the judge teased them by saying, "Looks like you two have this under control. What am I doing here?"

Roger laughed. "You have to make it legal, Your Honor."

He grinned sheepishly. "Oh yeah! It does work like that, doesn't it?"

At the conclusion of rehearsal, minus the secretive groom-and-company entrance dance, everyone returned to the Hudson Theatre for rehearsal dinner.

While dinner was being served, the wait staff came around and filled everyone's glasses with wine. Roger stood up and addressed the twenty-two people gathered around the table. "Guess I'll get this party started," he began. "First off, I'd like to thank all of the groomsmen and bridesmaids, as well as all of our family members, for helping Lauren and I prepare for our wedding. Without all of you, nothing would have gotten done. Dr. Hanson," he tipped his glass to his future father-in-law. "Thank you for your financial contributions and for helping to make mine and Lauren's dream wedding come true. And thanks to both you and your lovely wife for raising such a loving, supportive, and beautiful woman and for allowing me the honor of making her my wife."

Randy acknowledged with a quick bob of his head. "It's our pleasure, Roger."

He paused for a moment, not only to gather his thoughts, but to find his composure because he was starting to get emotional. He cleared his throat then turned to his bride and said, "Lauren, you have changed my life in so many positive ways, I don't even know where to begin. As I sat and thought about what I was going to say to you tonight, I had a difficult time finding the right words to express how much you mean to me. I know our life together won't always be perfect, but no matter what life throws at us, I find comfort in knowing that we'll hold hands through it all and come out standing tall. Every day for the rest of my life, I will wake up not only to your beautiful face, but to the sound of your breath on my neck, the warmth of your lips on my cheek, and the touch of your fingers on my skin. I'll always love you, Lauren." He swallowed hard to remove the sentimental lump in his throat before he lifted his glass. "Here's to my bride: she knows everything about me, yet loves me just the same."

Everyone toasted with him.

Jason stood up and addressed the group. He had to get in his two-cents too. "Alright everyone, enough mushy gushy kissy stuff. I'm going to take the floor now."

"Oh no you don't," Roger said. "Sit back down."

"Hey now," Jason said. "This is my show for once. You need to take a back seat and let me do this."

Roger leaned back in his chair and let Jason have his fun.

Jason began his speech. "For those of you who don't know me, I'm Jason Preen, and I have the wonderful fortune of being Roger's Best Man. Many years ago, during casting calls for Newsies, I had the joyful privilege of meeting Roger. I remember that day very clearly. I saw him tap dancing around the empty warmup studio. I figured he was one of the dancers I was auditioning with, until I heard him sing. And let me tell you, this guy has got a voice. He introduced himself, and since then, our friendship has developed into one of trust and genuine respect. I can honestly say that Roger is my best friend and a man I trust with my life. Because I care about him, I wanted to make sure he hooked up with the right person. But truth be told, when Roger and Lauren first started dating, I had my doubts. I badgered him about it, and even tried to reason with him. Fortunately, Roger isn't one to listen to reason. He dodged my bites and didn't let a badgering hound like me get in the way of his happiness. And I'm glad he didn't, because Roger and Lauren truly bring out the best in one other. They encourage each other's curiosities, support each other through the tough times, and cheer each other on." Jason raised his glass. "If you'll all join me in raising a glass to our happy couple, Roger and Lauren. May the joys you share today be the beginning of a lifetime of great happiness and fulfillment. Congratulations."

"Thank you, Jason." Roger raised his glass. The rest of the room followed suit.

Unexpectedly, Peter rose from his seat. Normally, Peter wasn't the type of person to address large groups or make sappy speeches, so when Roger saw him standing there with a wineglass in his hand, a sentimental lump filled his throat. "Pete, what are you doing?"

"Usually you're the one who takes center stage. Right now, it's my turn." Peter began, "My name is Peter Zellers. I'm the older, wiser brother of the groom. You older brothers in the room will know what I mean when I say you never expect your younger brother to grow up. Somehow, mentally, Roger will always be the little guy curled up beside me in my bed at night because he's afraid to sleep alone after watching a scary movie. Then one day, I turned around, and this little kid is starring in his first play, going on his first date, graduating from high school, and making quite a name for himself in his world of theatre. Roger's talent gave him the upper hand in life, but he never let it get to his head. I'm proud of him for that."

Roger almost lost it. The connection he had with his brother had always been strong. Since Roger's biological father wasn't around, Peter took it upon himself to guide his younger brother through the trials of life and protect him from anyone who did him harm. He cheered for him during performances, encouraged him when he lost hope, and taught him a few life lessons along the way.

Peter continued, "Roger, take Lauren's hand."

Roger did as he asked.

"Place your other hand over hers."

He did that too, but was unclear about where his brother was going with this.

"Now, remember this moment and cherish it, because this will be the last time you'll ever have the upper hand."

The room exploded in laughter. Even Roger got a chuckle out of this.

"Congratulations, little brother. You kept your head even while you lost your heart."

"Thanks, Pete."

Chapter Twenty-Nine

June 3rd, the day Roger had been waiting for, the day that had been the focal point of his and Lauren's lives for the last five months, finally arrived. As the sun came up, Roger rolled over, but he didn't feel Lauren's warm body in bed next to him. "Honey?" he called out.

Lauren bounded into the bedroom. "Good morning." Roger's tousled hair and the sleepy look on his face made Lauren giggle. "Tired?"

It was 7:00 A.M. and Lauren was already dressed in a purple flowered blouse and a pair of white shorts, exposing her sexy legs. Obviously she'd been up for a while. "Why are you up so early?"

"I'm getting my hair and makeup done this morning, remember?"

Roger did remember, but his brain wasn't fully functioning yet. "I knew that."

Lauren leaned over the bed and kissed him. "Wake up, Sweetie."

Lustfully, he watched as she grabbed her purse. The shape of her butt and the curviness of her legs and waist drove him crazy. But he and Lauren had made a pact not to have sex the night before their wedding. "You do know, don't you, that not having sex so we can save it for our wedding night is torturing me right now."

She laughed at him. "We both agreed to this, remember?"

"Yes. I remember. But putting me through this agony means you are in serious trouble tonight." He winked at her suggestively.

"And you'll have to wait until tonight."

He groaned, wishing he hadn't agreed to this.

"I have to go. What time are you meeting the florist?"

"9:00," he replied. "I'll bring all the bouquets over to the Ambassador. You ladies can sort them out from there."

"Sounds good."

"Next time I see you, we'll be exchanging vows."

This thought made her smile. "Yes we will."

"I love you, Lauren."

"I love you too. See you later." She kissed him goodbye then headed out the door.

While Lauren and her bridesmaids were getting their hair and makeup professionally done, Roger and his groomsmen gathered at his apartment to quickly run through their entrance dance before they put on their tuxes. They helped each other with boutonnières and hopped in a limousine to the Ambassador Theatre.

Roger stared blankly out the car window and constantly fiddled with the cuffs on his shirt. Peter began to sense that his younger brother's nerves were on edge. Since Roger performed in front of thousands of people every night, Peter assumed he had surefire strategies to help alleviate this problem. Today, however, none of his strategies were working.

"You okay, Rog?" Peter asked.

Roger snapped out of his trance. "What?"

"Are you okay?"

"I'm fine."

Peter knew better. "No, you're not. You're nervous. I can tell."

Jason recognized Roger's edginess and interjected, "It's okay to be nervous. This is a big day for you."

"I'm not nervous," Roger insisted.

This made Jason laugh. "Yeah, and I'm Mikael Baryshnikov. It's going to be hard for you to slip a ring on Lauren's finger if your hands are shaking, but I know exactly how to cure that." Jason flipped through the music on his cellphone and chose the perfect song for this occasion. "This will help."

'Bohemian Rhapsody' began to play. Roger loved this song. He couldn't resist belting the lyrics every time he heard it. "Dammit, Jason."

"You know you want to," Jason tempted him.

As Jason suspected, Roger couldn't resist. He sang out loud and proud. The rest of the men chimed in, attempting to harmonize. They were horribly off key, but right now, Roger didn't care. They were having a good time, and it was helping him relax.

When the men's limo pulled in front of the Ambassador, security was already on guard checking admittance tickets and double checking the guest list. They were thirty minutes early, which was good, because this gave them time to situate themselves for their big entrance. Roger set the box of flowers on a table inside the entrance of the theatre then he and Jason rushed to get the music cued on the sound system.

The Justice of the Peace also arrived early, allowing Roger time to explain the entrance dance to him. Upon hearing this, the judge chuckled then took a seat and waited.

About ten minutes before the ceremony was scheduled to begin, Lauren and the other women pulled up in their limo. Lacy ran inside and told Jason to take Roger somewhere away from the entrance so Lauren could walk in without him seeing her. He quickly complied, and Lauren headed back to one of the dressing rooms.

When all the guests were seated, the security guard closed the doors to the theatre. They were ready to begin. Roger and his groomsmen positioned themselves in the back. Each slipped on a black fedora and a pair of aviator sunglasses while Carmen waited for the cue to start the music.

With bouquets in hand, the bridesmaids took formation in the lobby outside the auditorium. Lauren and Randy stood side by side in the rear of this lineup. Lauren had him hold her bouquet so she could straighten his boutonnière.

"You look beautiful, Baby."

"Thank you." She looked up at his misty eyes. "Daddy, don't cry."

"I'm alright." He offered a reassuring smile. "You're marrying a wonderful man. He treats you the way you deserve to be treated, with respect and love. I couldn't ask for more than that." He handed the bouquet back to her. "I love you, Honey, and I'm very proud of you."

She hugged him tightly. "I love you too, Daddy."

When everyone was in position, Lacy came out and gave Roger the signal, who in turn slipped on his white gloves and gave Carmen a thumbs up. The ceremony began.

To Lauren's surprise, the song 'Gangnam Style' came on, which made the auditorium echo in laughter. Slanting her eyebrows, she said, "What is going on?" She peeked her head inside to have a look. "Oh my god, what is he doing?" Roger and his groomsmen danced their way up to the stage, all wearing fedoras, sunglasses, and ridiculous white gloves. "And what is he wearing?"

Roger took center stage surrounded by his groomsmen, who danced around him to a well-rehearsed, cleverly choreographed number. This little dance routine had creative moves with funny inter-actions between the men. They danced around the stage like synchronized swimmers in a pool. This lighthearted routine entertained their guests and added a much lighter feel to their wedding.

At the conclusion of the song, the entire theatre rolled with applause. The men broke formation, laughing together as they removed their sunglasses and hats and took their positions on the altar.

Roger carefully placed his gloves inside the hat and laughed at the crowd's reaction. "Did you see their faces?"

"Oh yeah," Jason replied with a chuckle. "That was great."

While Roger's back was turned, the women made their way into the auditorium. Jason tapped Roger's arm to get his attention. "Rog, look."

Still grinning from his posse's unexpected entrance, Roger turned around. The playful smile on his face transformed to a look of complete adoration and love. Lauren, clinging to her father's arm, strolled in wearing an asymmetrically-draped trumpet style gown. Roger was completely blown away; no words could describe how he felt right now. Lauren was the most beautiful woman he had ever seen. He couldn't take his eyes off of her.

The women paraded down the aisle one by one, which allowed Roger to see his beautiful bride in more detail. The pearl-beaded tulle on her gorgeous dress was detailed with intricately embroidered sequin and rhinestone beadwork. This, along with the delicate floral lace appliques, created a stunning wedding gown that was a special and unique piece of art. It had an elegant sweep train, and the neckline accentuated her bust. The waistline hugged her slim and curvy figure, adding just the right amount of sexiness mixed with glamor. The bracelet and matching diamond drop earrings she had on accessorized the dress perfectly. Her hair was held up by a scrolled pearl cluster and Swarovski rhinestone crystal hair comb. Her white one-and-half-inch heeled sandals featured stunning rhinestone embellishments, which added understated elegance to her look. Her toes and fingernails were painted in a French manicure.

Roger's heart pounded and his chest heaved, trying to recapture the air that had completely escaped him. The only word he could muster from his lips was, "Whoa."

"She's beautiful," Jason whispered, just loud enough for Roger to hear him. "Absolutely beautiful."

Jason's analysis did not do this moment justice. Roger stared down the aisle, his eyes locked on Lauren. "She's gorgeous."

All the bridesmaids took their position while Lauren and her father stopped short of the altar. Roger used this brief moment to step forward and shake Randy's hand. "I promise I'll take care of her," Roger assured him.

Randy had no doubts. "I have complete trust in you, Roger."

Releasing his grip, Roger faced his bride. "You're absolutely stunning." He offered his hand and carefully led her up to the altar.

Roger and Lauren wrote their entire wedding. They only needed the Justice of the Peace to officiate it and sign off on the marriage license to make it legal. But before they started, the judge gave an introduction. "Ladies and gentlemen, today we gather together to celebrate the marriage of Lauren Hanson and Roger Zellers…"

The entire time the judge spoke, Roger's eyes fixated on his bride. He had never in his life seen anyone so glamorous. He couldn't believe that this elegant and gorgeous woman standing next to him was about to become his wife. The judge's introduction continued, and Roger heard maybe five words of it— the part about trust and togetherness, and something about enhancing life's joy. He wished things would move along so they could get to the good part.

After a five minute introduction, the judge said, "Today, Lauren and Roger have chosen to engage in the covenant of marriage and dedicate their lives to one another. Please join them now as they exchange their wedding vows."

Finally! Time for the vow exchange. The moment he had been waiting for.

Lauren went first. She handed her bouquet to Lacy, took both of Roger's hands in hers, and gazed into his eyes. "I, Lauren Marie Hanson, take you, Roger Alan Zellers, to be my husband, my partner, my best friend for life, and my one true love. I will cherish you and love you more each day than I did the day before. I will trust you and respect you, laugh with you and cry with you. I will love you faithfully through good times and bad, and I will stand beside you and uplift you. Today, I give you my hand, my heart, and my love for as long as we both shall live."

Roger smiled at her. This woman standing before him was his love, his inspiration, and his purpose. No matter what happened in their lives, he knew with all his heart that Lauren was the one woman he could always trust. She was the one he could depend on, and the one who would always be by his side, offering support and encouragement. He was truly blessed to have her in his life. Now was his time to tell her.

"I, Roger Alan Zellers, take you, Lauren Marie Hanson, to be my friend, my partner, the mother of my children, and my wife. I will be yours in times of plenty and in times of want, in times of sickness and in times of health, in times of joy and in times of sorrow, in times of failure and in times of triumph. I promise to cherish and respect you, to care for and protect you, to comfort and encourage you, and to love you and stay with you, faithfully, for all eternity. Our love is a bond too strong to break, and through our union, we can accomplish more than we ever will alone. I love you, Lauren, and together, we will share our love with the world."

The love he felt for this woman could overcome any obstacle, climb any mountain, and cross any ocean. Together, they were invincible.

The judge said, "May we have the rings please?"

Jason reached into his pocket and pulled out two wedding rings. He handed them both to Roger, who in turn handed his to Lauren.

This time Roger went first. He took her left hand in his and recited the ring exchange speech he had written. When he was finished, he gently, and with the most genuine touch of love, slipped the ring on Lauren's finger.

She reciprocated with the same.

Throughout the ceremony, the love and devotion Lauren and Roger displayed toward one other brought heartfelt tears to many of their guests. There was no doubt they were in love.

The judge proclaimed, "Until now, Lauren and Roger, you have spent each moment of your lives as separate individuals. But from this day on, your lives shall be shared and spent as one. I now pronounce you husband and wife. You may…"

But Roger didn't wait. Before the judge even gave him permission to do so, he wrapped Lauren in his arms and kissed her.

The entire theatre celebrated with cheers and applause.

The judge introduced them as Mr. and Mrs. Zellers, but instead of holding hands and walking out together, Roger picked Lauren up and carried her out of the theatre. He gently set her down on the sidewalk, and they both crawled inside the limousine. Immediately, he closed his eyes and moved in to kiss her, this time drawing out the embrace and making it more intense.

After collecting required signatures, the Justice of the Peace followed Roger and Lauren outside. He cleared his throat to get their attention.

Reluctantly, Roger broke away from his bride. "Yes, Your Honor?"

"Thought you might want this." The judge handed Roger their marriage license.

"Yes, Sir. Thank you very much."

"Congratulations, and best of luck to you both."

"Thank you, Your Honor." As the judge walked away, Roger happily held up the legally signed document. "It's official."

Lauren giggled excitedly. "Yay!"

The wedding party scrambled out of the theatre and gathered by the limousine. "Quit kissing and move aside," Jason teased as he forced his way into the limo, almost sitting on top of Roger. "You have your whole life to kiss her."

Jason's comment made Roger laugh. He and Lauren scooted over to make room for the others.

The wedding party and immediate family members spent the next two hours shooting photos at various locations. Brandon had selected a variety of areas within Central Park in which to take romantic wedding pictures and fun group shots. For sentimental reasons, Lauren and Roger had requested the front of the Ambassador Theatre and the middle of Times Square with all the Broadway billboards in the background as two location to capture a few poses.

After ninety minutes of running around like busy bees posing for pictures, they all reported to the Hudson Theatre reception venue. The band was warming up, the cake had been delivered and placed atop a clear crystal-footed cake plate, and the caterers were busily preparing their meal. The theatre staff had kept their word. The table centerpieces were carefully placed on each table, and the entire room looked festive. While Brandon set up his camera, family members sprinkled a bunch of fresh rose pedals over all the tables and placed a rose tip on top of the cake.

It was now 1:27 P.M. The red carpet entrance had been lit and guests started to pile up at the door. The wedding party and family members took their seats while Lauren and Roger hid backstage, where they would wait until all the guests were seated inside. Jason, Nathan, and the groomsmen took position inside the door to act as ushers while the security guard positioned himself outside the door to check tickets, controlling entrance to this private reception. At exactly 2:00 P.M. security opened the velvet barriers, and guests made their way inside.

The same musicals that were represented on the cake were also represented by Playbill covers on each table. Upon entrance, guests could sit wherever they chose, as long as the two *Phantom of the Opera* tables were left open for the wedding party and immediate family.

Backstage, Roger leaned against the wall, his lips locked with Lauren's. Holding her like this was comforting and warm. He was the happiest man in the world. "You are absolutely gorgeous. This dress is fabulous."

The emotion filled day finally got to Lauren. Tears flooded her eyes.

"And the tears begin," he chuckled in delight, knowing she was crying for joyful reasons.

"This is the happiest day of my life."

With the gentlest touch, he cupped his hand on her cheek. "Mine too. I love you." A delightful thought came to him which made him chuckle. "Mrs. Zellers."

She smiled beautifully. "What was up with that Gangnam Style dance?"

Roger had to laugh. "Did you like that?"

"Yes," she said. "That was so funny. Did you throw that in at the last minute?"

"Actually no. It had been planned for a while. We had to sneak in rehearsals whenever we could because we didn't want anyone to find out. You can thank your sister for that."

Lauren dropped her jaw in surprise. "Lacy?"

"Yup. She choreographed the whole thing."

"It certainly gave our wedding guests something to remember."

"That it did."

Announced as Mr. and Mrs. Zellers, Lauren and Roger finally joined the festivities. They enjoyed dancing, drinking wine, eating hors d'oeuvres, and socializing with friends and family.

An hour into the reception, a woman outside the theatre insisted that she be allowed inside. When security asked for her ticket, she could not present one. The security guard then checked the guest list. The woman's name was not on it. The guard refused to let her in, at which time she became hostile and demanding.

Peter, being a law enforcement officer and not wanting his little brother's wedding disturbed in any way, saw the commotion and shuffled over to the security guard to see what was going on. "Everything alright?"

The security guard proceeded to explain the scenario.

Peter made a mental note of this then went into the reception hall to tell Roger. "Hey, Rog. There's a woman out here swearing she knows you and insisting she be admitted into the reception. Yet she doesn't have a ticket and her name isn't on the guest list."

Roger suspected this would happen and was glad he and Lauren had planned ahead. He walked with Peter over to the door to get a peek at this unwanted guest. The moment he saw the woman's face, his stance tightened. "Dammit. What is she doing here?"

"Do you know her?"

"Unfortunately, yes. That's Melinda."

Peter gave her a brutal and unfriendly stare. "That's your ex?"

"Yup," Roger said, his voice hoarse with frustration. "Lauren and I have a restraining order filed against her."

"She needs to go then. Want me to get rid of her?"

Roger nodded. "Please."

"Will do, boss." Peter spoke with the security guard and together they rectified the situation.

At this point in the celebration, Jane handed her husband a folded up piece of paper. He grabbed it from her and stepped up front to the stage. The band ceased playing and the crowd settled. All eyes were now on him. "Good afternoon ladies and gentlemen. I asked for an autocue for my speech today, as I have a memory like a geriatric goldfish lately, but I was told that the budget had been stretched to capacity and any extras would have to be paid for out of my pocket. Knowing this made me realize that my wife handing me this piece of paper was good enough."

Chuckles spread throughout the reception hall.

"For those of you I have not yet had the privilege to meet, I'm Dr. Randy Hanson, Lauren's dad, and my wife Jane and I would like to welcome you all here today to celebrate the marriage of our daughter and Roger. A warm welcome to Rogers's parents, Gary and Sharon, his brother Peter and family, and all of our relatives and friends. I know a lot of you have travelled considerable distances to be here. Thank you all for coming. When I first started organizing this speech, I was told to keep it short, to avoid smutty jokes, and to try and remember names. I will do my best to heed that advice and get right to the point."

He unfolded the paper in his hand and smiled at his daughter before he continued. "I could say a few embarrassing things about Lauren, but seeing as she lived with me for eighteen years of her life, she probably knows more gossip about me than I know about her, so I have called a truce. I would, however, like to share one particular story with you. When Lauren was six years old, she went out to buy a small ice cream from the ice cream van. She returned with a double cone of strawberry and vanilla, hundreds of sprinkles on top, and the whole work of art was covered in strawberry sauce. I didn't get any change. It was at this point when I realized my daughter had expensive taste."

This story made Lauren's face flush, but their friends and family enjoyed it.

"Last Christmas, when Roger asked me for Lauren's hand in marriage, I remember thinking, I hope he picks the hand that keeps dipping into my pocket." He downed a glass of water, cleared his throat, and carried on. "Every father hopes his daughter will find a reliable, sensible, respectful, and considerate partner, and as much as you try not to interfere in their lives, you always hope your children will make the right choices in life. Lauren chose Roger. In Roger, I believe Lauren has met her perfect partner. Although we have not known Roger long, both Jane and I think he is everything one could hope for in a son-in-law. He has many good qualities, not least of which is an ability to appreciate the finer things in life. After all, he did marry our daughter didn't he? I have found that Roger is reliable, sensible, respectful, and considerate, and as this closely matches my own values, I think Lauren has made an excellent choice. I welcome Roger to the Hanson clan."

Roger replied by saying, "Thank you, Sir."

"I know you will be able to keep my daughter in the lifestyle in which she has become accustomed."

"I'll certainly do my best."

Randy continued his speech. "I would like to leave you with this thought. The quality of love and the duration of a marriage are in direct proportion to the depth of the commitment by both people involved. Commit yourselves wholeheartedly and unconditionally to the most important person in your life—each other." He held up his wineglass. "Now, if you would be upstanding, I would like you all to raise a glass for the health and happiness of the bride and groom, Lauren and Roger."

The entire theatre raised their glasses.

When Randy returned to his seat, Jim faked a cry. "I'm touched, man. Way to make the wedding emotions flow."

Randy was clearly unimpressed by Jim's lack of tact at such a solemn event. "Shut up, Jackass. This is my daughter's wedding."

"Seriously though, nice job, Bud."

"Thank you." Randy turned to Jane and asked, "Any tears from anyone?"

"A few." And some of them came from Randy. "I see one guilty party right here."

Randy tried to hide his emotions. "I always knew this day would come but never expected it to get to me like this. I now understand why your father said the things he said to me and cried at our wedding. I wish my dad was here to see this."

Jane reached over and squeezed his hand. "I know, Sweetie. I wish Mom was too."

When the group settled and wineglasses were returned to their positions on the table, Roger's father stepped up to the microphone.

"What is he doing?" Roger said when he saw him.

Lauren turned to look. "Looks like he's going up to say something."

"He told me he wasn't making a speech."

Gary stood on the stage and tapped the microphone, which caused feedback to squeal through the reception hall. "Sorry," he said. "Unlike Roger, I'm not used to standing in front of a microphone."

One of the band members adjusted it for him.

"Roger was not expecting me to stand up here to-night, and quite frankly, I wasn't planning to, but I have something I'd like to say." He took a quick sip from his glass. "When I married my wife, I had the wonderful privilege of gaining two incredible sons. I didn't know Roger until he was six years old, and when I first met him, he wasn't quite sure what to make of me. I would like to say he and I share many similarities, but that's just not true. I'm a sports enthusiast. He loves theatre. I prefer Sci-Fi. He likes the classics. I enjoy classic rock. He sings show tunes. The list goes on and on. One thing we do have in common is that we both hoped that one day he'd marry a funny, smart, beautiful, loving woman, just like his mother. Today, that dream came true. We love Lauren as much as we love our boys. She's like a daughter to us. We couldn't be happier in Roger's choice for a wife. I'm sure Peter and Amy will join Sharon and I in formally welcoming Lauren into our family. We wish them every joy and happiness in their future together." He raised his glass and everyone took a sip to commemorate the happy couple.

Roger was beyond touched. He stood up, pranced up to the stage, and gave Gary a hug. Truly a bonding moment for the two of them.

Jason took the microphone off the stand. In a fun, announcer–type voice, he heralded, "And now, ladies and gentlemen, the moment we've all been waiting for. Drumroll please." With drumroll pattering, Jason held his hand out to Roger and Lauren, prompting them to stand up. "Straight from the heart of Manhattan, seen dancing together for the first time as husband and wife in this one night only event, I proudly present to you the stars of our show tonight, Roger and Lauren Zellers."

Roger removed his suitcoat, took off his cufflinks and stuffed them in his pants pocket, then rolled up his sleeves. He pulled one red rose out of Lauren's bouquet and whispered something to the band. As the lights dimmed and the spotlight came on, Roger took Lauren's hand, handed her the rose, and they assumed position on the floor.

Instead of the traditional bride and groom slow dance, Roger and Lauren danced the tango. No one expected this, but then again many things about this wedding were unexpected. Jason thought it was great. He laughed and watched them with a huge smile on his face. Obviously they had been practicing together for some time.

At the end of the dance, Roger dipped Lauren back and kissed her. The entire theatre applauded. They certainly didn't disappoint when it came to making their wedding entertaining.

Throughout the evening, Roger saw many of their guests utilize the photo booth, and surprisingly more dug through the fun boxes on the tables playing with the toys inside. The dance floor quickly filled and people laughed, celebrated, and enjoyed this fun-themed wedding party. Roger couldn't have been more pleased. Their wedding was a huge success. But the biggest success was that he now had Lauren as his beautiful wife.

Roger stood with a glass of wine in his hand staring at his bride. Brandon, the photographer, was right next to him, changing the battery in his camera. "I have to say, this wedding of yours was the most fun I've had in a long time. Thanks for inviting me."

"You're welcome," Roger replied. "Thank you for taking pictures for us."

"It's my pleasure. I'm seriously considering expanding my photography business to weddings."

Roger was glad to hear that. "That's great. I can't wait to see the shots you've captured."

"I'm gonna need a few weeks to sort through and process all of these pictures."

"Of course," Roger replied. "No hurry. Lauren and I are going to be out of town for the next two weeks anyway."

Brandon changed his camera lens and fiddled with the focus knob. "You cutting the cake soon?"

Roger checked his watch. "Shouldn't be too much longer. Want to give everyone a chance to finish dinner first."

The cake cutting ceremony was a fun event. Lauren peeled the little *Phantom of the Opera* mask off the cake and stuck in on Roger's nose. He pulled it off and set it aside. Together, both controlled the knife. They carefully sliced their cake and fed a piece to each other, getting frosting all over their faces. Roger even went so far as to lick extra icing off of Lauren's fingers.

While the theatre staff dished up cake slices and served everyone, wedding guests demanded that Roger take the microphone and sing. Feeling pressured, and knowing that the hordes weren't going to let up until he satisfied their demands, Roger gave in. "Okay, okay, I'll sing, but Lauren's coming up here with me." He held his hand out and directed her to join him on stage. "Honey, will you sing with me?"

The guests encouraged her with cheers and whistles.

Timidly, she agreed.

Roger pulled two chairs onto the stage. Lauren sat in one, he sat in the other. He moved the microphone down, positioning it between them, then leaned over and whispered in her ear.

The theatre fell silent. Without musical accompaniment, he began to sing 'All I Ask of You' from *Phantom of the Opera*. After a few measures, Lauren chimed in. Her strong, beautiful voice resonated through the theatre. This was the first time anyone had heard them sing together, and this duet was absolutely breathtaking. They harmonized perfectly.

Moments later, Roger knelt down on one knee. Lauren rested her foot on his leg and he lifted her dress, exposing her thigh. Men in the room wolf whistled as Roger lovingly caressed her leg, well past the garter belt. This display was sexy and alluring, and by the look Lauren was giving him, some speculated that Roger was fondling in places he probably shouldn't have been. Then, making sure to seductively rub his hands back down her leg, he removed the garter and threw it over his shoulder. It landed right at Jason's feet.

All the single women, and even some young girls, swarmed around Lauren, hoping to catch the lucky bouquet. As soon as everyone was gathered, Lauren turned around and tossed the bouquet behind her. Gabby was the lucky recipient. When Lauren saw who had it, she turned her gaze to her brother and laughed.

The limo chauffeured Lauren and Roger away, and Gabby brought the bouquet over to Nathan. "Did you see?" she asked him.

371

"I see it. Nice catch. You'd be good at stealing passes on the court. I think you almost knocked that lady over."

"Maybe she should have moved out of my way."

"Wow!" Nathan teased her. "Getting a little aggressive there, aren't you Gab?"

"If someone tries to take something I want, then yes."

Nathan found this incredibly amusing. "That lady almost took an elbow to the face. You girls can really get into cat fights over those flowers, can't you?"

"Don't you know the tradition?" she asked him.

He lifted a shoulder. "Should I?"

"You seriously don't know?"

"Why would I know that?"

She rolled her eyes, disgusted that he didn't know the significance of the flowers.

"I'm sorry," he protested. "I don't stay up to date on wedding etiquette."

As guests began to leave, Gabby loaded gifts into the car.

Nathan grabbed a few and helped her. "Are you gonna tell me what it means or leave me hangin'?"

She snorted at him, but didn't acknowledge his question.

"If you'd explain it to me then maybe I'd understand why you girls fight over it." Images of the bouquet battle flashed through his head. It gave him the giggles. "I have to admit, that was probably the funniest damn thing I have ever seen. I'm surprised blood wasn't drawn."

She swung around with her hands on her hips. "The tradition is that the woman who catches the bride's bouquet will be the next to get married."

No wonder she was throwing such a fuss. He had blown it off as if it were some sort of game, but obviously Gabby catching the bouquet meant more to her than that. Now that he knew the significance of this, he felt like a jerk for teasing her. "I'm sorry. I didn't know."

"You laughed about it like it was some sort of joke," she complained. "Do you think marrying me is funny?"

That was not at all what he said. She was blowing this way out of proportion. "I never said that."

"Then why were you laughing?"

"I told you already. I didn't know what the whole bouquet thing was all about. To me it just looked like a bunch of women fighting over a few flowers."

She stuffed the boxes in the car and disappeared inside.

He trailed behind her. "Had I known how important it was to you, I wouldn't have teased you about it. Cut me some slack here." He gently grabbed her arm and turned her body so she was facing him. "How many weddings have I been to?"

"You went with me to my dad's wedding. You should have known," she declared.

"Honestly, Gab, I wasn't really paying that much attention."

She sneered at him, throwing cold stones with her eyes.

The more he opened his mouth, the deeper hole he dug himself into. He was to the point where he felt like no matter what he said, it was going to bury him further. "What do want me to say? I didn't know, okay? I'm sorry."

"Do you even pay attention to things like that?" Gabby argued.

"What's that supposed to mean?"

She growled at him and stormed off.

Nathan called out to her, "Gab, come on. Don't be like that. I'm sorry." Although he wasn't entirely sure what he was apologizing for.

Gabriella slinked further away.

Nathan stood there baffled, wondering what the hell he did that pissed her off so much.

Jane had never witnessed Nathan and Gabby squabble before. When she saw that Nathan was upset, she stepped closer to him. "Everything alright?"

"What did I do to deserve that?" Nathan protested.

"What happened?" Jane asked.

"Gabby is mad at me because I didn't understand the significance of the bouquet catching cat fight. Now she thinks I'm some sort of insensitive ass for not paying attention to things like that."

"Maybe she's trying to hint something to you, Honey," Jane suggested.

"Hint what?" Nathan asked, not fully understanding. Then it clicked. "A ring? Is that what she's trying to tell me? That she's ready for a marriage proposal?"

Jane gently grazed her hand across his shoulder and went to help take down decorations.

Nathan let out a big sigh. Hoping to make amends, he walked up behind Gabby and gently kissed the nape of her neck.

"Stop it," she insisted.

Nathan did it again.

"Quit doing that."

"You're right. I should have paid more attention to small details like that, then I would have known the significance of the flowers and could have supported you in your excitement." His hand wrapped around her waist and gradually worked its way to her tummy. "You know I love you," he whispered in her ear. "And I do want to marry you, but we need to have consistent flowing income before we go there, Gab. You know that."

"I start my teaching job in August," she reminded him.

"I know. But you won't see your first paycheck until the end of September." He took her hand and drew her nearer. "I don't want us to rush into marriage if we're not financially ready for it. With my medical school schedule, I honestly don't know how many hours I'll be able to work at Dad's clinic. I think we need to wait until you get a steady income and I figure out what my schedule is going to look like." Not wanting her to feel like he was blowing this off, he offered an alternative. "Tell you what. Since we're both looking at apartments off campus, why don't we just get one together? That will give us time to examine our finances and figure this out."

Her smile beamed across the room. "Really?"

"Yes."

Gabby clasped her arms around his neck and brought her lips to his. His tall, toned body and her small frame morphed into one.

When Jane saw that they had resolved their differences, she continued to clean up, leaving the young couple to carry on with their business.

Chapter Thirty

Lauren and Roger stopped by their apartment to drop off her dress and his tux before they picked up their luggage for the Bahamas and returned to the Hudson Theatre Hotel to claim their bridal suite. Passion brewed quickly, and it wasn't long before intense breathing, moaning, and gasping echoed though the room. Making love to Lauren was intensely hot. The chemistry between them was erotic. The sound of release Lauren emitted, the sensation of her naked body pressed against his skin, and the pleasure radiating from his pelvis to all parts of his body completely fulfilled him. Lauren's breathing quickened, and her limbs tightened around him. Simultaneously, he felt his own tension rising. Climax was imminent, and there wasn't a damn thing he could do to stop it. His strength gave out and he collapsed on top of her. Still connected, with their sweaty limbs tangled together, his racing heart gradually began to slow down.

Panting, Roger kissed his wife on the lips. "Mmm," he moaned seductively. "You are amazing."

She released a pleasurable sign and relaxed her muscles. "Only because I'm with you."

He nibbled on her neck, slowly working his lips up to her ear. His eyes closed, enjoying the sensation of being this close to her.

They repositioned themselves, forcing them to disconnect. Roger rested on his side with Lauren spooned in front of him. With her naked back pressed against his chest, he leaned on his elbow and propped his head up so he could see her face. "Today was an incredible day."

"It was." She gripped his hand with hers. "And I have a handsome, sexy husband to show for it."

He touched his lips on her shoulder. "Since you're my wife now, there are a few things you should know."

"Uh oh," she teased him. "What deep, dark secrets have you been hiding?"

He tittered at her banter. "It's nothing bad. When we get back from our honeymoon, we need to set up a joint bank account. I have a secondary account as well, one I never told you about."

"Oh?"

"It's an emergency account, and the funds are not to be used unless all other resources have been exhausted and it becomes absolutely necessary. There's quite a bit of money in there."

"How much?" she asked out of sheer curiosity.

"A little over $600,000."

This was astonishing amount of money. "Wait a minute." She sat up. "You have an account with over a half million dollars in it?"

"We have an account, and yes. I also have a life insurance policy for $500,000 should, God forbid, anything happen. I'm going to add you as my beneficiary and set up a policy for you when we get back."

Lauren released an exasperated sigh. "We have so much to do. I have to get my name changed, we have to get our marriage license turned into the county courthouse, bank accounts set up…There's more to do after the wedding than planning the wedding itself."

Roger laughed at her analysis.

"Oh sure, you laugh. But you have it easy," she complained. "You don't have to change your name on everything."

"No, I do not. One of the advantages of being the groom instead of the bride," he teased.

"Speaking of which, I wanted to ask you something about my stage name. You're the expert on this sort of thing."

"I don't know about that."

"I'm serious," she said. "Everyone knows me as Lauren Hanson. I've performed under that name, and that's how the professionals in this business know me. Advice on this?"

He turned the question back to her. "What do you want to do?"

"I don't know. That's why I'm asking you."

"Well, it depends," he said. "You have a couple of options as far as stage name goes."

"Like what?"

"You could stick with Hanson and have no affiliation with the name Zellers at all."

"No. I'm proud to be your wife. I don't want to hide that."

He was glad she opted out of that. "I'm proud to be your husband too. You know what a lot of women in this business do? They hyphenate their stage name."

"Hanson-Zellers?"

"It's certainly something to consider," he advised. "If you hyphenate your name, people who know you as Hanson will see that it's still you, but at the same time they'll know you're my wife. Honestly, Honey, you're just starting your career. It's not going to matter what name you choose. But if you seriously want people to know that Lauren Hanson and Lauren Zellers are the same person, you might want to hyphenate your stage name. It's up to you though." He hoped she would use his name, but he wanted her to decide what was best for her. Trying to persuade her a bit, he offered one more suggestion. "You could just go with Zellers. Legally, and in my eyes, you're Mrs. Zellers. But I'll support whatever stage name you decide to go with."

She rolled onto her back and brushed the hair off his forehead with her finger. "Thank you, Sweetie."

"There's one other thing I need to discuss with you," he said, looking down at her. "I had a conversation with your father today. Since you are my wife now, and you are my financial responsibility, your father is no longer paying for school for you."

This was not news Lauren expected to hear. Why would her father abruptly cut her off like that? And if her father wasn't covering the costs of school, how was she going to pay for it? "He told you that?"

Roger explained, "No. He debated it with me, but in the end I was far more persuasive than he was. We're married, and the expenses we have are our shared responsibility, which includes Juilliard. I told him we would cover your tuition. I was quite insistent about this, Lauren, and your father had no choice but to give in."

Picturing Roger and her father debating over finances made her giggle. "I bet Daddy put up quite a fight though."

"He tried, but I won that debate."

Chapter Thirty-One

In the morning, they departed from LaGuardia Airport and traveled to Miami, where they had a two-hour layover before they caught their connecting flight to the Bahamas. Neither one of them had ever been to the Bahamas before and were excited about this adventure.

The Island of Great Exuma was truly an idyllic getaway. The landscape was absolutely gorgeous, and the weather was perfect with soft breezes and warm, non-humid temperatures. Some of the lushest vegetation they had ever seen blanketed the island. Mango and papaya grew wild. Pink and red hibiscus, yellow trumpet-shaped flowers, and sweet smelling plumeria enhanced the scenery. Poinciana flowers were in full bloom with their vividly orange blossoms. Many lignum trees, with glossy green leaves and abundant purple and blue flowers, lined the roads. Bougainvillea in many colors, strange brown fruit of the tamarind tree, coconut palms, and mangroves added to the richness of plants in this area. And birds—there seemed to be birds everywhere. A flock of West Indian flamingo and a few egrets flew overhead, and warblers and sparrows twittered away. The shoreline had golden beaches with sand as soft as flour, and the water was an unbelievably clear aqua-marine. Everything was laid-back. No high-rises, no taxis, no crowded streets.

Lauren happily surveyed their surroundings. "Roger, look at this place. It's gorgeous."

"Yes it is," he agreed.

"And it's so romantic."

"That's the idea." He gave her a suggestive wink.

Deep within the peaceful waters of Emerald Bay, Sandals Resort brought unprecedented luxury to the easygoing rhythms of the Bahamian Islands. This privileged enclave was specifically designed to be a romantic getaway for couples. The Bahamian-style architecture of elegant villas and suites harmonized with nature. Roger and Lauren fully anticipated being able to indulge in a world of heavenly togetherness, where endless beaches, intimate restaurants, and exotic gardens allowed for perfect interludes of exceptional privacy and romance. They could stroll along serene garden pathways, wade in hidden grotto pools, or dive into the deep blue sea. Roger hoped, that for at least part of their trip, they would dive under the covers as well.

He reserved an elegant and romantic honeymoon beachfront suite located in the calm of the resort's expansive lawns. Their walkout one-bedroom suite had an oversized bedroom and a large living room decorated with shell inspired décor. The two rooms were separated by French-style doors. The master bedroom had a plush king-size bed, and both the living room and bedroom featured large patios with teak beach chairs for sunning. An outdoor dining area with a double hammock gave them a private place to enjoy a romantic meal by sunset or lie together, undisturbed, to view the stars at night. Both patios offered sweeping views of the beach and Emerald Bay. It was truly paradise, and the perfect place to spend their honeymoon.

Roger reclined on the bed, hoping to entice Lauren to join him. "This is cozy. And big. Lots of room to roll around."

But she was too interested in checking out their magnificent accommodations, starting with the bathroom. "Rog, look at this tub."

He got up to check it out. The luxurious bathroom had a large soaking bathtub. Already he was getting ideas about what they could do to each other in there. "We're going to have to try that out tonight," he suggested, hinting what he had in store for her later.

She journeyed back into the living room area, where a bottle of wine and two wineglasses waited for them, along with a serving tray full of small fruit-topped tarts. She picked one up and ate it.

Roger crept up behind her and wrapped his arms around her waist. She picked up another fruit tart and fed it to him. But as she did, he sucked on her finger with a lustful gaze. "Mmm. Sweet and juicy." He chewed the tart and swallowed then slowly moved his hand up her shirt. "I know something else sweet and juicy I wouldn't mind getting a taste of." He sensuously nibbled on her neck while his hand wandered up to her breast.

All day, the only thing Roger seemed to have on his mind was sex. Every comment he made, every look he gave her, and every touch he initiated had some sort of sexual undertone attached to it. Lauren knew what he was thinking. He had made it pretty obvious. "The wine?" she guessed, knowing damn well that wasn't what he meant.

"No. Not the wine." He grazed his tongue across her neck, trying to seduce her.

She picked up a bunch of grapes and held them in front of his face. "These grapes?"

He took them out of her hand and set them back on the tray. "No, not those either. Let me give you a hint." He reached down and unfastened her shorts. One hand moved up to her tummy while the other snuck its way into her panties. He fondled around in there as he nibbled on her earlobe. Every touch was provocative and sexy. She easily became aroused. When he moved his hand up her bra, her nipple hardened between his fingertips. "I want you," he whispered.

He removed her blouse. As her silky skin was exposed, he offered kisses across her shoulder and collarbone, slowly making his way to her lips. He enticed her with his tongue while he moved his hands up the middle of her back to unlatch her bra. He slipped the straps off her shoulders and suckled on the soft flesh underneath. Lauren threw her head back. He worked his way up her neck and moved his kisses back to her lips while he lifted her off the floor and carried her to the bed. He gently eased her onto the mattress and crawled over top of her.

She unbuttoned his shirt, taking it one button at a time, starting from the top. When the last one was released, she slid the shirt off and let it fall on the bed.

He clasped both of her hands in his and held her arms over her head; his naked chest rubbed against her breasts. This sensation was a definite turn on. He forced his pelvis against hers, hoping she'd respond.

She thrust her hips, telling him she was ready.

In response to her cue, he moved his hands down and slipped her panties over her hips. She helped by kicking them off the rest of the way.

Roger watched as she unbuttoned his pants and slowly pulled the zipper down. He loved it when she undressed him. It was erotic and sexy. She rubbed her hand across his skin then slid his pants down to the floor. He responded by caressing the length of her leg, from her ankle up to her thigh. He placed his hands under her buttocks and slid her down to the corner of the bed. He stood on the floor and aligned his pelvis with hers. He used his body to spread her legs then gently placed his hand on her knee, giving it a soft kiss before he eased in. To him, penetration was the best part of sex. He liked to make this part last longer by teasing her a little before he slid all the way in. It built up pressure and increased desire, which made her want it more. He could tell Lauren liked it, because she moaned in ecstasy and cried out to him. He tried to make that feeling last as long as possible.

When the sun went down, Roger and Lauren dressed in evening attire and enjoyed a romantic candlelight dinner at the hotel's elegant Italian restaurant. After dinner, they returned to their room for the night. Lauren slipped out of her clothes and into a silk robe while Roger popped the cork on a bottle of wine and poured two glasses.

"Honey, I was looking at this brochure earlier and thought we'd check out this area called Three Sisters Rock tomorrow," Roger suggested. "We can go snorkeling and look at some tide pools. The concierge said there's a nice beach over there, and at night, you can view a pretty amazing sunset."

She stepped out of the bedroom and into the living room, tying her robe around her waist. "Sounds great."

Roger picked up both glasses and handed one to Lauren. She took a small sip. To allow fresh air into the room, he walked over to the patio door and opened it widely. He stepped outside and looked up at the nighttime sky. Many stars and constellations could be seen. "Wow!" he said, beholding this heavenly scene. "Come out here and look at this view."

She stepped onto the patio and stood by his side. Her arm went around his waist, his around her shoulder. "It's beautiful," Lauren said.

"I love New York, but it's nice to be able to look outside at night and see stars instead of headlights and billboard signs." The waves lapped in the background. It was such a relaxing sound. "Can you hear that?" he asked, loving the noise vacation his ears were getting.

She squinted her eyebrows. "I don't hear anything except the waves."

"I know," he concurred. "That's my point. It's great." He sat in the hammock and propped himself up. "Sweetheart, come sit with me."

Lauren willingly joined him.

They lounged together listening to the waves, gazing at the stars, and enjoying this quiet bonding time as they sipped on wine. As soon as Lauren's glass was empty, she hopped up to refill it.

"What are you doing?" Roger asked her.

"Getting another glass. You want one?"

"I haven't finished this one yet." He held up his glass to show her.

She tipped hers upside down. "Mine's empty."

"Then by all means, get another glass."

When she returned, she had not only a full glass of wine, but also a bunch of grapes in her hand.

"What's that you've got there?" he asked, curious as to what she planned to do with those.

"You want some grapes?" She handed him the bunch and crawled back into the hammock.

"Do I get to feed them to you?"

"If you would like."

385

"Oh, I definitely would like." He picked one off the stem and stuck it in her mouth. As he did, she enclosed her lips around the tip of his finger, sucking on it erotically. He gave her a seductive glance. "Someone feeling provocative tonight?"

She held his hand and kissed the tip of each finger one by one.

This sensation gave him tingles.

She gulped her wine, chugging down half the glass. "Do you think I'm sexy?"

His head flinched back. "What kind of a question is that? Of course I do. You're beautiful, sexy…" He took another sip of his wine then popped a grape in his mouth. "Why would you ask me that?"

She tried to explain, "I get the feeling that people see me as a cute, sweet, innocent girl, but I don't want that image. I want other husbands to be jealous because Roger has a hot wife."

Although he found her comment amusing, she had a good point. In public, she was modest and discreet. But even in her modest attire, Roger thought she looked hot. Other men noticed too, but Roger didn't mind. If they were jealous because his wife was gorgeous, that was perfectly fine with him. "Oh, believe me, Honey, you are most definitely sexy. After seeing you in that wedding dress yesterday, I can pretty much guarantee that no one doubts your sex appeal. That dress looked hot on you."

Lauren giggled. "Really?"

"Oh yeah. I had a hard time practicing self-restraint yesterday, especially after seeing you in that dress. It definitely turned me on. But you always turn me on."

Lauren downed the rest of her wine. When her glass was empty, she set it on the table next to Roger's. "Get up."

"Why?"

"Because, I want a bath." She hopped to her feet and held her hands out to Roger.

He seductively raised an eyebrow.

"Come on." She pulled him out of the hammock and led him inside, closing the patio door behind them.

While Lauren flipped through the music channels for some appropriate mood music, Roger drew a hot bath, putting bubbles in it. As the tub filled up, he poured two more glasses of wine and carefully placed them on the edge of the bath. When the tub was full, he turned the water off and sprinkled it with rose pedals, leaving the whole room swathed in the sweet scent of roses. He stripped down naked and crawled inside the steaming water. "Lauren, Honey," he called to her. "Come join me."

She came into the bathroom and saw Roger sitting in a tub full of bubbles and rose petals, holding a glass of wine in his hand. This scene made her giggle.

He sipped some of his wine and held the other glass out to her. "I have some wine for you, but you have to come in here to get it."

She untied her robe and let it fall to the floor.

With a lustful eye, Roger watched her sexy, curvy, feminine, naked body slowly crawl into the tub with him. When she settled in, he handed her a glass. "So, what shall we toast to?"

"To love?" she suggested.

"To marriage," he countered.

"To us," she submitted.

"To us and our life together," he added.

They gently clanged their glasses together and each one took a drink, at which time Roger set his glass on the edge of the tub and pulled Lauren onto his lap with one leg on either side of him. "This is nice." He rested his hands on her hips and gazed at her beautiful face. "Sensuous. Intimate."

He tried to take the wineglass out of her hand, but she quickly chugged the rest of it, dribbling it down her chin. Lauren wasn't much of a drinker. The fact that she was downing glasses of wine like this amused him. "You feeling ok?"

"I feel fine. Why?"

"I think you might have had a little too much wine tonight."

She tittered at his comment. "You know what I want?"

"What do you want?" he questioned, curious to know what was on her mind.

"I want you to wash every inch of my body."

This sounded extremely sensual. "Every inch?"

She nodded. "Every inch. And if you do a good job, I'll give you a reward."

Lauren often initiated sex, but this was far beyond anything she would normally do. Either the alcohol was getting to her or she felt dirty tonight. "Are you drunk?" he teased.

"No."

He eyed her with a sideways grin. "Are you sure?"

"I'm fine." She meandered her finger down the middle of his chest then thrust her pelvis into his.

"Ok, let me rephrase that. Are you feeling horny then?"

"What do you think?"

She had a certain sexiness in her voice, something he'd never heard from her before. Trying to entice him, she stuck her finger in her mouth, licked it seductively, and slowly pulled it out. Whatever she was doing, it was getting him excited. "I think it's a little of both," he deduced.

She reached into the water and handed him a bath sponge covered in bubbles. "Be a good boy and do as you're told."

He liked this spicy, kinky side of her. Maybe now that they were married, she felt more loose and adventurous, or maybe she felt particularly frisky tonight. He really didn't care what the reason was, he was going to comply with her request without question.

Roger and Lauren spent their days hidden away in their own private straw-roofed Balinese gazebo in a quiet area on the beach. They ordered tropical drinks and fruit trays to take with them and curled up in each other's arms on the comfortable cushion beds inside the gazebo. They took mid-afternoon naps and enjoyed the barefoot elegance of oceanside dining, where they sank their toes into the soft white sand under a Caribbean thatched roof as they indulged in local specialty seafood. They explored the natural wonders of the islands and strolled across secluded beaches.

Snorkeling and swimming in the turquoise waters around Three Sisters Rock was an incredible experience. Many of the islands' shores were made of limestone rock, which extended into the sea, presenting countless crevices, ridges, and holes to explore. These structures created an ideal habitat for various marine life, as it provided not only hiding spaces from predators but also protection from the powerful tides. Creatures abounded in this area of the Exuma Islands. Crabs and sea urchins hid under ledges while sea anemones and limpets attached themselves to the rocks. Sea plants swayed in the sea currents, and a wide variety of colorful fish swam around the rock formations. Closer to shore, Roger and Lauren observed peacock worms, rock oysters, blue crabs, and clubbed finger coral. The tidal pool revealed common hermit crabs, snails, urchins, and starfish. It was a spectacular, watery paradise.

Roger rolled up his khaki pant legs and unbuttoned his white short-sleeved cotton button-up shirt, exposing his chest to the sun and air. Lauren's light, breezy, pastel yellow sundress flapped in the soft summer breeze. They had their arms around each other, each carrying their own shoes, as the waves came onto the shore soaking their feet, ankles, and toes.

Lauren kicked the water, getting Roger wet.

"Hey," he retorted with a frisky, evil eye. "Don't start something you can't finish, Mrs. Zellers."

She smiled playfully. "Oh yeah? And what is Mr. Zellers going to do about it?" When the next wave came, she splashed him again.

"Alright. You're gonna get it."

They both dropped their shoes on the sand and Lauren took off down the beach with Roger chasing her. He grabbed her from behind and brought her down into the wet sand with him, right as a wave came to shore. Both of them got drenched. They rolled around on the sand for a while, her trying to escape, him tickling her as they both laughed. When he was finally able to get a good grip on her, he picked her up and carried her into deeper waves.

"Don't you dare," she warned.

"Remember who started this." He dropped her in the water.

She came up for air and splashed him. He laughed and splashed her back then lifted her out of the water

390

and carried her onto shore as a man carries his bride over the threshold. She put her arms around his neck and drew him closer.

Roger eased her onto the soft sand. He lay down next to her and propped himself up on his elbow, leaning over top of her. He gazed into her hypnotic green eyes. While he cradled her head in his hand, he gently placed his other hand on her waist. When the tide came up and washed over their legs and feet, Roger closed his eyes and kissed his bride. It was a picture perfect scene.

After a quick shower and dinner, Roger and Lauren decided to see what kind of nightlife the resort offered. They found a night spot that appeared to be hosting some sort of amateur Karaoke Night. Roger turned to Lauren and grinned. "Wanna check it out?"

"Yes."

They strolled inside, hand in hand, and took a seat at a table near the front. Most of the people stepping up to the microphone couldn't sing very well, but then again, it was amateur karaoke. Singers browsed through the song choices, stopping at the first one they knew. Then they'd grab the microphone, stand on stage, and follow along with the karaoke monitor, singing off rhythm and off key.

Roger hadn't sung karaoke in years, but he had that itch to be on stage. As karaoke was about to close, he and Lauren took their turn as the last performers of the evening. When they got on stage, Roger snagged two bar stools—one for Lauren and one for himself. He set them side by side on the stage. There was a second microphone nearby. He removed it from the stand and handed it to Lauren. When he found 'Tonight, I Celebrate My Love', he cued up the song and took position on the barstool next to Lauren, grabbing the second mic.

The song began to play and the room fell silent. Lyrics scrolled across the screen, but the young newlyweds knew the song so well that instead of following the monitor, they faced each other and sang from the heart. Their powerful voices rang out in beautiful harmony, expressing intense emotion and meaning every word that left their lips. Their rendition didn't sound like amateur karaoke at all. It was perfectly pitched and beautifully harmonized. Hotel patrons poured in to get a peek at who was singing this amazing duet.

When the song was over, Lauren and Roger embraced in a kiss. The entire room applauded. Roger put the microphones back in their stands and the DJ changed Karaoke Night into an all-night dance party. Several people came over and introduced themselves, wanting to know more about where Roger and Lauren learned to sing, how long they'd been performing together, and complimenting them on their beautiful voices. It quickly became apparent that these two were professionals.

Most big name performers on Broadway, like Roger, were well-known in the local Broadway community and among theatregoers, but the average Joe who had no connection with theatre generally had no idea who they were. Theatre was Roger's life. He thrived on pleasing audiences, but never became involved in Broadway theatre because of money or fame. He didn't necessarily like the recognition associated with being a leading man on Broadway and tried to keep his personal life as far away from the stage as possible. Unlike world-famous actors and musicians, Roger could walk into the streets of Manhattan and carry on with his life without being mauled by fans or under constant scrutiny of the tabloids. The further away he was from all of that the better. He was glad his name stayed local. He had a local base of loyal Broadway theatre fans, but to most people, Roger Zellers was just an average guy.

On their final day in the Bahamas, Roger and Lauren got out from under the covers, ate a refreshing breakfast of locally grown, fresh-sliced guava and mango, then gallivanted out to the beach and found a group of people playing beach volleyball. Roger was a good volleyball player. He could spike rather well and had a pretty powerful serve. He was also quite competitive. Lauren had never seen that side of him before, but enjoyed witnessing the athlete in him.

For lunch, they visited a local bar and grill. Roger ordered a soup called souse, a simple broth made with onions, lime juice, celery, peppers, and meat. He and Lauren split an order of lobster wraps, and they tried a plate of Conch Fritters, which were fried balls of chopped conch mollusk dipped in spicy calypso sauce. This dining experience of local cuisine was refreshingly tasty.

This bar and grill specialized in a local cocktail called Paradise Punch. It contained Campari orange, light rum, coconut rum, and pineapple juice. Roger wasn't a rum drinker and he didn't normally like mixed drinks, but to experience the culture, he decided to see what this local punch was all about. When it was brought to the table, he took a sip. Immediately, he puckered his face, as if he had eaten something sour.

Lauren laughed at the funny face he made. "Not good?"

This local 'punch' definitely packed a punch. "It's really potent. You'll get you plastered quick drinking that." He handed her the glass. "You want some?"

She turned her nose up. "No thanks."

He opted not to drink the rest of it.

Roger overheard other resort guests talking about The Exuma Banks side of the islands, which had two beautiful beaches and an abundance of gorgeous fish. Roger and Lauren decided to check it out. They spent the afternoon among sea turtles, marine birds, and fish of every kind. They even saw some fascinating land animals, like endangered iguanas and a small mammal called the Hutia, which was a member of the rodent family and looked like a small beaver minus the tail and large teeth.

On the beach, they discovered something called stromatolites—rare prehistoric rocks that were alive and grew like coral reefs. Roger found these unusual formations fascinating. "These are just odd," he declared.

"Why?" Lauren asked.

"Are they rocks? Are they not rocks? What the hell are these things?"

"They're fossils, Sweetie," Lauren clarified.

"According to this," he read from the brochure he had in his hand, "they're some sort of lime-secreting bacteria that produce oxygen. That doesn't sound like a rock or a fossil. Sounds more like some kind of plant." He poked it with a stick.

Lauren laughed at him. "It's not road kill. Why are you poking at it?"

"Because it's weird."

"So? You thought Ruth Porter was weird. You gonna poke her with a stick?"

"Why would I do that?" he asked, thinking that was a ridiculous suggestion, although it was kind of funny. "You know, maybe if I do poke her with a stick she'll quit making that god awful, high-pitched screeching sound she makes all the time. Whoever told that woman she could sing must have been deaf. She sounds like a damn mandrake."

Roger's sarcastic analogy made Lauren roll with laughter.

"I'm serious. I honestly think a rutting zebra is more on pitch than she is. She's probably the most annoying person I've ever been forced to be in a room with for an extended period of time."

"I've heard worse," Lauren stated.

"That sucks for you then. Do me a favor, next time we're anywhere near her vicinity, take my hand and run the other way as fast as you can. I really don't know if I can handle being subjected to that again."

Lauren held Roger's hand and together, they continued their adventure along the beach.

Fish weren't the only thing that liked to swim in these waters. There was an area along the beach where the scrub met the sand. Some pigs were lying in the scrub, but as soon as these pigs heard the dull vibration of a boat engine, they rose up from their naps and swam out to greet the incoming vessels. One of them even tried to hop into the boat.

Roger got a kick out of watching these swimming pigs. He decided to be brave and venture out to greet one.

"Roger, what are you doing?" Lauren asked.

"I want to pet one."

"That thing is gonna bite you."

"It is not. It's just a pig, Lauren. They're not vicious creatures." He crept up to the animal and squatted down to its level. "Here, piggy, piggy, piggy."

Lauren laughed at him, thinking he was nuts.

He held out his hand, trying to coax the animal to come closer. The pig snorted and moseyed toward him. When it got close enough to touch, Roger patted it on its rump. "See, he's a nice pig." The pig snorted contently, seeming to enjoy the human contact. "Maybe we should get a pet pig."

Lauren stared at him as if he had lost his mind. "I think all this sun is frying your brain. We are not getting a pig."

Roger put on a pouty face and hung his head playfully. He didn't really want a pig and wasn't really sad, but he pretended like the pig was. He looked at this creature and said, "Sorry, little piggy. The wife says no." He patted it one more time then stood up to rejoin his wife.

Lauren started giggling.

"What?" Roger asked, wondering what was so funny.

"It's following you."

Roger turned around. Sure enough that pig was right behind him. "Great, now it won't leave me alone."

"It was your idea to mess with it."

He tried to shoo it away. It happily snorted and continued to walk toward him. "Go away piggy."

Lauren couldn't stop laughing. "He likes you."

Roger clasped Lauren's hand and said, "Let's run. His little legs will never keep up."

Together, they ran off the beach. When they got a good distance away, they both looked behind them and the pig was nowhere in sight. Roger chuckled over this incident. "This shall forever be known as the swimming pig fiasco."

As the day came to a close, they stood with arms around each other on the soft white beach viewing the spectacular sunset. "This vacation was the most fun I've ever had," Roger remarked. "We need to come back here again. The Bahamas is definitely on my list of favorite places to visit. And the entire experience was even better because I got to spend it all with you." He gazed at his wife with a content smile on his face. "I love you, Mrs. Zellers."

She smiled back at him. "I love you too."

When the sun finally faded into the water, Roger used the opportunity to steal a kiss.

Chapter Thirty-Two

Ah. New York City, that thriving metropolis. The cauldron of activity that crackled with energy—bodies barreling in all directions, fluid, noisy, glittering with neon and gargantuan flashing electronic billboards—the cacophony of unmitigated and unmistakable sights and sounds. Honking horns, an abundance of yellow taxis, flashing lights, skyscrapers, and the smell of street corner hotdog carts greeted Roger and Lauren upon their return. The city seemed to be on steroids this morning, and everyone had about two dozen cups of coffee before breakfast. They were definitely back to reality. It was time to shake off the vacation sand from the lackadaisical rhythms of island life and reestablish some discipline.

Aside from getting her name legally changed on both her driver's license and her social security card. Lauren and Roger planned to spend the afternoon going to the bank, talking to the insurance agent, and taking care of other marriage business. But before dealing with all that craziness, Roger strolled down the street a few blocks and met Jason for a cup of coffee at Starbucks.

As soon as they saw each other, they greeted with a handshake and a hug. "Hey, Rog," Jason said rather boisterously. "Welcome back!"

"Thank you."

They stepped up to the counter to order. "How's it feel waking up every morning being a married man?"

Roger smiled the biggest smile Jason had ever seen. "I love being married. I am so happy, Jason. I can't even describe it."

"I can tell. You have a huge smile on your face." They grabbed their cups and claimed a table. "Your wedding was badass. Everyone I talked to said they had a fabulous time. It was entertaining and funny as hell. Definitely a memorable experience."

"That's what Lauren and I were going for. Saw you and Bailey smooching away."

Jason grinned bashfully. "A little."

That was an understatement. "A little? You were all over each other. Things must be going pretty well."

"Let's put it this way," Jason explained. "You weren't the only one having sex on your wedding night."

A canny smirk crept onto Roger's face. "Is that right?"

"Yup. I'd almost forgotten how intense it was."

"What do you mean?"

"It had been five years."

Roger bowed his brows. "You haven't had sex in five years?"

"Think about it, Rog. How many serious relationships have I had since we met?"

"One. I mean you've dated, but…"

"Exactly. I don't sleep around, and the last woman I was with was Cassandra. That was five years ago."

This made sense, now that Jason mentioned it. "Well, congratulations then!"

"Thank you," Jason replied with a chuckle.

"But seriously," Roger declared. "I'm glad things are going well with you and Bailey."

"So far so good. How was the honeymoon?"

Roger took a sip of his coffee. "Imagine having an hour long orgasm while angels massage your shoulders and the Mormon Tabernacle Choir sings the concluding refrain from Carl Orff's Carmina Burana over and over until the sky shatters."

Jason almost rolled out of his seat. "That good, huh?"

"The Bahamas were incredible, and the weather couldn't have been more perfect. Think it stayed about 78 the entire time we were there. It was absolutely gorgeous."

"Did you two actually get out of your room?" Jason teased.

"We got out. You know, I never thought it was possible to have too much sex, but clearly Lauren and I have disproved that theory."

"Why?"

"I have severe muscle fatigue. Both of us are sore and…" he gritted his teeth and squinted his eyes in pain. "It's a little tender down there. Think we might have overdone it. When it gets to the point where you experience more discomfort than pleasure then it's time to give it a rest."

Jason remarked, "That explains why you're walking kind of funny."

"Our honeymoon was unbelievable. We really spent some quality time together, and I learned a few things about my wife that I didn't know before. It was bonding and intimate on many levels."

Jason tried to imagine the intensity. "That's great. I'm really happy for you, Roger." He held up his coffee cup. "Cheers."

Roger tipped his cup and took another drink.

Monday morning, rehearsal began for *Crazy For You*. The cast had choreography to learn, songs to practice, comedic scenes to act out, and lines to memorize before for the scheduled premiere August 1st.

Roger loved being able to work with his wife on this production. Even though Lauren only had an ensemble role, she was still with him every day during rehearsal and even shared several scenes with him.

After a week of rehearsals, Lauren was called in to talk to the director. Roger waited outside wondering what was being discussed behind closed doors. When Lauren emerged, Roger immediately approached her. "What was that all about?"

"The director wanted to talk to me."

"Well, I figured that." He looked over at the director's door. "What were you talking about?"

"He wants me to understudy for the role of Polly.

Roger's jaw dropped to the floor. "Seriously?"

Lauren bit her lip and nodded.

Roger took her in his arms and lifted her off the ground. "Alright! That is wonderful news."

"It looks like I have lines to memorize now."

"I can help you with that," Roger said. "Polly has a few solos and some dance scenes you'll need to work on too."

"I know," Lauren replied. "I'm excited, but the chances of me actually playing her on stage are pretty slim."

"You never know," Roger encouraged her. "Things do happen. I've had understudies cover for me on quite a few occasions. I was out for two nights once because I had laryngitis so bad there was no way I could have done the show. I couldn't talk, let alone sing. I've gone out of town, had family issues come up, and twisted the crap out of my ankle right before a show and had to sit out a night. It happens. Not that I wish anything bad to happen to Sienna, but realistically, she will most likely miss at least one performance."

"That's true."

"I'm proud of you, Sweetheart. Nice job." He grabbed their bag and threw it over his shoulder. "Working as an understudy is going to add more to your salary, at least it should."

"I know," she said with a smile.

"We'll schedule a meeting with my union rep."

Prior to this production, Roger insisted that Lauren join the Actor's Equity Association, of which he was a member. The Equity was a labor union that represented the world of live theatrical performers. They negotiated wages and working conditions and provided a wide range of benefits to their members, including health and pension plans. Now that Lauren was a member, wage negotiations would flow much smoother.

"Which reminds me," he said. "I called the AEA about your medical card. They said they mailed it. Should get it either today or tomorrow."

"Good, because I need to have my prescription renewed. After this week, I'm not on Daddy's insurance anymore."

"Is he going to call it in, or do we need to find you a new doctor?" Roger asked.

"No, he'll call it in. I just need to give him the insurance information."

"The Tony's are next weekend."

Lauren had completely forgotten. "Oh, that's right."

"You haven't looked at dresses yet, have you?"

"No. With the wedding going on, trying to get my name changed, and this show, I forgot about it."

Trying to keep her from having some sort of stress-induced anxiety attack, he did his best to calm her. "It's okay. Just make it a point to do that."

"I'll go with Lacy tomorrow."

The Tony Award production team asked Roger to put on the mask one last time to sing 'Music of the Night' as part of a Broadway musical montage for this event. Of course he agreed. Being a part of this gave him the opportunity to be the Phantom one more time. Although he didn't have a Tony nomination, simply because he wasn't in a production eligible for one, his performance in *Phantom of the Opera* earned him several honors: the Theatregoer's Choice Award for Best Actor in a Musical, Viewers' Choice Theatre Award, a Drama Desk Award, and the Critic's Choice Theatre Award for Outstanding Actor in a Takeover Role. Aside from the Tony he already had displayed on his fireplace mantle, he now had four other awards to show off. Not too shabby of a showing.

The night before the premiere, the Imperial Theatre buzzed backstage with the last full dress rehearsal of *Crazy For You*. Roger warmed up by loosening his arms, stretching, and tapping out some basic rhythms. As he stared out at the empty seats, the lead actress, Sienna Montoya, hobbled into the theatre on crutches. Roger stopped dead in his tracks. "Oh no, Sienna, what did you do?" He trotted down the stairs and met her in the aisle.

"Nice, huh?" she huffed. "I was mountain biking with my nephews, and I crashed and burned."

Feeling her pain, he winced. "Ouch! Is it broken?"

"Yes. Right before the premiere too."

"Oh, man," Roger sympathized. "That sucks."

"There is no way I can do this show hobbling around like this," Sienna explained.

"It would certainly be interesting to see you try though. I mean, I guess we could do our dance scenes with crutches."

"Roger, get real."

He had to laugh. "I know. I'm just teasing you. How long?"

"At least six weeks. Maybe longer. It depends on how it heals."

Roger shook his head. "Damn!"

Broadway always had a backup plan. And in this case, Lauren was the backup plan. She had rehearsed this role and prepared for it in case something like this happened. But ultimately it was up to the director to decide whether or not the understudy was ready to take over or if the show was going to be postponed to try and find a new lead.

After speaking with the director, Sienna opted out of the show for obvious medical reasons. She hobbled over to Roger and said, "Guess who's taking over the lead? This is her shot, Roger. Get her through this." She smiled at him and left the theatre.

Roger knew exactly what that meant. He rushed into the director's office to confirm this information. "Hey, Darryl."

The director looked up. "Oh, hey, Roger."

Roger didn't beat around the bush. "Is it true?"

"Is what true?"

"Lauren's taking over as lead?"

"She's the one who's been preparing for it. I was about to call her in here."

Roger knew how much this opportunity meant to Lauren. He excitedly rubbed his palms together. "Oh, Darryl. I would love to be a part of that conversation."

"Why?"

Roger thought it was obvious. "So I can see the look on her face when you tell her. She is my wife."

"I am aware that she's your wife. But instead of being part of the conversation, how would you like to do the honors and tell her yourself?"

"Oh, yes," Roger declared, grinning devilishly. "Please."

"Just do it quickly because we need to get rehearsal started."

"Yes, Sir." He immediately trotted off to find Lauren. When he saw her, he took her by the hand and led her into his dressing room.

"Where are you taking me?" she asked.

"You'll see." As soon as they stepped inside, Roger put his hands on her shoulders and had her sit down.

"What's going on?"

He grabbed a foldup chair, turned it around, and sat straddling it. He folded his arms across the back and looked her in the eye with a mischievous grin on his face.

He stared at her like the big bad wolf eyeing Little Red Riding Hood. It kind of creeped her out. "Why are you looking at me like that?"

"I have some good news and some bad news," he began. "I'll give you the bad news first."

She reached out and touched his arm. "Wait a minute, you are up to something. I can tell by that sinister grin on your face. What kind of mischief did you get into?"

Acting innocent, he defended himself. "Me? When have I ever gotten into mischief?"

She cocked her head. "When haven't you?"

"True enough. But what I'm about to tell you has nothing to do with me."

Interest piqued and she became more curious. "What is it?"

"As I was saying, the bad news. Sienna broke her leg and can't be on stage."

Lauren gasped. "Oh my god. Is she okay?"

"She'll heal, but she's out of commission for a while. Now the good news." He was so excited, he could hardly contain himself. "You are playing lead at tomorrow night's premiere."

Her anticipatory smile quickly faded. "That is not funny." She stood up and began to walk away.

Roger grabbed her arm and stopped her. "I'm not joking, Sweetheart. I just got out of Darryl's office. He's putting you in for Sienna."

Lauren froze. The reality of what Roger had told her hadn't quite sunk in.

"Did you hear what I said? You are playing the female lead in tomorrow night's premiere!"

Slowly, she turned around, trying to process this information.

"Me?" she asked, not so sure she believed him.

The look on her face made Roger laugh. "Yes, Lauren, you. This is what you've been waiting your whole life for, Honey. Your big break, your opportunity to shine on that stage. You are making your Broadway debut tomorrow night as a leading lady. My leading lady."

When the significance of this finally hit her, her knees gave out like Jell-O. Unable to support her own weight, she collapsed on the chair. Her hands started to shake, and her breathing became so erratic, Roger thought she was going to hyperventilate.

"Breathe, Honey," he chuckled, not because he thought it was funny, but because her reaction was not at all what he expected.

Lauren looked like she'd seen a ghost. She stared at Roger but couldn't speak.

Trying to get her to calm down, he used his voice to soothe her. "Calm down. Just breathe."

She took a deep breath, followed by another and another. Roger felt her pulse rate go down, and the color gradually returned to her face.

Finally comprehending all of this, Lauren said, "I made it."

"You certainly did. Tomorrow, your name will be up in lights and the whole world will get to hear your beautiful voice echo across that stage." He squeezed her tightly, excited to share this moment with her. "I'm so proud of you, Honey. Now, you need to go change and report to the stage. We have a show to do."

She quickly left his dressing room. Roger grinned from ear to ear and prepared himself for rehearsal.

Rehearsal ran fairly smoothly, and the cast was impressed with how easily Lauren slipped into the lead role. Having Roger right alongside her helped significantly. Throughout the initial production stages of this show, Roger and Lauren had practiced together, both during and outside of rehearsal. Part of that practice involved preparing her for the possibility of taking over. This required Lauren to refine her tap dancing skills. Roger coached her along and helped her perfect the tap numbers. Based on her performance today, it was obvious she had been practicing. Overall, the dance routines were in sync, the songs had been well-rehearsed, and they were ready to open.

When they got home from rehearsal that evening, Roger took Lauren's hand and stood in the middle of their living room in dance position.

"What are you doing?" she asked.

"Practicing that last dance scene. Some timing issues need to be more precise."

She agreed with him. "Good idea."

Roger took the lead, guiding her through the dance. They made a good pair, flowing together and connecting with every step. He floated happily as he twirled her across the floor. He tipped her back in a graceful motion and leaned forward to kiss her, much more passionately than the scene called for. When he decided the scene was over, he stood her up and smiled. "We're ready." He picked up her cellphone and handed it to her. "Call your parents. Tell them that the show they are coming to see has a new leading lady. You are going to be brilliant."

Chapter Thirty-Three

Premiere night! Roger thought back to his debut performance on Broadway. A gamete of emotions ran through his head that night—excitement, anxiety, exhilaration, nervousness. He knew Lauren had butterflies in her tummy and her nerves were in overdrive, probably on the verge of being completely shot. He was a bit worried about her.

After dressing in his costume for the opening scene and tying his black tap shoes onto his feet, he headed to Lauren's dressing room to check on her. The nametag *L. Zellers* hung on the door. Seeing this made him smile. He softly knocked. "Lauren, it's me."

She recognized his voice right away. "Come in."

He peeked inside. "How you doing?"

She paced around the room, anxiously fidgeting with her costume.

Sensing her anxiety, Roger closed the door so they could have more privacy. He took her in his arms and tried to settle her nerves. "Look at me," he insisted.

She tipped her head, followed by a long sigh. "I'm nervous."

"That's natural. But channel that nervous energy into your performance tonight. Make it powerful and make it stick."

That didn't help alleviate the butterflies.

"The biggest thing you need to remember tonight is to have fun. The audience will see that you are enjoying yourself because it will reflect in your performance. Don't stress about fundamentals. You are well-prepared for this. Go out there, do what comes naturally, and have the time of your life. Let the energy from the audience flow through you. Take it all in."

She listened closely to his advice. "I will."

"Tonight is your night, Lauren Zellers, and you," he tapped her on the tip of the nose with his finger, "are going to be amazing."

She giggled at his flirtatiousness, and her beautiful smile brightened the room.

"There's that smile I love." Roger had a major dance number in the opening scene and needed to loosen up and get wired for sound before he took the stage. "I need to warm up, but I'll see you on stage shortly."

As he was about to exit her room, Lauren called out to him. "Roger?"

"Yes?"

Grateful for his encouraging words, she said, "Thank you."

"You're welcome. Now shine like the diamond you are, my sweet."

In the morning, Roger sipped on a cup of coffee while he skimmed through the entertainment section of the New York Times looking for reviews from their premiere. What he found was more than he anticipated.

Crazy For You is colorful, bubbly, brilliantly choreographed, dynamically staged, and beautiful to look at. It is an alive expression of sheer joy. Roger Zellers is a fantastic leading man. His portrayal of Bobby Childs is brilliant. He excels both in dance and duet with the wonderful Lauren Zellers, whose rendition of 'Someone to Watch Over Me' is powerful and exceedingly lovely to listen to. Between Lauren Zellers' powerful voice and Roger Zellers' leading dance moves, this show is energetic, fun, and entertaining to watch. Well done to all the cast!

Roger beamed as he read the review. Lauren was going to be pleased to see this.

Now that Lauren had a lead role, Roger wanted to make sure she was getting the proper credit and pay associated with it. He called Darryl and arranged to have a meeting with the production team to discuss her contract. Since he knew the business end of Broadway and knew how to talk to production executive big wigs and contract negotiators, he insisted on being present when negotiations occurred.

Before they walked into the room, Roger turned to Lauren and said, "I'm going to warn you. This might get ugly."

"Why?" she asked.

"I don't play games with contracts. That's why I want to be in the room. I know how to talk to these people, I can negotiate with them, but when I do, be forewarned, you may see a side of me you won't like very much."

She wrinkled her forehead. "What are you going to do?"

"If they don't give you what you deserve, I'm going to get in their face. I won't let them jerk you around, Lauren. I want to make sure you're getting paid what a lead actress should be getting paid, and I won't rest until they give it to you."

Her jaw tightened and her muscles became tense. "This doesn't sound very fun. What if they won't negotiate? I don't want to lose this show, Roger."

"You won't." He put his hands on her shoulders, offering reassurance. "But you're going to have to trust me."

Kenneth Kingsley, a contract negotiator from the Actors' Equity Association, stepped into the hallway and shook Roger's hand. "Roger Zellers, it's a pleasure to see you again."

"Pleasure is all mine, Mr. Kingsley." Roger introduced him to Lauren, and they made their way into the conference room.

They situated themselves around a conference table along with the show's director and a representative from the Broadway League. Under no circumstances was Roger intimidated. He came prepared and confident. "Good morning, gentlemen," he stated with a charming smile.

The Broadway League representative began the conversation. "What can we do for you, Roger?"

Roger explained the situation. "Contract negotiations."

"We've already set your contract. You signed off on it," the league rep reminded him.

"I'm not talking about mine. I'm talking about Lauren's." He pulled out her contract and turned to the page where it stated what role she was portraying in the show. "Right here it says she was cast as an ensemble member, then later…" He flipped the page and pointed out a contract amendment. "We added understudy pay."

"That is correct."

Roger closed her contract and tossed it in the middle of the table. "This contract is no longer valid. We need a new one drawn up."

The league rep narrowed his eyes. "Mr. Zellers, this contract is perfectly valid."

"No, it isn't," he refuted. "She is no longer an ensemble member. She has a leading role. I want a contract that indicates that."

The director stepped in at this point. "Gentlemen, my lead actress had an accident and broke her leg. Therefore, she was unable to perform. She and I decided it was best for her to terminate her contract. At that point, Mrs. Zellers stepped up from understudy and took over as lead."

Roger added to the argument. "Lauren is the one who performed at the premiere, her name is on the program, and she is listed as the lead on all publicity for this show. We're drawing up a new contract listing her as the lead."

The league rep agreed. "We'll take care of it."

"I want it done before the show tomorrow night," Roger insisted. "And she needs a pay increase associated with a leading role."

"We'll offer 2K."

Roger shook his head, insulted by that offer. "That's not enough."

"She's new to the industry," he claimed.

Roger firmly disputed this statement. "She's good, and she deserves better than that. I want 3.5."

The league rep countered, "We'll go 2.1."

"You read the reviews. Critics are raving about her. We're going to sell out tickets for this show and pack this theatre every night. I want 3.5."

"She has no prior experience."

Roger disagreed. "She has formal training from Juilliard and years of stage experience."

"Amateur stage experience."

"She has off-Broadway professional experience with the West Avenue Musical Theater Club where she's played several leading roles. She's playing a lead now. Not a supporting role, not an ensemble role, a lead. And it's not just acting. There's dancing and singing involved. How many people can you find who have the talent to do all three? This is a full blown, all-encompassing production, gentlemen. Lauren Zellers is a triple threat, and she deserves more than what you're offering."

"In that case, we'll go 2.2," the league rep offered.

That offer was insulting and completely unacceptable. Roger quickly became impatient. "This show officially opens next week. Let me see you find an actress who knows the part as well as she does who is prepared to take over the lead. You won't find one. Lauren stepped up to the plate. She is the lead for this show, and she deserves equivalent pay to what other lead actresses receive."

Roger certainly wasn't joking when he said this could get ugly. He was being flat out stubborn, and Lauren began to fear that maybe he was pushing too hard.

Roger was not known for backing down in a contract negotiation, but Kenneth knew he was being unreasonable to request that much for a newcomer to the business with no prior Broadway stage experience. He had to step in. He pulled Roger aside to talk privately. "She has no experience on Broadway, Roger. You have to work with them."

"You've seen her resume. It's a lead role, Kenneth," Roger opposed, frustrated. "I know 3.5 is higher than what new people usually get, but I'm using it as wiggle room. She deserves at least 3K. She was bringing in 1,900 as an ensemble member with understudy responsibilities. Boosting her salary by only $300 a week is a joke. I know for a fact that lead dancers make more than that."

The contract negotiator agreed. "True. Their offer is low."

"I'm not backing down on this," Roger insisted.

"I know she's your wife," Kenneth stated, "But you have to give them something to negotiate with."

Roger glared at this man, refusing to back down. "2.2 is unacceptable. I'm not giving into that. She deserves more."

"I'm not saying to give in, but you do have to negotiate. You know this business well, Roger. You have to give them something to work with. Counter offer, and I think they'll be willing to give the 3K you want."

Roger rubbed his hand across his chin, contemplating Kenneth's advice.

"3K is good for a newcomer," Kenneth reminded him. "You can't deny that."

Roger took a deep breath. "I'll counter, but I want the contract drawn up and signed by tomorrow afternoon."

"I'll arrange it."

Roger and the union rep returned to the table where Roger laid it on the line. "Alright. Here's the deal. She has professional, specialized training at Juilliard. She has voice and dance experience. She received rave reviews at the premiere. She has prior professional stage experience off-Broadway, and she did her duty as an understudy and was willing to step in and take over the lead at the last minute with no prior warning. You all know that lead roles require more work, more media contact, recording and extra appearance responsibilities, and more rehearsal hours, along with eight performances a week. She was making 1,900 as ensemble. I think it's fair to expect a significant pay boost for taking over a lead role in a major production like this."

"What are you offering?" the league representative asked.

Roger countered, "We formally change her contract over to lead actress and boost her up to 3K. The rest of the contract stays intact."

The committee pondered over this, discussing amongst themselves. Finally, the league rep offered, "We'll offer full contract, 3K a week, mindful that she follow all rules and regulations stated in her current contract. She'll perform eight shows a week according to schedule, maintaining full duties of the lead role."

Roger looked over at Lauren, wanting her approval to proceed.

She nodded, indicating her agreement.

"Do you have any questions? Any comments?" the league rep asked her.

"No, Sir."

"We'll have a revised contract drawn up for you." The league representative reached across the table and shook Lauren's hand. "Congratulations."

"Thank you."

Roger added his last words, "We want that in writing by tomorrow."

"We'll have it ready for you to read over and sign after tomorrow's rehearsal."

Roger smiled cordially. "Thank you. Much appreciated."

The room slowly cleared, leaving Roger and Lauren alone. She questioned his actions, confused by what she had witnessed. "What just happened?"

"What just happened was I got you 3K a week for doing this show. For your first Broadway production, that's exceptionally good."

"You seriously told them to find another actress to cover the lead? You could have cost me this job."

He fully denied this accusation. "At no time was your job in jeopardy, Honey. You can't let these people walk all over you. What they were offering was ridiculously low. No lead actresses makes that, new to the business or not."

"You're ruthless, aren't you?" she commented with a chuckle.

"I told you I can get ugly when it comes to contract negotiations. You need to get the most you possibly can out of these people. They make huge profits from these shows, but they wouldn't make any profits at all if it wasn't for the actors and actresses involved, and they know that. If you're good, you deserve to be compensated."

"Wow," she stated. "I'd hate to see you negotiate a contract for yourself."

Roger laughed. "That's easy. I just dangle my Tony Award over their heads. What frustrates me about this business is that a big name actor, who's really not a stage performer and can't sing or dance, can come in here and flash his name and viola, he's landed a 120,000 dollar a week contract simply because he's a name. Who cares if he's got talent? These people may be good on the big screen, but some of them have no business being on Broadway. They should just stay in movies and TV and quit corrupting my stage."

"They have a right to audition too," Lauren responded.

"I know they do," Roger agreed. "I'm not disagreeing with that. But it pisses me off when I go into the same audition as that guy, have smoother dance moves and a crisper voice, but because he is a bigger name than I am, he'll get the part over me. Happens all the time."

"That's not fair."

"It's all about profit, Honey. If you don't have the talent to draw in crowds or aren't a big-name star who can fill the theatre, then they're not interested. That's why this business is rough. There are 700,000 performers in this city fighting over 50,000 available roles. That leaves a lot of people constantly looking for work and forced to carry day jobs to pay the bills. If you get any kind of role on stage, especially a principal or lead, you're one of the lucky ones."

"I never thought about it that way," Lauren said.

"Why do you think I'm looking for work well before my current contract expires? I want to lock in a new contract and avoid having a lapse. I could go several months between shows otherwise. That's a lot of money lost. That's also why I don't like signing more than a twelve-month contract. Unless they're long running productions, most shows close within twelve to eighteen months from the time they open. I try to get out of it before it closes. That gives me time to look around and find a good show instead of taking the first role that comes up simply because I'm out of work and desperate. It's also good practice not to limit yourself to one type of role. The more varying types of roles you do, the more versatile you become as a performer. Producers and casting directors need to see that you can spread yourself as an actor and are capable of putting on whatever kind of show is necessary to sell tickets and get butts in the seats."

Lauren never really considered this aspect of the business before. "I am glad I have you here to help me figure all of this out. This is so much more complicated than I imagined."

"Just takes experience, Sweetheart. I'll help you. Eventually you'll get the hang of it."

Lauren was having the time of her life performing on Broadway. This was the realization of a dream she had always hoped to achieve, but playing the lead required a lot of prep work and time commitments. With eight shows a week, it would be next to impossible to balance performances, extra appearances, rehearsal schedules, and a fulltime class load. Knowing this, she was faced with the most difficult decision of her life. She sat on the sofa trying to weigh all the options.

The contemplative look on her face made Roger wonder what she was thinking. "What's the matter?"

She lifted her chin. "I don't know what to do."

"About what?" He took a seat next to her.

With a disheartened frown, she said, "How am I supposed to be in a Broadway show and go to school full time? I can't be in two places at once. If I'm in class all day then have an 8:00 performance every night, I'll have maybe an hour between class and the time I have to report to the theatre. By the time the show is over, it will probably be close to midnight before we get home. I guess I could study then, but when am I supposed sleep? I have to be well-rested and prepared to get up at 6:00 in the morning for another day of classes. How do I manage all of this?"

He didn't want to tell her what to do, but tried to give her insights from his own experience. "I've been in your position, Honey. And ironically I was your age when this exact same thing happened to me."

She thought back to the conversation she and Roger had about his debut on Broadway. Wondering how he handled this she asked, "How did you decide what to do?"

He did his best to guide her. "The cold hard truth about this industry is that not many people get a shot at being on stage. Talented people spend their entire lives trying to get on Broadway and never make it. Getting on stage, even as an ensemble or a swing, is very difficult to achieve. If you are one of the lucky ones, it's an opportunity you probably shouldn't pass up, because you may not get another chance. This business is brutal and extremely competitive. Along the same lines, Juilliard is a tough school to get into. It's selective, and no one offers better voice, dance, and theatrical training than they do. But," he rebutted, "both require full commitment. The amount of homework, studying, and performance prep involved with Juilliard is grueling. Not only is it an advanced curriculum, it also requires extra time with rehearsal schedules and performances. Being a lead on Broadway requires no less of a time commitment. It's a full time job. You will have rehearsals during the week as well as two matinee and six nighttime performances. There are press appearances involved, charity events, interviews, cast recordings, and other commitments that come up when you are a lead in a major production."

Lauren began to fiddle with her wedding ring.

"Realistically speaking, there aren't enough hours in the day to successfully take on both. You will run yourself ragged and pure exhaustion will catch up with you. And if you are in class, at rehearsal, studying, or doing a show from 6:00 A.M. until midnight every day, how is that going to affect our marriage?" He looked her in the eye and earnestly stated, "I would like to spend some time with my wife once in a while."

She stared at her hands with a dazed look on her face.

"No one can tell you what to do, Lauren. I just want you to fully see all of the implications of this. The bottom line is you're going to have to make a decision. It's going to come down to priorities. Which one do you want more?"

Lauren carefully pondered over everything he said. "I love being at Juilliard. It's something I've always wanted. But performing on Broadway has been a dream of mine my whole life."

"And now you're living that dream," Roger reminded her. "Do you really want to let that dream slip away?"

"No."

"I know how hard this is. I've been in your shoes. However, this decision has to be yours. Just know that no matter what you decide, I will support you as best I can. But you are going to have to choose, because in all honesty, Sweetheart, there is no feasible way you can do both."

After working hard on applications and auditions and gaining invaluable insights and experience from the school, Lauren chose to leave Juilliard for Broadway. This decision was a sting in the tail for her, and one she didn't take lightly. She and Roger discussed it wholeheartedly, weighing the positives with the negatives. The option of going back to school after her contract was over was not completely off the table. Granted, she would have to go through the application and audition process again, but she left that possibility open.

"What about my father?" she asked.

"What about him?"

"How am I supposed to break this to him?"

Trying to ease Lauren's worry, Roger said, "You're dad's a reasonable guy."

This was a true point. But she was still apprehensive. "He's going to be upset that I'm quitting school."

"He has to understand your reasons though. He knows you've waited your whole life to be on Broadway. If he cares about you, as I know he does, he's going to be happy that you're living your dream," Roger explained. "I like your dad. He's a good man, and he's a supportive father. He knows you just got your big break. He'll understand."

When Randy found out Lauren was leaving Juilliard to dedicate her time to this show, he wasn't really surprised. Deep down he figured she would get her shot at the Broadway stage sooner or later, and he knew his daughter well enough to discern that she wasn't going to turn an opportunity like that down. He always hoped she'd finish school first, but as Roger suspected, Randy understood her reasons for leaving. She was going to be a star!

Chapter Thirty-Four

Gabby was only weeks away from starting her first teaching job. To prepare for this, she spent the majority of the summer attending staff-development, shopping for teaching supplies, looking over her Kindergarten curriculum, and pre-writing lesson plans. She was thrilled about her career choice and couldn't wait to get started.

Nathan was busy prepping for medical school. He purchased books, which were ridiculously overpriced, and stocked up on spirals, binders, highlighters, and pens. He bought a lab coat and goggles for science labs and a second lab coat for clinical work. This coat had a nametag attached, *Nathan Hanson, Medical Student, UWSOM*. He had to wear this anytime he had hands-on clinical experiences at a medical facility. That way, he would not be mistaken for a licensed physician.

Since mid-June, Nathan had been taking a Human Anatomy class. This was a fifteen hour a week fast-paced class, the majority of which occurred in the laboratory dissecting cadavers. This class was specifically designed as an introduction and provided a broad understanding of the structural organization of the human body with the intent of providing a foundation for physical examination and assessment. All beginning medical students were required to take this course the summer prior to their first year. Between this class and working in his father's clinic, Nathan's summer was full.

Around the middle of August, Nathan received his fall semester schedule—Biochemistry, Immunology, Cell Physiology, Microbiology and Infectious Diseases, Microscopic Anatomy, a class specifically on the Musculoskeletal System, a class called Medical Information for Decision Making, and between four to six hours a week of hands-on clinical training. When he saw how full his schedule was, he raised his hand to his temple and leaned against the door frame. "Holy shit."

"What's the matter?" Gabby asked.

He handed her his schedule. "I'm going to be in class or in a lab for eight to ten hours a day, every day. This is insane. Dad told me this was gonna be rough, but damn."

"It doesn't look that horrible. You'll still have your evenings free."

"Not really. I'll be working a couple hours a day and have four hours of studying a night, minimum. I have to eat and take care of personal needs at some point during the day. If I'm lucky, I'll get five hours of sleep every night."

Gabby handed his schedule back to him. "You can do this, Nathan. I'll be right here to support you."

"When are we supposed to spend time together?"

Gabby laughed. "Don't worry about me."

But he was worried. Gabby was important to him, and he didn't want to neglect her. "I'm not just going to blow you off, Gab."

"You won't. That's what weekends are for. I'll be busy during the week anyway. You need to focus on school right now."

Nathan wondered how he was going to juggle all of this. When his father was in medical school, he carried a full course load, worked a part time job, and had a steady girlfriend, yet he managed to survive. Feeling overwhelmed, Nathan sought his father's advice.

"That's pretty standard," Randy said, scanning over Nathan's upcoming schedule while he munched on fish tacos and coleslaw. "Looks like you're going to learn a lot your first year."

Nathan put his schedule back in his pocket. "How did you do all this? Ten hours a day of classes, working, studying, and you and Mom started dating when you were in medical school. Where the hell did you find the time?"

"It's all about prioritizing," Randy explained. "You have to sneak in study time whenever you can. Every time I had a break between classes, I utilized that time to review lecture notes. I worked in the clinic from the time class was over until about seven or eight then grabbed a quick bite to eat and spent the rest of the night studying. I was able to get in a few more work hours on Saturday, which left Saturday evenings and Sundays free. Sunday mornings were set aside for studying, but the rest of the day was for me to do with as I pleased."

"I'm worried that after being in class all day and studying all night, I'll take my stress out on Gabby. I don't want to do that to her."

"She'll be alright. Gabby's always supported you, and she knows how important this is to you. She'll do what she can to help you get through it."

"This is a lot to put on her," Nathan said, feeling guilty about the insanity of his schedule. "Studying is time consuming, and it takes me a long time to read and comprehend a chapter's worth of information. I'm never going to have time for myself or for Gabby."

Randy offered his son some sound advice. "One of the things that really helped me, and I'm sure Jim, Bruce, and Mandy would attest to this, was group study. Not only did it give all of us time to review and help each other, but it relieved stress. We could vent our frustrations and share some bonding time while we worked together toward a common goal. You need a strong support system."

"How did you manage to get everyone together all the time?"

"That's what Sunday morning was for. We met diligently every week. It gave us an opportunity to reflect on what we had learned the previous week and gave us time to prepare for the following week. The weekdays were dedicated to self-study, that way we were all prepared for Sunday's group session. We made our study sessions fun though. We'd take turns providing snacks, we made up study games, had team competitions. Little things like that helped all of us get through it."

Nathan liked the way that sounded. "How'd you determine who was in your study group?"

"It was my Anatomy lab group. We started together. We went through it all together. We ended together. We became very close in the process, and to this day we are all still good friends."

Nathan knew Dr. Bruce Buckman, Dr. Amanda Buckman, and Dr. James Ryan, three of his father's good friends, all of whom went to medical school with him. He assumed these were the people his father was referring to. "So it was you, Jim, Bruce, and Mandy?"

"Actually, there were originally six of us," Randy corrected. "One failed out, the other one quit, which really upset me because when she left, she only had one more year of classes to finish before clinicals. We could have helped her get through it, but she opted out. She's still involved in the medical field, she just isn't a doctor. And we all still keep in touch with her. That's my friend, Sarah."

"The EMT," Nathan remarked.

"Yup."

"What about the other one?" Nathan asked curiously.

"His name was Steve Hall. I have no idea what happened to him. We didn't part on very good terms, I'm afraid," Randy admitted.

"Why not?"

"He and I had a severe personality conflict. Steve caused problems most of the time, and since he didn't contribute much to our study sessions, we collaboratively chose not to have him in the group anymore. Not long after that, the JMP asked him to leave."

"Oh man. That sucks," Nathan said.

"I kinda blame myself for that. He was a douchebag, so I didn't make a conscience effort to help him, even though I knew he was struggling."

Nathan couldn't say that he blamed his father for that. "If the guy was an ass, I wouldn't have gone out of my way either."

Randy laughed at Nathan's bluntness. "And I didn't. But because I didn't, he failed out of medical school."

"Obviously you and Mom made it through this," Nathan ascertained.

Randy grinned. "Yes we did. It took a lot of patience on both our parts, but we made it. And you and Gabby will too, if you're both willing to work at it."

Nathan felt better after talking to his dad. "There's something else I wanted to talk to you about."

"What's that?" Randy said, gulping down his coffee.

"It's about Gabby. I know she wants to get married and…"

Randy immediately put an end this conversation. "That is not a smart decision right now."

"Hear me out."

Although he didn't like where this conversation was headed, Randy folded his arms across his chest and listened to what his son had to say.

"I want Gabby to know my intentions are good."

"Meaning what, exactly?"

"I get her a ring. That doesn't mean we plan a wedding right away. We can wait for that part. But at least she'll know that I'm serious when I say I want to marry her."

By the look on Nathan's face, Randy knew his son had something else on his mind. "And?"

"Well, a lot of what we decide to do is going to depend on you."

Randy didn't see the connection. "What do I have to do with you and Gabby getting married? Whether I agree with the decision or not, I'm not going to stop you if that's what you want to do."

"It's med school, Dad."

That didn't clarify anything. "What about it?"

"There is no way Gabby and I can afford to pay for medical school tuition on a teacher's salary."

"I told you a long time ago that if you got accepted into medical school, I would pay for it. That is a promise I intend to keep, whether you and Gabby are married or not. You can't let cost of tuition be a deciding factor. But you do need to seriously consider your schedule at the moment and whether or not Gabby's salary will support both of you."

"I know," Nathan concurred. "And those are things she and I will discuss, but I at least want to give her a ring. She's waited long enough."

Randy completely understood where his son was coming from. He didn't necessarily agree with his timing on this, but he was going to support him. "Have you picked one out?"

"Yes, but I have about two more weeks to save up before I can get it."

"Saving is good. Don't put yourself in debt over an engagement ring," Randy warned.

"I wasn't planning on it. But I do need to talk to Mom because I need her help."

"She'll be home this afternoon."

Nathan set his napkin on the table and got up to use the restroom.

"Nathan?" Randy said to his son.

"Yes, Sir?"

"Be responsible and be smart about this," he advised. "Don't let this distract you."

"It won't, Dad. Don't worry."

After lunch, Nathan drove over to his parents' house to speak with his mother. She greeted him with a huge hug. "Hi, Sweetie. How's school?"

"School's going well," he replied. "Busy as hell."

"It's medical school, Nathan. You knew it wasn't going to be a cake walk." She offered him a cookie and a glass of milk.

He took a bite and sat on the living room sofa. "Mom, I need your help with something. I need any pictures you have of me and Gabby together, clear back to eighth grade. Prom, graduation, basketball games, birthday parties, anything at all."

"Why? What's going on?" Jane asked him.

"It's for a project I'm working on."

She knew he was up to something. "What kind of project?"

Nathan completely trusted his mother, but he didn't want to give away what he was doing. "I'm trying to gather memories she and I have made together. Little things that helped our relationship grow. Any pictures you have would be helpful."

"Alright, I'll look tonight," she stated.

"It's a surprise though. You can't hint anything to Gab. Call me when you have the pictures, and I'll come pick them up."

A few weeks later, Nathan and Gabby snuggled on the couch watching a movie. They paused briefly to gather refreshments. "You want a soda, Sweetie?" Gabby offered.

"Sure."

She stood up and stepped into the kitchen.

While she was out of the room, Nathan reached under the couch and pulled out a red scrapbook with white lace ribbon and a red rose on the front. He sat it on the cushion beside him.

Gabby came back with two sodas in her hand. She handed one to Nathan. "Here you go."

"Thanks, Babe."

She saw the scrapbook sitting on the couch. "What's this?"

"I want to show you something." She sat down beside him, and he placed the book between them so they could look at it together. He opened the cover to the first page.

On this page, Nathan had pasted Gabby's eighth grade school picture right next to his. Above them, in fun red puffy letter stickers, he spelled out, *Nathan and Gabby sitting in a tree, K-I-S-S-I-N-G.* There was also a big red lips sticker attached to the page. This made her giggle.

"Turn the page," he said.

She flipped the page over. This page was titled, *First Comes Love.* Throughout this section were various pictures of the two of them over the years, ranging from eighth grade basketball games and Gabby's sixteenth birthday to high school Prom and college graduation. They looked at these pictures together, laughing and reminiscing over the memories they had shared together. Nine years of memories were pasted in this book.

As they approached the end of the scrapbook, Gabby said, "We've shared so much together."

"Yes we have, but there's one more page."

Gabby couldn't wait to see what was at the end. When she turned the page, what she saw made her jaw drop. The title, *Then Comes Marriage* was printed on the top. In the middle of this page, tied on with a white lacy ribbon, a 14K white diamond engagement ring sparkled in front of her. Underneath the ring, in the same puffy red letter stickers, Nathan spelled out, *Marry me?* She looked over at him, teary-eyed. "Nathan."

He gazed at her pretty face. "You didn't answer the question."

She placed her hand on his. "Oh, Sweetie. You know I will."

The huge smile he displayed spoke volumes. "I love you, Gab."

"I love you too." Their lips interlocked in a sweet embrace.

431

Nathan untied the ribbon that held the diamond detailed ring in place and grasped it between his thumb and forefinger. "You have to let me do this. Gimme your hand."

She gladly held out her left hand.

Nathan carefully slipped the ring on her finger. "Now we are officially engaged."

Gabby admired the ring he had given her. "This is beautiful."

"Keep your hand out like that so I can take a picture." He pulled his cellphone out of his pocket and snapped a picture of Gabby's hand with his camera. "There," he declared as he put his phone away. "We'll print that picture and attach it to this page."

Gabby closed the scrapbook, impressed with the unique proposal he crafted. "Did you come up with this idea yourself?"

"Yes I did. Mom helped gather all the pictures, but the idea was mine."

She held the book against her chest and hugged it. "This is the most romantic thing you've ever done. Thank you, Sweetie."

"No," he retorted. "Thank you."

"For what?"

"For saying yes."

She smiled blissfully. "You knew I would."

"I did, but it was still nice to hear you say it."

The next day, Nathan shared the news with his family. Despite Randy's concern that Nathan might have been jumping into the marriage boat prematurely, everyone was excited for them. Lacy was home for vacation when this news was announced. Even though she was happy for her brother, a dark cloud hung over her. She went up to her room and closed the door.

Jane could tell something was bothering her. She followed Lacy upstairs and knocked on the door. "Lacy, Honey."

"Come in, Mom."

Jane stepped inside. Her daughter sat cross legged on the bed hugging her pillow. Lacy didn't usually get emotional and didn't let things get her down. She was also not much of a crier. When Jane saw tears in Lacy's eyes, she knew something was wrong. "Honey, what's wrong?"

"It's just that…" She squeezed her pillow a bit tighter. "Lauren's married now and Nathan is engaged. I want to experience that closeness with someone. I want to find love, but how can I when I don't even have a boyfriend."

Jane gave her daughter a hug. "You're still young. You have lots of time."

"Every guy I've ever dated was a selfish jerk," Lacy sniffled. "All I seem to find are men who only care about themselves. They start off acting like they care about me, but as soon as they get me into bed, they disappear. I'm tired of being treated like a possession or an overnight stop."

"Not all men are like that. There are some very nice and respectful men out there."

She set her pillow down. "How am I supposed to find one if I can't maintain a relationship long enough to fall in love with someone or have him fall in love with me?"

"You haven't met the right man yet," Jane replied, offering her motherly advice. "When you meet him, you'll know. Nothing will be able to keep you apart. He'll want to spend every waking moment with you, he'll shower you with affection, and you'll know from his actions that he loves you." She placed her hand on

Lacy's arm. "The right man will turn up someday. Be patient and wait for him."

After comforting her daughter, Jane reported outside where her husband was watering plants and flowerbeds. "I'm worried about Lacy."

"Why?" Randy asked.

"Lauren and Roger are married. Nathan and Gabby just got engaged. She's upset because she doesn't think she'll ever find Mr. Right."

Randy found this amusing. "She's twenty years old, Jane. Why would she be worried about that?"

She scowled at her husband's lack of understanding.

Realizing that he had just inserted his foot in his mouth, he said, "You didn't think about that at her age did you?"

"All young women her age think about that."

He turned off the water and rolled up his garden hose. "Wait a minute, you mean to tell me the whole time we were dating you were scoping me out as potential husband material?"

That question didn't merit an answer.

Trying not to be on the receiving end of his wife's evil glare, he said, "It must be a woman thing then, because I can tell you right now that when I was her age, commitment was the last thing on my mind."

"I know what was on your mind," Jane scolded him. "And that's why Lacy's upset."

"Twenty-year-old men think about sex, Jane. It's what guys do."

"Randal," she rebuked, not impressed with his comment.

"What do you want me to do? Tell her that guys don't think about sex? I'd be lying if I told her that."

Jane questioned his previous response. "And by the way, Dr. Hanson, there are guys out there who have more on their minds than sex. I know for a fact that's not all you think about."

"At the age of twenty it was," he admitted.

Jane redirected the conversation. "She's feeling down because she's afraid she'll never find love."

"Then maybe she's looking too hard."

"What are you talking about?"

"A lot of people find love when they're not really looking for it. I did."

"Meaning what, exactly?"

He explained his thinking. "When I met you, the last thing I wanted was to fall in love with you. I had way too many things going on in my life at the time, was too focused on myself, and didn't want to commit to a serious relationship." The look on his wife's face told him she was irritated. He had to try a different approach. "But…" He took her hand. "As I got to know you, I found myself wanting to spend more time with you. It wasn't long before I fell head over heels in love with you. Was I looking for love? No, not at all. Was I hoping to find my future wife? No, I wasn't. In fact, marriage was the furthest thing from my mind. You haphazardly walked into my life, cocked attitude with me, and spiked a damn volleyball at my head."

She laughed remembering that day.

"My point is that if you are deliberately seeking love, you may miss it when it walks in because you're too busy looking the other way. I wasn't looking for it, so I was able to see it when it hit me. And it hit me hard." He put his hand on his head. "Right in the head."

Jane moved closer to her husband and wrapped her arms around his waist.

He reciprocated. "Lacy has her eyes so fixated in one direction that Mr. Right is going to walk right in front of her and she won't see him."

"Maybe you should go talk to her," Jane suggested.

"And say what?" Randy scoffed. "Lacy doesn't like talking to me about men. She doesn't like talking to me about much of anything. She and I have always butted heads."

"Maybe this can be your chance to connect with her."

Randy let out a big sigh. "She's not even going to let me in her room. She has a 'Dad is not allowed' sign on her door."

Jane thought this was a silly thing for him to say. "She does not. She's not sixteen anymore. She's a young woman who needs her father."

"Any advice I've ever given her has been insignificant in her eyes. It's gone in one ear and out the other. She's not going to listen to me."

"Try," Jane insisted. "You keep telling me you wish that you and Lacy were closer. This will be a good bonding moment for the two of you."

"What if she wants to talk about sex?" Randy feared.

"I thought you were an expert on women's sexuality? You're a gynecologist. You counsel women on those matters all the time."

"She isn't one of my patients. She's my daughter."

"Then use your counseling know how, be her father, and to talk to her. Your daughter needs you." She released her grasp on him and walked back into the house.

He knew his wife was right, but he feared where the conversation with Lacy would take him. He didn't feel comfortable discussing these matters with his daughter, but more importantly, he didn't want Lacy to feel uncomfortable about it. Inhaling deeply, he toughed it out and headed up to Lacy's room.

Wrapped up in Gabby's arms, Nathan fought to regain air. "Gab," he panted as he kissed her. "I wanna talk about when we want to get married."

Nathan always seemed to bring up unusual topics of conversation immediately after sex. She didn't understand why he did this, it was just part of who he was. "You want to talk about that right now?"

"Yes." His pounding heart slowly relaxed and he started to breathe more regularly. "We both want to wait until we are financially stable, and I'd like to get my feet wet in med school before we take that step."

Gabby nuzzled in closer and rested her hand on his chest. "So what did you have in mind?"

He put his arm around her, drawing her closer. "What about next summer? I won't have any classes, and you'll have your first year of teaching behind you by then. That will give us a year to plan it all, which is plenty of time. And with the summer months not so insane, we will have time to go on a honeymoon. That gives us the whole school year to situate our finances, save money, and try to find a place to live that is more suitable to married life. What do you think?"

"You're thinking June or July?"

"Yes." Then a brilliant idea came to him. "Maybe on the beach."

He was just full of romance lately. A beach wedding sounded incredible. "That would be so romantic."

"Wouldn't it?" he confirmed. "I bet we can make that happen."

She snuggled in a little closer. "This dream is finally coming true for us."

"Yes it is." He kissed her lovingly on the lips. "I told you I was going to marry you someday. I'm sorry it took so long to make it happen."

She peered up at him. "We weren't ready, Nathan. You know that."

"I know, but…"

Gabby cut in, "If you would have tried to propose to me before we were ready, I would have told you to wait. I'm glad you didn't try to rush this sooner."

Nathan grinned. "Really?"

"Yes. It will be much better this way."

The guilty feeling he'd been carrying slowly faded. He squeezed her tightly against his body, loving the path they were taking. "I love you, Gab."

"I love you, too."

Chapter Thirty-Five

Fall was Randy's favorite season. He loved the crispness in the weather and the changing hue of the leaves. The colorful fall foliage intermixed with picturesque images of Lake Washington, Puget Sound, and Mt. Rainier made Seattle a truly stunning, quintessential experience to anyone lucky enough to visit there this time of year. To commemorate this season, Randy decked out his house and his clinic in harvest décor, pumpkins, and festive fall-colored chrysanthemums.

Randy was known for having a sense of humor. He utilized this gift to get a few smiles and laughs from his patients. He carved and decorated a pumpkin to resemble a woman delivering a baby. He did this by placing a small pumpkin inside the hole of another and topped them with a pumpkin face that looked like it was grimacing in agony. He used carrots for arms and legs and put a hospital cap on its head. To top off the look, he wrapped an admittance band around its wrist then placed it in a delivery position atop a rolling supply cart. He wheeled his creation in front of the bulletin board where all the photographs of babies he had delivered were displayed. Next to his masterpiece he wrote, *Made by Dr. Hanson.*

When Randy's partner saw this, he busted a gut laughing. "Nice, Randy."

Randy grinned devilishly. "You like that?"

"That has to be one of the most creative jack-o-lanterns I've ever seen. That will certainly get a few laughs."

"That's the idea." Randy checked his appointment schedule and saw that he was booked all day. If he was lucky, he might have time for lunch today. "Looks like I better snag some coffee now or I won't get any at all."

"I'm packed too." Greg read through the file of the first patient he had scheduled that morning. "Are the girls coming home for Thanksgiving this year?"

"Actually, we're all going to New York."

"Thanksgiving in New York, huh?"

"Yup."

"That's a busy place to be during the holidays."

"Oh, I know," Randy said. "Crowded and crazy. Speaking of which, both Lauren and Roger are performing in the Macy's parade this year."

"Are they? I will have to check that out."

"She is definitely making her mark in that city."

"That's what she's always wanted though," Greg reminded him.

"Oh, I know it is. She's fulfilling her dream, and I'm proud of her for that." He stepped into his office to grab a cup of coffee before he began his busy day of appointments.

"What time did you tell everyone to be here?" Lauren called out to Roger from the bedroom.

He stepped into the room wearing only a pair of jeans. "Four o'clock. Why?"

Lauren had that panicky look in her eyes, like she was about to lose it. To keep her from freaking out, Roger offered an alternative. "I can have them come later if you want, but I figured four o'clock would give us plenty of time."

Aside from the two of them performing 'I Got Rhythm' with the rest of the cast from *Crazy For You*, Lauren and Roger were also hosting Thanksgiving dinner for the entire family this year. "It's going to take three hours to cook the turkey."

They had previously prepared several dishes. However, the turkey still needed to go in the oven, potatoes needed to be mashed, gravy needed to be whisked, and corn bread needed to be baked. The dinner table hadn't been properly set yet either. Roger didn't understand why she was throwing such a fuss over this. They didn't have that much left to do. He put his arms around her, trying to get her to relax. "We have plenty of time. If we don't dawdle around afterwards, we should be home by noon. The meal will be ready and the apartment will be all fancied up before anyone gets here. We'll work together on this. You stay focused on the big stuff. Let me handle the details." He slipped on a red polo shirt and tucked it into his pants. It was now 6:30 A.M. They had to be at the parade site no later than 7:30 to put on costumes, get wired with microphones, perform sound checks, and warm up for their performance. "If we don't get moving, we're going to be late."

Lauren quickly finished getting dressed.

It was chilly outside, but at least it wasn't snowing. Since Roger had performed outdoors many times, he offered Lauren some professional advice. "Performing outside is a lot different than being on stage, especially when it's cold. Keep your muscles lose and warm or you're going to cramp up. Bring a cup of lemon tea with you to keep your voice from giving out. In the cold, your throat will dry out quickly."

She frantically grabbed her jacket and gloves and gathered all the things they would need for the parade. Roger watched as she stumbled around, acting as if she was overwhelmed with the scheduling of their day.

"Honey, you really need to relax."

"We have so much to do," she said.

"It's not that much," he tried to explain. "Take one task at a time. Right now, focus on the parade performance. When we get back, we'll divvy out tasks between us. Everything will be fine. This is what happens when you're involved in a major production. You have performance commitments you have to attend to as well as personal things that need to be taken care of. You can't let it throw you. Just go with the flow."

"How do you balance all of this on a day like today? Ugh! I didn't realize all the media coverage and photo shoots and extra rehearsals and performances that occurred in preparing for an event like this. It's been crazy."

Roger had to laugh. "Welcome to Broadway. This is what happens when a show is successful, which is why I told you to keep your days open for the next couple of months. It's not just about performances. There are other commitments, especially this time of year." Not wanting to burden her with more stress, but knowing she would find out sooner or later, he said, "Did I tell you that both of us have been invited to perform at Rockefeller this year? I thought we'd do a duet. And the Broadway League is holding a Broadway Live concert on New Year's Day and we've been asked to attend."

She stopped what she was doing. "Are you serious?"

"The Today Show also asked us to interview with them next week."

Her stress level was quickly growing, and she felt like she was going to burst. "What do they want to interview us about?"

"The show, our experiences on Broadway. They're supposed to call me tomorrow to give us a heads up on some of the questions they're going to ask. They specifically asked for both of us to be there. I honestly think they're more interested in you than me."

"Why?" she asked, not understanding why the Today Show would care about her at all.

"Because you're the new leading lady on Broadway, and the public doesn't really know anything about you. They're curious."

"But you said not to share personal information with the press."

"You don't share intimate details, no. You share enough to satisfy their curiosity and alleviate speculation. We'll look at what questions they want to ask and come up with appropriate responses. I've done several interviews. They're not a big deal." He looked at the clock again. They were officially running late. "Honey, we really have to go. Are you ready?" He grabbed his coat, the apartment key, and his cellphone.

"Yes."

"Good." He kissed her. "Let's go. We'll grab some tea on the way."

This was Lauren's first time hosting Thanksgiving dinner. She wasn't nervous about it, but she did want everything to be perfect. When they finally got home a little before 12:30 that afternoon, she began to prep the turkey for roasting then worked on peeling potatoes and mixing up corn bread.

While Lauren prepared dinner, Roger started on the table setting. Entertaining and decorating was not something he was lackluster about, so he went all out, making harvest colors reign supreme. He started off by spreading three beige burlap-patterned tablemats on the middle of the dining table. In the center one, he placed a large amber-colored vase full of branches, each covered in orange, red, and light brown leaves and berries. On either side of the vase, he strategically positioned two square-shaped amber-colored candles, one taller than the other, and surrounded the base of each with these same berry-covered branches. With all the wonderful hues of the harvest season, Roger chose to layer every place setting to blend the colors. Every setting had a similar, but slightly larger beige burlap placemat. Overtop each one, he layered a large white dinner plate, small white bread plate, neatly folded white linen table napkin, and an amber-colored square glass salad plate. To complement the look, he placed a ripened Comice pear on top. He placed silver stemware and both a long-stemmed crystal flute and amber-tinted wineglass at each setting. He accented the table with several white tea candles, which flickered inside glass amber-colored mini tumblers. This created an amber and yellow colored glow throughout the dining area. Spread across the credenza, he scattered a layered array of orange, yellow, and amber leaves, topped off with a harvest fruit bowl full of assorted mini pumpkins and gourds. This organic look added just the right touch of the season.

He stood back to examine his colorful creation. It was festive and elegantly layered. "Sweetheart, come out here and tell me what you think."

Lauren dried her hands with a dish towel and came out to have a look. "Oh wow!"

"Is this what you were going for?" he asked, hoping his wife was satisfied.

"Roger, this is beautiful. The pear is a nice touch."

"Good. The table is done then. Living room to go."

She returned to the kitchen to finish food prep while he worked on the coffee table and fireplace mantle.

Roger and Lauren combined their culinary talents and came up with a dinner menu to please the family's palate. Their menu consisted of roasted turkey, mashed potatoes with fresh dill, turkey gravy, sautéed green beans and mushrooms, citrus zest cranberry sauce, lemon maple squash, grape and pecan salad topped with cinnamon, and homemade corn bread. For dessert, they prepared old fashioned apple crisp, pumpkin pie, peach cobbler, and peanut butter pie topped with hot fudge sauce. They had a fresh vegetable tray with a variety of dips, a bowl of mixed nuts, and crackers and cream cheese laid out for people to snack on at their leisure. Their guests would not leave hungry.

Around 3:30, they had everything ready. The apartment smelled incredible, and it looked extraordinarily festive. Taking in the delicious aroma of the turkey, Roger declared, "Now I'm hungry,"

"Is the wine chilling?"

"Yes, Ma'am," he replied. "Both bottles. Just need to uncork and pour."

"Good, because Mom just called. They're on their way."

"Fantastic!" Roger boasted, anxious to get this family party started. He reached into the mixed nuts and pulled out a peanut, popping it into his mouth. "Told you we had this under control."

After enjoying a mouth-watering Thanksgiving meal with the family, Roger felt like a stuffed turkey. It was a good thing he didn't have to perform tonight, because if he did, he would have been tapping around on stage like an uncoordinated elephant.

The family sat around the living room conversing with one another about various topics. Peter prompted Roger by saying, "A lot of these Broadway shows go on to become movies or live TV productions, but some of the people they cast into those roles can't dance or sing. If they ever invite you to participate in something like that, you should definitely take them up on it, Roger."

"I have no desire to be on TV or the big screen. I'm a stage performer," Roger explained. "Those movies aren't about the musical score or the choreography. The actors can get away without being able to sing and dance. No one cares. People buy the movie and watch it anyway. But if you come to a live Broadway show and the performers can't dance and sing, the show gets bad reviews and loses ticket sales. Broadway is more about showmanship."

"But you're a good actor," Peter rebutted. "In Phantom, you took a creepy, deranged, psychopathic killer and made me feel sorry for the bastard."

Roger laughed. "That's because we stage actors have to put a hundred percent emotion into every performance. There's no doing the scene over if it isn't believable. There's no 'oops I forgot my line. Cut please and let's start again.' There aren't any computer animated special effects, no photo cropped scenery. It's live. That's the difference between Hollywood acting and Broadway acting. If they want to record a live stage performance and sell it on DVD, that's fine. I'll be a part of that. But I'm not packing up shop and going on location somewhere to film a movie when I know that the stage production will be better. It's not just that though. I don't particularly want my name to be world-renowned. I enjoy my privacy too much. Some people like having their name plastered all over national tabloid magazines. I don't."

"I don't blame you," Peter agreed.

"When you think about it, Pete, how many Broadway performers who stick solely to live stage are considered big name stars?" Roger asked.

"None that I know of," Peter said.

"And that's the way I like it. I'll keep my name limited to Manhattan, thank you very much."

With the addition of Peter and Amy's new baby, Roger now had three nephews. Gabriel was seven, Matthew was five, and the youngest one, Joseph, had just turned four months. Trying to get their uncle's attention, Gabriel and Matthew ran up to him screaming, "Uncle Roger!" They each grabbed one of his hands and tried to pull him out of his seat.

"Oh no! I'm being mauled by munchkins!" Roger teased them.

As they tugged and pulled on his arms to get him up, they begged, "Play something!"

"Alright, alright," Roger gave in. With his nephews by his side, he walked over to the piano and pulled out the bench. He sat down, and they both took a seat on either side of him, dangling their little legs. "Hmm. Shall we play Lion King this time?"

"Yay!" they exclaimed. "Pumba!"

Roger placed his fingers on the keys and began to play, singing as he did. "Hakuna matata, what a wonderful phrase…"

While Roger played, the boys sang as loudly as they could, bee-bopping on the bench and giggling.

In a deep Pumba voice, Roger sang out, "When I was a young warthog…"

The boys yelled, "When he was a young warthog!"

Roger snorted like a pig then he and the boys continued singing together. Roger's silliness with his nephews was positively adorable to watch. Their cute bonding moment made everyone laugh.

Roger's nephews adored him, and he really seemed to enjoy his time with them. They folded paper airplanes together and played Go Fish. Roger let them put on some of his theatrical hats, helped them make fun paper turkey snoods, and chased them around the apartment making gobble noises. He also played peek-a-boo with the baby.

Jane enjoyed watching Roger interact with his nephews. "He's really good with children."

Peter responded to this comment. "Oh, he's great with the boys. Uncle Roger is their favorite person. The fact that he bribes them with money and overindulges them with candy might have something to do with it, though." He looked over at his little brother, who was still playing piano and singing with Matthew and Gabriel. "He's always wanted to be a father."

Cradling the baby on her shoulder, Amy directed her attention to Lauren. "Have you two talked about having children?"

Lauren replied, "We both want children, but we've never discussed when."

"Roger is a good man," Amy said. "He'll make a wonderful dad someday."

As soon as everyone left, Lauren and Roger cleaned up the kitchen, sealed up and refrigerated leftovers, loaded dishes into the dishwasher, and hand washed wineglasses. Roger blew out the candles on the dining room table and reflected on the evening. "Not bad for our first Thanksgiving."

"Nope," Lauren agreed. "It was a fun night."

He placed his hand on his overstuffed belly. "Ugh, I'm so full, but man that was good. You make a mean peanut butter pie, my dear."

"Thank you, except that was my mother's recipe, not mine."

"Regardless, it's very tasty." He turned off the light in the dining area and kicked off his shoes, relaxing on the sofa. "We're going to need to do our show tomorrow to burn off all this food we ate tonight."

Lauren dried off her hands and hung the towel by the kitchen sink before she joined him on the sofa. The table lamp next to them was the only light glowing. "You were so adorable with your nephews today. They really love their uncle Roger."

"They're good boys." He put his arm around her and got more comfortable. "It's such a joy to see their smiles and hear their giggles. Always look forward to spending time with them."

Lauren curled her legs and leaned into his chest. "You will be a great daddy someday."

"Someday," he declared as he kissed the top of her head. "When we both feel ready."

"We could start thinking about that," Lauren proposed, wondering how Roger was going to react to her suggestion.

He asked for clarification. "What, having kids?"

"Yes."

Roger was at the peak of his career. Lauren was just starting hers. She no longer had school to contend with, but they both had rehearsals and show schedules to work around. They'd only been married for five months, which wasn't necessarily bad timing. After all, there were no guidelines written anywhere dictating when a couple should decide to start a family. That was an individual and personal decision. If they got pregnant now, the baby wouldn't come until after their first wedding anniversary. Plenty of time. But making this decision was going to depend a lot on Lauren. She couldn't be in this production once her pregnant belly started to stick out. Then again, that was going to be the case no matter what show she was doing. Now that he considered all of this, any time a baby was involved, there were going to be challenges. It was simply a matter of what they wanted and whether or not they felt ready. "Are you saying you want to have a baby?"

"I'm throwing the possibility out there. What do you think?"

Roger grinned at this prospect. "I definitely want to have kids. And I certainly won't mind trying to get you pregnant," he said in a seductive voice. "But are you sure you're ready for that?"

"I think we should start thinking about it," she told him.

"When you start to show, you're not going to be able to be on stage, unless the part specifically calls for a pregnant woman," Roger explained to her. "Polly can't be pregnant."

"I know, but I won't start to show right away. We'll have time."

He wanted her to understand how pregnancy might potentially affect her career and tried to get her to see this from all angles before they made any life-changing decisions. "You just started your career, Honey. Hypothetically speaking, if we were pregnant right now, you'd start to show around April. It won't even be a full year into the production."

"Is that a bad thing?" she asked.

"Not necessarily. It's just not a whole lot of experience under your belt."

She wondered what he was getting at. "Will that affect me getting a job later?"

"Not if we play it right," he reassured her. "We'd have to terminate your contract, but that's not hard to do. Kenneth will work with me on that. It's been done before."

"Would they close the show?" she asked, wondering how that worked.

"Don't know. Depends on if they feel like replacing you. But I think that when you go, I'll leave too. I can find another show to do. They may close it or they may do a cast change. We'll have to wait and see." Roger could tell she was seriously considering all of this, but he wanted to know what she was thinking. "We have to weigh all of this very carefully before we decide if we're going to do this right now, Lauren. I want to have a baby with you, but in all honesty, it's going to affect you more than it affects me. I'm not the one who has to carry the child."

She sat in deep thought, weighing the pros and cons.

"Talk to me, Honey. What are you thinking?" He gently rubbed his hand across her tummy. "Are we going to make a baby, or do you want to wait? I'm fine either way. Just need to know what you want to do."

She placed her hand over his. "Let's have a baby."

He was thrilled, yet surprised by her decision. "Alright. We'll go off the pill and let nature take its course."

She bit her lip suggestively. "Sounds good."

He raised an eyebrow at the sexy look she gave him. "This is gonna be fun. Can't wait to get started."

The following night, the entire family gathered together to see *Crazy For You*. This show, staring Roger and Lauren Zellers, was a musical love story. The way it simultaneously spoofed and celebrated classic Broadway productions was hilarious. It had innovative choreography, a lively company, and superb dancing. Roger and Lauren were both able to display their amazing talent. Roger showed off his smooth, elegant tap moves, emitting explosive percussive rhythm. His voice was strong and powerful, as usual, and his fun-loving personality shined through on the stage. Lauren's voice was just as beautiful, and she could really belt it out.

Randy enjoyed watching this show. It reminded him of classic Broadway back in the thirties when stars like Fred Astaire and Ginger Rogers used to shine on the stage. He was most impressed with seeing Lauren on the big stage. Her solo performance of 'Someone to Watch Over Me' echoed off the walls and brought loud applause throughout the entire theatre. Her performance made him a very proud dad.

At the curtain call, Lauren and Roger both received a standing ovation, which lasted several minutes. From the reaction of the audience, it was obvious that theatregoers were crazy for Lauren. Her Broadway dreams had come true, and she was a show-stopper.

"Damn!" Nathan said. "Lauren has an intense stage presence, and holy crap she can sing."

"She's always had a beautiful voice, but I didn't know she could dance like that," Gabby added.

"She's gotten really good. I'm impressed with how far she has come in her dancing skills. I've heard that tap is one of the most difficult styles of dance to learn."

"It is," Lacy confirmed. "Not everyone can do it. I'm not very good at it, but Roger is the best in the business, and he's been working with her."

"I can tell," Nathan remarked. "He is the best tap dancer I've ever seen. He makes it look so easy."

Jane expressed her opinion. "He is quite the showman, and he and Lauren blend well together."

"They do," Lacy added. "Lauren is a powerhouse vocalist, and Roger is literally the best actor on Broadway right now, with scores of credits. New York theatregoers love seeing them together."

"I can see why," Nathan said. "I'm not usually into musicals, but this rocked!"

After the show, the family met Roger and Lauren backstage, at which time Randy presented Lauren with a bouquet of roses. "You were outstanding, Baby. I'm so proud of you."

"Thank you, Daddy." She took the flowers from him and set them on the vanity.

"Isn't she spectacular?" Roger boasted. "She steals the spotlight."

"I'm gonna have that song stuck in my head all night now," Randy proclaimed with a chuckle.

"That's good. Means it made an impression on you."

"You were incredible," Randy said. "Both of you were. What a fabulous performance."

That same weekend, Columbia University dance students paired up with Brooklyn's Academy of Music to put on a contemporary holiday show called Bonne Fêtes. Lacy had a choreographed number in this program. After spending an afternoon watching the Knicks/Clippers game at Madison Square Garden, Roger, Lauren and the rest of the Hanson family went to Miller Theatre to watch Lacy perform in this show. This festive performance put everyone in a holiday mood.

Because of performance commitments, Roger and Lauren celebrated Christmas with Roger's family in Owego rather than traveling out of the state. Their first Christmas together as husband and wife was a memorable experience. They even bought a tree ornament to commemorate the event.

Chapter Thirty-Six

6:00 A.M. on a Monday morning, Roger heard Lauren get out of bed and head into the bathroom, where she threw up. After a toilet flush, she turned on the shower water. He rolled over and tried to go back to sleep.

When she finally came out of the bathroom wrapped in a towel, the expression on her face revealed that her physical wellbeing was subpar. "You alright?" Roger asked.

She shook her head. "I feel like crap."

"I heard." Roger sat up and stretched. "Why are we prolonging this?"

She dug through the bureau to get undergarments. "Prolonging what?"

"You're several weeks late, and now you're throwing up the minute you get out of bed in the morning. We need to buy a pregnancy test and check this out."

"You might want to put on some clothes first. Would hate to have to bail my husband out of jail for running around naked down the streets of Manhattan. That would be very hard to explain to the family."

He grinned drolly at her witty, sarcastic comment. "I wasn't planning on streaking through Manhattan. New York City already has one naked cowboy. We don't need another one." He popped out of bed and grabbed her from behind, which made her scream. "When I get back, I'll treat you to breakfast, with clothes on."

"Sounds yummy."

Roger hopped in the shower, got dressed, then headed to the drug store. He came back with not one, but two pregnancy tests.

Lauren laughed when he took them out of the bag. "Why did you get two?"

"Second opinion." He turned one of the boxes over and read the directions on the back.

Giggling at him, she picked up the urine stick. "There's only one way to find out." She walked into the bathroom and closed the door.

Holding the other box in his hand, he followed her, waiting outside for her to finish. When she was done, she set the test strip on the counter. Although he was excited about the high possibility that they could be pregnant, Roger was a little anxious that the test would indeed come back positive. He stared at the test strip, waiting for something to happen. Within minutes, the area at the end began to turn pink. He instantly fumbled for the box to find out what that meant.

While Roger tried to decipher the results, Lauren already knew what it meant. She held her test strip out to him and cried, "I'm pregnant."

"We're pregnant?"

"Pink means pregnant." She pointed out the color change. "It's pink."

A huge smile crept onto his face. He drew her into his arms and smothered her with kisses. "This is incredible! I'm going to be a daddy!"

The first person they called was Randy. Roger did the honors. "Hello, Dr. Hanson. How are you this morning?"

456

"Exceptionally well, thank you."

"I have a medical question for you," he asked.

"Alright. What's up?"

"I was wondering if you could recommend a good obstetrician in the New York City area."

"I know of one. He and I did our residency together. His name is Robert Scalafani. Why do you need an obstetrician?"

"Because you are going to be a grandfather." Randy's end of the line fell silent. Roger wasn't sure if his father-in-law was in shock or upset over hearing this news. Trying to get clarification, he attempted to regain Randy's attention. "Dr. Hanson?"

Randy finally spoke up. "Lauren's pregnant?"

"Yes, Sir, she is."

"Did you confirm this?"

"Yup," Roger explained. "Took two home pregnancy tests. Both came back positive."

"That's great news." He moved his mouth away from the phone and told his wife the good news. Ecstatic screams followed. When Randy came back on the phone, he advised, "You need to get her in to see Robert as soon as possible."

"We intend to. Do you have contact information?"

"He's in Brooklyn. I'll get you the phone number. Hold on."

After receiving contact information for Dr. Scalafani, Roger thanked his father-in-law.

"Give him my regards when you see him, and let him know Lauren is my daughter," Randy advised. "Make sure you get her some pre-natal vitamins. She needs to start taking them right away."

"Will do." Before ending the conversation, Roger handed the phone over to Lauren so she could talk to her parents.

In the morning, Lauren awoke to Roger towering over her with a glass of orange juice in his hand. "Good morning, Mommy," he said softly when he saw that her eyes were open.

She stretched and sat up.

He leaned over and kissed her then handed her the glass. "Here. You and baby both need this."

She took the glass and drank.

Roger sat on the bed next to her. "Let's see if we can get you in to see this Dr. Scalafani either today or tomorrow."

"We're not going to have time today. We have two shows to do. We're going to have to schedule it for tomorrow morning if we can."

He lovingly patted her on the thigh. "I want to be as involved in this pregnancy as possible. That means going to doctor's appointment, ultrasounds, anything at all like that. You get to experience things I don't because you're carrying the child, but I don't want to miss anything. I want to bond with baby too."

"You can have some of the nausea I've been feeling the last couple days if you'd like. I'll gladly give that to you."

"If I could take it from you, Honey, I would."

She suddenly felt ill. She held her stomach, scurried out of bed, and hurried to the bathroom.

Unfortunately, Roger had to listen to the unpleasantness that followed. He hoped this phase didn't last very long.

Before taking Lauren to her first obstetrical appointment, Roger met Jason for coffee. While sipping on his latte, Jason said, "I still can't believe it."

"Believe what?" Roger asked.

"That you're going to be a father."

"I'm psyched," Roger declared, bouncing around as if he'd already had several cups of coffee.

Jason laughed at his overly-zealous response. "I can tell."

"You know I've always wanted to have a family, Jason."

"Yes, but I figured you'd enjoy marital bliss for a while before you jumped into parenting. You guys didn't wait very long. You've only been married for nine months."

"We're on the nine month plan," Roger teased. "Married nine months, a nine month pregnancy. We have a system down."

"Were you guys trying to get pregnant or was this a contraception malfunction?"

"Oh no, we planned it."

"How's she feeling?"

Roger sympathized with Lauren's current misery. "She's been waking up the last few days with the toilet being her best friend. Kinda gave me a complex this morning. Nothing like starting the day with sex then having your wife throw up afterwards."

Jason found this hilarious.

"She got a little light headed yesterday between performances, but once she drank some water and sat down to rest for a few minutes, she was fine for the rest of the night."

"Did you get a due date yet?"

"No. Gonna head to the doctor in about an hour."

"Cool," Jason replied. "I'm excited for you. Still shocked over the whole thing, but excited."

"Thank you. We're excited too."

When Roger took Lauren to the doctor that morning, he went into the exam room with her. After performing the initial exam, drawing blood, checking uterus size, measuring the girth of Lauren's abdomen, and looking at a due date calculation chart, the doctor determined that the baby was expected around October 14th. They figured she was probably between five and six weeks pregnant. When they had a sonogram done, Roger's excitement level escalated. Generally, the fetal heartbeat started beating twenty-two days after conception. However, it was much too small to be heard using a Doppler. Therefore, doctors frequently used ultrasounds to confirm pregnancy and measure early fetal heartbeat. Roger hoped that when the image of their baby appeared on the screen, they might hear the heart beating.

The doctor took the tip of his pen and pointed out the small peanut-shaped embryo. "See? Baby's right there." He waited for these first time expectant parents to react. That was his favorite part.

Seeing their baby's image for the first time was more of an emotional experience than either one of them imagined it was going to be. Roger got teary eyed. "There's a baby in there."

The doctor chuckled. "Yes there is."

Lauren said, "Baby's so tiny."

"Yes, but baby will grow quickly at this stage," the doctor said. "We'll do another ultrasound in about seven to eight weeks. You'll see a lot of growth between now and then. Let me print out a couple of these to take with you."

While the doctor was busy doing that, Roger looked down at Lauren, who had imaging gel all over her tummy. He grabbed a paper towel and helped her wipe it off. "Wow. This is quite the experience."

She fastened her pants and sat up. "Wasn't too thrilled about them sucking blood out of me though."

The doctor interjected, "Not generally a favorite among my patients, but it's for yours and baby's health. We're going to do some screenings and run some tests to ensure everything's okay."

Roger liked this doctor. He was down to earth, easy to talk to, and very cheerful. He had a way of making uncomfortable situations, like pelvic exams, more bearable. He was just as excited as they were about this baby, and he gladly answered any questions they had. Roger felt comfortable having this man take care of his wife and his unborn baby during this vital time.

"Here you go," the doctor said, handing Roger three sonogram images. "Baby's first photographs."

"Thank you very much." Roger handed the images to Lauren. "Oh, I almost forgot. We were supposed to send a hello your way from an old friend of yours."

This sparked Dr. Scalafani's interest. "Who might that be?"

Lauren replied, "My father. Dr. Randal Hanson."

Robert Scalafani grinned hugely. "You're little Lauren Hanson?"

"Uh huh."

"Dr. Hanson highly recommended you," Roger stated.

"He did, huh?" the doctor chuckled. "I'll have to shoot him an e-mail and thank him." He looked directly at Lauren. "I haven't seen your dad in years. How's he doing?"

"He's doing well," Lauren said. "Still has his practice in Seattle. He mentors medical students and provides them with clinical OB/GYN experience. Nathan is in medical school now."

The doctor's forehead wrinkled. "Is he?"

"Uh huh. He goes to UW."

Dr. Scalafani shook his head in disbelief. "Wow, I remember when all three of you were little. Last time I saw Randy was at a conference in Seattle. You and your sister had to be five or six and your brother was probably eight or nine. What are you doing in New York?" he asked her.

"Came here for school. I attended Juilliard."

"She's a lead actress on Broadway now," Roger added with a grin.

The doctor's eyes widened. "It that right?"

"My first show," she said proudly.

"She's spectacular," Roger boasted. "If you get a chance, you should come see the show, staring yours truly and my leading lady here."

"You're in the show together?"

"Yes we are," Roger explained.

"Which one?"

"Revival of Crazy For You at the Imperial Theatre." Roger reached into his wallet and pulled out two orchestra level tickets, handing them to the doctor. "Here. Complimentary tickets."

The doctor grinned and took the tickets from Roger. "Thank you. My wife and I will have to check it out."

"Please do. It's a great show."

Even though they couldn't see it, baby was growing quickly. Arms and legs were expanding and beginning to take shape, and baby's fingers were starting to separate. Facial features were forming as well. The baby's spinal cord and brain were growing at an exponential rate, producing about one-hundred new brain cells every minute. Their baby was becoming stronger and more vital. Although the fetus could move its limbs, it would still be a while before Lauren would be able to feel these movements. Since baby's bones were hardening, the doctor recommended that Lauren increase her intake of calcium-rich foods.

By the end of the third month, the baby measured nearly two and a half inches and weighed about half an ounce. To Roger, this didn't sound like a lot, but Dr. Scalafani reminded him that the baby had more than tripled its size in two months. It was quite an amazing achievement. The ultrasound image clearly showed a baby with moving arms and legs. Not only were Roger and Lauren able to see the baby's heartbeat, they heard it as well. What a difference a few weeks made.

"Baby looks great." He moved the transponder to get a clearer image. "Next time you come in, we're going to have to run some tests on you, and you're probably going to feel like a pin cushion."

"Ugh! Really?"

"Yes, but don't hate me," he chuckled. "These tests, although they may be a tad uncomfortable, are necessary to monitor your baby's development and identify any risks for birth defects. I'm also going to give you a glucose screening to check for gestational diabetes."

Roger grew uneasy. "Is this something we should be concerned about?"

"Rest assured that the vast majority of test results come back perfectly normal. But we have to run the screenings just to be safe. We're getting into the second trimester now. You're a third of the way there."

When the doctor put it that way, the reality of pregnancy really kicked in. The first trimester went by quickly.

Realizing that they only had about six months left until the baby was born, Roger and Lauren decided it was probably a good idea to start buying essentials.

They spent their off day shopping for a crib, dresser, changing table, and other necessary furnishings and started to plan out the theme of their baby's nursery.

Changing out the guestroom to make it into a room suitable for baby was a huge chore. They had to remove the double bed from the room, as well as other bulky furnishings, and lug them out of the building. The awkward and heavy baby furniture needed to be moved in, and the crib needed to be assembled. To complete this back breaking task, Roger instilled the help of his dear friend, Jason Preen.

"Jason, I need you."

"I appreciate the love, but I have a show to report to in an hour," Jason reminded him.

"I know, I do too. But tomorrow morning, I need you to come over to my place."

"Why?"

"Lauren and I had a bunch of baby furniture delivered this afternoon and I'm going to need help moving it. I attempted to put this crib together today and failed epically. I need your help."

Roger's lack of crib assembly know-how made Jason laugh. "Sure. I can help you out, but can I bring Bailey with me?"

"Of course," Roger replied. "She and Lauren will keep each other company."

"What time?"

"9:00ish?" Roger suggested.

"Alright, but you owe me breakfast," Jason demanded.

"I'll have it waiting for you when you get here."

"Sweet."

"Thanks," Roger said. "See you in the morning."

"With bells on. Break a leg tonight, Rog."

"You too."

Roger had apple fritters, yogurt, fresh fruit, freshly brewed coffee, and orange juice waiting in the kitchen when Jason and Bailey arrived. He greeted them at the door, gripping Jason's hand firmly. "Hello, Mr. Preen."

Jason wasn't as enthusiastic. "You do realize that I don't work until I eat."

"It's in the kitchen," Roger chuckled.

Bailey walked in behind Jason. "Hi, Roger. It's good to see you again."

"Good to see you too."

Over the last several months, Roger had become better acquainted with Bailey Metcalf. She was a kind-hearted person with a fun sense of humor, and she treated Jason with respect. Most importantly, Jason liked her. The two of them complemented each other, and they had a lot in common. Lately, they seemed to be inseparable and spent almost every free moment together. As Jason walked past Bailey to grab a fritter and a banana, he winked at her flirtatiously. In response, she winked back then joined Lauren in the living room.

Roger had never seen Jason this happy. It was a refreshing change. "So, you and Bailey."

"What about me and Bailey?" Jason took a bite of his apple fitter.

"Been spending an awful lot of time together."

"Things are getting serious."

"How serious?"

"We're moving in together."

Roger gulped down his orange juice. "Is that right?"

"Yup. She brought a bunch of her stuff over yesterday. She's gonna move more this afternoon."

"That sounds pretty serious."

Jason leaned against the counter top. "And what about you with all this baby business, knowing you're going to responsible for the life of a little person. That has to be frightening."

"I'm excited about becoming a father, but, yes, being responsible for this tiny person who is totally depending on me to provide for him is a bit scary."

"I can't even imagine trying to bring a child into the world right now. What a huge responsibility." Jason turned his head to Lauren, wondering about the severity of her pregnancy symptoms. "Is she feeling any better?"

"Actually, she is. No more morning vomit fests."

Jason chuckled. "That's good."

"We had another ultrasound done last week. Got to see baby moving and heard the heartbeat."

"Bet that was neat," Jason proclaimed.

"Makes it very real, that's for sure. We can't see external signs of the baby yet, but hearing that was reassuring."

"Bailey and I want to get you guys something for the baby," Jason said, wanting to help out his friend. "What do you need?"

"I honestly don't know. We're still trying to figure all of this out. I've been instilling the help of my brother in that domain. But based on all of the advice we've received, it sounds like babies need a lot of crap."

Jason laughed. "Where's this crib that's kicking your butt?"

Roger set his glass in the sink and the men headed to the spare room.

Chapter Thirty-Seven

Gabby came home from a training session to find Nathan sitting on the floor in the corner of the bedroom staring at a framed photograph. Worried about him, she set her school bag down and sat by his side.

The picture in his hand was taken back in high school; it was an image of him and his childhood friend, Mike. Mike and Nathan had known each other since they were six. Growing up, they were the best of friends. They played basketball together in the peewee league, were on the same team in junior high and high school, and were roommates in college. The summer before Nathan's sophomore year at UW, Mike had a difficult time dealing with some personal issues and ended up taking his own life over it. Losing his best friend was devastating for Nathan. Since that time, he had learned to adjust to life without Michael, but occasionally, certain incidents or events would trigger an emotional reaction.

Nathan turned away from the photo, biting back tears. "When Mike and I were kids, we always said we'd have each other's backs. I specifically remember an incident back in fifth grade when a bully started pushing people around and picking fights with everyone. He tried to start in on Mike, and I

467

coldcocked the guy. Knocked him on his ass. I got in serious trouble for that and ended up in the principal's office, but I wasn't about to let some jerk mess with my friend. When the principal questioned everyone about the incident, Michael took the rap for me, even though I told him not to, because he knew how angry my father was going to be if he found out I was fighting at school. And since he'd already been punched by the guy and looked like he'd been in a fight, the story was convincing. He ended up getting a two day suspension and had the discipline incident added to his permanent record, but the bully never messed with him or me again. I had his back and he had mine." He set the photograph on the floor beside him. "I always thought Mike would stand next to me when you and I exchanged vows. He was supposed to be my Best Man." His shoulders slumped. "Who's going to be my Best Man now?"

Gabby gently placed her hand on Nathan's arm, offering him comfort. "We don't have to have a line if you don't want to, Nathan. I'm sure we can have the ceremony with just the two of us standing up there."

"That's not fair to you. You want to have your closest friends up there with you, I'm not going to deny you that. I'll find someone, I just don't know who."

Gabby tried to help him. "Have you thought about Elliot?"

Nathan puckered his brow. "I think Elliot's a cool guy, but no. I don't want him as my Best Man."

"What about Andrew? He's always been a good friend, and he was there for you when you needed him the most."

"That's what I was thinking." He looked down at Mike's photograph again. "I miss him."

"I know you do." Hoping to get his mind on something else, Gabby suggested, "Let's do something fun."

"Like what?"

"You like airplanes. Let's go to the Museum of Flight."

Gabby knew him well. Looking at airplanes, jets, helicopters, and spacecraft would definitely improve his mood. "Sounds fun."

Gabby rose to her feet and extended both arms, helping Nathan off the floor.

University of Washington medical students were affectionately coined as the "Weary Whitecoats." With disillusionment written all over their faces, they were often seen trudging around campus carrying lab coats. They were mentally fatigued and suffered from callouses on their index finger where they had continuously jammed it into the sleep button of their alarm clock.

After another eighty-hour week of sitting through difficult classes, working in his father's clinic, performing clinical skills, writing lab reports, and studying, Nathan drug himself through the door. He dropped his backpack on the floor by the doorway and collapsed on the couch. His energy tank was depleted, and he had absolutely none left in reserve. His first year of medical school was nearly finished, but burnout was creeping in. He was running on fumes, functioning off four hours of sleep. He could no longer keep his eyes open. Exhaustion kicked in, and in less than two minutes, he was out.

Gabby came home from a late planning meeting and found him completely zonked out on the couch.

With the excessive stress and anxiety he'd been facing lately, she left him there to rest.

Despite suffering from severe exhaustion, Nathan stayed true to his passion. At no time did he develop negativity or throw in the towel. He worked hard and maintained his dedication even though some around him had given in to the frustration. Gabby was proud of him for that. The strong support system he had contributed greatly to his survival and sanity. His friend and former teammate, Andrew Garibay, helped him burn off steam by setting up basketball games for him to participate in, which always helped him relax. His parents offered financial support, and his father, in particular, imparted advice and offered personal insights into Nathan's experiences, encouraging him every step of the way. His study group served as a venting venue, and they supported one another academically. Most importantly, Gabby offered patience, love, and an immense understanding of his dedication.

The delicious aroma of spaghetti sauce woke Nathan. Still fatigued, he stretched and sat up with an unpleasant groan.

"Uh oh. There's a grizzly bear in my living room," Gabby teased him.

"Don't start singing the bear song please," Nathan begged. "I don't think I can handle going over the mountain and through the forest today. I might have to grab a shotgun and shoot that damn bear."

Gabby could tell Nathan was tired. He became grumpy and overly sarcastic when he didn't get enough sleep. She tried to cheer him up. "You'll leave poor Booboo without his Uncle Yogi if you do that."

"You really need to get out and talk to adults more often." In his sleep deprived state, he remembered something he wanted to ask her. "Why is there a plastic tub full of toilet paper tubes in the bedroom?"

"Don't throw those away. I need them," Gabby declared.

"What for?"

"We're making tube rabbits for the letter R next week. Don't use the bag of cotton balls on the bathroom counter. I need them for the rabbit's tails."

Gabby's creativity never ceased to amaze him. The funny stories she would tell about her five-year-olds always brought a smile to his face and could make even the longest, most challenging day more bearable. "Tube rabbits with cotton ball tails? I'm afraid to find out what kind of song goes with that."

She giggled at him. "Would you like me to sing it for you?"

"Not today," he grumbled.

"You're going to bed early tonight," Gabby insisted. "You've worked too much this week."

"I'm not gonna argue with you on that." He rested his weary head on her shoulder.

Gabby ran her fingers though his hair. "I brought something home for you."

"What is it?"

"Watch this for a minute and I'll go get it." She handed him the spoon she was using to stir spaghetti sauce then went over to her school bag and pulled out a stack of papers. "My students made something for you."

"Your students? Why would they make something for me?"

"I told them you were learning how to be a doctor and had some big tests coming up next week. So they drew pictures and made cards for you as encouragement."

"Really?" He handed the spoon back to Gabriella and took the stack of papers from her. They were held together with a paperclip. He looked through the adorable child drawings of doctors, most of which had notes written in phonetic Kindergarten spelling. His favorite drawing was of a lanky figure with exceptionally long arms, tiny legs, and an oversized head. He appeared to be wearing scrubs and a long white coat. Around his neck was a detailed drawing of a stethoscope. This cartoonish-looking doctor's face had a huge grin, large eyes with long camel-like eyelashes, and brown hair sticking straight up. He had purple sneakers on his feet. Above the drawing, the child wrote, *Good luk doktr*. This picture made Nathan laugh. He held it up to show Gabby. "This is awesome! Who's this creative one? That's a pretty detailed drawing for a Kindergartener."

"That's Penelope. She's my little artist."

"I can see that." These adorable pictures reaffirmed that the hard work and long hours he dedicated to medical school were worth the sacrifice. Apparently these young children thought he was a pretty important person.

"I know how hard you've been working and how stressed you've been. You needed a pick me up."

Nathan paper clipped the drawings back together, except for Penelope's, which he hung on the refrigerator with a magnet. "These are great, Gab. Thank you."

"You're welcome. Now, go wash up for dinner."

Chapter Thirty-Eight

Toward the end of May, Lauren's baby bump started to show. It wasn't noticeable when she was dressed, but when she was lying on the bed naked, Roger could see it.

"My clothes are too tight," she complained.

"I keep telling you to get maternity clothes. Take Lacy with you. I'm sure she'd love to go shopping."

Lauren was at the point in her pregnancy where she had to admit the truth. In a few weeks, her clothes wouldn't fit at all. That included costumes for the show. "I won't be able to do this show for much longer."

Roger rolled his hand over her tummy. "Are you ready to have a conversation with Darryl and Kenneth?"

Reluctantly, she agreed. "I think we need to."

"Alright. I'll give Kenneth a call."

"Have you decided what you're going to do yet?"

"I'm not renewing my contract."

"I'm sorry," Lauren apologized, releasing tears for no apparent reason.

"Don't worry about it. I have a couple of gigs set up. We'll be fine."

"This is all my fault."

"Sweetheart, do not apologize. Actors and actresses leave for various reasons all the time, it's not a big deal. And it's not like we're throwing it at them at the last minute. As soon as we found out we were pregnant, we told Darryl. He knew this was coming." Her emotional state fluctuated quite often lately. One minute she was happy, the next minute sad. He figured it was the pregnancy hormones running rampant. To reassure her, he gave her a hug. "This is all your fault, huh?" he laughed at the absurd assumption she made. "Are you trying to tell me that you got pregnant without me? Because the last time I checked, it took two to make a baby."

She giggled at his bluntness. "That's not what I meant."

"We decided to have this baby together, and we are in this together. We're going to do what's best for our family."

That afternoon, Roger and Lauren sat with Darryl and Kenneth to discuss Lauren's departure from the show. Roger made it very clear that when Lauren's contract ended, his was as well. The show was successful, had a huge net profit of millions of dollars, and had earned several Tony nominations. Since it was going to be difficult to continue the show with both of their leads leaving at the same time, the Broadway League made the decision to close the show, setting a closing date for June 25th.

Roger fully intended to be available in October for Lauren's due date and didn't want to get involved in anything long term. He did, however, arrange to participate in a few events that would earn him some extra cash. The first of these was a tap number at the Tony Awards with his Folley ensemble from *Crazy For You*. Another gig he was asked to participate in was a one night only Broadway Live Concert. Returning to classic theatre, he signed up to be a part of a three-day summer Shakespeare Festival in Central Park. He also agreed to record a song for a Broadway benefit Christmas album entitled, Carols for a Cure.

He committed to a short term contract performing in *White Christmas* during the holiday season. This show would only be open for three weeks, from December 1st until December 23rd, but rehearsals weren't going to start until November. That would give him plenty of time to help Lauren with their newborn and allow him ample baby bonding time.

Now at twenty weeks pregnant, Lauren had an obvious belly bulge. Her clothes didn't fit, which forced her to wear either pants with elastic waistbands or maternity attire. Yet she had a difficult time finding anything that looked flattering on her. The dress she picked out for the Tony Awards this year was an elegant black evening gown with an embellished design and crisscross back. She looked glamorous and stunning in this dress, at least Roger thought so.

He knew she was self-conscious about her pregnant tummy, so he made it a priority to tell her how beautiful she was. Pulling up to the red carpet, he cradled Lauren's tummy with his hand. "You're glowing."

She placed her hand over his. "This dress doesn't fit right. It makes me look pregnant."

He laughed at her. "That's because you are pregnant. Unfortunately the press is going to zoom in on your pregnant belly instead of focusing on the reason we're here."

She grinned. "The Tony's."

"Yes, the Tony's. And our show received five nominations."

This year, Lauren was a star in her own right. Both she and Roger received nominations for Best Performance By a Leading Actor/ Actress in a Musical. Even though neither of them won in their respective categories, the musical received Best Choreography, Best Revival of a Musical, and Darryl won for Best Direction. Lauren was a little upset that she didn't win, yet Roger wasn't that concerned. He was proud of the show, and knew that he and Lauren were involved in an extraordinary production. Five nominations, three Tony wins, impeccable critic reviews, and loud applause for Roger and the Folley Girls during their tap dance performance of 'I Can't Be Bothered Now' indicated how successful this show was.

Roger pointed all of that out to her. "I didn't win either, but that's okay. We won't win every time. I'm just honored that we both received a nomination. The show received five total nominations and won in three categories. That says a lot about the quality of this production. We were both involved in something incredible, and you received a nomination for your debut on Broadway. You should be proud of that. When I debuted in Newsies, I didn't get a nomination. Kudos to you. That's contract bargaining power for sure."

The next day, photographs of Lauren and Roger were plastered all over social media, accompanied by a caption. *Soon-to-be parents, Roger and Lauren Zellers, stylishly sashayed across the red carpet at the Tony Awards at NYC's Radio City Music Hall on Sunday. Roger was nominated for Best Performance By a Leading Actor in a Musical for his portrayal of Bobby Childs in Crazy For You. Lauren received her nomination for portraying Polly Baker in the same production. Unfortunately, both lost out. The Broadway stars are expecting their little one this fall.*

Many people at the Tony's commented about how elegant Lauren looked that night. This article and the fan comments that followed confirmed what Roger already knew—Lauren was beautiful, and pregnancy seemed to draw out her beauty even more. "See, Honey, I told you, you looked stunning last night. It's all over the internet."

Brandon Schaefer was the regular photographer for large social events like this. Since he and Roger were friends, Brandon offered to give Roger copies of the shots he captured on the red carpet. "Brandon said he'd send a few pictures our way."

"Why would we want pictures of my pregnant belly at the Tony's?"

"Because it was your first nomination as a leading actress on Broadway. That's memorable. Also because you looked gorgeous. I don't know why you were so self-conscious. People complimented you all night. Many came up to me personally and told me how lovely my wife looked."

Lauren stepped out of the bedroom dressed in a pair of grey leggings and one of Roger's white dress shirts with the sleeves rolled up and the top two buttons unbuttoned.

Roger did a double take when he saw her. "Never knew my shirt made such a sexy maternity outfit."

"Your shirts are comfortable right now. They're baggy and don't feel tight on my tummy."

"Looking at you right now is exactly the point I'm trying to get across to you." He stood behind her and positioned his hand on her bulging belly. "You are gorgeous, Mrs. Zellers, no matter what you wear."

She smiled at his flattery.

He sent loving kisses down her neck. "We're going to have to be a little more creative in the bedroom. Your tummy kind of got in the way last night."

She giggled. "That was a little awkward, wasn't it?"

"I'm not complaining," Roger declared. "We can work around the tummy issue. It'll give us a chance to play with different positions. I'm just glad you still want to."

She didn't understand why he said that. "Why would I not want to?"

"Some women, when they're pregnant, lose that drive. I'm glad you're not one of them. Don't know if I could handle going nine months without being intimate with you. I'd have to take a lot of cold showers."

Their sex life as a married couple was no daily Kama Sutra, but it certainly wasn't dull either. They got wild under the covers at least twice a week, and even with Lauren being pregnant, that didn't subside much. Roger knew that as she got closer to her due date, and for several weeks following giving birth, this would not be the case. He was convinced that having a newborn in the house was going to severely lower both of their libidos, especially once sleep deprivation kicked in. He soaked up the passion and relished every intimate moment while they still had the energy to do it.

The final performance of *Crazy For You* was June 25th. They had a huge cast party that night, which ended up turning into a baby shower for Lauren and Roger. With the closing of the show, Lauren planned to take a hiatus from the stage, at least for a while. Roger, on the other hand, planned to make a few small appearances here and there until rehearsal for *White Christmas* started. In the meantime, he had a bit of time on his hands. He used this down time productively by preparing the baby's room.

After much discussion and debate, they opted for a Lion King theme in the nursery. They purchased a comforter, window treatments, crib sheets, blankets, and bumpers with Simba and Nala printed on them. Above the chestnut brown crib, he hung a mobile with plush lion cubs who looked like they were chasing after dangling butterflies. Roger bought a couple of shelves to hold a set of stuffed animals they bought from the Disney Store, including Simba, Nala, Timon, Pumba, Rafiki, and Zazu. The lamp on the dresser had a ceramic Simba for the base with a brown jungle print lampshade. For the walls, they had several embroidered Lion King wall hangings, some of which were handmade by Roger's mother. But before they could decorate the room, Roger needed to paint it.

He moved all the furniture to the middle of the room and covered it with a plastic drop cloth. He slipped on a pair of old jeans and a tee-shirt then grabbed the blue painter's tape, paint rollers and rolling pan, and several different types of polyester filament paint brushes. He spread a blue tarp across the hardwood floor and began the task of painting.

He was in the middle of covering a wall with neutral beige paint when his cellphone rang. He set down the paint roller, wiped his hands with a rag, and carefully reached for his phone, trying not get paint all over it. "Hello?"

"Hello, Roger. It's Philip Powell."

Philip Powell was the director Roger worked with during his time in *Les Misérables*. Roger hadn't spoken to him in years. "Hey, Phil. How you been?"

"Doing well. I see you've been busy."

"Yup," Roger concurred. "I try to stay that way."

"Congratulations on another Tony nomination," Philip said, trying to butter Roger up for what he was about to ask him.

"Thank you. Would have been better if it was a win, but such is the nature of the business."

Philip didn't beat around the bush. "Heard you were available."

"I'm not currently under contract. Why?"

"I'm in a desperate situation and I need you," Philip said to him.

"What's going on?"

"My lead quit unexpectedly."

"Get a new lead," Roger suggested.

"It's not that simple. We open in five days."

That was definitely a problem. "What about the understudy?"

The director explained the situation. "The understudy was in a car accident last week and is still in the hospital. I'm not going to be able to find anyone who can learn the part that quickly, and I really don't want to push the premiere back, that's why I called you. I need you, Roger. You know Valjean well."

"Valjean, huh?"

"Yes. Will you help me out?"

Roger considered the implications of this. "The thing is, my wife and I are expecting. She's due in less than four months. If I accept this, it's only going to be until the first of October. I need to be available for her."

"That's perfect. It will buy us some time."

"When did you say the premiere was?" Roger asked, wanting clarification.

"Friday. Will you be able to pull this off in five days?"

"I should be able to," Roger explained. "I already know the part, I'll just need to rehearse on stage a few times. But let me talk to my wife before I commit to anything. Are you going to be at this number for a while?"

"Yes."

"I'll call you right back." Roger discussed this with Lauren and they decided that he would accept the part, but only until they could find a replacement. Roger wanted to be available for Lauren as her due date came closer.

He called Philip back and accepted the offer, which meant he had a major part to prepare for in a very short amount of time. Dress rehearsals started Monday morning. Between now and the time the baby arrived, Roger was going to be exceptionally busy.

When he finished painting the walls of the baby's room, he came into the living room and dug through a box of old musical scores, scripts, and sheet music.

"What are you doing?" Lauren asked when she saw him dump everything out of the box.

"Looking for my score for *Les Mis*. I know it's here somewhere."

Lauren placed her hand on her tummy and giggled.

Roger turned his head. "What?"

"Come here."

He ambled over to her, and she put his hand on the side of her pregnant belly. "Can you feel it?"

Roger didn't feel a thing. "Feel what?"

"The baby kicked me."

"Really?" He felt more purposefully now. When the baby kicked, a joyful smile lit up his face. "I think there might be some tap dancing going on in there." He rubbed his hand across her bulging belly, searching for more wiggles and kicks.

Chapter Thirty-Nine

"Baby looks great. Heartbeat is strong." Dr. Scalafani moved the ultrasound imaging device to the other side of Lauren's belly to get a better look. "All ten fingers and ten little toes are wiggling around just fine." Before he moved the device again, he asked, "Did you want to know the gender of this baby?"

Lauren and Roger looked at each other, confirming what the other was thinking. "Can you tell?" Roger asked.

"Yup. Have a perfect view right here." The doctor highlighted the defining organs. "It's a boy."

Sure enough, Roger and Lauren could clearly see the identifying parts. Roger grinned proudly. "I'm going to have a son."

"Yes, Sir. A bouncing baby boy. Congratulations."

"Another grandson for your parents," Lauren remarked.

Roger was perfectly fine with that. "I think they were hoping for a girl this time, but I'm thrilled."

The doctor gave his last bits of advice. "We're only a few months away. Nutrition and exercise are important at this stage. And if you haven't yet, you might want to consider signing up for Lamaze classes."

"Alright," Lauren said, heeding her doctor's advice. "Am I clear to fly this weekend?"

"You're clear, especially since your dad will be around. Just make sure you drink plenty of water on the plane. Try to claim an aisle seat if you can so you can get to the bathroom easily. Be sure to walk around and stretch. If you're immobile for too long, you are at increased risk for developing blood clots, and we don't want to go there." He wrote something on a piece of paper, signed it, and handed it to her. This paper stated her expected due date and gave her medical clearance to fly, just in case there were disputes at the boarding gate. "If for some reason there's a problem and your dad needs your chart, have him call me. I'll gladly send him whatever he needs."

"Thank you, Doctor," Lauren said.

"Have a safe flight, and congratulate your brother for me," Dr. Scalafani concluded.

"I will. Thanks again."

Roger shook the doctor's hand on his way out. "Let's go home and finish packing."

In the morning, they were heading to Seattle for Nathan and Gabby's wedding. This was a much anticipated event in the Hanson family. For ten years, those two had been the best of friends, and for the last seven, they had been a fully established couple. After all that time, the two of them finally committed to marriage.

Much to Nathan's relief, he completed his first year of medical school. He was beginning to believe that he might actually make it through this. It was going to take work and it wasn't going to be easy, but he was going to make it. Gabby had a good first year of teaching, for the most part, and confirmed that she had taken the proper career path. Throughout the school year, Nathan and Gabby had saved enough money to make a down payment on a house. Over the summer, they signed the mortgage paperwork and moved into their new home. Currently, they were painting walls, buying furniture, and making it look more like home.

As they gathered last minute items for their wedding, Gabby asked, "What time are Roger and Lauren flying in tomorrow?"

"I think she said 4:30. I honestly don't remember. I'll have to look at the e-mail she sent me. We're supposed to meet Mom and Dad at the airport at 4:00 to pick them up. Dad wants to take everyone out to dinner afterwards."

"I'm excited to see her. I can't believe she's going to have a baby."

"Lace says she looks good," Nathan stated. "Obviously she hasn't had any problems with the pregnancy or else the doctor wouldn't have cleared her to fly."

"Do they know what they're having?"

"As of the last time I talked to her, no. She did say they were going in for an ultrasound. Maybe they received some news."

Lacy was the first person to greet Roger and Lauren at the airport. She hadn't seen her sister in over a month and desperately missed her. Lacy hugged her tightly then put her hand on Lauren's tummy to see what changes had occurred with the baby since they last met.

When Jane saw her daughter, she immediately greeted her with a hug. "You look fantastic, Honey. Look at you."

Nathan had to tease her. "Nice tummy, Sis. You do know that if you have sex without contraception, you're probably going to get pregnant."

She playfully smacked his arm. "Shut up, Smartass."

He wrapped his arms around her and squeezed. "It's good to see you."

Randy looked Lauren over before he said anything. She was beautiful, especially with a pregnant belly. Still in shock that his baby girl was going to be a mommy, he said, "Hi, Baby."

"Hi, Daddy."

"You look great. Robert's been taking good care of you."

"He's a good doctor. I like him."

"I knew you would." Randy gave her a huge hug. "What news did you get from the sonogram?"

Roger handled this question. "We're having a boy."

The family had a brief moment of celebration before heading off to baggage claim.

Nathan and Roger took up the rear. Nathan was in one of his smart aleck moods and felt the need to give Roger a hard time. "I bet it's satisfying to know that your boys can swim."

Roger chuckled at Nathan's bluntness. "It certainly boosts the male ego a bit."

"I'm not sure if I should congratulate you or be creeped out over the fact that it's my sister you impregnated," Nathan teased.

"Just doing my husbandly duty. Anything worth doing is worth doing right."

Nathan had to laugh.

The night before their wedding, Gabby and Nathan snuggled in bed together. Nathan had his arm around her and Gabby rested her head on his chest with her hand between his pectorals. He gently combed his fingers through her hair. "You know what I was thinking about?"

"What?" she asked, kissing his naked chest.

"Eighth grade English class. I used to sit kind of catty-corner behind you. You didn't know it at the time, but I could see everything you wrote from there. All I had to do was glance to my left."

"Were you copying me?"

"No. But I remember once when you had your notebook open, you drew a heart and wrote my name inside. Underneath, you wrote Gabby Hanson."

Gabby covered her mouth with her hand. "You saw that?"

"I did. I never told you though. Ten years, Babe. After dreaming and drawing little hearts, you'll finally be Gabby Hanson." He kissed her forehead as a token of his love for her. "Did you know that you were the first girl I ever kissed?"

"I was?" he giggled.

"It wasn't a real kiss, it was more like an oh-my-god-we-won-the-game celebratory peck on the lips."

Gabby laughed remembering that day. "I remember that. What were we, fourteen?"

"Yup. We just sat there and stared at each other for a minute, not quite sure what to do." Nathan chuckled. "And then there was our first real kiss."

Gabby recalled how sensuous and romantic their first kiss was. "That was our first date."

"Yes it was. And you're an incredible kisser, by the way."

"How do you know, if you've never kissed anyone else?"

"Because I know how I feel when I kiss you." On that note, he interlocked his lips with hers.

486

"The first time I ever danced with a boy was with you, at the eighth grade dance."

"You were my first too," Nathan admitted. "You and I have experienced many firsts together. First kiss, first date, first dance, first love." Then a thought flashed in his head that made him laugh. "First time I ever saw a girl naked. I'm sorry about that, by the way. I did not mean to walk in on you."

Gabby busted out laughing. "Oh god, I forgot about that."

"It was embarrassing," Nathan declared. "When you're fifteen and you walk in on a naked girl trying to change into her swimsuit, it's a bit shocking. Three years later, I saw you naked again when we lost our virginity together." Thinking about this brought chills.

"Who would have thought, ten years ago when I first saw you, that you would have turned out to be my husband?"

"Tomorrow, Gab," Nathan said excitedly. "We've waited a long time for this."

"We have," she agreed.

"Which reminds me," Nathan explained. "I did my homework this time."

She had no clue what he was talking about. "What homework?"

"I researched wedding traditions. Last time we were at a wedding, you got upset with me because I didn't know the customs."

"Nathan, are you still hung up on that?" she asked, feeling guilty for jumping on him about insignificant things. "That was over a year ago."

"My point is," he said, "I'm prepared this time. And I will have you know that we have broken almost every traditional wedding custom."

"Like what?" she asked, looking forward to hearing his insights on this.

"Let's start with your white dress. Brides wear white to symbolize purity and virginity. I know damn well you aren't a virgin. I'm also not supposed to see your dress before the wedding. We broke that one too. It looks beautiful on you, by the way. And apparently, we aren't supposed to see each other the night before the wedding. Not only are we together right now, but we're sharing a bed," he said with a smartass snicker. "So much for that tradition."

"Oh, so you've become an expert now?"

"No, I just find it funny how some of these ridiculous traditions got started. Take the white representing virginity bullshit. I've never known any woman who hasn't had sex at least once prior to her wedding. My mother wore white and she wasn't a virgin. Lauren wasn't either, and neither are you. Who came up with that?"

"I don't think it's used to symbolize virginity anymore," Gabby explained.

"That's good, because a bride wearing white because she's pure is the biggest lie ever told." Nathan went on a rampage now. "I was reading about the history of that tradition and they made it sound like every woman who was getting married in white had never had sex before. Yet every guy was experienced and was supposed to take his new bride into his bed and introduce her to all the carnal pleasures of sex, as if he were some kind of expert. Hypothetically speaking, if that were the case, who the hell was he having sex with prior to marriage that gave him all this experience if every woman out there was supposedly a virgin?"

Nathan's philosophical reasoning had Gabby fighting desperately to muffle giggles. He was deadly serious and obviously had been thinking about this for some time. He rambled on and never gave her a chance to respond.

"You know what I think it is?" he stepped on his soapbox again. "I think every woman back then was just too damn scared to admit that she had engaged in the pleasures of sex because she didn't want her father to find out and risk ruining the family reputation. Either that or she was terrified people would stone her to death for being a slut. It could have been that she was trying to hide it from her future husband too, that way he would think he was the only man who had ever claimed her as his sexual property, as if any guy would be naïve enough to really believe that his wife was a virgin when he married her."

"Sweetie," Gabby said, "White symbolizing virginity dates back hundreds of years. It's virtually obsolete now."

"Those people were stupid to believe it in the first place. And I suppose a groom who wore white was a virgin too?" He fake coughed, "Bullshit! No one has sex for the first time on their wedding night, I don't care what they say."

She moved her lips to his ear and slowly worked her way down his neck.

Nathan closed his eyes, soaking in every touch. "God, that feels good."

Her plan to distract him worked. She found his lips, and they fused together, tenderly at first. To spice things up, Gabby moved in with her tongue. In response, Nathan cradled her face with his hand and moved in perfect sync with her, offering just enough of a tease to entice her to want more. The kiss was sensual and sexy, with delicious essence.

When they came up for air, Nathan said, "You drive me wild when you kiss me like that."

She eyed him seductively. "Maybe that's the idea."

"I'll take it."

Gabby snuggled into him and released a worrisome sigh.

Wondering what triggered that response, Nathan asked, "What's that all about?"

"I hope my mother doesn't cause a huge scene tomorrow."

Nathan hoped not too.

"Every time we have a function where my mother is invited, she always causes a big commotion over ridiculous things."

"No offense, Gab, but I'm afraid I'm going to be one of those husbands who doesn't like his mother-in-law very much," Nathan admitted.

"That's okay. I don't like her either."

Nathan rubbed his fingers through her hair. "I'm sorry about that."

"Why are you sorry?"

"Because your parents haven't been there for you when you needed them. I was hoping your dad would come through for you, but he's disappointed me. He seemed all gung ho about being involved in your life, but when push came to shove he didn't take much interest in your life at all. It's like he wanted the emotional bond with you, but didn't want to have to earn it."

Gabby agreed. "Your parents are more supportive and loving than mine are."

"That's the way they are, Gab. They've always liked you." Nathan grinned. "And the good thing is they will legally be your family now."

"I know," she declared. "I'm so excited about tomorrow."

"So am I, Baby. So am I."

Nathan kept his promise about getting married on the beach. They booked a place called the Shilshole Bay Beach Club. This was perfect for their needs because it provided the romance of the beach right on the waterfront of Seattle.

Their wedding wasn't fancy, just a casual celebration to commemorate their relationship and celebrate their love for one another. Their wedding party, with only Andrew as Best Man and Lacy as Maid of Honor, dressed in comfort. Nathan wore khaki dress pants and a short-sleeved white Guayabera wedding shirt, untucked. On his feet, he wore slip-on khaki canvas beach loafers. Gabby's dress was a strapless tea-length gown that draped down longer in the back. The entire thing was made from lightweight croqueted lace with white cotton lining underneath. She had on pretty white lacy sandals with her toenails painted in a French manicure, matching her fingers. The only jewelry she wore was a pair of delicate pearl earrings. Lacy's lightweight yellow beach dress was accented with dangly yellow earrings and open-toed sandals. Andrew was dressed exactly like Nathan.

The flowers they chose represented a mix of summer brightness. Both Gabby and Lacy had multi-colored bouquets in hues of yellow, purple, and pink intermixed with greenery and wrapped in pretty yellow and pink ribbon. Smaller bouquets of the same hues were placed in the center of each reception hall table. Several rows of white foldup chairs lined the beach, leaving an aisle in the middle for Gabby to walk down.

At the end of the aisle, a flowered arch served as an altar for Nathan and Gabby to exchange vows.

When Nathan and Gabby sealed their union with a kiss, all 147 guests cheered in celebration. This landmark wedding was ten years in the making. It was truly a celebration of life-long love.

The décor inside the reception hall was just as light and airy as the ceremony. The table settings were completely white, other than the silver flatware and linen napkin in mix-and-match hues of yellow, purple, and pink. Each setting was accompanied by a long-stemmed crystal clear champagne glass.

During the reception, guests had the joy of viewing a slideshow with various photographs timelining Nathan and Gabby's developing relationship, beginning with eighth grade and working all the up to the week before their wedding. It was an adorable presentation, receiving many laughs and awes from their guests.

For their first dance as husband and wife, Nathan and Gabby chose the first song they ever slow danced to. With all eyes on them, Nathan took Gabby in his arms and they gently swayed across the dancefloor. Their eyes never once looked away from one another. They were deeply lost in the moment, and deeply in love.

With the gentlest touch, Nathan cradled her cheek with his hand. "I love you, Gabriella."

Gabby touched his face. "I love you."

He held her close, savoring every moment.

Jane watched them, whimpering. Never before had she witnessed such an adorable and sentimental testament of endearment, affection, and love. "That is the sweetest thing I've ever seen."

Randy put his arm around her. "What is?"

"Seeing Nathan and Gabby like this. Look how lovingly he holds her, and do you see the way he looks at her?"

His wife was getting all blubbery and emotional over something that happened between Nathan and Gabby on a daily basis. "Janey, he always looks at her like that, and he's always held her that way. The boy is in love with her. He has been from the day they met."

"Usually they're talking about basketball or stuffing food in their mouths. I didn't know Nathan was romantic like that."

"Give the kid some credit, Babe. He does have his father's blood. I'm sure he learned a few tricks of romance and charm over the years."

She playfully smacked his arm. "You are far from charming right now, and you're ruining this moment for me."

Randy just laughed at her.

As the last notes of the song played, Nathan leaned in, closed his eyes, and kissed his bride. The reception hall applauded, but Nathan completely blocked them out. Nothing existed except Gabby. They stood in the middle of the room happily joined together as husband and wife.

The cutting of the cake was the part of the wedding Nathan looked forward to the most. Their cake was three-tiered lemon cake covered in white frosting with a staircase of pink, purple, and yellow flowers creeping from the bottom to the top layer. He couldn't wait to smear brightly colored frosting all over Gabby's face. But by the time he had a slice in his hand, she beat him to the punch and wiped frosting on his nose. Her quickness made him chuckle. He reciprocated by feeding a slice to her, getting more cake on her face than in her mouth.

Before the bouquet throwing and garter removal, Lauren's face became flush and she started fanning herself.

Concerned about her condition, Roger asked, "Sweetheart, you alright?"

"It's really hot in here," she complained.

"Let's get you some air." He supported her with his hands and carefully escorted her outside.

As Roger walked Lauren out of the room, Randy noticed that her gait was wobbly and weak. "Wonder what's going on with Lauren," he said to his wife.

Jane looked toward the door and saw what Randy was talking about. "I don't know."

Randy set his napkin on the table. "I'm gonna check on her."

When Randy stepped outside, Lauren was leaning against the building. Her face was ghostly white. "Daddy?" she called out to him.

He gently put his hand on her shoulder. "I'm right here, Baby. What's going on?"

The world around her started to spin. "I don't feel well."

Randy looked over at Roger. "Sit her down."

Roger gently supported his wife to help her sit.

Randy squatted to Lauren's level and reached down to check her pulse. It was slower than it should have been.

Both Lacy and Nathan had now noticed this scene and came out to see what was happening. Worried about his sister, Nathan asked, "What's going on? What's the matter with Lauren?"

Randy reached into his pocket and pulled out his car keys, handing them to Nathan. "Run out to my car and grab my medical bag. Be as quick as you can."

Nathan took the keys and ran off.

Seeing that he was worried, Randy turned to Roger and calmly said, "Go inside and grab a bottle of water."

"Alright." Roger rushed inside.

Randy focused his attention to his daughter again. "Lie down, Honey." With Lacy's help, he had Lauren lie on her left side, hoping to get the circulation flowing properly again and keep her enlarged uterus from compressing any veins, making her condition worse.

Moments later, Nathan returned with Randy's medical bag. Randy immediately opened it and pulled out a thermometer, a portable blood pressure monitor, and a stethoscope. He checked Lauren's heartbeat first. Normal. He checked baby's heartbeat next. That too sounded strong. No trauma to the baby. He did a quick check of her blood pressure. It was a little low, but nothing to be alarmed about. He draped his stethoscope around his neck then checked her temperature. It was slightly higher than normal, but not enough to be worrisome.

Roger hurried back with a bottle of water. "Is she alright?"

"Did she say anything to you before you walked her out here?"

"She said it was hot in there," he answered.

Lauren's color slowly returned and she seemed more alert. "How much water has she drank today?"

Flustered, Roger drew his shaky hand up to his temple. "I don't know. Four or five bottles maybe."

"Looks like she got a little overheated," Randy explained. "Lowered her blood pressure and made her feel woozy."

"She's going to be okay, right?" Roger asked, still worried.

"She's going to be fine. Just a little dizzy spell. We need to let her cool down a bit and allow her blood pressure to return to normal." Randy commended Roger, proud of his quick reaction time. "That was a good call to bring her out here." Randy placed his hand on Lauren's shoulder and asked, "Are you still feeling dizzy, Honey?"

"No," she replied.

"Sit up for a minute," he advised. "Slowly."

She followed her father's directive and sat up.

He took the lid off the water bottle and handed it to her. "Drink this."

Lauren grabbed the bottle from her father's hand and drank almost half of it.

Roger sat next to his wife and held her hand, relieved that she was ok. "Is this normal?"

Randy reassured him, "It's not uncommon. Right now her cardiovascular system is pumping a lot more blood per minute than it was pre-pregnancy. This makes her heart rate go up. At this stage of her pregnancy, her blood vessels dilate and her blood pressure gradually decreases. If she stands up suddenly, doesn't get enough to eat, doesn't drink enough water, or overheats, it could leave her feeling lightheaded or dizzy. It's nothing to be alarmed about." He hoped Nathan was paying attention. "Are you listening to this?"

"Yes, Sir," Nathan replied, giving his father his full attention.

"Instead of kissing your wife all day, maybe you'll actually learn something," Randy teased.

Nathan laughed. "I'm listening, Dad."

Seeing that Lauren downed a good majority of the water, Randy asked, "How you feeling?"

Lauren replied, "Much better."

She looked one-hundred percent better too. "Sit here for a few more minutes to make sure the spell is completely gone, then you need to eat something. How much have you eaten today?"

"I had yogurt, oatmeal, and a bowl of fruit this morning. A glass of milk, a chef salad, and a granola bar for lunch, and I ate dinner here."

"Good. Make sure you're eating properly, and I'm not just saying that because I'm a concerned dad. Right now I'm being a doctor."

She nodded in understanding. "I know."

Randy gave Roger instructions as well. "Make sure she eats."

Roger found this comment amusing. "Oh, she can definitely eat, Sir. That's never been a problem for her."

When the excitement settled and medical supplies were returned to their proper place, Nathan returned to his wife. Randy, Roger, Lacy, and Lauren went back inside with the rest of the guests, who were ready for the garter and bouquet toss.

After the joyous celebration was over and the guests cleared, Nathan and Gabby walked hand in hand on the beach. They were both barefoot, and Nathan had his pant legs rolled up. "Was our wedding everything you dreamed it would be?"

Gabby squeezed his hand. "I have everything I've ever dreamed of right here."

He curved his arm around her waist and she rested her head against his shoulder. "We couldn't have planned a more perfect day," he said. "The weather was absolutely gorgeous."

As they strolled along the beach, Gabby saw a stick. She picked it up, drew a large heart in the sand, and wrote Nathan's name in it.

Nathan took the stick from her and drew a second heart connected with the one she had drawn. "Okay, Babe. You can write it for real now."

She knew exactly what that meant. He handed the stick back to her, and inside the heart Nathan had drawn, she wrote Gabby Hanson. Right below the two interconnected hearts, Nathan etched the date. When he was finished, he pulled out his cellphone and snapped a picture.

"Page one of our new scrapbook, the day we started our life together as husband and wife." The sun left an orange glow over the water. Nathan gazed at his beautiful bride with a huge grin on his face. "I love you, Gabriella Hanson."

"I love you too, Dr. Hanson."

He laughed when she said that. "Don't jinx it. I still have three more years before I earn that title." He embraced his bride and slowly drew her lips to his. "Forever and always, Gab."

"Always and forever."

As the sun made its final descent, their lips interlocked in a passionate kiss.

Back at the Hanson home, Roger and Lauren changed out of their wedding attire into cooler, more casual clothes. Roger gently placed his hand on her tummy. "You scared the hell out of me today," he said, still shaken over her earlier medical incident.

"Sweetie, I'm fine."

"You were pretty incoherent, Lauren. I was worried." He offered soft kisses down her neck. "I'm glad your father was there."

"Daddy's good at that."

"Good at what?" Roger asked.

"Being there when you need him." She looked up at Roger. "You're good at that too. Thank you for being there for me today when I needed you."

"I'll always be here for you."

Lauren felt the baby push against her skin, which made her giggle.

"What?" Roger asked, wondering what she found so amusing.

She moved his hand to the other side of her tummy. "Can you feel it?"

Roger held his hand in that spot and felt a bump push against his hand. "There he is," he beamed. "He's letting us know he's in there."

"Uh huh," Lauren said. "He does that a lot."

Roger used this opportunity to talk to her about his fears associated with parenting. "I'm excited about becoming a father. But in all honesty, Honey, I'm a bit frightened by all of this."

"Why?"

He took in a cleansing breath. "Our lives are about to drastically change. Our son will become our first priority."

"I know," she said.

Feeling overwhelmed, Roger expressed what was on his mind. "I want to be a good father, and I want our son to be happy and have positive memories of his childhood, but I don't want to spoil him or give him everything he wants. I want him to grow up to be respectful and disciplined and responsible for his actions. I don't want him to be afraid to take risks, but at the same time I want him to be aware of the consequences if he makes the wrong choices, and accept those consequences. I want him to pursue his dreams and I want to support him in every way I can. I want so many things for him." He gently kissed Lauren's shoulder. "Where do we even start?"

"It's a lot to think about," she replied, feeling just as frightened and overwhelmed as he was. "Parenting is a big responsibility, and it's a little intimidating."

"It is," he agreed. "It's scary to think that this tiny person is going to rely on us to provide for him, to guide him, to instill morals and values in him that will stick with him his entire life. I don't want to screw this up."

"Even the best parents make mistakes along the way. My mom told me it's a lot of trial and error."

"Guess we'll find out soon enough, won't we?"

"Yes we will," she confirmed. "And I'm sure, together, we'll figure it out. Our baby will develop and grow and we'll have to adjust as we go. But I'm excited about it. It will be a learning experience for both of us, and a wonderful adventure to share with you."

Talking about this, and knowing Lauren felt the same way he did, made Roger less apprehensive about parenting. "Gary was a loving father to me when he didn't have to be. I want to be as supportive as he was."

"You are a caring and compassionate man, Roger, and you're going to be a wonderful father."

"I hope so."

Chapter Forty

Lauren was now within days of her projected due date and was seeing the doctor weekly. She hadn't experienced any signs of labor yet, but two days before her 39-week appointment, she experienced some mild, sporadic contractions. They weren't really bothering her, and she didn't think much of them, but she told Dr. Scalafani about them anyway to ensure that everything was alright.

After doing a checkup on Lauren, the doctor said, "Everything looks great. Baby is strong and healthy. We are almost there."

Lauren put her hand on her protruding belly and hobbled off the exam table. "I'm gonna run to the restroom before we go," she said to Roger.

"I'll be here."

When Lauren stepped out of the room, the doctor said, "Call your father-in-law and tell him three things: plus two station, 4.2 centimeters, ninety percent effacement. He'll know what that means."

Roger eyed the doctor, confused by this medical lingo. "Mind telling me what that means?"

"It means she's close."

"How close?" Roger wondered.

"I doubt she'll make it to her next appointment."

Roger suddenly felt weak. "Are you serious?"

"Yes. Might even be today."

"Today?"

"Very high possibility," the doctor confirmed, chuckling at the terrified look on Roger's face. "I would suggest you keep an eye on these contractions she's having, and if you have to go out, don't go far, and make sure you have your phone turned on."

Roger was excited about becoming a daddy, but now that they were this close, reality sank in. "This is going to get intense, isn't it?"

"Let me put it this way, she's going to need you more now than she ever has before." In an attempt to comfort this new dad, the doctor said, "Call your father-in-law. He'll offer you some advice. I'll probably see you later this week. Enjoy the rest of your afternoon."

"Thank you, Doctor."

Dr. Scalafani grabbed his laptop and stethoscope and exited the room.

Upon returning home, Lauren felt fatigued. Ever since the doctor gave her a pelvic exam, these small contractions she'd been having seemed to be more prevalent. They weren't really painful, more of a discomfort than anything. Yet after several hours, they were become more and more uncomfortable and didn't seem to be going away. Hoping to alleviate the discomfort, she went in the bedroom to lie down for a while.

While Lauren was napping, Roger called Randy, worried about the development of these contractions over the last three hours. He wondered if they were those so-called Braxton Hicks contractions he'd heard about or if this was the start of the real deal. "Hey, Dad."

Randy instantly noticed the worried tone in Roger's voice. That and the fact that Roger called him dad, which he rarely did, had him a bit concerned. "Hey, Roger. Everything alright?"

"I'm not sure," Roger said. "I took Lauren in for her weekly exam today."

"How did that go?"

"Dr. Scalafani wanted me to tell you something. He said you'd know what it meant."

"What did he say?" Randy wondered.

"Something about plus two station, ninety percent effacement, and 4.2 centimeters."

This information seemed to excite Randy. "Really? What time was that?"

"Her appointment was at one o'clock this afternoon."

Randy looked at the clock. It was 1:33 P.M. With the three hour time difference, Lauren's appointment was about three and a half hours ago. "Has she been having any contractions at all?" Randy asked, trying to gain more information.

"Actually, that's the reason I called," Roger explained. "Over the last couple of days she's been getting small contractions that seem to go away if she lies down, but right now they're not going away."

"Intensity?" Randy asked.

"At first they weren't bothering her, but since we've been back from the doctor, she says they feel more intense and she keeps complaining that they're getting worse."

This sounded promising. "Are they consistent?"

"They hadn't been, but now I don't know."

"Hmm, I wish I could see her contraction spikes."

"She was fine this morning. Why would she suddenly develop more intense contractions?"

"Sometimes pressure put on the cervix from a pelvic exam can push labor along. It's nothing to be worried about. Do me a favor though. Start timing these contractions to see if they are consistent, and have her give you a ranking on intensity, zero being no pain, ten being unbearable. Do this for about an hour then call me back."

"She's sleeping right now," Roger declared.

"Let her sleep then. She's going to need her strength. But keep me posted. I'm going to have Jane start checking airline reservations."

Randy's urgency made Roger think this was the real deal. "Whoa! Wait a minute. Do you think she might be in labor?"

"With her contractions suddenly becoming more severe like that, I'm certainly not going to rule it out."

Realizing the actuality of all of this, Roger started to panic. "Damn."

Sensing Roger's anxiety, Randy offered his advice. "This is normal and natural. You need to keep Lauren as relaxed as possible. That is your job right now."

Roger, being a first time dad and new to all of this, wasn't sure how to react. "We've taken Lamaze, but level with me here. How bad is this going to get?"

"The first stage of labor is the easiest and the longest, especially for a first pregnancy. But once these contractions start hitting hard, things could get pretty intense. I'm not going to lie to you. It is extremely difficult to watch your wife go through that kind of pain. She may say things she doesn't normally say, she may scream, she may cry, she may swear. But you need to remember not to take any of it personally."

"Oh Jesus." Roger held his hand up to his head, not prepared to deal with this.

"I know this is scary, especially since this is your first and you're not really sure what to expect, but you have to stay calm for her. Help her focus on breathing, remind her of all of those Lamaze techniques you guys have been practicing. She needs you to keep it together, Roger."

"I can have them give her something for the pain if it gets to be too much, right?" Roger begged. "Please tell me she can take something for the pain."

"Yes," Randy reassured him. "There are options. But that's a decision Lauren has to make, not you."

"So if she opts not to take pain killers, there's not a damn thing I can do but sit and watch this torture?" Roger reasoned.

Randy laid it on the line. "You need to keep her relaxed and help her cope with the pain. That is your job."

Roger didn't like this at all. "This sucks."

Randy sniggered at Roger's reaction. "Women have babies every day. You're going to be alright, and so is she. Think about holding that baby. It makes all of this very worthwhile."

"At what point do I say enough is enough and bring her in?" Roger wondered.

"Consistent contractions, coming at predictable intervals, lasting for extended periods of time. About five to six minutes apart or less. She'll be uncomfortable and in pain. Bring her in then."

Roger was quiet on the other end, trying to soak in all of this. He and Lauren had prepared well for this, but now that the painful reality of labor had hit, he was terrified and apprehensive about it. This definitely did not sound like a good time. He was going to have to muster up every ounce of strength he had to help Lauren get through this.

Randy was worried about him. "Do you have someone there as a support system for you? Your parents? Your brother?"

"I can call and have them start heading down here," Roger suggested.

"You might want to do that. Jane's looking at flights to New York now, but she probably won't get there until tomorrow. I can't leave right now, but I'll be there in a few days. I suggest you call Lacy. That will give you and Lauren some additional support."

Roger agreed that was a good idea. "I will."

"You two are going to be alright," Randy told him. "Be there for her, Roger. Help her focus. She needs you now."

"Yeah."

"When she wakes up, time her contractions and call me back."

Lauren didn't last many hours past that point before Roger brought her to the hospital. Lacy met him there. With Lacy close by, he and Lauren would have some family support until the parents arrived.

By now it was almost 8:00 P.M. Lauren's contractions were getting more intense, coming at closer intervals, and lasting for longer periods of time. She had been in active labor stage for almost three hours now. Roger did his best to help Lauren relax and deal with the pain through the Lamaze techniques they had worked on. He offered back rubs, held a moist washcloth up to her head, sang to her, rubbed her hands, and fed her ice cubes. So far Lauren did not want pain medication. In fact, she was very persistent about not using pain medication. Roger tried to support that decision.

506

However, doing so was making him a nervous wreck. He didn't show it on the outside, but inside he held a gamete of emotions—anxiety, nervousness, fear, excitement, and worry. Seeing Lauren in pain like this was almost more than he could handle. But he remembered his father-in-law's advice and pictured their baby. That image made it all a little more tolerable.

"Breathe, Honey." Roger helped Lauren find a rhythm that would get her to relax through these strong contractions. He held her hands and guided her through breathing, encouraging her to inhale and exhale slowly and consistently. "That's it. Nice and slow."

She tried to focus, but the pain was too intense. The extreme pressure in her pelvic area and back made her wince. With an agonizing look on her face, her hands began to shake. "I can't do this."

"Look at me," Roger encouraged, trying to make eye contact. He feared she had hit the final, most painful stage of labor. The torturous pain she was going through made Roger want to cry. He couldn't stand to watch this. "You're doing great, Honey. We're almost there." He was about to fall apart, but knew he had to be strong for her. He held her hand, and she squeezed as hard as she could.

At this point, Dr. Scalafani walked into the room. After a quick pelvic exam, he checked her contraction spikes on the fetal monitor. "Alrighty," he said cheerfully. "Let's have a baby!"

He called Pediatrics and had the nurses start setting up for delivery. They helped Lauren get into position and draped a white receiving blanket over her chest. The doctor gowned up and took his position at the end.

Roger, who was now breathing heavier, looked over at Lacy with a panic-stricken expression. Lacy offered reassurance by touching his hand. He squeezed then they each took position on either side of Lauren, ready for the big show.

After about ten minutes of pushing, baby's head eased its way out. The doctor suctioned the nose and mouth then helped guide the shoulders and torso. Roger could now see his son's face, which brought tears to his eyes.

The doctor clamped the cord and handed Roger the scissors. "Would you like to do the honors?"

Roger took the scissors in his hand and snipped.

The doctor made a sweeping motion, placing the infant on Lauren's chest. The entire room reveled in that first illustrious cry.

The pediatric staff give the newborn a brisk rubdown and placed ointment in his eyes to prevent infection. They wrapped him up in a blanket and gave him a blue knitted hat to prevent heat loss while the doctor worked on cleaning up Lauren.

Roger and Lauren nuzzled forehead to forehead, feeling exhausted, exhilarated, and overwhelmed. Roger had held his emotions in for the last four hours and could no longer suppress them. The tears came. "He's beautiful," he said to his wife, feeling more joy than he could ever remember feeling. "I'm so proud of you, Sweetheart. You were amazing."

"So were you. You were the perfect coach."

"You are superwoman," he said. "I could not have done what you just did. I love you so much."

"I love you too."

The pediatric staff did a workup on the baby then returned him to Lauren. She sat up slightly and held the infant in her arms. Together, she and Roger nuzzled him, beginning the bonding process with their beautiful baby boy.

It was October 7th, 8:43 P.M., seven days before her original due date, and they had a healthy baby boy. He was twenty inches long and weighed seven pounds, three ounces. He had a fuzzy patch of brown hair on his head and pretty hazel eyes. They named him Jacob Michael Zellers.

After eating a full meal and attempting to nurse the baby, Lauren finally rested. Roger stood guard and watched over both her and the baby. He was tired, but couldn't sleep. Too much adrenaline coursed through his veins throughout the day, and he needed time to let it subside before attempting to get any shut eye.

He peeked into the crib. Jacob's eyes were wide open. Trying not to wake Lauren, he picked up the baby and cradled him in his arms. He gently kissed his son's forehead and brought him over to the recliner in the corner of the room. He reclined back into the chair, unbuttoned his shirt, and unwrapped baby from his swaddle. He nuzzled the infant on his chest, supporting him with his hands. Covering the baby with the blanket, he took a moment to cuddle his son one-on-one. As he snuggled with this tiny infant, he began to sing a lullaby. It wasn't long before both he and Jacob fell asleep.

After a semi-restful night, Lauren was a little sore, but Tylenol seemed to ease her discomfort. Trying to figure out how to nurse the baby was a bit challenging, but Jacob finally learned to latch on. While the baby ate, Roger pulled out his iPad and sent emails to their friends and family members, attaching a few pictures he had taken. For the opening line he wrote, *The most amazing thing happened last night. Lauren and I became parents! Meet the newest member of our family: Jacob Michael Zellers. Born October 7th, 8:43 P.M.*

Several people stopped by the hospital to visit. Jane flew in from Seattle, Roger's parents drove down from Owego, and Lacy stopped by after class. Jason and Bailey came over on their way to dinner. They brought the happy new parents a bouquet of blue, white, and yellow flowers with a floating Mylar balloon attached.

When Jason saw the baby, he got a good look at his face. "Wow, he looks like you, Rog."

"We noticed that too." Roger tried to hand the baby to Jason. "You want to hold him?"

Jason hesitated with this task. "I don't know."

"It's ok," Roger teased him. "He doesn't bite."

Jason hadn't been around many babies, but he did his best to support the infant with his arms. Holding this tiny human made him grin. He was a cute little guy, wearing a tiny blue knitted hat with his forehead all crinkled up. "Hey, little one." He looked up at Roger. "You created this adorable thing?"

"I know. Amazing, isn't it?"

"It's pretty spectacular. You deserve a Tony for that performance."

"I don't want a Tony. I have Jake. That is all the reward I need." Roger grabbed his camera and snapped a picture of Jason holding Jacob.

Before Randy left to catch a flight to New York, he met Jim for coffee. Jim waited a long time for this moment and could no longer resist. With a big shit-eating grin on his face, he handed Randy a gift bag.

"I don't even want to know what's in here," Randy said, hesitant to open the bag.

"Dude, you knew this was comin'."

Randy carefully peeked inside, half expecting a snake to jump out.

Jim laughed at his friend's reaction. "Be afraid. Be very afraid."

Biting the bullet and preparing himself for imminent torture, Randy reached into the bag. Inside was a package of Oreos and a coffee mug with the words, *World's Best Grandpa*. Taped to the cookie package, Jim attached a note: *Welcome to the OLD side. We have Oreos!* Randy had to admit, this was funny.

"Now you can have Oreos with your coffee and be reminded every day that you're an old fart."

"Gee, thanks," Randy mocked.

"But seriously, congratulations, man."

"Thank you. I'm looking forward to meeting my grandson."

Chapter Forty-One

Right before Roger was scheduled to begin production of *White Christmas*, he met Jason for coffee. He was bleary-eyed with saggy eyelids and didn't carry his normal energy level. Instead, he lethargically dragged himself into the coffee shop, looking like a zombie.

Roger's drowsy state made Jason laugh. "You look like hell."

"Gee, thanks." Roger gulped down his coffee, hoping the caffeine would kick in.

Trying to sympathize with his friend, Jason asked, "Sleep tank empty there, bud?"

Good assumption. "Sleep? Oh, you mean that wonderful nightly activity that involves closing your eyes and remaining horizontal for eight hours? I don't remember what that is."

Jason figured as much. "Baby keeping you awake?"

Roger yawned and took another sip of his coffee. "He's not a bad sleeper. He just wakes up every three hours wanting to be fed. We never get consistent sleep. We try to nap during the day when Jacob naps, but quite honestly, having a newborn is a relentless harsh awakening, and the challenge of adjusting has been severely amplified by sheer exhaustion. We're both a little frazzled, and I'm just flat out tired."

"I can tell," Jason said, feeling pity for his sleep deprived friend.

"I love my son dearly, but I want to hug my pillow right now. Lack of sleep has severely hijacked my brain. I'm in a mental fog. Yesterday I spent an hour searching for my keys when they were sitting on the table right in front of me the whole time. And a few days ago, I caught myself dozing off in the middle of a conversation," Roger chuckled. "I apologize ahead of time if I start snoring. Don't take it personally."

"I won't. Don't worry." Jason took the lid off his cup and stirred in some sugar. "When do you start production for your new show?"

"Tomorrow morning."

"You gonna make it?" Jason chuckled.

"I'm chugging along." Roger stared at his coffee cup. "I've been drinking way too much of this lately."

Jason set a gift bag on the table. "Bailey and I bought you something for the baby."

Roger reached into the bag and pulled out a Yankees outfit, a stuffed dog that lit up and played lullabies, and a blue onesie tee-shirt imprinted with *All the world's a stage, and my daddy is the leading player*. "These are great, Jason! Thanks."

"Bailey picked out the puppy."

"Love the puppy. Thank her for us." Roger carefully slipped the objects back into the bag.

"Speaking of which," Jason paused briefly and looked Roger in the eye. "Bailey and I got engaged last night."

Roger almost choked on his coffee. "What?"

"Bailey and I…"

"I heard what you said. I'm just surprised." He shook Jason's hand firmly. "Congratulations!"

"Thank you. Will you do the honors for me?"

"Definitely. It's payback time." With a devilish look in his eye, he rubbed his hands together and gave an evil laugh.

Roger's devious intent made Jason laugh. "Wow, either you are more sleep deprived than you thought or the neurotic Phantom side of you is coming out."

"I owe you one for humiliating me at my wedding," Roger justified.

Jason defended himself. "I was just screwing with you and you know it."

"Oh, I know, and now it's my turn to screw with you. And you, my friend, are going to get it hard."

The two men looked at each other and grinned.

After getting a string of six week vaccinations, Jacob felt kind of yucky. Therefore, Roger and Lauren opted not to travel for Thanksgiving. Since Roger was involved in *White Christmas*, and it was set to open to the public the following week, the Broadway League promoted the show by having Roger sing 'I'm Dreaming of a White Christmas' during a holiday special. Lauren stayed home with Jacob, watching the show from her living room. When Roger appeared on camera, Lauren narrated for the baby. "Look, Sweetie. There's Daddy!"

The baby cooed and kicked his legs.

Lauren and Roger often filled their home with music, from Queen, the Eagles, and Journey to Andrew Lloyd Webber, Tchaikovsky, and Gershwin. Jacob loved music. Whenever Roger played the piano or he and Lauren sang, little Jacob expressed his pleasure through coos, lip smacks, and jerking arm and leg movements. It was almost as if he was dancing and singing along.

514

They had a nice quiet dinner at home for Thanksgiving that year, sharing their meal together by candlelight while Jacob took a nap. Everyday life with a baby was much different than the life they lived before Jacob was conceived. Those pre-baby days sometimes seemed a distant memory. They were overjoyed about the arrival of their son, but exhausted and stressed by the new demands of having a baby in the house. They remained honest with each other about their feelings, talking frankly about the weird changes having a baby brought.

Going through this transition made Lauren and Roger forge a new kind of intimacy with one another. Over the last six weeks, despite the fact that they were tired beyond belief, they focused on loving one another by cuddling, hugging, massaging, or simply holding hands. During Lauren's postpartum checkup, she renewed her prescription for the pill. However, it would take time for them to reestablish in her system before they hit their peak effectiveness. Roger prepared for this and bought a box of condoms.

After tucking Jacob in for the night, Roger and Lauren cuddled on the bed, kissing. It wasn't long before cuddling turned into a full blown make-out session. Between breaths, Roger proclaimed, "I want you in the worst way." He squeezed her buttocks and pulled her onto his lap.

"Do we have condoms?"

Letting his hands roam all over her body, he panted, "We're covered."

They stripped each other, and Lauren assumed the position by straddling his lap. Roger slipped on a condom and eased in slowly, releasing with a moan. He let her control pace and depth, trying not to cause her any discomfort, until they established a pleasing rhythm that felt good for both of them. After six weeks of not engaging in sex, Roger wanted to make it last as long as possible.

At the conclusion of their long awaited session, Roger held Lauren in his arms, feeling an intense bond with her. "I talked to Marv and Gloria yesterday and got some intel about a remarkable production coming up."

"What is it?"

"Singin' in the Rain."

"That sounds right up your alley."

Getting her to see this from his perspective, he said, "The female lead would be perfect for you. I think you should read for the part and audition with me."

"I can't do a show right now."

He begged to differ. "At some point you're going to have to get back on stage. Don't want people to forget about you."

"What about Jake?" she asked, legitimately concerned.

He offered her a logical solution. "What if we look into hiring a professional caregiver or a nanny?"

"I don't want to leave him."

"Believe me, Honey, I didn't want to leave him either. But at some point, you have to get back on stage and remind people about your talents. Can't stay idle for too long."

A sigh escaped her lips, worried about leaving their baby with a sitter.

Roger tried to reason with her. "Jake's going to be fine. We can't put our lives on hold just because we have a baby. Parents have to carry on with their jobs and everyday tasks. There's nothing wrong with hiring a professional, experienced caregiver to take care of him. We'll look for someone who's specifically trained to handle infants. I'll ask around. I'm sure one of my connections knows someone who's good." He kissed her shoulder to ease her mind. "I really think you should audition for this. Production doesn't start until February. Jacob will be four months old then."

Roger had valid points. Jacob would be older then, and she did need to get her name back out there. "When are auditions?"

"They're holding auditions next week. They'll want to hear you voice range and see what kind of dance moves you have. Since we're auditioning for opposite roles, I'm sure they'll want us to read together." He nuzzled his chin into her shoulder. "You in?"

She nodded in agreement. "I'm in."

"Good. I'll pick up the scripts and scores tomorrow." He glanced at the clock with a chuckle "I'm guessing we'll get two solid hours before he wakes up."

Laughing at their relentless on and off sleep patterns, Lauren replied, "Probably."

"I'll get up with him first. You can take the second shift."

They kissed goodnight then snuggled under the covers to try and get at least a few hours of sleep before Jacob woke up.

Chapter Forty-Two

Roger resolved to make more of an impact on society by increasing his contributions to charitable organizations. With the weather quickly turning colder, he and his co-stars from *White Christmas* decided to organize a coat drive for kids, hoping to get New York City to donate new or gently used winter coats to children in need. Good Morning America offered to help them promote this program by giving them a snippet of time to talk about it. In return, they would perform for the audience and television viewers. Not only did this help needy kids, it also publicized the show.

The first performance of *White Christmas* was at the Marquis Theatre that night. Once this coat drive performance was complete, the cast had one more rehearsal prior to tonight's premiere, which was already sold out. From now until Christmas, they would perform twenty-two full-length shows. Roger was definitely going to stay busy.

He returned from rehearsal with two written copies of the script and musical score for *Singin' in the Rain*. He handed Lauren her copy then greeted her with a kiss. "Hi, Sweetheart. Where's Jake?"

"Sleeping."

Roger headed toward the baby's room.

"Don't you dare wake him up," Lauren said, giving Roger the evil eye. "He's overtired and cranky today. He needs a nap."

"I'm not going to wake him. I just want to peek."

Jacob was Roger's pride and joy. He loved that little boy and showed pictures of him to everyone he knew. He was always on the floor playing with him, talking to him, or singing to him. He loved to snuggle with Jacob and insisted on being involved in feedings, bath time, and diaper changes.

Satisfied that his son was napping peacefully, Roger came back out to the living room carrying a box wrapped in pretty pink paper. He handed the box to Lauren. "I got you something today."

She drew her lip between her teeth. "Ooh, what is it?"

"Why do you always ask me that? Do you really think I'm going to tell you? It's much more fun to watch your reaction when you open it."

She ripped off the paper and removed the lid. Inside, a silver charm bracelet had seven charms dangling from it: a theater mask, a rose, a heart, a tiny diamond ring, a pair of wedding bells, a palm tree, and a baby onesie with the name Jacob engraved on it.

"Now before you say anything," Roger said. "Each one of those has special significance." He held the bracelet in his hand and went through each charm one by one, starting with the theatre mask. "This one represents how we met." He moved on to the rose. "Our first date." He touched the heart-shaped charm and grinned at her. "Our first kiss."

She remembered that night very clearly. Thinking about it gave her chills.

He continued with the tiny ring charm, followed by the wedding bells and palm tree. "The day we got engaged, our wedding, our honeymoon, and…" He held the onesie charm between his fingers. "Little Jacob."

Each charm held sentimental value for both of them. Lauren couldn't believe Roger went through the trouble to pull together such a thoughtful gift.

"Notice there's room for more as our family grows and we experience more milestones together." He clasped it around her wrist. "I wanted to do something to signify the important events we've shared together. Each one of these led to the other. If the first one wouldn't have happened, our precious Jacob wouldn't be here."

She held him in her arms and kissed him tenderly on the lips. "I love it. Thank you."

"You're welcome."

"I made dinner," she said to him.

"I know. I can smell it."

"Are you hungry?"

"Starving," he replied.

"Good. It'll be ready in a few minutes." She released him and headed toward the kitchen.

Even though Jake was too young to understand what was happening, Roger and Lauren enjoyed spending Christmas with their baby. Jake's first Christmas was even more special because Roger and Lauren invited the entire family to join them. The Hanson's flew in from Seattle. Peter, Amy, and the boys flew in from Baltimore, and Roger's parents drove down from Owego. For five days, Roger and Lauren hosted fifteen people. They took everyone shopping along Fifth Avenue, making sure to stop at FOA Schwartz so the boys could play with the big piano and experience the childhood splendor of that magnificent place. They showed the family the gargantuan Rockefeller tree, built a snowman in Central Park, and took the boys to Macy's to talk to Santa. Having kids around at Christmastime significantly boosted the energy and excitement level. Seeing the holiday from a child's point of view gave Roger and Lauren an entirely different perspective. Roger had an absolute blast.

Part of the celebration involved the adults piling into cabs and going to the Marquis Theatre to watch Roger's show. This was the final performance of the season. Since Roger's mother had already seen it, she happily offered to stay behind and babysit.

Hosting Christmas ended up being less of an undertaking than Roger and Lauren originally thought it was going to be, mainly because Jacob's care was taken over by grandparents, aunts, and uncles, at least until they returned to their hotels for the night. Sharing the magic of New York City with family, and witnessing the joy and excitement on his nephews' faces made this one of the best Christmases Roger could remember.

With the coming of the new year, Roger made a conscious effort to hold true to his resolution. Aside from his usual charitable contributions, one of the first activities he took part in was a Broadway benefit concert at the Palace Theatre. This five day concert series, organized to raise money for St. Jude's Children's Hospital, featured composers, musicians, and more than one-hundred stars of Broadway who volunteered their time to come together to perform a collection of songs from various Broadway shows. The show featured renowned Broadway performers, along with the Muppets and cast of Sesame Street. Performers gave solo and group performances and the

Muppets had cute skits in between. They topped the whole show off with a huge closing ensemble, which included a major tap dancing number, featuring both Roger and Jason. They televised the entire event and made into a two-hour DVD. The full concert was released by Broadway Records, and all proceeds went directly to the hospital. It was a huge success. With ticket sale proceeds alone, they raised over two million dollars.

Shortly after this benefit concert, both Roger and Lauren received callbacks for *Singin' in the Rain*. This pre-production stage involved more readings, more voice auditions, and showing off snippets of dance routines. After several weeks of back and forth return callbacks and repeated readings, both were offered lead parts. Contract negotiations proceeded.

Roger went in the room with Lauren, but wanted her to bargain through her own contract this time. "A good rule of thumb is to ask for five-hundred more than you made last time. Since you made 3K for the last show, ask 3.5 for this one. Try to get more if you can. You have Broadway experience now plus a Tony nomination to hang over them. You shouldn't be getting any less than that, in fact they'll probably offer you more."

"Should I start higher?" she asked, wanting a little guidance.

"Don't go ridiculously high, but high enough to allow some wiggle room."

Roger sat through Lauren's contract negotiation, listening intently but saying nothing. He wasn't planning to interfere unless they deliberately denied her what she was worth. She started her bargaining at 4K. They countered with 3.8. Lauren found this reasonable and closed the deal. The whole process was fairly quick and painless. Not bad for her first time. Roger was able to get 9.5K for his contract, making $13,300 between the two of them. Pretty darn good for a week's work. That would definitely boost up the saving's account…and buy a lot of diapers.

With a new show set to start production next month, it was time for Roger and Lauren to search for a qualified nanny. Roger took the proactive approach and used his connections. He networked with colleagues and sent out a bulk e-mail, asking for any insights or recommendations about fulltime infant caregivers.

While whisking eggs in a bowl, Roger received an unexpected phone call. He stumbled to locate his phone. "Hello?"

"Hey, Roger," the cheerful caller said.

Although the person on the other end of the line knew him, Roger didn't recognize the male voice speaking to him. To put this conversation into meaningful context, he kindly asked, "I'm sorry, who is this?"

"Edwin Ashley."

Roger knew Edwin. They worked together in *Memphis* many years ago. "Edwin! I didn't recognize your voice. How you been?"

"Doing well. Congratulations on the birth of your son."

"Thank you."

"With a new baby in the house, no doubt you've been busy," Edwin added.

"Yes, but I like it that way. Keeps me on my toes. What's up?"

"Heard you were looking for a nanny."

"Yes, we are," Roger confirmed. "We're starting rehearsal for a new show next month and need someone to keep an eye on Jake for us. They must be willing to watch him during the day while we rehearse, but switch to evening hours when we actually start performances."

"I think I can help you with that," Edwin said. "My daughter is an experienced nanny, and she's worked with Broadway performers before. She knows all about performance schedules."

This was encouraging news. "How much experience does she have?"

"Over ten years. She's CPR and First Aid certified, has had a thorough background check, and is state licensed."

This sounded too good to be true. "Does she have experience with infants? That is something very specific Lauren and I are looking for."

"Yes she does."

"Can we meet her?"

"Of course."

Roger collected contact information and arranged to meet with Kara Ashley that afternoon. Kara had a pleasing disposition and many years of experience with infants. It turned out that she had worked mostly with Broadway performers and professional musicians. She was familiar with the way show scheduling worked and was willing to adjust her schedule to meet their needs. She would provide her own transportation, do mild household chores, and she was only going to charge them twenty dollars an hour. She offered references and showed them her CPR certification and nanny license, as well as background check information. Her resume was impeccable, and her references were positive and solid. Overall, she had everything they were looking for. They let her interact with Jacob for a while to see how they connected. Jake seemed to like her.

Later that night, Lauren and Roger openly discussed this important decision. "Well, her references are good, and she was recommended by a source I trust," Roger said.

Lauren read over Kara's resume again. "She seems to have everything we want and she was good with Jacob," Lauren added. "He even cooed at her."

"And twenty dollars an hour is really reasonable. A lot less than I anticipated." Wanting to know what his wife was thinking, Roger asked, "Shall we give her a try and see how she does? We can start small, just a couple hours at a time, then slowly ease her in. It might make the transition easier for everyone."

"That's a good idea."

"We can use the time she's with him to take a breather, get some groceries, or have a date night. It will allow us to spend some time together without having to worry." Roger could see the gears moving in Lauren's head. He knew she was seriously considering this. "So, what do you think? Shall we give her a call in the morning?"

Lauren grinned. "Yes."

Finally! They found someone they both liked. Roger breathed a sigh of relief. "See? I told you not to worry."

Chapter Forty-Three

Now that Nathan had a year and half of medical training and several clinical experiences under his belt, Randy put him to the test. When Nathan came into the clinic one afternoon, Randy poked his head out of an exam room and said, "Nate, can you come in here for a minute please?"

Nathan dropped what he was doing and followed his father into the room.

Randy stood by the counter skimming over a medical chart. "I have another patient coming in. I want you to take vitals on her."

This was a request his father had never given him before. He wasn't sure how to react. "Me?"

"Yes. You do know how to take someone's temperature, use a stethoscope, attach a blood pressure cuff, and record a pulse rate, don't you?"

"Yes, Sir."

"Then get vitals on this patient. I'll monitor you."

Nathan nodded in compliance, excited that his father trusted him enough to allow him to practice these skills on his patients. As Randy was about to leave the room, Nathan called out, "Dad?"

Randy glanced up. "Yes?"

"Thanks."

"Just focus on what you need to do. If you do a decent job and don't screw this up, then you can thank me."

But Nathan didn't screw it up. He performed his duties quickly and thoroughly. More importantly, he was accurate. When Randy finished his examination on the patient, he called Nathan into this office.

Nathan stepped inside and closed the door. "Yes, Sir?"

"Sit down," Randy insisted.

When Nathan heard his father's gruff tone, he thought he was about to get lectured. "Did I do something wrong?"

"No, not at all. In fact, you did well. I'm impressed."

Nathan breathed a sigh of relief. "Thank you."

"You've really learned a lot. I'm proud of you."

Dr. Hanson was one of the most selfless physicians Nathan ever had the privilege to work with, and he had proved to be more than just a father to him; he was also a role model and a mentor. Hearing his father's compliment made him feel more confident. "Thanks."

"I called you in here because, if you're interested, I'd like to give you more responsibilities around here."

"Like what?" Nathan wondered.

"Like helping my nurse collect vitals on patients. I talked to Tammy, and she is more than willing to allow you to do that on the days you're working, supervised of course. She will handle the other duties, but that one, I'd like you to tackle for a while."

"Won't that slow you down and put you behind schedule?"

"Not significantly. It takes two minutes to collect vitals. It won't make a huge impact on my schedule, and I want you to practice."

Nathan liked this plan. Getting some extra clinical experience would only benefit him in the long run. "That sounds good."

"And I want you to start coming to work in your lab coat with your UW badge so my patients know who you are. From now on, I'm going to treat you as I do the rest of my clinical students, which includes enforcing the dress code. You are to wear proper professional attire at all times."

"Yes, Sir."

Randy removed his stethoscope and set it on his desk. "Did you get your semester grades?"

"I did."

"And?" Randy asked, waiting for an answer.

Sounding disappointed, Nathan replied, "I barely squeaked by with a B in Ethics. That class kicked my butt."

Randy completely understood. "A lot of that is based on judgment calls. It takes experience to master it. You'll get more into that next year when you start clinical rotations. I can help you."

"There are a lot of decisions doctors have to make that can really affect people's lives. It's frustrating when you're doing all you can for a patient and they refuse treatment, or the family fights you on every decision you make. Then the pharmaceutical companies try to get involved by pushing their prescription drugs at you insisting you try them out on such and such a patient. Then there are insurance issues. Don't even get me started. I could go on and on about that craziness."

Randy had to laugh at his son's cynical attitude. He was starting to sound like a doctor.

"It seems to me that as doctors try to treat patients, there's always some opposing factor that gets in the way. As a physician, I want to do what's right for my patients. But I've discovered there is a fine line between what's morally right and what's medically sound."

"Welcome to the world of medicine, Son."

"I have my first batch of OSCEs next week," Nathan said.

The Objective Structured Clinical Examination, or OSCE, tested a variety of clinical skills. They included communication skills, physical examination skills, clinical reasoning, and clinical knowledge. A typical OSCE involved the medical student interviewing or examining a standardized patient who was taught to act and respond in a standard way. They also had to complete a set of written exercises and computer simulations. For second year students, OSCEs were administered over two blocks of time—one in January and a second in April. Each subsequent exam was longer and more challenging, and growth was expected to occur between each one.

"If what I saw today is any indication, you're going to rock it, Kiddo," Randy encouraged his son. "Have Gabby bring her pompoms and cheer you on."

Nathan had to laugh. "I don't think so."

Chapter Forty-Four

Rehearsals for *Singin' in the Rain* were some of the most demanding Roger could ever remember having. The choreography was challenging, yet extremely fun to do. He and his co-star, Noah, spent hours upon hours rehearsing together, and individually, for their tap number called 'Moses Supposes'. Aside from Roger's solo dance performance of the title song, this particular song was one of the main dance routines in this musical. This number was jam packed with body movement while tapping out sweet, swinging rhythm. This was dancing in its essence—all the style, core twisting, rhythm, and yummy goodness that would get audiences begging for more.

During a rehearsal session, the entire cast laughed as Noah and Roger went through the scripted comedic part of their scene. Everyone had seen them run through this part and sing this song together many times before, but had yet to see them perform the choreography together. This was the first time they attempted the entire sequence with everyone watching. Both were very capable tap dancers, young men in great shape with many years of modern dance training, which was good because this number was quite a workout with its high-energy choreography.

Dressed in tee-shirts, dance pants, and tap shoes, Roger and Noah gave it a go, complete with bench props and full orchestra accompaniment. When they began the tap sequence, the cast and crew watched in awe. They both captured the mannerisms of their characters so well. When Noah missed a step, the two men laughed, but they kept going. After spending painstaking hours working on this routine, there were very few mistakes. The guys were technically spot on and down to the details of the original movie production. Pretty darn good for a first go at it. When they concluded with their final note, the cast and crew applauded, whistled, and cheered.

The director gave them a standing ovation. "Phenomenal performance! Very nicely done, gentlemen. I think Gene and Don would be proud."

Roger and Noah gave each other a high five as they panted to regain air.

This particular cast and crew had a bold and playful energy level, and they were fun to work with. All of the people involved were enthusiastic and dedicated to this project, and all worked with one goal in mind, to stay as true to the original as possible and put on one hell of a show. There would be singing. There would be dancing. There would be rain. And most of all, this show told a wonderful story—a love story. That was, after all, why Roger's character was singing.

They only had one more week before the premiere—a week of large-scale, full dress rehearsals using all props, projections and effects, including the full sound system at their designated venue, the Gershwin Theatre.

Lacy reported to the Gershwin Theatre to see her sister and brother-in-law perform in their opening night of *Singin' in the Rain.* This theatre, located in the Paramount Plaza building in midtown-Manhattan, was named after famous composer George Gershwin and lyricist Ira Gershwin. It had the highest seating capacity of any Broadway theatre, with 1,933 seats. Since tickets sold out quickly, Roger arranged to get Lacy a front row seat, right where the action was.

The Art Nouveau style theatre was packed by the time Lacy got there. She found her seat and settled in. A man scooted in next to her and sat down. After adjusting and getting comfortable, he smiled at her and said, "I'm looking forward to this show. I'm a huge Roger Zellers fan. Did you see him in Phantom?"

"I did. He was spectacular."

"It's exciting to see him and his wife doing another show together. I'm glad she's back on stage. That woman has a powerful voice, and those two are extraordinary together."

"Yes, they are."

"I saw both of them in Crazy For You. Did you get a chance to see that one?" the man asked.

"I've seen every performance Lauren has been in, even before she debuted on Broadway."

This man raised an eyebrow. "You did?"

"Uh huh. I've known her my whole life."

"You know Lauren Zellers?"

"I know her quite well." She held out an open palm. "I'm Lacy Hanson. Lauren is my twin sister."

With a look of pleasant surprise, this man shook Lacy's hand. "I'm Max Chamberlain. Pleasure to meet you." He examined her facial features. She had chestnut brown hair and deep green eyes, similar to

Lauren's. "Wait a minute, that means Roger Zellers is your brother-in-law."

"Yes he is," Lacy confirmed. "Would you like to meet him?"

Excited about this prospect, Max replied, "Oh man, I wish I could."

"I'm going to see them after the show. I could introduce you," she suggested.

"You're joking, right?"

"No. I'm totally serious. Can you stick around for a while?"

"Yes. Of course! That would be incredible."

The cast and crew of *Singin' in the Rain* had huge shoes to fill. Everybody knew the movie title, but the fans were not disappointed by the Broadway stage version. As a matter of fact, they were amazed at the production surprises. Broadway had everything imaginable on stage for this show—silent movies, amazing choreography, an incredible ensemble for vocals, and rain.

The scene where Roger was dressed in a suit and fedora, hanging from a lamp-post and swinging his umbrella in the wild joy of new love, had a Broadway style rainstorm pouring into the theatre. Roger stomped through the puddles of water in gloriously saturated ecstasy making big wet splashes. He soaked not only himself but any theatregoer who happened to sit in the first row 'splash zone.' The entire sequence was the most joyous musical sequence in the entire production. Roger loved this scene. Even though he was soaked afterwards, it provided him with a tactile medium he didn't normally use while tap dancing, and he got to kiss Lauren right before the dance sequence.

The climax, when Lauren's character fled from the stage while Roger revealed to everyone that he loved her, was a bravura romantic scene. And because Roger and Lauren loved each other in real life, the scene was even more heartwarming. When they kissed in the final moments, it made Lacy tingle.

After the show, Lacy led Max backstage, making her way through the cast and crew members who bustled in every direction. When they arrived at Roger's dressing room, she knocked on the door.

"Who's that knocking on my door?" Roger sang out from behind the closed door. "If you've come seeking cookies, Lauren and I ate them all."

"Roger, it's me," Lacy said.

Roger recognized Lacy's voice and opened the door. "Hey, Lace," he greeted her with a big hug. "How's my favorite sister-in-law?"

"Where are these cookies you were talking about?" Lacy asked.

Roger handed her a box of assorted Schmackery's cookies. Great after-show munchies to satisfy the sweet tooth. "Here you go. Take your pick."

Lacy reached in a grabbed one.

Roger also offered one to the man standing next to Lacy. "Hello there. Would you like a cookie?"

Max reached in to grab one. "Thanks."

Lacy introduced them. "This is Max Chamberlain. He sat beside me during the show."

Roger extended a friendly handshake. "Hello, Max. I'm Roger Zellers."

Max couldn't believe he was standing up close and personal with one of the biggest stars on Broadway. "I know who you are," he proclaimed. "Huge fan. Loved you in Phantom."

"Thank you." Roger showed them inside.

Lacy took a seat on the sofa. "By the way, thanks for soaking me during your rain scene."

Roger laughed at her. "It is called Singin' in the Rain for a reason."

"Did you have to deliberately aim for me?"

"Did you not read the disclaimer that said the first two rows were potential splash zones?"

"That's why you got me a front row ticket isn't it? So you could get me wet."

"Darn! You uncovered my secret." Roger winked at her with a playful snicker. "You looked like you could use a shower. I was kindly offering my assistance."

"Thank you so much for your consideration," she refuted mockingly.

Roger offered Max a cup of coffee and a chair so they could chat for a bit.

After about an hour of mingling with cast members of *Singin' in the Rain* and having a friendly conversation with Roger Zellers in his dressing room, Lacy escorted Max out of the building. "It was incredible to meet him, to actually sit down and have a conversation with Roger Zellers in his dressing room. That was awesome!"

"I'm glad you enjoyed it. It was a pleasure meeting you, Max."

Lacy quickly dismissed him, but he was not as willing to dismiss her. "Hey now, hold on. No one's ever done anything like that for me before. At least let me buy you a cup of coffee to express my gratitude."

"Coffee?" Lacy questioned his intentions.

"Yeah. Let me treat you to a cup of coffee or a drink or something."

"Coffee sounds good," she confirmed.

"Can I call you?" he asked, hoping maybe they could exchange phone numbers.

"Sure." She gave him her number, not thinking he was serious, before they parted ways.

Lacy wasn't expecting Max to call her. Most men who asked for her number never did. But unexpectedly, the following morning, Lacy answered her phone and heard Max's voice. "Max. I'm surprised you called."

"Why? I told you I would. I'm still holding true to that invitation, you know."

"Really?" she asked, surprised by his faithful gesture.

"But instead of coffee, I was kinda hoping you'd have dinner with me instead."

"Like on a date?"

He chuckled. "Yeah. I'll pay and everything."

She found his comment amusing "Sounds fun."

"Great!" he exclaimed. "The only problem is I'm about to head to the firehouse and won't be available until Monday night."

"Firehouse?" she asked, wondering what he meant by that.

"Yes. I'm a New York City firefighter. Engine 76 Company in Manhattan."

"Oh wow. You're like a real life hero."

"I don't know about that, but I do fight fires, rescue people from burning buildings, and educate the community about fire safety."

"That's cool," she relied. "Much more exciting then what I do."

"And what's that?" he asked.

"I'm a dance and choreography student at Barnard School of Dance at Columbia University. I'm about to graduate."

"Maybe we can hit the dance floor after dinner. But then again, you'd dance me under the table and I'd look like a floundering fool. Not a good way to make an impression."

"It would be fun tough," she added.

"Yes it would," he said. "Are we on for dinner and dancing Monday night?"

"Yes," she agreed.

"Good. I'll call later to work out details, but right now I have to go. Duty calls."

"Be careful."

"I always am. I'll talk to you later, Lacy."

Curious about Max now, she searched for his firehouse. It was located on West 100th Street in Upper West Side Manhattan, fairly close to the university. Hoping she could talk to him, she decided to stop by. Both giant firehouse doors were wide open with the fire trucks prepped and ready to go. Lacy peeked her head into the garage and saw a fireman standing next to the engine reading some gauges and writing down notes on a clipboard. "Excuse me," she said.

The firefighter looked up. "Yes, Ma'am. May I help you?"

"I'm sorry to bother you. Obviously you're busy, but I'm looking for someone."

Hastily, he set down his clipboard. "Is this person lost?"

"No," she clarified. "I was told he was a firefighter here. His name is Max."

"He's in the back. Would you like me to get him?"

"If it wouldn't be too much trouble."

"No trouble at all." He faced the back of the firehouse and yelled, "Hey, Max!"

"Yeah?" Max hollered back.

"Come here for a minute. There's a woman out here looking for you."

Max stepped out from behind the back of the fire engine. "A woman?"

"She's about five foot seven, long brown hair, green eyes."

Max knew that description. "I'll be out in a minute."

This firefighter returned to Lacy. "He says he'll be out in a minute."

"Yes, I heard. Thank you."

"Anytime." The fireman picked up his clipboard and went about his business.

Holding a brown paper bag in her hand, Lacy waited outside the firehouse.

Moments later, a young, physically fit firefighter with strong arms came out wearing his blue fireman uniform. It had a *FDNY, Engine 76, Upper West Side* patch sewn on the side of the arm, and on the front of his shirt was a fire department badge and a nametag with the name *Chamberlain* printed on it. "Hey, Lacy. Wasn't expecting you to stop by."

She sized him up, lusting over his gorgeous body. He looked incredibly sexy in that uniform. "Nice uniform."

"You like it?"

"Yes. I love it."

He raised an eyebrow at her statement. "Hmm, I may have to wear this around you more often then. Which brings up a point. What are you doing here?"

"I have something for you." She handed him the bag she was holding. "Roger wanted me to give this to you."

He opened the bag to reveal a ceramic *Phantom of the Opera* mask with Roger's signature on it. He took the mask in his hand and stared at it in total shock. "Seriously? He's giving this to me?"

538

She pointed to Roger's signature. "He even signed it for you."

Max grinned from ear to ear. "Wow! This is incredible. Tell him thank you for me."

"I will."

He looked up at her. "You came over here just to give me this?"

"Well," she admitted. "I also wanted to see you."

He flashed a flirty, sexy smile. "Good. Because I've been thinking about you."

"You have?"

"Just this morning I was saying how much I was looking forward to seeing Lacy's pretty face again. And look, here you are. It's good to see you."

"It's good to see you too."

As they stood outside talking, the station alarm went off. Max looked behind him. "I have to go." He rushed inside calling out, "I'll call you later."

Lacy stood on the sidewalk in front of the firehouse and watched the entire company of firefighters, in under thirty seconds, slip on their turnout fireproof pants and insulated waterproof boots then quickly hop inside Engine 76. With sirens blaring and lights flashing, the red engine pulled out of the station and raced down the street while the firemen buckled up their fireproof coats. The ladder truck rapidly followed. It was a fascinating spectacle.

Chapter Forty-Five

On their date, both Lacy and Max were quite talkative. Lacy shared her hobbies, her passion for dance and choreography, and told him all about her family in Seattle.

He listened attentively, trying to learn as much about her as he could. "You're father's a doctor?"

Lacy nodded. "Uh huh."

"Bet that's an exciting job."

"My brother, Nathan, is also into medicine. He's in his second year of medical school."

"Ooh," Max said, sympathizing with the enormous amount of stress involved in that undertaking. "I've heard those medical school programs are tough."

"They are," Lacy concurred. "But he's doing well. Are you much of a college basketball fan?"

"I am," Max replied with a huge smile on his face.

"My brother used to play for the University of Washington."

Max knew that team. Washington was the number one ranked college basketball team in the nation two years ago. They made it to the finals that year, and for the first time in Husky history, they walked away with the championship trophy. He remembered that game well. It was a huge upset for Duke and made national sports news headlines for months. "The Huskies?"

"Yup. He was on the team that won the national title a couple years ago."

"That game was crazy." Max recapped the details of the game. "During a loose ball, Washington's point guard got bashed in the nose by an elbow and they had to stop gameplay to clean blood off the floor. It wasn't broken, thank goodness, but he was out for a good chunk of time. When he finally came back in the game, the Huskies gained the lead and walked away with the title."

Lacy got excited that Max knew who her brother was. "That was Nathan."

"The guy who got nailed in the nose?"

"Uh huh," Lacy reiterated. "He was Washington's starting point guard for three seasons."

Max was impressed. "Damn! That must have been an incredible experience for him."

"Definitely," she replied. "He had a sore nose for several days after that game though."

Max chuckled. "I bet. That was one of the best basketball games I've ever seen. He was a good player."

Lacy agreed. "He still is."

As the conversation progressed, Lacy learned a few things about Max. He was twenty-five years old and lived in Brooklyn. Apparently firefighting ran in the family; his father was the Chicago Fire Chief. Max took the firefighter's service examination at age nineteen and was quickly accepted into the New York City Fire Academy's eighteen-week training program. Upon induction, right before his twentieth birthday, he remained a probationary firefighter until he turned twenty-one, at which time he was appointed to a position as firefighter Fifth Class. From there, he worked his way up the ranks of the New York City Fire Department and was now in his fourth year. He worked two consecutive nine-hour day shifts, then was off for forty-eight hours, after which he worked two consecutive fifteen-hour night tours. He was then off for seventy-two hours. While on duty, he and his fellow crew members lived and ate together at the firehouse. This made firefighting a unique type of work because firefighters were together constantly while working. They were coworkers who behaved like roommates, and ultimately like a family.

He proceeded to tell her about the hazards, dangers, and potential life-threatening aspects of his job.

"That sounds scary," she replied.

"It's the nature of the job. Fighting fires is what I do. It's what I love and something I'm not willing to give up."

Even though it sounded risky at times, she thought his job was exciting. "That is an incredible thing you do for people. You are to be commended, and certainly respected for the service you offer the community."

Her response made him smile. Many times Max had gone out with women who, as soon as they learned about the risks involved with his work, immediately walked the other way, not wanting any part of it. Lacy was different. She actually seemed to support his job choice. He really liked her and wanted to proceed with building this relationship in hopes that it might develop into something more serious later on down the road. Making it very clear what his intentions were, he laid it out for her. "I'm having a good time tonight, and I'd like to see you again, but you need to understand that my job has risks. If you don't think you can handle the dangerous situations I'll be put in, it's ok." He reached for her hand. "I want you to be totally honest with me. If you don't want to be a part of this, I completely understand, but please say so now, before we progress this any further. You won't be the first woman to walk away. They'll be no hard feelings whatsoever." He gently rubbed his thumb across her wrist. "Am I going to see you after tonight?"

She touched his hand. "Yes."

"This isn't gonna be too much for you to handle?"

She shook her head confidently. "Nope."

"Does that mean you'll meet me for pie tomorrow night?"

"I like pie."

"I like pie too. And I know a great place to get some."

At the end of their date, Max walked Lacy up to her room. "Thank you for sharing dinner with me," he said.

"Thank you for inviting me. Dancing with you was really fun."

Her comment made him chuckle. "Yeah, I bet. I'm sure it was hilarious as hell, considering I can't dance." As they stood outside the door, his gaze wandered to her lips. "I guess I'll see you tomorrow."

"I'm looking forward to it." Lacy was the kind of woman who wasn't afraid to make the first move. Instead of waiting for Max to take action, she moistened her lips and kissed him.

Without hesitation, he kissed her back, soft and tender at first, gradually increasing the intensity. Her kiss was delicious, and he wanted more. Much more. But he restrained himself and slowly pulled away from her. "Goodnight, Lacy."

"Goodnight, Max."

He gave her one last kiss before he left.

Chapter Forty-Six

Max and Lacy texted and talked on the phone almost daily. They spent time together often and got to know each other quite well.

One afternoon, shortly after Max reported to the firehouse, Lacy heard an announcement on the radio about a huge chemical fire blazing in a west Manhattan high-rise. The blaze utilized all nearby companies and was declared a six alarm fire. She turned on the news to try to get a clearer picture of what was happening. The images she saw were horrifying. Fire trucks, police vehicles, and EMS units were everywhere. The building was aflame and people were injured and crying. It was total chaos. She carefully viewed the fire trucks on the scene and saw Max's company. Then, right before her eyes, the building exploded, which led to a structural collapse. Several fire department signals were called out. Through dating Max, Lacy had become familiar with some of the signals the New York Fire Department used. As she watched the news' coverage of the horror, she heard them announce the dreaded 10-66 signal. If a 10-66 was transmitted, it meant firefighters were missing.

The news reporter announced that this blaze had turned into a nine alarm, very dangerous and deadly fire. Already two firefighters had been killed. Three more were now missing in the attempt to put out the flames. Lacy kept her eyes glued on the TV screen hoping to catch even the slightest glimpse of Max's face or the back of a turnout coat with the name Chamberlain on it. Men from his company held hoses trying to douse out flames. Others had axes and wore oxygen tanks, looking like they were about to enter the burning building, but there was no sign of Max.

Three hours into the incident, she still hadn't seen or heard a word from him. She began to worry that something tragic had happened.

When the incident was finally over, Lacy received a much awaited phone call. "Oh god, Max, it's good to hear your voice," she cried. "I was so scared."

"These kinds of situations happen. Our company, our battalion, we're a family. We all look out for one another. That's the way we work. We do whatever we can to keep each other safe. We even saved a few lives today."

"But you're okay?" she asked, hoping he wasn't hurt. "You're not hurt?"

"I'm fine," he reassured her. "And no one in our battalion is missing or injured."

She breathed a sigh of relief. "Thank goodness."

"I'm tired, hungry, and desperately need a shower. But I wanted to call and let you know I was alright."

"Thank you."

"We're heading back to the station now, but I'm still on duty. I'll text you later."

Knowing he was safe made her rest a lot easier.

When Max saw Lacy later that night, she jumped into his arms and embraced him with a desperate grip. He chuckled at her rampant enthusiasm. "Why the death grip? I can't breathe."

"I almost lost you."

"No you didn't," he corrected. "I told you I'm fine." He saw the worried look on her face and tried to ease her anxiety. "Things got a little hairy there for a while, but it wasn't anything we couldn't handle. We're trained to deal with situations like that. My company is one of the best in the city. We work well together as a team, and we don't take unnecessary risks."

"Don't scare me like that," she insisted.

"I didn't scare you. The over-exaggerated news coverage of the incident scared you." He looked her in the eye and seriously stated, "I'm going to be in situations like that. We've talked about this."

"I know, but when I saw your company on the scene and heard that firefighters were missing and dead and saw no sign of you anywhere…You can't expect me not to worry," she argued.

"I'm flattered that you're concerned about my safety."

"I care about you," she declared.

"And I care about you." He slipped his arms around her waist. "In fact, there's something I needed to talk to you about, but I wanted us to be face to face to do it."

"What is it?"

He proceeded to tell her, "I've never met anyone like you. You're kind, affectionate, caring, spunky, and you're fun to be around. You never cease to make me smile. Over the last six weeks, you have managed to pull on my heart strings. And you've pulled so hard that you've made me completely fall for you."

Hearing him say that made her breath escape her momentarily. She stared at him, but didn't say a word.

Max became a bit worried when she didn't respond. Concerned now that he had jumped the gun by admitting his feelings, he tried to fish some kind of a response out of her. "Lacy? You going to say something?"

Their eyes met in the most intimate glance the two of them had ever shared. Hoping she had heard him correctly, she asked, "Did you just say that you've fallen for me?"

"I did." With a loving touch, he cupped her face in his hands and pulled her lips to his, fusing together as one. This kiss was not like a kiss they normally shared; this was much deeper. It was sensuous, profound, passionate, purposeful, showing his deep devotion and affection for her with every ounce he had within him. His hands slid down her back and crept their way to her butt.

She tightened her grip around his neck and wrapped her legs around him.

He held her up by supporting her bottom with his hands while he pushed her against a nearby wall. Things were getting hot, and he was getting excited. But they were in public, not the most appropriate place to put on this kind of lustful display. People were now staring at them.

"Lace," he said, panting between lip locks. "We can't do this here."

"Where do you want to go?"

"Somewhere more private." Offering a quick solution, he said, "Let's go to my place."

She willingly agreed.

They hopped on his red 1966 pinhead softail Harley Davidson and drove through Manhattan, across the Manhattan Bridge, and into Brooklyn to the Brooklyn Heights Apartments. Immediately, they went up to the fourth floor, kissing in the elevator on the way. This was Lacy's first time in Max's apartment, but she didn't even notice the interior layout because they went straight to the bedroom. Max pushed the pillows off the bed and let them fall onto the floor. In one quick motion, he removed his shirt and tossed it behind him. As he and Lacy made their way to the middle of the mattress, their playful caressing quickly turned into foreplay. With his chiseled abs, sculpted pecs, and strong muscular arms, she had to have him now.

Max moved his hands up her blouse and unfastened her bra which, along with her shirt, quickly came off. While Lacy reached down to slip off her pants, he unfastened his belt and unzipped his pants, letting them fall to the floor. He moved in closer, feeling her breasts brush against his skin. Unable to resist her any longer, he reached down and pulled her panties off. Their bodies locked together as one. The lustful longing that followed was intense, erotic, and loud.

When the task was complete, their sweaty bodies collapsed into each other. Max lay on his right side, panting while his heart rate slowly subsided. Lacy propped herself on her elbow, turning her body to face him.

Max had a tattoo on his left shoulder. Lacy touched it, trying to get him to reposition himself so she could get a better look at it. "I didn't know you had a tattoo," she said.

He slanted his arm. "Yeah."

She closely examined the elaborate details. The tattoo itself was in the shape of a fireman's cross. FDNY was printed on the top of the cross. The bottom had the date 9-11-01. On the right side was a picture of a fire hydrant, and the left side had a ladder intersected with a pike pole. In the middle of the cross wan an image of the Twin Towers with a fireman's hat in the foreground. After carefully examining it, she concluded it was a 9/11 memorial tattoo. "That's really cool."

"I had that done about four years ago. All the guys in my company have one." He flexed his muscle. "Pretty sexy, huh?"

"Definitely." She moved her mouth to his and their lips interlocked.

Chills flowed down his back. Intrigued by her flirtatiousness, he raised his eyebrows suggestively. "You make it very hard to resist you."

"Maybe that's the idea," she replied.

"Are you trying to seduce me?"

"Is it working?"

"Yes." He pulled her close and tasted her delicious mouth once more.

"What made you decide to become a firefighter?"

Max opened his eyes. "The desire to serve."

She wanted more details. "What does that mean?"

He tried to explain. "I protect those who are in danger, those in times of need, and I serve human society. There is no feeling in the world like walking out of a burning building, carrying someone in your arms, and knowing that you just gave that person another chance at life. It's a proud endeavor to save a life."

"It's brave, noble, and heroic," she added.

He disagreed, "I don't do it to be a hero. I do it because I find satisfaction in it. The guys in the firehouse, we look out for each other. Each one of us would lay down his life for the other. We protect each other, celebrate together, and mourn losses together." He paused to gather his thoughts, feeling the loss of the recent events. "The New York City Fire

Department lost two fireman in that explosion today. We haven't lost a firefighter in three years. When something like that happens, it doesn't just affect one company or one battalion, it affects all of us. Firefighters stick together. We try to save lives, that's what we do. It's what we live for. Sometimes it's what we die for."

"Did either of them have families?"

"One of them was married and had three children. The other had recently gotten engaged."

Lacy got a little teary eyed. "That's terrible."

"Unfortunately it happens," Max stated, feeling the lump in his throat from losing two of New York's bravest men. "But it was no one's fault. They just happened to be in the wrong place at the wrong time. There is always the possibility that I may die in the line of duty, Lace. But that's not going to deter me from doing what I love. That's my sacrifice to make."

"I feel bad for those families. And I worry about you when you go out on runs like that."

"I know, but you can't live in fear every time the alarm goes off at the firehouse. You just need to believe that my company is going to do whatever needs to be done to get all of us home safely." Trying to ease her fear, he said, "I trust these guys with my life, Lace, and they trust me."

"They sound like great guys."

"We're like brothers." He chuckled as a thought came to him. "They're all pestering me at the moment."

"Why?"

"They've been trying to hook me up for a while now. They've seen me texting you and they know we've been seeing each other; they're curious. They want to know who Lacy is. I was thinking maybe sometime next week, you could come over to the station for a bit so the guys can meet you. Once you get to know them, you'll learn to trust them as I do."

"I would love to meet them."

"Good." He changed the subject. "What time are your parents coming tomorrow?"

"2:30 I think," she replied, anxious not only to see her family, but also to finally graduate from college.

"Are they flying into La Guardia?"

"No," Lacy corrected. "Newark."

"How are they getting in from the airport? Do they need a ride?" Max offered.

"Roger and Lauren are picking them up."

"Cool." He snorted under his breath, thinking about what was in store for him tomorrow. "I get to meet the parents tomorrow night, huh?"

"Are you nervous?"

"Should I be?" he questioned.

"I don't think so," she reassured him. "They're going to love you."

"Let's hope so."

Lacy quickly scanned the simple, yet effective decorating in this room. He had dark mahogany bedroom furniture, a plain white comforter and simple brown and white throw pillows. The huge bedroom window had an amazing view of the East River, the Brooklyn Bridge, and the Manhattan skyline. "So this is your apartment."

Realizing that this was the first time Lacy had ever been here, Max laughed. "Welcome to my humble abode. You're free to look around if you want." He kissed her softly. "Or we can just lie here together a little longer. Whatever you feel like."

She eyed him seductively. "Think I like the idea of lying here in your arms a little longer."

"You'll get no complaints from me."

Chapter Forty-Seven

For the last four years, Lacy had been a dance student at Barnard Dance School. Technically, Barnard was under the umbrella of Columbia University, but it had its own core, endowment, and application process. Not only was Lacy graduating from New York City's Ivy League school, she was also receiving a dance degree from one of the top ten dance colleges in the country.

Because of the affiliation with Columbia, Barnard students were included among and considered to be Columbia University students—their diplomas and transcripts stated such. Barnard and Columbia University students also participated in the same graduation ceremony, and Lacy couldn't wait to walk that stage.

The entire Hanson family flew into New York for Lacy's graduation. Nathan had just finished his second year of Medical School and planned to take full advantage of this down time before he had to go back to prepare for boards.

Baby Jacob was now seven months old. He was sitting up, crawling around, and could turn his head to his name. He had three teeth and was eating soft foods in his high chair with the family. He loved games like itsy-bitsy spider and peek-a-boo, and would bop and giggle excitedly every time he heard music. He made a wide variety of expressions with his face, from big grins to frowns, and communicated vocally by making different sounds—laughter, blowing bubbles or raspberries, and babbling in chains of consonants. Dada and nomnom were two sounds that seemed to have a consistent meaning. By using the context in which they were used, Roger and Lauren were able to determine that dada referred to either Mommy or Daddy. He didn't seem to differentiate between the two yet. Nomnom was something he always said when presented with food.

When Lauren and Roger met Randy, Jane, Gabby, and Nathan at the airport, baby Jake was with them.

As soon as Randy saw his grandson, he grinned. "Wow! Look how big he's gotten."

"And we're mobile now, Grandpa," Roger said. "So watch out."

"Uh oh. Is he getting into everything?"

"Not too bad. He has some kind of fascination with my tap shoes though. I don't know if it's the shiny tips on them or the color or what it is, but he loves to play with them. I took them away from him the other day and he started screaming."

Randy busted out laughing and looked directly and Nathan. "Sounds like a baby I used to know."

Nathan defended himself. "I did not scream like that."

"Oh yes you did," Randy corrected. "You were convinced that every spherical-shaped object in the house was a ball for you to play with. You'd throw a fit if we took them away from you."

Jane cut in, "Actually, Sweetie, your father is right. The Christmas after your first birthday, we couldn't put ornaments on the bottom of our tree because you would pull them off and throw them across the room."

Roger tried not to laugh.

"You got your first basketball hoop for Christmas that year," Randy said. "It's been a love affair ever since."

"Not such a bad investment then, was it?" Nathan said.

"It certainly was not."

Roger and Lauren dropped the Hanson's off at their hotel to get checked in before they all met at Carmines Italian Restaurant to celebrate Lacy's graduation. Lauren and Lacy went inside to secure a table while Roger and Max waited for the Hanson's to pull up.

Max openly expressed his anxiety. "Lacy tells me not to be nervous tonight. Based on your experience, can you give me some pointers?"

Roger helped him out. "The Hansons are a wonderful family. Hospitable, understanding, open-minded. They're delightful to be around. Dr. Hanson was a little standoffish when I first met him, but that's to be expected. I was dating his daughter, and he didn't know me. He can be a little intimidating sometimes, but don't take it personally. Strike up a conversation and give him time to get to know you. He really is a cool guy."

"What would be a good topic to start with?" Max asked, begging for any kind of advice Roger could offer.

"For Dr. Hanson? Sports cars are the way to go. Fishing and basketball are good conversation starters too." Roger chuckled at Max's desperate look. "Don't worry about it, and don't act like you're trying to make an impression. He'll see right through that." Roger put his hand on Max's shoulder. "You're a great guy, Max. Just be yourself."

When the Hanson's cab pulled up, Max cordially greeted them, making it a point to introduce himself. "Good evening, Dr. Hanson. I'm Max."

Randy shook his hand. "Lacy tells me you're a firefighter."

"That's correct," Max replied. "Been with the New York City Fire Department for four years now."

"Already we have something in common."

Max didn't see it. "What's that, Sir?"

"We both save lives. Good man." Randy patted Max on the shoulder then walked into the restaurant with his wife and kids.

Roger was completely taken by surprise by this interaction. "When I first met him, he didn't say two words to me. He sees you and instantly blurts out compliments within the first minute. What did you say to him?"

"I have no clue."

Chuckling, Roger said, "Well, that ice was easy to break. This will be a piece of cake for you."

Over dinner, Lauren remembered something she was supposed to pass along to Lacy. "Lace, I almost forgot to tell you. I spoke to Jason the other day. He told me they're seeking dancers for the production of Dirty Dancing that's coming out on Broadway in a few months. Open casting calls are next week." Lauren pulled a card out of her purse and handed it to Lacy. "He thought you might be interested and gave me information for the dance studio where they're holding auditions."

Lacy took the card from her, appreciating the gesture. "Thank him for me."

"I will."

Later that night, Lacy went over to Max's apartment. They snuggled on the sofa together with the lights low, watching a movie and munching on popcorn. Max gently rubbed her hand. "You going to audition for that show?"

"I don't know."

She hadn't said anything about it since Lauren brought it up over dinner. Wondering how she felt, he tried to get her to talk about it. "It might be a good experience for you."

"Maybe."

She was far than enthusiastic, and he sensed she wasn't really interested in it. He probed further to get her to say what was on her mind. "But…"

She shrugged. "I don't know. I just see everything Roger and Lauren go through. It seems like they deal with a lot of crap—contracts, rehearsal and performance schedules, publicity. I really don't want to be involved in all of that."

Good. She was opening up and talking about it, and she had valid points. "You're saying auditioning is a no then."

"Broadway's always been Lauren's dream, not mine. I just want to dance and share the joy of dance with others. I don't want all the recognition or the spotlight of being on stage," she explained. "Lauren keeps encouraging me to take auditions, but it's just not what I want to do."

"Did you ever tell her that?" Max asked.

"She's my sister. I don't want to hurt her feelings."

"No, but she does have a right to know how you feel. It won't hurt anything to let her know that you have no desire to be on Broadway. I'm sure she'll understand."

"It's not just that," Lacy said woefully. "I'm also kind of sad."

He didn't follow what she meant. "About what?"

"Lauren and I used to be so close. But now she's a star on Broadway, she's married, has a baby…it's not like it used to be. It's hard because she's my twin. I feel like a part of me is missing."

Max could see why she felt that way. "She's busy, Lace. She does have a baby in the house, and she's a working mom and a wife. And like you said, she has a lot to deal with as far as Broadway is concerned. Life gets in the way sometimes."

She stared at her hands. "We just don't seem to share the same interests anymore. When we were younger, Lauren and I were inseparable. We did everything together."

"You and Lauren may be twins, but you are two totally different people, Babe. It's those differences that make both of you unique. You're individuals with different personalities, different interests, and different goals in life. There's nothing wrong with that. Did you ever stop to think that she might feel the same way you do? When's the last time you and Lauren sat and talked, just the two of you with no one else around?"

"Before Jacob was born," she replied.

"Maybe you need to have a girls' day to just hang out with your sister," he suggested. "You should call her tomorrow and set up a time to do that."

Meanwhile, back at the Zellers household, Lauren had just put Jacob to bed for the night. As soon as he was settled, she returned to the living room where Roger was relaxed on the sofa with his feet up, flipping through channels on the TV. She sat down next to him. "He's finally asleep."

"Good. He had a busy day today. He was a tired little guy." Roger wasn't finding anything he liked so he handed Lauren the remote and opted for a book instead.

Lauren turned off the TV and set the remote on the table. "I miss my sister."

Roger chuckled, "You saw her tonight."

"That's not what I mean."

It was obvious that his wife wanted to talk. He closed his book to devote his full attention to her. "What are you thinking?"

"I know I just saw her, but it's not the same. She and I used to share everything together. We talked all the time, we always spent time together, we were close. I haven't spent any quality time with Lacy in months, and we haven't really talked much. I feel like I've been neglecting her. A huge part of my life is missing."

Roger knew how connected Lauren and Lacy were, and if Lauren was feeling this way then obviously there was a problem. "What do you want to do about it?"

"I want to spend more time with my sister."

"So why haven't you?" he asked.

"Jake."

"What about him?"

She didn't answer.

"Honey, if you want time to hang out with Lacy, just say so. Jake and I will share some daddy-son bonding time so you can relax and unwind with Lacy." He teased her by saying, "I am capable of taking care of my son."

"I know you are."

"Then that's not an excuse." He picked up her cellphone and handed it to her. "Call her. Set up a time to get together."

558

Lauren shook her head. "Not right now. She's with Max. I don't want to disturb them."

Good thinking. "Oh, yeah. That would not be good. Wouldn't want to interrupt anything," he laughed. "Call her in the morning then."

She agreed that she would.

Jacob enjoyed the freedom of mobility. He was starting to pull himself to a standing position and cruise along the furniture. Roger was convinced he would take a step on his own any day now. He also attempted to use a spoon and was quite adept to picking things up, but toys scattered all over the living room floor had become a problem. To correct this problem, Roger and Lauren set certain boundaries for Jacob and taught him how to pick up his toys when he was finished playing with them. They guided him along in this developmental growth stage and purchased a large woven basket. Not only did this get Jacob's belongings off the floor so they weren't tripping over them, it would also provide a central location within the living area for Jacob to keep his toys and allow him to clean up after himself.

While Lauren was getting ready for an outing with her sister, Roger put some of Jacob's toys in this basket. "Jakey, come here. Daddy wants to show you something."

Jake crawled over to Roger and sat on the floor. "Dada."

"We're going to put your toys away." He handed Jacob a toy car then walked over to the basket. "Toys go in here."

Jacob rolled the car toward his father.

"No," Roger said, handing it back to him. "It goes in the basket." He picked up a toy to show him.

"Watch Daddy. Toys go here. Come put the car in the basket, Jake."

Jacob stared at the car for a minute. "Dada."

Roger squatted next to the basket, trying to entice Jake to come to him. "Bring it to Daddy."

With the car in his hand, Jacob crawled over to Roger and handed it to him.

"You do it," Roger directed him.

Jacob dropped it in the basket.

Roger applauded, praising his son's efforts. "Good job. Now go get the ball."

Jacob toddled over to the ball and picked it up. "Ba!"

"Yes, that's a ball."

Jacob pulled himself to his feet, using the sofa as leverage. He held on and looked at his dad. "Ba."

"Put it in the basket, Jakey."

Jacob let go, trying to balance. He was wobbly, but he stood by himself.

Roger urged him, hoping he'd take a step. "Come on. Bring Daddy the ball."

Jacob tried to take a step, but fell on his bottom. He frowned, giving Roger sad puppy dog eyes.

"Honey!" Roger hollered to Lauren, who was in the bedroom. "Come out here! You're going to miss it!"

Lauren quickly scampered out to the living room, wondering what Roger was yelling about. "What's going on?"

"Watch this." He focused his attention on his son again. "Bring the ball to Daddy, Jakey."

Jake held the ball up. "Ba."

"Yes, bring it to Daddy."

Jacob used the sofa to pull himself up again.

"Watch him," Roger said to Lauren with a huge grin on his face. "Come on, Jacob. Bring Daddy the ball."

Jacob made a second attempt to walk the ball over to the basket. This time he took three steps before he fell on his bottom.

Lauren screeched in excitement. "Oh my god, he's walking!"

Roger grinned proudly. "He's trying."

Lauren over exaggerated her applause. "Yay! Good job, Jake."

Jacob handed the ball to Lauren. "Mama."

"Thank you, Sweetie."

Roger picked Jacob up and hugged him. "Good job, buddy. Daddy's proud of you." He kissed his son on the cheek and set him back down on the floor.

"He's putting his own toys away," Lauren said.

"We're getting there. It's going to take time and a lot of patience, but he can do it." Roger reached into the cupboard and pulled out a box of teething cookies, handing one to Jacob. "You want a cookie?"

Jacob gripped the cookie in his hand. "Nomnom."

Excited that his son was attempting to walk, Roger said, "He's gonna take off any day now."

Lauren smiled. "I can't believe he took three steps. Our baby is getting big."

"I know. This year has gone by fast."

Since Lauren was out with Lacy, Roger had the baby all day. After feeding Jake, giving him a bath, diapering him, and getting him dressed, Roger prepared the diaper bag for an outing.

He met Jason at Central Park. When Jason saw Roger pushing Jacob around in the stroller, he said, "Well, well, the Zellers boys."

"Yup," Roger replied with a smile. "Thing One and Thing Two."

They strolled through the park for a while before stopping at a playground. Roger pushed Jacob on a baby swing for a while then spread a blanket out on the grass under a tree. He pulled some toys out of the diaper bag for Jacob to play with. One was a plastic car. Roger rolled it around on the grass making car noises, which made Jacob giggle. Jason found it amusing how both the baby and Roger equally enjoyed this activity beyond all reason.

When Jake started to get fussy, Roger had him lie down on the blanket. He handed him a bottle, and Jacob held it in his hands and drank. His eyelids became heavy.

Roger put the toys back in the diaper bag then sat on the grass and leaned against a tree. He crossed his ankles and gently placed his hand on Jacob's tummy.

Jason sat on the opposite side, leaning back on his hands, enclosing Jacob between them. He grinned at Roger. "He's a happy baby. You and Lauren are doing a good job."

"We're trying. It's been a lot of trial and error, but we're figuring it out." Roger looked down at his son, who had now fallen asleep. He took the bottle away and left him there to rest. "He's such a joy in our lives. I can't imagine life without him."

Roger had more fun at the Tony Awards that year than he ever remembered having at this event. The host was hilarious, the audience was enthusiastic, and the performances were entertaining. He even got to perform 'Good Morning' from *Singin' in the Rain* with both his hilariously funny co-star, Noah Krazinski, and his wife, all three of which had received nominations for their performances.

The cast and crew of *Singin' in the Rain* celebrated when the musical won Best Musical Score, Best Choreography, and all three main stars received a Tony for their individual categories. The musical walked away with five total awards, sweeping the floor for the year. It was an incredible night full of memories and music.

Aside from the two new additions to their fireplace mantle, Roger had Brandon create a large canvas portrait of his family, which was taken at Conservatory Garden in Central Park. They posed in front of the Burnett Fountain with pretty pink blossoms in the background. Once Brandon had the photo enlarged, Roger and Lauren hung it on the wall above the fireplace, accenting many awards and one white ceramic Phantom mask sitting on the mantle.

Chapter Forty-Eight

This slow-pace of July was a relaxing change after one of the worst semesters Nathan ever remembered having. Aside from his regular class schedule, he had to gather up the motivation and stamina to study for his boards, which tested everything he had learned the past two years of medical school. The United States Medical Licensing Examination, or USMLE, was administered to all medical students during their second year. This was an eight-hour, computer-based exam consisting of over three-hundred multiple-choice questions. It was divided into seven blocks of forty-six questions each. Questions included audio and video clips, and each block had to be finished within an hour. This particular portion of the exam tested their knowledge of basic medical sciences, such as Pathology, Pharmacology, Anatomy, and Immunology. This was the hardest and most important examination Nathan would take during his career. It determined if he was competent enough to practice medicine.

All summer, Nathan anxiously awaited the results of this exam. He checked the USMLE website daily, yet no scores had been posted. While browsing the internet one afternoon, he looked again. Finally, the much anticipated scores were ready to view.

Nathan skimmed through his results and breathed a sigh of relief.

Gabby overheard him. "What?"

"They finally posted board results."

She grew nervous for him. "How'd you do?"

The corners of his mouth slowly lifted. "I passed."

She gave him a celebratory hug. "Congratulations, Sweetie. I knew you could do it."

"Thanks. I got a really good score too. I needed a 188 to pass. My score was 236."

"That's good."

"I'm happy with it, especially since the first time I took a practice test I only got a 208."

"You've worked hard on this. I'm not surprised you did well."

Third year clinical rotations were the heart and soul of medical school and the reason why Nathan went to medical school in the first place. The third year primarily consisted of clerkships, in which the medical students were required to complete six-week rotations through various specialty areas—Family Medicine, Obstetrics and Gynecology, Pediatrics, Psychiatry, surgery, and a twelve week rotation in general medicine.

Nathan's first rotation was general medicine, which involved eight weeks of inpatient and four weeks of outpatient experience at various Seattle sites. During this rotation, he participated in the care of hospitalized patients. The purpose of this was to refine his skills of history-taking and physical examinations and learn how to care for the acutely ill. Daily rounds and conferences acted as training sessions, and students were given hands-on experience in use of the written and computer-based patient management system.

Half way through this rotation, Nathan pulled Gabby onto his lap and kissed her tenderly on the lips.

"You've been so patient with me, Babe. I know I can be a bear to live with sometimes."

Gabby giggled at him. "But you're a sweet, cuddly bear."

"I never would have gotten this far without you."

"We'll do whatever is necessary to get you through school, Nathan." She touched his face, which was predominant with stubble. "When's the last time you shaved?"

"Friday. I'm boycotting shaving on weekends. I have to dress professionally and wear a tie and be clean shaven Monday through Friday. Weekends, I'm gonna be a bum."

"You're not only a sweet and cuddly bear, you're a fuzzy one too," she teased him.

"But the fuzzy bears are the most snuggly, and the ones you want to take to bed and squeeze," he winked seductively.

"I wouldn't mind taking my bear to bed and snuggling with him."

He grinned. "Really?"

"Really," she affirmed.

"Sounds like someone's coming onto me."

She straddled his lap and wrapped her arms around his neck, kissing him with succulence and purpose.

He placed his hands on her hips and scooted her closer. "You better watch it. You know what kissing me like that does."

"Prove it." She dared him with a feisty grin.

Was she challenging him? "Prove it?"

"Yeah, Hotshot. I hear an awful lot of talk coming from those lips but don't see much action."

She was challenging him. "Oh, you're looking for action are you?" He picked her up, right from the position they were sitting, and carried her into the bedroom. "I'll show you more action than you can handle, Mrs. Hanson."

Chapter Forty-Nine

One long, hot summer night, Max and the members of Ladder 22 and Engine 76 were working an average night tour. By midnight, the company had a good meal and several routine runs behind them, and the neighborhood seemed to have quieted down. However, there was a hatred fomenting that turned to murder shortly after two o'clock in the morning.

A flammable liquid was spread throughout the interior stairway of a three-story apartment building, and a fire was released on the sleeping residents. At 2:06 A.M., the computer at the firehouse spit out a phone alarm for a fire at that address. As the rigs pulled out of quarters, the dispatcher assured them that, from the volume of calls they were receiving, a working fire was in progress and police were on the scene.

The short distance from firehouse made it a fast response time. As Engine Company 76 and Ladder Company 22 pulled up to the three-story, non-fireproof, multiple dwelling, heavy smoke spewed from every window and a raging inferno engulfed the interior stairway. The ladder apparatus set up near the fiery building while Max and the rest of the Engine 76 Company formed an inside attack team from the first floor. They performed a victim search. A man in great distress yelled from a second-floor room. A central fire escape was attached to the building, but the flames in the hallway blocked the victim's exit to it. Someone had to reach him. Engine 76 was able to charge a line and advance up the flaming stairwell long enough for Max to get to the second floor. But a new problem soon became evident. As Max headed into the room to pull the victim out, he heard his commanding officer, Captain Matthew Cochran, report that the interior stairwell had been completely burned away eliminating their exit. This interior rescue just advanced from a degree of difficult to impossible, and time was running out. With the fire escape blocked by a wall of flames, the only way to get the victim out of the burning building was through the window.

The intense heat and excessive smoke in his lungs caused the victim to panic and collapse to the floor. Without hesitation, Max dove headfirst into the room. The high heat conditions pushed him to the floor, however the thick smoke made it hard for him to locate the victim quickly. Crouched down on his hands and knees, he searched the room, calling out, "Fire Department! Yell if can hear me!" He eventually found the man, but his removal required Max to carry this 175-pound body over his shoulder and stand up to get him to the window. By now, the already intense heat in the room was quickly building up, and thick, acrid smoke seemed to roll across the ceiling—indication of an imminent flashover. If a flashover occurred, temperatures in the room would reach 1,500 degrees Fahrenheit and the room would burst into flames. It meant death to any person trapped in the room, civilian or firefighter. Search and rescue attempts would be over. Max had about two seconds to get himself and the victim out of the room before it completely ignited. He quickly carried the victim out the window to the ladder truck. Right as he and the victim descended down the aerial ladder, the predicted flashover occurred. The fire now consumed the entire top floor.

After rescuing the 60-year-old man from the inferno, Max returned to his company to help fight the flames from the interior on the bottom floor. As he reentered the burning building, he heard a child's voice screaming and crying. Directing his company, he hollered, "There's a child over here!"

"We got ya, Max!" His company careened water into the adjacent apartment.

"I'm going in!" Max went inside a smoke-filled apartment calling out, "Fire Department! Is anyone in here? Yell so I can find you!"

"Help!" The child coughed and gagged, struggling to get air.

"I hear you! Keep yelling!" Max followed the weak cries on the first floor, crawling to a rear room engulfed in smoke. He found a child hiding in a closet, trapped amid the smoke and confusion of the burning building. The young boy was crying hysterically, gasping for air, while holding a whining puppy in his arms. "Fire Department," Max called out to him. "I'm here to help you." He helped the boy out of the closet, giving him directions. "Hold your puppy nice and tight, okay?"

The child coughed again, choking on smoke.

Giving assurance to the boy, Max said, "I'm going to get you out of here." He picked the child up and cradled him in his arms, sheltering him in his flame retardant coat. The child gasped, unable to breathe. Max removed the facemask from his breathing apparatus and gave it to the child. "Close your eyes. Don't look."

The child complied.

With the child wrapped in his arms, Max raced out of the flame-filled room that flashed all around him at 1,000 degrees. He carried the boy and his puppy toward the front of the building, knowing it was their only means of escape. Sucking in smoke and intense heat from this inferno, Max rushed toward the light of the exterior door. When they made it safely out of the building, the medical team immediately attended to the child and the puppy. He had saved this child's life.

Knowing the child was now in safe hands, Max stepped over to the side of his 76 Engine truck. He leaned over and coughed, spitting out black mucous from his lungs.

The Engine Pump Operator from his company came over and put his hand on Max's back. "Max?"

Coughing still, Max replied, "I'm alright."

"You took in some smoke there, bud. You need to get checked out."

Max reported to the EMS truck. After holding an oxygen mask on his face, getting his right hand wrapped for a burn, and being evaluated by the medical team, they decided to keep him at the hospital for the rest of the night, just to be safe.

He called Lacy first thing in the morning and told her what happened.

Before she went to work that day, she stopped by to see him. She opened the door to his room and peeked inside. "Hey."

Max sat up in bed reading Sports Illustrated. When he heard her sweet voice, he looked up and smiled. "Hey, Babe."

Lacy sat on the bed next to him. "How you feeling?"

Max shrugged it off. "Sucked down a little smoke, but I'm fine. They have me here for precautionary measures."

His hand and wrist were bandaged in gauze. "What happened to your hand? Are you burnt?"

He held up his injured hand. "A little. It's not bad, though."

Lacy hugged him. "You saved that child's life."

"And his puppy."

"I'm so proud of you. That was so brave."

"Just doing my job." He slowly drew his lips to hers.

The men from his company poured in carrying plastic covered Tupperware containers. Trying to ruin the romantic moment, they all shouted, "Maxy!"

Max grinned, forcing him to break away from Lacy. "Hey, guys."

His captain, Matthew Cochran, gave him a high five. "We know how tasty hospital food is and knew you were dying to eat it, so we brought you breakfast."

Two of the guys from his company handed him plastic containers. The contents were still warm. "Mmm," Max said, looking forward to eating a home cooked meal from the official 'chef' at the firehouse. "Did Martin make this?"

"Oh yeah."

The savory aroma of Martin's special recipe scrambled eggs and homemade hash browns permeated the room. "Makin' my mouth water."

"After seeing the juiciness we walked in on, looks like your mouth was already watering." Matthew grinned at Lacy. "Hello, Lacy."

She smiled back at him. "Hi, Captain."

"They gonna let you outta here today?" his captain asked.

"I hope so."

"Before you report back to the firehouse tonight, the Division Chief said he wants to see you."

Max nodded. "Yes, Sir."

"Enjoy your breakfast, Max," Matthew said. "We wanted you to know that we're all behind you."

"Thanks."

As soon as his company left, Lacy said, "Maybe the chief wants to give you an award for bravery."

Max let out a long drawn out sigh, not sharing her excitement level. "I don't think so. Most likely, I'm going to get my ass chewed."

"Why? You saved that man and a little boy. Why would he be angry about that?"

"It's more complicated than that," Max tried to explain. "I broke safety protocol. At no time should I have taken off my facemask and given it to that child."

Lacy now feared that instead of being recognized for his noble life-saving act, he was going to be lose his job instead. To her this didn't seem fair. "Is he going to fire you?"

"I don't know. But I had to do it, Lace. The kid couldn't breathe. He was gagging and choking and suffering from smoke inhalation. He needed air. He could have suffocated to death. I couldn't let a little kid suffer like that."

She loved his moralistic longing for doing what was right, even at his own personal sacrifice. He was such a good and honorable man.

Taking responsibility for his actions, Max said, "If he wants to fire me, then I'll stand up and take the consequences. But I have no regrets about what I did."

Before Max started his next shift, he reported to the Division Chief's office as directed. He dreaded what was about to happen. Sitting and waiting to be reprimanded by the chief was taxing on the nerves. Fidgeting with his hands, he took a deep breath and sputtered his breath as he exhaled.

Finally, the secretary called Max in. "Mr. Chamberlain, the chief will see you now."

"Thank you." Hesitantly, he stood up and walked into the chief's office. "You wanted to see me, Sir?"

"Close the door," the chief of division demanded.

Max complied. He stood in front of his Division Chief's desk, waiting for this man to get in his face.

As Max feared, the chief let him have it. "Chamberlain, what the hell is wrong with you? How are you supposed to do your job and bring people to safety when you are sucking down smoke and don't have enough air to get yourself out of a burning building, let alone the victim? Do you know how many god damn safety protocols you broke in that inferno last night?"

Max defended himself. "It was a life or death situation, Sir. The child couldn't breathe. He needed air, and he couldn't wait. I wasn't about to let him die in my arms from smoke inhalation when I could have done something to prevent it. I had to protect him. I had no other choice."

"I don't give a good god damn what you feel you had to do. You put yourself in immediate danger. That was risky and ignorant on your part. I should fire your ass right now."

Realizing he needed to shut up before he angered this man further, Max simply replied, "I understand, Sir."

"But," the chief added. "The powers above me seem to think that your actions were some kind of meritorious act of bravery, and they want to commend you."

Max squinted his eyes, questioning this statement. "Sir?"

"The department seems to think you've earned a Valor Award."

To entitle a firefighter to a Valor Award, the act under consideration had to involve a degree of danger characterized as great personal risk—an individual act of personal bravery in conjunction with initiative and capability.

The chief tossed Max's service file on the desk. "After carefully looking over your service record from the last year, I have no choice but to promote you to First Class. Congratulations." He placed a First Class insignia bar on top of the file then leaned back in his chair and folded his arms across his chest. "You're on duty, Chamberlain. Get the hell out of my office and get to work."

"Yes, Sir." Trying not to show emotion, Max took the insignia off the chief's desk and left his office.

He reported to his firehouse where his Engine Company and the Ladder 22 Company were all in the garage doing workups and inventory on their trucks. When Max pulled up, they paused what they were doing. Matthew broke the silence, "Well?"

Max grinned. "I got First Class."

They congratulated him then Max joined them in completing their tasks.

Things were pretty slow in the firehouse that night. Max utilized this down time to call Lacy. He knew she had been worried and would be glad to hear the good news.

"What did the chief say?" she asked, fearing the worst. "Is it bad?"

"Well, as I suspected he pulled me into his office and ripped me a new asshole. Then he threatened to fire me," Max stated.

Hoping that hadn't actually happened, Lacy asked, "Oh god, he didn't, did he?"

"No, he didn't. But the New York City Fire Department is giving me a ribbon of commendation for saving the lives of those two people, and the chief gave me my fifth year promotion."

Relieved, Lacy celebrated with him. "That's fantastic, Max. I was so worried."

"I was too, but all's good. There's an award ceremony later in the year where they'll recognize me. I'll get my ribbon then."

"That's wonderful. Congratulations!"

"Thank you. What do you say we celebrate when I get off? We'll have dinner and maybe go see a show. What do you think?"

"Sounds great," Lacy agreed.

Lacy had never seen Max's full dress uniform before. When he pulled it out of the closet to add his First Class ribbon insignia, she finally got a chance to admire it. His dress uniform was a double breasted navy blue dress coat. Each brass button down the front was embossed with the letters FDNY. His jacket cuffs had matching buttons. Above the left side breast pocket was his metal FDNY badge. Centered on the right was his nameplate, along with various ribbon insignia. He currently had two ribbons: an Engine Company 76 insignia with red, white, and yellow stripes, and a purple and black FDNY 911 memorial with the number 343 printed on it. He now added his blue First Class insignia, which indicated five years of service in the New York City Fire Department.

Sewn on the left shoulder sleeve of the jacket was a Fire Department, City of New York patch. On the right was a reverse field American flag patch with a silver border. His coat's lapel had two pins, a silver bugle horn and an American flag. The collar of his light blue dress shirt had two silver FD pins poked through it, one on each side. They were oriented in such a way that the base of the letters were perpendicular to the tip of the collar. A navy blue necktie draped around it, and a pressed pair of straight-legged navy blue trousers hung neatly on the hanger underneath.

Lacy marveled at all the shiny pins and buttons. "I've never seen you wear this."

"I only wear it for special occasions." He picked up his navy blue bell crown service cap and put it on her head. "Looks sexy on you. Did you decide what show you wanted to see tonight?"

"You know what?" she claimed. "I haven't seen Wicked yet. Have you?"

"No." Max returned his uniform to the closet and took the hat off Lacy's head. "Is that the one you want to see?"

"Yes."

"Alright." He took her hand and pulled her toward him. "Shower with me?"

"Shower sex?"

"Hey, I'm open for sex anywhere you want." Lacy was wild in bed—sexy, enticing, shameless, and open to pretty much anything. They had christened every room in his apartment at least once. It seemed like she wanted it all the time too. Max wasn't complaining though. Lacy was the best he'd ever had. "Ever had sex on a firetruck?" he asked.

She puckered her lips, enticing him. "Ooh, that could be fun."

Raising an eyebrow, he replied, "I might be able to arrange that."

Chapter Fifty

Clinical rotations were going well, and Nathan was learning a lot. He loved the hands-on experience he gained from working with patients. His second rotation, Obstetrics and Gynecology, was directed by his father. Nathan had only seen his father work within his own clinical setting. This time, he was going to witness the teacher side of Dr. Hanson.

Six medical students were in this OB/GYN rotation together. Randy met with these new third-year students to do a brief overview about what to expect during this rotation and familiarize them with the hospital facilities at Swedish Medical Center, specifically the Maternity Ward. He started off in the conference room, informing them that within this six-week placement, each of them would be required to have a total of forty-eight hours of on-call status, where they would need to be available for a 24-hour timeframe to assist in any deliveries or emergency situations that came up during that time. The two 24-hour on-call days had to be spread out throughout the rotation.

Each medical student was assigned to a different attending physician for outpatient work, but all of them had to spend a full day at the hospital once a week to participate in Grand Rounds, seminars, hospital rounds, observe and assist in surgical procedures and obstetrical emergencies, and discuss gynecological related issues. Randy specifically made it a point not to have Nathan placed with him for this rotation. Nathan had already worked with him in a clinical setting, and Randy wanted his son to stretch his experience and see another doctor's perspective. But as far as inpatient care, surgeries, and emergency situations were concerned, Randy was glad Nathan had the opportunity to learn from him.

After touring the Maternity Ward and introducing all six of them to the L&D nursing staff, Randy brought them back into the conference room to educate them on a particular obstetrical procedure, which they were going to observe and take notes on later. Each would then have to prepare a written report on the procedure and present it at the end of the day. He also assigned them each a unique OB/GYN case and expected them research it, come up with a diagnosis, and prepare to discuss possible treatment options with their classmates during the next week's seminar.

Randy liked to make Grand Rounds an open discussion forum rather than him lecturing the medical students. His philosophy was not to sugar coat the medical experience or give them a bunch of fluff. He wanted to expose them to as much real life, practical physician work as possible, which meant assigning them obscure cases where they had to find unknown answers. He also expected them to work closely with local obstetricians on real cases, hold on-call statuses, and update themselves on new developments in the field. They practiced simple skills and procedures, and once a new skill was learned, he expected his students to perform it from there on out.

Nathan really liked his father's approach and was excited about this rotation. He came home that evening ready to research the obscure gynecological case file he had. "This is gonna be awesome, Gab."

"What is?"

He draped his white lab coat over the back of a dining room chair. "This OB/GYN rotation. I love the way my dad handles this. He gives us hands-on experience, and he's challenging us with unusual cases. I get to experience what it's like to be on-call and will actually observe and assist in surgeries, C-sections, and deliveries. It's gonna be so cool."

Gabby loved Nathan's enthusiasm. He was in a much better mood since he started clerkship rotations and wasn't stressed about classes or exams. He really enjoyed working with patients. "That's great, Sweetie."

He took his stethoscope off and set it on the table. "How was school?"

Gabby giggled. Boy did she have some stories to tell him tonight.

Several weeks into this rotation, Nathan presented a synopsis of a case he had and explained his diagnosis and opinion about it. He felt confident about his presentation and thought for sure his father would be impressed.

But as soon as he was finished with his analysis, Randy asked, "Where's your evidence?"

Nathan didn't understand. "What?"

"Your evidence. You were quick to mouth off your opinion but what medical evidence do you have to back it up? I want proof."

Trying to defend his statement, Nathan argued, "I presented the case where similar symptoms were present."

"That was a solitary case, and not all the symptoms matched. I need to see more profound data and more case studies if you want me to accept your opinion on this. You didn't search deep enough."

Offended that his father felt that way, Nathan pushed back, "I showed you my evidence."

"You showed me one case, which I'm not convinced displayed the same symptoms as the one I presented to you. You have no evidence. No one will trust your word if you don't justify your professional opinion with solid proof." He addressed the next medical student. "Ms. Crawford, show us what you have please."

"Yes, Doctor."

Nathan stared at his father, fuming. Randy totally disregarded what he said, negated his opinion, and blew him off right in front of his classmates. He'd never been so humiliated in his life.

Over the next week, Nathan continued to work on this case but had a hard time finding supporting evidence. He was convinced this case didn't have an obvious diagnosis or treatment, and the case was so obscure, very little was known about it. His father obviously assigned him this case to try and trip him up. He also nitpicked small things and was quick to criticize. Nathan didn't like the way he was being treated and decided to confront his father about it.

Randy was organizing some files and setting up the laptop and LCD projector when Nathan waltzed into the conference room forty-five minutes early. Randy smiled when he saw him. "Hey, Nate. Why are you here so early?"

"I need to talk to you."

"What's up?" Randy said, wondering what was so important.

Nathan laid it on the line. "Why are you giving me cases that are next to impossible to find answers to? It's like you're deliberately making this harder for me than for everyone else."

Randy didn't like this accusation nor his son's disrespectful tone. "Oh, is that what you think?"

"Yes, that's what I think," Nathan snarled and folded his arms across his chest.

"Did you really expect me to make this easier on you just because you're my son?"

"No. I'm expecting to be treated fairly," Nathan complained.

"And I suppose you think you're being treated unfairly?"

"Yes, I do. I think you're giving me the hardest cases, being overly critical of my comments and opinions, and treating me like crap."

Randy dropped the files on the table and stared at his son with a harsh, scolding glare. "I am not going to candy coat this for you or lead you to believe that medicine is all fun and games. This is the reality of it, Son. Cases can be hard to solve and research difficult to find. People will constantly question your reliability and expertise as a physician. If you think for one second that every single patient or family member or fellow physician is going to trust your medical judgment, you are gravely mistaken. That is not the way medicine works. Cases are not always easy, patients are not always cooperative, and quite frankly you are not always going to know the answers. I am helping you see the cold, hard reality of what this profession encompasses. I'll be damned if I'm going to fluff this up for you and let you take the easy way out. I could not, on my good conscience, send you down the easy path and allow you to settle for mere mediocrity when I know you are smarter and more capable than that. So don't hand me this poor Nathan crap. Grow some balls, be a damn doctor, and deal with it. This is the meat and potatoes of medicine, Son, and I'm going to challenge all of my students. You are no exception to that. If you aren't willing to dig into it and get your hands dirty, then get out."

Nathan had never heard his father say anything like that to him before. This speech left him speechless.

Randy made his point clear. He eyed his son, not feeling the least bit sympathetic. "Are you going to step up to the plate, or are you walking home? Make up your mind now, because I don't have all morning to debate this with you."

Nathan looked his father in the eye. "I'm stepping up."

"Then take the damn heat and suck it up," Dr. Hanson commanded. "Am I clear?"

"Yes, Sir."

"Good. Now let's go grab a cup of coffee before the others show up."

His father issued him a tough wake up call, and surprisingly, Nathan was grateful his dad had knocked him off his pedestal and snapped him into a much needed reality check. He set his bag on the table and joined his father at the coffee shop.

Chapter Fifty-One

Jake's first birthday ended up being more of an aggravation than originally planned. Aside from Jacob deciding halfway through his party that he was going to be cranky and start screaming and throwing a fit, he also managed to spill his cake on the floor, getting sticky blue frosting all over the expensive Oriental rug, which was very hard to wash out. He walked away pretty heavy in the toy department though.

Max was gliding around from person to person striking up conversations and having a good time, yet Lacy avoided him all day. He wondered if he had done something wrong or said something that upset her. He couldn't recall anything, yet she seemed distant and wasn't really talking to him other than superficial surface talk. He thought maybe she was just busy trying to help Lauren with Jacob's party, but he wanted to be sure.

When Lacy stepped into the kitchen to grab paper towels, Max followed her. He shoved his hands in his pockets and questioned her recent behavior. "Have I done something to upset you?"

She denied this statement. "Why would you think that?"

"Because you've hardly said two words to me all day." He tried to get her to look at him, but she wouldn't do it. "And you won't look at me."

"It's your imagination."

"Is it?"

"Yes. Everything's fine."

Max didn't believe her. "Then why won't you talk to me?"

"I'm busy, Max." With a wad of paper towels in her hand, she returned to the living room.

When the party was over, Max walked Lacy up to her apartment door. She was quick to step inside. Max took her by the hand and stopped her. "You're doing it again," he said. "Walking away instead of talking to me. What's going on, Lacy?"

"Nothing."

"Come over to my place tonight and we'll talk."

She shook her head. "I can't. I have things to do."

"Like what? What is so important that it can't wait until tomorrow?" he wanted to know.

She avoided the question. "Max."

"I'm serious, Lace. What is so important?"

She refused to answer him.

Concerned about her silence, he suggested, "Stay with me."

She wavered for a moment before she said, "I really need to get things done."

Obviously, she wasn't going to change her mind. "I guess I'll see you tomorrow then." He leaned in to kiss her, but she didn't get into the kiss like she usually did. Instead, she quickly broke away and closed the door.

His heart ached over the distance between them. He didn't understand why she was acting this way, and for some reason she wouldn't tell him. He hoped that by morning she'd be in a better mood.

Roger couldn't help but notice the tension between Lacy and Max. He hoped Lauren knew what was going on. "What was up with your sister today?"

"What do you mean?"

"She was kind of cold and distant with Max and didn't really talk to him. Is everything alright?"

Lauren placed a glass in the dishwasher. "She's thinking about breaking up with him."

"What?" he stammered. "Why?"

"She doesn't think he cares about her."

"That's ridiculous. Of course he does."

"She thinks their relationship is purely physical."

"Max doesn't believe that. He told me he's crazy about her."

"Really?" Lauren put soap in the dishwasher and pushed the start button. "Because he's never said that to Lacy."

This statement didn't make any sense. "He's never told her?"

"Max has never once told Lacy that he loves her, and she feels like she's wasting her time with him."

Roger held his hand over his mouth and chin. "I can't believe he's never told her."

"She was hoping he'd at least acknowledge that he has some sort of feelings for her, but he hasn't. She's convinced they have no future together."

"Max is going to get sideswiped if he doesn't fix this."

At the firehouse the next day, Max was pretty quiet. Normally he was a cheerful, energetic, and talkative, yet today he was mopey and kept glancing at his cellphone as if he was expecting an important phone call. At 3:00 P.M., he sat at the kitchen table, sulking. Matthew sat across from him and encouraged him to talk. "Hey, Max."

Max gave him a half-hearted smile and checked his cellphone again.

"Expecting a call?"

"Why do you say that?"

"You've been staring at that thing all day."

Max set his phone on the table. "I was hoping I'd hear from Lacy. I texted her about five hours ago, but she still hasn't answered me."

Matt could tell by Max's gloomy demeanor that he was upset about something. He offered a listening ear. "Everything alright?"

Max shrugged. "Honestly, I don't know. She's been distant lately. I asked her if she was mad at me, but she denied it. She doesn't want to talk, she refuses to look at me, and when I kissed her last night, she acted like she didn't want me touching her. I can't figure out what I did, and she won't tell me." Max let out a desperate sigh. "I'm starting to fear that our relationship may be in jeopardy." He looked at his captain, feeling heartbroken. "I don't want to lose her."

"Did you tell her that?" Matt asked.

"Tell her what?"

"That you don't want to lose her. That you don't want her to go. That you want to be with her," Matt explained.

"Of course I want to be with her. I love her."

"Does she know that?"

"What? That I love her?" Max questioned.

"Yes."

"She knows."

"How can you be so sure? When's the last time you told her?"

Max hung his head.

The fact that Max didn't respond had Matt concerned. "Have you ever surprised Lacy by sending flowers? Or cooked her favorite meal and served it to her by candlelight? Ever strolled down the beach holding hands or watched a sunset together?"

"Lacy's never expressed an interest in any of that stuff."

Matt shook his head. Not only had Max not been telling Lacy that he loved her, he hadn't made a conscious effort to show her either. "You can't assume that Lacy knows how you feel. She needs to hear it from you. You need to tell her you love her, and show her every day by the things you do. Let the world know that you're proud to be with this girl, because if you don't, she's going to assume you don't care, and you are going to lose her, Max."

That's why Lacy had been so distant and uncaring toward him. He had been taking her for granted. Now that Max understood this, he began to panic. "Shit."

"You can still fix this." Matt handed Max's phone to him. "Call her, Max. Tell her you love her. Reassure her that you want to be with her and you don't want her to leave."

Max stared at his phone.

"The phone isn't going to dial itself," Matt teased him. "My guess is she'll be completely over the moon that you've finally mustered up the courage to tell her how you feel. You'll never know if you don't make that call." The captain got up and left the room.

Max took a deep breath and tried to piece together what he was going to say. When he finally pulled his thoughts together, he stepped out back for more privacy and dialed Lacy's number.

When her sweet voice answered, he said, "We need to talk, Lace. I know you've been distant toward me lately, and…"

She quickly interjected, "Max, don't."

"No, listen," he insisted. "There's been distance between us, and I know why. I wanted to say I'm sorry."

The other end of the line fell silent.

Max continued, "Baby, I love you. I've always loved you. My life became complete when you walked into it. I want to be with you and shower you with love and affection and always be by your side. I haven't been showing you how much you mean to me, how much I want us to be together, how much I love you. Tonight, right now, that changes."

Lacy started to cry.

Max had never heard her cry before, which made him feel awful. If he would have just stepped up and told her how he felt, all of this could have been avoided. "I am so sorry, Baby. I should have told you every day and showed you every second how much I love you. You're beautiful, and I never told you. You're affectionate and compassionate and kind, and I never told you. You're the funniest, smartest, sexiest, most talented woman in the whole world, and I never told you." He scoffed at his own stupidity. "What the hell is wrong with me? I am in love with the greatest woman on earth, and I was too damn stupid to let her know how much she means to me."

Lacy managed to giggle through her tears. "You are a little dense sometimes."

"Which is why I need you to give me a good firm kick in the pants," he admitted. "I love you, Lacy."

Max finally got it through his thick head that she needed to hear how he felt about her. "That's all I wanted, Max, was for you to say it. All you had to do was say it."

Feeling like a total idiot, he agreed with her, "I know, I know. I should have said it every day, and I will from now on. In fact, I won't just tell you, I want to show you. What do you say, when I get off, that you and I grab some dinner fixings and a bottle of champagne, put on a little mood music, and share a nice quiet candlelight dinner together. No one else around, just you and me. We'll make dinner together, sip on champagne, and slow dance right in the living room. We'll spend quality time together and talk. What do you think?"

Admiring his effort, she agreed. "I'd love that."

"It's a date then."

They talked for about ten more minutes before Lacy said, "I know you're on duty and you're probably busy."

"We're not really doing anything right now," Max returned, trying to keep her on the line. "I can still talk."

"Well I can't, because I have a 4:00 jazz class to teach," she joked.

She had a good point. It was almost 3:30, and he didn't want her to be late for work. "Alright."

"I'll call you when I get home tonight," she said.

"Good, because I want to hear your beautiful voice."

"Can't guarantee how beautiful it will be."

He laughed at her comment. "I love you, Lacy. So much."

"I love you too. I'll talk to you later, Max."

As soon as he got off the phone, he went online and ordered a bouquet of flowers and had them delivered to Lacy at work.

Matthew came up behind him to see what he was doing. "Everything okay now?"

"Yes." He turned around and offered a smile of gratitude to his captain. "Thank you, Matt. I can be as thick as molasses sometimes."

"Just a little." Matt chuckled. "I'm glad you two were able to work things out. Even after eight years of marriage, my wife needs to hear that I love her. Let her know you care. Shelter her, stand up for her, compliment her, listen for those verbal and non-verbal cues. She'll usually let you know what she needs, but you have to pay attention. Show her you love her, every day."

"I intend to."

Chapter Fifty-Two

The excitement level in New York City doubled once November rolled around. The weather began to get colder, averaging from the low 30s to mid-50s. With Thanksgiving, Christmas, and New Year's Eve right around the corner, New York City tourism was sky high. Such events as the Macy's Thanksgiving Day Parade, Radio City Music Hall's Christmas Spectacular, the Rockefeller Center Christmas Tree Lighting ceremony, New York City Ballet's performance of *The Nutcracker*, the Lighted Boat Parade in New York Harbor, the New York Pops holiday celebration, West Village Chorale's annual Handel's Messiah Sing, and the Gray Line New York Holiday Lights tour made this magnificent city a holiday lovers destination from November through January—which also explained all the crowds. T'was the season of celebration in New York.

"What did Roger and Lauren need us to bring tomorrow?" Max asked as he and Lacy made last minute plans for Thanksgiving.

"We're not bringing anything because I'm going over there in the morning to help her keep an eye on Jake and prepare dinner while Roger's at the Macy's Parade."

"Macy's?" Max asked, concerned about the rampant hordes of people present at that event. "That's a crazy tourist trap place to be. What the hell is he doing there?"

Lacy explained, "He and Noah are performing 'Moses Supposes' in front of the crowd."

"Those two did a fabulous job with that."

"Which is why they're doing it at the parade," Lacy said.

"Yeah, but Macy's is mass hysteria. There are millions of people over there. He's gonna get trampled to death."

"He does it almost every year."

"That's crazy." Max buttoned his uniform and tucked it in. "What time are you going over there tomorrow?"

"Around 8:30."

Max was working a night tour, which meant his shift wouldn't be over until 9:00 A.M. the next day. And after two night tours in a row, he was going to be tired. "Should I just meet you over there when I get off?"

"If you want. You might want to get some sleep before you come over."

"Good idea. I'll take a power nap and change first. What time is dinner?"

"Three."

Max sat on the edge of the bed and slipped on his black work shoes. "I'll be there."

"Please be careful tonight," she pleaded, concerned about his safety.

He stood up and grabbed his wallet, his cellphone, and his keys. "I'd be more concerned about Roger being in the midst of those teeming crowds tomorrow morning than I would about me." He kissed Lacy goodbye. "Don't eat all the turkey without me."

Lacy giggled. "We'll wait for you."

"Make sure to lock the door on your way out."

"I'll take care of it. Go to work."

"Alright. Love you, Lace. I'll see you tomorrow."

"Love you too."

Roger and Lauren invited Jason and Bailey over for Thanksgiving along with Lacy and Max. Everyone had been diligently working to prepare dinner and everything was ready, but Max hadn't shown up yet. "Hey Lace, is Max coming over?" Roger asked.

"Yes. He just texted me. He had to work a night tour last night and only got four hours of sleep, but he is on his way."

"A night tour?" Jason asked, wanting clarification as to what exactly Max did for a living. "Does he work for Gray's Line touring company?"

Lacy said, "No, he's a New York City firefighter."

"Oh, wow," replied Jason. "A firefighter, huh? That's cool. Did he work all night?

"A fifteen hour shift," Lacy explained. "He didn't get home 'til almost ten this morning."

Jason questioned Roger about this. "You never told me he was a firefighter."

"You never asked me what he did for a living."

When Max finally arrived, Roger introduced him to Jason and Bailey.

"It's a pleasure to meet you," Max said, offering an open palm. He took in a big whiff. The apartment emanated with the heavenly aroma of turkey, gravy, sweet potatoes, and baked goods. "Man, it smells so good in here. I'm starving."

While the holidays in New York seemed chaotic and full of crowds, holidays in Seattle weren't that much different. Wonderful holiday displays put an attractive bow on this already picturesque city by the sea, and like New York, there were numerous Christmas shows and events to select from. Among the most popular Seattle Christmas events were the tree lighting celebration and the holiday parade. If you wanted to treat yourself to a Christmas show, the Pacific Northwest Ballet's *The Nutcracker* was always a favorite. Also similar to New York was Seattle's Christmas Ship Festival, the presence of live stage productions such as *A Christmas Carol*, and the Seattle Symphony's holiday concert. Despite the similarities the two cities shared during the holidays, the Emerald City shined in many different ways.

Winterfest was a celebration unique to Seattle. This Christmas event lasted from Thanksgiving until December 31st. Visitors could enjoy free concerts, tasty holiday foods, and a variety of family-friendly activities. The overall atmosphere was festive, and capping off the five-week festival was the spectacular Space Needle fireworks display on New Year's Eve.

Another celebration was Yulefest. With this event, Seattle transformed the Heritage Museum into a Nordic Christmas marketplace filled with special Christmas crafts for kids, shopping booths, delicious Nordic food, and entertainment with music and folk dancing. The University of Washington Music Department put on their Carol Fest concert, and the Trans-Siberian Orchestra toured through Seattle this time of year.

This year, Randy and Jane had all of their kids with them for Christmas, as well as a few additions, namely Roger, Jacob, Gabby, and Max. Their family was growing, and they were thrilled to spend Christmas together and experience it all with Jacob.

Jacob had several words in his repertoire now: mama, dada, nom-nom, ball, up, bye-bye, nana, and uh-oh. During this trip to Seattle, he learned a new word—papa—which everyone figured meant Grandpa from the context in which he used it.

Randy spent a good amount of time down on the floor with Jacob, playing with him, talking to him, and laughing at his cute baby giggles. Randy bought him a fuzzy blue stocking with Santa on it and had Jake's name embroidered on the top. He hung it on their fireplace mantle right next to his. It was adorable watching Randy interact with his grandson. They really seemed to connect with one another and communicated in their own little way.

Randy gave Jacob chocolate milk, introduced him to Oreos, and played hide and seek with him throughout the house. They watched *Rudolph the Red Nosed Reindeer* together, and when a dusting of snow covered the ground, they bundled up and went outside to play. Randy thoroughly enjoyed being a grandfather and was absolutely in love with that little boy.

Shopping downtown with Jacob was a fun pursuit. The tree-lined streets, glowing with festive Christmas lights, fascinated him. He loved all the sparkles and bling, and the abundance of ornaments and decorations left him entranced.

As the family walked downtown together, Randy carried Jacob on his shoulders. When they saw a man in a Santa suit, Jacob squealed in excitement.

"That's Santa," Randy said with a smile. "Santa says, ho ho ho!"

Jake babbled then started to laugh.

"We need to take him to see Santa," Randy suggested.

Lauren agreed. "We should."

After breaking for lunch, the family took Jake to visit Santa. Santa made himself a comfortable home at Nordstrom in downtown Seattle. Roger pulled out his camera, and the others snapped a few with their cellphones. When Jacob decided he'd had enough, he held his arms up to Randy and whimpered, "Papa, up."

Roger and Lauren looked at each other and gasped. They had never heard Jake say that word before. "What did he say?"

Jacob outstretched his arms. "Papa."

Randy grinned the widest smile. "Ha! You all heard that. He called me Papa." He picked up Jacob, who clung to his grandpa's neck.

Jacob and Grandpa had definitely connected. This melted Lauren's heart. "Looks like you have a buddy, Dad."

"Oh yeah, he's Papa's boy."

That night was Christmas Eve. After feeding himself finger foods and getting a bath, Jacob toddled around downstairs in his yellow ducky footie pajamas holding his stuffed Elmo. He dug through the bag of toys Lauren packed for him and pulled out his *Elmo's Merry Christmas* book. With his book in his hand, he toddled over to Grandpa. "Papa."

Randy looked down at the child. "You want to read the book?"

Jake crawled on his grandpa's lap and leaned against his chest, hugging his stuffed Elmo while Randy read this book with him.

Halfway through the story, Lauren glanced Randy's direction and saw that Jacob was sound asleep. "Dad, he's sleeping."

Randy peered down at Jacob. His eyes were closed and his neck was kinked to the side, struggling to hold up his heavy head. Randy closed the book and kissed his grandson's head.

"You want me to take him?" Lauren asked.

"No," Randy said, adjusting himself slightly so both he and Jacob were comfortable. "Let him lie here for a while."

Lauren grabbed Jacob's blanket and covered his legs. She leaned into Randy and whispered, "You're such a wonderful Grandpa. Jake adores you."

Randy gently put his hand on Jacob's tummy. "He's a good boy."

Lauren kissed her son's head, then kissed her father on the cheek. "Thank you, Daddy."

About forty minutes later, when Randy could no longer feel his left arm, Roger put Jake to bed.

Randy shook his hand to regain feeling in his fingers. "Tomorrow's going to be fun with Jacob here. We haven't had a little one around at Christmas in a long time."

The Christmas tree was loaded with sparkly wrapped presents, many of which belonged to Jacob. Roger shook his head in disbelief. "For a one-year-old, he sure made out in the gift department, didn't he? How are we supposed to get all of this stuff home?"

"We'll toss it in a box and ship it to you," Randy suggested.

Roger laughed. "Great. More toys for me to trip over."

"Cherish these moments, Roger," Randy reminded his son-in-law. "They don't last forever. I miss hearing my babies' footsteps running down the stairs at 6:00 in the morning, eyes filled with wonder as they peek under the tree to see what Santa brought. Kids bring more joy to the holidays."

"Oh, I know. When we had my nephews last Christmas, it was great. I can't wait 'til Jake gets a little older, then he can truly enjoy the magic and splendor of this holiday."

The day after Christmas, the Zellers family had to return to New York. As the family walked toward security, Jacob peered over his father's shoulder and waved to Randy. "Papa. Bye-bye."

Randy was thrilled that he had the wonderful privilege to bond with his grandson, but he was sad to see them leave. Living so far away, he didn't get to see Lauren, Roger, and the baby very often. The precious time he did have, he cherished. He waved back to Jacob. "Bye-bye, Jakey. Papa loves you."

Jane put her arm around Randy, knowing this moment was pulling at his heart. "How you doing, Papa?"

Randy smiled. "I'm gonna miss that little guy."

"I think he's gonna miss you too."

Thinking about Jake made him chuckle. "He calls me Papa. That's so cool." He turned his eyes to Jane and gave her a kiss. "Come on, my dear. Let's get some lunch. Clam chowder is calling my name."

She took his hand, and together they exited SEA-TAC airport in search of a good chowder shop.

On the way to Century Link Field to catch a Seahawks game, Randy poked at a bobbing hula dancer attached to the dashboard of Jim's Jeep. "What the fuck is this?"

Jim pushed Randy's hand away. "That's Leilani. Quit pokin' at her."

"You named your dashboard ornament?"

"She's a hula goddess, Dude," Jim corrected. "You're damaging the bodaciousness of her rhythm."

"You have got to be joking? She's a plastic doll." He poked at it again, messing up her rhythmic dance.

"Quit fuckin' with her, man. You're a pain in the ass. How does Jane put up with your obnoxiousness?"

Randy had a hard time maintaining a straight face. "My wife finds me irresistible. She can't help herself." Randy shifted in his seat and gulped down the last of his coffee. "Right now she's slightly envious of me."

"Why?"

"Because while the kids were here for Christmas, my grandson clung to me the whole time and called me Papa. He only has a few words in his vocabulary right now, and I find it flattering that Papa is one of them. Not Grandma. Papa. Made Jane jealous."

"He calls you Papa?"

"Yup."

This brought a smile to Jim's face. "That's cute. Told you bein' a grandparent is awesome."

"I love it.," Randy replied. "I just wish Lauren and Roger lived closer so I could see Jake more often. He's growing like a weed, and we're missing it."

"I know what you mean. I'm glad Maddie is close by now. I actually get to watch my granddaughter grow up."

"They don't stay babies very long," Randy sighed.

"No they do not. Speakin' of babies," Jim changed the subject, "I have an awesome ER story for you."

"Oh really?" Randy asked, anxiously awaiting the story Jim was about to tell. His ER stories were the best.

"Yesterday, a young pregnant woman, probably nineteen or twenty years old, was brought into the ER for vaginal bleeding. She wore a pad in and sure enough it was saturated with blood. So I'm thinkin' oh, crap. I try to find fetal heart tones while Jill is attempting to get her OB on the phone. The OB finally showed up and gave her an ultrasound to check for placental abruption, you know the standard procedures. Once cleared, the OB gave her a cervical exam. When the doc spread the labia, the cause of this woman's vaginal bleeding was painfully obvious. She had deep puncture wounds from a penetrating bite that was gushin' bright red blood."

"What?" Randy asked. "Who bit her?"

"That's what we asked her. She claimed she had no idea what we were talkin' about. Many stitches later, the vaginal bleeding was cured. The baby was thankfully fine, but the patient still refused to explain what had happened."

Randy had a story to tell too. "I had to call security upstairs last week."

"In the Maternity Ward?"

"Yup. It was crazy. A young patient of mine came in laboring. I've had extensive conversations with this young woman about her birth plan. She was pretty adamant about being able to labor naturally, and she hoped the father of the baby would show up and be supportive. The first part was definitely going to be a go, but getting a supportive dad to show up when he hadn't been involved for the past seven months might not go as well. The L&D nurses got her set up and moved her to a room with access to a Jacuzzi tub. I guess my patient must have taken care of the second part of the plan because a couple of hours into labor, the father of the baby showed up. I came upstairs to check her progress, and to put this mildly, the guy looked rough. As her labor progressed, it quickly became obvious that this dad was one of those guys who handles crying, screaming, and probably any uncomfortable situation by acting like a jackass. He started yelling at her to 'just get the damn epidural,' making her irritable. When I got her alone, I asked if she wanted him to leave. Big tears appeared in her eyes because she knew her plan wasn't working. I told her all she had to do was give us the signal and he was out of there. I stuck around for a while to see what was going to happen and to make sure he didn't do anything stupid. All it took was two more contractions of him acting a fool and she wanted him gone. I went in to try and get this guy to leave, which was quite a fiasco in itself."

Jim wondered how this went over. "Why do I have the feeling this didn't end well. What happened?"

"I very calmly told this ass that he was agitating my patient and asked him to leave. He didn't take it well. After all, how dare I take this experience away from him? He loves her so much...blah, blah, blah. You know, all the stuff that being completely absent through the pregnancy clearly indicated. It quickly turned into a shouting match, at least for him. By now there were three nurses and one of our techs in there with me trying to ease him toward the door. Now mind you, Jim, he's a big dude who could have easily picked up both of my nurses and run off with them, one under each arm. To alleviate any potential problems I had the nurses call security for help. Minutes passed. Still no security. The shouting continued. The five of us herded the guy in the right direction while he spewed off threats about how we all better watch our backs. Then he went all Terminator on us screaming, 'I'll be back'. We finally managed to get him to the elevator, and who was standing there? The security guard."

"Nice of you to show up, Dude," Jim commented.

"Exactly! We called him up there STAT and he took his own sweet time and got on the elevator with seventeen other people."

"Dumbass."

Randy continued, "It gets better. Now, we get strange calls to L&D all the time from people asking for weird and completely non-L&D related things, but I talked to Leanne later and found out that about four minutes past bar closing time, the phone rang. Guess who it was? Asshole, who was obviously intoxicated, was whining about how sorry he was and had the gall to ask Leanne for a ride home."

"You're kidding?" Jim asked.

"Nope. So Leanne, being a good sport, asked the guy where he was and called him a cab."

"What a fuckin' assmunch."

"Guy was a total loser," Randy argued. "I've never had to call security up to L&D before. On the plus side, my patient got half the delivery she wanted, and probably a little closure."

Jim couldn't help but laugh. "That's always a bonus."

Chapter Fifty-Three

In a hurry to get out the door, Roger frantically searched the apartment for his cellphone. "Honey, did you see where I put my phone?"

"If you put it within Jacob's reach, it could be anywhere."

Roger ripped pillows and cushions off the couch and dumped contents out of containers. "Jakey, did you take Daddy's phone?"

"Dada bye-bye?" Jacob replied.

"Yes, Daddy has to go bye-bye. What did you do with my phone?"

Lauren called out, "Jake, come see Mommy."

Jacob toddled off while Roger continued his desperate search. About a minute later, Jake returned with Roger's cellphone in his hand. Roger stopped his search and looked at his son. "Where did you get that?" He took the phone from the child.

"Mama," Jacob replied.

"Mommy had it?" Roger questioned.

Lauren stepped into the room. "You left it on the bathroom counter again. I had Jacob bring it out to you." She gave him a gentle kiss. "You need to keep better track of your phone, Sweetie. You're always losing it."

Roger gave a mirthful laugh as he carefully slipped his phone in his pocket. He was on his way to audition for the Broadway stage adaptation of Disney's classic animated film *Aladdin*, hoping to take on the title role for the upcoming summer production. He had been involved a Disney show before with *Newsies* and was familiar with the way Disney handled stage productions, which was always very professionally done and creatively innovative. *Aladdin* was one of his favorite Disney movies. Roger was especially intrigued by this role not only because it involved the usual acting, singing, and dancing he was so good at, but also because he would get to play with sword props and fly on a magic carpet, Broadway style. Definitely a fun time.

"What time is your audition?" Lauren asked.

"1:30." He checked his watch to see what time it was. "I have to go. Love you, Honey." He gave Lauren a kiss goodbye. "I'll see you in a few hours."

When Roger came back from his audition, he was ecstatic, not because of what happened while he was there, but because of news he had received. He couldn't wait to tell Lauren. "What is your favorite movie?"

He already knew that answer to that question. "*Ever After*. You know that."

"Yes I do. But guess what I found out today. The musical version has been touring nationally for about twelve months now. It's become so popular that they want to move it to a bigger stage, the Broadway stage," he said with a huge grin.

Lauren's mouth gaped open. "Are you serious? They made that into a musical?"

"Yes, Ma'am. But there's more. Apparently the woman who plays Danielle de Barbarac for the national tour is not going to be involved in the New York production. They're looking for a new lead to bring this to Broadway, and I know the perfect woman for the part."

"Who?" Lauren asked.

Roger laughed at her. "You. It's your favorite movie, you know the characters well. They're having readings and auditions within the next week or two."

"Where did you hear this?"

"I ran into one of the production managers of the show today." He handed her a piece of paper with a name and a phone number on it. "I told the producer that you might be interested, and he wanted to make sure you knew about this."

Lauren took the piece of paper from him.

"They have a Tony award-winning director leading it up. They already have some of the casting secured, but like I said, they need a female lead. They've been searching for one for a while and ta-da." He did a dance motion to point to her. "That's where you come in."

"When do they start production for this?" she wondered.

"Don't know," Roger admitted. "The production manager has all the information. He wants you to call him."

She turned to him for advice. "What do you think I should do?"

He thought it was obvious. "Call him. You can't pass this up, Honey. This role is perfect for you, and the production manager was excited when I told him you might be interested."

She bit her lip in anticipation, enthusiastic about this possibility. "Do you really think I have a chance at this?"

Roger put his arms around her. "I think you are going to blow them away. Make the call. Talk to them. You have nothing to lose."

Eagerly, she grabbed her phone and made the call.

Chapter Fifty-Four

Another school year came to a close, and Nathan had successfully completed three years of medical school. Only one more to go. He awoke to the sun shining in the bedroom window, casting a celestial glow about the room. Birds happily twittered outside. Gabby was wrapped in a towel, fresh from the shower. She reached into a dresser drawer to pull out her undergarments. She was beautiful in every way. Nathan wanted to touch her, but could barely reach her from where he sat. He stretched his arm out and pulled her onto the bed with him.

"I'm trying to get dressed," she said.

"And I'm trying to prevent you from doing it." Their lips interlocked for a brief moment. "I've been thinking."

"Uh oh," she teased. "That's why I see smoke coming out of your ears."

He snickered at her sarcasm. "I'm serious."

She sat on his lap and wrapped her arms around his neck. "What's on your mind, Superstar?"

"You know how you told me that you're getting that baby itch, but we've been waiting for me to decide I'm ready?"

She wondered where he was going with this conversation. "Yes?"

"I'm ready."

Gabby couldn't believe those words just came out of his mouth. "Are you serious?"

"This is my last year of med school. I'll start my residency next June. If we plan this right, you'll have the baby next summer. It'll be perfect. What do you say? You wanna make a baby with me?" he asked with a flirtatious smile.

Gabby hugged him tightly. Tears of joy filled her eyes. "Thank you, Sweetie."

"You're welcome. I love you, Gab."

"I love you too."

After grossing over twenty million dollars for the Broadway League, the production of *Singin' in the Rain* closed. Both Lauren and Roger had other productions set up, but before they began rehearsals for those, they had about two weeks of down time. Peter and Amy planned to take their boys to Walt Disney World in Florida for vacation. Roger and Lauren decided to take Jacob and join them.

Roger was just as excited as the kids. He hadn't been to Disney World since he was a child and hadn't been on vacation with his brother since before Peter got married, which was almost twelve years ago. On their first day, they had a fun-time breakfast buffet with Disney characters and were able to meet and get their picture taken with Mickey Mouse and Buzz Lightyear. Following breakfast, they enjoyed gaming in a virtual, 4D shooting gallery with Toy Story characters. They also experienced the thrill of racing on the Tomorrowland Speedway and had lunch at Pizza Planet Arcade. After lunch, they explored Fantasyland, and Uncle Roger bought each of the boys a mouse ears hat with their name embroidered on the back. By nightfall, the boys were worn out, so they took a break to watch the spectacular Fantasmic show, which took them into the colorful imagination of Mickey Mouse as the Sorcerer's Apprentice fighting evil villains. With its immersive effects, pyrotechnics, laser lights, a cast of fifty costumed performers singing beloved Disney tunes, and one million gallons of dancing water, it was quite the extravaganza.

The minute they returned to the hotel, the kids crashed.

Roger opened a bottle of raspberry sparkling water and took a seat on the sofa. He kicked off his shoes and sat back to relax from the exhausting day they had.

"You should book a gig doing a show like that," Peter said. "Dressed up like Mickey Mouse, singing and dancing on stage."

Roger took a drink from his bottle. "It's funny you say that, because I recently landed the lead for a Broadway Disney production."

"Which one?" Pete asked.

"Aladdin."

Peter's boys had watched *Aladdin* several times a week. He knew that musical well. "You get to be a street urchin."

"Yup, then rub a magic lamp and sweep into an exotic world full of daring adventure. I get to ride on a flying carpet and play with swords too."

Pete got a kick out of Roger's description. "That definitely sounds like something you will enjoy. Congratulations!"

"Thank you. The boys had a blast today."

"Looked like you did too." Getting more comfortable, Peter joined his brother on the couch. "You obviously have another job lined up, but now that Singin' in the Rain is closed, what's Lauren gonna do?"

"She's locked into the lead role in a new musical called Ever After. They're supposed to start the production process sometime in September. I'm proud of her. She's come a long way in this business."

"She had you to guide her," Peter reminded him.

"I can't take the credit, Pete. She's done this all on her own. Her talent got her into these shows, not me."

"You know she has to kiss prince charming in that, right?"

Roger shrugged, blowing off this comment. "It's a stage kiss. I've done stage kisses before. In fact, I have to kiss my counterpart in Aladdin too. It's no big deal."

"That doesn't bother you, knowing your wife is going to be kissing someone else?"

"It's acting, Pete," Roger clarified. "There's a big difference between a stage kiss and the way Lauren kisses me. I don't kiss actresses on stage the way I kiss my wife. They are definitely not one and the same. You'd have to be an actor to understand."

"To understand what?" Lauren walked into the room and sat on Roger's lap.

Roger greeted his wife with a sensuous kiss. "I'm explaining to Pete the difference between a stage kiss and a real kiss."

Lauren said, "A real kiss makes you tingle, you do it because you want to. A stage kiss is different. You only do it because the scene requires you to. There's no emotion attached to it. It's kind of like kissing your dog. Sure, he's cute and cuddly, but you wouldn't want his tongue in your mouth."

Pete rolled with laughter.

"That pretty much sums it up. Good one, Honey." Roger put his hand between Lauren's knees. "Is he asleep?"

"He's out," she confirmed.

"Good. It was a long day for him."

Pete interjected, "Let's take the kids to Adventure-land tomorrow. There's a treehouse there for the boys to climb on, and there's even a Magic Carpet Ride that I'm pretty sure Roger won't mind riding with Jacob."

"Oh hell no," Roger agreed. "I'm all for it."

Peter laughed at his brother's enthusiasm.

In August, Nathan began his fourth and final year of medical school. This last year of rotations was important, not only because it wrapped up his clinical training, but also because this was the year he would take the second part of the USMLE exam, which would make him an MD and direct him toward his residency. His clinical work this year was more advanced. He had four weeks in Emergency Medicine, four weeks in neurology, and four weeks in chronic care. He also had four weeks of selectives, which meant he could choose from a variety of clinical options. He chose Orthopedic Sports Medicine, focusing specifically on knee and shoulder surgery. The rest of his time was used to study for boards and prepare for his transition into residency.

August was also the time of year when Gabby prepared to return to the classroom. She spent a week in staff development and a few days sorting through her classroom materials. The day before school started, she woke up feeling ill. This, along with the fact that her period was three days late, made her wonder if maybe she and Nathan had gotten pregnant sooner than they expected. Since Nathan was doing his ER rotation at the time and was working overnight shifts at the hospital, he probably didn't notice she was late. Keeping this a surprise would be easy. With that in mind, she made a trip to the drug store and bought a pregnancy test. The result came back positive. She stood in the bathroom staring at the test strip for a while. She didn't want to jump to conclusions, so she waited another three days and tried again. The second one also came back positive. With tears in her eyes, she covered her mouth with her hand. She couldn't wait to give Nathan the news.

She came up with a cute and creative way to tell him. She used the scrapbook idea Nathan started when he proposed to her and built on it. She purchased a photo album, and on the first page creatively arranged the words, *First comes love, then comes marriage, then comes baby in a baby carriage*. Underneath, she cut out three funny Pacman looking figures and glued googly eyes on them. She pasted them on the page and drew little tails on each one with a Sharpie marker. Below them, in bold black letters, she wrote, *One made it!* She taped the two positive pregnancy tests down on this page, one on each side. She planned to give this to Nathan as soon as he got home from his shift that night.

When Nathan trudged through the door, Gabby shuffled behind him and covered his eyes.

He chuckled at her. "What are you doing?"

"Sit down and close your eyes. I want to show you something."

With her hands over his eyes, how was he supposed to walk over to the couch? "Gabby, I can't see anything."

"That's why you need to sit down." She led him to the sofa and helped him sit. "No peeking. Keep your eyes closed."

Thinking she was crazy, he replied, "Mind telling me what's going on?"

"You'll see."

Nathan waited impatiently. "Gab."

"Just hold on." She pulled the scrapbook out from where she had hidden it and set it on his lap, taking a seat next to him. "You can open your eyes now."

He stared down at the book. "What am I supposed to do with this?"

"Open it, silly."

He turned to the first page and his jaw hit the floor. He didn't have to go any further and didn't need an explanation to figure why she was in such a lively mood. "Are you serious?"

She beamed with excitement.

Nathan combed his fingers through his hair and looked at her, stumbling for the right thing to say. "You're pregnant?"

She bobbed her head.

Shock quickly turned to joy as he began to laugh. "Holy shit. We're gonna have a baby?"

"Uh huh," she replied. "We're gonna have a baby."

He squeezed her tightly. "This is fantastic."

"So, you're happy?"

"I'm ecstatic." He looked down at the positive pregnancy tests. "I wasn't expecting it to happen this quickly though."

"It only takes one time, Nathan," she reminded him.

"I know, but I guess multiple times upped the chances." He winked seductively then gazed into her eyes. "This is great, Babe. I'm very happy."

They confirmed the results with Nathan's father. "Yup. You're definitely pregnant," Randy said. "Looks like about five weeks, from what I can tell. We'll confirm with an ultrasound. Let me snag the portable imaging machine and we'll have a look. Nate, come out here with me for a minute please."

"Yes, Sir." Nathan gave Gabby a kiss before he joined his father in the hall. "What's up?"

Baffled, Randy stared at his son. "Was this planned?"

"Yes."

Randy seriously questioned Nathan's logic behind this decision. "What the hell were you thinking?"

"What do you mean?"

"Son, you are in medical school. You're going to start your residency in less than a year. Do you know how much time and energy that requires?"

Nathan argued, "Yes, Dad, I'm well aware of the time commitment involved. But everything in our lives has revolved around my schedule and my goals and has been focused on me. Now it's Gabby's turn. She wants to have a baby, and I'm not going to make her wait any longer."

Randy rubbed his chin.

"Dad," Nathan said. "This is your grandchild. I thought you'd be happy."

"I am, Nathan. I am. I just…" He offered his son some serious advice. "I hope you and Gabby are not trying to take on something you're not ready to tackle. Babies are a huge responsibility."

"Gabby and I have discussed this in detail. We know what we're getting into. This is something both want, something we are both excited about."

"Alright. Then I'll support you. Let's take a look at this baby, shall we?"

Nathan grinned. "Absolutely."

She was indeed five weeks pregnant. Randy predicted that her due date would be in April, a couple months shy of summer vacation. Not quite what they planned, but close enough.

Chapter Fifty-Five

About ten weeks into the pregnancy, Gabby had severe pain in her lower abdomen. At first she thought maybe she had to go to the bathroom, but when she sat on the toilet, her panties were blood stained. She screamed in horror. "Nathan!"

He charged into the bathroom. "What? What's wrong?"

Gabby sat on the toilet shaking.

"Baby, what's wrong?" Nathan asked again, insistent that Gabby tell him.

She stood up and showed him.

Bright red blood had turned the toilet water ruddy. She was badly hemorrhaging. Trying not to panic, he said, "Get dressed. I'm taking you to the hospital." He immediately called his father, who in turn called Jane. She agreed to meet them at the hospital to offer support.

After getting Gabriella checked in, Randy did a full workup on her. She was still cramping up and bleeding, expelling clots up to five centimeters in size. He ran an ultrasound, and much to his dismay, the heartbeat had ceased. He analyzed all the data from the tests then pulled Nathan into the hallway, dreading what he was about to tell him.

Nathan had enough experience and training in obstetrics to know the surefire signs of miscarriage, and Gabby had all the typical symptoms. This situation looked horrifically grim. "Please tell me this is not what I think it is," he begged.

With a heavy heart, Randy stared at his son but didn't say a word.

Nathan didn't like the look on his father's face. He knew it meant bad news. Filled with heartache, he raised his hand to his forehead and closed his eyes, fighting to hold back tears.

Randy hugged his son. "Nate, I'm so sorry."

Nathan did something he hadn't done in a long time—he cried on his father's shoulder.

Offering whatever comfort he could, Randy held his son and let him release his emotions.

Several minutes passed before Nathan was able to muster up the strength to look his father in the eye. "How the hell am I supposed to tell Gabby?"

"Do you want me to do it?"

"No," Nathan maintained. "She's my wife. She and I are in this together. I'll tell her." He took a deep breath to calm down. "Give me a minute."

"I'll be here if you need me." He left Nathan alone to pull himself together.

Jane stepped out of the elevator and saw Randy standing in the hall with a sorrowful look on his face. She approached him with a hug. "Hi, Sweetie. Where's Nathan?"

"He's trying to compose himself," Randy replied.

That didn't sound promising. "Why? What's going on?"

Randy told her, "Gabby's miscarrying. She doesn't know yet. Nate's about to tell her."

"Oh god." Further down the hall, Nathan sat on the floor, leaning against the wall with his elbows on his bent knees. He hung his head and stared at his hands. "How is he?"

Randy wished she could take away Nathan's pain. "He's hurting, which is to be expected. He and Gabby are gonna need a lot of support from us."

After pulling himself together, Nathan stood up and tread carefully into Gabby's room. He hid well what he was about to tell her by entering with a smile. "Hey, Baby."

She smiled back at him. "Hey you."

"How you feeling?" he asked, hoping she was at least feeling better physically.

She rubbed her tummy. "Crampy."

Nathan slowly crept closer.

Gabby noticed his puffy, blood shot eyes. "What's wrong?"

He sat on the bed and took a cleansing breath, exhaling heavily. "Honey." He tightened his lips, dreading what he was about to tell her. "You're having a miscarriage. We lost the baby."

Gabby's heart plummeted to her stomach. She began to breathe erratically, then the tears came.

They huddled together and wept. Feeling as much misery as she did, Nathan tried to console her.

Randy and Jane didn't hear anything for several minutes, which made Jane wonder what was happening. "Has he told her yet?" she asked her husband. "Can you see anything?"

Randy peeked into the room. What he saw tore him apart. Nathan and his wife desperately clung to each other, grieving over this overwhelming loss. He released a heavy sigh and backed away from the door.

"Looks like he just told her." Glancing back at Gabby's room, he muttered, "Be strong, Kiddo."

After several minutes, Nathan was finally able to pull himself together. When he walked into the hall, Jane instantly greeted him with a hug. "Oh, sweetheart. I'm sorry."

Nathan stood in disbelief. His emotional state of mind was still shaky. "Do me a favor, Mom. Go in and sit with Gabby, please. She needs someone with her until I get back in there. I don't want to leave her alone."

"Alright, Honey." Jane smiled sympathetically then headed into Gabby's room.

With a dazed look in his eye, Nathan held his hand up to his forehead. He desperately needed the doctor standing in front of him to be a supportive father. "I can't believe this is happening."

Randy knew his son needed him. Offering solace, he gave him a hug.

Finding comfort in his father's arms, Nathan buried his face in Randy's shoulder and let the tears freely flow. "Gabby's completely devastated, and I don't know what to say or do to help her get through this."

"This is devastating for you too. Don't pretend like it's not." Randy wished there was something he could say to ease his son's heartache. "It's okay to feel sorrow, and it's okay to cry. You and Gabby lost a pregnancy. That's not an easy thing to deal with." He put his hands on Nathan's shoulders and offered the best advice he had. "This is one of those difficult times in a marriage when you need each other the most. Lean on each other, Nathan, and talk. For god's sake, talk about your feelings."

Nathan wiped his eyes and inhaled deeply, trying to calm down.

Randy reassured his son. "Your mom and I are here for both of you, you know that."

"I know you are. Thank you."

By morning, the majority of the physical trauma was over. The emotional aftermath, however, took much longer to heal. One thing Nathan and Gabby did to help them cope with this tragic incident was plant a yellow rose bush in the front of their house as a tribute to their lost pregnancy. This growing, blooming beauty was their way of remembering their little one. It also helped them move on and gave them closure, allowing themselves time to grieve.

Saturday morning, Randy picked up a single yellow rose from the flower shop and drove to the cemetery. He didn't invite anyone else to come with him because visiting time with his father was something he preferred to do alone. He removed a few dead leaves from his father's gravestone and sat down in the grass. "Hey, Dad. I haven't stopped by to see you in a while." He swallowed the lump in his throat. "A little angel came to join you this week. We don't know if it was a boy or a girl, but it was definitely a Hanson. Your great grandchild." He hung his head and a tear fell onto the ground. "Nate and Gabby were heartbroken over the loss of their baby, but they find comfort knowing their little one is with you now. I can't imagine the pain of losing an unborn child." Randy took in a big breath to choke down tears. "But you know, they're tough kids, and they'll bounce back. Knowing Nathan, I wouldn't be surprised if they tried to get pregnant again soon. He's stubborn that way. I wish you could see him now. You'd be so proud. He's damn good, dedicated, knowledgeable; the kid knows his stuff. He's called me out on a few occasions, and he's really found his calling in orthopedics. He's become such a compassionate, responsible man, and he's a good husband. Jane and I are really proud of him."

Randy stayed and talked to his father's gravestone for a while, jabbering on about happenings in all of their lives. Before he left, he stared at the yellow rose in his hand then carefully laid it on the ground against the gravestone. Slowly, he rose to his feet. "We miss you, Dad. Look after the baby for us."

A little over a month after the loss of their pregnancy, Nathan came home and handed Gabby a dozen red roses. "Let's try again."

His bold statement threw her off. "What did you say?"

"Let's get pregnant again."

She stared at him, not sure how she felt about this.

"Every time I got knocked down in a game or you fell off the top of the pyramid, what did we do?"

"We got up and kept going."

"Every time we fell behind on the scoreboard or the other team overpowered us on defense, what did we do?"

"We pushed through and kept fighting," she replied.

"And every time the curriculum became challenging or the task seemed impossible, what did we do?"

"We kept trying."

"Exactly. And why? Because you and I are not quitters," he explained. "We don't give up and we never, ever go down without a fight." He pointed toward the bedroom door. "We are going into that bedroom. We're going to strip each other naked and have the wildest, most intense sex we've ever had."

His energy and determination were certainly inspiring, and his pep talk made her laugh. "You're crazy."

He set the roses on the coffee table and pulled her off the couch. "Come on. Let's make a baby."

Chapter Fifty-Six

Gabby went the entire month of November without starting her menstrual cycle. She felt nauseous almost every morning, her breasts were overly sensitive, and fatigue had set in. She knew what those symptoms indicated, but tried to hide them from Nathan.

By the middle of December, her symptoms became more noticeable, and she could no longer hide them. Nathan questioned her secrecy. "If you were having pregnancy symptoms, why didn't you tell me, Gab?"

Her shoulders tightened and she blinked rapidly, looking at him with fear written all over her face.

That's all he needed to see. He took her in his arms and held her close. "I know you're scared," he remarked. "I am too. But we can't ignore this."

They drove to the drug store and picked up a pregnancy test. Gabby followed the directions and nervously watched, waiting for the results to turn up. When the plus sign appeared, she started to cry.

Nathan hugged her, knowing exactly what she was thinking. "It's gonna be okay. Babe."

"What if…"

He forced her to look at him. "Everything's going to be fine. You'll see." To ease her mind, he kissed her on the lips. "Let me talk to Dad. We'll make an appointment and go from there."

Nathan met his father for lunch the next day. In the middle of a conversation about basketball, Nathan abruptly changed the subject. "We took a pregnancy test yesterday. It came back positive."

Randy knew this was bound to happen. "That's good." Or so he thought, until he saw the fearful look on Nathan's face, which immediately made him question his original statement. "Isn't it?"

"We're happy about it, but…" Nathan was open and honest with his father. "Gabby tried to hide the symptoms from me, and she refuses to announce it to anyone. She's terrified that something is going to happen. And quite frankly, Dad, I am too."

Randy tried to reassure him. "That makes sense, but living in fear is going to cause unnecessary stress on the baby, and we want to avoid that. The sooner we get her pre-natal care, the better. I need to see her as soon as possible. Can she come in this afternoon or this evening?"

"I think so. I'll have to text her and find out, but I'm sure she can stop by after school."

"Find a way to make it happen," Randy insisted. "I'll work around her schedule, but I want to see her today."

"Yes, Sir."

Randy could tell Nathan was tense. "Let's take it one day at a time."

Gabby met Nathan and Randy at the clinic later that evening. The minute she saw Dr. Hanson, her eyes welled with tears.

He gave her a hug. "Relax, Sweetheart. Let's take a look and see how we're progressing. We'll make a plan from there."

First, he took a urine sample to confirm pregnancy and test for signs of a bladder, urinary tract, or kidney infection. Then he checked her weight, height, and blood pressure and listened to her heart. Everything looked and sounded great. He performed a full pelvic exam, checking for changes in the cervix and the size of her uterus to confirm the stage of her pregnancy. Based on this information, and the date of her last period, he figured she was around eight to ten weeks. He pulled out his due date calculator to confirm. "Let's see here. Looks like we're about nine weeks right now," he said. "Full term is July 16th. I want to run an ultrasound to check everything out. We'll look at the heartbeat, measure the size of the baby, then I'll draw some blood. We're going to check everything: Rh, hemoglobin, protein count, varicella, STD's…"

Affronted by that comment, Nathan cut in, "Dad, she doesn't have an STD. I'm the only person she's ever been with."

"I don't care. I'm gonna check anyway." Randy redirected the conversation back to Gabby. "Have you been taking any medication?"

"No," she replied.

"I know you don't smoke, but have you been drinking at all?"

"No."

Randy wrote a few things on her chart. "Have you been using any kind of birth control?"

"Not really."

He peeked up from his file. "Not really? What does that mean? Did you go back to taking the pill? Were you using a condom? Have you been abstinent?"

Nathan rolled his eyes. "Really?"

Randy snarled at Nathan, annoyed by his constant interjecting. "Dammit, Nate. If you're going to keep interrupting then get out of my examination room."

Nathan bit his tongue.

Returning to his conversation with Gabby, Randy rephrased the question. "Have you been using any kind of birth control at all while engaging in intercourse since the miscarriage?"

"No," she replied.

Nathan interrupted again. "She's pregnant, Dad. Isn't the answer to that question kind of obvious?"

Clenching his jaw, Randy reprimanded his son. "Are you an obstetrician?"

"No, Sir," Nathan admitted.

"Well, I am. And I have been since before you were born. I don't need you trying to direct this from the back seat. Do you want me to be thorough and make sure we are not overlooking anything?"

"Of course I do," Nathan said.

Randy pointed to a chair across the room. "Then sit in that chair and shut up."

Gabby found this amusing. "You better listen to him, Sweetie."

"See?" Randy said, teasing Nathan. "Even your wife knows better."

Nathan sat down without speaking another word.

Gabby just giggled at him.

They examined the ultrasound image. The embryo's heartbeat was a regular flutter. This was a very good sign. "Excellent. About 160 bpm, Randy said. "That's very strong." He took a crown to rump measurement. The baby was twelve millimeters in length and was estimated to weigh about .04 of an ounce. "Good size. Growing nicely." He snapped several pictures from different angles before he had

Gabby wipe imaging gel off her tummy. "Baby looks fantastic. Nice and strong."

"So we look good?" Nathan asked for confirmation.

"Yes. Looks very good. I want to see Gabby every week to take measurements and track baby's growth, at least until we get through the first trimester."

Hearing this put Gabby more at ease. "Thank you."

"We're gonna get you through this," Randy assured her with a hug.

Over the next three weeks, the baby developed normally and grew stronger every day. When Gabby came in for her weekly exam, Randy performed several tests on her. He gave her a full pelvic exam and ran an ultrasound scan. The fetus measured 2.8 inches and weighed fourteen grams. He examined the amount of amniotic fluid, the position and appearance of the placenta, and performed a detailed scan of the baby's anatomy—obvious elbows, distinguishable feet, hands and fingers. The head and brain appeared to be developing normally. The baby had a visible stomach and bladder, and the umbilical cord was inserted correctly. The spine was clearly seen, which ruled out any possibilities of spina bifida. Randy even ran a Doppler to examine the baby's blood flow. Everything looked normal.

Gabby and Nathan eyed the ultrasound screen and saw their tiny baby kick out. Of course Gabby couldn't feel any of these movements yet, but seeing their baby move was very reassuring. Smiling blissfully, Nathan said, "Wow! Active little one."

Randy chuckled. "Yup. But that's good. Fetal movement is what we want to see. An active baby is a healthy baby."

At this stage in the pregnancy Randy performed a few precautionary procedures, including testing for chromosomal abnormalities. He drew a small sample of blood and thoroughly examined these lab results. Every scan, every test, every measurement he took was perfect.

"Baby is really strong," he stated confidently. "Everything looks great." Once the first trimester was complete, the chances of miscarriage were slim. And as strong as baby looked, it was highly unlikely that any complications would occur. "We made it through the first trimester. Only twenty-eight more weeks to go. You'll probably start feeling a bit of movement and you might start to show later this month. We're gonna cut down your visits to once a month now until you get closer to your due date." He closed his tablet and grinned at both of them. "Congratulations!"

Gabby and Nathan looked at one another, and together, they breathed a sigh of relief. They were out of the danger zone. "We made it," Gabby said.

"Yes we did."

It was January 11th. What a wonderful way to start the New Year.

"Mommy," two-year-old Jacob called to Lauren from the bathroom.

Lauren came in to see what he wanted. "Yes, Honey?"

He stood up proudly to show her what he did. "I go potty!"

Sure enough, he had used the toilet. "Good job, Sweetie."

"I show Daddy," he announced with a huge smile.

Lauren giggled, thinking that was just what Roger wanted to see. "You need to wipe and wash your hands."

"Otay." He attempted to clean himself up.

Lauren returned to the living room, snickering under her breath.

Roger asked, "What's so funny?"

"Jacob wants to show you something."

Roger looked up from his magazine. "What is it?"

"Go see for yourself."

Roger set his magazine on the table and stood up. When he entered the bathroom, his son was standing on a step stool at the sink, attempting to wash his hands. "Hey, Jakey."

Jacob turned his attention away from the sink, spraying water everywhere. "I go potty!"

Roger shared in Jacob's excitement. "You did?"

"Uh huh. I go poopoo."

"Good job." Jacob had managed to get water and soap everywhere. Roger tried to redirect him. "Pay attention to what you're doing. You're getting water all over the place."

Jacob giggled. "Oopsie."

"Yeah," Roger corrected, not finding this amusing. "Oopsie." He grabbed a towel off the towel rack and handed it to his son. "You need to clean this water up."

"No!"

Roger raised his eyebrows, surprised by his son's defiance. "Excuse me?"

"Mommy do it."

Roger shook his head, upset that his son was acting like this. "Mommy is not cleaning up your mess. You are."

"No!" Jacob crinkled his face and threw the towel on the floor.

Pointing at the towel, Roger demanded, "Pick that up."

"Me no want to."

"I don't care what you want. Pick that towel up right now."

"No!"

Trying to remain calm, Roger picked up the towel and handed it to his two-year-old. "You are cleaning up this water. And since you don't want to listen to Daddy, you have lost your playtime at the park today."

Jacob threw himself on the floor and screamed.

Roger immediately carried the child into the living room and sat him in a chair. "You sit here until you calm down. Then when you are done throwing a fit, you are going to clean up that water you got all over the bathroom. I'm not doing it, and Mommy isn't doing it. You are."

Jacob grabbed the towel and threw it on the floor, sulking.

Roger left it there, and left Jacob to wallow in the misery of his tantrum. In an attempt to release frustration, Roger took a calming breath before he stepped into the bedroom where Lauren was. "Damn, that kid is stubborn," he complained.

"What was he screaming about?" Lauren asked.

"He sprayed water all over the bathroom. When I asked him to clean it up, he told me no several times then proceeded to throw a temper tantrum. Now he's sitting in a chair to calm down."

Lauren had a hard time maintaining a straight face.

Although Roger was angry and annoyed, he did find this incident humorous. "Terrible twos in full swing. Peter warned me about this stage."

"You didn't clean it up did you?"

"No! He's going to do it. And then he's going to take a nap because he's being a cranky ass."

Lauren was proud of the way Roger handled their son. Sometimes parenting was challenging for him, but despite that, at no time was Jacob allowed to get away with disobedience. Roger wasn't afraid to discipline the child. He did not tolerate talking back or temper tantrums. "Good. He needs to take a nap anyway."

"Two-year-olds are tough. I hope this phase passes quickly, because this is going to get tiresome."

Lauren's cellphone rang. When she saw it was Nathan, she rushed to answer it. "Hey, Hotshot!"

"Hey, Sis. What you up to?"

"Dealing with my two-year-old. He's being a pain, kinda like you were when we were kids," she teased.

"I wasn't that bad."

"You got yourself grounded more than Lacy and I did," Lauren reminded him.

"But Lacy got the evil eye and was on the receiving end of Dad's wrath more than both of us combined," Nathan added.

This made Lauren laugh because it was true. "What's up?"

"Have some good news."

"Oh? What's that?" she asked.

"Gabby's pregnant again."

Knowing how heartbroken he and Gabby were over the loss of their first pregnancy, Lauren sympathized with her brother. "How do you feel about that?"

"We're happy. We were nervous about it at first, but Gab just finished her first trimester. We're golden," he said happily.

"Really? She's been pregnant for three months and you're just now telling me?"

"Gabby didn't want to tell anyone until she knew we were ok," Nathan justified. "If it makes you feel any better, you're the first one I've called."

"Ok. That gets you out of the doghouse. When's she due?"

"July 16th."

"Congratulations, Nathan. Keep us updated please," Lauren insisted.

"We will." As soon as Nathan got off the phone with Lauren, he called Lacy and told her the news.

Chapter Fifty-Seven

"What?" Roger's entire body tensed up and his face suddenly fell. He nervously paced around the living room with his hand in his pocket as if he was trying to make sense out of what the person on the other line was telling him. "Is he alright?"

Lauren overheard part of the conversation, but couldn't figure out who he was talking to or what they were talking about. From his posture, it was obvious he was concerned.

"Ok," he stammered. "I'll make arrangements and book a flight over there tonight." Roger frantically searched for a pen and scratched some notes on a piece of paper. "Thanks, Mom. I'll let you know when my flight gets in."

When he hung up, Lauren asked, "What's going on?"

"Pete's been shot."

Lauren completely understood now why Roger was so flustered. She gasped in dread. "Oh my god."

"He's alive, thank God. No vital organs were hit. He has a nasty bullet wound through his left shoulder though. He's in surgery getting the slug removed right now." He immediately booted up his laptop to book a flight. "I have to get to Baltimore."

Lauren agreed that was a good idea. "Yes, please do."

From gate to gate the trip itself was only about an hour. By the time Roger arrived at the hospital in Baltimore, Peter was out of surgery. Roger spotted Amy in the hallway and immediately approached her. "Amy."

She turned to his voice and greeted him with a hug. "Roger, I'm glad you're here."

"How is he?"

Amy explained what happened. Apparently, Peter had been shot in the shoulder by some hoodlum with a .22 caliber handgun. Luckily a .22 was a relatively low-powered weapon, as far as firearms went. The bullet passed through the shoulder without hitting any arteries, and fortunately lacked energy to penetrate bone. It did manage to lodge itself, however, but the doctor was able to get in and remove it. Peter suffered tissue damage to the left shoulder, which would definitely incapacitate him for a while. The doctor said he would need at least two months for tissue recovery, with full rehabilitation taking approximately six months. Discharge from the hospital would occur in five to seven days, barring no blood loss or infection occurred.

"Is he awake?" Roger asked, hoping he could see his brother.

"Yes. And he'll be so happy to see you."

When Roger peeked his head into Peter's room, Pete was sitting up in bed hooked up to an IV and wearing a sling. "Hey, Pete."

Still groggy from the anesthesia, Peter smiled at his brother. "Hey, Rog."

Roger pulled a chair over to his brother's bed. "How you feeling?"

"Sore." His shoulder hurt like hell, and needless to say, he was pretty pissed off. Despite the fact that he was in severe pain, hilarity ensued. With a chuckle, still maintaining his sense of humor, Peter bellowed, "Asshole shot me with a .22. A fuckin' .22. Can you believe that?" he complained, not happy at all. "What a piss poor, wussy ass excuse for a weapon. If he had to take a shot at me, you would think he would have at least used a gun with some balls."

"You're lucky he used a .22," Roger claimed, thankful that his brother was alive. "Anything bigger could have done some serious damage. Did you at least take him down?"

"Hell yeah," Peter boasted. "We did a massive drug bust, and he's going to do some serious jail time. Not only did I catch him in the act of dealing, now he's tacked on another major felony for shooting a police officer."

"He's screwed."

"Pretty much," Pete concurred.

Roger looked his brother in the eye. "When Mom called and told me you'd been shot, the most horrific thoughts popped into my head."

Pete shook his head. "Leave it to Mom to make a mountain out of molehill."

"I'm glad you're ok. I have to admit, Pete. When I heard you took a bullet, I feared the worst."

Peter shrugged it off, although he couldn't actually shrug because his shoulder was in too much pain. "I'm alright. I'll recover." Then Peter said something to his brother he had never said before. "Dad would have been really proud of you."

Roger always felt disconnected when a conversation about their father came up. Everyone in the family spoke highly of Andrew Zellers and shared positive memories about him, yet Roger had no memories. All he had were stories people told him. "My job isn't nearly as important as yours. I don't protect the citizens of this country or save lives or keep bad guys off the street."

"No, but you have amazing talent. Talent no one else in the family has," Peter told his younger brother. "Dad was an accomplished piano player though. Did Mom ever tell you that?"

"No."

"He was extraordinary. I have many memories of him sitting in front of the piano pounding away, very much like you."

For as long as Roger could remember, his mother kept a piano in the house, which he thought odd considering no one in the family could play it except him. "That's why Mom had a piano. It was Dad's, wasn't it?"

"Yup," Peter confirmed. "I'll never forget when you were five years old. You got curious about it one day and started plucking at the keys. We were amazed that even though you'd never touched the thing before, you could immediately play songs by ear in perfect key, as if you'd been playing for years. Mom and I both stared at each other, absolutely astounded by what we had heard. It was right after that when she signed you up for piano lessons. To you, the music came naturally and you picked it up quickly." Peter smiled at his brother. "You are so much like Dad in many ways, Roger."

"I wish I'd known him. You guys always tell me stories about him, yet I have no idea what any of you are talking about. I feel out of the loop. I don't have the emotional attachment to him that you have, Pete. I didn't mourn his loss because I never knew him. I feel heartless in that regard."

"You shouldn't feel that way," Peter reassured him. "It must be hard for you when we all share memories about Dad, memories you never had the opportunity to experience with him."

Admitting how he felt, Roger said, "I'm in a happy marriage, I have a career I enjoy, and I love being a father. I'm constantly surrounded by positive people, have very loyal and supportive friends, and I know my family will always be there to love and support me unconditionally. Yet I feel like a part of me is missing, a part I don't know how to find."

Peter understood. "You know, I have some video footage, family gatherings, holidays and whatnot. Several have Dad in them, and a couple in particular have footage of him and Mom when she was pregnant with you."

This made Roger smile. "Really?"

"Mom gave them to me a long time ago. Maybe seeing them might help you find what you're looking for," Peter suggested.

"It might."

"I'll have Amy send them to you." Pete glanced at his shoulder and laughed. "I would do it myself, but I'm afraid I'm going to be incapacitated for a while."

"So it seems," Roger teased. Then a thought came to him. "Do you have the plot number where Dad's grave is?"

Although Peter was surprised his brother asked this question, he was glad Roger was trying to find some sort of emotional connection with their father. "Section 67, Site 1205. Why?"

"Think I might pay him a visit."

In the morning, before heading back to New York City, Roger made a side stop in Washington, D.C. He took the metro and reported to the hallowed grounds of Arlington National Cemetery on the Potomac River, directly opposite Washington. The rolling green hills of the cemetery were dotted with over 8,500 majestic trees. These trees, many of which were hundreds of years in age, complemented the intimate gardens found throughout the 624 acres of the cemetery. This impressive landscape had a diverse collection of ornamental plants that served as a backdrop and tribute to the service and sacrifice of every individual laid to rest within this national shrine. This historic landscape was a living memorial and a natural beauty.

Roger's first stop was the Welcome Center located next to the cemetery entrance. He picked up a map at the information desk then popped into the bookstore and bought a bottle of water. As he walked out the door to the cemetery, rows upon rows of upright white marble headstones stared at him. He exhaled heavily, slightly apprehensive about what he was about to do.

As he skimmed over the map trying to locate his father's gravesite, a man dressed in an Arlington National Cemetery Tour Guide shirt walked up to him. "There's a tour set to leave in twenty minutes, if you'd like to join them, Sir."

Roger lifted his head. "Thank you, but I'm not interested in a tour."

"Can I help you with something?" the man asked, trying to offer assistance.

"I hope so. My father was buried here over thirty years ago. I was trying to find his gravesite."

"Do you know the plot number?"

"Yes," Roger said. "Section 67, Site 1205."

"I can take you there. Follow me."

"Thank you." Roger followed this man to the far end of the cemetery. A white marble gravestone had a cross engraved on the top along with the words *Andrew Zellers, New York, Lieutenant, US Air Force.* His date of birth and death followed. "This is it. Thank you."

The tour guide looked twice at the name on the stone. "Wait a minute, Lieutenant Andrew Zellers was your father?"

"Yes, Sir."

Puzzled, this man stared at Roger. "Peter?"

The fact that this man knew Peter's name made Roger a bit uneasy. "How do you know my brother's name?"

"You're not Peter Zellers?" this man asked.

"No," Roger replied. "Pete is my older brother."

This man instantly developed a huge grin. "Oh my. Can this be? You're the baby Sharon was carrying."

Not only did this man know his brother's name, he also knew his mother. "Who are you, and how do you know my mother?" he asked, curious as to how this complete stranger knew so much about his family.

This man explained, "Your father and I served together in the Air Force for years."

"You knew my father?" Roger asked, wanting to know more about this man.

"Yes. I knew him quite well." He offered Roger a handshake. "I'm William Scott, retired Air Force Colonel."

"Roger Zellers. It is a pleasure to meet you."

"I can't believe you're standing here. The last time I saw your mother she was pregnant with you, and Peter had to have been six years old."

Roger updated him. "Pete's a Lieutenant in the Baltimore Police Department now. He's married and has three boys."

"Is that right?" the man replied, overjoyed by that news. "And what do you do, Roger?"

"I'm a performer on Broadway. I've played the lead in several major productions."

"Talented, like your father." This man took a closer look at Roger's facial features. "It's amazing how much you look like Andrew. Spitting image."

"People tell me that all the time."

"He was a good man," Colonel Scott told him. "And a good friend. I have wonderful memories of your father."

"If you have a minute, would you mind sharing a few with me?"

"Not at all."

Together, the two men sat on the lawn right next to Lieutenant Zeller's gravestone. Thrilled to have the opportunity to meet the child Andrew Zellers never knew, Colonel Scott shared many stories with Roger, laughing as he told them. "He was so excited about becoming a father again. Two days before the accident, he found out you were a boy."

"He did?"

"Yes, and he was overjoyed. You have a family?"

Roger twirled his wedding ring around his finger. "I do. My wife, Lauren, is a performer on Broadway too. She and I have a two-year-old son."

"How's your mom?"

"She doing great. Loves being a grandma. Spoils the boys rotten."

The colonel laughed. "Sounds like Sharon. Did she ever remarry?"

"Yes she did. An aeronautical engineer named Gary Pennington. He works at Lockheed Martin designing high performance military helicopters and aircraft. He's a wonderful man, and has been a very loving and supportive father to me and Pete."

"Good," the Colonel said, satisfied that the family seemed happy and content. "I'm glad to hear that."

The men chatted for a while longer before Roger felt his phone buzz in his pocket. It was a text from Lauren. He turned to this man and said, "Thank you so much for your help today and for sharing memories of my father. Since I never knew him, stories people tell me are all I have."

"It's been a pleasure, Roger. I'm glad I had the opportunity to share them with you." They shook hands and parted ways.

Roger replied to his wife's text, snapped a picture of his father's gravestone, and glanced down at the map. Before he left, he stopped at The Tomb of the Unknown Soldier, which stood atop a hill in the plaza overlooking Washington, D.C. The white marble sarcophagus had six wreaths, sculpted on each side of the tomb. Inscribed on the back were the words: *Here rests in honored glory an American soldier known but to God.* He snapped a few pictures of the cemetery and its many monuments, saving this experience so he could share it with Lauren when he returned home. The day had given him some perspective, personal connection, and insights into who his father was. It was well worth the stop.

Chapter Fifty-Eight

At twenty weeks gestation, Gabby had a small baby bump protruding and was starting to feel fetal movement. After a long day at work, she relaxed by lying across Nathan's lap on the sofa. Just for fun, he reached over to the table and grabbed his stethoscope. He lifted Gabby's shirt and placed the metal bell on her abdomen.

She cocked her head. "What are you doing?"

He put the stethoscope in his ears and probed around a little. "Ssh. Don't talk, Gab. I'm trying to listen." He was able to hear the faint sound of baby-to-be's heartbeat, which made his lips quirk up.

"What are you grinning about?" she asked.

He held the bell in place and transferred the earpiece to her. "Listen."

Gabby listened carefully. She heard a fast, faint thumping sound. "What is that?" she asked.

"Baby's heartbeat. You hear it, right?"

Gabby listened more intently, but it had already faded. "Aww, it went away."

"Baby probably moved. Still kinda early to hear it consistently with a scope. We'll try again later." He set the stethoscope on the table then placed his hand on her tummy. "You're getting a bump."

"I know," she concurred.

"We really need to think about getting baby's room ready. I'm sure I can get Andrew to come over and help me, but we need to decide what we want to do."

"That depends on if the baby's a boy or a girl."

"Do you want to find out?"

Gabby nodded. "I'd like to know. Wouldn't you?"

"Yes. Twenty weeks is about the time to see it too."

The following evening, Nathan asked his father if he could borrow one of the portable ultrasound machines from the clinic. Randy allowed him to use it, but insisted that he return it first thing in the morning. "If you break that, you're replacing it," Randy warned.

"I know. I won't damage it, I promise. I just want to borrow it."

Randy handed it to him. "You know how to use that, right?"

"Yes. I've been fully trained, remember? You're the one who trained me," Nathan reminded him.

"Just be careful with it. That's 34,000 dollars' worth of medical equipment in your hand, Nathan."

"I'll be careful. Don't worry."

When Nathan got home that night, he was anxious to have a peek at his baby. He had Gabby lie on the couch while he booted up the ultrasound machine. "Time to get gooey," he teased as he gelled her up.

"That stuff feels funny."

"It's fun to rub it all over you though." He held the probe in his hand and grinned at her. "You ready to check this out?"

"Uh huh."

He placed the transducer on her abdomen and began to look around. "Look, there's baby's face," he said, showing her a clear image of baby's facial features. "Hi Mommy, here I am."

This made Gabby giggle.

Nathan moved the probe and saw the heart beating steadily. "Heart looks good, Babe. Nice and strong." He was able to get an image of baby's arms, hands, and tiny fingers. He carefully counted them all. "And we have ten fingers." When the baby made a fist, they both laughed. "Guess baby doesn't want us counting fingers." He moved the transducer again and caught a glimpse of a foot.

"Aww," Gabby said. "The feet are so tiny."

Nathan was more interested in the toes. "Ten toes as well," he confirmed. When he moved the probe to the left slightly, the image he saw brightened his whole face.

"What do you see that I don't see?" Gabby asked him.

"Hold still for a minute." He froze the image to show her. With the stylus, he traced around two long shapes, side by side, and wrote *leg* on each one. "Ok, these are baby's legs." On a rounded shape connecting them, he wrote the word *rump*. "This is baby's bottom. But this is what I want you to see." He circled an appendage in between. "Do you see this?"

Gabby squinted, trying to make out what it was. "What is that?"

"You don't see it?"

"It looks like a bunch of dark shadows to me. How do you make sense out of any of this?"

Nathan pointed it out to her. "Look, Babe. These are little boy parts. See? That is a scrotum and there's an appendage sticking out." He drew an arrow pointing to it.

Gabby gasped, "We're having a boy?"

"Yes. Can you see it?"

Now that Nathan pointed it out, she could see it plainly. "Uh huh."

Nathan tittered in excitement. "We're having a boy. This is great!"

When Nathan returned the ultrasound machine the next morning, he told his father. "Well, we're having a boy. Saw it plain as day last night."

Randy smiled. "Really?"

"Yup. I'm jacked!" Nathan could hardly contain his excitement.

"I can tell." Randy took the machine from his son. "Are you available this weekend?"

"On Sunday I am. Why?"

"Let's go fishing," Randy suggested.

Nathan loved that idea. He and his dad hadn't been fishing together in a while. "I'll bring breakfast."

Fishing on Lake Washington in the spring yielded Coastal Cutthroat Trout, a few Rainbows, Largemouth and Smallmouth Bass, Yellow Perch, and Black Crappie. And if they were lucky, they might walk away with a prized Sockeye Salmon.

Before sunrise Sunday morning, Randy stocked up on bait, checked the lines on the two fishing reels, and pulled both his and Nathan's tackle boxes out of the shed. He grabbed a small cooler and packed a large lunch bag with snacks. When he was finished, he sharpened and honed his fillet knife, loaded the boat, and filled it up with gas.

Nathan arrived at his parents' house carrying a portable drink carrier with two cups of Starbucks coffee and a paper bag. He set the bag and the drink carrier on the kitchen island. "I got you a Caffè Mocha and a breakfast sandwich."

"Perfect." Randy took his cup out of the cardboard carrier and sipped from it. "Your mom doesn't let me eat that stuff."

"I know. That's why I bought it for you." Nathan pulled two egg and sausage sandwiches out of the bag and gave one to his father.

"Thank you."

After chowing down breakfast, they hit the water. While Randy slowly and patiently reeled his line in, trying to wiggle his lure for a curious fish, Nathan changed his bait. "Since Gab and I found out we're having a boy, we've been looking at prospective names."

"Find anything?"

Nathan cast his line out then reeled in to tighten the slack. "We've already chosen one."

"Do tell."

"Daniel Mark Hanson."

Randy's face tightened up, and he had a hard time holding back the waterworks. "You used Grandpa's name?"

"Yes, we did."

"That's great," he said, approving of their choice. "That's really great."

That evening, after staking claim to their daily catch, Randy hopped in the Jag and reported to his father's marble grave marker. He approached the grave site with a smile on his face. "Fish were biting like crazy this morning, Dad." Randy squatted down closer to the ground. "Nathan out-fished me again, dammit. If you would have gone with us, you could have shown the punk kid how an old pro catches a trout, but instead he had to show me up with that big ass bass he hooked." Randy poked around at the grass. "Guess what? He and Gabby came up with a name for their little boy.

647

You're not gonna believe this. They're naming their baby after you—Daniel Mark Hanson," he said joyfully. "Now this papa will have two grandsons, Jacob and Daniel." He removed a few stray leaves from the marble stone then rubbed his father's name with his finger. He closed his eyes and took a deep breath, exhaling slowly. "I miss you. I wish you could have been here today. The fish were calling your name." He leaned a *World's Greatest Fisherman* plaque against the gravestone and slowly stood up. "I love you, Dad. There will never be a better fisherman than you."

Chapter Fifty-Nine

One of the perks of being a New York City firefighter was the four weeks of paid vacation Max earned every year. With the warmer weather, longer days, budding trees, and chirping birds, Max decided to take one of his weeks to get some much needed R&R. He also planned to spend some quality time with Lacy, who scheduled her vacation at the same time.

The two of them explored New York City together. Central Park in spring was a great place to people-watch, see weird dog breeds, listen to street musicians, or share a picnic lunch on Sheep Meadow. Strolling through the park allowed Max and Lacy some together time to explore outdoor art, including Eva Rothschild's 20-foot-tall steel structure that rose over the plaza like a ten-legged spider. Central Park's Conservatory Garden was a flowery paradise. Another romantic Eden was the Shakespeare garden, which featured blooms from the bard's poems. For a view overlooking the garden, Max and Lacy walked up to the long, curved Charles B. Stover Bench, where they could whisper to each other from its far-away ends. They never imagined that exploring Central Park could be so much fun.

In the evening, they strolled along the iconic flower-lined stretch of Brooklyn Heights Promenade and enjoyed the view of the skyline. The Brooklyn Bridge and the Empire State Building were clearly visible. As the sun went down, Max took advantage of the opportunity and stole a kiss under the moonlight. He held Lacy in his arms and took in the sweet scent of her hair. It smelled like mangoes. "Mmm," he said. "Your hair."

She combed her fingers through her hair. "What's wrong with my hair?"

"Nothing. It smells wonderful. You've smelled wonderful all day."

"I think it's all the flowers."

Max begged to differ. "No, it isn't the flowers. It's you. You smell amazingly sweet, and your lips taste sweet. In fact, they're pretty damn intoxicating. I'm convinced you wear tainted lipstick."

Lacy giggled. "I do not."

"You must, because every time I kiss you, you pull me under your spell and I can't escape." He grazed his hands across her cheek and pulled her mouth to his, making the passionate kiss they shared last as long as possible.

Their next stop was Coney Island in southwest Brooklyn. Coney's boardwalk linked exciting, colorful amusements to the sweeping calm of the ocean. It offered an ideal spring respite from the hectic and steamy city. With nearly three miles of sandy beaches, Max and Lacy were able to catch some rays and catch the court for a game of beach volleyball. Afterwards, they spent a few hours at the New York Aquarium, where they experienced eerie moon jellyfish, fierce sharks, and adorable black-footed penguins. They watched the sea lion show then stopped and ate world famous Coney Island hotdogs. In the afternoon, they rode the Cyclone, the least confidence-inspiring roller coaster in the world, then crashed into each other on bumper cars. Max also played his hand at some amusement games and won a large stuffed Dalmatian wearing a firefighter's hat, which he gave to Lacy.

"He's cute," Lacy said, carried this huge plush puppy under her arm.

"What are you going to do with that?" Max asked. "It's huge."

"Set it on my bed. That way when we can't be together, I'll still have a firefighter sharing a bed with me."

"Don't know what good a stuffed dog will do if you ever have a real emergency."

"He'll be there for me to hug." She took Max's hand and walked the boardwalk with him. "I think I'll name him Max."

Lacy had cute qualities about her—small quirks, facial expressions she would make, her love of a good beer, and her cute collection of stuffed dogs—that drew a smile on Max's face every time. She was everything fun, anything unpredictable, and always supportive. Being with her made him happy and gave him something to look forward to every day.

At nightfall, they took advantage of New York's enviable views by grabbing a drink at a rooftop bar. The scenery didn't get much better than at 230 Fifth, where an unobscured view of the Empire State Building and a luxurious environment filled with leafy fronds, palm trees, candles, and space heaters was an ideal spot for a casual boozefest.

They enjoyed a few drinks together, and by the end of the evening, Lacy had gone beyond her plan of 'just getting buzzed'. Her love of a good beer got the best of her today. She was exceptionally giggly and very ditzy. And right now, she had a difficult time staying on her feet. Noticing that she was drunk, Max lovingly pulled the beer bottle out of her hand and set it on the bar. "I think you've had enough." He helped her stand up. "Come on. I'm taking you home."

They took a cab to Max's apartment building, where he carefully helped her walk to the elevator. She laughed at everything and kept tripping over her own feet to the point where she almost fell. "Be careful, Babe," Max chuckled at her clumsiness. "You're gonna hurt yourself."

She looked around. "Where are we?"

"We're at my place. I'm taking you upstairs." He pushed the button on the elevator.

She clumsily threw her arms around him. "Ooh, are you taking me to bed?" She kissed him and began to fondle around the button and zipper of his pants, totally coming on to him in the lobby.

He resisted her. "Lace, you've had too much to drink. You need to sleep this off."

She slipped her hands into his back pockets and thrust herself against him. "I want you to bring me upstairs and take me."

Her inappropriate sexual prowess caused several people in the lobby to stare at them. "Babe, not here. People are watching us."

She tried to unbutton his shirt.

He moved her hands away. "Honey, we can't do this here."

"You don't want me?" she asked, feeling rejected.

"Yes," he reassured her with a kiss. "But not here." The elevator door opened and he helped her step inside.

As soon as the door closed, she reached her hands up his shirt and caressed his chest, hanging all over him like a leech. She kissed him amorously, tried to remove his shirt, and attempted to unfasten his pants.

He fought hard to resist her. "Lacy, stop it."

"Why don't you want me?" she slurred.

"I didn't say I didn't want you. I just don't want to do this if you're drunk."

She reached into his pants and began to rub, trying to stir up arousal. "Take me."

The elevator stopped on his floor and he had to hold her up to walk down the hall so she wouldn't fall over. "Come on. Let's get you to bed."

When they stepped into his apartment, Lacy stripped her clothes off. With her naked breasts exposed, she pressed her chest against his. "Stick your cock inside me, Max. I want to feel you fucking me."

Max raised his eyebrows, shocked by the obscene words that just came out of her mouth. Apparently she was one of those people who became sexually aggressive when she was drunk. Max wasn't sure if he should laugh at her insanely perverse tone or be offended by it. "Lacy, I am not going to have sex with you when you are drunk." He helped her to the bedroom and sat her on the bed.

While he searched for a clean tee-shirt, she slid down to the edge of the bed with her legs spread wide open, totally exposing herself to him.

"Here, put this on." He turned around to hand her the shirt and this sexual, almost pornographic display, took him by surprise. "What the hell are you doing?"

"Take me now!" she demanded.

He picked up her panties and handed them to her. "We are not doing this tonight. Put some clothes on."

She buried her face in her hands and sobbed.

Max rolled his eyes. "Why are you crying?"

"Because you don't want me."

Knowing her drunkenness had caused this emotional state, he firmly, but lovingly said, "Lacy, listen. I think you are very sexy, and I want you all the time. But I am not going to be an ass and take advantage of you in this condition. If you were sober, I'd make love to you right now. But since you're not, I refuse to have sex with you." He kissed her forehead. "Now put some clothes on. You need to go to bed."

He stepped out of the room to get her a glass of water. By the time he returned, she was lying on her side passed out. He set the glass on the dresser and covered her with a blanket. Once she was tucked in, he brushed her hair off her face, kissed her cheek, and left her there to sleep.

Lacy awoke in the morning with a horrible taste in her mouth. Her head throbbed, and she felt nauseated. Max's grey FDNY tee-shirt was beside her on the bed. She slipped it over her head and put on her underwear. As soon as she was dressed, she made her way to the living room.

When Max saw the repulsed look on her face, he had to laugh. "She's alive."

"Ugh," she scowled.

"How you feeling this morning?" He stirred milk into his oatmeal and took a bite.

"Crappy."

He gently touched the tip of her nose. "You, young lady, had way too much to drink last night."

She sat in a kitchen chair, folded her arms on the table, and rested her head on her hands. "I am never drinking again."

He ate his oatmeal right in front of her. "Do you remember anything about last night?"

She groaned.

"Do you remember coming on to me in the lobby?"

She lifted her head and looked up at him, totally embarrassed. "I didn't really do that, did I?"

"Yes, and then you tried to take my clothes off in the elevator and insisted that I have sex with you. I'll save you the embarrassment by not telling you what happened after that or what you said to me."

Humiliated, she plopped her head back down. "Oh god."

"Actually if was kind of funny. You got pretty aggressive with me."

Feeling like an idiotic fool, she apologized. "I'm sorry."

"Don't worry about it. Guess we now know what too much alcohol does to you." He took another bite of his oatmeal. "If it's any consolation, despite your insistent efforts, I didn't touch you last night. I slept on the couch."

"You did?"

"Yes," Max reassured her. "That would not have been consensual sex. It would have been an asshole taking advantage of his drunk girlfriend. Not my style."

Grateful for his gentlemanly ways, Lacy smiled appreciatively. "Thank you."

"You want some oatmeal?" he offered, pushing the bowl her direction.

She cringed at the thought. Even the smell was making her gag. "No."

"More for me then."

Over the past year, Roger and Max had spent a great deal of time together because of the twins. During this time, they discussed sensitive issues, watched and debated over football, basketball, and baseball games, and loved to attend sporting events together. Roger, Max, and Jason donned jeans, sneakers, and Yankees garb, and headed to the ballpark for the opening game of the season.

Yankee Stadium—the cathedral of baseball. Cold brew, kosher hot dogs, and hot garlic fries provided a warm welcome as they found their seats right along the first base line above the Yankees' dugout. They were so close to the field that they could smell the dirt and Kentucky bluegrass. They saw the detailed pinstripe grass pattern of the baseball field, heard the flags and pennants flapping in the wind, and heard the baseball smack against the mitt every time the players tossed the ball back and forth.

"These seats are awesome, Rog." Jason settled into his chair and set his plastic Yankees cup full of Heineken draft beer in the cup holder.

Roger took a seat next to Jason. He had a Goose Island Honker's Ale, which he took a drink of before he set it down. "Got a good deal on these tickets. Having connections has its perks."

"Sweet," Max replied, taking a seat on the other side of Roger with a full cup of Budweiser in his hand. "Can't beat the view."

Aside from watching the game with his best friends, Roger was called to deliver the official start to the Yankees home game with the national anthem. He quickly wolfed down his hotdog because he had to report to the field to set up. "I'm gonna head down. Save my seat, and don't drink my beer."

"You're gonna be shit outta luck if you leave it up here," Jason teased.

"Well, I'll know who to blame if it's missing then, won't I?" Roger replied. "I'll see you guys in a bit."

Carefully, he squeezed out of the stands and headed toward the field.

"Break a leg," Jason called to him.

Max and Jason ate the rest of their hotdogs and garlic fries while Roger got situated down by the field.

About fifteen minutes later, the players exited the practice field and a microphone was placed behind home plate. Roger stepped onto the grass and waited for the announcer.

"Your attention please, ladies and gentlemen. Will you please rise, remove your caps, and direct your attention now to the microphone behind home plate." The announcer introduced Roger, at which time he removed his Yankees baseball cap and took position at the microphone. With his right hand over his heart, he sang, "Oh, say can you see…"

During the presentation of the flag, Max held his hand over his heart like everyone else. Since he was a commissioned NYC firefighter, Jason wondered why he did this. He was under the impression that all military, police officers, and firefighters saluted during the National Anthem. Apparently he was wrong.

Roger belted out the last line of the song and it echoed through the entire stadium. The crowd cheered and applauded at his performance then the flag was removed from the field. The entire stadium returned to their seats. While the first pitch was announced, Jason questioned Max about what he witnessed during the presentation of the flag. "As a firefighter, you don't salute during the National Anthem?"

Max clarified this misconception. "It depends. When in uniform, we salute during the Pledge of Allegiance and the National Anthem. We also salute during the raising and lowering of the flag, when a flag passes in a parade, ceremonial occasions, Pass and

Review of a fallen firefighter's casket, or when a fellow firefighter's funeral caisson passes. And if we've been saluted by someone in uniform, it's common respect to salute back. But when I'm not in uniform, I don't salute at all. It's United States Code and firefighter mandate. If I would have come to the game in uniform, I would have saluted. But who comes to a baseball game in full dress?" Max questioned. "When I'm not on duty or involved in a formal ceremony, I don't wear it."

"Makes sense," Jason replied.

"By the way, you're not the only one who's asked me that."

Roger reported back to the stands. "So what'd I miss?"

Max told him, "Only the best rendition of the National Anthem I've ever heard. Thanks for keeping it trite and true. Nice job."

"Thanks." Roger spied his beer cup to make sure it hadn't been tampered with. "You guys didn't mess with my beer did you?"

"No," Jason replied. "Although Max was thinking about it."

Max chuckled. "But I decided against it. It's not right to steal a beverage from the man who's honoring our nation in front of all these baseball fans. There's something sacrilegious about that."

Roger picked up his cup and took a drink, moistening his throat and sucking down the savory hop flavor. As he swallowed, he curled his lip, not liking the way it tasted. "Ugh, it's warm. I need a new one." He put it back in the cup holder and went to the vender to get another one.

Max and Jason looked at each other and laughed.

The Yankees were playing the Red Sox. Since these two teams were massive rivals, the crowd was noisy and a little rambunctious during this game. By the end of the sixth inning, the two teams were tied.

During the seventh inning stretch, Jason got up to use the restroom. "You guys need anything while I'm up?" he cordially asked.

"I'm good," Roger replied.

"Nah, I don't need anything," Max said.

"Okay. Be back a bit." Jason crawled out of the stands and headed to the men's rooms.

Max leaned back and took another sip of his beer. "I was gonna tell you something the other day when I saw you, but Lauren was there."

"Tell me what?" Roger asked, wondering why Lauren being there mattered.

"I bought a ring for Lacy."

Roger's face perked up in joy. "Like an engagement ring?"

"Yeah," Max replied. "I got it last week but haven't had a chance to tell you. I didn't want to say anything with Lauren there because she would have overheard."

Roger completely understood. Anything Lauren knew, Lacy knew, and vice versa. Keeping this information from Lauren was definitely better. "That's cool. When are you going to ask her?"

"Was hoping to do it sometime next week. I have a plan on how I want to do this, but Lacy has to be at the right place at the right time for it to work."

"Anything I can do to help?" Roger offered.

"Not unless you can get Lauren to take Lacy out to lunch at a balcony restaurant or bar when I happen to be on duty and not in the middle of a call. Which is pretty unlikely, so I may have to rethink this."

That whole circumstance seemed next to impossible, yet Roger had a plan. "I actually might be able to arrange that."

"Really?" Max asked, not seeing how this was possible.

"They wanted to have lunch together sometime next week anyway. Lauren's tired of going to the same places all the time and keeps asking me to give her names of new places they can try. Why don't I just suggest one for her?" Roger hinted. "You have a place in mind?"

"Seriously?" Max said. "You would do that?"

"Sure. Name your poison. Where would you like me to send them?"

Max suggested, "Café Nicole."

"Ah," Roger grinned. "By Times Square."

"Yes."

"I can do that." Curious as to what Max was planning, Roger asked, "Why does it have to be on a balcony? What are you going to do?"

Max explained his plan.

Roger thought it was fabulous.

"You can't hint to Lauren what's going on," Max told Roger. "If she suspects anything, she's going to tell Lacy and the whole plan will be ruined."

"Oh, don't worry. She won't have a clue." Roger was determined to help in whatever way he could. "Get your company to help on your end and I'll handle the girls."

They high fived each other and set Max's plan into motion.

Chapter Sixty

After breakfast, a quick workout, and a shower, Max reported to the firehouse ready for duty. The morning was kind of slow. They had a couple of routine calls then killed time running drills. Around 11:30, Max texted Lacy to check in and make sure the plan he and Roger had discussed was in place. *Mornin' Babe! Whatcha doing?* he asked her.

Going to have lunch with the girls.

So far so good. He probed further to get more information. *Cool. Cool. Where you going?*

Cafe Nicole

Roger had done his homework. *That's a great place. What time?*

Meeting them there in about an hour.

Max checked the time on his watch, hoping they wouldn't get any major calls in the next hour or so. *You should get a balcony seat. It's a gorgeous day*, he suggested.

We were going to.

Sweet! Have a beer for me, and don't get drunk this time, he teased her.

Shut up!

Her reaction made him laugh. *GTG back to work. Luv you.*

I love you too.

Max spoke to the guys in the firehouse and they initiated the plan.

Lacy met her sister and some of their friends on the second-floor balcony of Café Nicole, which was a restaurant in Manhattan located inside the Novotel New York Hotel at 52nd Street between Broadway and Eighth Avenue. The outside terrace offered dining high above Broadway, overlooking the lights of Times Square. The café had a French flair, serving light lunches and cocktails.

While the girls sat and talked, Lauren admired the necklace Lacy was wearing. It was a crystal heart pendant displaying the firefighter's Maltese cross. The fine multi-faceted heart design was embedded with a handcrafted image of a waving American flag. It dangled on a silver chain. "I love that. Where did you find that?" Lauren asked her sister.

"Max gave it to me."

Lauren examined the details on it. "When you see Max later, tell him Jacob absolutely loves the fire hat he gave him. We have a hard time getting him to take it off."

"I'll let him know."

The girls were enjoying a peaceful lunch when the calmness of their soiree turned a little more exciting. Two fire trucks pulled up in front of the building—Manhattan's Engine 76 truck and the Ladder 22 truck. The 100-foot aerial ladder on the 22 truck extended right up to Lacy's table on the seventh floor balcony, startling not only her and her girlfriends but the other diners who were sitting up there. Max, wearing his navy blue on-duty uniform, climbed up bearing a dozen red roses. He leaped onto the balcony.

Lacy stared at him, wondering why in the world he was climbing the ladder up to the balcony. "Max?" she questioned, thinking he had lost his mind. "What are you doing?"

Max handed her the roses then reached into his pocket for a small box. In front of Lacy's sister, her friends, and in the presence of all these startled and delighted diners, he opened the box and got down on one knee in front of her. He looked Lacy in the eye and said, "I love you, and I want to spend the rest of my life with you. Will you marry me?"

Lacy couldn't believe this was happening. She stared at the ring in Max's hand then met his glance. She could see by the expression he carried that he was deadly serious.

"Marry me, Lacy."

With trembling hands, she said, "Yes."

Max took the half-carat, princess-cut diamond out of the box and slipped it on her finger, and they embraced to the applause of the entire café.

Delighted, Lacy said, "You're crazy."

"About you. I'm also on duty and have to go back to work. I'll call you later." He hopped back over the balcony onto the ladder and made his descent. "I love you, Lace," he called to her as he disappeared out of sight.

When he made it to the bottom, all the guys from his firehouse stared at him in anticipation, wondering what went on up there. "Well?" Matthew finally asked. "What happened?"

Max grinned. "You are looking at an engaged man."

They all congratulated him, recoiled the ladder, and returned to the duties of their borough.

When Max got home from work that evening, Lacy was dancing around the living room with ear buds in her ears working on some kind of choreography routine. Luckily, she hadn't seen him walk in. He slipped his truck keys in his pocket then slowly crept behind her and touched her arm. She jumped about a hundred feet in the air and screamed. Her reaction made him laugh.

She took her headphones off. "Dammit, Max! Don't do that. You scared the hell out of me."

"Sorry, Babe. Wasn't trying to give you a heart attack." He greeted her with a kiss. "You ok? You jumped so high, you almost hit your head on the ceiling."

"I'm fine." She eyed him curiously. "I can't believe you did that today."

He gave her a crooked grin. "Weren't expecting that, were ya?"

"No. A ladder truck was very clever, I have to say."

"It seemed appropriate." He fixed his eyes on the ring on her finger. "Do you like it?"

In complete amazement that he would even ask that, she held out her hand to eye the diamond she was wearing. "I love it. It's gorgeous."

"You and I have a wedding to plan."

Excited about this, Lacy drew her lip between her teeth. "Yes we do."

He untucked his work shirt and removed his shoes to get more comfortable. Wondering what she was doing when he walked in, he asked, "So, what're you working on?"

"Some moves for the dance parade."

The NYC Dance Parade celebrated the diversity of dance. This parade featured exuberant energy, music, and dance in all its forms, from Bolivian folk dancing and the waltz to Hawaiian hula and Roller Disco. Even children participated. Amongst beautifully crafted floats, live bands, and DJs, the parade chronologically honored the history of dance from ancient to contemporary. All in all, over seventy different dance styles were performed by close to 10,000 dancers. The parade ended with the Dance Fest in Tompkins Square Park, where visitors would enjoy free choreographed dance performances and would be able to take free dance lessons.

"You're performing in the dance parade?" Max asked, reaching in the refrigerator for a cold beer.

"As are some of my dance students. We've been working on this routine for a while, but I'm tweaking it a little."

"What kind of dance are you doing?" He popped the top off the bottle and took a drink.

"Do you want me to show you?" Lacy offered.

"Please." He sat on the sofa to provide her with an audience.

She blasted the music through the whole apartment and proceeded to give him a private show.

Max loved to watch Lacy dance. The way her body moved when she danced was seductive and alluring. While she performed this dance routine, she slowly made her way to his lap. This solo performance quickly turned into a dangerously enticing private lap dance, which got him excited. He had a feeling this was not the routine she had choreographed. This was more like an exotic pole dance, and he was the pole.

He reached out and touched her. "Damn, you are hot."

She straddled his lap and dipped her head back, exposing the nape of her neck.

He set his drink on the table and licked her salty skin. "You're not doing this for the parade crowds I hope."

"Nope," she affirmed. "You're the only one who gets this show."

"Lucky me."

Chapter Sixty-One

On May 23rd, the University of Washington's School of Medicine held a hooding ceremony to recognize their graduates. Nathan sent out announcements for this event and gave tickets to family and friends. He purchased his professional regalia of traditional black doctoral gown, black tam, green-colored hood, and gold tassel then picked up a purple stole of gratitude, which he planned to give to his parents as a token of appreciation for of all they had done to make his success possible.

This formal ceremony involved speeches, honors and awards, introduction of graduates, and investiture of doctoral hoods, at which time Nathan would officially be given the title M.D. All graduates would then participate in the administration of the Hippocratic Oath and recessional.

Nathan arrived to Benaroya Hall wearing black dress slacks, a white dress shirt, black tie, and black leather dress shoes. He carried his cap and gown in his hand. Once he got to the floor where the other graduates were, he slipped his gown on.

"I'm so proud of you," Gabby said, straightening his collar.

"I couldn't have done this without you, Babe. You've supported me from day one."

She gave him a kiss. "Are you ready to give your speech?"

"Yup. Dad has no clue."

Every year, fourth year medical students nominated fellow classmates, faculty, and clinical staff members for various awards. Nominations were tallied and consolidated by the Student Affairs Office, and an election ballot was posted for final consideration. Results of the election were announced during the graduation ceremony. Randy did not know this yet, but he had been voted by the medical students to receive the Distinguished Teacher Award. The award recognized clinical faculty members and basic science professors the students felt had been excellent teachers. This honor carried with it a $5,000 monetary award for classroom and teaching use. This recognition was presented by a student. This year, Nathan was chosen to do the honors of presenting this award to his father

Gabby gave her husband one last look. "You look great, Sweetie."

"Thank you."

"I'll finally get to call you Dr. Hanson."

Nathan cocked his head. "My dad is Dr. Hanson."

"Yes," she said. "But I'm not talking about him. I'm talking about you."

"I can't believe this is happening. This has been my dream since I was eight years old." He gently rubbed her pregnant tummy. "I'm gonna head over. I'll see you in a few hours."

Nathan reported to his designated area. His father stood nearby. Randy had attended every UWSOM graduation ceremony since he became a clinical professor with the University of Washington many years ago. This year, he attended the ceremony not merely as a staff member celebrating success with his students, but also as a parent.

"Hey, Dad," Nathan said when he saw his father.

"Hello, Nate. How are you feeling today?" Randy knew exactly how he felt. He remembered all too well the pride he felt when he finally graduated from medical school and received his MD.

"I feel fantastic," Nathan replied. "Relieved, excited...I can't even describe it."

Randy gave his son a hug. "Congratulations, Nathan. You have worked exceptionally hard for this, and I'm very proud of you."

"Thank you, Sir."

"Oh no," Randy insisted. "Professionally, we are equal. At no time are you required to call me sir."

"I call you that because I respect you," Nathan replied. "I've always respected you. I know I didn't always show it, and I was often a pain in your ass, but I am very grateful for everything you've done for me over the years. All the support you and Mom offered, you never stopped believing in me."

Moved by Nathan's heartfelt sentiments, Randy stumbled for the right words. "I always thought the day I graduated from medical school was the proudest moment of my life. Yet that was nothing compared to the day you were born. Watching you grow up, seeing the amazing young man you've become, the loving husband, the caring soon-to-be father, that makes me proud too. But hooding my son and being here today when he receives his MD is by far the best experience of my life."

Nathan started to get emotional. "Alright, stop before you make me cry. I don't need to be all blubbery today."

When Nathan was announced as Dr. Nathan James Hanson, he grandly paraded across the stage, accepted his graduation envelop from the Dean, then walked over to his father. Randy, in turn, picked up Nathan's green hood and instructed him to turn around. Nathan took in a big breath and faced the crowd. Randy reached over his son's head, draped the hood around his neck, and carefully laid it flat in the back. He held his hand out to Nathan and said, "Congratulations, Dr. Hanson."

But Nathan didn't accept his handshake. Instead, he gave his father a huge hug. "Thank you, Sir."

When the last graduate crossed the stage, the Dean said a few words then introduced Nathan, who stepped up to the podium and took claim to the microphone. "Welcome ladies and gentlemen, parents, family members, friends, and fellow graduates." He waited for applause to subside before he continued. "Becoming a physician has been a challenging journey, yet it's been a dream all of us have fought to achieve. Along this journey, we had setbacks, discouragements, and frustrations. We also celebrated many successes and received encouraging words from the people who helped us achieve our goals. None of us would be here today if it wasn't for great teachers who not only educated us but shared with us their passion and love for medicine, challenged us to rise above any expectations we ever had for ourselves, and offered us support and encouragement every step of the way. As we traveled down this road together, there was always one teacher, one amazing physician whose name popped up over and over again. This man pushed us, not only to meet the challenges set before us, but to exceed them. He provided us the most intense, hands-on, thought provoking clinical experience and gave us all the critique we needed to improve, the praise we needed to stay motivated, and the encouragement we needed to succeed. That man has been voted by this year's graduating medical class as an outstanding mentor and devoted teacher. His caring attitude, along with the high expectations he set for all of his students, has earned him the much deserved honor of being the recipient of this year's Distinguished Teacher Award. I am very honored and pleased to announce an exceptional physician, who is not only a mentor and teacher to all of us, but has always been a supportive and loving father to me. Dr. Randal Hanson."

All the guests cheered and applauded as Randy stood up. The medical students gave him a standing ovation.

Randy gave Nathan a hug. "You didn't tell me about this."

"Of course not. It was supposed to be a surprise. Congratulations, Dad." Nathan stepped down, allowing Randy to stand behind the podium and accept his award.

Nathan used the few weeks of down time he had to set up the baby's room. To no one's surprise, he and Gabby chose a basketball theme.

To help decorate, Nathan called on a former teammate and old friend, Andrew Garibay. They painted the walls medium grey, which matched the unique white and pewter-colored baby furniture Gabby was lucky enough to stumble upon from a work colleague. They accessorized the furnishings by purchasing white and grey crib bedding. Brighter colored basketball décor was incorporated throughout the room. Nathan draped an orange basketball-patterned fleece blanket over the baby's crib and spread a UW basketball rug on the floor in front of the door. He placed a basketball-base lamp with white lampshade on the dresser and hung a few basketball decals on the wall, including one with Daniel's name on it. Between the two windows, he hung a basketball-shaped clock on the wall. Grey and white striped curtains adorned the side of each window with a middle orange curtain between them. To top off the look, Nathan hung a large pewter cylinder light fixture from the ceiling and placed a plush basketball and two stuffed grey Huskies on a shelf.

When they were finished, Andrew scanned the room, impressed with their creative craftsmanship. "You know, this is a badass room. I never had a room like this when I was a kid. This baby is stylin'."

"It does look pretty cool. Thanks for your help." Nathan and Andrew knuckle bumped. "I have a feeling it's going to quickly fill with toys from my parents. I see how they treat my nephew. That kid has way too much crap."

"Good to know your child is loved and cared for by so many people." Andrew took a seat on the floor in the newly decorated nursery. "You're only about a month away from becoming a father. That's scary shit."

Nathan sat next to him and crossed his ankles. "I'm excited, but knowing the tiny person Gabby is carrying will depend on us for everything he needs, that's a big deal."

Andrew couldn't have agreed more. "There is no way I'd want to take on fatherhood right now. I'd be nervous as hell if I was in your shoes."

"I am a little nervous. Caring for a newborn is a big responsibility. But Gab and I have talked about this extensively. She and I are on the same page as far as parenting goes and that alone is going to make this easier for both of us. We're excited to take this on together. It's a new chapter in our lives. I am not, however, looking forward to what Gabby has to go through in order to bring Daniel into the world. I hate to see Gab cry, let alone see her in pain. It's gonna kill me to have to watch that."

Andrew cringed. "That's gonna suck. Is your dad doing the delivery?"

"That's the plan. He's been her OB from the start," Nathan replied. "She wants to try to do this without pain meds, but I don't think she realizes how intense this is going to get. Gabby has a really low pain tolerance. I have a feeling that halfway through this, her birth plan is going to end up in the toilet."

"She'll be alright. It's not like she'll have to do it alone," Andrew reminded him. "You'll be there with her."

"For sure. And after my son is born, I'm going to be totally involved. I'm not afraid to shelf some of my freedom and routines to give time to my baby. I really want to develop that relationship with him."

Chapter Sixty-Two

Aside from becoming a soon-to-be first time dad, Nathan was going through other changes in his life, namely his first day at University of Washington's Orthopedic & Sports Medicine Residency Program.

In the morning, Gabby greeted him with a kiss. "You ready for this?"

"This is what I've been waiting my whole life for. I'm actually a practicing physician now." Nathan pointed to the letters MD on his name badge. "See? My badge even says so."

Giggling at the prideful face he wore, Gabby said, "I see that."

Dr. Nathan Hanson slipped his cellphone in his pocket, grabbed his stethoscope, and draped his lab coat over his arm with his car key dangling on his index finger. "Wish me luck today. If you have any problems, text me please."

"I'm not going to have any problems."

"I'm just saying. My phone is in my pocket if you need me." Reaching his hand down, he softly rubbed her tummy. "Take care of baby Daniel while I'm gone."

"I will."

"Love you, Babe." He left her with a kiss before he confidently walked out the door.

As a first year resident, Nathan's rotation schedule fell into four week blocks: orthopedic trauma, rheumatology, ER, burns and plastics, pediatric surgery, general surgery, and EVATS, which included two weeks of vacation, one week of coverage for someone on vacation, and one week of independent surgical skills. He also had mandatory monthly meetings. Every other Monday, an attending physician gave a two to three hour lecture on a topic in their specialty. A nationally recognized leader in orthopedic surgery was invited to a lectureship every year to lead discussions and offer their expertise. This lectureship gave residents the opportunity to present difficult and unusual cases to a renowned member of the orthopedic community. Nathan would also have to meet with an attending in the cadaveric dissection lab several times a year to review anatomy and surgical procedures. Throughout the year, the residency director scheduled appointments with each first year resident to discuss progress and issues pertaining to the program. Needless to say, Nathan would be busy his first year, and he would receive a wide range of experiences and opportunities to practice and learn orthopedic skills.

Nathan's first day as a working physician began in the conference room, where a team of senior residents and attending physicians discussed the patients on the floor. Names, medical conditions, and management decisions flew by him left and right. He frantically penned down information and rummaged through manuals, trying to make sense of the information. By noon, he was overwhelmed by contorted papers sticking out in all angles from his clipboard. He took a brief bathroom break then shoved half a sandwich in his mouth before he made his first rounds.

With his pocket pharmacy booklet, pocket diagnostics, and a medical terminology pamphlet in his possession, he strolled from room to room throughout the hospital's labyrinthine hallways reciting his meticulously practiced monologue. "Good afternoon, Mr. or Mrs. So-and-so. I'm Dr. Hanson, and I'll be your physician while you're here at University Medical Center."

Throughout his twelve hour shift, Nathan was able to independently examine patients, answer their questions of care with the help of senior residents, and establish enduring and meaningful relationships. When evening set in, he sat down at a resident-designated computer to document his patient encounters. While he typed his notes, he reflected back on his day and quickly came to the realization that holding the title MD meant nothing without experience. Although he was amazed at how much he had done, he still felt unfit to make real medical decisions without his senior physicians' input.

Because of his extenuating circumstances, the Dean of the College of Medicine, the director of the residency program, and the hospital director all sat down with Nathan and had a meeting. The purpose of this gathering was to discuss the EVATS rotation, in which two weeks of earned vacation was granted during Nathan's first year of residency. With the impending birth of his first child, Nathan tried to get permission to take his vacation time early. This would allow him to be available during delivery and the first two weeks of his son's life. He knew he hadn't officially earned the time yet and was basically asking for an advance on this vacation time, but he hoped his request would be granted. If it was, he wouldn't have any vacation time the rest of his first year. But to be available for Gabby when she went into labor and get much needed bonding time with his son, Nathan was more than willing to make that sacrifice.

University Medical Center was flexible with him regarding this situation. After an extensive conversation and working out small details, Nathan was granted the two weeks he asked for on a pending status, which meant his two weeks would begin the day he called and said his wife was in the hospital. Nathan could now rest easier knowing he had the freedom to be available for his wife when she gave him the word.

July rolled around, and Gabby began to feel small, periodic contractions. In anxious anticipation, Nathan had his phone in his possession constantly.

Randy was grilling burgers on the Fourth of July when he looked over at Gabby lounging on the beach with Jane. He watched her for a moment and noticed something different about her. Wanting Nathan's medical opinion, he asked, "Does it look like the baby's dropped to you?"

Nathan turned to look. Now that his father said that, the baby was sitting lower on Gabby's abdomen. "Yeah, it does."

"When she came in last week, she was dilated to three centimeters and about sixty percent effaced."

"I know. She told me." He took a sip from the beer in his hand. "She had a hard time sleeping last night."

"Did she?" Randy wondered.

"That's the third time this week. She keeps getting contractions, but as soon as she rolls onto her side, they go away."

"I think she's close, Nate."

"How close?"

"Wouldn't be surprised if we had a baby this week."

Nathan wasn't sure if he was excited or terrified. "You think?"

"Baby will come when he's good and ready, but based on the contractions she's having, and the fact that she's dropped and has started to thin and dilate, wouldn't surprise me at all."

Waking briefly from a night of peaceful slumber, Nathan rolled over to put his arm around Gabby. She wasn't lying next to him. Thinking she was in the restroom again, he called out her name. "Gab?" She didn't reply. The bedroom door was closed, but from the gap underneath, he could see a light on in the living room. Apparently, she was having another sleepless night. Still groggy, he stumbled out of bed and slipped on a pair of basketball shorts. He entered the living room and squinted his eyes, trying to block out the brightness of the lamp. Through the glare, he saw Gabby lying on the sofa with her hand on her tummy. "Hey, Babe. What are you doing out here?"

She turned to his voice. "I can't sleep."

"Again?" He sat on the sofa and rubbed her feet. "That's the fourth time in the last week."

"It's these stupid cramps. They're really bad tonight, and lying down isn't helping."

Nathan raised an eyebrow. "Really? Is it one consistent cramp or a series of cramps that come and go?"

"They come and go."

"How far apart?" he asked, wondering if she'd been timing them.

"I don't know. I'm not staring at the clock. I'm trying to make them go away."

Nathan checked the time. It was nearly 1:00 A.M. "How long has this been going on?"

"A couple hours."

"Why didn't you wake me up?"

"It's nothing. Go back to bed."

But he didn't want to. "Are they worse than they were last night?"

"They aren't any better," she countered.

"Time them for an hour. See how many minutes it is between each one."

Gabby saw no cause for alarm. "Nathan."

"I'm serious, Gab. If they're consistent, and the intensity is growing from what they've been, then we need to monitor this. Sounds like you might be in labor."

In an hour's time, her contractions consistently occurred about every five to six minutes and lasted for a solid thirty seconds each. She wasn't in tremendous pain yet, but they did cause discomfort.

Nathan knew what this meant. "Alright, Babe. I'm gonna hop in the shower. Call Dad and tell him what's going on."

"It's two o'clock in the morning," Gabby reminded him.

"Yes, I am aware of that. Call him anyway," Nathan insisted. "He's on-call tonight. He'll have his phone on. Tell him about your contractions, and inform him that we're heading to the hospital."

When Randy's phone went off, he grumbled under his breath before he answered it. "Dr. Hanson,"

"Hi, Dad," Gabby said. "I'm sorry to wake you."

Recognizing Gabby's voice, he sat up. "It's alright, Sweetheart. What's going on?"

"Nathan wanted me to call you. I'm having contractions."

He rubbed his eyes to wake up a bit. "How far apart?"

"Five minutes right now."

That was close. He probed for more information. "On a scale of one to ten, one being no pain, ten being unbearable, what's the intensity of the contractions?"

"Probably a five or six," Gabby replied.

Yup. She was in labor. "Let me talk to Nathan."

"He's in the shower."

"Is he taking you to the hospital?"

"Yes," Gabby replied.

"Good. Have him call me when you guys get there."

When the conversation was over, Randy stretched and turned on the bedside table lamp.

This awakened Jane. "Do you really have to have that light on?" she groaned, trying to hide her face under the pillow.

"Gabby's in labor." He knew that would spark her interest.

She peeked her head out. "Really?"

"Nathan's taking her to the hospital soon." Tired from a broken sleep cycle, he yawned. It was 2:07 A.M. "I need to head over there." Bleary-eyed, he got up and headed toward the shower.

Jane rolled over and moaned. "I'll put on a pot of coffee."

"That would be great. Thanks, Babe."

Nathan packed up the car and drove Gabby to the hospital. They had her checked in and moved up to Labor & Delivery in a little over fifteen minutes.

While recording vitals on Gabby's chart, one of the Maternity Ward nurses asked, "Has your obstetrician been notified?"

Nathan grinned. "My father is her OB, and I already called him."

"Who's your father?" she asked, wondering who this young man was.

"Dr. Randal Hanson."

"You're Nathan Hanson?" she asked.

Obviously this woman had heard his name before. He outstretched his hand to her. "Dr. Nathan Hanson." He emphasized the word doctor.

"I'm Janessa Williams. Pleasure to finally meet you, Dr. Hanson. Your father talks about you all the time. Is he on his way?"

"He's awake," Nathan chuckled. "Not sure how alert he is if he hasn't had coffee yet, but I'm going to call him again to see what the plan is."

Nathan's cell number popped up on Randy's phone. "Hey, Nate. What's up?"

"Are you heading over here?" Nathan asked, hoping his father was on his way.

"Soon. What's her dilation?" Randy casually sipped on a cup of coffee to try and wake up.

"I don't know. I didn't check her."

"What nurse is on duty tonight?" Randy wanted to know.

Nathan didn't understand why that mattered. "Janessa's in here with us now."

"Let me talk to her for a sec."

Nathan handed his phone to the nurse. "My dad wants to talk to you."

The nurse held the phone up to her ear. Nathan only heard one side of the conversation, but at the end, the nurse appeared to be in agreement with whatever his father said. She handed the phone back to him and Nathan resumed his conversation with his father. "What's going on?"

Randy replied, "The nurse is gonna check Gabby then call me back. Mom's in the shower. She wants to come, so I'm waiting for her before I head over. How's Gabby doing?"

"She's uncomfortable," Nathan replied. "Her contractions are painful. Not to an unbearable level yet, but I have a feeling that's not going to last long."

"Has she asked for anything?" Randy asked, knowing she probably would.

"No."

"If she wants something for the pain before I get there, have anesthesia come upstairs. Since you're a physician, you can authorize that," Randy clarified. "I'll sign off on it later."

"Yes, Sir."

Remembering the massive bombardment of emotions he went through when Nathan was born, Randy asked, "How are you doing?"

Nathan was totally honest. "Right now, I'm okay. When the action comes and things start getting intense, that may be a different story. I've assisted you in deliveries before, but it's a lot different when my wife is going through it."

"I completely understand," Randy affirmed. "Hang in there, and keep Gabby as comfortable as possible."

"I will," Nathan replied. "And Dad?"

"Yes?"

"Please get here before the baby comes. I really don't want to make this delivery."

Randy laughed. "Don't worry. I'll be there. I've never shown up late. Take care of your wife please. I'll be there soon."

Nathan tried to keep Gabby comfortable, which became more difficult the further she progressed, and she seemed to be progressing rapidly. The nurse claimed she was dilated to six already, and it was only 3:45. Labor was progressing quickly, which was fine with Nathan. He didn't want to drag this out.

Gabby had resorted to panting, but during the next set of contractions, the pain became unbearable. She screamed in panic.

Nathan held her close, trying to calm her down. "I'm right here, Babe. You're doing great."

"I can't do this." She desperately gripped his arm, digging her fingernails into his flesh.

Certain that she had broken the skin and left bruises on his arm, Nathan asked, "Do you want something for the pain?"

Gabby bobbed her head.

Randy waltzed into the room far too joyfully. "Good morning. How are we doing?"

Nathan was not as cheerful. "She's ready for anesthesia."

Randy stood next to Gabby and touched her shoulder. "We'll get you something to take the edge off, alright?"

Crying, Gabby begged, "Please."

Randy called anesthesia then scrubbed up and slipped on a pair of latex gloves. He checked Gabby for dilation. She had reached seven centimeters. "Wow. We are moving right along, aren't we? At this rate, it won't be too much longer."

Another hour passed, as did another cup of coffee, before Gabby was fully dilated. She progressed through labor at lightning speed. Pressure started to build and she felt the urge to push. Randy checked her one more time. This time, he could feel baby's head at the base of her cervix. She was ready. "Alright, Nathan. Let her push. Pediatrics is on their way."

Nathan proceeded with his father's orders. Prompting his wife, he held her hand and directed, "Next contraction go ahead and push, Babe."

"It's time already?" she cried, anxious to get this over with but scared about the delivery process.

"Yup, you went fast. This will be over soon."

Randy positioned himself by Gabby's feet, ready to catch baby while the nurse handed Nathan a white receiving blanket. Wanting Nathan to get the most out of this experience, Randy offered, "When baby makes his appearance, I want you to grab him and bring him up to Gabby. His daddy is gonna do the sweep."

Nathan loved this plan. "Sweet! Thank you."

Baby Daniel made his appearance at 5:07 A.M. on July 6th. Randy suctioned out his nose and mouth then handed Nathan the scissors. "Here you go, Son. Nice clean snip."

Nathan had done this many times before, but this time it had more significance. This was his child. After making the cut, Nathan gently wrapped the baby in a blanket and placed him on Gabby's chest. An illustrious wail filled the room.

Gabby looked down at her son. The happiest tears flooded her eyes. "Nathan, look at him."

"He's beautiful," Never in his life had he felt as many emotions as he had at this moment. He was a father, and his son was the most beautiful baby he'd ever seen. He had Gabby's blonde hair and his dark grey eyes. After witnessing his wife give birth, Nathan was convinced he was married to the world's toughest woman. She had super-human strength, and she was his hero. He kissed Gabby's forehead. "You did great, Babe. I'm so proud of you."

While Randy finished his workup on Gabby, Nathan intently watched the pediatricians clean up baby Daniel and run an APGAR test on him. He weighed in at seven pounds, nine ounces and was twenty-one inches long. The pediatrician diapered him and put a blue knitted hat on his head then gently placed him in Nathan's arms. "Congratulations!"

Nathan looked down at this tiny person. He couldn't believe this beautiful baby boy was his own flesh and blood.

Jane put her hand on her son's back. "Proud moment, isn't it?"

"Yes, it is," Nathan said, getting weepy. "He's perfect."

Jane smiled at him. "He's a beautiful baby, Nathan. Now let Gabby hold him."

Nathan carefully brought the baby over to Gabby, who sat up wincing. She cradled her baby in her arms. "Oh my god, he looks like you."

Nathan grinned proudly. "Except for his blonde hair."

Randy removed his latex gloves and scrub shirt and disposed of them. "He looks almost exactly like you did when you were a baby, Nate." He washed and dried his hands then joined Nathan and Jane at Gabby's side.

Nathan sisters didn't know Gabby had gone into labor. Realizing this made Nathan laugh. "Guess we should call Lauren and Lacy."

Jane pulled out her phone. "I'll call them."

Since no one was currently using it, Randy arranged for Gabby to get the suite of the Maternity Ward. It was more comfortable, more private, and had a better view. Once they were settled, he looked over at Nathan, who happily held his child. "You want some breakfast?"

"Yes," Nathan said. "But I don't want hospital food. I eat enough of that during the week."

Randy could easily relate. "I'll make a taco run."

Breakfast tacos, one of Nathan's favorite things. And after the busy morning they had, he was starving.

When Randy returned forty-five minutes later, Nathan snatched the taco bag from his father's hand. "Gracias, papá."

"Hey now, don't get grabby."

Nathan reached into the bag and pulled out a foil wrapped delicacy. "I am starving."

"Share those with Gabby. She needs to eat too," Randy insisted.

By 8:00 A.M., Nathan and Gabby had a meal, and baby Daniel had done well for his first time nursing. He had a full tummy and his first diaper change. It had been a long and tiring night, and all three of them were ready to crash.

Before Jane and Randy left, Randy pulled Nathan into the hallway. "You did well today, Son. You were calm and supportive."

"Today was the most exhilarating, emotionally draining, joyous, and proudest day of my life. I am completely in love with that little boy. I didn't think love at first site was possible."

Randy understood. "Until you have children. They change your outlook on everything."

"No kidding," Nathan confessed. "Daniel is an amazing little miracle."

"Becoming a father is pretty intense, isn't it?"

"That's an understatement," Nathan replied. "Intense doesn't do this experience justice, not in the slightest."

Randy remembered all too well. "From now on, things will be very different for you and Gabby. You have a baby boy who needs you."

Nathan was more than willing to give his son anything he needed. "And I will gladly provide for him."

Randy placed his hand on Nathan's shoulder. "You sound like a dad."

Nathan grinned proudly. "I am a dad."

Randy reached behind the nurse's station and pulled out a baby blue gift bag with a basketball printed on it. He handed it to Nathan. "I got you something."

Inside was a book called *The New Dad's Survival Guide* and a tee-shirt that read, *He shoots! He scores!* The basketball analogy made Nathan laugh. "This is awesome. Thanks!" He gave his father a hug. "And thank you for sharing this with us today."

"I kinda didn't have a choice. I am your wife's doctor."

"Even if you weren't, I know you would have been here."

"I wouldn't have missed this for the world." He hugged his son tightly. "Congratulations, Nate."

"Thanks."

When the excitement settled down, Jane and Randy left the hospital, leaving Nathan, Gabby, and baby Daniel alone for a while to bond and take a much needed nap.

Chapter Sixty-Three

Fall brought about change in the weather and change in responsibility and family structure as Gabby and Nathan adjusted to having an infant in the house. Both were thrust into the life of being full time working parents. Gabby returned to the classroom, and Nathan resumed his residency duties.

Since Jane's sports psychology work was done on an as needed basis by appointment only, she was able to set her own schedule. Because of this, she agreed to look after baby Daniel during the day while Gabby and Nathan were at work. Daniel was growing and changing daily. He learned how to grab things and roll over and was beginning to recognize people's faces and voices.

On the opposite end of the country, Lauren awoke feeling lousy. She dashed to the bathroom and threw up. Hearing this horrible sound made Roger roll over with a groan. After a late show the night before, it was far too early to be awake, especially when awakened by such unpleasantness. "You okay, Honey?"

She returned to the bedroom holding her stomach. "I feel horrible."

Roger sat up and leaned on his elbow. "Are you coming down with something?"

"I don't know. It might have been that chicken wrap I ate last night."

"Hopefully it's out of your system now."

"I hope so."

They ate breakfast, cleaned up the apartment, then took Jacob for pizza and playtime at the park before returning home.

That evening, when Nanny Kara showed up to keep an eye on Jacob, Roger and Lauren headed down the elevator together. Roger turned to her and asked, "Are you feeling any better?"

"I'm fine now. But the last few mornings I've felt like crap, especially right after I wake up."

Roger chuckled, not because he found it funny that his wife was ill, but because he was certain he knew what the issue was. "Are you sure you're not pregnant? We have gone a couple of months now without any form of contraception."

She hadn't thought about that. "It's possible."

He reached over and held her hand. "We should probably check it out, don't you think?"

Lauren agreed.

"We'll stop by the drug store on the way home."

They grabbed a cab together and headed off to their respective theatres.

In the morning, Lauren woke up nauseated again. While she was in the bathroom praying to the porcelain gods, Roger slipped out of bed and grabbed the pregnancy test they bought the night before. He walked over to the bathroom and knocked on the door. "Honey?"

She groaned grumpily. "What?"

He cracked the door open and handed her the box. "Here."

She leaned over the toilet and threw up again.

He placed the box on the counter, closed the door, and left her to vomit in peace.

About twenty minutes later, Lauren stepped out of the bathroom wrapped in a towel with a pregnancy test strip in her hand.

Roger sat up. "What's it say?"

She handed the strip to him. "See for yourself."

A bright blue plus sign revealed the results. "Told you." He set the test strip on the bedside table and grabbed Lauren by the waist, pulling her onto the bed with him. He positioned himself over top of her, both happily grinning about expecting their second child. "Guess we're paying Dr. Scalafani a visit."

"I'm sure he misses us."

Roger pulled her into his arms and interlocked his lips with hers, passionately searching every inch of her tongue and mouth. He removed her towel, exposing her naked body. He was still nude from the previous night. Now that she was too, he could feel her feminine flesh rub against his skin. He eagerly caressed her entire body, paying special attention to sensitive areas. He eased in with long, slow strokes, soaking in every luscious sensation.

In the middle of the act, a tiny voice called out, "Mommy?"

Roger closed his eyes and gritted his teeth, trying to suppress his rampant desire.

Lauren bit her lip, hoping Jacob didn't hear them. "Yes, Sweetie?"

"I hungry," the little boy said from behind the closed door.

"Alright, let Mommy get dressed, then I'll get you some breakfast. Go in and go potty."

"Otay."

Hesitantly, Roger flopped onto the bed. Being forced to stop in the middle of sex was definitely grounds for a cold shower this morning. He groaned in frustration. "Dammit! That was really bad timing."

"Sorry, Sweetie." Lauren got up and slipped on her robe.

"It's not your fault." Roger released an exasperated sigh. "I'll make sure he's hitting the toilet. He still needs to work on his aim."

Before Roger got up, Lauren leaned over and whispered in his ear, "We'll make up for it tonight."

He eyed her with a seductive grin. "Sounds good to me."

While Lauren was in the shower, Roger stepped out of bed. He slipped on a pair of sweats then headed into the other bathroom. Jake was standing on his little footstool so he could reach the toilet. Enthusiastically, Roger announced, "Hey, Buddy. Everything going ok in here?"

"I go potty." The child proudly pointed to what he did.

Sure enough he had gone in the big boy potty, and he didn't make a mess this time. "Great job. Don't forget to flush."

Jacob complied.

"Wash your hands with soap. Sing the ABC's while you make bubbles."

Jacob moved his stool over to the sink, turned on the water, and washed his hands, which was an activity they never had a problem getting him to do. The child loved water.

Roger tried not to laugh as his son loudly sang the alphabet song. "Make sure you rinse all those bubbles off and wipe up any water you get on the counter or floor, please."

"Otay, Daddy."

"I'll be in the kitchen when you're done. What do you want for breakfast?" Roger asked.

"Waffles!" Jacob exclaimed.

"Alright. Take care of business quickly, please. No playing in the water."

"Otay," Jacob affirmed with a giggle.

After confirming their pregnancy with the doctor, Roger and Lauren had to tell Jacob. They bought two books, one called 'I'm Going to Be a Big Brother' and another titled 'Waiting for Baby.' They sat on the sofa with him, and Roger started the conversation. "Jakey, Mommy and I have something to tell you."

Being the inquisitive boy he was, he wondered what was going on. "What?"

"You know how Uncle Nathan and Aunt Gabby just had a baby?" Roger reminded him.

"Uh huh. Baby Daniel."

"Yes, baby Daniel," Roger confirmed. "Well, Mommy and I just found out that we're having a baby too. You're going to be a big brother." Roger waited for Jacob's reaction.

Not fully understanding this concept, Jacob looked around the room. "Where is the baby?"

Lauren put her hand on her tummy. "The baby is inside Mommy's tummy."

Jacob wrinkled his forehead. "Mommy, why you eat the baby?"

Roger tried not to laugh. Although he found Jacob's comment amusing, Jacob was serious "She didn't eat the baby, Jake. That's where babies grow."

Jacob lifted his shirt and looked down at his tummy. "I grow a baby too?"

"No," Roger explained. "Only mommies can grow babies."

Jacob put his hand on Lauren's tummy. "The baby in there?"

Lauren touched Jacob's hand. "Yes, Sweetie. The baby has to grow for a long time."

Jacob kissed Lauren's tummy. "I love you baby."

Lauren and Roger looked at each other and smiled. So far so good. They read the two books to him and talked a bit more about being a big brother. Jacob had a lot of questions, but they did their best to provide answers for him. When Roger and Lauren were done discussing this with him, it was time to spread the word to family members and friends. They let Jacob make the announcement—a great big brother job.

Not long after announcing the impending birth of their second child, Roger and Lauren held a birthday celebration for Jacob's third birthday. Instead of being excited about his own birthday, he spent the majority of the day talking about his baby and how he was going to be a big brother. Hopefully that feeling would last.

Daniel was a few days shy of being four months old. He was able to support his head and chest with his arms while lying on his stomach. It looked like he was doing push-ups. He had recently figured out how to roll from his back to his front, and vice versa, and had enough lower body strength to stretch out his legs and kick. His hands could open and shut, come together, swipe at colorful dangling objects, and grab a toy or rattle, all of which went straight into his mouth. He smiled and giggled, and his personality was beginning to surface. He was a curious, gregarious, and determined little one who was fairly easy to entertain. While he was on his tummy, rolling a ball about two feet in front of him led to hours of entertainment, and he was able to coordinate his hand and eye movements to reach for it. Daniel had a small basketball that jingled when he shook it. This toy fascinated him. Every time it would make noise, he would stare at it in serious contemplation and examine it as if to say, what's this colorful round thing and why does it make noise when I shake it? Easily, he kept himself entertained in his crib when he first woke up in the morning. Gabby put a shatterproof mirror in there and he would stare at the most amazing sight in the world—his very own face— while giggling and squealing.

Taking him on expeditions always offered entertainment. Gabby and Nathan often took him for walks and watched him respond with glee as he saw leaves move and birds fly or listened to the sounds of dogs, cars, or anything else that made a noise. This baby loved noises, loved to make noise, and slept better around noise.

They slowly weaned him away from breast milk to formula, simply because Gabby couldn't accommodate pumping and breastfeeding when she was teaching full time. Because his growing tummy could hold more, Daniel was able to sleep for six or seven hours at a time, which translated into a good night's sleep for Nathan and Gabby. They had a pretty set routine in place now, and Nathan very much enjoyed being a daddy. Some of his most treasured moments were the times he spent with Daniel.

Nathan lounged on the sofa watching basketball with Daniel lying on his chest, nuzzled on his shoulder. He gently rubbed his son's back as he supported him with the other hand.

Gabby came home from a trip to the store to find her two boys lying on the couch. "Hello," she sang out.

"Hey, Baby."

She greeted Nathan with a kiss. As she did, she noticed that Daniel was sleeping. "How long has he been asleep?"

"Not long. He has a full tummy and a clean diaper. He and I were watching the game when he crashed. It's been maybe twenty minutes."

"Do you want me to put him to bed?" Gabby offered.

"No. Just leave him. He's fine hangin' with dad. I'll lie him down in a bit." Nathan reached for the soda can next to him. "We got a wedding invitation in the mail from Lacy and Max. It's on the table if you want to see it."

Gabby grabbed the red foil lined envelope off the table. The invitation itself was printed on light grey parchment paper. The firefighter image on the right-hand margin was dressed in his black and yellow fireman's turnout suit wearing his black hat. Standing next to him was a bride in a white gown and veil holding a red bouquet. "These invitations are cute."

She proceeded to read the inside. *Dr. Randal and Mrs. Jane Hanson request the honor of your presence at the marriage of their daughter, Lacy Nicole to Firefighter Max Savon Chamberlain, son of John and Jennifer Chamberlain, Saturday, December 20 at four o'clock in the afternoon, Sixty-Ninth Regiment Armory, 68 Lexington Avenue (between East 25th and East 26th Streets), New York City, NY. Dinner reception immediately following.*

She flipped to December on the calendar. "The Saturday before Christmas?"

"Yup," Nathan grumbled, disapproving of the date Lacy and Max chose. "Convenient for you. It'll be your Christmas break. Tight for me though. I'm going to have to catch a flight Friday night and return home on Sunday. I told Lacy I didn't have any vacation time, but she didn't seem to care. You can fly out before me if you want."

Gabby didn't like that plan. "I'd rather travel with you, not ahead of you, especially with an infant."

He was glad she chose that option. "Good. I wanted to travel with you too." He snarled under his breath, trying to figure out why his sister planned this the way she did. Lacy never was the logical one in the family. "The airports are going to be packed right before Christmas, and if the weather is shitty, all the flights are going to be delayed. What the hell was she thinking? Who gets married right before Christmas?"

"Your sister. And you are going to support her, Nathan," Gabby scolded, shocked by his negative attitude.

"I intend to. I just don't think she thought this through very well. We told her not to do this so close to Christmas, but of course she didn't adhere to our advice, as usual. That really shouldn't surprise me. This is Lacy we're talking about."

Gabby gasped, appalled by his critical comment. "Be nice to your sister. This is her wedding. Why are you being mean?"

"I'm not being mean. I love my sister, and I like Max. But think about it, she's in New York. The weather there tends to be nasty in winter, and that close to Christmas, the airlines are going to be overbooked. She didn't consider travel difficulties for her guests when she planned this. We better secure a flight and hotel now or we may not get there at all."

"I'll book a flight," Gabby suggested.

"Check flights into Newark first. If there isn't anything available, then go into LaGuardia. Try to avoid layovers in Chicago if you can. I don't like that airport. It's always crowded and notorious for cancelling flights. A direct, non-stop flight would be better."

Gabby laughed at his pickiness. "Anything else?"

"Yes, get a decent hotel. Better yet, find out where my parents are staying and get a room in the same hotel," Nathan suggested.

"Geez, Nathan. I should call you Dr. Pickypants," she teased him.

"I want to avoid hassles. People get bitchy when they travel, and around the holidays it's going to be worse, especially if the weather's bad."

"The only one who seems to be bitchy is you," she teased him.

"No I'm not. I just want to make our travel experience with an infant run as smoothly as possible, not only for us but for Daniel. The last thing we need is to be stuck in Chicago for ten hours with a fussy baby. Daniel will be miserable, we'll be miserable, and everyone around us will be miserable. If we can get a direct flight, we'll avoid that hassle."

Gabby was able to find a non-stop, roundtrip flight from Seattle to Newark. It was scheduled to leave Friday the 19th and return Sunday the 21st. "Sweetie," Gabby called to Nathan from kitchen table. "Can you come over here for a minute?"

Since there was a break in the game, Nathan laid Daniel on a blanket to finish his nap then came over to see what she had found.

"I found a flight, but it's expensive."

It was an overnight flight that left Seattle at 7:20 P.M. Friday and would arrive in Newark at 3:18 the next morning. The return flight left Newark at 9:15 A.M. Sunday and would arrive back in Seattle at 12:22 P.M. The problem was it was $643 per person. "Screw it. Just book it," he insisted.

Gabby looked at him like he was insane. "It's thirteen hundred dollars."

"I am aware of that. A direct flight is going to be easier though, don't you think?"

"Probably," she agreed. "But that's a lot of money."

"I'd rather spend the extra money and avoid having to switch planes or getting stuck somewhere. Book it, Gab."

Not wanting to argue with him, although she thought this was crazy, she booked the flight.

Nathan and Gabby planned to split the cost of a hotel room with his parents. However, finding a room in Manhattan around Christmastime that would accommodate everyone was challenging. It didn't help that Randy was exceptionally picky when it came to hotels. Generally, he refused to stay in any hotel with less than a 4-star rating. After weeks of searching, they finally found a one-bedroom suite at the Hotel Marquis Marriott in Times Square. This suite featured a master bedroom with one king-sized bed, a separate living room with a pull-out sofa bed, a dining area that accommodated four adults, and a fully equipped kitchenette complete with coffee maker, a definite necessity for Randy. It wasn't the fanciest hotel in Manhattan, but it would definitely serve their purposes and accommodate the five of them for the two nights they were in New York. Randy reserved this room and Nathan paid his father their half.

With reservations secured, Nathan felt more comfortable about making the trip to New York. Now he could relax and celebrate this joyous occasion with Lacy, his future brother-in-law, and the rest of the family.

Chapter Sixty-Four

"Max," Lacy said as she checked final arrangements for the wedding. "Did you go get fitted for your tux yet?"

"I don't need one," he told her.

What was he planning on wearing at their wedding then? "What do you mean you don't need one?"

"I'm getting married in full dress, Babe. The guys are wearing their blues too. All's good."

This made sense. And actually she was glad he chose to get married in his uniform. She loved to see him in full dress. "Oh, good."

Since this was a fireman's wedding, the firefighter's theme they were going for fell into place accordingly. Aside from the firefighter wedding invitations Max and Lacy sent out, they were able to book the reception hall at the Sixty-Ninth Regiment Armory, the same location where the New York City Fire Department held all of their medal ceremonies. To decorate for this event, they picked out fun firefighter décor and chose red and yellow, the colors of fire, as their wedding colors. These colors, along with black and brass, adorned the reception hall abundantly. Right inside the front entrance, a bright red, life-sized ceramic fire hydrant welcomed guests. Two rolled up firehoses leaned against it. In front of those, a pair of fireman boots and a black firefighter's hat added flair to the already hospitable area. Aerial ladders leaned against the walls, linked together by dramatic swags of red and yellow tulle. Aisles were lined with fire-tinged flowers and tulle-draped fire hydrants, and small fire truck toys were spread throughout the hall.

Every table in the reception hall was dressed in traditional white linen tablecloths with a shimmering yellow runner down the middle. White china plates, silver flatware, and alternating red and yellow linen napkins adorned every place setting. A wedding favor box wrapped in red and yellow ribbon was placed on top of every plate. Inside each box, a smoke detector (batteries included), red fire truck lollipop, firefighter's cross keychain, diecast Matchbook fire engine, fire hydrant cookie cutter, Lego fireman, Dalmatian novelty candle, and a bottle of bubbles in the shape of a fire extinguisher served as gifts for wedding guests. Each table setting also had a crystal champagne glass.

The centerpiece of each table was a black plastic firefighter's hat with the words *Max and Lacy Chamberlain* printed on the front. A shiny black firefighter's boot full of red and yellow fire-tinged roses accompanied each hat. Every table had a place card, held up by a toy fire truck. Printed on each place card were the words to a different fire related poem or saying. A red crystal bowl on each table offered several fire-themed candies: Atomic Fireballs, Redhots, Life Savers, Cinnamon Fire Jolly Ranchers, and Hot Tamales. Guests could reach in and grab these at their leisure.

Their red velvet wedding cake hidden in demure white icing was decorated with fancy red and yellow frosting. The cake top featured a bride standing with a bouquet in her hand and a fireman groom, dressed in his black turnout gear, climbing up a ladder on the side of the cake carrying a fire hose over his shoulder trying to reach his bride. Instead of the traditional cake cutting knife, Max and Lacy cut their cake with a fire axe.

They opted for a traditional reception menu, but added a firefighter's twist by choosing menu items with fire related names—Fire Roasted Tomato Pasta with Shrimp, Flame Broiled Chicken with Garlic Roasted Red Potatoes, and Tossed Fire Salad, which included lettuce, jalapeno peppers, tomatoes, Anaheim pepper, red onion, and cilantro. With the meal, they served Autumnal Fire beer and various types of fire-related mixed drinks—Chimney Fire, Blue Chimney Smoke, Goblet of Fire, Forbidden Smoke, and Smoked Martinis.

As far as music went, fire-titled songs filled their playlist. Instead of the traditional limousine, Max secured the service of an out of commission fire engine to transport them to the armory.

His groomsmen, all firefighters he worked with, wore full dress uniforms. Lacy's bridesmaids wore yellow dresses with red and yellow rose bouquets. Lacy's dress was traditional white, but to add flair, she tied a red and yellow sash around her waist. Her bouquet included red-tipped fire roses and calla lilies in shades of red, orange, and yellow. The bunch was tied together with red and yellow tulle swag. Her wedding garter was made from satin flame fabric with a Maltese cross dangling from the middle.

Max and his groomsmen stood at the altar with the Fire Department Chaplain, whom Max had com- missioned to perform the ceremony. Patiently, yet anxiously, he waited for his bride to appear. Jacob, who acted as ring bearer, toddled up the isle wearing a red firefighter's hat. He ran up to Max and handed him the red ring pillow, which brought about a few laughs. Max directed him to the fireman standing next to him. The Best Man took the pillow and Jacob joined his father.

The bridesmaids marched in two by two, Lauren and Gabby among them, followed by the flower girl. She walked down the aisle carrying a red bucket full of red and yellow rose pedals, tossing them on the floor along the way. Finally, Max saw his bride. Her elegant gown and long, flowing hair, held in place by a hair clip, immediately brought a smile to his face. She exemplified beauty.

With a bouquet in her hand, Lacy clung to her father's arm as she strolled down the aisle. When they arrived at the altar, Max anxiously awaited the hand of his bride. But before Lacy released her grip on her father, she looked up at him with misty eyes.

"Alright now, none of that," Randy insisted.

She hugged him tightly. "I love you, Daddy."

Randy had a hard time containing his emotions. He and Lacy always had a rocky relationship. It seemed they were never on the same page and did not see eye to eye on most things. The fact that she was clinging to him like this melted his heart. He loved his daughter so much, but the entire time she was growing up and maturing, he was convinced she hated him. They butted heads constantly, but not today. "I love you too, Sweetheart, and I'm very proud of you."

"Thank you, Daddy." She squeezed him with a death grip, not wanting to let go.

Max stepped forward and offered Randy a firm handshake. "Dr. Hanson."

"Max."

"I promise I'll take care of her, Sir."

Randy completely trusted this man. "I know you will."

Lacy wiped her eyes and kissed her father's cheek before she took Max's hand and joined him at the altar.

As Lacy and Max exchanged vows, Randy's eyes watered. Over the course of five years, the Hanson family had grown by leaps and bounds. Randy and Jane gained a daughter-in-law, a son-in-law, and two grand-children. And now Lacy was making that lifelong commitment and settling down. Within minutes, another son-in-law would join the family.

When the chaplain pronounced Lacy and Max as husband and wife, Randy watched his daughter kiss her new husband. He let out a sigh. His job was done. All of his children had left the nest and had families of their own now, a new generation of Hansons. Everything Randy and his wife set out to do for their children and everything they hoped their children would accomplish had been achieved. Nathan pushed himself as an athlete and a student, became an outstanding physician, and married his high school sweetheart; he was now a devoted father. Lauren's Broadway dreams became reality, she married a supportive man, and was a loving mother to a sweet little boy, with a baby girl on the way. Lacy had pursued her dance passion and was now spreading her love of dance to future generations, and despite her heartaches and the doubts she held about love, she finally found the man of her dreams. Max Chamberlain was a selfless, fun-loving man who was very compatible with their daughter.

After being pronounced as husband and wife, the men from Max's firehouse, donning full dress blues, made an arch by holding pike poles in the air. Max and Lacy strolled underneath to the applause and cheers of the wedding guests.

During the reception, laughter, joy, and happy conversation filled the room. Randy gave his traditional father of the bride speech, after which, he and Lacy took the floor for the traditional father-daughter dance. Randy had only danced with his daughter one other time, at the daddy-daughter dance back when she was in high school. This was truly a sentimental moment.

"You look beautiful, Baby," Randy said to his daughter.

Lacy smiled at him.

"I'm sorry if I embarrassed you during my speech."

"That's okay," she assured him. "It's not like you didn't say anything that wasn't true." She gave him an apologetic glance. "I'm sorry, Daddy."

"Why are you sorry?"

"For all those times I argued with you and talked back and slammed doors in your face. I constantly questioned you and gave you so many reasons to get upset with me."

Randy snorted under his breath. "You and I are more alike than you think."

"How?"

"We are both pigheaded and opinionated."

This made Lacy laugh.

"You're a strong woman, Lacy, and you don't put up with people's crap. That's a good quality to have because you don't let people push you around. I get on my high horse sometimes and need a violent kick when my pretentiousness escapes. You called me out many, many times. You questioned my opinion and demanded explanations. You didn't just take my word, you expected me to justify myself."

"I was argumentative," she explained.

"But you knocked me down a notch when I needed it. You know who you remind me of?"

"Who?"

"Your mother."

Lacy's eyes became misty. "Really?"

"Yes, so much. Your mother has put up with a lot of crap from me over the years, but she always calls me on it, always makes me justify my opinion, and has no qualms about telling me when I'm wrong. That woman has knocked me off my pedestal more times than I care to admit to. I get arrogant and often think that my opinion is the only one that matters. Mom sees it, she questions me about it, and has on occasion slammed a door in my face when I refused to overcome my pigheadedness. She keeps me in check."

Lacy giggled.

"It's one of the many things that I love about her. She's not afraid to put me in my place. She's a strong woman who speaks her mind, just like you. You are the only one of the kids who had the courage to question me. You demanded justification when my opinion and stubbornness had no firm foundation. Max is very lucky to have such a strong, assertive woman who's not afraid to question authority." Randy flashed a crooked grin. "I'm sure you've put him in his place before."

"A couple times."

"I guarantee that he appreciated it. A long time ago, you and I had a conversation about relationships. It was right after Nathan and Gabby got engaged. You were convinced you'd never find the right man and were ready to give up. Do you remember?"

She nodded. "Yes."

"Do you remember what I said to you?"

"Yes, you told me to stay true to my high expectations, never to give in, and advised me not to settle for the first man who came along. You said I had to pay attention because Mr. Right would appear when I least expected him, I just had to be patient and wait for him."

"Do you recall what your response to me was?"

"I promised you I wouldn't marry for the wrong reasons. That I would wait for the right man and never settle for anything less than what I deserved."

"And you stuck to it. I'm proud of you for that, Lace. Max is a wonderful man. He loves you, respects you, and treats you the way you deserve to be treated. The first time I saw you two together, I knew it was only a matter of time before this day would come."

"I love him," she replied with a smile.

"I know you do," he confirmed. "And obviously he loves you. You and Max have a good foundation, Baby. Now build on it and make it stronger."

"Thank you, Daddy."

"You're beautiful from the inside out, Honey. Don't change who you are, because that is who I love, and the person Max loves."

Lacy hugged her father tightly. "I love you, Daddy."

"I love you, too, Baby."

As the father-daughter dance ended, Max cut in. "May I?"

"Of course." Randy moved out of the way and allowed Max to occupy the floor with his bride.

Thinking about the day's events, Randy looked at his wife. Jane was his purpose, his reason for living. Now that the dancefloor was open to all wedding guests, Randy offered his hand to Jane. "May I have this dance, Mrs. Hanson?"

Jane placed her hand in his. "Absolutely, Doctor."

He helped her stand up and led her out to the floor.

She rested her head on his shoulder. With a satisfied tone in her voice, she said, "We did it."

Randy wrapped his arms around her and exhaled with a heavy heart, somewhat saddened over the fact that his kids had left the roost, yet proud of the adults they had become. "Yup. The kids are happy and everyone had a good day." He looked into Jane's eyes. "Life with you has been an adventure, an adventure I wouldn't trade for the world. Every morning, I thank God for giving me another day with you. You are the best mother, wife, and friend a man could ask for. Without you in my life, I am nothing. You have made my life complete. You have given my life purpose, and I have learned and grown so much because of you. I'm glad I decided to go to Santa Cruz all those years ago. Ever since that day, my life has never been the same." He pulled her close and kissed her. "I love you."

"I love you, too."

Taking a break from dancing, Randy occupied a table. Jacob was in the chair next to him, coloring on a piece of paper. "Hey, Jakey."

"Hi, Papa." He held up the picture he had drawn. "I made a picture for you."

Randy examined the drawing. Jacob had drawn a Christmas tree full of gifts. The round, red person he drew looked an awful lot like Santa Claus. "This is great, Jake. You excited about Christmas?"

"Santa's coming soon."

"Yes he is. I hope you've been a good boy."

"I'm always a good boy." He started singing, "You better watch out, you better not cry…"

Randy scanned the room. Roger, Lauren, Lacy, Max, Nathan, and Gabby bopped around the dancefloor, laughing and having a blast together. Seeing the kids bond like this made him grin.

Jim snagged a chair next to Randy. Taking a sip from his beer, he said, "This is one hell of a party, Dude. It's good to see all the kids together again."

Randy replied with a sigh. "It's hard to get everyone together. They have their own lives now."

"Yup," Jim reassured him. "But they all made great lives for themselves."

"That they did," he replied. "I'm proud of the adults they've become."

"The kids comin' home for Christmas?" Jim asked.

"Nathan and Gabby will be, but Lauren and Roger are spending Christmas in New York with his family, and Max and Lacy will be on their honeymoon."

"The only one we'll have home this year is Jalene."

Randy shifted in his seat and picked up his beer. "You guys want to come over for Christmas?"

"Can we bring our dog?"

Randy flinched his head. "When did you get a dog?"

"Jill and I adopted a beagle. We're picking him up when we get back to Seattle."

"A beagle?"

"Yup. We named him Kahuna."

Randy found this amusing. "Why does that not surprise me?"

"He's a cool poochie. Well behaved. Housetrained. He wears a green bandana around his neck. He's stylin'."

"I bet he is," Randy teased. "Stylin' just like you."

"Damn straight, Bro." Jim took another drink from his beer. "You wish you had my sense of style."

Randy laughed, "Oh yes. It's my ultimate goal in life."

"So can we bring the pooch?" Jim asked again.

"Yeah. Can't guarantee Fingers will approve, but..."

"I'm pretty sure he can hold his own against that damn parrot. It'll be fun to spend Christmas with my best bud."

"Yes it will." Randy tipped his beer bottle. "Cheers."

"Cheers, Dude."

They toasted then enjoyed the rest of the celebration with the family.

Epilogue:

In the spring, Lauren and Roger had their second child, a girl named Sophie Rose. They both continued to perform on Broadway and both remained active in the Broadway Cares/Equity Fights AIDS foundation.

Jacob became interested in music, dance, and theatre. He was a natural entertainer, chasing the dream of performing on the big stage, not unlike his parents. To encourage this talent, Roger and Lauren put him in dance classes, gave him voice lessons, and enrolled him in junior theatre. The youngster made his Broadway debut at the tender age of eight when he played the title role in *Pinocchio*, singing and dancing in front of large crowds, and eating up the audience's reaction.

Little Sophie was more interested in visual arts. She loved to paint, draw, and sketch on anything she could find. Roger and Lauren fed this creativity by putting her in art classes, buying her an easel, and constantly keeping her stocked in art supplies. She also had a natural knack for playing the piano, sharing her father's talent. She picked it up quickly and was able to read music before she could read. Roger gave her weekly lessons, allowing her to improve her skills and increase her musical repertoire.

Nathan and Gabby completed their family with three boys, Daniel Mark, Michael Jonathan, and Luke Alexander. All three boys loved sports. Two were involved in little league and one was a natural on a basketball court, just like his father.

After completing his five-year residency program, Dr. Nathan Hanson became a board-certified orthopedic surgeon specializing in total joint replacement, ligament reconstruction, arthroscopic and reconstructive surgery of the knee and shoulder, general sports-related orthopedic injuries, and sports medicine. He was a member of the Arthroscopy Association of North America, as well as a certified member of the American Academy of Orthopedic Surgeons. His clinic, Momentum Physical Therapy and Sports Rehab Center, offered the full spectrum of care devoted to the diagnosis, treatment, rehabilitation, and prevention of sports injuries and conditions that affected the body's muscles, joints, and bones. Two other orthopedic physicians and three physical therapists were located on site.

Gabby continued her career as a teacher, teaching Kindergarten, then first grade, and eventually moving to third grade. She was given many leadership positions and was voted teacher of the year twice.

Max and Lacy were blessed with two girls, Lyndsey Malia and Melody Liann. Max was a dedicated father, and even though he was a manly firefighter, he never hesitated to have tea parties, play with Barbies, or attend his daughter's ballet recitals. After ten years with the New York City Fire Department, he was promoted to Lieutenant and became shift leader for his company. He was actively involved in the New York City

Firefighter's Fill the Boot Drive, which helped raise money for burn victims and their families.

Lacy continued to teach dance classes and regularly choreographed concerts and music videos within the New York City area. Every year, she was involved in the Fire Island Dance Festival and the Hudson Valley Dance Festival, both of which were charity fundraising activities that raised millions of dollars for AIDS victims. Her name quickly spread throughout New York City. She became a highly acclaimed lead choreographer and one of the main organizers for the Annual New York City Dance Parade and Festival.